THE SORRY TALE

A STORY OF THE TIME OF CHRIST

BY
PATIENCE WORTH

COMMUNICATED THROUGH
MRS. JOHN H. CURRAN

EDITED BY
CASPER S. YOST

NEW YORK
HENRY HOLT AND COMPANY
1917

THE QUINN & BODEN CO. PRESS
RAHWAY, N. J.

PREFACE

THE story of the invisible author of *The Sorry Tale* was told in the book entitled *Patience Worth: a Psychic Mystery*. It seems sufficient here to present a brief statement of the facts in relation to that phenomenal personality. She came to Mrs. John H. Curran, of St. Louis, Missouri, one evening in the summer of 1913, as Mrs. Curran sat with a ouija board on her knees, and introduced herself as "Patience Worth," with the declaration that she had lived long ago and now had come again. From that time she has poured out a continuous stream of communications, conversational or literary, including hundreds of poems, numerous parables and allegories, several short stories, a drama, and two novels. All of her compositions are distinguished by the archaic form of her language, which is, however, not the same in any two of her larger works, there being important dialectal variations that make each one quite different from the others in this particular, and the archaic quality as well as the dialectal form varies as much in her minor productions and in her conversations. Yet upon all of them is the impress of a single creative personality. Each and every one of them bears the imprint of Patience Worth.

Mrs. Curran, through whom all of this matter has come, is a young woman of normal disposition and temperament, intelligent and vivacious. She receives the communications with the aid of the mechanical device known as the ouija board as a recording instrument. There is no trance or any abnormal mental state. She sits down with the ouija board as she might sit down to a typewriter, and the receipt of the communications begins with no more ceremony than a typist would observe. Mrs. Curran has had no experience in literary composition and has made no study of literature, ancient or modern. Nor, it may be added, has she made any study of the history, the religions, or the social customs of the period of this story, nor of the geography or topography of the regions in which it is laid. Her knowledge of Palestine and of the beginnings of the Christian religion is no greater, and probably no less, than that of the average communicant.

Patience Worth began the writing of this story on the evening of the fourteenth of July, 1915, and some time was given to its transmission on two or three evenings of every week until its completion. In the early months she proceeded leisurely with the task, usually writing 300 to 1,000 words of the story in an evening, and, in addition, poems, parables, or didactic or humorous conversation, as the mood or the circumstances prompted. As a relief to the sorrows of *The Sorry Tale* she started another story which she called *The Merry Tale,* and for months the composition of the two stories continued alternately. Often she would work at both on the same evening. But as *The Sorry Tale* progressed she gave more and more time to it, producing on many evenings from 2,500 to 3,500 words of the tale in a sitting of an hour and a half or two hours. In one evening 5,000 words were dictated, covering the account of the Crucifixion. At all times, however, it came with great rapidity, taxing the chirographic speed of Mr. Curran to the utmost to put it down in abbreviated longhand. The nature of the language made it unsafe to attempt to record it stenographically. At the beginning of the story Patience had a little difficulty in dropping some of the archaic forms she had previously used, and which she continued to use in her other productions and in her conversation; but this difficulty seemed to disappear in a few weeks, and thereafter there was never a change of a word, never a pause in the transmission, never a hesitation in the choice of a word or the framing of a sentence. The story seemed literally to pour out, and the amount of her production in an evening appeared to be limited only by the physical powers of Mrs. Curran. " Ye see," she said once to a visitor who inquired about this ability to write with such pauseless continuity, " man setteth up his cup and filleth it, but I be as the stream." As in all her work, it mattered not who was present or who sat at the board with Mrs. Curran. Whether the *vis-à-vis* was man or woman, old or young, learned or unlettered, the speed and the quality of the production were the same. From start to finish some 260 persons contributed in this way to the composition of this strange tale, some helping to take but a few hundred words, some many thousands. Parts of the story were taken in New York, Boston and Washington. Each time the story was picked up at the point where work was stopped at the previous sitting, without a break in the continuity of the narrative, without the slightest hesitation, and without the necessity of a reference to the closing words of the last preceding instalment. These words were often read for the benefit of those present, but Patience repeatedly proved that it was not required by her.

For some weeks before the beginning of the story Mrs. Curran had received intimations of its coming and of its nature: " 'Tis sorry tale (a tale of sorrow) I put a-next," Patience said on the fifth of July.

"Aye, a lone-eat tale. Ye ne'er do to know an eat like to a lone. Be ye lone (alone) eat doth bitter." It was as " the sorry tale " that she ever afterward spoke of it. On the evening of the ninth she entertained a company of twelve persons and in the midst of her conversation she exclaimed: " Hear ye a song! " and presented the following verses referring to this story and the material she desired for it:

> *Wind o' the days and nights,*
> *Aye, thou the searchers of the night,*
> *Lend thou to me of thee.*
>
> *Sun of the day, a-bath o'er Earth,*
> *Lend thou of thee to me.*
>
> *Rains of the storm,*
> *A-wash of Earth's dust to a-naught,*
> *Lend thou of thee to me.*
>
> *Sweets o' the Earth, the glad o' day,*
> *Lend thou of thee to me.*
>
> *Prayers o' the soul, the heart's own breath,*
> *Lend thou to me of thee.*
>
> *Fields of the earth, a-gold o' harvest-ripe,*
> *Lend thou to me of thee.*
>
> *Dark o' the nights, strip o' thy robe,*
> *And lend o' thee to me.*
>
> *For I do weave and wash and soothe*
> *And cloak o' one who needeth thee,*
> *A one o' His, a-stricken,*
> *A one whose soul hath bathed o' crime,*
> *And Earth hath turned and wagged a nay to him.*

Two persons besides the Curran family—Mr. and Mrs. Curran and Mrs. Pollard, Mrs. Curran's mother—were present on the evening of July 14, two persons under whose hands Patience had expressed a wish to begin the tale. There was a certain solemnity to the occasion, a feeling that something of profound significance was to be inaugurated. Solemnity is quite unusual in the meetings with Patience, whose exuberant humor is one of her most charming qualities, and who, however serious she may be, loves not a long face. But on this night there were no flashes of wit. On the contrary, it was for a while a tremorous, hesitating, faltering Patience, almost overcome by the task upon which she was entering.

"Loth, loth I be," she said. "Yea, thy handmaid's hands do tremble. Wait thou! Wait! Yet do I to set" (to write). For a moment the pointer circled slowly about the board recording nothing until it picked up the murmur: "Loth, loth I be that I do for to set the grind" (the circling motion of the pointer). And then, for the first and only time in the long experience with her, she asked for a period of quiet. "Wait ye stilled," she said. "Ah, thy handmaid's hands do tremble!"

For three or four minutes there was no sound in the room, and then, as if in reality from out the silence of twenty centuries, as if actually from out the darkness of the greatest night in all history came the plaintive cry of Theia, "Panda, Panda, tellest thou a truth?"

There was no further hesitation in the delivery. Without another pause, except by Mrs. Curran for rest and discussion, the story proceeded rapidly, and about two thousand words were received on that evening. The first thing noticed was the great difference in the language and the atmosphere from anything previously written by Patience. Next was the knowledge displayed of the people and the time and of the topography of the country. The language retained some of the verbal and syntactical peculiarities of Patience, the same freedom from grammatical restraints, but it was not the language of her other works, nor that which she used in her conversation. Her other productions of a narrative nature had been redolent of medieval or Renaissant England; the atmosphere of this was truly Syrian and Roman. But the knowledge shown was and is most puzzling. I do not undertake to say that there are no errors of fact or condition, no anachronisms. I merely assert that after much study and research I have been unable to find anything that I could so term with certainty. There are some things upon which no authority accessible to me gives any information. There are some variances from history, profane and sacred, but these are quite evidently intentional and with definite purpose. From the beginning to the end of the story Patience seemed to be absolutely sure of herself. Discussion of mooted points brought no comment from her and no modification of her statements. Several times she condescended to clear a doubt by later putting an explanation into the text, but in doing so she emphasized the original assertion. The interesting question arises: If

Patience is, as she says, an Englishwoman of the seventeenth century, where did she get the knowledge and the material for this story? It is a question that gives rise to many speculations, but apparently she answers it for herself in the words of Theia to Tiberius in the garden of the imperial palace at Rome: " ' Thy hand did reach forth and leave fall a curtain of black that should leave a shadow ever upon the days of Theia. And the hand that shall draw the curtain wide and leave the light to fall upon thy shadows shall be this! ' —and she held her hand high."

I have described the trepidation of Patience at the beginning of the story. Several times in the course of the composition she gave expression to this feeling, which seemed to grow out of a profound sense of personal responsibility. " Thee'rt a-wind of a golden strand," she said one evening. " This be the smile of Him that turneth back unto the past. The hand of thy handmaid shaketh at the task. This lyre singeth the song of Him. Think ye the hand of me might touch athout (without) a shake? 'Tis a prayer I'd put that the very shaking of this hand should cause a throbbing of the air of Heaven and set aflow the song unto the Earth." And at another time she said: " This holied tale be the love of me. Yet 'tis a sorry put (a work of sorrow), for woe is me that I do tell of the woes of Him." Again she remarked, by way of introduction to an evening's work: " Athin (within) the put (the story) be much of Him, and this tale be dear, dear unto me. Ye see, I be at put (at the writing) as though 'twere me upon thy earth. Yea, for how may a one tell unto his brother that that he knoweth as the dear wish of him unless he be as the brother of the flesh of him? " And then, further to voice her feelings, she gave this poem on Jesus by the Sea:

> Calm eyes a-look 'cross sea.
> The seething waters lap 'pon sands
> At feet of Him. The day, a-bathed of blood,
> A-soundeth 'mid the soothing of the sea's soft voice.
> Earth, old, olden, yea,
> And yet so youthed, so youthed!
> And He a-sit, calm-eyed, years youthed,
> And wisdom olded past the tell.
>
> And lo, His voice a-mingled there
> With silvered tongues of speaking waves.
> The rolling waters lapped
> The very murmur of His prayer.

And e'en this day, methinks,
'Tis tongued unto the earth.

The sand's soft clung about the feet a-bared
That still should trod 'pon stones a-sharped.
Yea, Earth e'en then did hold the greenéd tree
That burst the sod for upping of the cross.

And lo, the voices of the Earth
Cried out and sounded discord
'Mid the heaven-song of Him.
And He a-walked Him from the sea's calm shore
And through the vale, the bittered cup to sup.

Methinks that there within the garden place
I see me of His holied self a-stripped.
No brother of the flesh might know of Him,
For God be God and man doth fear to know.
And Earth doth stand it, still a-crying out
Against this song of love.
And yet, I do to see Him sit,
Calm eyes unto the sea
And wisdomed past the tell.

Upon still another evening she said: " Look ye! The side that flowed red doth weep fresh drops, e'en unto this day. Yea aday! And this shed of the tides (times) agone but bought of the then, and yet He, smiling, sheddeth ever, yea, ever. The every day seeth the weeped drops. Think ye then that this hand would set these drops gushed, or yet touch them that fell and be dust that they stir in their holy, athout (without) a tremor?

" Ah, men of Earth, look! look! Amid thy day stalketh He. Yea, and thou mayest see His drops aflow e'en upon thy byways. Yea, and what doest thou that the drops be stopped? He be the oped chalice that poureth the cleansed flow ever, ever, ever. Think ye that they who fall, bathed of blood, be stopped athin (within) their own flow? Nay!—born anew athin (within) His own. Yea, His arms cradle seas. Yea, and His hands plucketh e'en the motes as His own. Yea, His treasures gleam. And I be a-telling thee—ah, joy!—much be His that He doth treasure that Earth hath cast as chaff. E'en though His vineyard showeth blight, still within His press, behold, naught save sweeted wines do flow!"

I present these expressions of profound devotion to show the sentiment that has unquestionably actuated Patience Worth in the production of this story. There is much within it to arouse discussion, but she has no fear. "Hark ye!" she says. "There shall be ones who shall tear at this cloth till it shreddeth, yet the shreds shall weave them back unto the whole 'pon love strands. For Love be the magic warp, and Love may ne'er die, but be born athin all hearts that sup the words."

C. S. Y.

CONTENTS

BOOK I
PANDA

CHAPTER I

"PANDA, Panda, tellest thou a truth? Panda, thou whose skin is burned to saffron from desert's blaze, look thou, and tell but truth! 'Tis Theia who wearyeth.

"Panda, the gods do forsake thee and Theia. Gods! In pity's name, gods! What, what does a word, a word sent of prayer, buy of gods? Gods! Panda, the gods are but the streaming tongues of priests.

"Panda, the earth doth rock and sick o'ercomes thy Theia. The earth doth rock like sagging slip of camel. The smell hath set it deep within the sick. Panda, speak! seest thou a burning torch or lamp that sheweth thee and me the way?"

"The dark doth lift not; but thou, Theia, canst see 'tis stars' light and yonder standeth, high and black, the city's walls. Canst thou then lean upon thy Panda and set ahead?"

"Nay, Panda, nay. But leave me rest and sit here beneath the stars that I may sing and pour the emptiness of this heart unto the night.

"Yon walls, Panda, shall shut the far land ever from thy Theia's tongue. Yea, hate shall step with Theia there within the walls and seal her lips, and seal their hate. The morrow, yea, Panda, I fear the morrow shall break upon the fruit of hate. Canst thou but step thee on and search thee for one to aid? 'Tis well upon me, Panda, and I weak and fail. The chill doth creep and eye doth shew a weary gray ahead, and haunting bright behind.

"Thou, Panda, thou and Theia, the waste of Rome! Rome, who holdeth carrion and decketh it with rose, and yet hath not a place for thee and me. Rome! Rome, white handed, and yet she leaveth Theia but the desert-burnt for aid. Panda, on!"

"Behold, a hut, Theia! A hut doth stand amid the dark, and fire's smoke spiceth the air! Wait, wait thee, Theia! Rest! for though 'tis Rome who dealt thee but a desert's scorch, 'tis sun that teacheth well; for he who parcheth knoweth well of pity. 'Tis then I go, and leave thee but to aid. Long, long hath the journey carried unto this.

"Hark, 'tis a step! Yea, the dark doth belch a formless mass.

"Who art thou, brother? What bringeth thee asearch?

"Ah, thou art a woman, a woman of the town! Theia, it seemeth the gods did hear and send a gentler hand for aid of thee.

3

" Who art thou, and yon city, what its name?

" She babbleth, Theia, a tongue not thine and mine, and sayeth 'tis Bethel—Beth—Bethel—lehem—Bethlehem."

" Panda, burn thou the name, yea, and scorch it deep, that thou canst bear it unto Rome with thee, and when time hath riped the hate, and when it hath bloomed and fruited, thou mayest pluck the fruit and bear it back and tell unto Rome its bearing place."

And Theia turned unto the woman and spake:

" Art thou a woman? A woman who suppeth tears and bitters of the earth for man? Hast thou a sordid hate that burneth thee till thou dost flame like sacrificial fire? Art thou the plaything of the gods, that sitteth throned and then walloweth deep in blood of bearing the folly of a man?

" 'Tis upon me! By all the gods, do hear, the birth of hate hath seized! Panda! Panda, thou youth of Rome, the gods do laugh! Her ears are stopped! And dark, dark doth party to the trick! "

And she reached her forth unto the woman, saying: " Here, here, see! or better, leave me thy hand! 'Tis gold."

And Panda looked upon this and spake: " There, there, Theia! She harketh to the metal tongue."

And Theia cried aloud: " Panda, leave me not! For when the dark doth take thee unto itself, then, then there shall die the hope of Theia, drowned in dark."

And she took up the hand of the woman, saying: " Here! Since thine ears do hear me not, set thy hand here unto my breast and I call the grinning brass of gods to hark, else I then shall spat upon their metal tongues.

" Ha, ha, ha! Panda, she knoweth! Ah, do thou follow and wait, Panda, wait until the hate doth cry aloud unto the earth! Come thou and follow, and when thou shalt seek the paths that followed thee and me to here, remember, Panda, remember! Thou shalt see. Thine eyes shall be unloosed! Thou art but a slave lad, and Theia, Theia, the plaything of the gods, who danced her path unto the King's * own door, and payeth for the peep! Ah, Panda, her eyes hold far o'ermuch e'en now, and 'tis what a sport for gods and kings to tear the rose to tatters! "

" Theia, I fear thou hast offended much the gods."

" Yea, Panda, and yet do I offend! "

And they went them up unto the hut of the woman and within. And Theia cried:

* " King " was a common title for the Roman Emperors in the Eastern provinces.—FARRAR-EWALD.

"The camel, 'twas sweet, Panda, to this, the filth! A throne! A throne, Panda, a throne of rags and a scepter of straw! A Psyche Jove did touch and for a play she fell, a Venus who walloweth of love. Yea, Panda, and look! Still the gods do play! Look! She hath a face like Dagon,* I swear! Panda, I fear lest her sides should show a scale!"
And she cried out: "Oh-o-o-e! Oh-o-o-e! Oh-o-o-e! Ha, ha, ha! That should wake their sleep!

"Panda, stay thee, that thou mayest bear back this tale of merry-make. Look! Look! Here! take thou this, the strands of me! 'Tis gold, 'tis gold! All, all the gold the earth doth hold for Theia. Take thou this! See! these hands of mine do pluck it out and offer it as price, that the tale may bear a token of the truth. Take it, take it, Panda! Take it and throw upon the fires of Jove! Take it, lest he fall jealous that it be spared to Theia—Theia, whom he hath stripped!"

"Yea, Theia. Yea, I wait thee and thy labor. Till morrow, Theia, till morrow, though 'tis a scourge that payeth Panda. I sit me here and smell the damp chill of the stone, that filth scent filleth me not."

"Ha, ha, ha! Thou art right, Panda, thou art right! The filth is Theia's gift—the incense, the burnt offering to the o'erkind gods."

And she looked upon the woman and murmured:
"She sitteth here and rocketh and watcheth and looketh like fish that lay beneath the sun; and eyes filmed, the chosen god for hate's-born! A goddess of filth!"

And again she cried: "Oo-o-eh! Oe-e! I chill! O-oh-e-e! 'Tis o'er, Panda, 'tis o'er! May Jove then strike me dead that I did finish of the bearing of Hate! Come thou, Panda! Come! the light hath dimmed the room. Come thou, and touch the hate-born! Come! Nay, nay! say not it hath died of hate's wine! Nay, say not! Ha, ha, ha!"

And the babe wailed and Theia cried out: "The wail! The wail! Theia is undone! Panda, touch thou with loving!"

And behold, she looked upon the hand of the woman.
"Panda, the gods do win! Panda, look! she hath a leper's hand! Ha, ha, ha! The dead hand! The whited! The fall flesh! But she hath touched not the Hate!

"Panda, thou shalt bear it yon within the city's wall and hide. Hide, hide, Panda, where there shall be plenty! Hide where chill shall flee! Hide, Panda, where thou shalt find a face of loving!"

"Theia, thou hast tempted the gods and digged a pit wherein we did fall. 'Tis a son, Theia, the son of——"
And Theia stopped his words.

* The god of the Philistines, represented as half fish.

"May thy tongue set stiffened, Panda! He hath not a name! Ha, ha, ha! He hath not a name! Hate, hate, hate shall follow him and earth shall swallow him, and I, Theia, shall follow him like shade doth follow bright. Leave me, Panda, leave me! Thou knowest the feast's-leave, cast forth, is fit for naught and cast to rot!"

"Theia, it shall be, it shall be. Yea, but Panda seeketh not Rome. At light, at light, he shall seek the city and bear thee, Theia, unto a townsman. Strip thee. The pack holdeth fresh robe. Theia, Panda's eyes are sealed unto thy mysteries and Panda's hands await thy bidding."

And Theia did this thing and spake: "Sick hath sealed my lips, Panda; sick doth mist the day's birth like hate-mist cloudeth the birth of him. I wait thee. I wait thee. Seek, seek thou! and come unto thy Theia."

And Panda spake in comforting: "It shall be, Theia, it shall be. But Panda shall be a brother unto him, and thee. Rome, Rome hath slaves that turn, and hate doth make them knaves, but to the King's blood, though it hath spilled afar, the slave of him doth bow.

"'Tis scarce light. See! Panda shall wrap thee well within this mantle that is the cloak of Panda, and bear thee and thy babe unto yon deep thicket that sheweth 'long the road. And then, and then, Theia, to city, that I bring forth an aid. No man hath seen thee and me abided here. 'Tis scarce spoke and thou art ready. Cling, and hold thee close the babe! So. Canst hold?"

"Yea, Panda, and yet the sick doth weary."

"These arms thy handman offereth. 'Tis but a score of leg's spans."

And they went from out the hut and unto the thick. And Panda looked upon the road's-way and cried:

"Fortune's god hath smiled, for yonder cometh men, men of Bethlehem. But leave thy Panda that he speak unto them and tell much, and naught. The walls have shewed in light and from o'er the hills the sheep-bleat soundeth and market murmur telleth 'tis close. They come, Theia—merchants, for they bear trays of fruits and greens. Three; and one white like to thee."

And these came upon the road's-way and Panda cried out:

"Hail! Hail! Hath thee aid for travelers awearied? Hail! Not thee and thee who babble much and unto me it meaneth naught! Thee, thou white-skin, thee! By the gods! what hath set thee so at wonder?"

And he of the white skin spake in answering: "Hail! Hail! Thou art a fool that thou speakest loud thy tongue. Who art thou?"

And Panda made answer: "But wind's chaff, blown by night to where we know not."

And the one spake: "What need art thou?"

And Panda made question: "The city?"

And the one laughed loud.

"Ha, ha, ha! The city! A babe town! Man, thy name!"

"Panda. What art thou then named?"

"Simeon,—named by fortune so, for Rome hath this heart. Wouldst thou start should I to speak 'Ajax,' the name Rome knoweth me by?"

And Panda stood in wondering, and Simeon said more:

"The city! Ha, ha, ha! The city! The babe town is full, o'er-full of wonders this dawning. Shepherds came with wonder-tidings and told of the star [1] that shewed and trailed a beard like a priest's beard, long and bright. Ha, ha! They searched the highways and byways and sought a babe. A woman, a traveler, and one Joseph, bedded in a manger, and she, named Mary, was with child and delivered there. And they sought and found the babe, and they tell of a vision of bright ones that sang and spake unto them. And they kneeled, and spiced the garments of her who bore the babe and kissed the hem of the swaddling-cloth. And they made obeisance and spake that o'er the sleeping babe and mother a light shewed like unto golden cloth. Ha, ha! Naught, lad, naught but a shepherd's dreaming o'er his flock. For Simeon went unto the manger place and brought fruits and greens that they might eat thereof, and, lad, the mother slept, and babe lay sleeping there upon her arm. And the shepherd's dream fell to naught, for lips, wreathed sweet with smile and mother-rest, was all."

And he spake more, but Panda stopped him.

"Ajax, Ajax, dost thou remember Theia, the King's slave from thy land, Greece?"

And Simeon cried out: "Theia, who danceth like the flames of Apollo's fires! Who hath the wings of Mercury at her ankles bound! Theia! Theia! Panda, the handman of the King's own chosen! Thee? Hath Rome shut from her breast thee, Panda, and Theia? Ajax, cast to pit and legs broken and left to rot—a play for Rome and kings! Rome! Rome, who drieth her breast to her own born! A harlot, who decketh her and leadeth her lovers but to death!

"Ajax, who breathed and loved the breath of Greece, and Theia,

---

[1] Numbers in the text indicate notes in the appendix.

the daughter of his land, and Panda who slaves, a saffron skin, a desert's child—we, the foster children of a harlot who smote the fathers and played at cast and catch of hearts!

"Panda, I swear Ajax shall be a one who beareth a twain of names: 'Simeon' the Jew and 'Ajax' who hath wrestled for Rome's play. Yea, Panda, and Simeon shall be as the name of him unto the Jews, and unto the Roman's the other."

And he started and spake: "Hark! A wail!"

And Panda said: "Yea, Simeon, or Ajax, which e'er ye be, 'tis Theia and her babe, who lie hid deep within the thicket yonder. Theia, the fallen; Theia, the mothered; Theia, who hath drowned within her tears and doth curse the gods of thee and me. Hath thee an aid, man, for such a one?"

"An aid ye seek of one whom thou canst see doth stand awry! A one whom Rome hath blighted and cast forth!"

And Panda cried him loud: "What hath Rome and thee and me, Simeon, to do at such a time? I tell thee 'tis Theia who hath a need of thee and me, and not the tonguing of thy tale and mine."

"Thou tellest me, Panda, that Theia, Theia, the chosen of the gods and kings, is yonder, and babed? Though Simeon doth limp and sag like one smitten, he hath still a heart that knoweth naught of such a blight. Come, and we do seek! Speak thou not unto Theia that 'tis I, Ajax. See! 'tis the beard of me that hideth him and maketh Simeon, the Jew."

And the voice of Theia cried from out the thick: "Panda! Panda! Panda! Faint doth seize! Panda! Panda, come!"

And they went unto her, and Panda spake: "Yea, Theia, yea, and I do for thee and thine at thy bid. See! the merchant man hath offered thee and me an aid. This, this, Theia, is Simeon, a herder and a vineyard's-man."

"Yea, maid, yea, and thou and Panda shalt come unto the house of Simeon and dwell thee within the shadow of the hills. Wait thee and rest here upon these, the mantles of Panda and Simeon, and we then shall go unto the hills and bring forth an ass and thou shalt lay thee upon twigs and branches, bound, and we shall bear thee unto there."

And Theia looked upon his face and spake: "Simeon! Art thou a Jew?"

And Simeon made answer: "Yea, a Jew who hath traveled far and knoweth thy tongue."

And she turned unto Panda and cried out: "Panda, a Jew! A

Jew! Then this is the land of Jews! What hath kept ye that thou shouldst tarry at such a time?"

"The town's word, Theia, the tale of Simeon here. It seemeth that within the walls a wonder did come as the word of shepherds who told of a star and vision and birth of one who was the King's own."

"What! What, Panda! Hast thou and Theia then suffered at the god's trick and hath a word then come before?"

"Nay, Theia, nay. This was the son of one called Mary and a man named Joseph, who traveled. And she was heavy with child and did bring forth within a manger that stood within a shelter place, one not walled. And shepherds came and sought the babe, and kneeled, and they were blinded by the golden light. Ha, ha, ha! But Simeon telleth 'tis but a shepherd's dreaming o'er his flock."

And Theia's eyes shewed bright, and she made word, saying:

"Who, then, is the King's own? Send thee unto them and say he lieth here! See! See! He lieth like a young rose-bloom; deeped the rose tint, yet unbloomed. Yea, yea, and time shall come when a brightness shall show from out the East, and sands shall gleam, and sun shall catch the glittering of the caravan, studded o'er with gold and set with jewels. And at the lead shall one ride upon a camel white as goat's milk, whose eyes shall gleam like rubies, and scarlet shall his robe show. And slaves shall march in rank on either side and wave palms and chant. Yea, yea, yet shall this be!

"And I, Theia, shall rise and unwind the robes of me and cast unto the winds and clothe but with the rose, wove and tied to garments with scented strands of reed; and sweet-steeped oils shall scent mine locks. And I, Theia, shall dance and set the air to dance at such an offering. Then shall Theia bend, and writhe, and flow, and sink, and rise, till it seemeth the sea hath sent forth her siren, and the sea's own life shall Theia show."

And she looked unto the babe and spake: "List thee, thou prince of the lands. I, Theia, swear unto thee it yet shall be!"

And she turned and said unto Panda and Simeon: "Go! go thee! and I shall pour out what thine ears should hear not."

And they went them on their way, and to the sleeping babe spake Theia:

"What had day to show that it broke to light? Such scent! 'Tis camel musk. I see, and yet mine eye hath not yet beheld within the wall.* Long, narrow streets, fly-swarmed, crawled o'er with fruit's-

* Within Bethlehem.

worm. Filthed merchants who peddle rotted greens, and figs the
worms do home within. No man whose legs shew shorn and oiled. No
maiden's flower-decked. The music but a babble. The ass ne'er
decked with rose-wreath for folly play, but prodded with pack. The
gods found play in turning days awry. Theia, Theia, who loved,
who loved afar, and whose flowers were plucked and cast not to her
loved! Theia, Theia, and thou, thou! Ah, Theia should hate thee,
and yet, what doth it mean to hate but the death of love? For every
hate was born of love. So, Hate, list thee!

"Hate is but a love-born, that dieth but leaveth still within the
heart, love. Thou art the flesh of Theia's dance, for she hath loved
and lived but dance. He, he whom Rome holdeth, he hath Theia's
love, though 'twas the King who played the robber of the store.

"Hark thee! Hark thee, thou child of Venus, a Cupid of her
court! They come, they come, to bear the King unto them,—the
shepherds who sought! For who knoweth that they seek not thee and
me to bear back to Rome? Else why, why didst thou and Theia
live?"

And she looked her high and cried out: "Gods, gods, if gods there
be, why doth silence ever answer thee? Gods, who ever hunger and
ne'er do feed them who bear their feasts! Gods who crave the firstborn and blight Rome's chosen youth! Gods, who smile them on, the
flesh of Rome's own rotted at their feet!"

And even as she spake came Panda and Simeon and they had
brought forth the ass. And Theia spake:
"Is it thou, Panda and Simeon? Then it is not afar, the hut?"

And Panda made answer: "Nay, Theia, nay, but 'neath the shade
of yonder hill."

And Theia spake more: "List thee! Say unto Theia that she
shall dwell without the wall, that Rome then shall be not shut away;
for though she knoweth me not 'tis Theia who knoweth her. Yea,
thou hast come and the ass standeth ready. Weak seizeth me. Canst
thou aid?"

And Panda did this thing, saying: "Yea, there, it is so. See,
Theia, the sky, the blue! 'Tis Rome's sky! See the sun! 'Tis
Rome's sun!"

And Theia spake in sorrowing: "Yea, Panda, but yonder walls
are not the walls of Rome."

And Panda said: "Theia, Simeon hath herds, and o'er the hill his
vineyards stand. But see! cloud showeth black and bellows as it
sags. Haste thee the ass, Simeon!"

But Theia looked her unto the coming storm and cried: "Nay! Nay! Stay ye here! Thus doth Theia defy the gods. For each crashing of their bolts shall she hurl a curse! Ha, ha, ha! A paltry blaze to that kindled at this heart! Crash thou! Beat thou! Send thou hail! Send thou thy hot breath, burned with lightning's birth! Hurl thou! Hurl thou, Ajax, thy bolts!"

And Simeon stood him in fearing.

"What! What! Standest thou pallid, Simeon? What! art thou afeared? See! I cast this stone straight unto the gods who hate the givers unto them! What can winds blow but o'er the earth and what snap but twigs? This tree of hate hath rooted past the blow of storm's rage! 'Tis clattering and chattering of gods who laugh at play."

And she turned her to the storm's blast and spake more: "I spat upon thy works, and hate and hate and hate thee! And cast thy beliefs and fears back unto thy hands!

"Gods! Gods! They need the trick lest they fall short of playthings, and thou, thou didst trick! Yet doth Theia win; for hath she not born a King?

"And yet the earth shall know! Yet the earth shall know! And he shall live and die a King! And earth shall know! Hear ye, earth shall know! I scream and defy thee! Earth shall know, yet though the days shall pass and time shall slip it on and on, yet shall earth to know, though thou art sure that thou hast won!

"Hear thee! Hear thee, gods of Rome! Gods of heavens! Gods of earth! Hear ye! Yet shall earth and man know he that was born is King!

"He shall come upon a camel white as goat's milk, and so shall ye know! Ha, ha, ha! Yea, and though Theia is but dust, still shall she win! For list thee, gods, gods, gods! Thy trick shall be thine own undoing; for storm's-lash shall loose the dust of her and she shall float and dance and know he hath come upon a whited camel! And she shall ever blow, and thou canst but blow, and what hath been dust shall ever be dust, and still shall Theia win! Ha, ha, ha!"

And even as she spake the spent storm died in rumbling. And she turned unto Panda and Simeon and said:

"See! hate and curse hath cooled the bolts, and rains but wash. The gods weep! What sort of men art thou that ye stand feared and shaken? See! Theia feareth not. Come! On, then!"

And upon their ways, Panda said unto Theia: "Theia, Rome hath lost a flower and it sorroweth. Wouldst thou deny it sup? The gods shall smite one who curseth and the flower shall wither, so that thou and Panda may bear it not back unto Rome from whence it came."

And Theia made answering: " Panda, list! When the gods do smite, I tell thee Theia shall play with their metal heads like discus! * Yea, and smite their fatted sides with cestus! † Theia yet shall win, for list! she seeketh a god of gods, who setteth o'er the brass of earth."

And they came unto the place where the hut of Simeon stood, and Theia spake:

" This, then, is the hut of Simeon. Ah, Theia loveth the spot, for Simeon's heart hath offered all. Yea, and Theia shall make it to show her loving. The hearth's-stones shall bake from Theia's hand, and though Theia hath danced and played for Rome, Theia's hands shall labor and work for Simeon."

And Panda said: " See ye, Theia, Simeon hath brought a lamb and put so that the babe shall sleep close and warm."

And seeing this thing Theia questioned: " What, Simeon, doth thy lambs bear for thee? Art thou a merchant of thy wares at Bethlehem? "

" Yea, and Bethlehem payeth much for what hath come from out her walls; since Rome hath cast me—nay, thee, forth, thou art welcome to the store of Simeon. Yea, Theia, but hark ye. The man who abideth without the walls hath reason. The hills bear flocks, and sheep are like one unto the other. Seest thou? "

" Yea, yea. Ha, ha, ha! 'Tis Theia who playeth such a game for gods' undoing. Who, who, yea, what man might deem a woman who wailed upon the hills might seek of his flocks? But, Simeon, Theia asketh price. Since we abide one with the other, then I speak, that ye know my heart."

" Name thou the price, Theia. Much worth 'twould be."

" Yea, price. And list! not god's metal. Nay, but thou and Panda shalt go unto Bethlehem with Theia and shew her unto this Mary, who brought forth, within a manger, a king. Hark, and tell to Theia, is this Mary of Rome? "

" Nay, Theia, nay, for shepherds spake of Mary of Galilee, and Joseph, a Nazarene."

" Still Theia doth ask the price."

" Then it shall be. When thou art cleansed and time hath come that thou art strong, then shall we seek within the walls of Bethlehem and bring thee unto the mother and the babe."

* The game of quoits.
† A covering of leather bands for the hands of boxers.

And Theia made question: "This king the shepherds sought, king of what domain is he?"

And Simeon spake in answer: "Tiberius Caesar needeth not to suffer one jealous pang. Nay, Theia, this, the shepherds say, is the King of the Jews."

And Theia looked afar and made word, saying: "Caesar, who cloaketh the kinsmen of the blood, though their robes do steep deep in iniquities; and cutteth off from Rome's lands the offender through the blood of him, and setteth afar Rome's daughter who played a part e'en 'gainst her heart's wishing! Panda, Caesar shall sup a bitter cup. Yea, and at the draining shall find bitterer dregs than he hath e'er dealt.

"What hath a noble of Rome to do with a slave who danceth? Much, and little. Much, till sweets have fallen, like leaves at cold-season; and little, at their falling. 'Tis Theia who would seek this Mary and he who is born the King. Here within this heart hath set a wish that Theia shall see. Thou art sure, Panda, the shepherds sought not him who sleepeth here?"

"Nay, Theia, nay. Rest thee till time doth ripe, and thou shalt seek this Mary and her babe."

And Theia made question: "What city, Simeon, standeth near this babe's town?"

"Jerusalem."

"Hear thou, Panda, Jerusalem of the Jews! A hateful sound it hath! Hath Rome men who rule o'er this city's laws?"

"Yea, a King, Herod."

"Then 'tis Theia who seeketh the court and setteth bitter within the royal cup. The gods strike them bold. 'Tis Theia who wrappeth bitter and hideth smite, and Theia who showeth the gods a wiser way. Simeon, thy pilfer shall fall as naught. For, hark ye! from out the very temples shall the temples' vessels go. Yea, at incense time, when prayer stoppeth the ears and busyeth the lips, then shall Theia smite. Yea, when the King hath supped and slept he shall wake stripped of jewels, and I, Theia, shall bear back unto this very hut the cups of royal fashioning— gold, wrought like to the lion who opeth wide his jaws, and he who suppeth putteth his lips within their ope; and yet like to the deer; cups like as this Theia shall bear unto thee and ye shall know 'tis the smite of Theia."

And Simeon spake: "Nay, Theia, nay, Herod hath favor of one Claudia."

"Ha, ha, ha! What! Think ye, Simeon, that Jerusalem might hold a one who doth equal Rome's favored? Nay. Doth she reek her with scent, then shall Theia seek a scent that sickeneth one who smelleth that of her. Doth she make her locks to shine like ebon's sheen, then Theia shall shower a golden dust o'er the locks of her and deck with purple lilies. Yea, and doth she dance for favor of the King then shall Theia dance, and lo, the dance of Claudia shall seem unto the King but camel's gait. Yea, Theia shall seek the King robed in film, with glowing limbs that shine like morning's stars. White, white shall the film show, and rose-kissed the limbs. Yea, and gold the locks that fall unto the hem like waves of sea the sun hath kissed. Yea, and close, and close, shall Theia hold her arms, and sway and sway, and run, and bound like unto a young kid, until the King hath drunkened upon the sight. And then, and then shall Theia unloose two white doves, tethered one unto the other with rose garlands, and she shall flee, led by them aflutter. And ne'er shall the King to know this, the siren who seeketh him. Yea, and at every coming from out the court shall Theia bear a price that ne'er was given. For list! she doeth this with breast that holdeth not a heart! I hate, I hate, ah!—see, see! The King hath grasped his scepter! Look thou! The babe holdeth Theia's fingers grasped, and hath waked!

"Simeon, what hath touched thy heart? Why weep? Rage but buyeth tears. Thou and Panda shall measure rage and love and hate, that I do deal but what is meet unto them who dealt unto me."

"Theia, Panda would bear thee and the King's own back unto Rome, but Panda feareth, feareth Rome; and here, doth fear thee."

"Ah, Panda, e'en the gods shall fear Theia! Yea, for Theia shall play with them, yea, she shall hang them upon one strand from out her head! Panda, what setteth thee at pity for gods, who dyed thee saffron and cast thee slaved unto a King, who gave thee unto his favored, a living toy? Panda, thou art like one who feasteth much upon a crumb and waileth at o'erfilling. Look! thy gods have set heavy upon Theia's limbs, and stilled her steps. Ah, Panda, it seemeth that Theia, could she but dance, might ease the aching here. Theia hath a coin she yet doth spend, a coin that buyeth bitter for the royal cup. See! these arms that hold the King's own should cast it forth and hold but love— he whom Rome doth hold, he whose limbs shine white as alabaster, blue-veined and oiled, he who smiteth and falleth all whom Rome doth offer, he who knoweth Theia not, but ever at the finish did Theia cast a rose and ever did he to step upon its bloom in token he did see, and fearing lest the King might see. How the heart of Theia fluttered at sight of him who walked like unto the lion, loose-limbed, and bowed most regal, like unto the lion who turned at finish of the feast and sneered. Ah, hark thee, hark thee, Rome! Thou holdest him and the love of Theia! Hark thee, hark thee, Rome! Thou holdest naught save evil 'mid thy nobles, but thou dost hold a noble 'mid thy citizens!"

And Simeon sunk, and Theia cried out: "Panda, what hath seized Simeon?"

And Simeon murmured: "Naught, naught. 'Tis but a faint. I suffer so. Naught. A sup from yonder well shall ease the hurt."

And he went forth unto the well. And Theia spake:

"Panda, list! The hurt of Simeon bathes within the well and washeth it to naught. Where, ah where, is such an well that thou, Panda and Theia, do bathe? Look! A stoned pit! And that the bath? Where marbles pinked the crystal drops and perfumes climbed upon the air, and rose-bloom cradled upon the sheen and danced and rose and fell as plash did send the drops adance! The flowers, the playthings, the lusts of court, did wallow thus; and smoking pots sent incense up that hung and curtained o'er the sight. Theia, Theia shall loose the girdle of her robe and sport within a sheep's track, aye, a stream that washeth Jews! More play for gods! What hath Simeon that we sup?"

"Wait thee, Theia! He cometh. And see! he steppeth slow and knee doth touch the earth at every step. Wait thee, and haste not the coming!"

"Panda, 'tis well the gods did leave thee a tongue. What did e'er spare thee that thou shouldst be the handmaid of thy Theia? Rome drank not the all of thee, and left to Theia one who comforteth.

"What, Panda, brought unto Rome him who sought favor of the Caesar? What drunkened the noble that he did cause the feastings and sports for favor of the kinsman and of all? Panda, why? What did Theia that she should be cast as purse to beggar, a gift to him who coveteth Rome and Caesar?

"Then, Panda, the sands, the camels, the swaying sick, and days and days that Theia knew not her Rome. And then, Panda, and then, back, but to be cast forth. And yet sick, sick she sought the arenas and him; and Panda, Panda, he was not! Simeon, what hast thou?"

"Branch; branch and leaf's-fall, that chill may warm. Aye, I sup. Sit thee at the door's sill, and Theia, stop thy hate and rest, and leave love to fill thy breast. Beneath the hearth's-stone there thou'lt find meat and barley bread. Panda, wouldst thou take this grain and set thee there beside the stones and grind?"

And Theia looked upon these things and spake: "Theia, Theia feasteth upon the barley bread that sheweth husks! Theia tasteth kid, the slave's meat!"

And Simeon cried unto her: "Stop! Stop! List! meat nor yet bread doth make the noble. These Jews, remember, Simeon is of them. Yea, Simeon is of the Jews and seeketh the hills for sheep, and limpeth, yet he curseth not the gods. I tell thee, Theia, hate hath eaten thee. Hark! A woman babed is like to a man who beareth past his carry. Hark ye, Theia! leave Simeon bear the babe and cast it unto Bethlehem that we may war the gods and thou mayest war unburdened."

"Nay! Nay! Nay, Simeon, 'tis Theia who would ne'er to believe this of thee. Nay, Theia shall lay the gods low with one hand loosed! So, thou art a man, indeed! A thief who plyeth trades of kill and treason! Thou wouldst fill thy land with Rome's waste! Come thou, Hate, thy mother mayest hate, but keepeth the hate of her. What sort of man art thou? Thou wouldst, then, that Theia cast her whelp? E'en a wolf would bed its whelp. I flee—ah, but weak sinketh me!"

And Simeon smiled him slow and spake: "See, Panda, her hate hath not a pure metal! There, Theia, rest! And see! Panda hath meal. The meat's smell and browning bread shall hunger thee. Long hath high sun past. See! the storm hath left a frowning at the west. Soon shall dark shut heaven away."

CHAPTER II

And days passed and Theia waxed strong. And they set them out upon a pilgrimage unto Bethlehem. And the " babe town " shewed gray. And as they came within the place, Theia made question:

" Simeon, thinkest thou that Mary hath traveled thence? "

" Nay, for men unto whom the shepherds spake told unto me that Mary was not yet readied for the journey unto Jerusalem. Nay, Theia, for at the eighth day she shall bear the babe and doves * unto the temple, and thou dost know 'tis but the third watch and day for thee. Nay, Mary abideth still within Bethlehem."

" Panda, look thou! Canst thou see, as doth Theia, the filth? And see! the beards and robes are not the robes and beards of Rome."

And behold, as they went them on their way unto the market's place Theia cried out:

" Panda, it is she—Mary, the undoer of thy Theia! Look! 'Neath the fig tree sitteth she! The light! The gold light! Look, 'tis there, 'tis there! Seest thou, Panda? The babe, the babe stirreth. Yea, fear clutcheth Theia! Fear seizeth Theia! 'Tis so. 'Tis so. Yea, Panda, see! she seeth not thee nor Theia nor yet Simeon! But look thou! And she, too, hath much to bear. And look! The light! The peace! Ah, she hath that that Theia was robbed of—love, much love.

" She sitteth regal. She hath born a king of citizens! And Theia hath born a king of nobles. Aye, and earth hath evil 'mid her nobles and nobles 'mid her citizens. Yea, and the noble hath much to envy of the King of Citizens, for the kingdom of him is earth, and no man sitteth o'er.

" Yea, and he who sitteth nobled sitteth upon a seat that tottereth and lo, the wolves of earth await the leavings of his feasts and lands, and e'en do sit and howl at either side of his very throne!

" Simeon, she is but a youth-bud! Yea, fear toucheth Theia, and chill creepeth o'er. What, what doth Theia dream? For like a dreaming cometh that that maketh fear. I tell thee, Panda, and thee, Simeon, yonder Mary and Theia trod upon a path that leadeth unto sorrow. Sorrows! Tears of them shall wash the earth and e'en the

* Luke 2:24.

17

ages! Yea, and yet the gods of her are not the gods of Theia. Ah, did
Theia leave this fearing riot loosed, she then would clasp the Hate and
flee. Yea, and yet what stayeth her?

"Mary hath born love and earth shall pay with hate. Yea, and
Theia hath born hate and earth shall offer back but hate. Hate, that
suffered at the hands of earth; the gift of earth unto the mother. Mary
hath born from love a hate. Yea, and Theia hath born of hate, hate.
For earth shall follow not with loving the bearing of this King of
Citizens. Nay, for Jews glut o'er a throne, and doth Mary to claim the
right of her own bearing, then falleth wrath. Yea, but hark! the
citizens of earth shall choose their king, and though the Jews do hate,
the earth yet shall love and claim its own! Yea, and Theia, doth she to
claim the rights of her own born, doth loose the wolves of Rome, and
bared bones would be the gift Rome left to her. Ah, sick, sick hath
seized Theia; for as at a dream's birth showeth a vision, and it telleth
'tis earth that giveth unto Theia such bared bones and hate through
ages! And yet, I swear, He shall come upon a camel white as goat's
milk, and so shall she to know the King hath sought his own. Yea, and
list thee, Hate! I lift thee up unto the God that sitteth o'er the brass
that grinneth senselessly, an offering that I do give unto Him, doth this
to come! Unto the very path's end doth Theia trod with her yonder.

"Nay, nay, 'tis not meet that Theia should speak with her! Nay,
Hate should ne'er look unto the face of Love. And yet, at path's end
Hate and Love do meet!

"Mary! Mary! Mary! Sorrow croucheth at thy throne! And
Hate dieth at thy feet! Ah, Mary, Mary, wouldst thou leave the Hate
to die without thy smile? Cast thou one bloom upon his bier. The
youth of thy days shine bright with loving, and Theia's darked with hate.
And dark shall cloud thy season's ripe! Ah, unto Him whom I do seek I
cry! Leave bright to creep unto the days of Theia that she knoweth
Thee by the token, the whited camel that cometh from out the
East!

"See, see, the light! Yonder lieth the King! Simeon, Panda, what
gods show such unto their people? No king hath borrowed of the gods
a heaven's robe of bright. This babe is King! Yea, and the regal robe
of Him shall gleam scarlet with earth's blood. Yea, and the crown He
weareth shall be jeweled with the hearts of men! Simeon, Simeon, Theia
hath been ever a one who did read the dreams of royal heads. More
doth she tell. The blood she hath born shall stain the ages! Yea, and
when the earth hath supped up and man hath forgot, then shall the drops
spring forth like tongues of fire and burn through the past unto the day!

Yea, and the dusts of Theia shall blind the gods who grin o'er Rome, and know the token hath been!'"

And they listed to her words, and Simeon spake:

" Panda, what manner of woman hath spoken that which doth sound as sorceress' chant?"

"Yea, Simeon, yea. Look! she standeth and drinketh of the sight! Who said unto her this was Mary? Dost thou see such an light as she sayeth?"

" Nay, nay. Panda, she dreameth o'ermuch. Hush!"

And Theia spake: "Hark, Simeon, leave thou to Theia the fruit thou bearest unto the market's place. Leave it Theia, that she doth offer unto her. For Theia's lips seem locked, and yet Theia would speak unto Mary. Hold thou the Hate, and wait thee. See! the grape hath moon's kiss upon its blue. So hath Theia's heart softed. A wine setteth this blood leaping up from Theia's heart that seemeth like love's first stirring. Hate withereth like husks and falleth but to leave the fruit."

And she went up unto Mary, and said: " Ah, Mary, Mary, what god is thine? Hath the whited camel showed to thee? Hath He come from out the East? Hath He kissed thy lips and left the god's kiss there? Yea, yea, thou hast found Him that Theia doth seek! This, this, thy babe, the kiss of thy god? See! Theia offereth thee of fruits."

And Mary harked and smiled but made no word. And Theia cried aloud: " Ah, ah, the gods do win! She hath not a lip * that mayest tell unto Theia of the God she hath found! I, Theia, do bend me low and kiss thy hem and pledge that Theia seeketh the God of thee who showeth unto her through thee. Upon His fires Theia shall cast her hate-born.

" Gods! Gods! Grinning gods! Grin on! For such smile as setteth here shall soothe the earth and stop thy claim. Unto thy smile of love-born doth Theia kneel. Ah! Ah! Ah! The light! The light! See, it batheth Theia! Simeon! Simeon! Panda! Help! 'Tis Theia who falleth prisoner to one smile! Were she to smile her on, then Theia would fall enchained upon a strand of golden smiles. Mary, thou and Theia yet shalt kneel beside the same throne! Upon thy path of loving thou shalt seek this throne. Yea, and Theia shall seek upon her path of hate. And yet, and yet, thou and Theia shall meet to mingle tears! Mary, Mary, the wolves of earth shall hound thee! And thy armor but a smile! Yea, and Theia shall war with hate, and yet thou and Theia shall meet, unarmed! Yea, Simeon, yea, Panda, Theia cometh."

And Panda spake: " Hath she spoken unto thee, Theia?"

---

* Meaning that Mary did not know the tongue of Theia.

And Simeon made question: " Hath she spoken with thee of Him who was born? For Theia, Bethlehem murmureth much."

And Theia said in answering: " Spake? Yea, spake. Yea, and nay. Yea unto Theia's heart, and nay unto Theia's ears."

And Simeon made that he go unto the market's place. But Theia held him.

" Nay, Simeon, not unto the market's place! Nay, unto the hills. The Hate sleepeth. Ah, that Theia might shed her tears like torrent's-sweep and wash the Hate and bathe yon Love. Simeon, what gods set o'er the Jews? Who spake that which the shepherds brought forth? What name doth such a god bear? "

" Theia, thou art seeking of the Jews—Jews thou hatest."

" Simeon, this Mary, what say ye, is Mary of the Jews? "

" Yea."

" And she goeth unto Jerusalem to offer up a fire? "

" Nay, Theia, thou hatest Jews; then why seek of Jews their god? "

" Speak, Simeon! Speak thou this god."

" Jehovah; God o'er all the Jews and all the earth. For hark thee, Theia, these Jews have scripts no man hath heard. This shepherd's tale hath sprung from script. Yea, and Jews set o'er all. Yea, and Theia, this God hath much of script that earth hath yielded up. Yea, even stone hath born it up. Yea, Theia, yea, and yet thou hatest Jews! "

" So? So? Time hath yielded up of this Jehovah? Simeon, Panda, Theia hath spoke the gods of Rome were but the streaming tongues of priests. Thou tellest the shepherd's tale grew from out the scripts. What, Simeon, meanest thou? "

" Theia, thou art seeking more of Jews! The tale is of a promised King, the seed of David. The King of Jews who should come, and star * should tell. Yea, and yet these shepherds, Theia, were not wise men, and script held promise of wise men who come from out the East.

" Yea, Theia, but this tale of wise men sprung from one who abideth in the temples of Jerusalem; a woman, ripe in years, who fasteth and prayeth much.† She hath a sooth-chant ‡ and waiteth until the King shall be born and brought to the temple for circumcision, where she shall speak it out before the high priests: ' This is He who is born King of the Jews.'

---

* Possibly based upon Numbers 24: 17.   † Anna. Luke 2: 36.
‡ A song of prophecy.

"Shepherds who went unto Jerusalem for the feasts of the Passover and feastings and sacrificings heard much of this. So, Theia, He hath been born, and shepherds come, but still the seeress hath spoken of wise men who shall seek."

And Theia made word, saying: "Wait, wait, and time telleth. Simeon, Simeon, what hath the earth a need of wise men? Theia telleth this is He. Come unto the hills that Theia layeth her upon their breasts and rests. How, Simeon, how cometh it that Jews claim such a God? Thinkest thou, He, Jehovah,² hateth Rome?"

And she spake in the chant of the see-woman: *

"Hark! Hark! Theia seeth more! He smiteth Rome! And layeth her as a wanton painted with blood and still a-smile in death! She tricketh him, and lo, he leadeth her on! Yea, and drowneth her within the pool of her own beauty! She shall drink from out this pool till drunk, and drown her drunkened.

"Go thee, Simeon and Panda, unto the vineyards where fruits await thy plucking. Theia would cast this robe she weareth this day and clothe within the smile of Mary, to rest, to rest! Theia would sit beneath the trees and clasp the Hate and dream a smile like Mary's."

And they went forth, and Theia spake unto the babe:

"List thee, list thee, Hate! He shall come upon a whited camel from out the East. Yea, it shall be so! He shall come. Yea, Hate, and Theia, thy mother, shall dance to meet the caravan. Yea, at the lead shall be the whited camel.

"Rome hath claimed for her own the love of Theia. Yea, Rome hath killed the flesh of Theia's love. What, what, by what right do gods and Rome claim that which Rome and gods can ne'er repay—life? For gods do shew no returning of them whom they do claim, and Rome decketh o'er the spot and seeketh new loves. This, the God of Theia, though she knoweth Him not, shall send the token, yea, the whited camel."

And Panda came, and Theia spake: "What! is it thou, Panda? Art come to hark unto thy Theia's tears and words of hating?"

"Nay, Theia, nay. Panda feareth that thou who makest bittered cups may drink from out the bitter and slay thyself. Simeon hath labored 'mid the fields and wearied much. Come! See! the brands glow and chill falleth without."

"Chill? Chill, Panda? The chill that filleth Theia's heart no fire may warm. Hate, the hate-born, should be the comforter, but lo, he but chilleth more; for Theia seeth much and knoweth hate shall fol-

* A seer, a prophetess.

low hate unto the end. Dreams shall fill with hate and dark the night's fair hours."

And they went upon their way unto the hut. And they come unto Simeon asleep, and Theia spake low:

"See! See! Simeon hath fallen to dream here while thou and Theia speak of hate and dreams. Panda, look thou! The moon showeth that that setteth Theia's fancy to riot. See! Simeon, whose beard hangeth black, looketh as a marble there. Panda, Panda, look! Theia dreams of one who walketh like a lion, loose limbed, and turns to sneer at finish of the feast! Look! Look! Panda, there upon the lips of Simeon there is such a sneer! Panda, Panda, the gods did seek me out e'en here without the walls of Bethlehem! Panda, hath Rome done this thing? Is he yonder, sleeping, he whom Theia loveth?"

And Panda looked afar and made no word. And Theia spake:

"Yea, this, this, Theia sayeth, is the work of Rome and Rome's gods. Panda, thou, and Simeon, Simeon who houseth 'mid the Jews and denyeth Rome, and Theia, who hath drunk from Rome's royal cups, shall seek within the walls of Bethlehem; for the Jew's god dwelleth not without the walls."

And she beat her hands one upon the other and cried out:

"It is he! It is he! Jehovah, it is he; he whom Rome hath smitten; he who holdeth Theia's heart! Panda, though he hath suffered much in flesh, Theia is smitten deeper far at heart.

"Theia, Theia, dragged amid the mires of earth and cast and supped; cast unto Rome's own and supped by Rome; she lieth stripped and broken like the blooms that marked the feast and fell, a foot-cloth for the drunkened. Hark thee, Panda! 'tis Theia who loveth much. The Theia who holdeth hate, for hate hath been her gift, doth flutter up from out the filth and rise like white mist of the early morn that flees the sordid earth. Yea, and Panda, this, the white-mist Theia, is the Theia of him who sleepeth yonder.

"Rome, and gods of Rome, shall fall into the hands of them she hath cast to earth, broken vessels of the feasting! This God, Jehovah, shall build back the break and offer unto earth and Rome a cup of bitters; yea, offer unto Rome the cup she broke at ribaldry. And from out Rome's nobles shall one, the hate-born, be set up through ages, the puppet for earth's mockery. Yea, and though ages roll them o'er to blot the stain, it still shall stand; for but Theia holdeth power. And time and time shall pass, and when it ripeth, then shall Theia wipe away the crimson brand! Yea, and hark, Panda! when the time is ripe, the earth shall stand full, yea, full of crime, and crimson shall run and bathe her sides.

And it shall be that Theia, then, shall reach through time and ages and wipe the stain away.* Yea, Panda, and Theia's words, spoken here without the walls of Bethlehem, shall harken unto this time and comforting shall fall to crimed; yea, and crimson shall dry.

" Yea, and earth's men shall speak much of this, and Theia's dust shall dance before the tabernacles and stop the tongues of them. Theia shall wring from earth's heart the every drop of Rome's wrong-shed blood.

" Simeon hideth, behind a beard and name, Rome's man, a borrowed citizen of Greece, the land of Theia! Rome named this man 'Ajax the Defier!' Yea, Ajax! Rome bowed her noble head to the strength of him, and plied and plied until the snapping of his legs! What gods, Panda, stand them a party to such? There, I tell thee, Panda, is a one, a God, who holdeth dear the broken of the earth, and 'tis He whom Theia seeketh; for He setteth right the broken.

" Say ye not to Ajax Theia knoweth him. Think ye, Panda, Theia would tear the heart of him out and play with its throbbing as hath Rome? Nay, nay. Love is but a cloak that decketh its wearer. Then 'tis Theia's love she casteth o'er him who sleepeth yonder as a cloak and offereth it as gift, without the thank.

" See, Panda, the Hate sleepeth. Yea, much doth babe sleep. Yea, this Hate sleepeth that he knoweth not the day. Wake him not. Nor him yonder. I cast me here upon the straw and wrap me in thy mantle. 'Tis right and meet; the noble's throne is builded but of straw."

* Apparently referring to the present time and this book.

CHAPTER III

AND it was night and dark. And storms arose, and lightnings licked the skies with fiery tongues. And waters washed the hills. Then did storm break and still fell o'er and about Bethlehem. Sheep, storm-lost, bleated, where, out upon the hills, they lost them. And Simeon slept, and waked with crashing, and sought the hills. And brought back unto the hut sheep of Simeon, and sheep of men. And he met upon his way a man, a fisher, one Peter, who offered of fish ³ that he might eat of lamb's meat. And Peter spake of the casting of the morn, and dragged a net and leaned upon a staff.

And Simeon said unto him: " How have ye come unto Bethlehem? "

And Peter answered: " Much word hath come from out the walls of Bethlehem. Anna of Jerusalem hath had visions that she sayeth come from scripts; and sayeth within Bethlehem the Christ is born. And Bethlehem murmureth much 'mong her people. The fishermen sent me unto her that I bear back that which she sayeth."

And Simeon made much of word and told unto Peter of the manger child, and Mary, and much he had heard within the market's place of Mary who was espoused to Joseph, and Joseph found she was with child before the coming of her unto him. And how this Joseph thought to put her away privily that the world know not of the shame of her, and how a vision showed, and he arose and took her unto himself and spake that he was the husbandman of her. For he was a good man and just.

And market men laughed loud at this. And Joseph walked among them at the market's place, and they did back their thumbs and shrug. And Mary followed, and o'er the face of her a light, for she saw not the earth, but looked afar.

And Peter marveled and made him on his way. And Simeon sought the hut with fish. Unto the door he stepped and halted there, and his eyes flowed loving from out their bright, and he did raise his hand toward Rome and spake:

" Rome, Rome, thou hast cast her from thee unto me. Where, then, is thy victory? "

And the babe, Hate, wailed.

From out the ash did Simeon draw forth coals, and place upon the glowing the fish he had cleansed, that Theia and Panda, who were waked, might eat thereof.

"Hath storm washed night away, Simeon?"

"Yea, Theia, and Panda hath waked and maketh ready trays that we bear unto Bethlehem. The grape hath dried and merchants make much price for such. Do ye go with us into the city?"

"Nay, nay, Simeon, should Theia seek Bethlehem this day she could hate not, for Mary bideth there. Theia seeketh Jerusalem with Panda at a later time. Yea, but Theia stayeth her amid the hills till Mary seeketh Jerusalem, for Theia would seek the temples with her that she heareth that which the scripts have promised.

"What! hast thou fish? Where, Simeon, hath fish found thee and me? Did rains then throw fish to earth?"

"Nay, Theia. Peter, a fisherman, sought Bethlehem at this morn with fish for the market's place, and made much of lamb, and hungered for lamb's meat, and offered fish for lamb."

"Then Theia eateth the sides of Dagon, and thus a god is undone. Simeon, tell of Jerusalem—the palaces, the temples, the streets, the men, the maids."

"Jerusalem hath temples. Yea, and priests that tell much that e'en they know not. Yea, and Theia, wert thou to ask Simeon of all Jerusalem what he held best, 'twould be Simeon who would say to thee the pool wherein at times the angels trouble the waters * and the lame and sick seek and are healed. Yea, Theia, Simeon would seek this pool, but Simeon limpeth much, and Simeon's faith limpeth, too."

"Simeon! Thou of the Jews, who claim the God, Jehovah, the God whom Mary knoweth! How, Simeon, how hath thy faith shrunk! Thou, thou Jew, speak and defend thy God! The gods of Theia have fallen to earth like hail and melted to dust. Build thou a pedestal of marbles pure and carve thee deep the word ' Jehovah,' and set thee up within the public places that He setteth thereon, that man may see. Yea, it shall be of stone, the pedestal, and builded up through ages. And the men of earth shall know 'tis the foundation of Him, Jehovah. And yet Theia seeth more, for sleeping 'bout the pedestal are babes. Then this is the God, for babes know Him. This Theia sayeth of the God who knoweth her not, though she doth seek Him out. Speak, speak, Simeon! He is thy God? Speak to Theia it is so, that we may know one the other's heart."

"Yea, Theia, I, Simeon, who know the gods the earth holds 'mong her men, do know but one, Jehovah."

* The pool of Bethesda. John 5:2.

" This, then, is the God of thee, Simeon? "

" Yea, yea, thrice yea, Theia."

" Simeon, what keepeth Theia from out Bethlehem? She hungereth much to go within the walls,' and yet feareth that she knoweth not."

" 'Tis but an evil dream, Theia. Thou hast left thy fancy rove and it hath led thee unto a where I know not. List! Panda hath the trays laden and o'erlaid of leaves that the winged hosts molest not the fruit. Come, Theia! Thy babe slumbereth, and we shall bring forth the ass and ye shall come with Simeon unto Bethlehem. Within the walls abideth a man and his household who knoweth Simeon and knoweth what the earth hath not yet learned—to keep silence. Unto Ezekiel and Rhea shall we then go and Rhea, who hath a heart that opeth as the heavens, shall leave thee, Theia, the storm-cloud, rove therein and spend thee till thou art pured and cleansed of thy hate. Yea, Theia, Rhea knoweth not thy tongue, and yet she speaketh all the tongues of earth, for she knoweth hearts."

" Then shall Theia seek this Rhea. Hath she a face of beauty, Simeon? "

" Nay, Theia, she is broad and deep, and comforteth much, like mothers comfort babes, them who seek, as thee. Panda, what causeth thine eyes to follow Simeon like one who loveth much and sorroweth deep? "

" Simeon, thou hast struck the reedbough and it telleth thee the marshes stand near. So, Panda standeth feasting much on dreams of days; and dreams pass swiftly, but to eat the heart and leave thee hungered more. They fill not the days but stride 'mid night. Panda, then, strides the night 'mid days, and the eye of Panda showeth."

And Simeon smiled and spake: " Should dreams, Panda, grieve thee, then wake. See! Simeon, laughs at dreaming. Simeon loveth waking and striveth but the day since the coming of Theia, and thou, Panda. What, Panda and Theia, might waking bring to thee and me? Let dreams fill the waking, since waking I do sleep, and sleeping I do wake. This, then, is a fancy's trap for thee! "

And Panda looked afar and made answering: " Simeon, thou speakest much and tellest little. Yea, since Rome teacheth then 'tis Rome's child who doth put the learning to the day."

" What, Panda, what meanest thou? Thou of Rome beareth unto Bethlehem but of Rome and do burden them of Bethlehem with Rome's learning. What hath Simeon to do with Rome? Panda, hath the dreaming loosed thy tongue? "

"Simeon, dreams but show a wry of naught, and lead not the heart to speak unto the day."

"Then go, Panda, and bring unto the hut the ass, for Theia goeth unto Bethlehem. Simeon shall seek the hill's shelter where sheep stand hid awaiting him that they do eat of the drying greens of earth. Within the caves of valleys stand they. Then at a later time shall Simeon bring unto Bethlehem a sheep slain, and sell unto the market's place, and he who buyeth of the meat thereof shall be the shepherd of the sheep, verily. For Simeon slayeth when sheep stand not for slaughter, but for wool. Yea, and Simeon suppeth with this shepherd at the eve. For Simeon hath Jew's learning. From out the priest's beard he plucketh hair to weave a sling with which to stone the people."

And Theia, who listed her, spake: "Simeon, thou sayeth this of thy God! Then Theia knoweth thee not. Theia would believe Simeon hath spoken but that the ears of them who list be filled. Unto Bethlehem thou shalt bear thy trays and Theia shalt seek the hills and loose the sheep the storm hath cast unto thee. Pilfer not such, for what mean sheep to gods? Strike thee rather deeper 'mong the nobled who think the gods stand within the hands of them. Theia shall strike and pilfer, but Theia doth ever stand her before this God, Jehovah, as one who smiteth but that He shall be the God of gods. Yea, she shall undo the Kings that He sitteth o'er."

Then did they to set them upon their ways unto Bethlehem. And the babe, Hate, slumbered deep. And they went up unto the house of Ezekiel, and Rhea came forth in greeting, and though the tongue of her spake not unto them, the smile of her spake loudly. And she took up the babe, Hate, and held him close unto the bosom of her, and he smiled. And Theia, the mother, marveled much. And unto the words of wooing of Rhea his lips moved and smiles stopped the wailing. For babes know not of tongues. And Theia who hated learned much that tongues tell not.

Then Simeon spake the words of the household man and told of Theia who abided with him and Panda, a man of Rome, a slave, who awaited the hand of Theia.

And these, the people of Bethlehem, spake among themselves that Bethlehem was indeed a place for travelers, for still abided there Joseph and Mary and their babe. And they told unto Simeon that while Mary sat without the living place, came forth the fowls of the air and sang them joyous. And she would reach forth her hand and lo, they would eat therefrom, though some were of the highest air. And she plucked flowers and dipped them within the well and held forth their cups filled with the waters of the well, and the birds drank therefrom. And they spake of her more, and said she stripped the flowers when they had drunk, and kissed the petals as they fell. And these were the flowers of the fields that grew late.

And Simeon spake and told unto Theia this, and Theia stopped him that she might speak what she did see.

"Yea, yea, and the late flowers and even the leaves of the trees shall blush ever through the ages at this time, blush for the kiss of her and the blood of Him. Yea, and when they drop, the memory of this shall set them blooming o'er the stalk that bore the leaves. Look thou! Theia kisseth this, a broken bough that showeth not life, and when men see the leaves and blooms forsaking of the boughs, then shall man know 'tis the kiss of Hate. Ah, Simeon, yea. And still Theia is undone by Mary, for o'er the stalks Hate hath kissed, moss and vines shall creep to hide the Hate."

And Rhea listed * and marveled that Theia spake like one who walked 'mid dream, and fell afeared and shrunk, and held close the babe and was loth to give unto Theia him who slept. And she touched the locks of Theia as one who toucheth fire. And Simeon spake unto them and said:

"Theia, this woman, hath much sorrow, for nobles put her from the lands of her. She suppeth bitters and speaketh bitters, yet I, Simeon, say unto thee, she hath hid the Theia thou shouldst know."

And Rhea oped her arms and took Theia and her babe therein. Unto Simeon she spake that they should come much unto her. And they went on their ways unto the market's place and bought of grain and cloth and fruits, and shoes of skins, for the feet of Theia were bared, but sandaled of grass. And rough cloth they made purchase of, that she might be as the people of Bethlehem and not as the nobles. There within the market's place did Simeon seek men who bought wool. And Panda and Theia waited him.

And the market's men wondered at her whose locks were gold, and drew them nigh and made words unto her. And she shrunk and clasped the Hate close, and they spake:

"This is a woman who looseth her girdle. Bethlehem holdeth much of these women."

And Theia knew not of the words of them and looked afar. And the locks of her fell 'bout her burning face, and over, like to a golden

* Listened. The archaic "list" is used for "listen" throughout the story.

shower; and the sun shone forth upon the gold, and lo, a gold light sprang up!

Then did they stop their tongues, for word that fell not to her * lacked much of spice. But one stood him near and taunted much, and parted the locks to see what they hid. But the eyes of her were shut and tears blinded, and her lips moved and she spake:

"Yea, from out the East it shall come; aye and the whited camel at the lead. It shall be so! Yea, Hate, it shall be so!"

Then came Simeon from out the market's men and listed unto the words of him who taunted, and stepped unto the place where he stood and made word.

And Theia harked not, but, wrapped within the locks that hung close, murmured on.

And Simeon, though he stood awry and stooped, reached forth and smote him who spake, and lo, the power of his smite did lay him low, to wallow 'mid mire. And Panda, who knew not the tongue of the molester, waked to wrath and followed with smites. And the word of Simeon waxed loud and rage shook him. And lo, the arms of him swelled in power, and he plucked forth a metal bar and bent it o'er his chest.

Then did the market's men draw nigh to look upon this man who stood upon withered legs and whose arms were the arms of the mighty.

And Theia oped her eyes and crimson bathed her cheek, and lights broke from out her eyes, and she made motion that she cast a flower, and lo, Simeon did set his heel upon a spot! And they looked one unto the other. And the market's men cast money and stopped their tongues.

And Simeon and Panda and Theia sought the roadways unto the hills. And they spake among themselves that these were the men who made merry of Joseph and she who bore the King. And Simeon spake that Mary, Bethlehem told, would seek the city, Jerusalem, at not the eighth day but upon the fulfilment of the cleansing, according to the laws for one who bore a man child. And this was forty days.

And Simeon bore much that men had told of Anna who abided in the temples and spake that she dreampt o'er the scripts and told that which she did dream as that of the scripts.

"For she sayeth, Theia, she hath a vision, and the priests hear much word."

"Simeon, what careth Theia for priests or this? Hath Bethlehem not made much sorrowing for Theia, and thinkest thou that Theia

* Word not understood by her.

seeketh Bethlehem once more? Nay, Simeon; Theia seeketh Jerusalem, but not the temples until the coming of Mary at the forty days. Theia tarrieth not without this Bethlehem, but seeketh Herod. Is this man a one who loveth much merry?"

"Not so, Theia. Herod lieth smitten sorely. For they of him whom he hath bathed in blood, he lieth so bathed."

"What, what, Simeon, what! Hark, Panda! Rome's hands, like snakes, creep 'mid these hills and befoul. Still would Theia seek Herod, that the last rest of him be as a fire's pit."

This they spake upon the hill's-way unto the hut.

And they came them unto it and did alight and go within to cast the buying of the market's place. And Panda brought forth the table of skin and they sat and reclined unto it.

And Theia suckled the babe at the breast of hate, that it wax stronger of hate. Then did she cry out unto Simeon:

"Simeon, this God, Jehovah, is long coming! At the morrow's come we set forth unto Jerusalem."

Then made they packs of skins, and Theia put therein linen, and skins, soft and shorn of wool, and bleached, that she would wear o'er the linen. And she brought forth the robe of mists, the white wool, thin, that hung soft and like clouds, the curling wool scarce held together. She brought forth the armlets of copper, set of jades, and ankle rings unto the scores. These Theia packed within skins, and waited morn.

CHAPTER IV

AND when the time had come, Panda and Simeon brought fresh
asses, packed with meats and dried fruits, that they might eat thereof
upon this journey unto Jerusalem. And they waited Theia, who spake
unto them and asked that they might go unto Bethlehem upon their way
and see the living place of this Mary.

(And this was the time that Theia waited for the God, Jehovah,
whom she knew not. But He sat upon the ass she rode unto Jerusalem
and followed them upon their way.)

And when Bethlehem was reached it was young day. And they came
unto a well and lo, one drew waters therefrom, and it was Mary. And
Theia watched her long from afar. And Mary cast back a stream unto
the well and listed her unto its laugh. Then sat she the water pitcher
upon her shoulder and drew her mantle close and walked most regal
unto the living place. And Theia spake:

" Simeon, seest thou this Mary and the casting of the waters back
unto the well? Hark ye! so shall Mary cast back that that she holdeth
most dear, unto the earth. Theia filleth the eyes of her upon this
Mary at her happiest hour, for when Theia and Mary meet upon this
path once more, Mary's tears and Mary's sighs and Theia's tears and
Theia's sighs shall men weigh. And there shall be enough of tears to
wash the heart of earth. And man shall weigh those of Mary, and leave
the sighing to dry those of Theia.

" Yea, but He cometh, Hate, He cometh. Thy mother, Theia,
sayeth He cometh from out the East."

Then stoned paths of mountains they set upon, and cooled beneath
the purpled trees where dark of thick leaves clustered deep. And
sought the pools, and journeyed on unto the walls of Jerusalem.

At the early hours of the day they came unto the wall where beggars
slept and dogs lay close unto their men.

And one whose hands showed swelled held forth in whining that they
cast alms. And Theia's hand did tremble, and she shut out the sight.

Then on within the walls and unto the templed place. And out
from the templed place crept incense smoke and the voice of priests

31

who chanted within the inner places. And Theia made much of the city, and asked of Simeon:

"Is this place the palace of Herod?"

"Nay, this, Theia, is the palace of Jehovah."

Then did Theia unloose the girdle that binded her mantle and spake unto Simeon: "Simeon, take thou this and cast unto the fires of Jehovah."

"This, Theia, is not the time for such. Nay, see! upon the temple's steps the merchants hover with wares. Hark unto the voices, and list thou unto the chanting of the priests. Panda, see! Theia hath love for Jerusalem, and hate for Jews!"

"Simeon, thou hast spoke a folly. Theia loveth not Jerusalem. Nay, but Jerusalem is the cup wherein Theia maketh bitters for the King. On, Simeon, on unto Herod's place, that thou shalt find a one who knoweth Theia's tongue. Claudia—seek out this Claudia! Theia would see her dance. Up unto the slave's place take thou Theia and Panda, for think ye the King careth that one should seek the slaves?

"See, Simeon! thou shalt take Theia as a sooth's-woman * unto Claudia. Yea, and Theia shall tell unto the Claudia much that shall set the women of the court at words. She shall coax this Claudia with fondle-words, until she danceth with joy. Then shall Theia beg that she dance for price. Simeon, no noble hath such a head as Theia's! For women slaves fear not a one babed. See! Theia bindeth her locks, so. And dust shall hide Theia's face. See! dust she spreadeth o'er. Panda, go thou and seek a staff; Simeon needeth that of him. Seek thou one without the walls, that no man see thee."

And Panda went him unto the outer wall and came forth staffed unto Theia, who took up the staff and went with Simeon unto the palace gates. There they begged alms, and Simeon set him aside the gates and Theia went within.

And the step of her fell regal; and she strode with head high and looked unto the slaves who lined the palace steps and waved palm branches. Black shone they against the white marble of the pillars. And blooms strewed o'er the stepping places, and fountains played that sent up sickening scent.

And unto the slaves' place strode she and stopped, for there upon the couches lay they, the King's chosen. Wide and fatted much; women whose fingers were dipped in saffron and whose locks dripped sweet oils. And they played with fans of feather that sent up winds of sweets.

* A fortune-teller.

And the flesh of them seemed ripe and o'er the riping. Yea, and the feet of them seemed o'er small to bear them up.

"Hate, Hate," Theia murmured, "this is the King's own chosen! This, the slaves' place, holdeth Claudia, the King's dance-woman. Which then is she? For none who wallow here might dance, save shake the fat of her!"

Then did the women of the place wake from out the sweet drunk of them, and spake one unto the other of her who sought. And Theia knew the tongue, and stooped and whined for alms. Then spake she:

"O daughter of the morn, who hath the trod of the antelope, and yet the wing of the fowls of air! From out the city cometh thy hand-woman that she tell thee of thy love.

"What noble hath 'mong his slaves such an one? O thou daughter of the morn, whose beauty drunketh the King's nobles. Unto her I speak!"

Then did Claudia arise and answer: "I, I, Claudia, the dance-woman of Herod, am his chosen. Yea, the daughter of the morn, for seeth thou such among his women here? The King feasteth upon Claudia's dance when his hunger beareth not the eating of flesh."

And Theia murmured her: "Yea, yea, and feasting upon thy dance he eateth much of flesh! Yea, yea, thou, thou, the daughter of the morn, whose curving looketh like unto the moon! Theia shall set thee a pace!"

Then unto Claudia spake she: "A goddess of the East art thou! If thou wouldst know thy dream's reading, go unto the slaves there and bid they bring forth a goblet that I drink therefrom, and thou. Then shall I dream dreams and see sees."

And Claudia brought forth wine, and Theia drank therefrom, and lo, the tongue of her was loosed, and in the see-chant * she spake unto Claudia:

"O woe to thee, thou daughter of Venus! For from out a city place shall come one who floateth like unto a dove and skimmeth like unto a swallow. Yea, and thou shalt kneel when she doth rise, for she eateth of fruits and leaveth meats, and suppeth wines and toucheth not honey's syrup, so that the teeth of her show like ivory. And see thou, thine show snagged! And the arms of her shall glint like alabaster, and thine art saffroned! The scent of her shall be like the perfumes of the summer's morn, and thine scentest like to camel musk! Yea, yea, and thou shalt go before the King and dance, and this one shall come and thy noble lord shall fall at the feet of her!"

* The monotone once affected by fortune-tellers.

And Claudia waxed wrathed and sought the King; and Theia followed her. Then did Claudia call forth slaves who made musics upon loud noised reeds and skins. And she stepped before the couch of Herod⁵ who lay sick, for this man was deep in taint of sin, and the limbs of him would bear him not. Yet the eyes of Herod shone lustful, and the hand of Herod shook, and he drank much and wallowed. And his beard was wet with many wettings that knew no washing away. Yea, and the locks of him had dropped in places from out his head. Yea, and the nails of his hands were broken and yellowed and sored about. And Claudia smiled upon this man and swayed her form and stepped like one aged.

Then did Theia set the lips of her, and cast the rough mantle that cloaked the wool robe, and lay the Hate and staff beneath the mantle at the pillar's side, and stripped the feet of her of the skin shoes, and caught up blooms and bounded within the smoke of the pots that lined the room, and danced to the music of her laugh! And the gold of her locks was loosed and flew like golden mists behind, or like to wings of gold.

And Herod drew him upon his elbow, and dragged his wasted limbs unto the floor of the palace and chattered laughter and watered much from out his lips. Yea, and Theia bounded unto the couch whereon he rested and smote his cheek! And he reached forth his hand that he might lay hold of her, and she bounded on.

And Claudia stood wrathed. And Theia laughed much and spake unto Herod that this was a camel-woman who had drunk her full for journey. And Theia spake her:

"Most noble King, I, thy slave, do bow unto thee."

And Herod wondered much, and thought him of the drinking of the feasts, and marveled much that 'mid a cup he made such buy! And he called that cups be brought that they might drink. And they brought forth locust wine,* honey-sup; and they supped.

And Claudia supped bitters from out the sweeted cup. Then did Herod drunken him and seek much of Theia, who ever bounded on till he slept.

And Claudia, fearing much this woman, wrathed upon her, and spake that when Herod waked she would seek audience and tell of the coming of her and that she had come babed.

Then did Theia laugh, and cast the rough mantle o'er her and fled from out the walls and unto Simeon and Panda, who waited her.

* Probably a spirit distilled from the bruised pods of the locust or carob tree.

And bared were the feet of her, and the babe made loud its wailing. And Panda, seeing Theia had fled from out the place, took up the babe and gave it unto Simeon, and took Theia within the arms of him, and they fled them on.

And slaves made seek, and questioned them about the place and spake that Herod sought this woman. For Claudia in her wrath had waked the King.

Unto the place of one whom Simeon knew they made way, the house of Flavius. And Simeon knew this man abided in Jerusalem. And when they had come to the spot where shadow showed, they tarried. And Flavius came forth from out the house and stopped, and feasted the eyes of him on Theia and looked with wondering upon Panda. And seeing Theia was babed he drew up his shoulders. Then looked he unto Simeon, who bowed o'er the babe, and he spake thus:

"Theia! Theia! Then Augustus hath drunk and thrown forth the vessel! Theia, look thou! Knowest thou not Flavius whom Augustus hath put, a Senator, unto Jerusalem, stripped of that that maketh men kneel? Yea, sent unto the place of Jews!"

And Theia looked upon him and cried out: "Flavius! Ah, Rome's children seek new lands that they die not at their mother's feet. Yea, Flavius, the mother hath not a loving for the sight of death! Ha, ha, ha! Think ye, Flavius, that Augustus drank? Not Augustus. Nay, he seeketh a kinsman to hold the goblet. Look, Flavius, look! The King's blood slumbereth there, and I say unto thee, the sire of him shall sit upon the seat of Caesar Augustus, for the itch of greed tickleth this man. Theia might set up in thanks that he who supped and supped but for one sup, and at the supping the potion set him low, but Theia knoweth that he, Augustus, shall cloak the chosen of him and cause a flowing of the blood of him to set aright his wrong. For from out the land of bondage cometh he at the bidding of Augustus. Then shall he, Augustus, who seeketh one who hath head, set him up and cause earth to acknowledge the flowing of his blood into this man. This is the word of Theia. Yea, and when he sitteth so, the Hate-child shall know not his sire.

"Theia! a purse thrown to him who took fancy to the steps of her! Yea, and when the time came when favor set upon this man, then was Theia taken back unto Rome; for Flavius, Theia was but the coin of Rome's hoard, where when e'en a beggar dieth, the pence of him then are Rome's."

"Theia, stop! This is not Rome, but Caesar. Yea, Theia, and

Rome, thy land and mine, shall send up greensward to cover Caesar's stains."

"Hark, hark thee, Flavius, unto Theia's words! The God of these Jews shall rock Rome's foundations. Yea, and the first rocking of her roots shall be when Theia shall offer up the Hate a sacrifice unto this God, in answer of the token, the whited camel."

"Theia, thou art a seer. Seest thou the road Flavius shall set upon?"

"Thinkest thou, Flavius, that Theia, who knoweth thee as one of Rome's noble citizens, might tell unto thee that that she knoweth? Yea, it shall be. Thou, Flavius, shall meet with Theia at the end of thy road, and Theia shall know thee not, for thou shalt rend the regal robe of Him born King of the Jews. This is the word of Theia. Flavius, hast thou left thy heart in Rome?"

"Nay, Theia, for Eunice hath come from Rome upon the arm of Flavius."

"Eunice, the heaven-eyed! Eunice, who danced with Theia! Ah, Flavius, Rome is good."

"Yea, Theia, yea. Rome is good, and Eunice hath not born a king's blood, but the child of Flavius. Yea, Theia, and this day hath she brought forth. Still the child hath not a name; then shall Theia speak the name of her."

"Flavius, hast thou a chosen name?"

"Nay, Theia, nay, it shall be as thou sayest."

"Then Flavius, Theia sayeth this shall be the name of her; Mary, not of Rome nor of Greece, but Mary; for Mary weareth the crown of earth."

"It shall be as thou hast spoken. Yea, but Theia, where hast thou heard this name? 'Tis not of Greece nor Rome."

"Thinkest thou, Flavius, Rome and Greece hold all that is good? Nay, I tell thee Bethlehem holdeth good, the good of earth's treasures, for though the earth hath emerald, yea, and ruby, yea, and onyx, earth holdeth one gem that like a drop of dew shall vanish, and yet I, Theia, say unto thee, this gem is earth's rarest."

"Theia, thou hast held thy power of cunger * with the gods."

"Nay, Flavius, Theia hath not a need for gods. She seeketh the God, Jehovah."

"What, Theia! thou of Rome speakest of the Jew's God!"

"Yea, yea, Flavius, since Rome holdeth gods that fill upon filth and leave the carrion of half-eat flesh of filth, then Theia seeketh one

* Magic.

who cleanseth. Yea, Theia loveth Panda and Simeon here, far o'er the gods of Rome."

And Flavius looked upon Simeon and asked of Theia: "Simeon! Is this man of the Jews?"

"Yea, but knoweth thy tongue and mine. Simeon, this man is Flavius of Rome."

And Flavius spake low: "Simeon! Simeon! So thou tellest Flavius this man is Simeon of the Jews! Theia, thou hast lied. The land of Rome held but one man whose shoulders set so, and whose eyes held fight's-fire. This man is Ajax! Hath he come back unto earth? I tell thee, Theia, I, Flavius, saw him felled by one who smote not with bared fist, but buried metals in his palms. Yea, and man, I tell thee, Caesar planned thy undoing."

And the eyes of Simeon flamed. And he caught at his breast and sunk. And Theia cried out:

"Flavius, he hath burst his mantle ope in wrath! Look! he sinketh, o'ercome! Panda, lend thy hand unto Simeon. Theia would that he should see not that she hath beheld his undoing. See! he waketh. Flavius, hold thy hand unto him. Speak thou words unto him. Make him to know thou holdest regard. Stand thou this man upon his limbs, though they be withered, for Rome holdeth not a one whose heart is stronger, though she putteth far more of worth upon flesh than hearts! Flavius, yonder man is yet Rome's strongest!"

And she knelt, and Simeon stirred, and she spake: "Simeon, thou hast waked? What o'ercame thee? What word did Flavius speak that wrought thee so undone?"

"'Tis naught, Theia, but the suffering of which I spoke to thee. Rome knew me as a slave, and thee as a king's slave who standeth e'en o'er a citizen, and I tell thee that we, Rome's own, are slaved by heart to Rome, and fall smitten at thought of losing Rome's plaudits."

"Then, Simeon, thou art of Rome?"

"Yea, and cloaked me in a Jew's robe. Theia, thou and Simeon for long knew naught each of the other, and yet knew all. By what chance did thy path of bondage and the path of Simeon meet in this, the Jew's land, where thou art thine and I, Simeon, mine?"

"Hark, Simeon, hark! Theia telleth but one word, and it answereth all—Jehovah."

And Simeon arose and Theia spake more: "'Tis time we sought the house of Flavius, that Theia see the babe that Eunice hath brought forth. Thou, Simeon, and Panda, shall stay within the house of Flavius. Then, Flavius, do thou to bring us to thine abode."

And Flavius spake: " 'Tis but right that ye should seek shelter while thou art abided in the city of Jerusalem, for Herod hath hunger for much that is not meat. Come then unto Eunice, Theia, for 'tis near the time that Flavius should seek the palace, and thou shalt sit and feast thy heart upon the heaven-eyed. Greece hath lost her daughters. Yea, but not the hearts of them. Yea, and doth Rome crush out their hearts then doth their feet make happy. Greece beareth women to set the blood of Rome clean.

" Make thee silent that Eunice waketh not doth she sleep. Ajax, step thee here within the shadow. Nay, wait thee! Come unto the parapet and wait thee there. Thou, ' Panda of woman's hands,' and Theia here—Ah, she waketh! Eunice! Eunice! Rome hath given up to thee thy sister! "

And Eunice cried out: " Theia! Theia! "

And Theia spake: " Go thou, Flavius, and wait without. Leave Theia that she speak out unto Eunice; for Theia's heart is o'erfull."

And Flavius sought Simeon, and Theia spake unto Eunice, saying: " Eunice, speak! What hath smitten thee? What set thy cheek whited? Yea, and thy hand! Maid, what, what hath beset thee? "

" Theia, say not unto Flavius thou seest the vine withered. 'Tis but a season of sun's fall and rise that Eunice stayeth, for the gods have spoken."

" Gods! Gods! Eunice, Rome's gods sing but lies. Yea, what hath thy days to do with gods or gods' singing? "

" Theia, thy laughing warmeth that of Eunice that freezeth up with fear."

" Fear not, sister of Greece, fear not. Theia, who loveth thee, hath sought a God and found His abiding place. Yea, and she shall take heed unto the spot. This God, Eunice, hungereth not for flesh nor metal nor high estate. Nay, He hungereth for thee and me. No man hath told this unto Theia, and yet, and yet, Eunice, He hath spoken unto the white-mist Theia that liveth 'neath this flesh. This God would do not unto thee this thing."

And Eunice, seeing the burden of Panda, made question: " What hath Panda? "

" The babe Hate, Eunice, the child of Theia and him who hath undone the gods who set o'er. For in the flesh Theia bore lay the gods' undoing; for Theia waked! "

" Thou who hast suffered, Theia, thou who hast eaten and drunk Rome's fullest, who hast suffered that there be no stone upon which to stumble upon the way that leadeth unto Caesar's seat! Hath a man

who suppeth when he hath hungered much and loned,* the right to
cast back the alms Rome offered as a balm to setting asunder that which
clung in loving? Doth a man o'erdrunk upon the locust seek new
scents? Theia, thinkest thou this man supped but for the supping, or
thinkest thou the cup held love's wine? Eunice would believe this."

"Ah, Eunice, thou wouldst believe well of Rome, and thou hast
supped of truth. Yea, but Caesar holdeth out a branch laden of fruits.
Thinkest thou this man might say him nay? What hath woman that
she may tie her faith? Woman slaveth as a plaything, else she burdeneth
with a pack unto the end. Eunice, this day shall stand like burning
brands upon the days to come, and the fires of these brands shall be
the blood of Rome and the blush of Rome's women. Yea, and men of
time that yet hath not come shall sneer upon an Empire who bathed her in
blood that she might wax whiter, and whose royal heads sold office for
lusts. O'er the slain bodies of Rome's women and youth, her chariot,
that beareth her to times hence, shall roll. Yea, and their dust shall
ne'er be buried, but up shall rise their hate and wrong and bathe the
days that stand them clean."

And she shewed unto Eunice the babe, and spake: "Look thou,
Eunice, this is the flesh of hate, and this flesh shall brand Rome in shame
through ages. Rome shall hide her treachery and dream this babe is dead
and dust, and earth shall know not more of him, and yet Theia shall
tell unto the earth this. And the time is then, and then, and then,
and not now.

"Look thou upon Panda, whose saffron skin is paled since scorching
of the sands. So, Eunice, doth the scorch then be shut away the
blush shall whiten. Hate hath fallen upon Theia and Theia hath basked
within a smile's gold and hate hath whited. Yea, but list, Eunice,
Theia hath born a living Hate, for she hath fed upon hate and the babe
hath sucked much of hate until his flesh is hate."

"What hath set thee undone, Theia? Thou shouldst fear the
gods that thou speakest so."

"Stop! Stop! No words of gods! He, Jehovah, hath love for
Hate. Yea, Hate shall crumble and spring from out its dust a vine that
shall climb up and up unto the seat of Him. He who nurtureth Hate
hath nurtured the seed of this vine. For He shall come upon the whited
camel. Yea, it shall be so!

"Thy babe, Eunice, stirreth. Leave thou Theia to look upon her."

And she looked upon the babe and chanted as the see-woman:

* Suffered with loneliness. "Lone" is frequently used for "lonely" in
this story.

"Mary! Mary! Mary! Sorrow croucheth upon thy path. Yea, but thy smile shall light the dark of ages. Shed thou thy smile upon her here, the child of Eunice. Mary, Mother, youth's mother, for love is youth; Mary, the bearer of His kiss!

"Eunice, this child hath a noble heritage, truth and love—not thine nor mine. She shall see His coming from out the East."

"Theia, hath taint set thee? Hast thou left thy reason flee?"

"Nay, Eunice, Theia's tongue speaketh sorrow for the crumbling, that the vine springeth. For Theia's sorrowing is Hate.

"Hark! Flavius! And Eunice, list! Ajax cometh. Say not one word that thou seest what Rome hath dealt unto him. Hark! Theia still loveth Ajax, and Rome cast him broken from out her walls with but shame as cloak. He who standeth victor of the arenas tore out the palms of him; for wrestling was poor sport with but one victor. Yea, and metal cutteth him who clutcheth. Yea, and Rome heard not her son's wailing. Eunice, this man is victor o'er Rome, for the man of him standeth touched not by Rome. Speak thou unto him. His face weareth beard and he hath hid 'neath a name, 'Simeon.' And ne'er until this time sought Jerusalem, that Rome's men know him not. For thy love of Theia speak unto him and tell much of what thou knowest of the time he trod the arenas. And speak not but that the time is so e'en now. Theia would speak so, but thou knowest Theia was not within Rome's walls at his going."

"It shall be, Theia, for Eunice loveth thee and thy loves, and thee and thy hates. Speak, speak, Theia, that thou believest the gods have lied."

"By the word of Theia, so speaketh she. Nay, kiss not this hand, Eunice. Bow thee unto Him, Jehovah."

And Simeon and Flavius came forth and Theia spake unto them:

"Ajax and Flavius, hath then the time been long? 'Twas feasting to her and Theia. Ajax, look thou! 'Tis Eunice, the heaven-eyed."

And she murmured unto Eunice: "Speak, speak, Eunice! See, he crimsoneth!"

And Eunice spake: "Ajax, Ajax, Rome's foundation, who holdeth Rome's men as Atlas holdeth up all of all! Speak unto Eunice, that she heareth the voice Rome loved. Speak, man, and look! the child of Flavius slumbereth upon this arm."

And Simeon made answer: "Eunice, Rome loseth her blossoms, thou and Theia! This breath and 'Rome' putteth wine unto the blood. Ajax standeth 'mid the pit, and smelleth scents, and heareth murmuring, and riseth up unto his utmost that Rome may know he

standeth her son. These arms burst out from 'neath the very skin.
Yea, Ajax hath fought man and beasts, and chooseth beasts. Yea, Ajax
seeth the multitude, and heareth musics, and seeth swaying lines of
slaves who dance o'er flowers; dance o'er earth that stains their white
feet crimson. And up windeth the smell of stale blood that creepeth
like Rome's treachery, and sicketh. For he who troddeth the arenas
knoweth this, and thou who trod 'mid the nobles, know 'tis true.

"Flavius, what hath Rome done unto thee? Did Rome but strip
thee and ne'er lay on the scourge?"

And Flavius spake: "Hark! Hark! Look unto her. Rome hath
withered the bloom. A slave, a dance-woman, whose strength bears
her not up, is worth unto Rome—what? And when Rome hath
supped up her blood, for she hath spat her life's blood, she casts her
forth!

"And Flavius spake o'er loudly, and thus the noble's displeasure.
Yea, much weighty speech of office hath naught but such for meat. Ha,
ha, ha! What a trick Rome hath done! A worthy trick! Cast babes
unto the pit. Theia, babed; Panda, slaved; Flavius, stripped and dealt
his death-blow through her yonder; Eunice, crowned with death;
Simeon, a man in irons! The Emperor should sleep him well and dream
of this. 'Twould be the cause for calling forth a seer, yea, and wake
him from out his comfort.

"Ah, Rome, thy sons hold thee dear, and the price they pay unto
their mother is the crushed hearts of them. Yea, they pluck forth their
hearts within their very hand, and crushing, bring forth thy blood, for
thy son's blood is thine. That Flavius should speak of Rome so, the
gods have willed."

And Theia made word, saying: "Stop, Flavius! Thou hast spoken
this was not Rome, but Caesar. Then speak not of gods. Gods are Rome's
and yet Theia sayeth Caesar is the god o'er gods in Rome. Thy King,
he who sitteth o'er Jerusalem, what a noble! An emptied vessel of
the gods! What think ye this Jehovah seeketh of Herod? I tell thee,
Flavius, Theia knoweth 'tis Caesar and Herod, and he who seeketh the
seat of the Emperor, and nobles of the land of Rome, that play with
brasses and fashion out gods whose throats are ever emptied and hungered for that of Rome's people that they hold most dear. These are
gods the hands of men have tortured out from metal. And what hath
Jehovah that He might fear such, when the fires of Him, the lightnings
of heavens, might melt their sides and run them back unto the earth
wherein He hid their very substance?

"Panda, go thou there and fetch forth wetted earth and fashion out a god that this man may worship him, the god of earth. For wetted clays are fitted for god's fashioning just so well as metals.

"And Theia seeth more: gods that were fashioned of clay stride the earth, and yet man seeketh metal gods! Yea, and He, Jehovah, shall send earth a God, and man shall pluck Him asunder. And time shall fashion from the words of Him a God, and earth shall worship Him. More Theia sayeth: Panda, and Simeon, and Flavius, and Eunice, and Mary, the babe of Eunice, and e'en the Hate, are of this God's land nobles."

CHAPTER V

AND Theia and Panda and Simeon bided them within the house of Flavius until the time when Mary should bring forth the Babe unto the temple and offer up the doves unto the priests.

And they set them, upon this day, upon the path unto the temple, and they waited at the wall's ope until Joseph and Mary should enter therein.

And lo, they came them. And Mary was seated upon an ass, and Joseph walked him beside, and Mary held close the Babe wrapped of cloth; and Joseph carried a basket of woven reed wherein the doves were put. Then went they unto the temple.

And it was so that Theia had sought not the court of Herod, but bided her with Eunice and her babe, for the breast of Eunice nurtured not and Theia fed the babe upon the milk of hate. And Theia made much of the gods who set a withering upon this sister of her land, for Theia, though she spake words of comforting, knew 'twas vain.

Of this she spake with them who waited with her, and when the time did come when Mary rode within the walls, the tongue of Theia was stopped and she shook as one that cold had smitten, and murmured unto Simeon and Panda, upon their ways, that that the see-woman within the walls of the temple had spoken was true. And the time was now when she and the priests would speak it so.

And Mary stepped from off the ass, and the head of her was high. Yea, and she held the Babe aloft. And they made them their ways within, nor knew they them who followed. And the way was darkened until the time, and lo, the sun broke forth and showed upon the Babe and she who bore Him.

And the woman Anna rose and came forth and spake: " This is the Christ! "

And the priests spake them: " Yea, this is the seed of Abraham. This is He of whom the scripts foretold."

And the eyes of Mary looked on high, and the face of her told not of that which abided in the heart of her. And the priests marveled at this woman, that she had born the seed of David and yet looked not upon herself with pride.⁶ For Mary spake no word, but kept within her heart much.

Then Theia, who watched afar, from the place of the Gentiles, spake unto Simeon: " Simeon, seest thou this thing? List thee! Theia sayeth from out the priests' mouths, and hers, the woman of the temple, hath fallen word that shall shake the throne of Herod. For list thee! there cometh from afar the see-men * from out the lands of the corners of the earth. Yea, for the God, Jehovah, hath set signs that these men know. For list thee! he who seeth, knoweth by the signs. Yea, long before the signs do come. For Simeon, He speaketh unto the in-man of him who sees. Yea, for earth holdeth few of men who see. The man of him who trods the earth seeth and the in-man † of him is blind. For this, the God of the Jews, setteth signs, and wipeth them out. So hark ye, 'tis but he who sees through the eyes of the in-man who knoweth the sign, e'en after it be wiped away.

" Yea, and through the in-man of these Jews who first set up the scripts, He spake. Think ye this, then, is a God who is but for one tribe? Nay, Simeon, this God is thine and mine, and knoweth Greece. This is the God that setteth Rome low, Rome who buildeth up gods she may melt to metals and form anew. Yea, Simeon, the abiding place of Rome's gods is o'erfull of gods. Hark, Panda! thou art far more god than they who set o'er the fires of sacrifice!

" More, more Theia sayeth: This God, Jehovah, hath spoken through the thunder and lightning, and He hath cast the earth up in quakes, and yet the men hark not. Yea, and now I tell thee He shall speak unto them through flesh, the flesh of Him whom Mary bore, and earth yet shall not hark. Nay, for Simeon, the in-man of earth is blind, and but the purge of blood shall make him see. This man hateth and that man hateth, yea, and the atoms of hate grow up and become a living thing. Yea, so it shall be that this building up of hate shall slay Him whom Mary bore, and it shall fall upon these Jews, and yet no man will have done the thing. So shall the sands of hate build up a stone that shall crush these Jews through ages. Yea, for blood shall bind up the grains and make thereof the stone. Yea, and when this Man shall say, ' I am the Son of Him,' then shall the hate-sand blow it up and blind these Jews until the blood be spilled!

" Oh, woe is me, Simeon! Would that Theia's wailing might be heard through time! Yea, but hark, it shall be! For earth shall bear up on high what Mary hath borne, and cast down the bearing of Theia. Yea, but earth hath need for dark and light; then Theia hath born a need if she but bore the dark. Yea, the passing of Theia into the night the earth shall not see. Yea, and more; when the day shall gleam, ever

* The Magi. † The spirit.

shall the dark follow. And all men await the day and care them not for night."

And Mary came forth from within and went upon her way, and Theia spake:

"Look! She hath gone! She who bore Him of Light! And Theia, who beareth Dark, is here within the temple. See! he, the Hate, lieth sleeping. The time is not ripe for his waking. Simeon, Simeon, thou art weighted down with the stone of hate, and Theia beareth at her ankles stones of hate. Yea, and the heart of the sleeping Hate is builded of the sands of hate. Yea, and this stone, the heart of him, shall be held up for the earth to cast to them she hateth, through ages. Yea, and Simeon, hark! the rain of Theia's tears and Mary's, and the flame of Theia's words and Him of Light, shall melt away the stone and burn to naught the living hate."

And Simeon spake unto Theia, saying: "Theia, thou livest within the dark. Cast ope thy heart and cleanse thee of thy hate, for though Simeon seeth not, he sayeth unto thee thou hast born, too, a king of citizens. Yea, and Theia, hear thou this: Simeon would offer thee of him but he would that that he offereth be whole, and that of him which be whole, the in-man of him, be thine. Yea, and Panda, thy handman, persecuteth the man of him and liveth with the in-man ever, else hate would wear him down."

And Theia looked unto Panda and spake: "Yea, and Panda, thou shalt wax fuller, with age, of the in-man. Yea, and men shall seek thee out and thou shalt tell unto them of the words of Him of Light. Yea, they shall seek thee with thy herds upon the hills. Yea, and thou shalt feed the people, and thou shalt seek this man Peter, who fisheth, and thou shalt be with the multitudes when He who was born of light shall cause much of little to show.* This meaneth little to thee, but Panda, Theia shall be not with thee and thou wilt say, ' So hath the word of Theia come to be.'

"Hark ye unto the chant that soundeth from out the inner place. Come! Flavius waiteth thee and me, and Eunice waiteth with her babe that Theia giveth suck unto it."

And they went their ways unto the house of Flavius, where Eunice waited their coming. And Flavius had not yet come from out the court of Herod. And they awaited him there.

Then came he with words of the dance, saying that Herod had sickened at the trippings of Claudia and had sent word unto the slaves' place that they should come forth, and each had danced that he might see.

---

* The miracles of the loaves and fishes.

Then had he cursed the sight of him that played false, else this dance-woman was the draining of his latest cup.

Then had Claudia shook with anger and wrapped her 'bout the neck of him, and Herod shook off the cling of Claudia.

And Flavius knew not this dance-woman Herod sought was Theia. Yea, and made much of the tale, and told unto them how Claudia had wrathed and spoken unto Herod that the woman who sought the courts was babed, and the face of her had shown dusts of travel. And she spake how this woman had told of the King's favorite who would come, and how the arms of her would be as alabaster and teeth as ivory.

Then spake she more that she had grown wrathed that this should be and sought the King and danced. And this woman had done this thing; cast from her the babe and danced like Spring who hath cast the Winter's robe.

And at the words of Flavius Theia mirthed. And she told unto them of that which had been. And even as Claudia had danced so danced she, and binded up her limbs that the steps be short. Then cast she free and shewed unto them the dance of Theia, the Dance of Doves. For she bended low like to a dove that circles 'bout its mate, and stepped her here and yon. Then spread she forth her arms, on which was hung the softest cloth, and spread it o'er the head of her and sailed upon the very air. So stepped she upon the very toes of the feet of her, and bounded up on high, and lighted as a dove alights to earth. Then fluttered she up unto each of them who saw, and 'bout and 'tween, and fell at last as the dove, at rest, the cloth o'er the head of her, and she a naught, so had she shrunk at the finish of the dance, and rested as the dove whose wing hovereth its head.

And Flavius pondered o'er this and spake that this was a thing for which Theia might fear the King. And Simeon's brow was deep of cloud. And Panda kept the tongue of him, and spake not, for he was the desert's child.

And it came to pass that they made them bonds one unto the other and Theia made known to them the thing next her heart. And Flavius, having not regard for this King, made him a party to the making of the bitters.

All these things were within Jerusalem and Jerusalem knew not of them.

CHAPTER VI

AND time came that Theia knew the tongue of the Jews. And Panda and Simeon spake unto the Jew men and Theia unto the women. And Simeon and Panda spake of sheeps and market's talk, and Theia spake of gods and Mary.

And the Jews knew the tribe of Mary and Joseph, and looked with wonder, and spake that this man, Joseph, was a one who wrought of woods, and Mary might bear but one, a Jew, who e'en though the blood of him might hold drops of nobles, still was but a Jew who stood not in ready for a crown.

And they looked with fearing upon Theia that she spake of this Babe as King, for they said she might well fear Herod were he to hear this thing.

And in the eighth month after the coming of Theia into Jerusalem, Eunice fell low and died. And Simeon and Panda, who had returned into Bethlehem, were summoned and came forth unto them, and they found Theia silent, and holding close that of which she spake not.

And when the putting away of Eunice was finished then came they back unto the house of Flavius, and Simeon spake unto them and begged that they bid Rhea and Ezekiel come from out Bethlehem unto them and dwell within the house of Flavius. And Theia said that this was the wish of her. And they came them and dwelled with Flavius.

And lo, at a time later, at the dawning of a certain day, they arose, and Theia had vanished into the night and left unto them the Hate. And when they had searched much and wondered much, and time had passed to the fullness of a fortnight, Panda spake unto Simeon, saying:

"Simeon, Panda hath that to speak unto thee that sickeneth him. Theia, Theia, thine and mine, hath the bright * spots! Yea, and she bid that I say unto thee, she would that that which she gave unto thee be whole, and she spake, ' Say thou unto him, Panda, all of Theia that be whole is the Hate. Unto Simeon deliver him.' "

And Simeon sunk, and lifted up his arms and cried: " Panda! Panda! Rome! Rome! Hark! thy brother and thy son sweareth that

* The leprosy.⁷

47

the sister of him be not forsaken! Panda, what is the life of Simeon
that but a skin's bright buyeth? Simeon seeketh out Theia and taketh
her unto him within the hills. Yea, Simeon and Theia, and the God
of Theia, abide them there."

"Yea, Simeon, but thou hast forgotten Panda."

And Simeon made answer: "Rhea hath a heart for the motherless;
then the babe of Eunice and the Hate shall abide beside her door.
Panda, as thou lovest her and me, speak! Where went she?"

"Simeon, I know not. She waked my sleeping that she might say
these things unto me and wrapped her mantle close and went her way
murmuring, 'Yea, yea, it shall be; He shall come from out the East.'
Little spake she else save word of Herod: that she, Theia, had spent her
coin within the court of Herod. Yea, she had drunk from out the
slaves' cups and set Herod at unrest. Yea, and Simeon, she laughed
much, and said that the journey of her unto Jerusalem was vain, for
the thing she sought to do was done within the walls of Bethlehem.
For Mary had borne the King's undoing. Yea, she spake more; that
this man, Herod, was but one King, and this, the bearing of Mary, was
the undoer of all kings. 'For the God, Jehovah, shall smite in His
name.' 'Say unto Simeon, Panda,' she spake, 'that Theia sought fruit
from off a dead tree. Say unto Simeon, Theia knoweth the smite of
flesh; then Theia knoweth Simeon more. Thou shalt say unto the Hate
his mother is no more, lest he seek her out.'"

And Simeon said: "Ah, Panda, thy words are sharp stones unto
Simeon! It shall be, then, that we make known unto Rhea that we
seek Theia, and I, Simeon, shall make price for the Hate's care, and
leave the babe of Theia here that Rhea shall pluck out the root of hate
and plant anew of loving. Yea, Panda, Simeon shall seek out Theia,
and Simeon feareth not the journey, for Simeon shall lean upon a staff.
Yea, Panda, he shall lean upon a staff, Jehovah! For be He not the
God Theia seeketh? For he who knoweth His name, the word
Jehovah meaneth Him.

"Panda, thou shalt wait Simeon here, and say unto them who
abide in the house of Flavius that the flocks of Simeon have called him
back to the land of Bethlehem. For Simeon knoweth that 'tis meet
that he see not these people, for Simeon's eyes would tell far o'er what
should be known. Take thou this coin unto Rhea and say as I did
speak unto thee."

And lo, when the dark hour fell, Simeon limped upon his way. For
when they did seek the ass, after the going of Theia, they found she
had ridden from thence. And Simeon made way through the dark and

rested him at day upon the way, that he might ask of them who passed had they seen the passing of Theia. And no man had seen.

And he came upon one who bided within Bethlehem, who spake that no woman had passed the walls save them who dwelled within the city and all men knew, save Mary, and Joseph was with her. And he told that no traveler came into the city, but that there had been a shepherd lad who was clothed in skins, and legs bare, and shoes of skin. And he had gone up unto the hills. And this lad, he said, was sick, for he was pale, and yet he strode not as a shepherd whose shoulders stooped, but regal; and he made no word to any man within Bethlehem but had sought out the abiding place of Mary.

And 'twas told that fruits stood fresh laid upon the door's ope at each morn. And this, the man spake, was setting the tongues of the city loosed, for this lad wore upon a skin's thong, so that upon his back it rested, a cross of wood. And the men of Bethlehem had thought this was a bow and so had spoken.

And Simeon made no answer, but made his way unto the hills, and the waters of his heart bathed the eyes of him. And when he had come unto the hut of him no life showed it there.

Then out amid the hills went he, and it was at the eve's hour when the sun holdeth rich gold. And Simeon sought the summits. And, lo, where earth had angered and hills bore tracery of her wrath in rugged stones and yawning opes, upon this bed of stones was flung, Theia! Theia, whose locks had loosed and melted them within the sun's gold! And the skins had parted o'er her breast, and there showed—the brand * of hate! And the throat of her was scarred with the binding of the thong. And she lay as one who had given up the ghost.

And Simeon flung up the head of him; and his bosom heaved and his arms reached forth; and he stepped unto where she lay and took her up and unto his breast. And she oped her eyes and spake, and saw him not:

"He shall come, yea, He shall come from out the East upon the whited camel."

And Simeon spake: "Theia, Theia, though Simeon hath but a broken staff to offer unto thee, 'tis thine; lean thou upon it."

And he set his lips upon the brand of hate, and murmured:

"See, Theia, if this be thy rose, then Simeon plucketh it!"

And Theia spake: "Simeon, Simeon, thou? Yea, yea. He cometh! This be the sign! He hath spoken unto the in-man of Theia. Yea, He cradleth Theia in the arms of Him! For Simeon, thou art of

* The leprous spot.

Him. Simeon, unto thee Theia sayeth she hath left the Hate unto earth and took up Love. Nor shall the eyes of Theia look upon that which showeth earth its lovely, but shall turn unto earth's crushed. Yea, for Simeon, he who plucketh but the perfect fruit, loseth much that be good, for though the smite hath fallen upon the fig, that part that be free of smite hath sweet, yea, sweet past the sweet of other fruits. Yea, man, thou wert sweet with love, but at the smiting of the flesh, unto Theia thou art sweeter far!"

Then came on the night's dimming of the sun's light. And there upon the hill's summit stood they, one clasped to the other. And they looked them afar o'er the valley, unto the place where the sun would show at the morn.

CHAPTER VII

AND Herod made much word unto the high priests, and called council with the scribes. And they spake that the scripts had foretold of the coming of this governor from out the land of Judea.

And Herod gnashed his teeth, and rent his robes, and said that the hand of him would smite the firstborn of the land. Yea, and he heard much at the coming of these men who rode them from afar; for they did ask of him: "Where is He who is born King of the Jews?"

And Herod held close unto his heart these words they spake, and said unto them: "Go thou and seek this child, that I may go forth and worship."

And within his heart he held much of evil, for Herod held naught but the undoing as the right for this King. Then set he forth and lo, the lands of Judea shook with wailing, for Herod plucked forth love from out the arms of women, for their babes were the root of love.

And the hand of the God of Theia smote him sore. Yea, and his rest was as a bed of fires, even so as Theia had willed.

And 'twas so that the babe, Mary, and the babe, Hate, fell unto the hands of Rhea. And Ezekiel, in fearing for his household, sought them a new abode; for 'twere the cunnings of them that had set the babes away so that no man knew of them; for Flavius was one who had been sent forth for the slaying.

And it came to pass that the son of Phethon had fallen; and Phethon had set this as the work of Flavius. And this man had coveted of Flavius the love of Eunice, and smote him when no man saw.

And there were murmurings that set upon the land of Jerusalem of this King that was born, and after the slaying they that did remain were in fear of Herod. And no man sought to come within the walls lest Herod hear of the flesh of him and slay it.

And when the time had passed that these wounds of the land of Herod were healed, then did Rhea and Panda and Ezekiel, with the babes, seek Bethlehem. And this was the time when the men brought forth the firstlings and slayed, and caused their blood to flow out upon the ground, where it was soaked up like unto waters.

Then did they bring forth the flesh unto the place where the priests

did will, and roast upon the fires, and they did sup deep so that no por-
tion of the flesh stood o'er the night's hour. Then cast they that which
did remain upon the fires that there be none left.

And Ezekiel made this feast with his tribesmen. And they abided
within the walls. And there was much word spoken, not aloud, of this
Mary, and the thing that had been within Bethlehem. For the fearing
of this King, Herod, was still upon them.

And Rhea heard from out the lips of them who were of her tongue
the word of how these men who spake many words of many tongues
had come, and unto this manger had brought forth precious gifts that
were for none save one of royal blood.

And Rhea marveled and remembered the word of Theia, and spake
not unto her people of what Theia had told unto her lest these of her
people should seek out Theia and slay her. For these Jews did hold a
sooth-seer as an evil. For had not the prophets spake this was an
abomination?

And Rhea set her hand unto the fulling of the flesh of these babes.
And lo, these Jews knew not them who abided within the hills. And
the going of Mary, who had fled with Joseph unto where they knew not,
was the source of much word.

Here abided in this land these people until the days had crept them
unto fortnights and the fortnights had crept them unto years unto the
time when these babes had reached the years of one and eight. And
the herds of Panda, who had sold himself unto Ezekiel, stood upon the
hills. And the seventh year had passed and Ezekiel had set him free
and had given him of his flocks. And at the every morn did Panda
drive them forth. And he was in the fullness of flesh and wise in the
tongue of these people.

And he ever sought, amid the hills, Theia and Simeon, and of that
which he found Bethlehem knew naught.

And he would go up unto the hills where the vineyards of Simeon
had stood and hold up on high his hands and wail unto the gods who
had forsaken him, and speak the name of his land, and murmur love
for Rome, his foster-mother. For Panda was the desert's burnt and
tracking of the sand's hot and scorch had sealed his lips. For he who
tracketh upon the sands speaketh unto the sand's waste and not unto
his brother.

And Panda sought out the hills and loosed his heart. And oft the
Hate child sought him there. And the lad was fair. Yea, and his
locks hung bright about his head, and his limbs gleamed strong, and
ever did he to dance his way.

And upon a day, up unto the hills went he, and there, upon his back, eyes up unto the sky and lips murmuring, found he Panda. And he spake out of a sudden unto Panda as he lay:

"Panda, wake! See, 'tis the Hate, Panda! Speak thou the name thou hast given unto the Hate. Speak thou the Rome name of him."

And Panda called the name: "Caanthus."

"Yea, Panda, so thou hast spoken it unto me. See! look thou! the limbs of me are strong as were the limbs of him. See thou, Panda, this stone! Watch how the strength of me shall set it within the bosom of the clouds. Look! I do pluck up the skin o'er the arms of me that the flesh shall fill up the place that showeth empty at the plucking. Yea, and Panda, at night's-time Caanthus * stretcheth forth his limbs that they grow in length that he may stride him abroad upon the hills and seek out thy sister, Theia.

"Panda, hark! Dreams trouble the rest of Caanthus. For Panda, it seemeth thy sister danceth within the place of his dreams. Yea, and I spake unto Mother Rhea and told unto her of this. And she said 'twas the seeking of thee among the hills that set upon a babe's shoulders the head of the aged. And I told unto her of the dancing of thy sister; yea, and Panda, she shutted up the tale.

"But it doeth no good unto me, for do I to shut out the light and lay me close that I sleep, there she steppeth. And Panda, she loveth me! Yea, and Panda, she telleth me of kings, and strange things showeth unto me. And she pointeth unto the East, where the sun seemeth to show. And Panda, 'tis strange! for thou tellest of her song of Him who would come from out the East. What, Panda! dost thou believe He hath come and borne her away from thee? Art thou my brother, Panda? What speakest thou unto Rhea? And why doth Rhea look unto her daughter and unto Mary and unto me, and the look of her is not the same one unto the other?"

"Thou child, trouble not o'er this. Nay, see! yonder ewe hath lost her lamb. Go thou! thy limbs are strong, and seek it out and bring unto me."

"Yea, but Panda, art thou my brother? For thou art not of the tribe of my father, Ezekiel. And Panda, time and time have I thought I, too, am not of his tribe."

"See, Caanthus, see! the sheep trod the lamb. Go thou!"

"Yea, Panda, and when I am come unto thee with the lamb, wilt thou tell of her, thy sister?—how the locks of her touched her hem and

* In reality the Greek name of Simeon.

gleamed like gold? Panda, she was not like thee, then, for thou art not lovely."

And Panda smote Caanthus with his palm and laughed, and sent him upon his way to seek out the lamb. And he came forth from the herd and bore up the trodden ewe's lamb, and sat him down upon the stones and held it close, and looked up unto Panda and stretched forth his arm unto the valley beneath and spake:

"Panda, come! rest thou here. Mine eyes are sharp for straying sheep. Do thou then to leave thy crook unto me and rest here and tell of her. For Panda, Bethlehem holdeth not such an one as thou sayest she was. And 'tis far o'er the living of the days of Bethlehem to sit and dream of her."

"Thou hast a tripping tongue, Caanthus; yea, thy tongue trippeth as doth thy feet."

"But Panda, art thou my brother?"

"Sit thou, Caanthus, sit thou. See! thou hast cast the lamb and it returneth unto the fold. Sit, and Panda shall tell unto thee of Caanthus, and Theia, his sister."

"Yea, Panda, of him and of her. He was strong; thou sayest so. See! I, Caanthus, so named for him, have power to bend this tree! Tell, Panda, tell of his smiting within the arenas. Panda, when I am come to the fullness of men, wilt thou take me then unto Rome?"

"Nay, nay, for he who cometh out from Rome leaveth his best."

"And did Caanthus love Theia?"

"Yea, yea; and his legs gleamed shaven, and his arms billowed up with strength as doth the sea, and his locks were black and glistened with man-strength, and he walked like unto a lion."

"Yea, and Panda, she floated upon the air like a summer's cloud. See! yonder white crest floateth so."

"Yea, yea, Caanthus; and he was victor ever."

"Panda, where wert thou? Didst thou, too, dance? Thy hand hath much tough within its palm. Panda, didst thou labor within Rome?"

"Yea, Caanthus, Panda labored; for his sister was but a slave unto the Emperor, and Panda was slaved unto him also."

"Yea, but it seemeth he would be loth that he loose such an one as thou."

"Yea, so Caanthus, but Panda may tell thee little lest it hurt the heart of him."

"Nay, nay, Panda! No more doth it hurt. Wouldst thou ne'er

tell unto Rhea did I tell thee of what the day of me did hold at the yesterday?"

"Nay. Speak thee, lad! What were thy doings?"

"Ezekiel slumbered, and Rhea was wrathed with Mary and her elder daughter, who, Panda, I love not, though she be my sister. Rachael hath much cunning that she turneth against Mary and against me. And 'mid the wrathing, Panda, Caanthus sought the wall where it opeth unto the roadway unto Jerusalem.

"And Panda, there beside the wall's ope was a one who wore skins, and he was lame, and he walked with arm about one who stooped. And she was seeking, as though she had lost much, for the eyes of her gleamed like unto the eyes of a wolf who seeketh out a lamb."

"What speakest thou, child? Where? Upon which path sought they?"

"I know not, Panda. But Panda, the earth oped and swayed and sick fell upon me. Yea, and I sought to follow, and the woman screamed aloud and fled. Fled, Panda; and I cast not a stone. And when she had gone up unto the thick growth of the hill's side amid the rocks, the skin o'er her head caught upon a thorn and slipped from off her head. And Panda, she had locks like gold, and they shewed like unto thy sister, Theia!"

And Panda got him from off the rock where he laid and took up his staff; and the blood of his heart stained his cheek.

"Panda, thou wilt say naught of this to Rhea, wilt thou?"

"Nay, nay, Caanthus! Nay, dost thou promise unto me ne'er again to seek, and yea, do ye break thy pledge."

And they set them upon their ways. And the sheep crept upon the hill's green until the white of their wool seemed but the clouds of fleece that crest the hill's brow. And they went them unto Bethlehem and Caanthus, seeing the men of the city, spake:

"Panda, seest thou these tribesmen and their children? Look! am I like unto these Jews?"

"Yea, Caanthus, like as one sheep unto the other."

And the Hate tripped him ahead upon the path, and swayed and bowed his way unto the house of Ezekiel. And they went them within. And Rhea stood over the grain's-meal where she made of breads that they might eat. And Rachael was weeping, and Mary stood, waxed strong in angers; and she smote Rachael and made loud word and spake:

"Rhea, she spat upon the bread that I did eat of. Yea, I flung out the bread unto the fowls. And Rhea, she sayeth swine should be my food! Am I then unclean that I eat of swine? Smite her, Rhea, smite thine eldest! Yea, lay her low, lest I, Mary, forget she be the sister of me!"

And Rhea looked not upon the wrath of Mary but shook of the grain dust and freed the meal of chaff. Yea, and plucked out the stones bits that grind them ever within the grain's-meal. Yea, then sought she dried fruits and sunk within the bread. And Rachael, seeing this thing, dried up her tears and sought the side of Rhea and made words unto her that Mary had much wrath and no child who smote her flesh * should eat a filling.

And the Hate, tripping upon his way, came within, and seeing this strode up; and anger flushed his skin, and he spake unto Rhea, saying:

"Rhea, mother, seest thou thy daughter's offense, and speakest not unto her? For Mary hath much to speak of the cunnings of thine eldest. Yea, and keepeth her word, for she knoweth thine ears are but for her.

"Yea, I, the Hate,—who hath named me so? Thy tongue and the tongue of my father, Ezekiel, telleth much at night's hours that mine ears do take in. Yea, and Panda and thou set shut the tales of my tongue. The very day of Bethlehem, Rhea, mother, seemeth not my day. Yea, I trod upon the stones of the streets of Bethlehem and blood stingeth the body of me and my head lifteth up and I feel, Rhea, mother, that I, Hate, might hold forth mine hand and they who walked my ways should bow them low. Am I then thy blood?"

And Rhea spake not, but Rachael, being deep in wrath, spake so:

"Nay, nay, thou art a Gentile dog! Thy mother a dance slave, and thy sire, who? Yea, thou hast not a name! Nay, thou art named Hate by thy mother. Yea, Hate! Hate! Hate!

"And Rhea hath called thee Hatte, that ye be not known as Hate abroad. Yea, and thy name is Hate! Hate! Hate!"

And the man-lad's eyes oped, and his cheeks burned crimson, and his breath stood still, and he murmured:

"Yea, Hate, Hate! This, then, is the thing that hath eat my days; the thing from which I fled at dark! Hate! Hate! Panda, hast thou kept this thing from me? Rhea, thy heart should weep! Hate! Hate! Yea, and e'en the babes of Bethlehem who know my paths, know Hate! Thou hast stolen love from Hate! Panda, lead thou me unto the hills. Yea, Panda, that I seek out a lamb and warm my

---

* Sister; but the word "flesh" is used generally for kin, often for a son or daughter.

breast. Yea, tell unto me of thy sister and her song. How, Panda, were the words? 'Yea, yea, He cometh from out the East.' Panda, thinkest thou He shall come for e'en the Hate?"

And they went them out upon the hill's way. And Panda oped his lips that he speak, and the Hate cried out:

"Nay, Panda, speak not! Thy very voice cutteth me. Nay, speak not! This heart! Panda, hath man e'er lost the heart from out his bosom? Nay, speak not! Leave the Hate's heart to die!"

And Panda leaned upon his staff in grieving and spake not. And the lad's lips whitened, and his hands smote one upon the other. So sat they. And the day sped on. And at a later hour the child spake:

"'Tis finished, Panda! Fill thou this empty breast, from out which the heart hath fled, with words of her. Who, Panda, who was the mother of the Hate? Panda, I fear much thy telling lest I hate the bearer of me."

"Nay, Caanthus, nay, thou hast love builded up in thee for her."

"Panda, the mother of the Hate—Hatte—Caanthus, she held not love, then she hath stolen love from Hate. Speak thou, speak thou, Panda, her name! Ah, Panda, the breath stifleth me! Speak thou, that I shall put upon my lips a curse—the first, Panda, the Hate hath spoken!"

"List thou, Caanthus! Thou art named for him, Caanthus of Rome. Thou art strong, thou art strong like unto him; yea, and thou lovest the love of Caanthus, Theia. List thee! Theia is thy mother's name!"

"Theia! Theia! Theia! Panda, stop thou! The earth, it slippeth away! Theia! Ah, Panda, hate thy sister? Nay, nay, love hath filled this empty breast. Her locks are gold, and she floateth as the clouds. Where, where, Panda? Hath He taken her unto Him, this one of the East? Speak, speak, Panda! What? Where? What shall Caanthus say and do? Take thou this hand and lead me unto the way. Theia is thy sister? Is this then true, or are thy words lies?"

"Lies, lies, Caanthus, lies. These lips are filthed with lies, and yet, Caanthus, Panda loveth and lieth for loving. Panda is but the slave of thy mother, Theia."

"Panda, Rachael sayeth 'who, my sire,' and giveth not his name. Yea, she asketh 'who'?"

"Hark, Caanthus! See thou! Panda's arms are oped to thee. Come thou and rest next his heart, that thou hearest of thy mother what is true. And fill thee well up with love, and leave not hate within thy breast. Hate thou the earth, not her! For she hath suffered much for thee."

"My father's name, Panda, speak!"

"List, Caanthus, list! When Panda, thy loved Panda, lived not among the white-skins, caravans swept o'er the sands, seeking out the goods of his lands. Yea, and Panda dwelled within a city that builded up her walls along the sand-sea's edge. Yea, and the mother of Panda, with the tribes of his people, made packs of spice—sweets and hots. Yea, and Panda wove baskets of grasses for their keeping.

"Yea, Caanthus, as these words fall from off thy Panda's lips he seeth this, his land, his sisters, yea, and his brothers, and his mother— deep, red-burned gold, blue locked, and ever at the every word the gleam of white teeth that showed at smile. And the babe, that ever seemed at the mother's breast; and the arm of her he ne'er did see empty. And the hand that was free—busy, busy at the weaving of baskets, and cloth that hung upon split reeds.

"And then, Caanthus, within the walls the caravans would squirm. And the babes who lived close unto the walls would sniff and tell of their coming e'en before they showed.

"And they gathered them about the wall's-gate, where palms rattled o'erhead, and the cloth of the palms shed upon the ground. For here, Caanthus, within this land, standeth palms that clothe them within a cloth of brown, and this slippeth beneath the trees. And the babes would take it up and cast it at the camels as they wallowed past. Yea, and laugh much at the noses of the beasts that hung o'er their very mouths.

"Ah, Caanthus, then would the caravans come within. And the packs squeaked at the loosing of the belts; and the men brought forth strings of bright bits, and metal, and cloth, stained crimson, and brass that looked like unto a man.

"And women rode upon the backs of the camels at other times. And they were not of the skin of Panda's people, but clothed them much and showed not their faces. And their hands were ringed of precious metal and jades and colored stones. And the women of Panda's land spake much of them, and oft bathed in sand and rubbed sore that they might be white. And they stood taking in much of the cloth and the borders of their mantles, that they might weave within their cloth. Yea, Caanthus, o'er the fires they heated much the pulps and leaves and barks, that they might make color thereof.

"And at the night's coming, the men of the caravans lighted fires, and sat them about, and spake their tongues. And the people of

Panda stood and listed to what they knew not. Yea, the women with babes astrided upon their hips, and the men who wove at eventide.

"And the moon would come up from out her bath of sand and leave the silver streaking o'er the sky. And the voices hummed, and the fires died, and the babes slept and drowsed, and them who waked wailed. And o'er these people hung the scent of palms and spice. And e'en the wood of sweets of which their sandals were soled, the sandal-wood, sent up sweet at damping."

"Ah, Panda, ah, this is not a lie! And thy mother, Panda, thy mother, tell of her!"

"Yea, yea, Caanthus. So lived the tribes of Panda, living 'mid the sun and sands and sleeping with night's sky for covering.

"Oft, yea oft, at night, when all slept, Panda would wake and list unto the sounds of his land: The slumber-breath of his sisters and brothers, the stirring of the camels, the rattle of their skin bindings, the whispers within the caravan, the howling of the wolves afar— and seek his mother's side! In the early hours, when the sands were damp, the babes would venture out and set prints of their feet therein, and, wide-eyed, wonder where this thing led.

"Yea, Caanthus, thy Panda hath stood so, and thought him the land afar, wherefrom these men had come, this land that lay beyond the sand, was the place where men were made. For the women told unto the babes that these caravans had brought them forth. Yea, and when the babes made sounds e'en before they spake, the mothers told unto the children this was the caravan-talk."

"Yea, Panda, these men came from out the East?"

"Nay, Caanthus, from the corners of the earth. And Panda lived so, unto the time when he went forth with his sire unto the plucking of the spice. And ever his mother would look upon his strength and beat her bosom, for these men of the caravans had oft done unto her people that which she feared.

"Then came a time when a noble's camels streamed within the walls. And the men of the city spake of a King and they called his name Caesar. And men with the camels wore strange garments of white, and bound round their legs, and o'er their mantles wore a square of cloth of heavy weave as cloak at night.

"And these men threw forth stones and branches that the lads of the city might fetch. And this was the play that Panda sought. And he stood tall o'er the lads who gamed, and threw swift, and ran swifter, and tied knots of many twists, and bore weights, and feared not. Yea, Caanthus, and Panda was but like to thee, one and eight.

And when the caravans left at deep of night's dark, while Panda slept beneath the sky, they laid hands upon him, and bore him unto the camels, and shut up his words."

" Panda, thinkest thou the night of Bethlehem holdeth such a thing?"

" Nay, nay; Bethlehem hath little in her nights and days."

" 'Tis well then, Panda. On!"

" Upon the sands these camels sunk their ways. Yea, and days and nights and days and nights, Caanthus, sand, sand! Ah yea, and Panda knew the babes came not o'er this. The men offered unto him fruits—dates and figs, and nuts of oil meats. And Panda wept, and did eat not. And they smote him, and spoke words he knew not, yet knew. For Panda knew this fruit was not offered in loving, but in fear of losing flesh. And they came them unto waters. And Panda knew not what sailed upon the waters. And they crossed o'er to other lands. And more they went upon camels, and then within chariots. And Panda knew not of these, though his people sold unto these men the horses of his lands.

" And Panda knew not the lands o'er which he came nor the tongues of this people. And he was brought up unto the palace of Rome, and knew the lash. And no brother found he there, for the eunuchs were black, and Panda gold. Yea, and Panda's days were Rome's, but Panda's nights were Panda's songs and Panda's tears. For the walls of the slaves' place echoed the songs of Panda's mother. And Panda's dreams were full of her white-toothed smile and blue locks and full arm."

" Yea, Panda, and tell thou unto Caanthus, was the bosom of thy mother soft? Oft, oft hath Caanthus plucked up the grass and heaped it high and pressed therein his cheek, and dreamed it was his mother's breast. What! Panda, art thou in tears? Nay, nay, shed not thy tears, for Caanthus shall seek her out!"

" Yea, yea, Caanthus, yea."

" Then tell thou of her, Panda. Tell thou of her, and of him who knew Theia, my mother. This King o'er kings knew her not? Then who, Panda, is Caanthus, and who his sire?"

" Rest thou, child, and list. There came a time when slaves were brought from out Greece. Slaves! And they wept, for their loved had been laid low beneath Rome's hand. And within one caravan that traveled not as them that swept the desert's sands, but grouped and scattered, and horse flesh drew them on their way, was one woman, who was babed. And she came forth, and Panda saw her cast unto the pit

for feeding, for she was smitten with a sickness upon the journey thence.
And thy mother, who was but a maiden, young as thou, had come with
this woman. And Caesar, seeing her, made it known that this child
should be slaved unto him. And he called forth thy Panda and gave
him unto her as her handman. Ah! and Caanthus, she shone as
pure as the star that riseth at the morning's hour, that thou hast seen
when thou hast sought the sheep hills with thy Panda.

"Yea, and time waxed until she was full of flesh and come unto
her beauty. And this time held much for thy mother, for she knew not
of the fate of slaves. And she danced through days and played the
hours away. And found the heart of Caanthus e'en before the going
unto the arenas. For he had come with the caravan that brought her
forth; yea, he was a youth of Greece.

"Then the babe of her whom Caesar had caused to be thrown into
the pit, had thrived and was called Eunice. And these two loved one
another much."

"Eunice! Then, Panda, Eunice, the mother of Mary, knew Theia,
and loved her e'en as Caanthus loveth Mary. Tell thou of their days,
the days of Rome. Did Theia dance?"

"Yea, Caanthus, ever Theia danced, as thou the child of her. And
Panda, within Rome, was known as 'Panda, the woman-hand,' for he
cared for these babes. The mother of Eunice had woed o'er leaving
Greece, her land, and the losing of them who builded up her house,
and put a blade unto her breast. And when Caesar had been shown this
thing, he made order that she be fed unto the pit."

"Ah, Panda, hath Caesar's dream a robe of black? Hath fear
followed him, and doth hate hide at dark's hour and set his legs
a-quaking?"

"Nay, nay, Caanthus, Caesar knoweth not lovely, doth it not cloak
in evil, and courteth evils as lovely."

"And Panda, is this the man of Rome—the man o'er men?"

"So; thou hast spoken truly, Caanthus, but hark! Time came when
men of kingdoms afar sought Rome. And a one, Tiberius, came unto
the place of Caesar, and thy mother, Theia, was brought forth with her
sister slaves, for the filling of the days with merry-make. And she looked
not upon these men, but danced with Eunice. And their eyes looked
afar unto the heavens, and their feet spoke of the seasons, and love, and
victors, and vanquished, ever on and on. And lo, Caanthus, this man
who had come unto Rome was filled as are the skins of wine. And
Caesar, who had woes o'er woes within his house, gave unto Tiberius,
Theia."

" What, Panda! gave Theia unto him! What meanest thou? For what did he this thing?"

" Caanthus, thou art to learn a slave is like unto a pence unto his holder."

" And did he bear Theia, my mother, unto his lands?"

" Nay, Caanthus, nay."

" Then did the sire of me lay him low?"

" Yea, Caanthus, yea. Wait thou!"

" Thou art long, Panda, long. Tell thou more and more, and tarry not."

" And this man, Tiberius,[8] had come at the calling of Caesar, and no man within Rome did dare to say he had seen his coming, for the time had not come when Caesar had need for him. And he called forth flesh * and sent him with Theia and men of Rome unto lands where no man knew. And this word reached far and angers raised up. Then did death set among Caesar's tribe and he caused word sent unto where this man abided and brought him forth, and thy mother."

" Yea, Panda, Theia—did she ride unto Rome at this Caesar's calling?"

" Nay."

" My sire, Panda—did he come forth and seek her out and stand before Rome's men to shew that she was loved as did Caanthus love Theia?"

" Nay."

" Then my sire is not my sire! Nay. Who then was he, Panda, that I may lay hold of his raiment and rend him naked before the tribes?"

" Caanthus, thy Panda may not tell unto thee his name, for he hath promised this unto Theia, thy mother. But hark! He is not a Jew, but of Rome, and more, he hath a noble's blood, and thou art his child."

" Panda, Panda, I, Caanthus, a noble? Then doth Caanthus say this thing: Caesar is noble of name and not of heart; then Caanthus shall be a noble of heart and not of name. Why, Panda, did not my mother seek the temple and offer prayers unto the priests? Yea, the rabbi telleth what should be."

" Within Rome, Caanthus, abideth many gods. They know not of the God of the Jews, and thy mother hateth Rome's gods, and sought a One who sat o'er."

" Thy word meaneth naught unto Caanthus. Tell thou of her. Did this man die, Panda, that I, his son, do know him not?"

* Horses.

"Nay, Caanthus, for when he had heard the word of Caesar the itch of greed ate his heart, and the slave, who had been the plaything of his barren day, was needed not. So, when he was bidden unto Rome, he spoke, unto them who bore unto him the word, of Theia and of thee. And Caesar, hearing this, sent forth Rome's men for her, and they set upon a journey to where she knew not. And thy Panda was her handman and all of Rome who followed her. And they set them afar, and lo, binded up her eyes that she see not. And upon waters and upon lands and upon greens and upon sands went they. Then, when they had come unto a wilderness, they unloosed the eyes of her and gave moneys unto Panda and left her, thy mother, and thy Panda, amid the rocks and hills—here, Caanthus, without the walls of Bethlehem! And this thing happened that this man might woo within his tribe and be not known as one whom Rome knew as a slave's love. Yet Rome hath love for these men, for he, Caanthus, was one who told not unto his hand what his foot stepped upon."

"Is this man he, Panda?"

"Nay, nay, nay, lad! He had much hate for thy sire."

"Thy tale soundeth as doth dreams seem, for that that seemeth right is wrong, when I do ask of thee. Panda, thou sayest Theia was within Bethlehem! then Caanthus loveth Bethlehem. Yea, and where is Theia, Panda?"

"Caanthus, Panda hath told thee much, and yet he may not tell thee more, save of her when she abideth within Jerusalem. For Theia hath sought not Bethlehem since her going from out Jerusalem."

"Panda, where was Caanthus when thou and Theia came unto this city?"

"Thou—thou—thou, Caanthus? The caravan had not yet come with thee."

"Theia, Panda, awaited the caravan, then?"

"Yea, yea."

"And she sang her song, Panda?"

"Yea, yea. 'He shall come from out the East upon the whited camel.'"

"Then He led the caravan that brought Caanthus forth?"

"Yea, yea, Caanthus, thou hast spoken the truth! And true and true she sung of His coming."

"Then she loved Caanthus. Rhea telleth of a one who dwelled with thee and Theia and Ezekiel within Jerusalem."

"Nay, Caanthus, we abided within his house, Flavius Marcus, the sire of Mary."

" Panda, where is he and Theia? "

" Flavius, Caanthus, the world holdeth dead and yet no man knoweth, for the man whom Jerusalem holdeth that held hate for him told naught, and Rome's men cared little. And we waited. And time came when Herod sought the lands with wolves for lambs, and Panda took thee and Mary and Rachael unto a well's pit and dwelled within until night's dark covered, when the house of Ezekiel fled."

" It seemeth, Panda, that Theia and her tribe fled ever! "

" Yea, and days and days, within a rock's ope * dwelled, until the fearing left the land."

" Meanest thou that Mary's sire dwelleth where ye know not? "

" Panda hath told all, Caanthus, his tongue may tell, for he knoweth not."

" And Panda, what was the time Theia abided within Jerusalem? And what sought she there? "

" Caanthus, thou hast spoken thou wouldst hear naught of gods. Thy mother sought the temples, as thou wouldst have her do."

" And did the rabbi tell to her the things she sought? Yea, Rhea hath told of him whom Herod feared, the son of Mary. And was He the King of the Jews, Panda? Yea, or did these men of the far seek out a noble of Rome? Thinkest thou my sire sent them forth? "

" Nay, and yea. He was the King they sought, for thy mother sought out the place where it was told. Yea, Simeon, whom thou knowest as Caanthus, and Panda and thy mother, sought the temple and waited the coming of Mary with this child, that Theia might hear it spoken and slay the hope within her heart."

" Then this was He, the King, Panda? And the caravan brought Him and me upon the night thou tellest of; for we knew earth, thou sayest, at the same hour. And they came from out the East for Him and not for Caanthus. Where is Theia, my mother? Panda, ah, Panda, tell, for it seemeth no hand may soothe this heart. Wilt thou take me, Panda, unto Jerusalem and shew unto me the place where these words were spoken? What, what, Panda, was the thing that drove my mother that she fled from me? Thou sayest she liveth; was this thing hate? And hath she named me so that I know? Ah, Panda, hold thou my hand. It burneth, and my heart leapeth, and 'tis not love! "

" Rest thee, Hatte."

" Speak thou not this name, Panda! Though Bethlehem knoweth Hatte, thou knowest Caanthus. Speak not this name, for Rachael

* A cave.

hath made it hateful unto me. Wilt thou, Panda, take me forth from here?"

"Nay, lad, the time is not come; but when it cometh, then seek thou Panda, and put thy hand in his, and Panda shall be thy handman."

"Panda, hark! Caanthus and thou shalt seek the hills where they show blue as the incense of the temples, and dwell there with no wall, amid sheep and earth, and not 'mid men."

"Yea, Caanthus, when the time cometh, it shall be. Unto Ezekiel thou owest thy labor until thou art come unto thine own. Then, Caanthus, then canst thou turn unto yonder sinking sun and hope for this day."

"Yea, Panda, yea, and the sun seemeth her hair of gold, and the white clouds the sheep, and the early stars her tears. See! I, Caanthus, am a noble! Then 'tis time this heart learn its task!"

And Panda brought forth goats and milked and put within the cup he wore, and broke up the bread that he took unto the hills, and they sat them down and eat thereof. And the sky-sheep fled the pastures of the night, and the gold sunk unto the treasures of the next of dawnings, and the stars showed thick, and thick, and thick. And it was night, and still they showed thicker, thicker, to light them upon their ways.

CHAPTER VIII

AND the day broke and up o'er the sheep's hills came light. And
Caanthus spake unto Panda 'mid the hush, saying:

"Panda, see thou, 'tis day! Come, then, we seek out the house of
Rhea. Yea, for though my breast be empty of love, she hath fed mine
hunger, and waxed the flesh of me strong."

And they arose; and Panda took up the sheep's crook and they
set upon the path unto the city. And Bethlehem lay like unto a babe
not yet waked; and the streets were damped of the night's kiss. And
the sheep went them ahead upon the way unto the wall. And Panda set
beside the roadway and awaited the going of Caanthus unto the house
of Rhea. And then went the lad within and sought her, the mother of
his days, within Bethlehem. And he spake unto her, saying:

"Rhea, Rhea, this is the time when Caanthus speaketh out the word
within his heart. Thou and thy tribe and Panda and the whole of
earth hath held away that that Caanthus knoweth now.

"Yea, for Panda hath spoken, and thou hast given out unto me the
name that Theia, my mother, did speak as mine, Hate. Yea, thou hast
cloaked the name within a word. Yea, thou speakest it Hatte, and
yet I say unto thee 'tis Hate. Yea, but this day doth Caanthus live
and slay the Hate. Rhea, mother, where, where is thy word to this?
Sayest thou naught unto Hatte? Speak thou and bid him gone, for from
this time he harketh not unto the name."

And Rhea angered much and spake unto Caanthus: "Is this thing
thou hast done right? For through the night have not I woed me much
that thou comest not? Yea, thy father hath sought within the walls and
e'en cried out unto the hills and no answer made ye! What meanest
thou? Speak! Speak!"

"Rhea, I bided in my father's house. Yea, for he is 'who,' and
'who' holdeth estate o'er the stars."

"Thy father! Speak, lad! Who hath told unto thee of him?"

"Panda. And Rhea, he is noble. Didst thou know Caanthus was
a noble's blood? See! these hands are of Rome's blood. And Rhea, I
am not of thy tribe. Nay, nor am I a Jew. For Panda hath spoken
it unto me. And Mary—where is she, Rhea? Hath she waked? Rhea,

mother, hath she waked? There is much to tell unto her of what hath filled up mine ears."

"Mary! Mary! Mary! Thou art ever seeking her! Rachael slumbereth, and Mary hath gone forth for waters unto the well. Speak thou unto Rachael and tell of this thing, for she hath much love for thee, Hatte."

"Who, Rhea, is this man 'Hatte'?"

And Rhea smote the lad in anger, and he drew him up and spake: "Rhea, this is Caanthus, smite or nay. Go! Bring forth thy flesh, Rachael, and leave Mary to rest beneath thy toiling of her. Thou art wearying the flesh and scourging the spirit. See, Rhea, she cometh, bended low! Look thou, mother! such hands were ne'er for burdens."

"Thou, Hatte, speak not so unto thine elders! Nay, when thy father cometh then shall I unfold unto him this of thy doing."

"So, Rhea, 'tis pity Caanthus casteth unto thy son 'Hatte.' Mary, Mary, art thou weary, and the morning's time scarce spent? Come, and Caanthus shall take thee unto his father's house. Come, come, Mary, sister! Rhea, thy mother and mine, hath much woe o'er her son 'Hatte.'"

"'Caanthus?' 'Caanthus?' Hate, I love not the name. Nay, I love thee as Hate. Who hath filled thee up with wonder tale, Hate? Hath thy dreaming shewed thee such a name?"

"Nay, nay, sister. Come unto the hills, for Panda waiteth there. Rhea, wouldst thee, for the love of thy son, 'Hatte,' give unto him a skin's full of vinegar,* for the cutting of thirst, and loaf, mother; for thou hast lost thy son 'Hatte.' Do thou this for the love of him."

"Yea, since this, child, is thy wish, go thou and Mary unto the hills. Hath Panda gone up on high, or waiteth he without the walls?"

"He waiteth, mother. Yea and hark! within thine arms hath the Hate lain and waxed strong. Yea, mother, and now leave him to die within them. Ope up thine arms and leave me in. And mother, say thee the word 'Caanthus' and love thou him."

"It is done, even now. Yea, for though Rhea hath of her own flesh, her heart is not full."

"Rhea, Rhea, at the coming eve wilt thou unlock thy lips and tell all, and all, and all, of her thou knowest, the mother of me? For deep, deep, Rhea, mother, within a spot I know not, where e'en when I say unto thee 'mother' there echoes deep and deep again, 'mother,' 'mother,' 'mother,' and gold locks do blind mine eyes. And think ye, 'tis but since the yesterday! And yet, it hath always been."

* A sour wine. Ruth 2:14. Matthew 27:48.

"What meanest thou, Hatte?"

"Nay, Mary, Caanthus."

"Caanthus. Yea, then Caanthus, did Rachael speak this unto thee, and is it a truth that Rhea is not thy mother? And 'who' thy sire? Who is this man 'who'? Art thou of his tribe?"

"Yea, yea and yea, Mary. Come thou! for Rhea hath ready the skin and loaf."

And they set upon their ways up unto the high wall that led unto the hills. And they came unto the ope and Panda had gone up. And Mary sought out the bright blooms, and Caanthus followed, and the path was but laugh and bloom. And they broke the loaf and eat thereof upon their ways. And Caanthus spake unto Mary, saying:

"Mary, look thou! yon shadow swayeth with the bending of the tree. Look, 'tis a-dance! Look! I, Caanthus, shall dance for thee."

And the lad was clothed not, save of skin and loincloth, and his limbs shone strong, and he bounded up and swayed and laughed and cast high the leaves and plucked the grasses. And at the high of his swaying, lo, a one watched afar as one of stone, and a voice cried out:

"Hate! Hate! Hate!"

And he harked not, but spake: "Nay, nay, nay! I am Caanthus. The Hate is dead! He hath died at his mother's hating."

And the watcher sunk. And the lad sprung forth unto her, and she cried out: "Nay, nay, nay! Come not unto me! See thou this!"

And she oped her breast. And the child spake not, but stopped and looked, and lo, the winds sprang up and loosed the locks, and he cried: "Theia! Theia! Mother! Art thou wounded deep?"

"Yea, yea, yea—deep! Nay, come not unto me! It may not be. For this, this, hath filled up mine arms."

"Ah, who hath wounded thee? Leave thou me to touch the spot that it heal of love."

"Nay, nay, nay, child! Not nearer, or thy mother fleeth."

"Then shall thy man-son follow! Ah, Mary, look, look! This is the mother of Hate—Hate, whom I did slay this day; and yet, Mary, what is this thing? For I do love Hate, and Caanthus is but a dream. 'Theia!' 'Theia!' 'Theia!' It soundeth as a song! And Hate, and Hate was the name she gave unto me! Then, Theia, mother, this is thy Hate! Ah, leave me come! Ah, leave me come! See! for time and time have I longed to press thy bosom. Ah, cast thou thy cloth and loose thy locks."

And she did this thing, and the Hate cried: "Yea, yea, as Panda hath told, they touch thy hem! Do thou to dance! See! see! thy son hath thy dance. Look, mother! I shall dance as the leaves of the trees, and thou shalt see. Come! Panda sayeth thy dance is like unto the summer's clouds; then mine shall be as the leaves that dance through loving of the cloud's-breeze."

And he swayed and swayed and held ope his arms. And Mary watched, and lo, Theia who had sunk, spake:

"See thou, my son, see thou! For thee thy mother steppeth." And she wrapped her in her golden locks. "See! this shall be 'the sun's rise and sink.' Watch thee! Yea, close!"

And she raised her then from off a rock's bosom and stepped to dance and dance. And at the "midhour's dance" the locks were burnt with high sun and gleamed gold and shewed as brands. And the child's bosom heaved, and his lips parted, and his steps followed. And at the "eve's coming," lo, she bounded on and on unto the thick and called back through tears:

"'Tis eve! 'Tis eve! And thy sun hath sunk!"

And the child stopped and looked unto Mary, who watched as one who dreamed, and he called unto the hills:

"Theia! Theia! Theia!"

And naught made answer, but deep, deep, deep echoed: "Theia! Theia! Theia!"

And he murmured: "Mother!" And he fell upon his face.

And Mary dried up his tears and spake unto him, though he listed not.

And the child arose as one who had lost his heart and sought for it within the path, for he looked upon the every side, and beat his hands one upon the other, and murmured:

"She hath a wound and 'tis deep, 'tis deep, and filleth up her arms, and her breast may not take unto it the Hate. Mary, Mary, take thou this hand and lead me forth unto Panda, that Panda shall tell unto me of her; for Panda telleth of her of golden locks and happy feet, and speaketh not of wounds! Ah, the eyes of Hate are filled up of this wound, Mary!"

And Mary took the hand of the Hate, and their feet sought out the path unto Panda. And their steps were slow, and dance had fled. And lo, they came upon Panda, who stooped o'er a lamb that the fold had trodden, and he held it up unto his breast and said:

"Thou art trodden so! Panda knoweth pity, for Panda hath lain beneath the feet of Rome's men!"

And seeing the Hate, who wept, Panda spake: "Caanthus, Caanthus, thou art named Caanthus for the love of Theia. Then dost thou weep?

Stand thou! Stand thou, lad! Hath not Panda told thee much of thy mother?"

"Yea, yea, Panda, thou hast told much, and yet thou hast spoken not of the wounds!"

"What meanest thou, Caanthus? Speak! Speak unto Panda and tell what meanest thou!"

"Panda, Panda, within the hills Caanthus died! And Hate hath come unto the day to live; for Panda, Hate hath hate! Yea, for the hills hold her, Theia, the mother of me, and Panda, her breast is not the breast that holdeth me! Nay, she hath spoken and sayeth 'tis full and shewed unto me the wound. And it gleameth as fires and ash. Yea, Panda, yea, so did it to gleam and burn the eyes of the Hate."

And Panda spake unto the lad and begged that he tell of the meeting with Theia and what had come to pass. But the Hate sat as dead and looked, with eyes that saw not, unto Panda, as a wounded dove. Then did Panda take him up unto him and speak of the love of Theia and of the dancing of the days of Rome. And the Hate spake:

"Nay, nay, nay, Panda, the dance hath died. Yea, she called unto me the day was o'er and the sun gone. Look, Panda, 'tis so! The sun hath robed within a dark cloud, and grasses that but a time agone were gleaming, studded o'er, and leaf that danced hath stopped and looketh sorrow.

"Panda, who, who is 'who'? Did Theia seek him out? Ah, Panda, he filleth up my wonder! See, Mary, see! the stones did cut the feet of Hate and naught but soft grasses did touch his flesh until this time. Panda, see! Mary hath tired o'ermuch and sleepeth. Panda, tell thou unto me where within these hills abideth she. And Panda, who hath wounded her? Ah, Panda, at every step of the dance of her she trod upon the heart of the Hate, for at each downfall of her foot the heart throbbed. Ah, woe! Ah, woe! O-h-e-e-e! Panda, the earth's bosom, too, is hard and cutteth me. Panda, Panda, where, where is the breast that welcometh Hate? Ah, Panda, where?"

"Here, here, here, Caanthus—the breast of Panda! For should Hate flee from out Panda's breast 'twould leave him lone."

And the child went unto the arms of Panda, and Panda let flow his loving. And Mary slept. And the fields were darkened from cloud, and the sheep lay, and quiet set upon the land, the quiet of the storm's birth.

Bellow-winds sprang up and tore asunder writhing clouds. Flash-torn and crash-roared sped on the storm. Trees reached out unto the coming drops and winds swept cool. And up the hill's side sped, upon the wings of storm, a one whose face was hid; one whose step was like unto a fallow deer; whose arms reached up unto the cool winds. And lo, the hands reached unto the locks and loosed them unto the wind, and shook them out and fled from their spreading. And 'mid the wailing of the trees and beating of the branch and trunks, lo, she sunk and fell and held close the arm's full of locks, and kissed their gold; and drops fell 'mid the bright strands.

And the storm broke and swept the hill's sides. And the one sat still, and rocked of grieving. And the dark and blue warred much; and the blue shone through. And the voice of the griever spake:

"Simeon, Simeon, thou water o' the desert's sands! Simeon! Simeon!" And the voice cried out: "Simeon! Simeon!"

And again the griever fled her on, ever calling.

And it was the eve's hour, when sheep wake for home paths.

And Simeon had slept upon his staff beneath a rock. And the sheep nosed 'bout and waked his sleeping. And he spake out:

"This is the storm's cease. And Theia, Theia, yea, Theia went unto the hills long and long."

And he took up his crook and limped, and chided the sheep. And they came upon the cot, and lo, a fire shewed from out the smoke's ope. But Theia shewed not. And Simeon harked and called and looked him ever, but found her not. And night came down and kissed the earth. And he sought up unto the spot where the Hate had stood and watched the dance. And there upon the earth lay Theia, with lips unto the spot where he had stood. And she murmured word:

"Yea, yea, it shall be! He shall come upon the whited camel from out the East. He shall come! Yea, yea, it shall be so!"

And wailing broke forth, but turned unto a song, for she wailed as music: "Jehovah! Jehovah! Jehovah! It shall be!"

And she cried unto the winds: "Take thou this, lest it stray, straight unto him! Yea, beat thou upon Theia and wrap her close, and fill up her arms, for she may not be unto thee unclean!"

And she plucked up the grass and leaves and crushed unto her breast.

And Simeon found Theia so. And he looked not upon her grieving, but spake of the storm and of the sheep and held forth his hands for her that she follow, and lo, the hands were binded up!

And Theia looked upon the hands of Simeon and wept. But no word spake he to her of this thing, but more of sheep and vines and vintage.

And they made their way unto the cot upon the path, wet and rough.

And Theia made word unto Simeon of what had been, and told of the Hate child, and spake:

"Simeon, Simeon, Theia's hate hath undone her, for she loveth Hate! Ah, Simeon, he is fair! Yea, and his limbs shone as one whom Theia loved, one of Rome, one whose limbs do ever shew unto her as then. Yea, Simeon, and his eyes, his eyes, his eyes hold love! Yea, and his arms, his arms reached out unto me—unto me, Theia, who would have cast him forth. And Simeon, Simeon, Theia could but say him, Nay! And his voice, Simeon, it spake out 'Theia!' 'Theia!' And it sounded soft and whirred as doth the panther whir at comfort. Yea, as doth Panda's. And Panda hath told unto him the name of Theia, for he stoppeth 'The-ia' as doth Panda. Yea, he breathed out the word. It ringeth as metal, Simeon, and cutteth this heart. Yea, Simeon, Theia hath seen the Hate and knoweth hate hath fled from out the wound the seeing dealt. What! What! Simeon, art grieving? Nay, nay, but the morrow and the morrow's morrow, yea, and morrows few, do stand between His coming unto me. For it shall be, and thou shalt see! Simeon, He shall come from out the East. It shall be."

And Simeon spake out unto Theia, saying: "Theia, what meanest thou? Hast thou spoken unto thy babe, or, speak ye! dost thou dream? Thou hast sought the hills in fearing lest thou shouldst see his face, and yet in hoping. Yea, it hath been, thou sayest, and yet thy heart crieth out in mourning."

"Yea, Simeon, for Theia's heart hath stopped its hate, and knoweth love. Yea, and doth the earth offer not unto its loving, then shall Theia keep unto herself that that the seeing of the Hate hath caused to flow unto her heart. Look thou, Simeon, upon Theia. See! Theia is smitten. Yea, her flesh is filth, and yet, ah, Simeon, the heart, yea the white-mist Theia, is not unclean! Nay, and Theia liveth within the day this Theia knoweth, and not the flesh day.

"He hath seen this, Simeon. I did ope up the breast of me and show unto him the smite. And music sounded, for hark, he spake unto me in song and begged that he be left for to touch the wound and heal of loving.

"And Simeon, I tell thee that 'tis Theia who shall turn the days of waiting and hate unto days of loving, and fill them up with the songs that have fled her lips. For 'tis come unto Theia, yea, a voice hath spoken unto her heart and telleth her she hath sought not in vain for this Jehovah. For lo, Simeon, hath Theia not born a hate that hath grown unto a love? For he standeth fair and strong, and Simeon, he showeth Theia's flesh and not the flesh of hate, and no god save this Jehovah might do this thing.

"Yea, yea, and yet it shall be. He shall come from out the East, and Theia shall know 'tis the token she hath found this God. Look thou Simeon! See! Theia throweth free the cloak of hating. Yea, and opeth up her arms unto Him, Jehovah, and danceth and singeth and 'tis the dance of love and the song of love. And Theia shall fill up the days so. For hark! Doth Theia hate? Nay, hate filleth not up her arms. Nay, Simeon, 'tis love that filleth her up of warmth and stirreth her heart."

And lo, she bounded up and danced, and the light broke out anew, and she sung as a child. And the flesh of her was whited upon the cheek. And she swept her up unto Simeon, who watched, and fell upon her knees and touched the hands of him, and wrapped them within her locks and wept. And Simeon's lips moved and they spake:

"Theia, what are the days of Simeon without thee? Yea, and what hath Simeon for hands were it not for thee? They but offered them unto thee and are worn for thy serving. Hath Panda come unto thee with the child?"

"Nay, Simeon, Panda hath lips that guard, and knoweth well the tricks of the Roman, who letteth not his word know its brother. Ah, Simeon, what a heart hath Panda, thy brother and mine! A saffron-skin, who yet hath noble's blood and the honor of the gods. What might Bethlehem know of Panda's seeking of the hills at dark that thy sheep go unto the market place? And what might Bethlehem care, that he bear unto the hill's-top of bread and grain, for eating at the waiting of the herds? Yea, Simeon, and Panda's lips told not of him, the flesh of Theia, unto her. Nay, for Panda knoweth what the heart's wound meaneth, and knoweth, too, that word chafeth. Then silence he offered unto Theia as a balm. Ah, Panda, then is the voice of Him, Jehovah, sounded out unto thee and me amid the wilderness."

And lo, even as she spake, Simeon sunk. And she cried out:

"Simeon, speak! Hast thou not a word for Theia? Speak, speak unto her! What, what hath stopped thy word? Ah! Ah! Oh-o-e-e-e! Oh-o-e-e-e! Simeon! Simeon! Hast thou forsaken me? Ah, the wilderness hath come upon me! Panda! Panda! Panda! Simeon! Simeon! Speak! Ah-h-h-h!"

And she sunk upon his form. And her arms held close the head, and her lips pressed close the lips of him, and she wailed amid the hills. And they mocked her back, and she raised her up and spread ope her arms and spake unto the airs that stirred:

"He hath gone! He hath gone! Yea, speed thou him upon his way, for he hath found the paths wherein the everblooms do spring. Yea, he hath gone, and I, Theia, shall dance of joy, for he hath fled from out the vale."

And she danced, and bounded, and swayed, and beat her hands one upon the other, and cast her locks out wide, and fled amid the shrub. And wailing broke anew upon the air and died as she sunk within the depths, as the child's wail as it sinketh unto the mother's breast.

And they who waited upon the hills afar, heard the wail-reft airs. And Panda harked, and stopped him at the sheep-cairns, and sent up his voice in shrilling. For he knew the wail of Theia, yea, well, well he knew! And he spake unto the Hate, saying:

"Go ye unto the house of thy mother, Rhea. Waken Mary and set upon thy ways, for Panda hath much to do within the hills. Yea, seek ye then unto Bethlehem and wait not for the coming of Panda."

And they did this thing. And when they had gone, Panda called aloud: "Theia! Theia! Theia!"

And the wailing ceased, and the voice of Theia rang out:

"Panda! Come! Come unto thy Theia!"

And it sounded as the lute of a shepherd that wailed at eve. And Panda went up unto the place and spake unto her. And Theia told unto him that that had been, and Panda sorrowed sore. And Theia stood mute, and pointed up unto the high hills where the hut of Simeon stood. And Panda looked unto her and murmured: "Theia, come!"

And she wrung her hands nd said unto Panda: "Seek not the place, for Panda, the flesh of thee, though it be slaved, is free. Yea, and there abideth a master, yea, a lord more mighty than Caesar, and his robe stinketh. Yea, and is builded up of rotted flesh. Panda, seek not this master, for he who goeth unto this place is slaved unto him."

And Panda stood and looked with hunger-eyes unto the high hill. And he tarried and spake more unto Theia, and told of the sheep that lay upon the hills below, and said that she might go beneath the night's mantle unto there and he would sit and wait the morn.

And the night came sad, and robed black, until the late hour, when, 'mid her quiet, at the deep of earth's sleep, she brought forth her jewel and set it upon the bosom of the sky. And the still was broken by the sorrow-breath of Theia. And Panda brought forth his pipe and whispered unto the night. And the notes sobbed and dripped with tears.

And the Day drank from out the Night's chalice, and drained the star-wine, and the cheek of morn burned with its gold. And Theia slept and Panda sat deep in thought. And he rose and stretched forth his hands and kneeled as the slave kneeleth before his master. And he rose and went unto Theia, at the day's-break, and touched her flesh and spake:

"Theia, Theia, come! Thy brother and mine dwelleth yonder upon the high hill, and he hath called through all the night."

And she waked and said unto Panda: "So, He hath come! Yea, He hath come, e'en though He hath not shown Himself unto me. And yet it shall be."

And Panda made answer: "Yea, Theia, yea."

And she waked from out her waking-sleep, and started up and fled, and called aloud unto Panda:

"Stand thou there and come not unto me, for thou art the herdsman of the sheep of Theia, yea, the lamb of her!"

And Panda said: "Nay, thy lamb hath a shepherd and the fold offereth unto him. Yea, and the ewe, who hath suffered that he be the lamb of her, shall take him unto her and make much of him, and thou, thou, Theia, art storm-lost and beaten, yea, trodden down. Thinkest thou that Panda might hear his lamb call out and heed not? This flesh, Theia, hath served as slave and Caesar hath cast it out. This master thou speakest of may not put the flesh of Panda as the slave of him, for he hath met with Panda, thou knowest, and knew him not, and claimed thee."

But Theia harked not unto him and spake that the Hate had need of him. And Panda told of the loving of the Hate, and spake that he would seek out the hills for Panda, and it should be that he should speak unto him and all should be well.

And they went them up unto the spot where Simeon lay as one who had fallen within a pit, broken, but arms and breast as a noble; as one who slept and dreamed of hosts, and victors, and of the rose! And the hands were wrapped. And the wrappings had loosed and showed the scarring; and within its shrunken flesh, pressed deep, a smitten bloom of dust; and 'bout the neck, upon a thong, a sandal small, was hung. And they came upon him so. And the sun had kissed his lips.

And Theia walked as one smitten, and stood wide-eyed and breathing out his name. And Panda stopped and looked, and went unto the thick and brought forth laurel, and wound a wreath, the wreath that crowneth victor.

CHAPTER IX

AND the days passed sorry. And paths shewed them trod from out Bethlehem unto the hills. And time set upon the lands. And at the going of Panda the Hate remained, and Mary. And lo, upon a day, the house of Ezekiel held much wrath, for Ezekiel spake unto the Hate, saying:

"Whither goest thou, and whither hast thou gone these days and days? Yea, from out the walls of thy father's house thou goest at the night's dark and yet thou speakest not unto him of thy going."

And the lad stood mute and hung down the head of him. And Ezekiel wrathed much upon him, saying: "What hast thou brought unto thy sire but sorrow?"

And the child spake, saying: "Yea, yea, sire, thou speakest a truth, for hark thee unto thy son! What may Hate bring unto the day but sorrow's tears? Yea, it seemeth the days of me, and them of me, lie wet of sorry-tears."

And Ezekiel wrathed hot upon him, saying: "Lo, thou art the son of a beggar, and thy mother, though she robed in royal dyes, is but a beggar of this land. Then what thinkest thou that thou mayest bring of good unto this house? Nay, Rhea hath much heart and little reason that she filleth up the house of her husbandman with desert's waste and Rome's offcasting. Did I not give of my folds unto Panda, and offer of my board unto thy mother, and ope up mine house unto the child of Flavius, and thee? Yea, a thankless son is like unto a wine yet within the fruit; he hangeth unto the sun and shrinketh, yea or ripeth, and 'tis not for thee to know whether it be the shrinking or yet the riping."

And the lad stood mute, and his eyes shot fires. And lo, Ezekiel forbade that he seek out the hills. For within the mouth of Rachael had grown words that told of the going at the dark.

And when the eve had come Ezekiel went forth for the seeking of his flocks and brought them unto his walls.

And the house of Ezekiel slept. And the hills shone white beneath the moon-kiss. And afar, at the late hour, there sounded out a pipe, clear, sorry-mellow. And lo, there came forth from out the wall of the house of Ezekiel a form that hovered at the door's ope and stood, and,

76

of a sudden, went forth as a lamb afrighted. And Ezekiel sent up his voice and called aloud:

"Hatte! Hatte! Stop thou! What hast thou beneath thy robe? Come thou unto me!"

And the child came unto him and stood. And Ezekiel put forth his hand and smote his flesh, and he but stood. And again did the hand of Ezekiel smite, and yet he stood, and no word came unto his lips. Then did Ezekiel bid that he shew unto him what was beneath the robe that he wore, and lo, he took him unto him and laid ope his mantle, and bread and vinegar shewed unto him. And Ezekiel lay scourge upon the Hate and raised up his voice and spake loud:

"Go! Go thou unto the hills! Yea, go from out thy father's house! Give unto him the bread thou hast pilfered from his store. Thou art the serpent of his days, yea, the smite-worm of his vineyard, and the bitterness of his cup. Go! Go!"

And the lad fell heavy beneath the blow. And he made word in voice that bore no tear:

"The bread! The bread! The bread! But give thou unto me!"

"Nay. Off ye! The swine of the land may feed and grow fatted upon thy sire's bread, but not thee!"

And the light of the white moon darkened, and when it broke forth, lo, the lad shewed not before Ezekiel. And the moon hid and shone in, fearing lest it see. And the high paths of the hills shewed the fleeing of the lad. And he sought out the sheep and laid him down among them to rest. And the night was still, save for the sheep's bleat and the pipe that sounded far. And lo, no answer made he, but laid him low and mute.

And the hours passed unto the lighting of the day, and at the early tide,* when but the shadow's shade did show, amid the still did sound the feet of travelers up unto the hill. And the lad awaked and harked, but spake no word.

And when they had come up unto the place where he lay, he watched in silence, for these were strangers upon their way to Bethlehem, a woman who rode upon an ass and one who followed. And before them walked a lad who sought the byways 'long the path.

And lo, He came upon the Hate and looked in sorrowing, for the eyes of him shot fires and the lips of him were mute. Yea, he looked upon the seeker of his woes in hating. And the lad who sought stretched forth His hands and oped up His arms and looked with sorry

---

* "Tide" is frequently used in this composition to express time, the old Anglo-Saxon sense.

eyes upon the Hate. And word came from off His lips: "Who art thou?"

And the Hate spake: "Who art thou?"

And the lad made answer unto him:

"I am thy brother, even as thou art mine."

And the Hate arose, and his bosom heaved, and his cheeks burned crimson, and he spake:

"Thou art the brother of my flesh? And thou hast spoken it? Then go thee unto thy father and mine, and tell unto him that his son seeketh him that he may lay ope his mantle unto all men, that they know that which he hath done unto his flesh and the flesh of Theia. Yea, go and tell unto him of Theia's wound.

"Hark! There soundeth step! Who seeketh? Is this man thy sire? Then he is the flesh that is the flesh of me. Nay, this is not my sire, for he hath forsaken me and taken thee unto him. Who then is he yonder?"

And the Seeker spake: "Thy Sire hath taken thee unto Him, even as He hath taken me. Yea, and He shall forsake me even as He hath forsaken thee. Yea, even as thou hast suffered, so shall thy Brother suffer, and even as thy mother is smitten in the flesh, so shall thy Brother's mother be smitten in the spirit. Yea, and even as thy Sire hath forsaken thee, so shall He come unto thee at the time when the darkness setteth."

And He went Him upon His way. And the Hate stood and watched Him sink within the thick growth down the hillside. And he sunk upon the stones and wailed aloud, and beat his hands one upon the other, crying out:

"Where hath He gone? Where hath He gone, that I may then to call unto Him. Lo, have I called upon the hills and sought upon the streets of Bethlehem and watched the travelers within the city and dreamed, and called, and where hath it then led?"

And he fled him down unto the hill's growth and called unto the lad. And lo, He stopped and came unto him. And the Hate held high his head and spake words, saying:

"Knowest thou that I am the noble's blood?"

And the Seeker spake: "Even so am I."

And the Hate said: "Yea, and knowest thou thy sire? For I know not the sire of me."

And the Seeker spake: "Even so, thy Brother seeth not His Father but knoweth Him."

"Thy words mean naught unto me. Goest thou unto thy father

within thy travel days, and wilt thou then speak unto him of thy brother?"

And the Seeker made answer: "Yea, I go unto the vineyards of my Father and thine. Yea, and He shall take thee unto Him even as He taketh me, for thou shalt come unto His house even as thy Brother."

And the Hate, seeing the woman who rode upon the ass, asked of her: "Is this thy mother?"

And the lad made answer: "Yea."

And the Hate cried out: "Then speak thou unto her and ask that she but leave me press her breast."

And the Seeker told unto the woman what the Hate had spoken, and she bid that he come unto her. And the Hate, whose eyes were wonderlit, came with halting step, and he whispered:

"What is thy name?"

And the woman spake: "Mary."

And the Hate cried out unto her: "Mary! And thou art the mother of Him! Yonder hill holdeth the mother of me, and she is smitten sore, yea, she hath a wound, and telleth me she may not take me unto her. Then wouldst thou, who lovest Him, but leave me press thy breast and love thee o'er, for her?"

And Mary oped her arms, and he fled unto their folds, murmuring: "Theia! Theia! Theia!"

And he drowned his tears in the smile of Mary.

And when he had ceased his tears, the Seeker spake unto him, saying:

"Thou hast come unto the breast of Mary, e'en as shall thy brothers and their brothers."

And the Hate lifted up his eyes and they shone with happiness, and he spake:

"Even as bread hath filled my hunger, so hath thy smile filled up my heart. Hark! Hearest thou the pipe? It is the pipe of Panda, and he calleth unto me. Yea, and I go me unto him that I bear of this happiness unto him and tell of thee unto her, that thou hast left me to shed my love for her upon thy breast."

And he fled. Light as the swallow's wing he stepped.

And the Seeker stood, and held high His hands and spake:

"Even as thou art lone, so shall I to be."

And Mary's lips shed smile that cloaked a wisdom.

And the Hate sped upon his way unto the spot where Panda piped. And when he had come close unto the place, lo, he came upon Theia, who stood beside a tree and wound about its roughened trunk her arms, and murmured, pressing close her lips unto its bark:

"Hate, Hate, I love thee!"

And he came upon her so and called: "Theia, here am I, thy manson! Ope up thy arms, for the flesh of me doth freeze for loving!"

And Theia, seeing him, made way unto the higher place where Panda waited and called unto him:

"Panda, see thee! the Hate hath sought thee here and thou hast told him of the folly should he seek thee here! Speak thou unto him, for I dare not to trust this tongue to speak word lest he hear that that is hidden within my heart."

And Panda ceased his piping and came unto him, and Theia went within the hut. And Panda made words unto the Hate and asked of that that had been. And the child told unto him of Ezekiel and his smiting, and that he had found the bread of his store pilfered and had set watch and found the thing to be. And Panda spake:

"Hatte——"

"Nay, Panda, the name she hath given me, Hate."

And Panda spake it so, and bid that he seek his father's house; for he told unto him that Ezekiel would ne'er send him forth, for Panda had left moneys within the hand of Ezekiel lest death should take him from the Hate. And even though Ezekiel had seen Theia with Panda in the hills, and told unto the townsmen of the thing and caused the stoning of Panda from out the city, yet he could ne'er do this thing.

And the Hate oped up his eyes and spake: "Panda, thinkest thou a noble might bow unto one such as he? Nay. And Panda, thou knowest that I, the Hate, have sought the tradesmen as they drive their flocks from o'er the hills about unto the market's place and have made price with them before their going within, that Ezekiel not know. Yea, and Panda, have I not given unto Rhea moneys that thy bread be bought?

"And Rhea knoweth this, Panda. Speak it, Panda, that I may abide me here. See thou, the sheeps hut them 'neath the rock that hangeth o'er. Speak, Panda, that I may lay me down with thy flocks. Yea, Panda, for e'en when I do stay me there within Bethlehem 'tis ever dark and ne'er a sun's gold save when I do look me unto this hill."

And Panda stood and looked unto the city and then unto the hut and wrung his hands. And he went unto Theia and they spake one to the other. And Theia wailed and her eyes started forth and her words came hissed:

"Panda, Panda, send thou him unto the city. Yea, Panda, in the name of thy love for me do this thing."

And Panda sat him down, and lo, age seemed to settle upon him.

And when he had set him long, and Theia had stood and beat her hands and wailed, and the Hate had waited, wondering and pleading from his eyes, Panda spake:

"Come thou, Hate, stand! Show thou unto Panda thy strength. See! run thou unto yon cliff. Yea, thou art even as a lamb. See thou, do raise this stone. Yea, thou art even as strong as Caanthus; is it not so?"

And Theia paled, and Panda spake: "Stand thou, Caanthus! Dost thou then love thy Theia?"

And the Hate made answer: "Panda, seest thou the sun that seekest here within the shade? Even so through the days do I seek her."

And Panda said: "Then, Hate, harken unto thy Panda. As thou dost say 'tis true, a noble should bow not unto such a man as Ezekiel. Then, hark! Thou knowest thy coming and going unto Bethlehem meaneth that Theia and thy Panda may live? Thou knowest, dost thou not?"

And the Hate answered: "Yea."

"Then, since thou art cast forth, and since thou knowest thy Theia hath not Simeon, then thou knowest 'tis thy love for her and me that must buy their bread.

"Dost thou remember at the market's place, where Rhea goeth that she may buy fish, a one who weareth beard and hath the name Peter? Peter knew thy Simeon and brought fish unto the hills until the townsmen knew; and Peter knoweth Panda. Then go thou unto the out-road of the city that leadeth unto the sea's town * and wait thee there until he shall come. Then go thou unto him and say thee: 'I am Hatte, the lad of Panda, and the flesh of Theia, who is smitten. And Panda hath sent me unto thee that I ask of thee; for Panda knoweth thou art a man who casteth young fish back that they do grow and do thereby pilfer not of the sea's store.' Canst thou do this thing, Hatte?"

And the lad stood mute, and Panda murmured: "Thou art strong, strong like Caanthus, and she needeth thee. The time hath come, Caanthus, that thou shalt set within the pit and wrestle for her."

And the lad raised up his arms, saying: "See thou, Panda, I am strong! Yea, I go unto Peter and speak as thou hast told unto me. What then, Panda, may this buy? He abideth not within Bethlehem. And think ye that I may bear bread from other land?"

"Nay, Hatte; Peter abideth but little way upon the out-road; for the fish come unto him that he beareth unto Bethlehem."

* Probably Joppa.

"Then, Panda, will this hill's dark show unto me at the eve's hour, and may I then stand and see the sun kiss it as it sinks?"

"Yea."

"Then do I to go."

"Yea, go, Hatte, and tell out thy heart unto Peter, for he is like unto the sea, for he hath dwelt upon the sea much and like it he knoweth man's sorrows and joys and knoweth that man casteth and catcheth much and naught. Then tell thou unto him of thy emptied net."

"And Theia, Panda, hath her wound healed?"

"Nay, Hatte, but thou mayst heal it much."

"Then do I to go."

And Theia came forth; for she had harked, and she spake: "Panda, thou hast ever treasures within thy pack."

And she looked unto the lad, and his lips moved: "Theia, mother, lovest thou me?"

And she murmured: "Yea! Yea! Where, child, hast thou abided since Ezekiel cast thee forth?"

And he told unto her of his going out of the city and seeking the flocks of Panda that lay below the high hill, and his hearing of the pipe of Panda that bid him come where he wailed. And how his heart had wrathed, and he had lain amid the sheep, and at the early morn the strangers he had heard, and the Seeker, the lad that had found him so and spake words he knew not, and that the lad was his brother; for He had told unto him this thing, and even though His sire had ridden upon an ass He spake that even as he, the Hate, He had seen not His sire, yet knew Him.

And Theia's eyes shot fires. And she asked of the lad was he a one such as the Hate? And the man, the sire of him, was he alone with the lad upon the journey? And the Hate told of Mary who rode and of her smile, but spake not her name. And told unto Theia of how he had begged that she leave him love her o'er for her, and how that she had done this thing and he had lost his sorrow in her smile.

And Theia spake: "Who was this woman, Hate, who?"

And he made answer she had called her name Mary. And Theia started up and cried:

"Mary! Mary! And Theia's flesh hath drowned its sorrow in her smile even as Theia did cast her hating 'neath her robe of love!

"Yea, Panda, hark! from out this child's lips shall fall words that shall set the priests in wonder upon their seats. Yea, He shall cast light upon the dark of this day. Yea, and the priests' words, that are as sheep that stay not within the fold but scatter them whither and yon, shall fall beneath this light He shall cast, as sheep who trod the home-way at the shepherd's touching of his crook.

"Yea, this child shall yet wear the crown. Yea, and earth shall weave it of the hating of her men. Yea, and hark! Theia telleth more. Even as a noble weareth jeweled band shall He wear this, the earth's crown, and it shall be the sign of the crowning of the King of Citizens. Yea, for from out earth's dust shall this crown grow up! Yea, and its jewels shall gleam crimson.

"Yea, yea, and he standeth there, the flesh of Theia, and he goeth unto the day that he be uncrowned! Ah, but Panda, hark, it shall be! He yet shall come! Yea, upon a whited camel shall He come from out the East, and it shall be! Yea, it shall be!"

And she waked from out her see-dream and spake unto the Hate:

"Go! Go thou, as thou lovest me, and ever know thy mother holdeth love here."

And she beat her hands o'er her heart's throb. And he went, fleeing and afraid.

And Theia sunk and cried out: "Jehovah! Jehovah! How long! How long!"

CHAPTER X

'AND the lad sped him down the hill's-way, and lo, he came upon the shepherds who drove their flocks unto the low lands for the dark-tide, lest they who sought the hills for sheep that bear not their shepherd's name, should find, and they should bear unto the heights wherein no man save them a-smitten traveled.

And he waited at the road's ope for the coming of Peter from without the city. And when the sun's ray had deeped unto a young wine's tint and eve crept it on, lo, there sounded the footfall of the market's men who came from out Bethlehem and sought their huts that lay amid the hills.

And a one came forth that leaned upon a staff and carried o'er his back a net wherein were put fish. And they sent up smell that reached before him as he came. And lo, the Hate arose and came up unto this man and spake: " Art thou Peter? "

And the man made answer: " Yea."

Then did the Hate speak him unto the man, saying: " I am Hate, the lad of Panda, and he hath sent me unto thee that I do ask of thee; for he sayeth thou hast wisdom of the sea and that thou dost cast unto the waters the young fish and keep but them of the full flesh and thereby do not pilfer of the sea's store. Yea, and he sayeth thou knowest man casteth of his net, and lo, doth catch naught. And he hath told unto me that I should tell out unto thee my heart. Yea, for unto thee should I bring the empty net of me and thou wouldst know."

And lo, Peter looked with pity unto the lad and laughed aloud and spake: " Lo, upon a child's shoulders standeth the head of Panda! "

And the lad but oped the eye of him and waited. And Peter looked with troubled eye unto him, and lo, his tongue was loth to word. And when he had waited long, then did he speak unto Hate and ask:

" Where, then, hast thou left Panda? "

And the lad made answer: " I know not."

And Peter spake: " Thou art not the lad of Panda."

And lo, the cheek of the Hate burned, and he cried: " Nay, sire, the tongue of me hath spoken false."

And Peter reached forth his hand and took the lad unto him, saying:

84

"Thou hast brought forth thy net, yea, but thou hast told not thy heart unto Peter. Since thou hast sought me out, then speak, lad, and tell of thy heart's full."

And the lad stood in wondering and mute. And Peter took him close unto his breast and set smoothed his gold locks and murmured low:

"There, there! thou hast sought out the shelter fold. Then rest thee, lad. Thou hast yet to learn Peter's ear hath ne'er trod the path unto his lips. Yea; then ope up thy heart and tell all unto him. Where hath Panda hid?"

And the Hate pointed him unto the high hills and spake: "Yon."

"And lad, hath he sought out this place to bide him alone therein?"

And the Hate made answer: "Nay."

"Then who abideth with him yon?"

And the Hate told unto Peter that Panda had sought the hill's height that he might be with Theia, who was smitten with a wound, and that Ezekiel had told this unto the tribesmen and they had sought him out and stoned him, that he return not unto the city. And how he, the Hate, had sought out the hill's places where Panda piped at the dark hours and bore bread unto him, that they might eat. And how Ezekiel had seen this thing and cast him forth, and of his going unto Panda. And that Panda had told him of Peter and that he should seek him at the road's ope at the eve's hour, and it had been.

And Peter closed up his eye and lay his thumb aside his nose. And he thought him long, and lifting up the Hate unto his shoulder looked deep into his eyes and spake:

"Seest thou Peter's eyes? Then look thee deep, for Peter shall ever see but what is right and meet for thee, and thou mayest ever lean upon Peter's staff. Yea, and thou then mayest come unto Peter with the full of thy net and tell unto him all of Panda and Theia. Where upon the hill do they abide?"

And the Hate made answer: "Up at the crest, e'en above the flocks of Ezekiel, where the trees and shrubs are thick. Yea, and Peter, list thou unto me, for Theia is smitten, smitten sore, and Panda sayeth that the love of me, then, must buy of breads that they do live. Yea, and Theia hath spoken it unto me that I should seek thee out and tell unto thee of her, for Ezekiel knoweth of Theia's abode and doth make much word unto the tribesmen, and Panda hath sore fear that they do seek them out where they are hid."

And Peter spake unto the lad and told unto him of his household, and that he then would seek out the high place at the eve's hour and make word with Panda, that there might be bread borne unto the place.

And the Hate told unto Peter of his meeting at this dawn's hour of the strangers who traveled unto Bethlehem, and that Theia had waxed wrathed that he had spoken unto them of her, and had asked if the sire of the lad did travel lone with him. And that he had told her of the woman who rode upon an ass, and that she had called her name Mary. And Theia, like unto the lad, had made word that seemed a naught unto his ears.

And Peter told unto Hate of Theia and of the lad who had been born within the city of Bethlehem at the time of his coming unto the day. And told of Simeon who had sat beside the market's place of Peter and had dealt of sheep and greens and fruits. And he, Peter, had sold unto the townsmen of fish that had come from out the far.

And they set them upon the road's-way unto the house of Peter, and lo, the earth was damped and the eve's sweet was upon the airs. And from out the flocks afar sounded the bleat of a lamb, and lo, the Hate stopped and harked and spake unto Peter:

" As thou lovest Panda and me, do thou but leave me seek out this lamb. 'Tis one that leaveth me to rest upon his wool as I do watch the folds. Yea, Peter, the eyes of this lamb thou hearest yonder have looked unto mine even as do the eyes of Theia."

And Peter suffered him to go up unto the place where it stood and bring it forth. And they set upon their ways, and the lamb followed at the side of the lad, and Peter leaned upon his staff and bent beneath the net.

And they stepped upon the up-way that led unto the higher valley, and lo, they came upon the house of Peter.

And at the door's ope sat a one who tied of nets, and he made musics as he slipped the wood bar between the strands. And Peter called unto the one and he harked not. And they came up unto the place where he sat, and Peter stretched forth his hand and touched the flesh of him, and he looked up unto them startled.

And Peter told unto the Hate of this, the son of him, who heard not. And he called his name Aaron. And the lad arose, and he was of the fullness of flesh, and yet as a babe.* And he shewed unto Peter the net wherein he had put dried leaves, and lo, he babbled much of the full catch. And Peter spake unto him of the moneys these should bring at the dawn and e'en did slip, from out the net, of leaves unto his own. And the Hate stood wide-eyed and spake unto Peter:

" Peter, is this thy son, and hath he a wound? "

* Full grown but an idiot.

"Yea, yea, thou hast spoken a truth, Hatte. He hath a wound, yea, a wound."

And lo, the Hate did slip him unto Peter and lay hold of his hand and look up unto his eyes and spake:

"Peter, even as Theia is wounded, and even as thou art the succor of her and of her flesh, so shall I deal unto this, thy son. Yea, even as the brother of my flesh shall I love him."

And Peter stretched forth his hand and rested it upon the Hate's locks and looked him long and long.

And the Hate made question: "Hath his mother, too, a wound?"

And Peter spake: "Yea, a wound so deep it hath laid her low. Even as thou, he is lone."

Then did the Hate to speak: "Peter, see thou! am I not strong, even as Simeon, whom thou didst know? Hath Panda told unto thee of Simeon and the love he bore for Theia?"

And Peter answered: "Yea."

And the Hate told all unto Peter of the pits and Caanthus, and how 'twas that Panda had called him by this name. And that he had come from out the hills that he might be the wrestler for Theia, as Panda had spoken.

"See thee, Peter! these hands are strong, and these limbs are strong, yea, and this heart is strong. Even as thy son shall I serve thee."

And Peter spake that it should be. And they brought forth fish and scraped their sides with stone and oped them up and hung upon the wood branch o'er the fire's smoke that they be fit for eat. And they sat them about the fires and ate thereof.

And Aaron sung musics like the wind of early season, that starteth up but to die and start anew. And he gathered up the leaves and laughed o'ermuch. And Peter sat, at the finishing of the fish, and slept. And lo, the Hate sat afrighted and beat his hands one upon the other and turned his face unto Bethlehem and the hills. And the lamb sought him out and lay beside him as he sat.

And the night came up from o'er the earth's curve, and lo, Peter waked and spake unto the lad that they should seek the hut. And they went within, and Peter shewed unto him the casting of nets upon the floors whereon they slept. For Peter was of the sea's land and, like unto the fishers, ever hungered for sea's smell. Yea, he hung at night's hour within a net that he sleep.

And when the hour was late, the Hate spake: "Peter, art thou wake?"

And Peter made answer: "Yea; what wouldst thou?"

And the Hate spake: " That thou wouldst leave me but go without the hut that I do look unto Bethlehem and see if there be a star that watcheth the high hill; for Peter, there soundeth the sheep afar and they are the sheep of the tribesmen of me."

And Peter made no word, for he slept. And the Hate went without and sat him down beneath the hut's wall and looked him deep and deep unto the night; and drops traced his cheeks. And he arose and went unto the fire's stones and raised a one high and cast it far and murmured: " I am strong, yea, I am strong like unto Caanthus."

And he dried his tears and went within.

CHAPTER XI

AND when the morn had come Peter waked the lads and said unto the Hate that they should stay within the hut that Ezekiel know not of his abiding place. And the Hate told unto Peter that the night had passed weary. For so did he to speak:

"Peter, fish be not alike unto lambs and sheep. Nay, for fish, e'en though they be live, do flee; and e'en at the lone hour 'tis sure the sheep shall seek and thou mayest feel a loving nose and soft breath upon thy hand. Yea, thy hearth is lone."

And Peter told unto him of the sea and brought forth shells that held the wave, and told of the salt's bite, and brought forth moss and weed whereon the babe-shells clung. And the Hate harked unto the shell and shook him nay, and spake:

"Peter, what lone it hath! The ewe hath far sweeter song."

And lo, Aaron came, and he laughed much and shewed unto the Hate a game of shell casting, for Peter had shewed this thing unto him. Yea, afar did he set a pebble and cast a flatted shell to cover. And the Hate did the thing he was shown. And Peter told unto him of the smiting of Aaron and that he, even as the Hate, had been strong and full of flesh unto his years, and the smite had fallen upon him as a fever. And he told of the thing that set within his day that he ever sought his brother, though he had none. And the Hate spake:

"Peter, then he hath found him! When Panda pipeth yonder, then wilt thou that I do go with him unto the spot? Yea, Peter, speak it yea, for Theia is lone, sore lone! Yea, and he may show her this, the casting of shells. Doth he, then, know of sheep?"

And Peter answered: "Yea, for he seeketh out the folds up the high valley."

"Then, Peter, should I give unto him a lamb and send him unto Bethlehem's road and bid that he make word that doth make the market's men to know 'twas a sheep of thine, would he bear of grains unto thee?"

"Yea, but he knoweth not reason. Still, the market's men know the son of Peter and would deal aright unto him."

"Then, Peter, he is the brother of me and doeth this thing, for thou knowest thou and Hate would be known, and Ezekiel hath words for casting unto Bethlehem."

And Peter spake: "Thou hast not this thing to do. Nay, thou knowest Peter hath told thee his ear troddeth not path unto his lips. Even so do Peter's feet trod hither and hence. Yea, and the step of him covereth the hence with hither and hither with hence."

And he bid that the Hate cast his woe and live but the hours of the day. And he shewed unto him Aaron who had spread his net and was drawing it forth to fill with leaf. And lo, he seined a stone and happied much. And the Hate set him about the fishing, too, and lo, the sea ne'er did give forth such a catch.

And when the sun stood high, lo, then came from out the high hill's path a one who cried out as he came. And he came up unto the spot where the lads gamed and called aloud:

"Hatte! Hatte! Come thou! Hast thou seen Theia? Lo, have I sought the hills and called in vain. Speak thou! Hast thou then seen Theia?"

And the Hate answered: "Nay, Panda, nay. Where hath she then gone that she should leave thee lone? Didst thou speak unto her at the going of me?"

"Nay, Hatte; at the eve's coming she sought the quiet where Simeon lay and bore leaf and buds thereto. And she sunk upon the earth and murmured o'er and o'er: 'Yea, yea, it shall be! It shall be! He shall come, yea, He shall come!' And Hatte, the words pierced even as an arrow here within thy Panda's breast. And when I had watched me long, lo, did I to flee, and at a later hour, lo, she came unto the hut, and her eyes were lit and she made words I knew not. And the mantle o'er her breast was ope, and she tore with both her hands at the cloth and spake:

"'Even so shall it be! He hath made the hate-flesh love, so shall He make the filth-flesh clean.'

"And she sunk and cried out unto Jehovah: 'So Thou hast done this thing! Yea, hark, for I do know!'

"And she shewed unto me that the bright spots had stopped, and said: 'Panda, 'tis this God that hath done this thing! Yea, that I do fill the days of me and guard the Hate. Yea, I have bathed within His days and cleansed me in the smile of Mary!'

"And she oped her breast and the bright was but as the young sun's flush. And Hatte, she hath fled! Yea, she spake that thou and Panda had borne afar o'ermuch, and that I then should seek Ezekiel and tell unto the tribesmen and bid that they seek the hut and see 'twas empty. And she told unto me of her bearing upon her shoulders, upon a thong, a wooden cross that she shewed unto Jehovah that she had supped the cup."

And the Hate spake: "Then, Panda, the coming of me unto Peter, as she bid, hath healed the wound?"

And Panda spake: "Yea, yea, Caanthus, thou art strong, for thou hast borne Theia and Panda upon thy back!"

"Yet, Panda, even so, she hath left me here!"

"Yea, yea, Hatte, thou still hast the pit to hold! For knowest thou not Ezekiel knoweth Theia and would suffer not that she return?"

And the Hate's tears flowed, and he spake: "Panda, her breast, then, is healed and I may not press its soft!"

"Yea, but thou, Hate, shouldst murmur as doth she, 'It shall be!' She spake of Jehovah, the God, and said: 'Panda, He needeth not the name these Jews have given unto Him. Nay, since He be God, then why needst thou and the people to call unto Jehovah. Nay, unto me then shall He be but God. Gods hath Rome named, and Greece; still there be but one God. Though ye know Him not, yet shall He be.'"

And the Hate spake: "Panda, thou hast spoken of the song of her, and thou tellest unto me that I should sing unto the day the song. Ah, Panda, 'tis burned within this heart of mine. Panda, speak, and tell unto me, where dost thou then go that thou seekest Theia?"

And Panda, seeing that Peter had shewed upon the up-hill, spake not but watched his coming. And the Hate wept and beat his hands one upon the other.

And the son of Peter came him up from his fishing of the day and laughed much and spake word that sounded much awry. And he told unto the Hate that they should seek of the hills that they find therein the brother of him. And lo, he would come then adown the hill's path with them and set the sorrows right. For he knew the tears of the Hate.

And the Hate spake: "Aaron, thou art the brother of me. Even so have I spoken it unto Peter."

And Aaron laughed as the young spring's winds that start up but to die. And he shewed unto the Hate the catch of the seine. And lo, when Peter had come up unto the spot, he oped up his lips and spake unto Panda:

"Panda, as thou hast loving for thy body seek not this spot."

And Panda told unto Peter of the fleeing of Theia and that she had told him of the healing of the bright spots. And bid that he come with him unto the hut that he see that it was lone and empty. And Peter told unto him of the tribesmen's word within the city, of the word of Samuel who sold of cloths beside the market's place, and that he had spoken of the going of the Hate from out of the house of Ezekiel and that Ezekiel had wrathed sore over his going.

And the Hate came up unto the side of Panda and Peter as they made words and reached forth his hand and plucked at the mantle of Panda. And Peter looked down unto the lad and spake:

"Panda, come thou within that we sup. For within have I stored of fish that be large and fit for eat."

And they went within and Peter brought forth the fish and they took them without the hut and set upon the wood's branch and set them down while they did heat o'er the fire's glow, and Panda spake unto the Hate:

"Hatte, look thou unto Panda and speak. Where hast thou put the lamb?"

And the Hate made answer: "Panda, the lamb hath rested at the side of me. Yea, but the night's hour did find me lone, lone, though I did press the cheek of me within its wool's-warm. Yea, Panda, upon its back the tears of me did flow."

And Panda said: "Peter, seest thou? This lad is sore loned, and Theia hath fled. What wouldst thou say that Panda and he should do?"

"Panda, Ezekiel hath made much word, and I tell thee 'tis best that thou shouldst bring from the high hills thy sheep and set them within the walls of the lands of me, that I seek out the market's men and make price. And thou shalt then take of the moneys and go unto Jerusalem with the lad. For within Jerusalem hath filth hid, and Jerusalem shall be no wiser for the coming of more of filth.

"Within Jerusalem is one Jacob, who hath a market's bin,* and he doth shew unto the city's people jewels and silvers, yea, and golds that look precious, and be not as they look. Yea, he hath much cloth like unto the cloth that Samuel doth offer unto Bethlehem. Yea, for he is the brother, the flesh of Samuel.

"Enos, the brother of him, hath a market's bin beside the place of him, and he doth fashion skins unto shoe. Unto them do thou to go and take thou the Hate. Yea, Panda, take thou the Hate from out this day, for 'tis told of Ezekiel that he hath spent the moneys that thou didst leave for the carrying of him, and cared little for the lad's day save when thou wert there."

And the Hate looked unto Peter and then unto Panda and spake: "Panda, is there not upon this earth a path or yet a city that hath wel-

* A stall.

come for the footfall of the Hate? What, Panda, doth it mean? Hath earth men who are as thieves who pilfer of their brothers' lands and e'en the mother of their flesh? For there seemeth, Panda, naught that hath come unto the days of me that hath been dealt in loving."

And he stood, and his lips moved, and he spake no word. And Panda looked unto him and shook the lad and said:

"Hatte! Hatte! What hast thou upon thy lips that thou speakest not loud unto Panda?"

And the lad looked afar and murmured as though in a dream: "I am thy brother, even as thou art mine. Yea, and He hath seen not His Sire, yet He knoweth Him. Panda, thou wise one, tell unto me what meaneth He?"

And Peter knew not the words the Hate spake, and went within the hut and brought forth nets that looked like unto sacks whose mouths were bound unto bended wood's branch. And he sat him upon his way unto the hills and spake unto Panda, so:

"Panda, thou shouldst take this lad with thee unto Jerusalem, as I have told thee. He hath the wander-eye and doth look e'en as doth Aaron."

And he went him upon his way, and Panda oped up his arms and spake: "Hatte, these arms would take thee unto them, but thy Panda hath yet to seek of cloth that he clothe anew. Go thou within and bring forth a mantle of sackcloth that be the robe of Peter and bring unto me and I shall cast the mantle of me, and e'en the skin-shoes unto the fires. Then, Hatte, thou shalt seek thy Panda's arms and Panda shall tell thee much, and right the wrongs that beset thy day."

And the Hate went within, and Peter came him down from off the hill's side, driving forth a ram. And upon its back he fitted a yoke and hung upon the yoke the fish sacks. And he went unto the hut and brought forth fish that he had set to salt within the sea's water.

And Aaron laughed much and filled up the nets with leaf and stone, and brought them forth unto Peter, and his eyes looked naught from out their depths, and his face bore smile that looked as pale sun that pryeth through the darked day.

And he called aloud unto the Hate, and the voice of him sounded out as a child's wailing, for he knew not the name of him. And Hatte came him forth and bore the mantle of Peter and it was of sack's-cloth. And he came him up unto Panda and spake:

"Panda, seest thou? Peter hath packed of fish for the taking unto Bethlehem and goeth him into the city's mart. Lo, have I then pilfered of his very hut to bring unto thee his raiment."

And Panda said: " Nay, Hatte, Peter goeth not unto Bethlehem, but remaineth here with thee and me, and Aaron seeketh the in-city with the pack of fishes for the mart."

And Peter came up from the ram's side, and salt clung unto his hands, and they were red of brine's soak. And Panda spake unto him, saying:

" Peter, it shall be as thou hast told me. Yea, for Hatte hath fetched from out thy hut thy raiment that I make clean. Then shall thy word be done."

And Peter said that Panda should take into Jerusalem fish that had dried beneath the sun and go within the market's place and set up a gaming of the shells among the market's men, and cast stones for moneys. For Peter knew of the hunger of Jerusalem that they be fed upon the follies.

And Panda listed him and made word of wisdom with Peter, and Aaron and Hatte spread seine for catch. Then did they seek the up-hills that they set Aaron upon the way unto Bethlehem. And the ram bore fish packs that dripped waters at the jolt, and it kept not upon the path's-way but eat of bud and branch that grew at the high places. And Aaron followed him ever as he did seek him off the path. And so they journeyed them unto the city's road.

And the steps of Peter and Panda and Hatte led back unto the hut. And Panda called unto the Hate and bid that he fetch of the sack's-cloth mantle. And he took from Hatte's hand the mantle, and went within the thick growth and clothed him therein, and came forth robed as a fishman.

And lo, the Hate sat him lone and wept. And Panda came up unto the spot and oped up his arms and took the Hate within them and made word unto Peter, saying:

" Peter, seest thou the lad? He mourneth much that we do leave the hills of Bethlehem."

And Hatte sunk upon the earth and cried out: " Panda! Panda! The hills do reach them out e'en as the arms of Theia. Yea, and think-est thou that when thou and the Hate seek out Jerusalem, then Theia will seem near? Panda, I know not why, but within this breast hath set up fires. Yea, what hath filled up my days hath been the love of Theia, and it hath gone with the passing of her. And lo, there hath set up a something that eateth as fires and maketh e'en the lovely day to sink unto a dark tide.

" Panda, thinkest thou that Ezekiel would tell unto the townsmen of thee and me? For Panda, surely within Bethlehem there shall be a one who holdeth love for thee and Hatte, who know naught as their home land save the hills of the outlands of the city.

"Speak thee, Panda, speak thee, and say that thou wilt not bear unto Jerusalem the Hate! Panda, thinkest thou that Theia hath fled? Speak, Panda! say 'tis not a truth, but that at the dawning I shall seek out the hills and find her loving o'er the trees and murmuring, 'Hate, Hate, I love thee!'"

And Hatte looked unto the hill's-way, and behold Aaron tarried him, and he spake unto Panda, saying:

"Panda, look ye! Aaron seeketh the bypaths and thereby doth waste his substance upon the losing of steps unto the path's right way. Yea, Panda, and he doth waste him much, for he laugheth merry at the words I speak unto him, e'en though he heareth not. And betimes, Panda, he doth make word that meaneth well. Yea, but this be but the telling of his brother that he deemeth doth bide him upon the high hills.

"Ah, Panda, 'tis woe that setteth me! Panda, thou knowest not the quiet time at the night's hour, when Peter slumbereth and thou mayest hear the sheep's bleat, lone, 'cross the valley's deep, and know 'tis the sheep of thy tribesmen, and thou art afar and lone! Ayea, Panda, lone!"

And the Hate sank at Panda's feet and cried him out loud, and clung unto the sack's-cloth that robed him. And Panda, seeing the lad sore sorried, sat him down and spake:

"Hatte, Hatte, thou art smiting the heart of Panda! Look thou, lad, speak and tell unto me, art thou strong? And art thou then willing that we set upon our ways unto Jerusalem?"

And the Hate spake: "Nay, nay, Panda, dost thou take the Hate from out the hills, then dost thou tear out his heart and leave him emptied of love! Yea, Panda, far and far would I choose that they did stone of this body than that they tear out this heart! Thinkest thou that Theia hath sought the roadway unto Jerusalem? Ah, Panda, speak!"

"Yea, yea, Hatte, Theia hath sought afar. For no man without the city yonder, save Peter, would offer of his store unto her, and thou and Panda may not lend an aid since she hath fled."

And Hatte's face lighted up with the light of loving, and 'mid his tears mingled smiles. And he oped up his eyes wide and showed them unto Panda, saying:

"Panda, Panda, look thou! See! these eyes have cleared their tears and dried up their streaming within thy word. See thou, Panda! I am strong, yea, strong like unto Caanthus! Aye, and thou mayest know that dost thou go unto Jerusalem, then do I go me even as doth thy staff, and upon me mayest thou then lean even as thou dost lean upon it.

"Yea, and Panda, from out the beards of the men of Jerusalem shall I pluck forth hair and weave me a sling for the casting of stones at the gaming, that so-by shall I coax of their moneys forth. Yea, for Panda, I shall seek me out a one who hath much and speak me honeyed word unto him, so-by plucking out the hairs."

And Panda laughed loud, e'en though his brow stood deep furrowed, and called aloud unto Peter and bid that he come unto him, for Peter sat at the mending of nets. And he arose and dragged upon the ground the nets, and they swept along the stones and leaves, and sent up a chilled sound. And Panda spake:

"Peter, speak! have I not told unto thee of the sorrow that bideth within the Hate's day, that he go from out the hills? And yet thou sayest, 'Go thou unto Jerusalem.'"

And Peter wagged his head and set his thumb aside his nose and spake:

"Thou, Panda, knowest the tongue of Ezekiel maketh much word, and much word ever holdeth sorrow. Then do I speak more; such words do set upon the path of man and doth he not speed him much, then 'tis word that o'ertaketh him and wreaketh sorrow."

And Hatte arose and came unto Peter and looked up unto his eyes and said:

"Peter, as thou lovest me, speak unto Panda and tell unto him of the going of Theia and say thee that thou believest that Panda and the Hate may stay within the hills. Speak, speak, speak! Peter, speak thee loud and say thee so!"

And Peter set his hand upon the lad's locks and spake: "Hatte, thou hast much to learn. Man casteth his net unto the sea and catcheth much, and little. Yea, and doth he catch him little, lo, then shall he make of a smile and set the net anew. Yea, thou hast set thy net within the hills and caught but tears. Then seek ye out the high seas and go thee upon thy way smiling."

And Hatte said: "Look thou, Peter! Upon the hill's-way cometh woe! Hark! Dost hear?"

And Peter looked, and Panda started him up, and they went them upon the up-way that they meet Aaron, who came swift. And lo, he came and fell at the feet of them and shewed unto them the stone's scars and made known of them that followed.

And up from the road's-way came the tribesmen from Bethlehem. And they bore stones and threw them up unto the spot where they did stand. And Peter spake:

" 'Tis time, Panda, that we go up unto the high place where Theia bided her. Yea, and thou mayest drive, then, thy sheep at the night's dark unto the downside and deep unto the valley. Yea, for the moon sheweth not and no man may see our going."

And Panda took up his staff and reached forth his hand that Hatte might follow upon the highway.

And Peter brought up unto his feet Aaron, who wept, and shewed unto him the coming of the tribesmen who climbed o'er the rugged hill's side. And lo, he went within the hut and came forth with skin's sacks and they were filled up of fish that shone of dry salts. And he bore a sack of lamb's skin wherein was put the moneys of his day. And they went them up unto the high hills, where in the thick growth they sunk from out the path of them that followed.

CHAPTER XII

AND they sought the hut of Simeon, and up o'er the stone's height where Simeon lay, they came unto the spot, and lo, o'er the dry earths, where sod did show it dead, lay leaves and buds of the young bush scattered o'er. And Panda looked unto Hate and spake:

"Hatte, seest thou this thing? Theia hath been!" And Hatte fell down upon the sods and cried:

"Theia! Theia! Mother, speak! Yea, thou winds from out the East, bear thou unto me of her voice!"

And Peter came up unto the spot and made word, saying: "Hatte, Hatte, speak thou not aloud, for Bethlehem, e'en though there hath been the birth of Love within her walls, holdeth not a love for them of the hills who bide them within the filthed hut of lepers. And 'tis but a stone's cast they would deal unto thee."

And Hatte oped up the breast of his mantle and shewed unto Peter and Panda the bared breast of him, and spake loud unto the airs:

"So be it, then! 'Tis better far, Panda, and thou, Peter, that Hatte be slain with the casting of stones, than he be left to sow the grain that shall wreak out his undoing!

"Yea, Panda, yea, hark! Like unto her voice there cometh, borne upon the hill's winds, hark! 'It shall be! It shall be! Yea, He shall come Him from out the East upon the camel white as goat's milk!' Yea! Yea! Panda, hearest thou? This man of the East is Him, my Sire. And He shall come, yea, He yet shall come and claim of His flesh!"

And he sunk upon his knee and plucked, from off the earth o'er the spot where Simeon lay, the bud, and smiled, and tears dropped from off his cheeks and fell upon the buds as dew. And he pressed thereon his lips and spake:

"Panda, her hands did pluck this branch."

And Panda looked unto Peter and stretched forth his hands and dropped them beside him, and heaved of deep breath and shrug. And Peter said:

"Panda, thy sheep stand them higher up within the stone's ope. Then shalt thou, at the deep of dark, seek out the spot."

And Panda spake: "Peter, thou art at seek of flesh and word of market's day, when look thou! here upon the sod doth lie a heart smitten. Yea, and thou speakest of sheep when thou mayest see the lamb is trodden down! 'Tis, Peter, as thou knowest, a shepherd's heart that seeketh out the lone lamb. Then hark! the sheep of Panda may fold and warm one the other and none of them have need for the heart of Panda. But Peter, this lamb that the gods of Theia and of Rome, and e'en of the Jews, did forget, hath warmth within the breast of Panda."

And Panda looked unto the Hate, who lay upon the earth o'er Simeon, and mists of tears-rain rose into his eyes. And Aaron made words that here within the high hills would he seek out his brother, and lo, he brought forth the fish-net Peter had brought unto the spot and set at fishing of the leaves. And Panda spake:

" Lo, who, Peter, is smitten sorer—Aaron, who hath woe within his day, or Hatte, who hath woe within his heart? "

And the Hate rose and drew him up unto his height and said:

" Panda, Peter, who are the gods of Theia? Ezekiel telleth of a Jehovah. Yea, and this god shutteth up his eyes and leaveth the tribes-men of Bethlehem, at the words of Ezekiel, to stone thee and me from out the city's men! Yea, and Panda, thou knowest thou didst tell unto me of the gods of Rome, who sat them upon their fatted sides and let the breaking of the limbs of Caanthus!

" Hatte knoweth not these gods! Nay, Hatte shall seek him out a sheep who hath borne a lamb and this lamb shall be not at the full strength of e'en one day. Yea, and Hatte shall smite this lamb and fell it at the blow, and laugh at the flowing of its blood, and shall look him then upon its death-eye and laugh and beat upon his bosom and say unto the four winds: " I am god, since this be the gods' play! '

" Ah, Panda, look not so! Nay, Caanthus is strong! Since these, the gods of Rome and the Jews, see him not, then shall he stretch him forth unto his height and cry aloud until the God of Theia heareth!

" Yea, but Panda, hark! Thou tellest of the dreams Theia hath told unto thee. So wait thee; e'en as a dream cometh unto me a path, long and dark. Dark, Panda, dark, until the flesh of me doth chill! And at the path's-way steppeth one, yea, one, Panda—ah, hold thou this hand, Panda! 'Tis Hatte! Hatte troddeth it! Yea, and he falleth ever, though he striveth on! Yea, and then, and then—ah, Panda, the slaying of the lamb!

" Panda, hold ope thine arms, that I may flee therein! Say thou 'tis but a dream, a dream, Panda! Speak! Speak! "

And Panda oped up his arms and the Hate fled unto their folds and wept. And Panda spake unto Peter, saying: " This is the son of Theia! "

And he sat him down and drew close unto his breast the Hate and murmured: " Hatte, Hatte, dost thou remember the tale thy Panda spake unto thee of his tribesmen? Panda's path was like unto this thou tellest of. Ever did Panda seek, and ever fall. 'Tis but the falling and the upping that beareth thee on upon thy path unto the earth. Yea, but Hatte, there cometh unto the earth's path an end, and He, the God of Theia, hath flung ope the light that thou mayest see at this, the ending of the path, for Theia hath spake it so."

" Speak thou His name, Panda; is He then my sire? "

And Panda spake: " Theia sayeth yea, thine and mine."

" Then, Panda, thou art of the flesh of me? Yea, and Simeon and Caanthus and Peter? Yea, and Panda, Aaron shall see?

" And Panda, this God, e'en though He shall slay the lamb, shall still shew unto it the light? Is this thing true, Panda? For think thee, the lamb of me is there at the hut of Peter, and the tribesmen may slay it with stones! "

" Yea, this thing is true, Hatte, true. Look thou deep unto thy Panda's eyes and see. For Theia telleth she hath found this God, and His tongue is the sweet sigh of the even's breeze, and His touch is its kiss upon the blooms. Yea, and His eyes are the stars, yea, and He setteth Him new stars, in fearing lest He see not thee and me! "

And lo, there within the deep thick did sound a breaking of the twigs, and soft bleat fell upon the airs. And Hate spake:

" See! See! Panda, He, the God of Theia, hath spoken unto me! The lamb, the lamb hath come! "

And he sunk upon the sod and threw his arms about the lamb's neck and wept, and murmured:

" Thou voice of the God of Theia, I do love Thee! Thou hast spoken from out the hills. Yea, and offered unto me the lamb of sacrifice, even as doth Ezekiel to slay for the god of him. Yea, the god of Ezekiel would crave of the men of earth slain lamb as sacrifice. And Thou, and Thou, dost offer it live and warm! See! unto Thee I offer of the plucking of Theia, the young bud! "

And he reached unto the casting of Theia o'er the sod that lay o'er Simeon and wove of the branches a wreath, and hung about the neck of the lamb. And Panda looked and smiled and murmured:

" The God is wise, yea, wise! He stoppeth the tongue of men with offering from Him."

Peter looked, and Aaron stood afrighted, and lo, the Hate arose and went up unto him and lay his arm about his neck and smiled and smiled and spake unto Peter:

"See thou, Peter, do I not smile as thou hast told?"

And he set at the fishing of leaves with Aaron that he dry his tears.

And Panda spake unto Peter, saying: "Peter, see! the sun hath sunk within the mists that rise. Yea, the morn broke it fair, and lo, the eve hath o'er-clouded it. Yea, even so shall be the days of Hatte there who smileth 'mid his heart's tears. Yea, hark! the dogs of Bethlehem bay upon the home way. Hatte spake wisdom, Peter. Where hath the Jew's god then hid, that he see not? Yea, and if Rome hath gods, where hath she hid their grinning? They seem, Peter, as dreams that fill up the night at the following of feasts. Yea, they sit them ever grinning at the tickle of tears.

"Peter, thy word of Ezekiel bore truth unto me, for thou hast spoken of the word of him that filled up the tribesmen and wreaked sorrow upon the days of me and Hatte there. 'Tis so, Peter, yea; and yon roadway, sunk within the night's coming, hath swallowed up their word and left the way that thou and Panda and Hatte and Aaron shall seek at the night's coming.

"Yea, look thou! Hatte casteth of the nets with Aaron, and thou knowest, Peter, the earth holdeth not a path that offereth of welcome for the foot of him. Yea, the tribesmen of his sire wallow fatted within gold's buy and thereby drown their follies in the wine's glow. For Peter, folly hath a whited face and 'tis but wine that maketh her to blush."

And Peter set his thumb aside his nose, and wiped it then upon his mantle, and spake:

"Panda, thou makest word that filleth it up with wisdom e'en as doth the sheep to fill upon the green herbs at the early hour, and thou knowest 'tis sheep that fill up o'er their filling, and do to lie them down and stir not. Yea, they be as dead.

"So thy words; they be naught unto me. Panda, thinkest thou the herds upon the high hill do wait thee? For see! the dark cometh and thou shouldst seek up unto the spot and see thee unto the driving of them down the hill's-way unto the roadway unto Bethlehem. Yea, and without the city's place there cometh upon the out-way a one, Enoch. And he seeketh the out-places that he see the shepherds before their going into Bethlehem. Then go thou unto this spot and wait thee there for his coming. Yea, within the word of thee set much wisdom, wisdom that be past the knowing of him that he know not e'en what thy word meaneth.

"Yea, and await thee, for Enoch will list him long and long, and look wisely unto thee, and then, Panda, at thy waiting that he make word unto thee, lo, he will then fetch forth purse and shew unto thee and shrug him and say: ' This for thy fold.'

" Yea, and then, Panda, thou shalt say thee nay, and lo, he then will fetch forth a money's sack and add unto the purse and offer unto thee, and Panda, thou shalt say thee nay. Yea, do thou this thing unto the thrice, then reach thee forth thy hand and seize the sacks, for dost thou tarry 'tis lost, Panda, 'tis lost!"

And Panda laughed loud and slapped his hands upon his sides and spake: " Peter, when thou art laid low and men do mourn thy going, beneath thy robe shall Panda put his hand and surely shall he find the purse! Yea, thy hand hath itched ever for the tickle of gold!"

And he called unto the lads who gamed, and the eve echoed back the calling. And lo, the words woed at their dying. And they came them unto Panda, the Hate and Aaron, who murmured of his brother who hid ever 'mid the hills. And Hatte said:

" Peter, list thee not unto Aaron; he babbleth, and see, 'tis Hatte that loveth him."

And he threw his arms about the lad. And Peter spake:

" See thou, Panda, look! Hatte batheth Aaron's wounds within his loving and he healeth."

And Panda looked unto Aaron, who stood tall and full fleshed, and watched the hands of him at their busy o'er the knots of the net. And they moved as the play-winds of the young season, for they ever flitted and stayed not at any task. And his lips smiled ever, and he shewed unto the day thereby that wisdom knew him not. And lo, his hands were full strong and the breast of him o'ergrown of hair and he looked as a man. And the eyes of Panda tarried upon the sight, and when he had looked him long, lo, he spake:

" Peter, 'tis hard, yea, hard to say the God is wise!"

And Hatte said: " Panda, 'tis thou who knoweth not wisdom, for see ye, Aaron hath been emptied that Hatte might be filled up. Yea, for hath not Theia sped her unto where we know not? Then hath He, the God of her, sent unto thee and me the lamb and Aaron to fill up with loving the emptiness."

And Peter spake: " Panda, still doth the tongue of me to chide thee! Seek out the high place and bring forth thy herds."

And Panda looked unto Peter, saying: " Peter, thou hast spoken of the herds and Enoch, that Panda should bear them unto him without Bethlehem at the early hours of night's parting. Peter, this thing may not be, for do I seek Bethlehem they do come forth to seek me. Nay,

Peter, it may not be. Panda hath not a caring for the days of him. Nay, but Panda hath a fold of but one lamb that setteth sore his heart."

And Peter spake: " Then, Panda, I shall seek Enoch for thee and make price. Hold thou this sack of the moneys of me, for Panda, doth Enoch see the sack, lo, will he go within Bethlehem with thy fold and the sack of me! Yea, for Panda, Enoch hath much of spittle, that he swallow thee. He maketh much word and thou art undone! Thou seest then, Panda, the wisdom that thou seekest him and make wisdoms past his knowing. Yea, but since thou speakest this may not be, then shall I seek me down unto the place, e'en while the light tarrieth as the shadow of the morrow."

And he took up the staff and cast the fish packs within the bushes and set him upon the highway unto the herd's cairns. And Panda listed him long unto the snapping of twigs and unto Peter who murmured upon his way. And Hatte sat him down and took within his hands the hand of Aaron and lo, the hand of Aaron was full so large as the hands of Hatte.

And Hatte laid the cheek of him down upon the hand of Aaron, and Aaron made words that Hatte shook him yea and nay in answering, e'en though no man held answer of such. And he spake unto Panda, saying:

" See thou, Panda, is it rot full measure of loving Aaron offereth unto me? For lo, he speaketh much that meaneth little, but Panda, 'tis ever true!"

And the night came it on slow, for dark had come but from mist's hug and sun shone dim e'en through the dimming.

And lo, at a time later there arose a murmuring far down within the thick and men sent up shouts, and lo, Panda stood him up and listed. And Hatte arose, and Aaron laughed. And Panda said:

" Hatte, woe is upon us! Art thou strong?"

And Hatte answered: " See thou, Panda, 'tis tall I stand and strong, yea strong! What wouldst thou?"

And Panda looked with teared eyes and smiled and spake: " Thy Panda goeth unto Peter, who hath sought the roadway unto Bethlehem. And harken thee, Hatte, thine ears will tell thee much. Seest thou? Aaron heareth not and smileth. Then, Hatte, await thy Panda with thine ears sealed, and smile."

And Hatte made answering: " Mine ears are sealed and the lips of me do smile. Go thou unto Peter."

And Panda sped him upon his way, and dreamed of the fleeing for stones cast by the men of Rome. And saw the white teeth of his tribesmen and the hand of his mother, busy, busy at the weaving of baskets;

and the arm ever full. And lo, the tears flowed down his saffron cheeks as gems set within the copper's burn.

And the path sunk deeper within the mists, for fogs arose, and the voices of the tribesmen seemed to die within its depths. And still he sped him on and called soft:

" Peter! Peter! Answer thou me!"

And lo, he fell, and at the falling his voice raised to a louder sound, and at the rising, lo, the tribesmen made louder their voices, e'en though they sounded far down the path's-way. And Panda stopped, for he heard deep breaths, and lo, at his feet lay Peter, smitten!

And Panda knelt beside him, saying:

" Peter, speak! What hath betided thee?"

And Peter looked him up unto Panda and spake:

" The sea hath calm. Yea, the craft is set."

And Panda wept, and Peter raised up his trembled hand and lay his finger beside his nose and spake:

" The sea hath calm. Yea, Panda,—art thou Panda? What then is this water? Nay, 'tis not red! Ah, nay, 'tis Galilee! See, the fishers come! The sea hath calm and the craft is set. Yea, but Panda, the seines of Peter he hath left within the hills. Yea, and they catch and haul but leaves. Tarry me not. I may not wait the seeking of the nets. Panda, care thou for them. See! the sun cometh o'er the water's way and staineth it crimson. The nets! Panda, Peter hath fearing they need his hand at mending; for they spill out the catch."

And Panda murmured: " Yea, yea, Peter." And Peter sunk within the arms of Panda and pointed unto the sky's arch and spake:

" The sea hath calm and the craft is——"

And so he was no more.

And Panda wept and murmured: " Peter, for thee shall Panda bear thy vessel through the day, e'en though it be broken. Theia sayeth the God is wise. So be it."

And as he rose up from the form of Peter the breast of his sack's-cloth mantle shewed stained, and lo, a stone whirred from out the depths of the bush and laid ope his cheek.

And Panda started up and sought the thick and spake: " Doth Panda stay him that he seek the gods or doth he seek out the lambs? Ah, thou God of Theia, will Panda ever be the slave?"

And Panda turned unto the up-way, and lo, there came from out the path the lamb of Hatte and it bleated loud. And Panda said:

" Yea, Thou hast spoken from out the hills. Yea, and Panda goeth unto the eweless fold."

And he raised up his arms and set his hands shut and shook them unto Bethlehem. And the tribesmen came up unto the place where Peter lay and laid hands upon his raiment and stripped him. And Panda, seeing from afar, where he stood upon a high point, bit his lips till blood flowed from out the wound, and murmured:

" Theia sayeth the God is wise. So be it."

And he spread ope his arms and made obeisance like unto a slave. And he turned and made way unto the high place.

And dark stood still to leave the sun to kiss the earth to rest. And within the gold light he came upon Hatte, who sat beneath the stone's brow and smiled. And upon his breast lay the head of Aaron who slept. And Hatte raised up his hand and made sign of silence and whispered: " Panda, see! I smile!"

And his eyes looked upon the cheek of Panda, and he started up and cried out:

" Panda, the God of Theia hath not done this thing?"

And Panda made answering: " Yea, Hatte, the God of Theia hath done e'en this, and 'tis right and meet it should be, for Theia sayeth this God is wise."

And Hatte reached forth his hand and touched the blood and kissed its stain. And lo, he stood and oped wide his eyes and swayed, and murmured:

" Panda, 'tis dreaming cometh! Yea, and the blood sicketh me, for Panda, 'tis the path long and dark and then—the slaying of the lamb!"

And Panda spake: " Hatte, e'en now the dark path is oped, yea!"

And Hatte stopped and asked: " Where, Panda, is Peter?"

And Panda answered: " Peter hath stumbled upon the path."

And Hatte spake: " Didst thou offer unto him an aid?"

" Nay, and yea, for Panda made offering of his hand, but lo, Hatte, the God of Theia hath lent unto him an everlasting aid. He needeth not thee nor Panda."

" Then Peter is no more! Panda, take thou this hand and lead thou me unto Jerusalem, for thou hast spoken that men of Rome abide them there and Theia hath sought the God of her within the walls of Jerusalem. Panda, Hatte loveth not this god of the Jews. Nay, for Ezekiel telleth of the smiting of the firstborn. Yea, and they make feasts unto such a god and call it of the name of the Passover! Panda, this god craveth sacrifice. This, then, is not the God of Theia. Nay, nay, nay! And yet, Panda, e'en though the God of Theia slew the lamb

of me, there is not within this heart the word to speak out nay unto
Him, for He, then, is wise, she speaketh. And thou hast told of His
loving, Panda."

And Hatte stopped and looked unto Aaron, and tears flowed them
o'er his cheeks, and he spake:

"See, Panda, Aaron smileth; then leave it so. For he knoweth
not sorrow and 'tis sweet to see such a one. Come, Panda, the hills are
empty. Yea, and there within the dark that hath set upon us, at a spot
that I do see not, she abideth, and she sayeth, Panda, ' Hate, Hate, I
love thee!'"

And Panda took up the fish packs that Peter had cast, and held
forth his hand wherein the money's sack of Peter lay, and spake:

"Hatte, thou and Aaron and Panda go forth upon a path whereon
no welcome waiteth, and fed upon the hand-work of the dead. Hark!"

And Hatte echoed: "Hark! 'Tis the sheep, Panda; they have lost
thee! Speak that Hatte may take upon the way unto Jerusalem the
lamb that he know of the flocks."

And Panda shut out the sheep's bleat with the hands of him o'er
his ears, and smiled unto Hatte and shook him "Yea."

And Aaron came up unto Panda, and it was dark and he dragged
the net. And Panda made signs of loving unto him and held forth his
hand, and Aaron followed smiling. And Hatte lay his hand upon the
lamb. So they sought the down-way o'er the hillside unto the road unto
Jerusalem. And it was dark, dark and still, still.

And at the deep of the valley-way, when they had traveled long,
Hatte spake: "Panda, hearest thou me?"

And Panda answered: "Yea."

And Hatte said: "Panda, I smile! Yea, I smile so long as the face
of me looketh toward Jerusalem and I dream not of the Bethlehem
hills. Look thou, Panda, see! do the shadows of their cheeks shew dark
upon the sky's gloom, or hath night shut them away? I dare me not to
look, lest the smiling die."

And Panda spake: "Hatte, the hills are green, and 'tis early season,
and the ewes have born new lambs, and the skies smile. Yea, and thou
mayest hear the piping of the shepherds o'er the hill's-way, and the dogs
bark. Yea, and look! the white mantles of the men shew within
Bethlehem and it seemeth but a city of whited sheep. Call thou—
Hark! E-e-e-u! E-e-e-u! See thou, the sheep come!"

And lo, amid the dark there sounded the patter-hoof of sheep! And
Panda stopped, and Hatte came up unto him and lay his hand within the
hand of Panda and spake:

"Panda, the God of Theia harked!"

And lo, Panda sent up the shout of the shepherd, and close up unto the flesh of him there came from out the dark the sheep. And Hatte spake:

"Panda, the weariness hath o'ertaken me, and see thou, the sheep have come. Thinkest thou, Panda, that the hour is here when thou and Aaron and Hatte may lay them down and rest? The eve's chill hath set beneath the mantle of me and, Panda, stingeth the cheek. Say thou we may then rest amid the herd."

And Panda answered: "Yea, Hatte, it hath come unto the time. The sounds of Bethlehem have died out and this, Hatte, is not the herd of Panda, nay, but a few sheep that fled in fearing."

And they went them within the rock's ope and lay them down. And Hatte spake when they had laid long and long:

"Panda, thinkest thou that Theia hath passed this way? For, Panda, this heart is chilled."

And Panda made answer: "Hatte, art thou strong?"

And Hatte spake: "Yea, Panda, yea. I do smile."

And the night sped on, and lo, at the waking of the morn, Panda, hearing the murmurings of Hatte, went up unto his side and touched the flesh of him, and lo, it burned, and the cheek shewed scarlet. And Aaron lay smiling the emptiness of his day, e'en unto the coming day. And Panda looked him long and stood turned unto the roadway unto Jerusalem and spake aloud:

"Jerusalem of the Jews! Beset by Rome and filled of filth! What hast thou for the cast awry? Unto thee Aaron bringeth his empty vessel, and Hatte beareth that of him, filled up o'erfull e'en now. Where within thy breast hast thou the rest for Panda, who beareth burdens unto thee?"

And lo, he sat him down and watched long and long the face of Hatte, and Hatte spake:

"Panda, 'tis the road and Hatte steppeth it! And then and then, the slaying of the Lamb! Hate! Hate! I love thee!"

And Panda started up and took unto his breast the lad and cried: "Wake thee! Wake thee! Hatte, speak unto Panda! Speak! art thou strong?"

And Hatte waked and murmured: "Weary, Panda, weary. Yea, speak unto Hatte that he may but lay and go unto the land of his dreaming wherein Theia danceth ever!"

And Panda reached forth his hand and shook Aaron that he wake, and Aaron stood forth from off the rock and went unto the nets and brought them forth. And Panda made known unto him that they should seek out the road and off unto Jerusalem. And he took up the Hate, who lay as a young lamb, long legs hanging limp, and so they set upon the road, the lamb of Hatte following. And the sheep, that came from out the night, set them ahead upon the way.

CHAPTER XIII

THE morn spread forth the golded tresses of the sun, and lo, a star still rested upon a cloud bar. And Jerusalem slept. The temples stood whited, and the market's place shewed emptied. Upon the temple's pool the morn-sky shewed, and doves bathed within the waters at its edge.

Beside the market's way camels lay, sunk upon their folded legs, and chewed, their mouths slipping o'er the straw, and tongues thrust forth to pluck up more for chewing. The hides shewed like unto a beggar's skull, hair fallen off o'er sores.

The day had waked the tribes, and narrowed streets shewed bearded men, and asses, packed. The temple priests stood forth upon the stoned steps and blew upon the shell that tribesmen come. From out the pillared place the smoke of incense curled, and within the stone made echo of the chants and sandals-fall of foot.

And tribes sought out the place, and lo, like unto ants they swarmed up and o'er the steps, to sit and make wisdom of the wording of the priests.

And merchants spread forth their wares upon the temple steps that they who came from out should see. Bent and shrunk like unto the skins of ox, they sat and whined, hands spread forth o'er the wares. Filthed hands bore fruits, and faces dead looked out from swathing of cloth; and they whined, and shewed sores and twisted limbs.

Beside the pool stooped women who put therein their hands and cast drops upon withered greens. One, dark and black-locked, held between her knees a youth of young years and searched within his locks for abominations, but stopping that she eat from off a fruit that lay beside. Within the market's place the merchants brought forth cloths and hung, spread wide o'er the bins, and shewed of breads and fishes and jewels and cloths and skins. And made word one unto another of the wares.

A beggar squatted at the road's skirt plucking at his scabs, and grinned unto the passers through his whines.

Within the walls the men of other lands came forth. And smells sent them up unto the day, scents of spice and fruits and filth. And the wall's gate had been oped since the light and the beggars came within like dreams unto night.

The patter of ass's hoof sounded upon the stoned street and brown-stained lad came after, shouting unto the market men: "Water! Water, that ye sup!"

And lo, upon the ass there hung two jugs of skin. And the man came forth and brought out bowls. And he loosed the jugs and sat them upon his hip that he pour forth. And they supped and wiped their beards upon their hands and their hands upon their mantles.

And there came from out the narrow street a maiden, who wore o'er her face a cloth, and she bore a tray of fruits and blooms. And upon her arms there shewed copper bands, and at her ankles they shewed, and the flesh of her bare legs was stained green with their touching. And o'er her breast hung a broad strand of black locks, and her bosom shewed dark beneath the white cloth that covered it. And within her ears hung hoops of metal. And she chanted of her wares and cast sharp glances unto the market's men. And the youths of the market's men called unto her and held up moneys, and lo, she cast down her eyes and saw them not.

"Nada hath tucked her heart within the blooms," said the market's men, and Nada shrugged and cast bloom unto the men.

And lo, the lad of the water jugs looked up unto her and the dark skin of her cheek burned. And the men laughed loud and spake:

"Nada hath loving for the white-skin of Rome. Yea, but the sun of Jerusalem hath darkened him. Lucius, thou knowest she looketh unto thee at the every day!"

And he shewed his white teeth in smiling. And lo, there came forth from out the bin that shewed of jewels that looked precious, a one bent, whose beard shewed long and black and who rubbed his hands one upon the other. And they called his name "Jacob."

And Nada looked unto him with frowning and spake:

"Thou Jew! Thinkest thou that seeking out upon the roadway thou mayest tempt the hoard of him? Lucius, he hath seen thee take of moneys and seeketh thee that thou shalt spend within the bin of him!"

And Jacob spread forth his hands and smiled and made words of lamentation, and spake of the jewels he had within his bin, that, should they seek, would rob him of his bread, so little did they bring and so much had he put forth for their buying. And Nada said:

"Lest then we do thee wrong we seek thee not!"

And there set up a murmuring among the men of the markets, for within the place there came a one who bore upon his breast a lad, a one

who dragged nets upon the streets, and sheep that hung close unto
their legs. And they looked unto him and spake:

"This man is no Jew! And the lad is a white-skin! And the sheep,
what man knoweth whose they be?"

And the men made as to do violence unto Panda, who stood firm and
spoke unto them with their own tongue. And they asked of him:

"Who art thou and whither goest?"

And Panda made answer: "Hath Jerusalem, then, the birthright of
all her men?"

And they raised up their voices against him and made loud noises
and said that he should be brought up unto the law's-men that he tell
unto them of his coming and going.

And Panda spake: "Knowest thou a man named Jacob?"

And they laughed loud, saying: "Thou hast indeed brought thy
bowl unto a dry well!"

And Panda said: "Then since Jerusalem offereth unto me no waters,
is it not meet that I should set beside the dry well and await thy sky's-
weep?"

And they wagged them that this was wisdom. And they went unto
Jacob, who rubbed upon cloth the brass of his wares, and they spake
unto him, saying: "There hath come a man who seeketh thee."

And Jacob made a noise like unto a swine and said: "Then leave
him that he findeth me!"

And they laid hands upon Panda and drove the sheep up unto the
bin of Jacob and spake: "This man is he."

And Panda said: "Thou art Jacob, thy tribesmen tell. I am from
Peter, who knoweth thy brother within Bethlehem. And Peter hath
bid that I seek thee out and say unto thee thy brother Samuel sendeth thee word bidding that thou shouldst leave thy household ope unto
me."

And Jacob rubbed upon the brasses and answered not. And Panda
looked and spake: "Art thou a man, or art thou a Jew?"

And Jacob looked unto the sheep and said: "The sheep, are they
thine?"

And Panda answered: "Yea."

And Jacob looked unto the lad Hatte, who hung about the neck of
Panda, and spake: "Is this lad thine?"

And Panda made answer: "Yea."

Then looked Jacob unto Aaron and spake: "And he who hath
naught within his skull, is he thine?"

And Panda made answer: "Yea."

And Jacob cried: "Out of Bethlehem there cometh no good! Samuel hath eat of swine! Thinkest thou then that Jacob doeth likewise, that he house a Gentile?"

And Panda spake: "Where, then, is Enos?"

And the tribesmen laughed and said: "Thou hast found the dry well at the finding of Jacob. Yea, and dost thou seek Enos, thou mightest as well press a stone that it give forth drink!"

And they told that no man bought of their wares and yet they had of the land's moneys and no man knew how this thing came. And lo, while this had been, Nada stood wide-eyed and looked unto Panda, and her lips moved and she came forth and spake in a tongue that no man knew. And Panda sunk upon his knees and whispered:

"The land of me!"

And the men of the market looked them in wondering and spake no word. And Nada reached forth her hand, thin and brown and cool, and laid upon the cheek of Panda that burned red and hot and shewed swelled. And Panda's arms tightened about the Hate until the flesh darkened, and he spake:

"Thy name! E'en as dreaming it cometh unto me as musics, for it shall be of the tongue of me. Speak thou it!"

And the maid made answer: "Nada."

And Panda spake it slow, "Nada!"

And she plucked at the cloth o'er her breast and tore from it bits that she dipped within the drops that dripped from out the skins Lucius had set upon the ass. And she laid the wet upon the bruised place and crooned "O-o-o-u-e."

And Lucius oped up the skin and went unto the market's place that he bring forth bowl that Panda drink. And lo, Panda reached up unto the cool cloth and took from off his cheek and laid it upon the burning brow of Hatte. And Nada smiled, and stripped cloth from off her mantle and wet, and let drops to flow o'er the Hate's fever.

And lo, there arose a loud noise, and Jacob ran forth upon Aaron, who, seeing the bright brass, had come up unto the place and reached forth that he take of it. And Jacob wailed and gnashed his teeth and tore at his beard and spake that Aaron was the son of a swine. And lo, he smote him upon the back. And Aaron stood smiling, wrapped with wonder o'er the shining bits, for he knew no man's wrath.

And Jacob reached forth with a thorn's branch and struck him o'er the cheek, and Aaron started up and made noises that sounded as the rumble of the thunders, and reached forth his hand and with one blow set Jacob amid the wastes of the market's street.

And the market's men made words of wrath at this thing, and Panda, hearing, spake:

" Lo, thou hast seen the fool undone by the wise man. Yea, but he who is wise and playeth the gaming of the fool seeketh his own undoing, for the fool knoweth well his game! "

And they spake: " This man hath wisdom." And they made them away that they lend not a hand unto Jacob.

And lo, there came forth a one who held out loaf and spake unto Panda, saying: " He who hath wisdom is the brother of me; then eat thou of this bread, for 'tis mine."

And Panda spake: " It shall be that brothers break the loaf together. So be it."

And he brake the loaf and eat thereof and offered unto him who brought it forth, saying: " Thou knowest brothers eat of the same bread and know one the other's name. I am Panda of the sands. Yea, and thou knowest no man hath a wish for sand. So, thou hast the tale of me."

And lo, the man spake: " I am Joel, whose father trod 'bout the grind-wheel's stone. Yea, and e'en now upon the feet of me is thick skin from the grinding. Yea, and thou knowest the men who seek of grain's meal care them not for chaff. So be it; thou hast the tale of me."

And Panda and Joel eat the loaf. And Nada looked, and Aaron stood darkened red and breathing loud. And Hatte hung limp 'bout the neck of Panda as he sat upon the stoned street. And Panda reached up his hand and lay back the golded locks, and Nada oped up her arms and spake in the tongue that Panda knew. And Panda loosed the arms of Hatte and lay him within the arms of Nada, and he sunk his head upon her bosom and murmured: " Theia! Theia! "

And Panda asked of Joel: " Hath Jerusalem a spot for sand's waste? "

And Joel answered: " Nay, no more hath she for chaff. Yea, but the beetle crawleth o'er the stone's damp and asketh no man. So be it."

And lo, Nada sat looking down unto the sleep of the Hate, and her hands soothed o'er his brow, and she lay her cheek against his and sat her down that she sway and soothe.

And Panda stopped and lifted his head high, and lo, his eyes looked not unto Jerusalem but unto the tribe's places of him, and he dreamed of the arm ever full, and the hands busy, busy ever. And he waked from out his dreaming with smile-spread lips and spake unto Joel:

" So be it, then; Panda crawleth o'er the damp."

And Nada held the eye of Panda e'en though he spake unto Joel.

And he stooped and touched the blooms that withered upon her tray, and his hand sought his mantle with bloom. And Joel smiled and spake:

"So be it, then. Whither goest thou?"

And Panda made answering: "I know not, for may man spend of sheep and buy with fever?"

And Nada oped up her night-dark eyes and loosed the cloth that hung o'er her face and wrapped the head of the Hate that sun reach him not. And her thin hands loosed the strands of her dark hair and spread o'er her face, and she spake:

"Thou hast told unto Joel thy name, 'Panda.' Panda, whither goest thou?"

And Panda answered: "Thou hast heard."

And Nada sunk her voice unto the whispering and made words, saying: "Thou shalt follow Nada, who seeketh out her sire. Yea, and thou shalt know him. See! Nada beareth bloom and fruits unto the market's place. Yea, for her sire weaveth upon the racks,* and steppeth not; for his legs bear him not. And within his walls abideth Caleb, who seeketh day amid the dark, for he seeth not. Yea, and he sitteth him at the door's ope and maketh that he smite oar unto the waters."

And Panda spake: "Thou hast this within thy walls and yet thou wouldst take Panda and his wastes within?"

And Nada answered: "Yea, for Nada hath lost a one like unto him who sleepeth here upon her breast. Yea, the brother of her flesh. Then unto dark bring thee dark and out from dark shall moon's light gleam."

And Panda asked of Nada: "What, then, is the name of him thou callest sire?"

And Nada spake: "Nadab. Yea, and he hath called the name of me 'Nada,' which, as thou knowest, be but the sheep † who hath no tail! The son of his flesh, who is no more, was named even as Nadab."

And Panda smiled and asked of Nada: "Is then thy sire a one who offereth his hearth unto the road's-spill?"

And Nada oped wider her eyes and laughed loud.

"Yea, for earth seeketh not Nadab; for no man who steppeth not among men knoweth men. And Panda, list! Nadab hath woven of a sacred cloth, one upon which the tribes offer words unto Allah. Yea, and within its weave there sheweth the days of Jerusalem. Yea, at its tie-end there shewed Nadab upon his withered legs. Yea, and he laugheth much and sayeth the tribes will know not, but deem this be a camel! And Caleb, when Nadab calleth unto him, bringeth forth bowls

* A rude loom for rug making.   † Nadab without the "b."

of color in which Nadab dippeth of the wool, and this cloth is woven of but the young lamb's wool. And Nadab at the night slumbereth upon this cloth."

And Panda spake of the Hate, who lay heavy within the arms of Nada, and Nada looked unto the eyes of Panda and made word, saying: "This lad is a white-skin. Is then his mother of the Romans?"

And Panda smiled and spake: "Nada, thy lips speak and yet they speak not thy heart. Thou wouldst know of me is this lad of my flesh? Nay; I have spoken it. And Panda dareth not that he ope his lips. What man, Nada, would seek from out his tribe's place 'mong men that know not his skin?"

"Then thou art of them whom Rome hath sought. Yea, Panda, Nada knoweth Rome eateth all the grain. Why, then, art thou cast forth?"

And Panda murmured: "The palms wave, the sands are cool, the women busy, busy at the weaving of baskets. Yea, and spice scenteth."

And Nada cried out, and Panda looked and spake: "Nada, by the love of Panda for this land, he sweareth he may not ope his lips."

And Nada said: "The palms wave, the sands flash, the caravans come, and Nada knoweth not more. Nadab hath reason that he seek not the streets, for Panda, Rome knew Nadab, and the flesh of Nadab is not the flesh of Nada. See!" And Nada stripped the flesh of her back and lo, scars shewed. "This thing was Rome's play!"

And Panda brake a wood bar in his naked hands, and he spake: "The lad slumbereth; and see! Aaron, the smile-waste, setteth at the nets."

And Nada said: "Ope thou thine arms and take the slumberer and follow Nada. Hast thou eat?"

And Panda shewed of the salt fish, and Nada smiled and spake: "There is bread of fruit as the bread of the land of thee. Yea, and figs."

And Panda cried: "Yea, yea," and took up the Hate. And Nada stooped that she bear the tray of withered blooms, and reached forth her hand unto Aaron and he came forth dragging nets, and looked unto the market's place and rumbled deep his voice.

And they sought the house of Nadab. And it was the hour when the sun hung o'er the temple's crest, and the light shewed red as fires of sacrifice. And within the priest's chants hummed and mingled with the tired whine of beggars and merchants 'long the way. And Panda spake unto Nada, saying:

"Nada, see! the blood Rome hath spilled staineth e'en the skies of Jerusalem and batheth the temples!"

And Nada spake: "Dark unto dark and moon's light flasheth! Yea, and blood unto blood buyeth the purging! Panda, Allah shutteth up his eyes."

And Panda murmured: "Nada, the god is wise."

And they went up unto the high gate and down unto the narrowed streets. And babes swarmed up and down and wallowed in the dusts. And the merchant men came, packed of their wares, unto this place, and the babes sought them as they came for the casting of withered fruits.

And the women came unto the door's ope and looked for the coming of their men, and lo, when they passed and were not them for whom they looked, they cast down their eyes and covered their faces.

And Nada went down such a street, and the babes called unto her for blooms, and seeing Panda and Aaron and sheep, stood wide-eyed and stared.

And when they had come unto the wall at the ending of the street, they came upon a house of stone, damp and shut. And Nada made word at the door's ope and knocked upon the wood. And there came a one who stumbled upon the way and whose hand steadied not. And she called his name Caleb. And lo, his locks were long and dark and his cheek bore scar, and his hands were thick and yellowed of old sores, and he carried a wood oar.

And Panda stopped and looked. And Nada came within and spake: "Caleb, hast thou found her?"

And Caleb answered: "Nay, Nada, for may man see the sun whose eyes are shut? Yea, and she hath gone unto the sun's land. Eunice! Yea, Eunice! But thy shadow lieth here!"

And he smote o'er his heart. And Nada touched the hand in loving and spake:

"Thou camel-man! what hast thou woven unto thy cloth? For see, thou art e'en now smiling!"

And Nadab held forth his hands, stained of color, and touched the locks of Nada and shewed unto her the new strand wherein was put an oar. And he laughed and said that the men of the tribes would see this thing a spear.

"Yet what matter it, Nada, that man see what be, or see what be not? For how be it that thou seest a thing and I do see it not?"

And Nada spake: "This, Nadab, is Panda, and he hath a lad who is sick, and one who is strong yet weak. Yea, and they go unto where they know not."

And Nadab laughed: "Then they are seeking out this spot, for no man knoweth it!"

And Nada made answering: "This man, Panda, will see ever right that that thou weavest."

And Nadab spake: "'Tis well. Then bring forth bread that we eat, and bear thou the lad unto the sheep's hide cast, that he may rest. And bring thou forth him who is strong yet weak, for man seeth him aright! And 'tis day that shall leave me seek the full of what he knoweth."

And Nada did this thing. And when the bread of fruits was brought forth, lo, they sat them upon the rug's-cast and eat from off a skin spread o'er the stones, and drank from bowls that were of clay. And they supped vinegar and dipped therein the bread of fruits, that the sweet sicken not. And Nada spake:

"Sire, within the city there is much word of one who hath sought the temple and sayeth it is the house of His Sire. And no man knoweth who this one be. And He is but a lad of young years, yet He hath spoken words unto the priests that hold wisdom past their knowing. Lo, He speaketh of leaves, and they do breathe and speak wisdom, He hath said. And the priests make words that this lad hath sick, yea, and is fevered, and yet they wag * 'tis wisdom he speaketh."

And lo, the Hate waked from out his fever and spake: "He then hath found his sire!"

And Nada said: "See thou! the lad is fevered much."

And Hatte came unto the place where they sat and cried: "Panda, take thou me unto the house of my sire, for He hath spoken that I do go unto His house even as doth He to go."

And Panda spake: "Hatte, 'tis not come unto the time when thou shalt go unto the house of thy sire."

And Hatte made answering: "Yea, Panda, but thou shouldst feel the burning of this heart that I seek Him out, for Theia sayeth He is nobled."

And Panda spake: "Hatte, robes of nobles clothe beggared hearts. Yea, and thou shouldst seek beneath the blue sky at the early dawn and come unto a field's-man who looketh up unto the blue and speaketh truth from out his eyes. And then, Hatte, thou shouldst speak thee loud, this man is he who is nobled!"

And Hatte spake as one who dreamed: "The hills! The hills, Panda! They stand dark, yea, and the men of Bethlehem have sought sleep and the sheep have laid them down at the rock's shelter.

* Nod the head in assent.

Yea, and the dark of night's purple hath stained the sky and 'tis lone, lone, Panda. Yea, the throat of me acheth, aye, and I—ah, Panda, wouldst thou take thy Hatte unto thine arms? See, he sorroweth! Yea, and yet he fain would smile for thee!

"Speak, Panda! dost deem the eve's star keepeth watch and standeth o'er the spot where Simeon lieth? Ah, say thee so! Say that thou seest it gleaming. Yea, 'tis a new star the God of Theia hath set!"

And Panda oped the arms of him and spake in soft words. And Hate sunk his head upon the breast of Panda and crooned in anguish. And lo, while the lips of Panda murmured unto Hatte, Nada went into the dark depths and brought forth lamps of oil wherein she sunk the sheep's wool and set them that they see.

And Panda's eyes looked unto Caleb, who sat beside Nadab. And when Nada had set the lamps, lo, she sat her down beside Caleb and broke the breads that he eat, and set her watch that he sup from the bowl and spill not the vinegar. And Panda looked long unto Caleb and asked not what or whom he might be.

And Nadab brought forth bowls of color and dipped therein the wool that it be dry for the next weaving.

And Nada told of the day of Jerusalem, and spake more of the lad who had sought out the temples, and of the mouthings of the priests. Lo, He had spoken that words should fill not the mouths of priests lest they be o'erfulled of words.

And Nada spake that 'twas so, for had she not sought the temple, and priests came forth and spake of that that was, and lo, it was not; and of that that was not, and lo, it was.

And Nadab laughed loud and spake: "Nada, thou art wise, yea, and even so the priests, for what be not for thee is for them, and what be not for them is for thee. Yea, and thou knowest even though a man feedeth his ass upon straw 'tis ever an ass, and doth his brother then feed his ass upon the rose even so is it still an ass."

And lo, the Hate slept, and Panda shut up his eyes, for he had looked long upon Nada, who dipped the wools into the bowls, and upon his cheek there gleamed drops. And Nadab brought forth a bowl wherein he set a burning and supped therefrom smokes, and Nada leaned o'er and stroked upon his head whereon no hair showed. And Nadab lay him upon the stoned floor upon a rug's-cast, and Caleb fingered o'er the oar.

And Nada sat dreaming o'er the smoke, and the voice of Nadab hummed: "'Tis early dawn. The spice is damped and scenteth sweet."

And Nada made answering: "Yea, the wall-opes show not yet the maids, for 'tis early, yea, and not yet time that they do wrap of veils."

And Panda murmured him: " Yea, and the steeds champ, and men seek out the fields, hung of baskets that they pluck. As brass they shew, shined of sweat. Their feet love the sod. The sun's heat hath not yet set the desert steamed. The babes wake and wail."

And Nada spake: " Yea, and o'er the golded moon's-crest upon the temple place the sun setteth gleam. The tribes come and chant of Allah, and beat their brows unto him."

And Panda stood him up unto his height and spake loud: " Yea, but this is Jerusalem and 'tis night's hour! Rome hath loosed her hungered lions that they eat the Jew's meat. Yea, and yet Rome hath homed thee and me."

And Hatte waked and said: " Panda, fearing hath sunk within my breast, for this god of the Jews hungereth ever, yea, and standeth him ever seeking. For do they not offer much unto him? And yet he hungereth! Ah, Panda, he but knoweth Jews; then where is the God of Theia? Panda, speak that when the day hath broke, I may seek out the house of my brother's sire."

And Panda spake: " Sleep, sleep, Hatte! Art thou strong? "

And Hatte made answering: " Behold, Panda, have I not lain long and no dreaming cometh? And dreams set a fright within this breast doth Theia not to dance therein. Ah, Panda, where, where within the vale, or yet upon the hills, is she? "

And Panda stroked his locks and told of the herds. And brought within the house the lamb, and Hatte lay his head upon its wool and slept.

And Nadab oped up the rug and stroked upon its soft, and spread it forth and sunk upon his knees and bowed down with flatted palms. And Nada did this thing, and lo, Panda cast him down with sobbing.

And they made the house shut, and night set them asleep. And 'mid the dark Panda arose and went unto the spot where Caleb lay and touched his scar and sat him there weeping, and spake:

" Rome! Rome! Thy son hath suffered thee to cast him forth and thou hast forsaken him! Yet Theia sayeth the God is wise. So be it."

CHAPTER XIV

Morn came unto the night and she bore a golded bowl. And Jerusalem knew not of what stood within her walls. The temple place stood oped. The priests slipped sandaled feet upon the stones.

Within the out-wall, upon a cloths' heap, there slept a one, a lad of young years, and the priest found this thing to be, at his coming forth to blow the morn-horn. And he laid hands upon the lad and waked Him that he speak of His doings.

And He oped up His eyes and looked upon the priest and spake wisdom. And behold, the priest sat him down that he list. And He bid that the priest speak of his wisdom. And this was done, and lo, at the finishing, He spake the words of the priest in things of earth that all men knew.

And the priest quaked, for he knew that in much word little wisdom was clothed. And he went unto the high priest and spake of the words the lad had made. And the high priest spake that wise men shewed not unto their brothers the empty of their measures. And more, that men knew wisdom by them who sought, and the fool sought wisdom where the wise man had found it to be.

"Then shew not unto the fool the fount."

And the men of Jerusalem came unto the temple, and the women sat within the out-places, and lo, amid the chant there came a lad who shewed fevered and asked of the road's-men of the way unto the house of his sire.

And the men wagged that woe was upon the babes, for at the temple place there had come a one who spake the walls were the walls of his sire's house.

And the Hate, hearing this thing, spake: "This is the brother of the flesh of me!"

And the men questioned: "What, then, is thy name?"

And the Hate answered: "Hatte; and the sire of me is nobled."

And they asked: "Then what art thou that thou art upon the street's-way?"

And Hatte made answering: "I go unto the palace of my sire."

And the men laughed loud and mocked him, saying: "Set him then upon an ass, yea, with the face of him turned unto the tail, for suredly he then shall find this noble that he seeketh!"

And the Hate stooped and plucked up stones and cast unto their mockery. And they made word 'mong their brothers of the child whose skin was white and was no Jew and yet laid claim unto the temple place as the walls of his sire.

And Hatte spake: "Hath the god of the Jews no spot within his land for Hatte? Then Hatte turneth unto his sire."

And he stood and swayed and spake: "He shall come! Yea, upon a whited camel, white as goat's milk, He shall come, from out the East. For Theia sayeth so!"

And the men stood back and spake this lad was sick. And one among them laughed much and made words: "Nay, 'tis folly-ridden he be!"

And they laid hands upon him and sat him upon an ass with his face turned toward the tail, and put within his hand a thorned branch. And he held him proud and spake:

"Do thou this thing! 'Tis but the brand that thou art fools, for I am nobled, and no man may stain a nobled blood!"

And lo, the ass laid down and moved not. And the Hate stood him up and spake: "So! seest thou? The God of Theia setteth thy wicked low!"

And he kissed the thorned branch. And the men stood back and shrugged.

And from out the temple, o'er the high steps, came a lad, and Hatte said:

"Seest thou? This is my brother! He hath spoke it so!"

And he looked long upon the man-lad who came, and started up and fled unto the house of Nadab. And sought Panda and told of the men of Jerusalem and the suffering at their hands, and of the lad of the temple, and cried:

"Panda, Panda, I fear! For amid His locks the lights shewed, and Panda, 'twas blood! blood!"

And Panda took him up upon his bosom and asked of the lad, and Hatte told of the hills at the early morn at Bethlehem and the coming of the lad, and said:

"Panda, this is He, and He said He sought His sire. And Nada hath spoken that He speaketh of the temple place and hath found His sire. And Panda, I sought, and the men of Jerusalem have laughed at the words of me!

"Hath Jerusalem a belly and no heart? The Jews, Panda, love one the other and no other loveth out of his tribe. Yea, their hoards do they keep within their mantle's sleeve and seal their hearts. E'en as the temple walls are builded up with stone and slime, so build they up a wall o'er their hearts, as strong 'gainst the seek of them who need."

And Panda looked him down upon the warring of the Hate and spake, and o'er his lips the smile of wisdom played:

"Hatte, thou art within Jerusalem. Thou art of her. Thy blood hath trod upon these Jews and shut their hands and hearts. Then cast thou stones at their learning?"

And Hatte looked him awed at the words that Panda spake and oped his lips in answering: "Panda, I know not thy word."

And Panda spake: "So be it, the God is wise."

And Aaron came from out the house of Nadab and stood smiling empty unto them and shewed beneath his mantle bits of brass and metals of the store of Jacob. And Panda, seeing this thing, spake unto Hatte:

"Look thee not upon this, for should men seek thee, be it so that thou mayest say I have seen not the thing, and speak true."

And Panda went up unto Aaron and took the brass and shook him "nay" unto him. And Aaron smiled and spread forth his net.

And Nada sung within the house, and the tongue of her words was the tongue of Panda. And Nadab sat within the door and slipped the reed between the binded woods whereon the rug was hung. And Caleb sat within the sun, and it shone upon his emptied eyes.

And at the eve's come there sounded out the voices of men who came unto the house of Nadab. And Panda sat with Hatte at the stone step that lay at the door's ope. And Aaron slept upon his net. And Panda and Hatte spake of sheep, and of the few of them that had followed.

And Panda, seeing the men and hearing their murmuring, stood up and awaited them. And they came up unto him, and seeing Aaron, who slept, laid hands upon him. And lo, Jacob was among them and he cried that Aaron was the thief who sought his stores and laid him low beneath the blows.

And Panda stretched forth his hand and spake unto them, saying: "See thou! this man who seeketh the lad hath wisdom. And he whom thou seekest, look! his beard sheweth, yea, and hideth his grinning. Look! he heareth not thy word, nor knoweth the why of thy coming."

And the men stopped within their very steps and looked unto Jacob. And Jacob rubbed his hands and plucked at his beard and shouted unto the ear of Aaron: "Thief! Thief!"

And Aaron offered unto him his net. And Panda looked wisdom

unto the men and they, seeing that Aaron heard not and knew not of the wrongs that Jacob chanted, raised up their voices against him and plucked his withered form up and bore it on high, and pulled at his beard and spake that he was one who sought fools, and he who sought fools was twofold more the fool.

And Hatte clung unto the robe of Panda and clutched the metal bits. And Panda looked unto Aaron, who laughed much at the going of Jacob. And Panda spake:

"Hatte, list thou! Wisdom the men of earth hunger for, and yet doth one man offer him of folly and another shew of the wares of wisdom, lo, 'tis one unto a score of them who seek that will take of wisdom."

And Hatte said: "Yea, Panda, the earth's men are goats that eat of follies e'en though the earth holdeth wisdom."

And Panda shook him "yea" and shewed of the brass bits and spake: "These did they seek, and took in their stead a Jew!"

And Hatte said: "Panda, I, Hatte, do hate these Jews!"

And Panda held up his hands in sign of silence and spake sharp: "Nay! Nay, Hatte! Thou art wrong. For Rome hath run her chariots o'er these Jews and set her signs within their very temples, and smote them for the saving of her own blood. For the Jew's heart is not sealed, but oped unto his brother and steeled 'gainst spears of Rome's casting. The sweat of Jews and the brawn of Jews have builded up their walls and temple places. Their priests are theirs; their temples filled with blood; their trust of priests hath led to fleeting of the lambs. Yea, the priests hold high their hands in supplication and lower them behind their backs for the drip of Rome's gold!

"Ah, yea, Hatte, and hark! these Jews hold afar more for Rome than Rome holdeth for them! When Rome hath crumbled down and mould hath filled her founts, still shall these Jews live! And yet, Hatte, Rome shall bow unto them!"

And Hatte swayed and spake: "Yea, yea, Panda, of the Jew's blood shall flow a stream that shall wash the earth."

And Nada brought forth the lamp and set the oils aflame. And the tribes sought their abodes. And Nadab brought forth a skin stretched o'er a nut's shell and beat upon its hollow, and Nada sat her down. And Panda and Hatte and Aaron sought the house. And Nada sung and swayed as one who danced, but not with her limbs. And she held within her hands pots of sweet herbs that burned and filled up the house with dream-smoke. And her eyes gleamed, and the teeth of Panda flashed.

And Hatte touched her hair and loosed its darked strands and kissed the soft and lay his head upon her breast.

And night shut Jerusalem away. Her walls slipped unto a naught within the dark. And sands shewed, and palms rattled. And the rattle of the armlets of Nada sounded as the caravans. And Caleb sunk asleep, and it was night.

CHAPTER XV

Morn bathed the hills of Bethlehem. And Rhea waked and sought the well, and Rachael sought her there and spake:

"Rhea, mother, knowest thou that Mary seeketh the up-way unto the hills?"

And Rhea made answering: "Rachael, thy tongue hath wrought woe before. Then speak not of this unto thy sire."

And Rachael spake: "Thou knowest that Hate spake words that meant unto thee and me a naught! Yea, his words set them not of worth that bought of e'en his bread."

And Rhea smote her and shook her body and sent her within.

And Mary sat at the baking of loaves. And her head was bent and her gold locks hung o'er her deep blue eyes. And her hands lay weak, and her foot shewed white beside the skin-sandal, and swaying, she made musics as the dance. And she ate of bread that she broke off from the loaf, and when she had eaten unto the half, lo, she spake unto herself, saying:

"This is the fulling of the share * of me. Unto the hills do I to seek."

And Rhea came within, and her mantle shewed wetted with the drops from off the water's jug. And Rachael followed and touched the flesh of Rhea and murmured:

"See thou, Rhea! she seeth not thee or me and hideth of her bread."

And Rhea held up her hand unto her lips and pressed thereon the sign of silence. And it was the time when they made morn-sup.† And Ezekiel came from off the herd-hill and brought forth three sheep, and spake that he should seek Jerusalem and bear unto the priests the sheep for sacrifice. For these were ones that had been born of the ewes at the appointed time.

And Mary harked her not but sat, her hands clutched unto the bread that was hid beneath her mantle. And Ezekiel, seeing this, spake:

"Come thou, Mary, what holdeth thee unto the bake?"

And Mary started up in fright and from out the sleeve of her mantle

* Completion of her share of the work. † Breakfast.

125

fell pence. And Ezekiel made loud word and stretched forth his hand unto Rhea, saying:

"Rhea, look thou! Thou hast oped up the household of me unto the offcasts of Rome and they have been but thieves and liars!"

And Rhea's cheeks dulled red and she bit upon her lip and cast down her eyes. And Ezekiel, seeing this, spake loudly:

"What sayest thou of these things? Shall thy husbandman leave Rome's waste to strip his lands and undo his household? They are Rome's waste! Filth, yea! The lad sought lepers and bedded with the fishmen!"

And Rhea spake: "Yea, and thou didst seek them even as did he, and cast stone at the lepers and deny bread unto babes! What, then, hast thou to say unto thy tribesman; that thou art a Jew and worthy of the name?"

And Ezekiel spake that Rachael should look not upon these things, and the men of Bethlehem were afraid lest the lepers come e'en unto the in of the city. And Mary, hearing, harked and went within the inner house. And Ezekiel wreaked anger upon Rhea, and Rachael looked unto her sire and wept. And Ezekiel waxed sore wrathed and when he had made much word, lo, he took up his staff and dug it within the earth in anger and went him up unto the market's place.

And when he had gone, Mary came forth unto Rhea and wept and told of a one who was old and had not bread and came unto the well where, it had been told, the King-lad had been much with His mother as she dipped the blooms. And he had spoken unto her, bidding that she go unto Rhea and speak and say unto her the name "Simeon."

And Rhea started, and looked unto Mary, saying: "Speak thou! Did this man walk upon lame legs?"

And Mary made answer: "Nay."

And Rhea murmured: "Then this man is not Simeon."

And Mary made answer that so had the old one spoken, that Rhea would shake her nay and that Mary then should shew unto Rhea this. And she held forth an armlet upon which were royal signs.

And Rhea was frightened much and bid that Mary hold silence before Ezekiel lest he wrath o'ermuch and past the bearing. And Mary asked of her that should she seek the well at the dark time would Rhea go there and speak unto the aged one. And Rhea, seeing Ezekiel come up unto the door's ope, made haste-word:

"Yea! Yea! Go thou and bake!"

And the day was much as other days of Bethlehem, filled of the coming and going of the sheep men and green-herbers. And it came unto the dark hour, and Ezekiel went unto the inn's place.

And eve was upon the lands, and Mary went up unto Rhea and spake it was the time. And Rhea set Rachael at the bruising of grain for the loaf of the morrow, and bade that Mary go unto the well and take thereto the jugs, and made seeming that her words were wrathed 'gainst her. And Mary did this thing, and Rhea cast cloth o'er her locks and followed.

And it was dark when they had come unto the place and one sat upon the well's stone and leaned upon a staff. And his garments were of cloth and skin. And Rhea came unto him and made no word. And Mary spake: "This man is Simeon."

And Rhea spake: "Nay."

And the one raised up his arms and cried out: "Yea, Simeon am I! For what earth knoweth of Simeon is hid within this heart."

And he plucked at the long locks that hung and spake: "Rhea! Rhea! Silence! Look thou!"

And Rhea came close and breathed the name: "Theia! Thou art unclean!" and made to start unto the town's-way. And Theia bended her and spake:

"Rhea, thou mayest know the word of Theia is true. Theia is cleansed! Yea, of flesh. Yet there within Bethlehem and Jerusalem are men who know of filth that be not flesh-filth! 'Tis from this Theia fleeth. Yea, within Jerusalem these men abide. And women of the courts of Augustus, e'en though he is no more."

And Rhea asked of Theia: "Knowest thou this thing?"

And Theia spake: "Yea, Augustus hath bidden much be done. And men speak within the markets that his chariot horses are spent and he scarce standeth that he flay them on. Yea, and they speak of a name that burneth Theia as coals!"

And Mary stood harking, and came up and offered unto Theia the loaf. And Theia laughed and took of the offered loaf and spake:

"Rhea, the hills hold what Theia feareth, for where is Panda and the Hate? Ah, Rhea, Peter lieth smitten upon the up-way! And with these hands did I cover him of stones.

"What think ye, that men who do this thing might slay a babe and one of wisdom's folly like unto Panda? For Panda loveth all men. Hast thou seen Panda?"

And Rhea answered: "Nay," and stood her far from Theia and bid that Mary come unto her side. And Theia spake:

"The hills have hid the woe of Theia and they have gone, stoned unto the earth's paths! Yea, the slaying of Peter was sup unto the thirsted for blood! And Theia went unto a rock's ope and bore of slain lamb unto the spot and waited her, and sought the house of Peter, and lo, 'twas loned. And men saw not the coming of Theia. And within the hut were skins and cloth and goat hide, and of this did Theia fashion out the raiment thou seest—cloth-bound 'bout the locks and goat's hair like unto the aged locks to shew."

And Rhea said: "Theia, ever doth thy word weigh it wise, far past the knowing of Rhea. Ezekiel loveth not thy tribesmen and wreaketh angers that I do house thy kind. What wouldst thou of me? For should Ezekiel seek and find not Rhea, lo, woe would set my days!"

And Theia looked afar unto the deep dark and spake:

"No rest shall bathe the limbs of Theia until the paths are oped and she knoweth the abiding place of Panda and Hate. Canst thou but leave of pence and bread that I do seek? For though fish were within the house of Peter, there shewed no pence. And 'tis weary that Theia hath fallen, for she hath sought Jerusalem, and drove thereto the sheep of Panda that scattered them o'er the hills. Yea, and the gods sought e'en the wilderness of the eve's-path unto there, for men seized of them and stoned Theia.

"And Rhea, thou seest there is no place within Bethlehem for Theia, and Jerusalem hath no hand within her wall that holdeth it not out for moneys. Thrice did Theia seek within the walls. Yea, at the loosing from filth, lo, there offered it unto Theia the freeing of her lamb. For Panda and Hatte sought but that Theia lives. Yea, and did Theia stay her within the eye-take of Bethlehem, lo, then the gentle shepherds would slay her lest she wolf upon their folds. For they know no cleansing of filth.

"Yea, and Jerusalem!—ah, Rhea, Rome hath blood within her city's place that knoweth Theia, and hungereth for sheep that they feed unto the gods. And send plea that they shut up the eyes of their tribesmen, that they see not their iniquities. Yea, and doth Theia seek with the lamb of her, lo, Rome's gods then would crave of its flesh.

"So, Rhea, seest thou that Theia's arms, though emptied of hate's brand, may not e'en yet take within their folds the Hate? Yea, doth Theia then set a blade to slay him? Lo, unto Jehovah doth she cry and plead that she be stood afar and see not. Look thou, Rhea! See! I offer unto thee this staff. Couldst thou then smite thy flesh with it and sit a-smile? Rhea! Rhea! Ope up thy heart and leave the warmth of it to flow within this, the chilled breast of Theia!"

And Mary came up unto the side of her who wept, and oped up her soft arms and covered the bended head and spake:

" Rhea, thou hast within thy day thine own. Look thou! she hath naught, and thou knowest no man of Bethlehem hath claim of me. Then ope up thy heart and give thou unto Theia the giving thou hast within thy walls; for thou knowest Mary is but the giving of the day. See! doth Mary stand she is but 'neath the hand of her, e'en as a staff. And Mary hath love, much love, that no day claimeth."

And Rhea spake her in breath-tone: " Yea! Yea! Ezekiel would say it so! "

And she put forth her hand and held therein pence and spake: " Unto the house of Peter until the morn-hour, then at the early light before the rising of the sheep, seek thou the roadway thence."

And Theia took of the moneys but harked not; for the arms of her were full.

And Bethlehem shut out the earth and lay wrapped of dark. And wisdom fled the wise men at their sleeping, and sought the fools' dreams. And day waked the fools who spoke wisdom and the wise men who spoke follies.

CHAPTER XVI

THE roadway unto Jerusalem shewed men and packs, oxen, yoked and packed, and herds creeping upon the way. And Theia and Mary sought after ones who set asses ahead upon the road. And these were men that had sought of flesh and market's filling from the cities near. And they came them from Zion. And seeing Theia they spake that one old should ne'er walk but be set upon an ass. And the babe, too, should seek not upon the long way.

And they came up unto them and made word that this thing should be. And Theia whined and cried of the babe that she did seek food and alms. And these men said that Jerusalem might cast alms, but asses-trod was all of theirs for the giving. And they shut upon their words.

And it was heat-day when they went within the walls. And one ran at the asses' side who carried jugs and cried: "Water! Water, that ye sup!"

And Theia held forth her hand and brought forth pence and took from out the jugs sup, and offered unto Mary of it. And the lad looked unto Theia and spake:

"Thy city's place—where?"

And Theia answered: "Afar."

And the lad smiled and said: "Yea, where the hair of goats grows upon the head!"

And Theia spake: "Lo, thy waters then batheth thine eyes?"

And the lad made answering: "Nay; Jerusalem sharpeneth the take-in of him who abideth within her walls."

And Theia looked unto the lad and spake: "Thy name?"

And he made answering: "Lucius."

And she said: "Then since thine eye seest afar o'ermuch, hath thy god set thy tongue sharped o'er its rightful sharping, or hath thy day taught thee silence?"

And the lad laughed loud and spake: "Should the tongue of Lucius set apace then would Jerusalem's market vanish as dew; for unto his ears the market's men speak o'ermuch! Yea, and he knoweth the greens that early dawn hath seen plucked and wetted that they shew fresh. Thinkest thou he singeth of such?"

And Theia smiled. And Lucius looked upon Mary and asked of her, and Theia answered, but told naught. And Lucius told unto her of the coming of many who bore babes. Yea, but yesterday had shewed one who bore a babe.

And Theia looked afar, but asked of Lucius: " What hath this babe of yesterday to do that thou shouldst speak unto me of it? For thou knowest not from what land it had come."

And Lucius spake: " Nay, and neither do I know from whence thou hast come! "

And Theia said: " From the land of the yesterday."

" Bethlehem," then spake Lucius.

And Theia looked wide-eyed unto him and asked who bore this babe. And Lucius made answering:

" A dark-skin, and sheep followed them within, and one who knew not the day of men but dwelled within the day of babes."

And Theia questioned: " And they went them where? "

And Lucius answered: " Thinkest thou a pence buyeth a man's word? "

And Theia smiled and spake: " This is Jerusalem! "

And within the market's place men called that Lucius bring forth drops that they sup. And Theia followed with Mary. And Mary spake unto the men, and seeing the golded locks of her they brought forth fruits and offered that she eat. And Mary held unto the hand of Theia.

And Theia limped upon the staff. And they went among the bins and stepped amid the gaming of the men and the whine-buy of the women. For lo, they would hold on high herbs and fruits, and the men of the market's place spake out their price. And the women wailed and begged and wept with dry eyes. And the men spake more of the wares and their words sung as the love of a babe sung by its mother.

And Theia looked upon this and sought after Lucius, who went unto all of the bins that he bring thereto waters.

And the men spake one unto the other of the doings of the Romans, but spake not aloud. And when the white-skins passed, lo, would the flesh o'er their knuckles whiten and their lips firm. And one spake:

" See! they trod upon the streets of Zion and metal rattle * soundeth when 'tis the Jews that trod but mantled! Yea, no Jew sheddeth blood save for the temple. Yea, Rome hath shaken the temple's pillars! "

And they spake word that bittered the name of Caesar.

* Rattle of weapons and armor worn by Romans, while the Jews were forbidden to bear arms.

And Theia heard of this, and looked upon the men of Rome who walked upon the ways e'en unto the temple walls.

And Theia of a sudden sunk! And this was at the bin of Jacob, and the voice of Jacob cried out:

"Behold, upon the way cometh he who hath sheep and the lad!"

And the men laughed. And Jacob shook his raised hands at the coming of them.

And Mary cried out: "Hate!"

And Hatte sprang forth, crying: "Mary! Mary! Hast thou seen Theia upon thy way?"

And Mary turned and held her hand unto the place where Theia had sunk and spake: "She lieth there."

And lo, they went unto the spot and Theia was not! And Hatte spake her name:

"Theia! Theia! Panda, come thou! Here hath come Mary, and she sayeth Theia is here within the walls of Jerusalem!"

And Panda came up unto the place and Hatte spake: "Panda, she hath gone! Why? Why, Panda?"

And Panda looked unto Mary and took within his own her hand and spake unto the Hate.

"Hatte, Theia is wise. Yea, and the God is wise. So be it."

And Hatte spake: "Thou sayest this thing, Panda, but Hatte oft wondereth how heavy of truth thy word."

And Panda spake unto Mary, saying: "Thou hast come with Theia?"

And Mary looked up unto his eyes and answered: "With the dance-woman whom Hatte hath shown unto me, yea."

And Panda asked: "When didst thou come from out Bethlehem?"

"At the dark and night through did we come."

And Hatte touched the locks of Mary and spake: "Thou shalt see Nada, who danceth and singeth. Ah, Mary, how she singeth! And Nadab, who hath not limbs and merrieth and weaveth the merry unto his cloth. Yea, he hath woven the lamb of me and sayeth the men of his tribe will say this thing is a cat of the wilds. And Caleb, who hath a voice like the summer's eve within the fields—soft, yea, Mary, soft. And he saileth seas and telleth of the waters, and roweth ever. Yea, but the house of Nadab smelleth of spice and not of fish! Yea, and Panda hath made sandals for Nada and woven within their skin his own locks. Is this not a truth, Panda?"

And Panda looked afar.

"And Mary, Nada weareth not these sandals but putteth them within her bosom."

And Panda stood tall and spake: "Thou hast spoken folly, Hatte!"

"Yea, Panda, and though thine eyes look tears, and thou hast sat silent like unto the stones, and men have sought thee for wisdoms, Panda, thou art full well fed upon follies."

And the lips of Panda spread of smile. And he stretched forth his hand unto Mary and spake unto Aaron and bid that Hatte come with him unto the house of Nadab.

And they went upon their ways, and lo, a murmuring set among the market's men and they spake one unto the other that this man had taken of babes that were of white skin, and no man knew what he had brought unto Jerusalem, or the land of him.

And among the bins there stood one whose name was called Joel, and he sent up word and seized upon one who stood bent and leaned upon a staff.

And the men of the streets came them up unto the place. And there were among them men of Rome and they, too, laid hands upon this one and tore ope his raiment and loosed the cloth that bound his head. And lo, they laughed loud; for o'er the stooped back of him whose raiment had lain ope streamed locks of gold.

And one among them laughed much and spake loudly: "This is the woman of Tiberius! Yea, and she hath either fruited or the fruit hath died green!"

And they mocked her, saying: "Surely Jerusalem hath need for the offcasting of the noble."

And they pricked her flesh with their blades' points. And she stood regal and spake no word. And one among them leaned close unto her cheek and offered that he press thereon, and lo, she struck him strong o'er the flesh of his cheek and left the stain of the smite thereon. And like unto a she-lion she sprung unto the bin wherein fruits were offered unto the men, and cast them unto the molesters, and their soft made havoc among them. And at the throat of him who taunted did she spring and claw with nails within his flesh. And her hair hung loosed. And they stood about her wondering, for no man knew where the next smite might be.

And she cried out: "Rome is o'erfull of fools and Jerusalem hath been o'errun with their follies!"

And the Jews made word one unto the other and a warring sprung up. And the Jews spake that no man might smite a woman. And they bid that these Romans tell of him who had claimed this woman. And the men of Rome laughed. And the Jews laid hands upon them.

And while this thing had been, lo, Theia had gone. And the men, seeing this, shrugged and left the spot.

And the dark streets that stood close unto the walls saw the fleeing of Theia, and upon the air her whisper hung:

"Yea! Yea! Yet it shall be! He shall come! Yea, He shall come!"

And upon the street's-way there came a woman, and Theia went up unto her and spake. And there followed her a Rome's man. And he ran up unto the place and called her name, "Theia," and his lips mocked the word.

And he made word unto the woman who stood waiting the word of Theia, and called her name Hebe. And she made answering and spake the name of him, Alexis.

And Theia turned and looked unto him and whispered the word: "Alexis! Thou? Then Rome knoweth thy finished work! Speak! Tell unto Theia that no man knoweth from thy lips the tale of her off-cast! Thou who hast seen her tears at thy leaving of her lands! Thou who hast spoken with him, the undoer of her day, say that thou hast told unto Theia's people that she hath died!"

And he smiled, and the smile was heavied of lust. And he held his toga up o'er his spreaded smile and spake:

"No man knoweth. Nay, Theia, no man! Yea, but Alexis holdeth shut his lips but for price!"

And he touched the flesh of her arms, and she shrunk as from lash and caught her hand unto her breast, and the breath choked at her throat and her lips breathed:

"Stop! Ah, stop! The God of Jerusalem sleepeth!"

And she wailed loud: "O Thou! Unto Thee of the East doth Theia cry!"

And Alexis spread forth his arms and made to take unto his breast the trembled form of her. And she grasped the blade of him beneath the toga folds and held it high, and smote!

And he sunk, and crimson flowed and bathed the hilt, and gushed o'er the hand of Theia. And her eyes started forth, and she kneeled and looked unto the stricken face, and her voice was hollow, and she cried: "Lo, hath Theia emptied one of Rome's filthed!"

And she swayed and spake as in a dream: "The blood hath sprung! Hate! Hate! The blood shall wash the tale from off Rome's mouth! Hate! Hate! I love thee!"

And she wiped her blooded hand upon the mantle of Alexis and spake more: "So shall the blood of Hate stain the mantle of Rome!"

And Hebe stood as one of stone, and her lips moved not, e'en though she strove to speak. And she looked upon Theia who knelt. And she saw upon the roadway there came men who sought Alexis. And Hebe raised up her hand and, moaning, pointed unto their coming. But Theia saw not, but rose and stood as one asleep.

And the men came up, and seeing what had been, laid hands upon her and binded her. And she waked and laughed mockery at them and kicked the body of him who lay dead. Then they smote her and tore at her locks, and the words of her came forth unto them:

"What thinkest thou thou mayest do? For shall the slaying of the body of me unlock the lips of him?"

And she spat upon them, and e'en though the hands of her were bound one unto the other, she shook her free and cast of her locks, and set at a dance.

And they bore her down the street's-way, and she danced and mocked. And the men of Jerusalem shook in pity; and the men of Rome laughed.

And they went them past the market's place, and Hatte saw this thing and called aloud: "Theia! Theia!"

And Theia sprang unto him and set the foot of her upon the pit of his stomach and laid him low!

And Panda stooped and took him up, and the lips of Panda oped not, but the whited teeth bit unto the flesh, and he breathed:

"Theia sayeth the God is wise. Where, then, is the wisdom of her words?"

And the Rome's men made curses that babes be left to run upon the street's-way. And they bore her on.

And Panda took the Hate and Mary and Aaron, who stood and had caused the waiting that he see the wares of Jacob, and they went them upon the way unto the house of Nadab.

And Panda spake aloud unto himself: "Is this, then, the path that Panda ever troddeth? Shall Panda ever be the slave?" ·

And he went unto the house. And Nada came forth and Panda spake of what had been and shewed unto her the Hate who lay still, sick. And Panda said the heat of Jerusalem's sun had caused him dreaming and smite.

"Yea, he standeth in the market's place and calleth 'Theia!'"

And Panda laughed. And Nada went within and bore the Hate and lay him beside the cross-legged Nadab, who wove and sheared the weaving.

And Nadab, seeing the flash of Nada's eye, took up a pot of color and daubed upon his face, and redded much the nose of him, and set greens upon his ears, and laughed and laughed.

And Nada spake unto Hatte, shewing of the face of Nadab, and Hatte lay long and spake not. And the eyes of him were wide. And Panda watched and waited, and when Nadab had wearied of the making of plays that he set the Hate at smiles, lo, Hatte spake:

"This thing is folly! Hatte hath drunk waters when he hath hungered, and said, 'Yea, I am fulled.' But this, Panda, was babe's play. Yea, and within Bethlehem Hatte hath lost his heart's aching within the soft wool of one lamb; but this, too, was babe's play! What Hatte hath seen sheweth ever unto him. This was no dreaming! Nay, Panda, nor yet the sun of Jerusalem!

"Whither have these men then gone with Theia? Panda, is the word of Him, the lad of the hills, true? Who is this man who abideth within the temples? Is He my sire? See! e'en though Hatte hath been seized with sick and fainteth, he would go up unto the door of the temple place and knock him loud and say unto them within: 'Let thou the son of this man within!'

"Yea, surely, Panda, if He abideth within and I, His flesh, go unto Him and tell of the doings of these men, He then will ope up His household unto Theia and her flesh. Speak, Panda, that this thing shall be!

"Panda, Hatte is old. Yea, old as Nadab! Yea, the rug of Nadab is no fuller of woes than the days of Hatte! What, what hath Theia done? Panda, she is fair. She doth naught but dance and love, and yet Jerusalem and Bethlehem and e'en He of the East hath forsaken her. See thou! without the door's ope sit the mothers of the Jews and within their arms their own, and no man careth, and yet, Panda, days and days and days and days of hunger-empty have stood between the arms of Theia and Hatte.

"No priest, no king, no man, Panda, hath a mighty-seat * the Hate might crave as the arms of her; and she—ah, speak, Panda! she did it but for loving, but Panda, she hath smote me!

"See thou, Panda! this heart gloweth with golds of love at the seeing of her, and is cut down.

"Mary, come! Weep not! See! Hatte smileth. Yea, he is strong, strong as Caanthus of Rome!"

And he stood forth tall and his arms raised he high and murmured: "Theia sayeth He is wise."

* Throne, or seat of office.

And Nada wiped the bright drops from her dark-hung eyes, and Panda looked afar, and he spake:

"Hatte, thou art to stay here within the walls and seek no man without, and speak not the name of Caanthus aloud."

And Mary stood wet-eyed, and looked unto the rug's-cast, whereon Caleb lay. And Caleb spoke, and the sea's rage had left him calm, and he knew not the day e'en though he held unto the oars, for within the sea's wrath had he lost the day, and ever that that had been lay buried there.

And he asked of the hour, and did the light show; and Mary, hearing the voice of him and seeing that the eyes were shut, stepped her unto the place and tried that she lift the lids. And she pressed her lips upon the scar, and her thin voice made word:

"What hath loned thee?"

And Caleb started up and sunk, with head bowed, and spake: "She hath gone!"

And Mary spake: "And thou art loned?"

And Caleb answered: "Yea."

And Mary said: "No man hath claim of Mary, Rhea hath spoken. And Mary hath much love and none of the day would of it. See! Mary giveth it then unto thee."

And Caleb spake: "Nay, nay, she hath gone!"

And Mary smiled and held forth her hand and made word, saying: "Then thou shalt take the hand of Mary, and Mary shall seek with thee."

And it was at the hour when the sun had sunk upon the top of the west wall and the streets were full of the come and go of the Jew's men. And them of Rome filled up the narrowed walks, and lo, the men of Jerusalem were suffered not to walk thereon, but set within the street's-way.

And Mary looked her out upon the way and shook her golded locks and spake: "Nay. Mary feareth that she seek, for Mary knoweth but sheep, and men who know of her, and this land is o'erfull of men!"

And Hatte murmured: "Yea so! this land is o'erfull of men. Panda, why hast thou sought unto Jerusalem?"

And Panda spake: "Hatte, this is the land of the meeting place of earth. Yea, thou shouldst know that the she-lion knoweth her cubs, for they bed them unafraid within her lair. So, what hath Panda to fear of Jerusalem? For Rome hath drowned her men's sins and Greece hath let her slaved to wander here, and e'en the land of Panda hath belched forth unto Jerusalem her offcastings."

And Hatte asked: "Do we then tarry us within Jerusalem, Panda? For Hatte would seek out the high city * where the tombs stand, and go unto the towers where, behind their shadows, hide the men of mantles that be not the mantles of Jews, nay, but men who wear blades and wave them before the Jews and set the Jews to crouch like unto dogs upon their bellies. Nadab hath told unto me that these men of Rome have loosed the sacred stones of the city's wall and left therein the scars that time and time will pass before the healing.

"Yea, and he telleth that the noble blood that setteth o'er Rome hath aged. Yea, and e'en at the prime of its flowing, lo, 'twas a one who lay at ease and looked not upon the work of his men.

"Panda, is then a man who doeth naught of good nor evil a better one than one that doeth but evil? Yea, and doth not the evil of his brother that he shutteth up his eyes that he see not, then weigh down his measure as his very own?"

"Yea, yea, Hatte. Thou hast spoken truth. But the God is wise, and the measure not thine!"

And Hatte stood and looked unto Panda and Nadab, who sat crosslegged and wide-eyed that youth should offer of wisdom unto the full-fleshed.

And Hatte spake more: "Mary, sit thee beside Caleb there, and hold thou the hand of Aaron, for he wearieth. Yea, but Hatte hath felt a flame that shall burn unto his in-man ever. Yea! Yea!"

And the youth's voice sounded as a metal that, heated, had fallen unto the cold drops.

"Hatte shall live upon the flesh of Jews. Hatte shall set the Jews within his heart as his people. Yea, Hatte hath hate for Rome! Yea, Panda, the sick creepeth! Hatte seeth Rome a youth's-man; yea, a war's-man; yea, and within his hand a goblet. Yea, a cup! Yea, and he drinketh. Ah—'tis the blood of Hatte!"

And Hatte fell, his long limbs asprawl! And he arose and his eyes blazed as fires and he cried:

"Ah, Thou of the East! The Sire of me! That I, Hatte, thy flesh, shall be thy worthy son! For who knoweth what tarrieth Thee? And Theia sayeth Thou shalt come."

And Panda rose and raised up his hands in the sign of obeisance, and Nadab wiped his eyes. And Nada brought forth the pots that smoked and sat her down. And Nadab brought forth the sacred cloth and spread it ope, and Nada lay her upon its soft glow and swung the pots. And Aaron wept, and Mary looked, and Caleb slept.

* The "upper city" of Josephus.

And Hatte spake more, saying: "Doth the men of Rome touch the flesh of her! Panda, what bursteth here?"

And he oped his arms and cried aloud:

"Oh, Thou! Oh, Thou of Theia! Send Thou thy hosts, yea, clothed of white, that they surge as the waves that Peter hath told unto Hatte of, and wash these lands!"

CHAPTER XVII

And night came upon the land, and tarried long within the day's hour. And when the light had come out from 'neath the dark mists, the city's ways shewed empty, and waters stood pooled within the stone's opes. The market's men came them, their mantles wet, and their legs stained of dust's wet. And camels dripped, and packs, skin-covered, shed drops o'er their sides. And babes came unto the door's ope and peered without and held their hands that they wet within the mist that fell. And smoke came from out the opes and hung close unto the street's-way, and men coughed. And asses backed their ears that the wet go not within, and shook their hides.

And within the Jew's bins at the market's place Jacob tucked up the mantle of him that it touch not the wet stones.

And there came one unto the market's place, and he called his name Enoch. And Enos spake with him. And Enoch was wet and stained, and carried, o'er his bended back, hides of sheep, and they smelled. And Enos spake unto Jacob, saying:

"Lo, hath Enoch come, and behold, he bringeth sheep's hides that we buy."

And Jacob looked unto Enoch and made no answering. And Enos shrugged and held high his hands, palms up, and swung his beard, and spake: "Thou seest, Enoch, Jacob hath no word."

And Enoch questioned: "What then? Shall a man bring forth goods unto him who buyeth and offer unto him and receive not e'en the answering?"

And Jacob looked not upon Enos, nor yet upon Enoch, and spake as though unto the men of the city:

"Should, then, a man who offereth that he buy, speak unto him who seeketh more than the price he offereth? This is a waste of word."

And Enoch oped up the skins and shewed unto Jacob that the wool stood thick and that there were seven and ten. And Jacob felt that they were as Enoch had spoken.

And Jacob spake: "What manner of man slayeth his sheep that he bear wool unto his market's men?"

And Enos held his fingers up unto his lips and spake him low:

"Jacob, Bethlehem's men know the ewes may not twofold * the herds o'er the day or night. Yea, and up upon the high places no man goeth, thou knowest, save him who be unclean. So, seest thou?"

And Jacob shook him "yea" and spake: "Bethlehem hath more ado within her place than e'en Jerusalem, for more hath come from out Bethlehem than Jerusalem knoweth. Yea, women who wear goat's hair upon their heads, and dark-skins that bear white-skin babes. Yea, and men who know not the day but know the glitter of metals! A thief! A thief! Yea!"

And Jacob rocked.

And Enoch spake: "Thou sayest a dark-skin? Then did his eyes look afar?"

And Jacob answered: "Yea."

"And the lad, was he fair?"

And Jacob spake him: "Yea."

And Enoch shewed fright, and Jacob lay his hands upon the great heap of hides and said:

"So! Jacob hath bought of thee these; for sayest thou one word then 'tis Jacob who opeth up his lips and speaketh what thou hast done! 'Tis no man o' wisdom who needeth that other men see for him! Yea, the wools of the sheep that followed the dark-skin bore the berries of the high place. And so thou seest here upon these. So!"

And he raised up his voice, and his eyes saw that no man harked, and yet did he chant: "Woe! Woe! This day then brought unto Jacob one who doeth wrong unto his brother! Woe! Woe! Woe!"

And Enoch begged that Jacob speak not loudly, and Jacob wept and spake louder. And Enoch cried: "Jacob! Jacob! Mercy upon thy brother!"

And Jacob reached unto his mantle and brought out mites unto the score, and held upon his oped palm, and spake:

"Of the store of Jacob wouldst thou take; for lo, may man weep and yet pay price unto the full? Nay. Of Jacob's tears hast thou taken. Then here, he offereth unto thee the full price he payeth. This or the oping of Jacob's lips. Which be it?"

And he cast unto Enoch the mites and cried out: "Off ye! Off ye! Woe, that Jacob looketh upon a one like unto thee!"

And Enoch made his way from out the market's place and Jacob lifted up the heavy pack of skins and brought them within his bin and moaned: "Woe! Woe!" And sat him upon the heap of skins.

And Enos laughed long and spake: "Lo, is then the God not wise

* May not double the herds in a day.

that He fashioneth thee, Jacob, of tender heart, and thy brother a one who slayeth of the lambs and fetcheth unto thee that thou mayest eat of flesh thy tender heart would not to slay?"

And Jacob sat upon the skins and spake of the woes of Jerusalem and the Jews. And he spake of the words that had come from out the city of Bethlehem that had set up the hate of Herod. And he said:

"Enos, thou knowest this man Herod is not of the Jews, and yet do the Jews await their Messiah. And thou knowest the splitting of the lands of Herod hath wrought but havoc among the Jews. Yea, and who, Enos, standeth beneath Rome's lash but Jerusalem?"

"Yea, Jacob would be filled up with Rome's plunder, that his people be venged. Yea, and Jacob knoweth much of Rome that no man of his blood knoweth; for Simeon * of the temple telleth unto the priests the woes of the land, and they do spill much blood and burn the fatted lambs that Jerusalem find favor with Jehovah. Yea, and yet these priests know much that, were lips oped, might set Rome to quake!"

And Enos spake of the lad that had gone unto the temple place, and told of the wording of Bethlehem of the babe that had been born therein, and of the wise men who came, and where shepherds had brought incense made of herbs, and gold that was but the hoarding of their sheep's price. Lo, had these wise men brought incense even as they within the temple place know, and gold that shewed as the royal jewels, and rubies, and jasper, made into cups and set of precious stones, and cloths that shewed dyes, purpled deep, and scarlet.

And this woman who had borne the babe lay and looked her afar. And Bethlehem knew of this thing, and e'en though Herod had slain the innocents, lo, here within the temple cometh one whose years would be as this babe's, and speaketh wisdom in babe's tongue that confoundeth the priests.

And this lad, men of the temple place said, had spoken unto His mother, at her coming, that was it not the time that He should be at His father's business? And spake of vineyards, and none stood within the temple.

And Enos spake: "Who is this lad? For within the city there is no Jew of the years of Him."

And Jacob swung his beard, and the winds spread the thin hairs and swept them unto his eyes, and he said:

"Thou sayest this lad is a Jew? Then the lad of white skin is not he."

And Enos answered: "Nay, the wise men asked of Herod and within

* Probably Simeon the high priest, son of Hillel and father of Gamaliel.

Bethlehem, 'Where is He who was born King of the Jews?' And yet this lad is of mean birth, though of the blood of David. Yea, and His mother was with child at her coming unto her husbandman."

And Jacob said: "This, then, is not he, for no King cometh him unpurpled."

And Enos said: "Yea, so."

And Jacob spake: "Enos, thou hast told that no Jew of the years of the lad shew within Jerusalem. Thou knowest there have been lads of these years."

"Ayea, but not of the blood of David, Jacob."

And Joel came from out the bin of him and spake unto Jacob and Enos and Enoch and the skins and asked: "What manner of man slayeth for wools?"

And Enos spake: "May not a man who buyeth wools and whose brother maketh show, buy of skins for the brother of him?"

And Joel smiled and said: "Jerusalem hath but one tongue, yea, and yet for her words there be the meanings of the whole tongue of the temple's steps. Yea, her men weep o'er sheep and weigh of tears."

And Jacob wailed of the man who had come from out Bethlehem and had done wrong unto his brother. And Joel held hard his sides and rocked, and he reached him high and plucked off from the bin of a market's brother a strong root and rubbed upon his eyes until they streamed drops, and he wailed: "Woe! Woe! Woe!"

And Jacob shook his head and said that no man knew of the woe at the heart of him. And Enos shut up one eye and shrugged unto Joel.

And Jacob stood him up and pointed unto the road's-way whereon Panda shewed. And Panda came bowed, and his beard lay upon his breast, and his locks hung black and heavy of drops. And Jacob spake unto Enos: "The dark-skin!"

And he spread cloth o'er his wares and watched the coming of Panda, saying: "Lo, the shadow of this man is but a thief!"

And, seeing that Aaron followed not, he stood and listed that he hear what Panda spake. And Panda came him up unto Joel and made word, saying: "Lo, doth the beetle crawl."

And Joel spake: "Yea, and no man seeketh chaff!"

And Panda held out his hand, and Joel touched it upon his brow. And Panda swept his mantle o'er his cheek and said: "Jerusalem hath ears upon the stones."

And Joel answered: "Yea, and Jerusalem's men wear ears within their feet-soles, yea, and within their beards!"

And Jacob shrugged unto Enos. And Panda spake: "Joel, thy brother hath sore woe and needeth counsel."

And Joel said: "Yea, man, and yet Joel may not leave his bin."

And Panda asked: "Will no man, then, take thy place therein?"

And Joel answered: "Yea. Lucius cometh later, yea, and Jerusalem hath already drunk o'ermuch, so then shall Joel bid Lucius that he await him and stay within the bins."

And Panda spake: "So be it. Then Panda awaiteth the coming of Lucius."

And he sat him down upon the skins of Jacob, and took up pebbles and cast unto the pools that stood. And Joel spake not, and Jacob spake not, and Enos spake not. And eyes stood upon Panda.

And the light broke and sun shone, and Panda arose and kicked the skins and spake: "Men have come at an early hour that they bear green skins!"

And he took up one that smelled and spread it ope, and lo, upon the back of it there shewed a spot that had been a sore and had healed. And Panda set his brows high and his fingers plucked the berries from out the wool. And Joel watched, and Enos made as though to set the skins away. And Panda spake:

"Folly hath broke loose; for what man slayeth his sheep for wool?"

And Jacob answered: "Thou hast heard of the high places. These sheep have come from out Bethlehem and woe hangeth o'er them; for Enos hath spoken no man goeth unto the high places save him that be unclean."

And Panda spake low: "So? Then, Joel, these skins be not fit for Jerusalem!"

And Joel wrung his hands and wailed: "Woe! Woe! Woe!"

And Jacob ran forth from the side to side of the bin and swung his beard and wept. And Panda spake, and his words came o'er the billow of laughter: "Joel, that thou and Panda shouldst see the brother of us buy of unclean skins!"

And he spake unto Jacob, saying: "Woe, brother! Thinkest thou that Panda might leave thee that thou doest wrong unto thy tribesmen? See thou! Panda and Joel shall bear these skins unto the out of the west wall and burn."

And Joel spake: "Yea, yea; for men shall surely know of their unclean, and who knoweth that the bright spot may not break upon Jacob!"

And Jacob, whose cheek shewed drops, arose and asked that they make low their voices. And Joel wailed louder, and men came up unto the bin and listed. And Jacob, seeing this thing, spake: "Thou hast spoken wisdom."

And he went unto the stone's ope within the streets and washed therein his hands in token that he was free of this.

And Lucius came with his ass packed of greens, and but one jug. And Joel told unto him of the need of Panda, and Lucius made fast his ass and said that he then would bide within the bin until the coming of them. And Panda and Joel stepped them down the street's-way. And Jacob shook his shut hand at their backs, weighted down of skins.

And Enos sat and laughed long. And Panda sunk his fingers within the ribs of Joel. And Joel smiled not but questioned:

"Then go we unto the west wall?"

And Panda answered: "Yea, just so straight as the east path leadeth thee."

And they sought the up-city and bought of blades; for Panda spake: "Lo, Joel, what man knoweth wool by its skin? Then do we set the skins free of wool and sell."

And Panda counted the skins, and there were seven and ten. And lo, he gave unto Joel one-half and one. And Joel spake: "This, Panda, is the heavy of the measure."

And Panda said: "Nay. No good cometh of the o'erfull measure; 'tis waste. Then unto the chaff goeth the waste."

And Joel made answering: "Yea, and upon waste the beetle feedeth."

And Panda laughed and spake: "So be it."

And Joel said: "Come thou, Panda, not unto the house thou hast abided in, but unto the house of Joel."

And Panda spake: "Why hast thou said this thing?"

And Joel answered: "Thou hast told of the ears of Jerusalem. Lo, man, there be eyes e'en upon the asses' tails!"

"Joel, thou art a white-skin. What, then, that thou shouldst seek of a dark one for thy brother?"

"Panda, would that Joel had within his breast a heart so white as thine! For from out thy eyes sheweth naught but good."

And Panda reached his arm about the shoulder of Joel, and Joel looked him down and asked of Nada. And Panda spake not, but looked him far. And Joel laughed.

CHAPTER XVIII

AND this was upon the way unto the high city. And they came unto the pillared hall of the Romans.° And men came from out the place and went within. And Panda looked him up unto the walls' opes, and Joel let the skins sink that he rest beside the place. And Panda sunk upon the skins he cast, and they wiped the drops from off their brows.

And it was high hour. And men spake the tongues of other lands. And Joel knew the tongue of the white-skins, and Panda listed and knew it, too.

And there came forth men who wore blades, and metals o'er their breasts and heads, and upon their forearms and upon their skins; and white shewed their skirts, and o'er their backs hung cloth that reached unto their knee's bend. And sandals wore they of strong skin, and thongs binded 'bout their legs.

And Panda murmured: "Ah, Rome! Rome! Still dost thou bite at Panda's heart!"

And these men went them down the street's-way. And Panda looked unto Joel and spake of what had been done unto Theia and how she had come unto the market's place and had worn goat's hair. And Joel stood him high and his cheeks burned. And Panda told of the things he had seen of the bearing of Theia by these men of Rome unto where he knew not. And Joel cried out:

"Goat's hair! And Panda, when they tore ope the head-cloth, gold locks streamed? Ah, man, and the hands of Joel did this thing! Panda, list unto thy brother! These hands shall be severed from off their seats doth he not undo this thing!"

And Panda spake: "He who doeth wrong and knoweth not payeth but from out his heart, Joel."

And they spoke of Theia, and Panda told unto Joel all, and Joel knew. And the going of this from out the heart of Panda unto the heart of Joel caused love to spring up.

And the hours crept unto one full and the half. And Panda of a sudden started up and pointed unto men who came. And these were the men of Rome's high seats, and there followed them the war's-men and they bore upon a skin, stretched, the body of one slain. And they passed

146

the spot where Joel and Panda sat, and Panda touched the flesh of Joel, saying:

"This is who?"

And Joel made answering: "I know not. There hath been word of the slain and it hath been spoken that the slayer was a woman."

And Panda tore ope his mantle. And the winds raised up the cloth o'er the dead face and Panda saw and gasped, "Alexis!" and shut his lips o'er the word.

And the Rome's men went within. And there stood at the gate's-way ones who bore spears and short broad-blades; and they stood them apart that these men go within.

And when they had gone Panda grasped the arm of Joel and spake: "Joel, Theia is there! This man thou hast seen slain is Alexis, whom Augustus sent unto Jerusalem and who was with Theia in the wilderness, and knew Panda and knoweth Theia e'en unto this day. For he held office high among the war's-men, but a one of the courts who was slaved, a woman, Virga, looked upon him much, and Caesar cared naught. But one of them o'er the war's-men coveted this woman. And love and war and office wrought thick as honey and mixed not; and Alexis was sent unto Jerusalem that Rome be rid of him. These men of Rome love and wed, yea, but the women of noble blood lay steeped of sweets, and 'tis the slaves that know the men's tongues, and fill up their hours. Nadab hath told unto me of the coming of Alexis, and Panda hath feared."

And Joel said: "This woman is fair, thou hast spoken; then these men will deal not with heavy hands."

"Joel, Panda burneth here within his breast in fearing the men Rome hath within these walls!"

And Joel questioned: "Hath this woman a honeyed tongue?"

And Panda answered: "Thou hast felt the mid-hour's sun of Jerusalem? It is even's cool beside the tongue of her! Yea, her words come as flames from out her. Yea, and within her breast is not the room for the hating she holdeth for Rome! Yea, Joel, Panda knoweth thy heart and putteth therein his dearest hidden word. Theia hath born a son for the noble blood of Rome. Yea, and he abideth here in Jerusalem!"

"Doth he know his sire?"

"Nay, and did his sire to know of him, 'twould be but the supping of the potion of death. Yea, the flesh of him would he to cause to be split unto the shreds of rags! Jehovah! Joel, what emptied hearts and fulled bellies [10] these Romans have!"

"Yea, and what fulled belly filleth a head!"

And Panda sat and plucked at his mantle, and his dark cheek gleamed ruby-red, and his teeth bit at his lips, and he spake:

"Rome hath ne'er built of a wall that shall hold Panda from Theia."

And Joel said: "And no man keepeth Panda's brother apart from him!"

And Panda stepped up unto the road's side, across from the wall's ope, and stood, and lo, at the earth's crust, at the in-wall of the pillared place, there shewed opes, and bars o'er the opes, and from out the bars there reached a hand, white and thin; and then its mate! And they locked, and a voice cried out: "O-e-e! Oh-e-e!" and died unto a mocking laugh.

And Panda shewed this thing unto Joel, who came up unto the spot, and they stood and talked of sheep, that the men at the gate's ope hear.

And they saw men of Rome go unto the out-door of this 'neath-place; and they brought Theia forth. And her mantle was stained of blood, and her hair hung long, and its locks at the ends were stained red of the blood; and her hands beat one upon the other. ·

And Panda, seeing this thing, rushed unto the gate's-way and tore ope his breast and screamed aloud. And the men that stood, pointed the lances unto his bared breast, and freed them their blades.

And the war's-men that bore her came up unto the gateway, and Panda cried him loud:

"This woman hath done naught! This hand hath struck Alexis!"

And they laid hands upon him. And Joel came up and spoke that he had set this man upon Alexis. And they took him within and brought Panda up unto Theia, who stood. And Panda cried out unto her, and she bared her teeth as a she-wolf and cried:

"The sun hath turned this man mad! Bear thou me within, that the dogs be fed!"

And she struck the cheek of Panda and called aloud: "Fool!" And the men of Rome bound her hands, and she held her head high and spake unto Joel, saying:

"Who art thou? This man is a fool and thou art his folly!"

And Joel looked unto Panda and spake not. And Panda swore by the gods of Rome that he had struck the blow. And they went them within.

And the head of Theia stood upon the arched neck, and the foot of her crept as the foot of the lion, and the sandal's slip sounded as the pad of the lion's foot. The hands, binded at the back, clenched, and the bosom panted heavy. And the men of the Rome's place cast the bodies of Panda and Joel unto the floor's stones.

And this was within the hall's arch where pillars stood, and steps led unto the in-chamber. Slaves swept silent to and fro, and virgins danced within, their heads woven o'er of beaded bands that rattled at the dance, and they made musics. And the black slaves brought forth bowls of fruits and jugs of wine, and chalices that they drink.

And the walls were hung of rugs and skins and precious stuff, and the mighty-seat was hewn of blacked wood and spiked of gold.

And there ranked at the sides seven black men, eunuchs, bared, who swayed of tufted grass that scented of the airs. And o'er the mighty-seat there shewed a golded sun, and there lay upon the steps up unto the spot a she-lion. And about the hall stood pots of brass upon tall legs.

And there came forth ones robed of white. And these were the vested virgins.* And they bore incense and set the pots ope, and lo, they smoked. And the virgins wailed and danced as the swaying vine about the curling clouds.

And the Man of Rome † sat upon the mighty-seat and slept.

And they that had borne Theia hence spake one unto the other, saying: "Why should we bring unto the Mighty a Jew? For hath not Rome dealt unto her war's-men power that they weigh and take of Jews?"

And one among them spake: "This woman is no Jew, for she hath spoken the tongue of Rome and knoweth much of the tongues of the streets; for the eyes of her shew this thing."

And they spake that they should take these transgressors unto themselves and before the senators,‡ and set them wording one with the other; for they said that thieves who spake one unto another wove nets and left of holes therein.

And Theia bared her teeth and thinned her lips in smile, and spake: "A Jew? Yea, and a woman! But dross for Rome!"

And she turned unto Panda and cried:

"Who is this man? A beggar of the temple's steps! And he who goeth with him but the pilfer-man of the emptied market who eateth rotted fruits?"

And they asked of her: "Art thou a Jew?"

* Not to be confused with vestal virgins. Apparently a dance of ceremony.
† If any dependence can be placed upon the dates assigned to the periods of rule of the Roman procurators, this should be Marcus Ambibulus or Ambivius, of whom history seems to record nothing.
‡ Probably the Sanhedrin.

And Theia made answering: "Yea, a Jew who hath lost her wares upon the streets of Jerusalem."

And Panda, who knew her words held Hatte within them, cried out: "Yea, yea, but suredly one man shall find thy wares!"

And Theia shrugged and spake: "Yea, but he who findeth thinketh 'tis but a copper cup and worth a-naught, and I say me 'tis pure gold and sapphired o'er, but no man shall know."

And Panda said: "Yea, yea, this then is true."

And Theia said: "Yea, and the dogs of the streets may drink from out this cup!"

And Panda cried out: "Nay, nay, for he who findeth shall suredly bear it unto a shelter place, e'en unto the temple!"

And the men of Rome, hearing this thing, spake: "What hath beset these of the streets?"

And Theia laughed, laughed loud, and spake: "What hath beset Jerusalem? Rome! Rome! Yea, and Rome besetteth them of the streets, for Rome's heel is upon the Jews! They look them unto the Jew's temple and curl of their lips and know not of the God that abideth therein. And then do they set their lance points within the temple doors and ope, and set the sign of other gods therein; for may not one god love another? Yea, and they look them unto the Jews and shrug and love them not. Nay, e'en as Rome despiseth the black-skins she slaves, so doth she hate the Jews. Yea, but worse; for Rome loveth of the Jews e'en so well that she slave them not, and yet so surely are they slaved as though chains held of their ankles.

"Ah, Rome! Thou hast of a breast, big, deep, yea, and empty! And these Jews do nurture by it! Jerusalem holdeth up a coin, yea, and the sun casteth of its shadow, and lo, the coin slippeth it unto the coffers of Rome, and the shadow, 'tis for the Jews. Yea, and more, e'en the sun forsaketh them!"

And the Rome's men harked, for they had heard not such a tongue as this of Theia. And she spake more:

"Rome, thou art full fleshed! Yea, and glut thee on! So time shall find thee a-wallowed of fats, and sick, and dead, and rotted!"

And they of Rome spake this was treason. And Theia said:

"Treason from the lips of Romans? Yea, but Rome dealeth unto them of her from off her lips, and from out her heart, worse!"

And Panda feared, and Joel plucked at her mantle. And Theia drew her up and spake:

"Thinkest thou a one who knoweth of the pit's beasts feareth them?

Lo, the measure tippeth with e'en the putting of a smile. Yea, but this shall hang upon a hair."

And the men took them within the inner place. And Theia stood and looked unto him who sat upon the mighty-seat. And the mighty one, e'en though he heard of the wording of the men and saw them they had brought forth, looked not but shut his eyes. And one among the Rome's men said:

"This woman knoweth much of Rome and hath made treason 'gainst her."

And the mighty one held shut his eyes and spake: "He who knoweth of Rome shall learn more."

And they told of what had been, and shewed of the blood stains and brought forth the body of Alexis that all men see. And lo, one among them stood forth and spake of his brother and that Rome had lost a one who stood 'mong her men as a star unto the heavens. Yea, and shewed of the smite wherein the blade had driven, and held up the stained cloth and turned the deathed eyes that they see. And made discourse in the weighty words of them of high office. And his brethren of high seat drew them unto a far place that they make word.

And he of the mighty-seat slept.

And they came them forth and spake that this woman should tell of what had been. And she laughed and said:

"Lo, did Rome offer of a cup, and I but cast its sup. Yea, 'twas filthed!"

And they said that her words made not a clearing,* and she spake: "No more do I."

And they said that within the hands of Rome stood that that loosed the lips.

And Theia said: "Yea, and within the hands of one of Rome was that that stopped of word."

And they brought forth the blade and shewed of its stained metal unto her, and she reached forth and kissed it and held it high and cried: "This is the key unto the treasure chest of Rome's nobled!"

And one among them spake: "Lo, hath this woman a tongue that Rome might envy, for she hath woven of cloths and binded us therein!"

And Theia spake soft words, and crept unto the dead Alexis, and crouched, and hissed, and held high the blade, and struck once more!

---

* Her meaning not clear; they did not understand.

And they seized upon her and lay blows, and Panda burst forth and cried that he had done this thing, and Joel said 'twas he, and each did swear unto his gods 'twas him. And the Rome's men looked one unto another and asked what then might be done.

And one among them went unto him of the mighty-seat and told unto him of what had been done, and asked that he give of his mightiness and do unto these as he would. And the mighty one waked and sat him, his head bent, and harked, and at the finishing spake:

"Lo, since there are three, and each sayeth he has done this thing, then bring forth three chalices, and one among them shall bear of a potion,* and offer unto them that each choose and drink."

And lo, they stood and spake: "Yea."

And Theia cried: "Ah, Rome! Thy play is here! Thy mighty one sleepeth and waketh but for the gaming! Then look ye, Rome's ones! Since this potioned cup be offered in play, 'tis a one of Rome who goeth unto the play at dance!"

And she plucked forth the mantle cloth of Alexis, stained, and held it high, and cast her blooded locks, and pawed of the stones as doth the charger upon the battled field, and screamed and laughed. And they sat them cold and frightened. And she plucked forth the blade and cut at her wrists and spilled blood upon the stones and wiped the stains upon her face and laughed and laughed.

And the mighty one wrathed, and spake that should she not choose of the potioned cup she then should be cast unto a pit.

And the slaves came forth, and there were three, and each bore of a chalice, and they walked them one beside the other. And the mighty one came forth and looked upon the three and spake that Theia should choose. And lo, she sprung and dashed the three unto the flags!

And they laid hold of her and smote her, and she laughed. And they brought forth more of chalices. And the mighty one went forth and chose of one and offered it that she drink.

And Theia looked unto Panda, and lo, the cloth of his mantle tore and his neck's cords stood out, and Theia spake:

"O thou of the streets of Jerusalem, art thou a shepherd?"

And Panda answered: "Yea, within the hill's place."

"'Mong thy sheep hast thou a lamb?"

And Panda made answering: "Yea, a lamb."

"And this lamb hath been chose as the lamb of sacrificing?"

"Yea, but 'tis not of this fold that shall be taken!"

* A poisoned draught.

And Theia spake and swayed: "He shall come! He shall come! Yea, upon a camel white as goat's milk. He shall come from out the East! It shall be! It shall be!"

And she drank, and laughed; for the taste was wine! And the laugh froze as she looked unto Panda.

And Panda laughed and lay his hand within the hand of Joel. And Joel took of the hand of Panda and lay it upon his brow.

And they offered of the cups. And Panda took and drank, and stood, his eyes started forth and hand reached unto the other.

And Joel spake: "But chaff!" And he drank and sunk, murmuring a-smile: "Chaff! Chaff!"

And Theia sunk upon the stones, her locks spread, and o'er the flesh of her the mantle, stained of the blood of Alexis. And Panda stood him tall, and his breast heaved, and his arms swelled, and his lips shut, and his teeth ground, and upon his brow stood drops. And he stood forth and went unto the fallen Theia and took her up and stood, his arms full of the casted play of Rome. And at the feet of him lay Joel, his arms limp, his eyes misted o'er, and lips smiled.

And the men of Rome stood them awed. And Theia stirred and her breath came as a moan, and she murmured her: "It shall be! It shall be!"

And as at waking she slipped her unto the stones, her knees swayed, and she spake:

"See, Panda, see! Is then the God wise? Yea, for He hath smitten not the shepherd of His lamb! Oh, thou of Rome, look thou here upon a one who lieth nobled. Yea, upon a stoned couch and drunkened unto death upon the bittered draught of Rome! Still doth he noble e'en the airs thou dost breathe!"

And Theia oped up her arms and held them high, and tears streamed down the stained cheeks of her. And she made words that sounded as musics, and the voice of her rose up unto a shrilled note, and cut at the airs like unto a bared blade, and sunk within the ears of them of Rome, and she spake:

"Ah, thou of the mighty Rome, how hast thou stoned of the nobled that thou makest play for thy high seated! Yea, upon the mighty-seat setteth he, the mighty one, and lo, he shutteth up his eyes and seeth not; for at the shutting, lo, he hath shut all of the earth that he knoweth as mighty. And lo, he who lieth here drunkened unto death hath shut of his eyes, and at the shutting hath seen that of the nobled that he who setteth upon the mighty-seat seeth never! Yea, never!"

And she kneeled her upon the stones and kissed of her stained palms

and lay them upon the brow of Joel. And looked her up upon high
and cried:

"O Thou of the East! Bathe Thou these hands clean! Yea, with
the blood shed from out the heart of him who lieth here. Yea, for
though he there hath shed no blood, still hath he sacrificed of his blood
for Thine own!"

And the sun's bright crept within and shone upon the gold locks
of her, and the stains darkened.

And he who sat upon the mighty-seat slept anew. And slaves came
them up and took of the body of Joel that lay and made that they bear
it away. And Panda spake unto the Rome's men and bid that they
leave that he bear the body of the brother of him out unto his land.
And they laughed and said that carrion was but for the casting and
brought no price, and 'twas well.

And Theia stood, and upon her flesh the hands of the men of Rome
held fast. And Panda's hands reached forth unto him of the mighty-
seat, and he spake:

"Thou hast taken of blood! Yea, and the thirst of Rome be satis-
fied. Then leave thou, with this thy men call carrion, the woman
yonder."

And the Rome's men made a loud noise, their voices raised unto a
wail: "Nay! Nay! Nay!"

And Panda spake: "What then, hath Rome hunger still?"

And they showed unto him the blood upon the mantle of Theia and
said:

"Then dost thou deem the slaying of the lion's cub be the slaying of the sire?"

And he of the mighty-seat stretched him anew for sleep and spake:
"Unto the pit!"

And Panda caught at the hands of Theia and his words came soft:
"Thou hast spoke the God is wise."

And Theia reached within her breast and sudden pressed within
the hand of Panda a skin sack and her words came softer than e'en the
breath:

"Doth Rome seek, then fat thy lamb upon this, and even as the
stoned bull that beareth of incense yonder so shall thy lamb lay."

And Panda spake: "The fields are green, yea, and lambs sleep
therein, and He is wise."

And they led her forth, and her words sounded, e'en at the last
step from out the hall: "It shall be! It shall be!"

And Panda heaved of his bosom and knelt that he bear of the

body of Joel thither. And the men of Rome set at word of the city's
ways, and among them no man seemed that he saw. And Panda took
up the limp form of Joel and stepped him out, and tears washed o'er
his cheeks. And at the gate's pass, lo, he came upon the skins! And he
unburdened him that he weep.

And lo, the eve had set, and the Jews sounded afar at the wailing
place. And Panda stopped of his ears and spake:

"So, Joel, the east way led unto this, thy journey's end."

And he took up the dead hand and pressed upon his brow, and he
stood and looked. And one came down the road's-way. And he
showed as a young youth. And Panda called out in the tongue of
the Jews:

"Woe! Woe unto thy brother!"

And he who came called clear: "Woe? Woe? Yea, woe's undoing
cometh."

And when he had come up unto the spot, lo, he saw the body of
Joel and oped up his eyes and spake: "Thy woe is done and no man
may set it then undone."

And Panda sat him down and spake: "Hark! the wailers moan,
yea, and it setteth the dogs that they do howl. Yea, and had this woe
within this heart of me a tongue, then would it sing it so."

And he asked of the youth: "What name hath Jerusalem known of
thee?"

And the youth made answering: "Samuel." And he bent him o'er
the form of Joel and spake: "What! This man, Joel, of the market's
way?"

And Panda wept and answered: "Yea."

And Samuel spake: "Then hath Jerusalem that that should set her
woed; for 'mong her men there showeth no man as he here!"

And Panda questioned: "Doth Jerusalem know this man?"

And Samuel made answering: "Lo, what be Jerusalem unto the
market's men but the market's place and them within its bins? Knowest thou Jacob?"

And Panda answered: "Yea."

And Samuel spake: "I am, then, the son of him."

And Panda looked him not upon the youth, but spake him soft:
"The son of Jacob! Then 'tis the fruit that hath of the tree's
sap." And he spake loud: "This man hath drunk from out the
street's pool and it hath held of that that hath slain him."

And Samuel asked: "What man hath seen this thing?"

And Panda answered: "No man." And he bit his lip and

stopped, and spake more: "Nay, no man, but Nada hath gone that she bring forth aid. Yea, and she hath seen this thing."

And Samuel bared of his teeth.

"What then! A woman seeketh with men that they bear of skins? Yea, and more, what bringeth thee unto the east way? For no market's place abideth beside the Rome's hall!"

And Panda said: "When man thirsteth and man offer of a cup, and still he thirsteth, doth man then still offer more of waters?"

And Samuel spake: "Nay, but doth man sup, then 'tis man that should bear back of the cup. I go me, then, with thee unto the house of Nadab."

And Panda stood him tall and o'er the sorrowed lips there broke a smile, and he spake: "Then bear thou these skins."

And Samuel cried: "This be the burden of an ox!"

And Panda spake: "Yea, but 'tis a man who hath not an ox that setteth his ass at the pack."

And Samuel took up the skins, and Panda stooped that he take Joel within his arms. And it was night's-come, and close unto the walls 'twas dark. And Panda went within the dark, and they made way unto the house of Nadab. And at the come unto its door's place, lo, the shutter was oped and within the oil lamp burned and Nada sung:

"*O tiny stars, spilled from the moon's cradle,*
Fear ye not, O fear ye not!
Thy mother sun shall come at dawn.
O fear ye not! O fear ye not!"

And this was spoken not in the tongue of the Jews but of the far land.

And Panda, hearing, spake answering in the tongue. And Nada heard not, but smote upon the fruits that she made unto breads. And Samuel said:

"He who maketh word and speaketh not his brother's tongue maketh treason."

And Panda spake: "Then 'tis thy tongue that shall speak and no word shall Panda put."

And Nada, hearing their voices, came forth and stopped, silent, for dark hid them from the eyes of her. And Samuel spake:

"Hast thou been up upon the east way?"

And Nada answered: "What man careth?"

And Samuel said: "Thy tongue speaketh and telleth naught. Hast thou seen Panda?"

And Nada looked her keen-eyed unto the dark, and the teeth of Panda gleamed, and she asked: "Who art thou?"

And Samuel said: "This is not thine answer."

And she spake: "Yea, the day hath been full of Panda."

And she held forth her hand unto Panda, who stood, and stepped unto him, and started, for her eyes saw that he bore of a one smitten. And Panda spake:

"Thou didst speak that pool's draught was fitted not for man."

And Nada said: "Yea, yea, yea."

And Panda questioned: "What, then tarried thee?"

And Nada wailed that Nadab had hunger and she had stopped that she set at the smite of fruits that she might set before him. And Caleb, then, had begged that he be fed. And Nada wailed sorrowing that she had tarried long.

And Panda spake unto Samuel, saying: "Thou art not a one that hath trod with the path of me, yet thou hast spoken my name."

And Samuel spake: "Yea, for Jacob hath told of the dark-skin whose teeth show white as wolves' and who hath cunning past them."

And Panda said: "Since thou hast brought forth these skins, bear them within."

And Samuel went within, and Panda followed, and the body of Joel sagged within his arms, and sweat stood upon his brow. And Nada stepped frightened after, and cast of rugs that Panda unburden him. And Samuel cast the skins and looked upon their pack and kicked at their binded thong, and spake:

"These skins—hast thou taken unto the market's place?"

And Panda answered: "Nay, these be the all of the store of Panda."

And Samuel said: "What wouldst thou for them?"

And Panda smiled and spake: "Lo, amid the dead's slumber breaketh smile! Yea!"

And he rubbed of his hands one upon the other, even as Jacob, and said: "Lo, these be skins of worth. Yea, tears, yea, and mites, yea, and woes hath day dealt unto them."

And Panda called him out the full of their price. And Samuel wailed, and Panda set thereon more of price. And Samuel spake: "Nay."

And Panda said: "Lo, doth man find of a spot that showeth it dry between two pools, then 'tis best he stand upon the dry and seek not unto the right or yet unto the left."

And Samuel brought forth coins and shewed. And this was the

full of the price first put. And Panda waited him long, and then reached forth, saying:

" 'Tis done, and woe! For yet shall tears wash upon these skins! "

And Samuel took up the binded pack and lo, it weighted him heavy; for the weariness of the long way up from the east way had set upon him. And he spake:

" Then the morrow shall find the bin of Joel empty. What thinkest thou, that copper pieces might be offered and he who offered them might buy at but small price? "

And Panda answered: " Lo, doth a man to slay of a bull, then 'tis his rabbi that biddeth that it be cold before 'tis eaten."

And Samuel spake: " Yea, but man's eye may covet that that he would eat."

And he bid that Panda speak did he know the time that this ridding of the bin of Joel should be, but Panda shook him " nay." And Samuel went him forth.

And Panda spake unto Nada, and wagged of his head unto Joel:

" Lo, hath coin bought of skins, and I tell thee, Nada, yet woe setteth upon the way unto the bin of Jacob! "

And he sunk him down and his lips broked in wide smiling and he shook of laugh. And his eyes rested them upon the body of Joel, and the lamp's flame set shadows o'er, and it seemed that the lips of Joel smiled. And Panda spake:

" Lo, Joel, thou didst to seek for blade. Yea, and this blade be bought, yet no price hath been given. Yea, Samuel beareth the bared blade unto Jacob."

And he told unto Nada what had been and asked: " Where hath Hatte gone? "

And Nada smiled and spake: " He sleepeth with Mary there."

And she pointed unto the in-place whereon they had cast them upon rugs.

And Panda oped up the tale of what had been done among the Rome's men, and spake:

" Nada, the lips of Panda hold much that might bring woe upon thee and Nadab."

And Nada asked of her whom she had seen, and told of the fevered cries of Hatte, and asked had this woman done wrong that Rome might reach o'er seas and yet o'er heights and smite?

And Panda looked deep unto the night-dark eyes of Nada and took her hand and lay it o'er his heart and spake:

" Dost thou then feel this throb? "

And Nada answered: "Yea."

And Panda spake: "Ever, ever, yea, unto the path's end, doth the heart of Panda lock his lips."

And Nada asked: "Panda, hath Hatte known of this wrong of her?"

And Panda made answering: "Nay. Nay, Nada, there be no wrong."

And Nada spake: "This, then, is the plucking of Rome, who smiteth though there be no wrong save that of her."

And she told of Caleb, and the smiting that men's words had shown had been, and of the flight of Nadab that he bear her hence, and their coming upon Caleb, who fell upon the stoned path within the wilderness. And at his ankles hung broken chains, and the flesh bled. And how Nadab had sold of rugs that he buy of a camel—and this had been packed of little—and one ass. And Nadab rode upon the camel pack and she upon the ass.

And this had been at the end of the sea's-way and land's-way that had led from Rome. And she spake of Nadab who wove of cloths there within Rome that the nobled be clothed. And that she was but a serving maid, the handmaid unto a handmaid. And of the seeking of the man of this maid, and the wrath that fell that she would not of him. And from the wrath of him grew the wrath of the handmaid. And the wreaking of the wrath that she be scarred and shorn of beauty. And her fleeing unto Nadab, whose house stood near and up unto the halls of Caesar.

And Nadab had not of bloods,* nor much of moneys, and lo, at her seek did he to weep. And this had been the time that he spake that they should seek new lands, for long had he longed that he go from Rome, and yet his legs would bear him not. So, then, the youth limbs of Nada should be as the limbs of him. And that Nadab had dreamed dreams that he had spoken he would weave into rugs, and that at the weaving of cloth, lo, the dreams beset him.

And Panda held unto the hand of Nada and sighed and shook his head "yea." And Nada went her on with the telling, and she told that Nadab had taken up this man Caleb, and Caleb had spoken of Rome and yet no name did he speak that they knew. And lo, he told of the seas and the arm-weary, and this, they had found, had been upon the blood † sea; for the waters had stained of the cloth of his mantle. The sands still showed of the "blood," and yet the lips of Caleb spake not the name of this water, but lo, he spake the name of Eunice and yet

*Kin.   † Red Sea.

of one called Mary, and told of the seeking unto the child-bed; and words babbled them unto naught. And woe had set him, for he sat at the day's hour and set his hand that he row unto this land. And this was the thing for which Nadab burned herb that he be healed.

And Panda murmured: " Unto the woed house cometh woe."

And Nada spake: " Nay, Panda, for the house of a man is like unto the sky, that welcometh all of cloud's fleet."

And Panda reached forth his hand and took therein the cold hand of Joel and held still the hand of Nada and looked him high and spake:

" Lo, the earth is big, wide, yea, big and wide, and yet thou and thou and me are but grains of grasses-seed, and yet this One o'er all, that Theia telleth of, hath found thee, thee and me that He meet * unto us."

And Nada's eyes glowed, and o'er their dark drooped the fringed lash and tears gemmed them o'er. And Panda stooped and pressed thereon his lips, and spake: " Lo, Panda hath brought unto thy house his emptied bowl."

And Nada spake: " Yea, but Panda, He whom thou hast said Theia knoweth, shall fill and fill and fill. Within Rome there abideth ne'er such One. Yea, and Jerusalem's gods hunger. Allah shemeth gold o'er the temple's moon and silvereth it at night. Yea, and yet his breast seemeth empty, too. Within thy land and mine men speak the name ' Allah! ' ' Allah! ' ' Allah! ' And this thing harketh not. And at whispers do they tell of what it be and no man telleth that which the other telleth." [11]

And Panda said: " Lo, the days have been but few, Nada, and yet look thou unto their † fulling."

And Nada spake: " Panda, this heart was shrunk, and at the drink-ing of woe it hath bigged; for maid may seek the market's place for flowers and fruits to bear, but Panda, 'tis a path that bringeth naught; for any maid may do this thing and fill not her hours save with the leering of the market's men. And Nadab hath woven and woven and woven, and dreams be few. Yea, the lad did he weave into his wools this day. Yea, and the lamb, he hath bordered it about."

And Panda stood, and his ears seemed that they heard not, and he looked unto Joel. And Nada saw, and she spake: " Panda, beneath a fig's bush at the wall's-out ‡ at eve of the morrow. Yea, these hands do set unto thine aid."

---

* That He bring us together.   † See how full they are.
‡ The gate.

And she went forth and brought a rug, and this was a one deeped of color, and she shewed it unto Panda and spake:

"This for the couch of Joel. For Panda, 'tis of the dower."

And Panda raised up his arms and sunk upon his knees and made obeisance. And Nada sunk upon the rug at the side of him and knelt her, too, and their locks mingled. And Panda rose at the finishing of the prayer-chant and spake:

"The days of Panda are empty, and he hath naught but these days, yet he hath offered unto any man, and unto no maid."

And Nada looked her down and spake: "Men care them not for the days of men. Yea, and maids may take not that that be not offered."

And Panda murmured: "Lo, the eyes of Panda shut."

And Nada spake: "Then the man seeth not, and the maid taketh thereof."

And Panda said: "So be it."

And Nada arose and went unto the in-chamber and came forth with pots, and sat her upon the rug and chanted, and lo, this was the chant of the dead.

And it was late hour and dark. And the smoke arose, and Panda stood, and Joel lay him stilled, his lips still in smile. And Panda knelt at the side of Nada, and his arms were about her. And the night came deep and hushed. And they arose, and Panda held his hand, palm unto the East, and lo, she held hers there, too. And she went within. And Panda lay at the side of Joel.

CHAPTER XIX

THE morn broke clear, and it was the time of sacrifice. And they slew of lambs and brought forth sweet oils and grain. Yea, and this was burned and set on the slow fires that burning be long.

And the priests came forth and made signs unto the East, and the smokes poured forth and scented of the airs. And within the market's place men came forth, and they looked them one unto the other and spake of what had been within the streets at the day's-light of the yester. And made word of the slaying of one of the Rome's men. And this thing they said had been done by the hand of one who wore goat's hair upon his head. And the hand of the man of the market's place had unclothed of his head, and lo, the long locks had fallen unto the earth and this man had been shown to be a woman.

And the sun came forth hot and set the stones that they sent forth sparks of heats dancing upon the air, and men sweat and wiped their brows upon their mantle sleeves. And it was the high hour. And the market's place sat it down that men eat of fruits, or whate'er their bins did offer unto the day, and they who had not that within their bins that did to offer for eat, sought out his brother and made buy of them.

And fruits lay stripped from their skins, and seed and skins lay upon the out-ways of the market's place. And meats hung blooded and swarmed of fly, and men waved of their arms that they drive from off and out them. The ass of Lucius sounded pattered from out the gate's arch and Lucius called him out: "Waters! Waters, that ye sup!"

And he came him up unto the bin of Jacob, and lo, loud words of lamentation sounded out, and Lucius stood that he hark.

And the voice of Jacob cried aloud: "Within the laws of Moses there standeth no law that dealeth unto such an unworthy son!"

And within, upon the skins'-pack, sat Samuel, who listed him, and lo, the jaws of him hung ope. And Jacob wailed, and the Jew's tongue of him sounded as the clatter of fowls, and he spake of the fool that plucked of his ass that he save of down. Yea, and walked him at the sea's edge and yet sought of pools. And he held aloft, unto the men who hung them o'er the bin's place, handful of brass and shammed precious stuffs, and cried him out:

"See ye, thou men of Jerusalem! Lo, aloft doth Jacob hold of his wares. Yea, and with one smile thou mayest take of him! Yea, a word thou hast that thou needst not, cast unto Jacob, and lo, these wares be thine!"

And one among them cried out: "Yea! Yea! Take that, it be a word!"

And he reached him unto the hands of Jacob and smiled him broad. And Jacob wailed and cried out:

"Lo, doth a man's tongue set him upon a folly path, 'tis ever the fool that followeth! Yea, and wares offered unto men by a woed man be but wares held; for lo, the tongue speaketh follies amid woes."

And he wailed and wept, and held close the stuff. And he bid that Samuel tell of what had been. And Samuel oped his lips and licked them o'er, and told of the high city and the meeting of the dark-skin who sat him upon skins, and of the woe that had beset Joel. That he had come upon them so, and the dark-skin had made word that told of what had befallen Joel, and lo, he held within his arms the body of this man, and there lay the skins. And these were all of the dark-skin's store.

So it had been that the dark-skin had asked that Samuel bear them unto the house of Nadab, and lo, these were skins that bore hair, and had he not bought of the dark-skin skins that bore hair at the price of them that bore not hair? What, then, beset his sire?

And Jacob held high his hands and shook his beard and wailed:

"Thou fool! Didst not thy sire buy at a price these skins at the early day and wept him o'er their buy? And lo, this man of dark skin, whose shadow is the thief, set up words wherein a pit was dug? And had he not then made it true that Jacob fell within the pit? And was this not enough that did the son, the very flesh of Jacob, then fall within this pit?"

And he raised his voice loud and spake:

"These skins hold un——!"

And his lips shut; for the eye of him saw the coming of Panda.

And the men of the market's place set up a loud laugh, and lo, Panda came him bowed, and the eyes of him raised not, and he came up unto the bin of Joel. And lo, o'er the wares showed the cloths that Lucius had spread at the going. And within the deep of the crowded place there sounded out the smite of Enos who smote of leathers o'er a stone. And Panda harked and looked him among the men, and seeing not that that he sought, he made word unto Samuel:

"Hath Lucius come?"

And Samuel shook his clenched hand and spake:

"So, thou art a wailer at the night's hour, but 'mid thy wails, lo, thou mayest make of price and sell of skins!"

And Panda's lips stood thinned, but at their thinning, lo, the cheek of him worked; for smile warred that it break. And he spake:

"Lo, doth the ass die and wolf hunger for its meat, then 'tis the wolf that opeth of its hide. So be it. He who eateth of meats first buyeth of the hide. Yea, and he who buyeth of hide o'er the dead, then buyeth woe."

And he took up a fruit and laid it ope and showed unto Samuel, saying: "See thou! Panda hath taken of fruits from out the bin of a man of Jerusalem."

And he went up unto the bin's edge and wailed, and wailed loud, and lo, the man of the place looked him long, and made naught of this. And Panda spake:

"See thou, Panda weepeth! See thou, take these tears as half the price!"

And he cast of a mite unto the market's man, and wept him more, and oped of the fruit, and lo, he did then to offer the skin unto Jacob, saying: "Skins be not fit for eating. Lo, they be unclean."

And Jacob oped his lips for word. And Panda looked him keen-eyed unto the eyes of him and spake: "Be this not truth?"

And Jacob took of the skin and the eyes of him showed wet, and he spake:

"So, thou hast spoken truth. Yea, what then? Shall I seek out thy son and offer unto him that that be unfit?"

And Panda spake: "The son of me be not, and he who be as the son of me is, as thou knowest, a fool. Then dost thou offer unto a fool and he take thereof it mattereth naught."

And he shrugged and went him hence, and sought out Lucius and spake:

"Come thou unto the pool yonder, Lucius. Panda hath word that the market's place needeth not."

And Lucius went him with Panda unto the spot, and Panda spake:

"Where standeth the house of Joel? And is this house the house of a Jew?"

And Lucius spake: "Nay, the house of Joel standeth without the wall at the East place. Yea, and 'tis but a hut of rock and builded up by the hand of Joel. And within there abideth naught of the blood of

Joel save a one of young years, a babe of one and nine. And this is the flesh of the blood of the sire * of Joel, and the name of her is called 'Indra.'"

And Panda spake: "This, then, is the household of Joel? Lo, doth Panda take woe unto a babe!"

And Lucius asked what these words told, and Panda spake: "Lucius, thou knowest of Nada?"

And Lucius spake: "Within the market's hot and filth there is but one flower. Yea, and this is Nada."

And Panda questioned: "What holdeth thy heart for Nada?"

And Lucius answered: "Man, Lucius beareth waters and Nada is but bloom. So be it. By what price doth water buy of bloom? Lucius feasteth of his eye upon the bright bloom and hungereth not. Yea, thou needst not bite at thy flesh, man."

And Panda started, and red stained at his cheek, and Lucius lay his arm 'bout the waist of Panda and laughed in loving. And Panda spake:

"Thou, Lucius, hast eyes, and lo, they are oped. 'Tis well."

And he took the lad up unto him and held him close and looked deep within his eyes and asked: "Thy measure—be it empty?"

And Lucius looked and answered not.

And Panda spake: "Thy measure—be it empty?"

And Lucius broke unto a smiling and answered: "Yea! Yea! Empty, and waiteth thy fulling!"

And Panda spake: "Lo, the fruit that Panda offereth is not sweet."

And Lucius said: "Lo, the market's men hold far o'er the measure full of sweeted fruits. Yea, they cast unto the out-roads the o'er-measure of sweet, at the eve's hour. Yea, and any man may take of this. So, seest thou? sweets may be not of worth. Lo, then offer of thy bittered or yet soured."

And Panda's eyes gleamed, and lo, he spake: "'Tis well. Thy tongue hath edge and thy wits are sharp."

And he told unto Lucius of all that had been, and lo, at the finishing he spake: "This is thine, Lucius. Do then as thou wouldst with it; for word sealeth not a man's lips."

And Lucius said: "Nay, thou speakest true; word sealeth not a man's lips, but the heart of him may shut them up."

And Panda bid that Lucius come with him unto the out of the east wall and unto the hut of Joel. And he made words of wonder-

* A niece of Joel's.

ing if Indra would stay her through the night's hour lone. And Lucius spake:

"Lo, hath she sat the hills the nights through; for Joel hath of flocks and Indra hath shepherded them."

And Panda went with Lucius up unto the high city and Lucius spake:

"Panda, 'tis meet that we seek the hills, for Indra will sit her there awaiting the coming of Joel; for lo, he hath these days and days done this thing. Yea, and he cuppeth of his hand and sendeth soft call unto her before his coming, and it soundeth so."

And Lucius cupped of his hand and showed this thing unto Panda. And at the come-up unto the spot whereon stood the Rome's place, the abode of the Rome's man, lo, Panda's eyes set them upon the stone wall and seemed that they eat them through. And naught showed but them of the gate's arch, and they within who walked them hither and yon. And Panda walked him slow and plucked at the mantle of Lucius, saying:

"Within these walls she abideth."

And Lucius, knowing from the lips of Panda of what had been, looked him long, too. And they passed on and made no word.

And it was eve's young, and heat hung the stones, and walls reached them forth their hot breaths and seared the flesh; and the brow of Panda shone and his arms ran drops. And Lucius spake that this was folly, for had he not left the ass of him within the market's place, and laden of drops?

And Panda smiled and murmured: "The plucking of the ass to save the down!"

And Lucius laughed loud, for the men of the market's place made much word of what had been and all men knew.

And they went them without the wall and walked within the sun's heat and beat them o'er. And at the down of the hill's place, lo, they followed of the path and up o'er the next rise. And Lucius lay his hand upon the arm of Panda and whispered: "Here."

And Panda cupped his hand and made a soft sound, and lo, there came back the sound e'en as the echoing of it. And there sounded as a bird within the thicks, and lo, there showed a one coming forth, small, whose dark locks hung wet of drops, and eyes shone of loving. And lo, the browned hands held close of leaves and branch that she had plucked, and she called: "Joel! Joel!"

And lo, Panda looked unto this maid of yellowed skin and spake unto Lucius: "See thou! yonder cometh babe unto woe."

And he held ope his arms and cried out, "Indra!" And she came forth, her hands bearing of leaves and plucked grasses, and her lips made no word.

And Panda bid that she come unto him, and she did this thing. And Panda made words unto her of the flocks and asked of the hut of Joel, and lo, she oped not her lips. And Panda spake unto Lucius:

"See thou! man knoweth no silence like unto the locked lips of the babe; for lo, beneath their silence no man knoweth what there be."

And Lucius spake: "There is a word that shall unlock these lips."

And he whispered unto the ear of Panda: "Joel."

And Panda asked: "Where hath Joel gone?"

And she oped her lips and smiled, but answered not. And Panda looked unto Lucius and spake:

"See! this is the wall that keepeth the heavens from the day of man; for did a babe to ope up its lips when it knoweth of days that man hath forgot, then might men know of heaven."

And Lucius smiled and spake unto the maid, saying: "Hath thy flock fed the hills well?"

And her eyes flashed and white teeth gleamed and she answered: "Yea." And lo, she oped the eyes of her wide and raised them up unto them of Panda, and Panda's shone of drops. And she oped her lips and spake not, but the brown hand of her plucked at the mantle of Panda. And Lucius spake: "She hath seen woe upon thine eyelids."

And Panda said: "What man might slay of a lamb without the tears, doth he to look unto its eyes?"

And his hand rested upon the black locks of the maid, and he asked of Lucius:

"See! this maid hath saffron skin, and Joel, thou knowest, hath white skin. How is this thing?"

And Lucius spake: "Yea, the flesh of Joel took of the saffroned unto him, a slave maid of the courts afar, and this is the stain of blood; for look! it be not saffroned but yellowed as sun."

And Panda spake: "Saffroned of the land of where?"

And Lucius spake of the East and that her locks hung straight and black.

"Yea, and her god hung him there. Look!"

And he plucked at the neck of the maid whereon hung, upon a silvered strand, that that showed as a god, alike unto the gods of far land. And lo, Panda took up this thing and looked thereon and spake:

"So! Thou, too, a god! And, like unto the gods that man filleth up the heavens with, hear not, see not, and know not of thine! Look, Lucius! hands rest upon fatted legs, and eyes that look not here nor yet there, but stare naught, and hands that reach them up ever, ever, ever empty, and craving that they be filled. Yea, and about the neck of the men of him doth he hang like unto a stone."

And Indra stood and listed and held high her hand that she take from Panda her god. And Panda took her up within his arms and told of the city's place and the markets and the men, and the things that stood within the walls, and asked of her would she come with him unto these things. And Indra stood and her eyes shone, but her lips spake: "Nay, for Joel cometh."

And Panda took up her hand and held it close and said:

"Lo, within the city, at the house of Nadab, where Nadab, who hath not legs, weaveth of rugs, doth Joel sleep. Yea, and thou mayest come with Panda, who will take thee unto him."

And Indra spake: "The sheep! Doth Joel sleep, then Indra shepherdeth them."

And Panda spake unto Lucius: "See! this that the maid hath spoken is true. Then, Indra, Lucius shall tend of the flocks; for lo, he knoweth sheep so well as he doth know his shadow."

And Indra spake: "Nay, for he knoweth not the note of Joel. See thou!"

And she cupped her hand and made a note, and lo, the sheep came through the thicks and up unto her. And she knelt and lay her arms about the lead sheep.

And she said that Joel had told unto her of the small gods that dwelt within the thicks, and spake that this was the note of them, and sheep knew of this thing and came, did a man know of these gods.

And she sat her upon the sod and her arms hung 'bout the sheep and they folded closer about and laid down. And she oped her lips and her eyes oped wide and her cheeks flushed and she told of the palace, the great hall that Joel had told unto her he should build that they abide therein. And pointed up unto the hut that stood and said he had told unto her that this was the little brother unto this place, and did they to wait, lo, would it grow and full and come unto this great hall.

And Panda looked unto Lucius, and Lucius stood, his throat swelled. And Panda stroked the hand of Indra and spake:

"This all hath come to be. Yea, Joel hath gone, that he do this thing. He hath gone unto a far land, and biddeth that thou shouldst love of me, Panda, for he hath spoken that he goeth that he build up this hall, yea, this palace."

And Indra smiled. " He hath spoken this should be, thou sayest? "
And Panda spake him, " Yea."

And Indra made word in answering: " Then take thou me, for doth the time be long, still doth Indra wait the coming of Joel; for he shall come? "

And these words sounded as a question, and Panda spake through the throat tight, " Yea."

And Indra pointed unto the flocks and asked: " These? "

And Panda spake: " Leave these unto the hands of Lucius, and come that thou shalt see the sleep of Joel, for he hath weary sore and sleepeth before the going."

And Indra said: " Joel sleepeth? "

And Panda spake: " Yea, and thou shouldst wake him not."

And Indra made answering: " So, then, it shall be."

And Lucius held forth his hand and took the hand of Panda and spake:

" Lo, hath Lucius seen of wisdoms of the priests and yet, Panda, Lucius sayeth this is wisdom that standeth the priests confounded! Yea, thou hast spoken unto this babe more wisdom from out thy heart than all the temple holdeth."

And Panda said: " Temples, Lucius, were builded up to hold wisdoms and not to give them forth."

And Indra sat and listed, her head upon the sheep's wool. And Panda stretched forth his hand unto her and spake unto Lucius more:

" Behold then, Panda goeth, and he leaveth the words he hath spoken within thy heart, Lucius, and he knoweth there 'tis locked."

And Lucius spake: " Yea."

CHAPTER XX

And Panda took the hand of Indra and they went them upon their ways unto the in-city. And it was the red-sun, and shadows stood deep at the out-wall, and men sat them without the gate's ope and wiped of the sweats of their brows, and talked their tongues and showed of their wares that the day had come unto the end and still no man had taken of these wares.

And Panda shewed unto Indra the street's ope unto the in-place at the gate's arch, and spake much that meant little. And lo, when they had come unto the street whereon the house of Nadab stood, Nada showed without the door's place where she waited the coming of Panda. And Panda raised his arm and made sign unto her, and she came forth. And Panda laid the hand of Indra within the hand of Nada and spake:

"See thou, Nada! Panda hath brought more of chaffs unto thy house."

And Nada smiled. "Since this be not the grains-grind, then 'tis well that it be the place of chaff."

And Panda asked of Nada what the day had dealt unto the household of Nadab. And Nada told of the waking of Hatte, and that he had wailed him o'er the going of Panda without the house of Nadab, and not a word unto him. And told of Aaron who had laughed him through the day's hours and that Hatte had builded, from out a wood's branch, a blade, that he swore he would smite the men of Rome.

And she spake her of the words the lips of Hatte had spoken of the child of the temple's place; for he had sought out the side of Nada and asked of the going of Him from the temple, and cried aloud, and had come unto Nadab and spake out that he had seen of this path, the dark, dark path, and then—the slaying of the lamb! And Nada spake that drops had stood upon his brow and he had clung unto the hand of her.

And Panda spake: "Nada, speak thou not of this thing."

And Nada spake: "Who is this One of the temple place he calleth the brother of his flesh?"

And Panda made answer: "Behold, there cometh within the walls of Jerusalem much that no man knoweth the answering of."

And he told unto Nada of this thing that had seized Hatte and the fearing that set his hours.

And Nada went within and held unto the hand of Indra, who wept. And Panda asked of the body of Joel, and Nada spake that she had wrapped it within the rug, the weaving of Nadab, wherein he had woven a dream that seemed not of the days of Jerusalem, nor yet of the days of Rome, but of the high place, the abode of gods.

And Nadab sat within the in-place and the smite of the reed-rack sounded upon its thudding, thinned. And he spake unto Hatte, saying:

"Hatte, thou hast learned of Jerusalem the tongues of the streets. The wicked of the hearts of these men hang upon their words."

And Hatte spake: "Yea, Nadab, thou hast spoken wisely; for lo, upon the temple's ways the men sit them, and lo, their mouths speak filths, e'en though the King o'er kings they do name as their own, this Jehovah, abideth within the very temple's arch. How then is this thing? For the brother of the flesh of me—for, Nadab, He hath spoken this be truth—sayeth His sire abideth there. Ah, then is the name of the sire Jehovah? This fear stoppeth the word, Nadab!"

And Nadab lay aside the weaving and oped up his thin arms and bid that Hatte come unto him. And he pointed unto the threads within the weave and spake:

"Lo, Hatte, did the weave of Nadab have tongue the airs would rock and men fall upon their very faces. Yea, e'en the loved of him would know what his heart locketh within its walls. Look! e'en within a rug is all of the heart of Nadab. So, 'tis well that man maketh of his days a loom and weaveth upon a warp of silence."

And Panda and Nada came forth from whence they had stood within, unto the spot where the voice of Nadab had sounded. And Panda saw that Hatte listed unto the telling of the tongue of Nadab, and he smiled and spake unto Nada:

"Nada, thou seest 'tis Nadab and Panda and Joel and Aaron and all of this household, that be as the dusts of the desert before the winds. No man knoweth when the winds shall rise nor yet when they shall sink."

And Hatte, hearing the voice of Panda, came him up unto his side and looked unto Nada who held unto the hand of Indra. And he asked of her. And Panda sunk upon the floor's flags, his legs tucked beneath his mantle, and took Hatte unto him, and held forth his hand unto Indra and spake:

. "Lo, Hatte, thou and Panda and Mary and Aaron are but chaffs. So, and loned; and Indra, this maid, hath lone like unto thee and me and them."

And Hatte spake: "Who, then, hath done this thing unto this maid?"

And Panda answered, saying: "No man, and yet thy Panda's hands are red."

And Hatte stood forth and raised up his hands and cried aloud: "This is the deed of Rome! What, Panda, hath locked the lips of the man who lieth there within the in-chamber? For at the high sun this day did Hatte seek and touch the flesh of him, and lo, it showed dark and cold, and the path showed and the sick crept. Panda, what is this thing? Mary wept at the sight, and within this breast did a thing break, and these eyes shut and Hatte knew not the day. Who is this man, Panda? It seemeth that yester's morn Hatte did see him within the market's place, and yet his limbs now bear him not up."

And Panda spake: "This thing is the going of man from out the living day."

And Hatte asked: "What then, hath he gone? and ne'er more doth he know of thee and me and the market's place and the days of Jerusalem?"

And Panda held the body of Hatte close and he spake:

"'Mong these Jews there are men who say that man goeth as thou hast spoken and ne'er knoweth of naught of the days nor yet the nights,* and yet there are them † that speak this thing is folly and look unto a far land, whereto they shall go."

And Hatte stooped him close and looked unto the eyes of Panda and spake soft unto his ear:

"Ah, Panda, the lips of yon man shew a smile far wiser than that that played them o'er at the yester's morn."

And Panda looked unto the eyes of Hatte and they shewed o'erbright and the cheeks of him burned scarlet. And Panda spake:

"See! Indra is loned and Mary soundeth without the door's ope. Go thou and bring them forth and seek out a spot whereon thou mayest sit and speak of hills and sheep."

And Hatte took the hand of Indra and spake: "Dost thou know of sheep?"

* The Sadducees.   † The Pharisees.

And Indra shewed her white teeth and answered: "Hark! dost thou hear a bleating afar?"

And she went her up unto Panda and spake: "He who watcheth knoweth not the note."

And Panda said: "At the dark shall we seek the spot and thou shalt go."

And Hatte cried him out: "And Panda, the eyes of Hatte shall look upon the wooled backs that shew amid the dark as white cloud upon the night sky? Out from the walls! Out upon the high place! Freed of Jerusalem, Panda, where Hatte may turn his eyes unto the Bethlehem roadway, and see amid the dark the far rise of the hills, and dream of the dance, the bound, the rise and fall of the feet of her, Panda, Theia! Of her who, Panda, the earth hath such a need for that, lo, they seek her out and leave not e'en the shadow of her that Hatte may rest within it! She danceth, Panda, ever, and it seemeth that she danceth with her heart lain ope and streameth scarlet at the every step; danceth, Panda, with light foot, and lo, the lips be frozen!"

And his voice sunk unto a hoarse empty: "And she smote her flesh! She smote Hatte! And Panda, list! Hatte hath seen the look that shewed within her eyes. Yea! The ewe looked so unto her lamb at the slaying!"

And Panda spake: "Hatte, go without. The eve cometh. Take thou Indra and out with thee!"

And he called unto Mary and she came within and Hatte made known unto her of Indra, and they went them unto the out of the door's-way. And Nada, who had stood and listed unto all that had been, came forth unto Panda and spake:

"Then thou seekest the out-walls with him who lieth yonder?"

And Panda shook his head "yea." And Nadab sat and the thud-ding of his racks still sounded out upon the airs. And Nada went unto him and spake:

"Sire, the light hath come unto its end. See! dark hath hung within the high of the chamber and light only lieth close unto the earth."

And Panda spake: "Set thy hands at rest, Nadab, and come. Nada, thou and Panda shall lend him aid and bring him forth unto the inner chamber. Panda hath word that he must empty unto thee and Nadab."

And the hand of Nadab hung upon the rack with love; and he spake:

"When, then, the light hath come unto its end, may the hand of

Nadab be found still at the rack. Yea, when at some hour when thou, Nada loved, thou fruit of the olive, and thou, Panda, Panda of truth, and Nadab, the shriveled fig of the greened tree, be not upon the earth's lands, lo, there shall sound out the thudding of the rack. Yea, like unto this the hand of Nadab causeth now amid the hours. And men of earth shall harken not; for they shall deem 'tis but the beat of branch or sound of other smiting of the day. And lo, upon the flag shall Nadab sit cross-legged and smite and weave dreams. Yea, and men shall set foot upon the dreams of Nadab and sleep upon the soft of this cloth, and lo, who knoweth but these dreams may set within their days, and be, for them."

And Panda's eyes deeped, and lo, they looked as though they looked not upon the day that then died, but unto the dawn of a day, a dawn afar. And he spake:

" Lo, Nadab, thy lips have spoken truth. What then? These days of me and these of the chaff may be the woof, yea the warp, for days to come."

And they laid hands upon Nadab and bore him hence unto the rug's cast. And Nada brought forth a taper lamp and set it high, and shadows played them o'er the flags and walls as flitting shades of days to come, warred of dark and light.

And Nadab brought forth from 'neath the rug's cast a casket, binded 'bout, and his slim fingers played at the binds and loosed of them. And he reached within and brought forth a dark stuff like unto the crumble of rotted wood,* and he left it pour back from out his hand unto the casket's ope, and lo, a sweet smell came forth.

And Nada went her forth unto the within and came back bearing of a brass bowl, and upon its sides there shewed the crescent [11] of the young moon. And Nadab reached forth for it and put therein of the stuff of the casket. And Nada put within it oil, and set unto this the wick, and it burned, and lo, smoke arose and sweeted the airs.

And Panda sunk upon the rug's cast and made obeisance, and spake: " From out thy lands and mine. Not of Jerusalem, not of Rome, but brown as the skins of thy tribes and mine and sweet with the earth of thy land and mine; for it grew therein."

And Nada made the chant of Allah, and the voice of Panda sounded as the murmurs of the sea, and hers as the gentle winds that cause the soft lap of young waves, and Nadab's like unto the hollow of the echoes within the shells.

And they brought this unto the end and made a thrice-obeisance,

---

* Possibly sandalwood or cinnamon.

and lay them prone. And Nada then took up the oils that had burned low and smoked much and still sent sweet, and set the burning out, and took the hand of Panda, and they went within where Joel lay, and she knelt and anointed him. And when this thing was done, lo, they went unto Nadab, and Panda spake:

"This then is the time."

And he sat him down, and Nada sunk at the feet of Nadab and lay her dark-locked head upon his bended knees.

And Panda took up the emptied bowl of brass and held it high and spake:

"Nada, Nadab, see! This bowl, the bowl of thy land and mine— empty! So, and yet thou fillest it of crumbled things: Aaron, whom the god hath sent with his bowl empty. Caleb!—harken thee, Panda speaketh—Caleb! Who hath spoken his name so? This man is a game of Rome! Played and ended! Smitten by the hand of one who coveted, and whose hand was sped by the glut of Rome. Within the walls of the Rome's hall at the east way, there did Panda see this man who smote. Yea, and she who stood like unto a smitten child, knew and feared."

And Nada spake: "Panda, how is this that thou knowest of Caleb when the lips of Nadab spake not and the tongue of Nada might not speak? For lo, they know not?"

And Panda spake: "Lo, hath Panda lay asleep beside the busied hands of Caleb as he 'rowed,' and his lips spake broken words. Of these hath Panda builded up much. This man lost of his flesh at the hand of Herod. Yea, and this 'Caleb' was Flavius of Rome, and one who stood armed e'en though he was of the high office; for lo, Rome casteth down the mighty. And this man, at the losing of his flesh, then, Panda doth speak, hath lain heavy hate upon Flavius as the slayer, when lo, the hand of Flavius smote not; for lo, within his household lay the babe of Eunice and the babe Hatte.

"And lo, this time was the time of blood, when the airs rung of the mothers' cries and the moans of the sires; when the pools of the streets shewed crimson and man crawled the flags that he slip not upon blood. Lo, within the walls there would sound out the thin cry of the babe, and lo, one went within and it stopped, and the voice of the mother took up the wail, bathed of anguish. And the women ran forth unto the street's-way and bore within their arms their dead.

"And the men of Judea swore venge upon the Rome's men, and the men of Herod who did this thing frightened much. And Eunice had gone from out the flesh, and there came a time when no man knew of Flavius and he came not, and the babes lay with no hand as their blood.*

"And Panda had of moneys that Theia had brought forth from out Rome, and this he held and binded him unto this man Ezekiel as his bondsman unto the seventh year, as is the Jew's law. Of him and his household thou knowest from the lips of Panda, and the woes of Bethlehem that befell the flesh of Theia, and the days of Hatte. Panda is as the chariot speeder who driveth woe, and lo, within his chariot doth babes and the weak stand.

"Much word hath Panda spoken of his days, and lo, he would tell of the days of Flavius. This man who smote him coveted of his woman, Eunice, and hate leadeth not a man aright. Nay, upon the very babe may he wreak his hate. For lo, a one of Judea had sought the house of Phethon and gone unto the house of him and slain of his flesh in venge, and this did he set as the deed of Flavius. Hate, hate, builded up woe. Lo, Flavius knew naught of this thing. That this had been, Panda found e'en at the time when Flavius came not, and yet no man knew of the going of Flavius, and this man shewed upon the street's-way and seemed that he would not of such.

"Yea, thou then mayest see the web stood but as the outstrands, and lo, the words of Flavius, the broken words, wove the 'bout and 'bout of it."

And Nada's eyes glowed, and Nadab beat his hands upon his knees, and Panda's voice hummed on:

"This is still not the all of it. For the babe, Mary, dwelled with Rhea at Bethlehem."

And Nada stood forth, her bosom heaved, and cried:

"Mary! Mary! She who came with the woman was called Mary! Then this is the flesh of Flavius!"

And Panda shook him "yea," and Nada beat her bosom and made that she tell all unto Flavius. And Panda held forth his hand and bid her stay, and spake:

"'Tis not fitting that word be made of this unto him. Thou knowest the broken twig must be bended straight before it flowereth. There, then, is naught save the filling of his emptied soul that shall bring forth his darkened day to light."

And Nada shook her "yea" and Nadab spake: "This dream shall I weave at morrow."

And Nada spake her it was well that no word be spoken unto Flavius, but that the day might deal unto him of truth e'en as the

* None left of their kin.

sand's grains do set up the desert's wide. Lo, should this wisdom come unto him grain by grain till all be well.

And lo, it was dark, for the taper lamp had burned low. And Nada went her, stumbled, unto the in-place and brought forth more of wicks and oils. And Panda stretched forth his arms at tire, and lo, sleep set his lips and he spake through sleep's tired lips and asked: "What hath the day dealt unto Aaron?"

And Nada spake: "Lo, he sleepeth there without and hath sunk upon his nets."

And Panda went unto the dark without and at the East there showed the white light of the moon, yet not upped, and the stars gleamed cool amid the heat's-beat hung upon the city's airs. And the breath of Aaron sounded out like unto the swine that noise at the dark hours. And Panda sought the spot, and it was at the stoned wall of the house of Nadab. And the stones burned hot of the sun that had shone the day through. And Panda touched the flesh of Aaron, and it was sweated o'er. And Panda spake:

"Ah, empty! empty! And yet here hast thou set a full within this heart."

And he touched the head where the long hair lay damp o'er the flatted brow, and slipped his hands o'er the mighty neck and o'er the long arms, whereon the flesh showed, in rise and fall, the might therein, and his lips made words:

"Lo, hath men of Rome such bodies, but ah, beneath their breast's skin no such an heart! For he who knoweth naught may take not evils."

And he pressed upon the brow of Aaron the hand of loving. And Aaron waked, and he looked up unto the dark and reached forth his hands unto the hand of Panda. And Panda spake unto the deaf ears: "Ah, Folly, the wisdom of thee! For lo, thou knowest not fear."

And Aaron clasped the hand that lay upon his brow, and made sounds. And Panda made that he lead him unto the taper's light. And Aaron took up his nest and went within, and the nets made sounds of metals upon the stones. And Panda started, and went forth and took up the seines, and lo, the wares of Jacob showed therein. And Panda shook his head, and the smile died, and he spake unto Nada:

"This thing breweth sorries."

And Nada spake that he had slept the morn through, and at the mid-hour, lo, she had found him gone, and at the one and one of the hours, lo, he had been there at the stones of the door's ope, asleep upon his nets. And Panda spake:

"Folly hath wisdom then."

And it was late hour. And at the out-wall that stood not upon the street's-way, Caleb sat, and the babes spake word that sounded unto the within. And Panda said that this was the hour that they should seek. And Nada spake:

"Nay; babes should see not this thing."

And Panda made answering that then should he call forth Hatte and shew unto him the wisdom that they go not without until the sun's up of the morrow. And Nada spake:

"Thou hast said unto Indra she might go unto the without with thee."

And Panda spake: "Lo, doth a man's lips speak falsely and he do this thing in wisdom, no man hath blame that he may lay."

And Nada said: "Panda, from off thy lips truth streameth, and thou hast bathed thee within the fount of wisdom, for lo, the priests know of the full of scripts and yet know not e'en the water's drops that fill the urn."

And Panda made answer: "Yea, yea, filled they be, and yet their words be empty."

And he went him up unto Aaron and held forth the bright bits of metals and shewed unto the eyes of him that he look him well, and touched of his flesh and shook him "nay." And made signs that this thing was wrong. And Aaron clapped his hands and laughed, laughed much. And he offered unto Panda that that he had pilfered. And Panda made that he weep, and Aaron offered once more of the bits. And Panda cast them out from the room's place and made signs that he was wrathed sore. And Aaron pointed unto the out where Panda had cast of the bits, and his eyes took on that that Panda had made that he shew unto him, and Panda knew that this thing had been done and Aaron had supped wisdom from that that held no word.

And Panda called unto Hatte, and Hatte made answering: "Aho! Aho-o-o-o! Panda!"

And Panda smiled; for this was the call of the sheep's hills. And he came him out from the dark and held unto the hand of Indra, and the sheep, the young lamb that had come from out Bethlehem with them, followed at their mantle hems, and Indra's hand lay upon its wool, and Hatte's lips smiled. And Mary followed, and within her hand the oar of Caleb, and Caleb's hand held she.

And when they were within, lo, Nadab spake unto Nada that she go and bring forth fruited bread and goat's milk that the babes sup. And Nada stripped her of her out-mantle and stood swathed of the winded cloth of the 'neath. And her limbs showed dark and sandaled, and the long mantle lay not o'er their curves, and her arms shewed round and warm, and she held them forth that she seek within the in-place where dark hung close. And she came forth bearing of an urn of dark stuff, earth, dry and fashioned unto the urn; and cups there were as bowls, and fruit-bread that smelled sweet. And they sat them down, and Nada gave unto each a bowl, and went her unto each with the urn and poured therein of milk and offered of breads, and brought forth salt and fish 'that shewed dry.

And Nadab held his hand high and made of the chant, the wail-voice of his lands, and cast of a crumb of the bread unto the airs and made thanks. And Panda looked and cast of the crumb, and Nada did this thing, and they did eat. And Panda spake:

"What, Nadab, is this that thou dost to cast of crumbs?"

And Nadab laughed and spake:

"Lo, Panda, this is one of the dreams of Nadab. For lo, did each man cast of a crumb unto the airs, and do this in loving, then might the hungered be fed and no one hunger."

And Panda broke of his bread and ate thereof and looked unto Nada speaking out: "This is truth."

And lo, the eyes of Indra hung sleeped, and her lips bowed down, and she looked unto Panda and listed not unto the words of Hatte nor yet Mary, who spake of that that had been among the Jews; for lo, did they to rise them up one against the other and smite much. And Panda's eyes turned unto Indra, and lo, the bread within her hand was uneat and the cup stood untouched, and her eyes showed wet. And she lay the bread upon the rug and set the arm of her o'er her eyes and wept. And Panda went unto her wailing, and Hatte lay about her his arm and spake soft words, saying:

"Lo, Indra, Hatte hath known this empty!"

And Indra spake but one word, "Joel," and turned her unto Panda, saying: "Thou hast spoken he sleepeth?"

And Panda made answer: "Yea, so, and thou shalt see; but wake him not."

And Indra spake: "Nay, nay, but take thou me unto him."

And Panda looked unto Nada, and Nada took up the lamp, and the wick was low and the light dimmed. And Panda took the hand of Indra and they went within where Joel lay, and Indra looked unto him and stepped her soft and spake: "Yea, yea, he sleepeth."

And Panda took her without, and Nada followed. And Indra's eyes showed wide and she clung unto the mantle of Panda and spake:

"Indra knoweth not the white of his cheek!"

And Panda said: "Weary, weary hath o'ertaken him. At the early hours doth he set upon his way unto the far lands."

And Indra murmured: "And he who watcheth knoweth not the note!"

And Panda spake: "List thee, Indra!" and he cupped of his hands and sounded the note.

And Indra spake: "Yea! Yea! The note of Joel!"

And Panda spake: "Then doth Panda seek thy sheep. Sleep thou, sleep!"

And lo, the eyes of her hung heavy and sleep had wearied of her limbs. And Nada sunk upon her knees, and the form of Indra crept close and hung as the vine that clingeth unto the wall.

And Nada arose and swayed beneath the heavied babe, whose arms hung limp o'er the rounded shoulders of her, and she lay her cheek close up unto the warm soft of the babe's cheek and set her lips upon the ear, hid of dark locks, that she murmur sweets of naught unto it.

And Panda's eyes gleamed, and he held high his hand unto the East and bowed him low. And Hatte touched his flesh and smiled and shook his head "yea." And Hatte spake:

"Lo, Panda, be it not a truth that man's lips may be set shut and yet he speak him loud?"

And he laughed and smote the flesh of Mary and shook his head unto Panda, wise. And they went unto the rug's-cast where Nadab still sat, and where Aaron laughed and played with crumbs; for lo, he had broken his bread unto bits and set them unto the rug as sheep, and took up of a bit of wood's splint and chided of the crumbs as though 'twere a shepherd's crook. And Hatte went up unto Aaron and looked upon the crumb herds and laughed; and went unto the lamb that lay beside the loom of Nadab and plucked of wool and set it unto a rounded woven ball, and made of the wool unto the score of these, and brought unto Aaron. And he lay him down upon his belly and upped of his legs, and Aaron sunk upon his side and rested him upon his bended arm, and they set ups of the rug's-cast where they did pluck it up, that hills be made, and each took of the wool-sheep and of the crumb-sheep and made that they herd of these. And Aaron still hung unto his nets, and his eyes, e'en though they busied at the sheep herd, strayed unto the out-place where Panda had cast of the metal bits.

CHAPTER XXI

AND Panda had sat him down beside Nadab and they made words of what stood that they should do. And Nadab shewed unto Panda Caleb who sat, and at his knee, Mary. And his lips told of wonder-tales that sounded as the days of Rome, and lo, amid the days of Rome, days of Jerusalem shewed. And he spake names that no man knew, and names that Panda knew and Nadab, and lo, he knew not; for his lips shewed the sick of his days.*

And Nada came forth and whispered that Indra slept, and Panda, seeing that all was well with the household of Nadab, made word unto Nada and Nadab, saying:

"Lo, this man Joel hath a bin within the market's place and no man hath he of blood's tie, and this babe hath not of years unto wisdom. What, then, should be done?"

And Nadab spake: "Nada hath sought not the market's place that she bear fruits nor yet blooms, for lo, the hands of her have stood busied that they tend the wander-flock."

And Nada said: "This thing is true, but lo, this man Joel hath ne'er supped of his market brother's hours nor yet hath he shared of his with them. What, then, Jerusalem knoweth not of, Jerusalem may not hunger for."

And Panda spake: "True, but Jerusalem knoweth not more of Panda than Panda careth that Jerusalem should know. And lo, even so doth Rome's men know more e'en than the Jerusalem's tribesmen; for 'mongst these men of the Rome's place are ones whom Panda knoweth, and who know of Panda, should their fat-weary † fall and leave their wisdom cup to flow. E'en this one that sitteth of the mighty-seat the weary hath set.

"What power or glory, Nadab, is there unto one who setteth of the mighty-seat that hath been left un-set by one ‡ who is unfit? It is folly that Jerusalem look unto this man as its own; and yet is there not one of its blood that a land may set unto its mighty-seat? Yea, and

---

* His lips (his speech) revealed the nature of his sickness—a diseased mind.

† Weariness of flesh.

‡ Evidently a reference to the deposed and banished Archelaus.

e'en though there be blood and it is fit, then 'tis Rome, yea Rome, that undoeth the god and setteth up a one. And yet e'en though the blood be unfit and driven hence, lo, doth the blood the gods kinged come it back and sit the seat. Woe, woe sitteth Jerusalem, mantled as the Roman."

And Nada said this stood as truth; for lo, did the very Jew's blood spat forth upon its kinged. And Panda spake:

" E'en the spat of the Jew in righteousness be afar more right than the blood of the unrighteous; for he who setteth this seat hath set thereon through the blood of the righteous e'en though he be not right. Yea, beneath the Rome's place there abideth one whose lips tell much, much of this man! Yea, at this, the sore trial of the flesh of her, did not this man sleep? For may not a Roman asleep try of a Jew's blood e'en so well as waked?"

And Panda's voice raised up and his words came loud: " What right hath man that he herd sheep e'en as though they be swine? For Rome holdeth these Jews dear, as the fill of the purse, and herdeth of them e'en as swine, when they sell and ask the price of sheep."

And Panda arose and spake: " The God is wise. She hath spoken it so. Then there shall be a time when the days shall fall as sheep beneath the shepherd's staff."

And Nadab said: " Thou hast deep of hate, Panda, within thee for the wrongs of this day, when lo, Nadab hath dreamed dreams of days that hold sorries, sorries past this knowing; for lands unkinged shall be as sheep unshepherded. And lo, from out the wrongs shall the shepherd's staff be builded up that shall chide them well unto the shelter-hill! "

And Panda made answering: " Nadab, the wisdom of Panda runneth dry beside the fount of thine."

And Nada smiled her upon them there, and Panda asked that she watch the play of Hatte and Aaron, that they hark not unto these words; for Aaron's eyes took in that that the ears of Hatte heard and did they to know of their going from without the house, lo, would they follow. And Panda told of the hut of Joel without, and the herds. And Nadab spake:

" Lo, doth the god of this man cast his wares unto the day, then 'tis for that that thou dost take unto thee of these, that this babe Indra fall not short of what the sweat of her flesh hath bought of Jerusalem."

And Panda said this thing was true and the flesh of Hatte might then be freed of the know of Jerusalem.

And Nada spake: "Then dost thou speak it that thou shalt seek without the walls?"

And Panda looked unto her and answered: "Yea, for there standeth the hut."

And Nada asked: "Who then shall abide within the bin of Joel through the day?"

And Panda spake: "The market's place knoweth Panda. Yea, and love abideth not there for the dark-skin whose shadow be as the wolf. Yea, but hark! Lucius hath watered the fevers of Jerusalem and worn unto the thick of the wood's bark his soles. Yea, for him hath Jerusalem cast but mites and shrugs. Then shall Lucius set him up within the bin of Joel, and abide without the walls. And the ass of him shall bear the greens from the hands of them who go within the walls at the early hours."

And Nada looked down and spake not. And lo, Hatte had wearied him, and Caleb had ceased his wording, and Mary slept. And Panda said that the rest-tide had come, and they sought out their resting places.

And when this was done, lo, Panda sought Nada and Nadab and they made ready the body of Joel. And Nada anointed his flesh of sweet oils and wrapped the body of him within the soft of the dower-rug. And Panda looked unto what had been done and spake:

"Who, then, goeth that he lend an aid?"

And Nada answered: "Aaron; for Hatte sleepeth and Aaron waketh e'en though he hath lain him down."

And Panda said this was to be. And Nada went soft unto the resting place of Aaron and bid that he come. And he arose and stood and looked and laughed, and took up the nets and followed. And they came them up unto the place where Joel lay, and Panda shewed unto Aaron that he should take up the burden. And Nada wept, and Nadab sat still upon the rug and looked and spake:

"Lo, youth hath given of youth that age might live, for why should youth crumble and age thrive?"

And Panda spake: "Lo, Nadab, earth hath need of rich soil that seeds spring and thrive."

And Nada oped of the door that led unto the wall's-way, and stepped her out.

And lo, it was the late hour, and the mid-moon stood it high and bathed the wall and whited o'er the pave and cast o'er the black locks of Nada a silvered mist. And she stood her still that Panda and Aaron bear forth the burden.

And they came them from within, and lo, Nada cast o'er her locks a cloth and made that she follow. And Panda and Aaron stepped them slow and Nada followed, stepped upon their shadows. And they made way through the dark places where they had come unto the street's-way, and no man shewed upon the paths. And Jerusalem slept, and the cocks crowed. And their sandals slipped soft o'er the stones, and at their stumbling, lo, Nada started in fearing.

And when they had come up unto where the markets stood, lo, there slept a one upon the stones, and he waked, and he was a one of Rome, but deep in cup. And he called forth for word that shewed them as of Jerusalem and asked, amid his drunken word, of their burden. And Panda spake:

" Lo, when a man slayeth of a sheep that he eat thereof, think ye he beareth not of the entrails without the walls? "

And this man spake: " Doth a fool seek the without with the within, then off ye! "

And Panda smiled and spake: " Lo, hath the lips of this man spoken follies straight that the sobered one might well set twist! "

And he looked unto Nada and shrugged, and they went them upon their ways. And Nada asked:

" Goest thou out by the sheep's gate? "

And Panda answered: " Nay, up and unto the east way."

And they set them ahead.

And when they had gone well upon the way, lo, weary o'ertook the limbs of Aaron and he made sounds unto Panda, and Panda spake unto Nada that it was wise they should seek out a dark place and set them that they rest therein.

And this was upon the up-way unto the east gate. And they lay the body of Joel down that they rest. And Aaron looked unto the moon's white and pointed him unto the dark that showed ahead and unto the shadows that hung unto the walls that stood not within the moon's light, and he made that they should seek out the way back unto the house of Nadab. And Panda shook him " nay " and pointed unto the up-way. And Aaron arose and made signs that he was wrathed at this thing. And Nada went up unto the side of him and lay her hand upon his flesh, and he stopped him of his wrath and sat that he rest.

And lo, the still of sleep hung o'er Jerusalem and no sound pierced the white light o'er the stilled airs save the step of them who watched.*

And Nada heard this thing and went up unto the side of Panda and spake:

* The Roman guards at the gate.

"Lo, Panda, hark thee, hark! for wisdom-fulled hast thou been and yet folly-empty. For look! how be it that thou dost bear the body of Joel without the wall? For lo, at the gate's-way are the men of the wall's watch. No man may set foot without this wall until the morrow's break."

And Panda spake him: "Lo, hath folly of tricks that set the wised at folly's sup."

And Nada said: "Lo, Panda, thou hast a full store of wisdoms. Yea, and yet but the beggars might of follies. So, how then mightest thou deal of follies unto Rome's men? For lo, Rome merrieth much o'er her own word and stareth as a graven stone at the word of her men. Yea, for the spill of blood tickleth the fat sides of Rome, be this blood the purse's fulling. And yet be this blood of one that is worth naught to her, lo, she seeth not this blood."

And Panda looked unto Nada and smiled, and the light of the moon shewed this unto her. And Aaron stood him up unto his full height and took up the rug's end of his burden, and Panda set him at the feet and they took it up and went upon their way.

And when they had come unto the gate, lo, there stood ones at the arch, and they came forth and made word that they tell of what they bore and where. And Panda set his back bent and said that they sought the out-way with rugs that had been of the store of him. And the ones of the gate's-way laughed and spake that he should shew this unto them.

And Panda lay the body of Joel down upon the earth and Aaron sat him at its side. And these men came forth and kicked of the pack and said this man was but a rug merchant and that should he then rest there beside the wall's place that they see the hours pass o'er him, he might go without at the day's break.

And Panda said this should be, and he made signs unto Aaron that he should lay him there beside the rug's pack. And Nada sat her down beside them, and Panda lay him there. And they spake of the days that had been since his coming from out Bethlehem, and that they were but few and yet full past the measure.

And these men of Rome, seeing that they spake among themselves, looked not upon them, but spake one unto the other of Rome's days and the days of Jerusalem, and of the words of the Jews that stood not as sweet words, nay, but bathed of hate.

And the moon sagged within the sky and set that it seek the earth and hide, and the hours grew late and dark hung. And the men that stood the gate leaned them upon the walls, and words stopped, and no sounds hung the air save the brays of the waking asses or yet the low of oxen that waked.

And the cocks crowed, and the men waked, and Jerusalem set upon its new day. And lo, the light tarried and mists arose and men stood not at seek for the woes of others but full of the woes of their own days.

And these men that watched at the gate's-way heard without the whines of beggars that waited the oping. And market's men that brought of wares from the without sounded out their voices unto the keepers of the gate, and they oped of the gateway. And their eyes were busied of the in-come and looked not unto the out-go. And Panda spake that this was the time they sought, and they sat them at the bear of the body unto the without.

And when they had come unto the gate's ope, lo, a one who rode upon an ass shouted unto the gate's man and asked did this out-go of Jerusalem then pass and not shew the within of the packs?

And Panda's eyes looked unto this one, and then unto the gate's man who harked unto his words, and lo, the face of the ass-strider shewed it merry and the face of the gate man shewed it woed. And Panda made signs unto Aaron that he leave the body lie upon the earth, and Panda went him up unto the Rome's man, and he who rode the ass came him up and spake loud words, saying:

" This man goeth from out Jerusalem with rugs and thou seest not. What then doth this thing mean? For verily, it seemeth that one who watcheth may shut up his eyes and see not the many who come within and set unto Rome's purse of the one share, and unto the gate's man's purse the two of the share, and no man knoweth. Yea, this is Rome's wisdom. But this man beareth of rugs without the walls of Jerusalem. And lo, this the in-coming unto the gate's-way was the task and greed's-fill of Rome. But the out-go of the wares of Jerusalem the Jews should know, and did no Jew then watch, then one without the walls should set him at the task of the abiders within the walls."

And the Rome's man lay hands upon Panda and bid that he show of the pack. And Panda stood him at the head of the ass and ran his hand o'er the rounded sides of it and spake:

" This ass is full and fatted much."

And lo, the ass's pack was full of greens. And Panda plucked forth of this and said the earth stood dry and had need of rains, and lo, e'en now the mists hung.

And he who rode upon the ass spake: " Yea, and one e'en now felt of drops." And the Rome's man spake of the pack and bid that Panda shew of it. And Panda said:

"Lo, yonder one resteth and the pack is still within the walls; so what then is this pack unto the gate's man until it outeth of the gate's arch?"

And Panda took up a stone and weighed it within his hand and took up another and weighed it, and yet another and weighed it. And this one weighed light, and Panda sought another and it weighed aright unto its brother's weight. And Panda sped one of these stones far and it sunk well unto the up of the road's-way. And all men saw this thing. And he who rode upon the ass spake, lo, this was a sling's throw. And he took up a stone and sped it out the wall's ope. And Panda turned him unto the gate's keep and held forth of a mite and spake: "See, thou hast left a stone of Jerusalem without!"

And he of Rome laughed and took up a stone and threw, and lo, it fell far short. And Panda laughed loud, and he who rode upon the ass slapped his sides. And Panda spake:

"This shall be a game! What sayest thou?"

And the man of the ass spake: "Lo, since the price of the withining of Jerusalem be not spent till the within be o'er, and I set me here upon the ass not yet within, then do I go without and set of the mark of the stone's throw, and he yonder may not take of price at the come within when this thing be done."

And he of the gate's keep said this thing was well, for might a man shut up his eyes e'en unto a gaming?

And Panda spake: "This then shall be, and he who speedeth of the stone past the throw of his brother, then shall his brother pay the price of the withining or yet the withouting."

And the man of the gate's-way said this was well but for one.

And Panda spake: "Yea, and he who goeth, lo, he sheweth not e'en of his wares."

And Panda spake more; should the stones fall at the even, lo, then should the man of Rome set the price. And he of the gate laughed loud and said this was that that could ne'er to be, for no man threw as his brother; but should the stone of Panda fall short of him who rode, then should Panda pay and throw anew with him. And should he fall short, then Panda should go without upon the price of Rome. And Panda said this should be.

And they stood them one beside the other and lay of a wood piece that they stand them even. And they made word among them of which should cast the first, and he of the gate said that since he had fallen short of the throw of Panda, that they should then throw with the throw of him. And they spake this was well.

And lo, he threw, and he who rode stepped upon the ground and unto the spot and threw his stone, and it fell short. And the one of the gate laughed loud and threw a new stone. And Panda looked keen-eyed unto its speed and sought him one and weighed it well within his hand, and swung his arms and made that he throw, and threw not. And the one of Rome saw that his stone had sped far and he looked unto Panda and took forth from his mantle his purse, a skin's sack, and waited that Panda throw.

And Panda spake him words that he who tickleth of his purse's sides might laugh it empty. And he drew him up unto the full height, and his eyes sought Nada, who sat still and waited. And he saw that Aaron watched. And he bit at his lips and the flesh of his fingers whited o'er the stone. And he drew a deep breath and sped it on, and it flew as a loosed bird and past the throw of the Rome's man. And Panda spake:

" Lo, did I speak that folly had of tricks that set the wise at the sup of folly."

And the one who rode took forth price, and the Rome's man shewed unto Panda that his eyes set shut. And Panda spake:

" Thou hast thrown the one stone. Look! wilt thou then cast anew that he who rideth go him unpriced within? See! since thy stone hath fallen short then throw thee anew."

And the Rome's man, who had supped of game, said this was well, for lo, had the in-come from out left the gate lone.

And they threw them once more, and Panda sped the stone first upon its way, and the Rome's man sped then the stone of him, and lo, it fell short, and he spake:

" Lo, doth a fool sup folly then doth he drink of folly's well."

And he turned his face unto the wall that they pass.

And Panda made word unto him who rode and spake that he had a pack that none lent aid for the bearing of save the lad who sat beside its cast. And he shewed unto him Aaron, and lo, this man made word that he should send this lad upon his way and that he would lend of aid.

And Panda asked of him what might be the name of him, and the one who rode spake his name, " Abraham." And Panda took up the skin's thongs that hung o'er the ass's head and hung o'er the arm of him, and Abraham walked at the side of Panda unto the spot where Nada waited.

And Aaron played with stones, and Abraham made words as they came upon Nada and Aaron that men of Jerusalem indeed slept deep that a man might go without the walls with such a pack and a woman and one who spilled folly from his lips. And Panda spake:

" Lo, the God is wise. Yea, this thing must be; for He hath set the wise confounded, and exalted the fools."

And Abraham spake: " Thy tongue hath wisdoms that set unto this, the ear of me, as the wisdom of priests. Yea, and man, this thing doth Abraham speak, that Jerusalem slumbereth is well; for lo, she harketh unto the priests and knoweth not; so, then, 'tis well that she wake her not; for there be naught for gain at waking."

And they came up unto Nada, and Panda made known unto Abraham of her. And Aaron held forth of stones that he offer unto the hand of Abraham, and Abraham spake:

" Lo, this man hath full flesh and less of wisdoms."

And Panda spake: " Yea, this is truth, and yet 'tis better far that one know and brother with fools who offer stones amid the day's light, than that he know and brother with the wise, who offer of stones beneath the dark hours."

And Abraham laughed him loud and spake: " This wisdom of thine setteth well unto the hours of man; for lo, thou dost strip them of words and offer but the meats of wisdoms."

And Panda spake: " Yea, yea, wisdom for feed unto the men of the days; and yet Panda hungereth! "

And Abraham looked unto the rug's-pack, binded 'bout, and spake him that this was a rug of rich weave. And Panda spake, " yea." And Abraham asked of the within of the pack, and Panda spake:

" Lo, it be full of outcast of the loom. Yea, outcast of the loom."

And Abraham spake: " Lo, no man casteth out of wools nor yet throweth he hence of warps."

And Panda shook him: " Yea, this be full of the outcast of the loom."

And Abraham took up the pack and made that he lift of it, and spake: " This be follies, not wisdom, thou art dealing! "

And Panda spake: " Hath not the casting of Panda, the man of thy road's meet, brought thee unpriced within? Then what wouldst thou—that Panda look within thy pack? "

. And he who rode spake, " nay."

And Panda made that he ope the pack of greens, and the one of the road spake: " Lo, wouldst thou bring Rome down upon this pack? "

And Panda made answering: " Lo, a man's tongue speaketh much of his brother, yet would he yoke of his brother's tongue."

And he bid that this man lend an aid unto the withouting of the rug's-pack and speak him not. And he told unto Nada of the stones casting, and how Abraham was to lend an aid. And Nada spake:

" Then, Panda, shall Nada go unto the house of Nadab; for lo, the morn hath broke and hunger shall set upon the babes and them within the walls that need."

And Panda spake: " Yea, this thing is fitting, and Aaron shall go with thee unto the house of Nadab, where thou mayest wait the coming of Panda."

And Nada looked unto the rug, and her eyes were wet, and she held forth her hand o'er the place where it lay and spake in her tongue, and no man knew of her words. And Panda sunk unto his knees and lay his brow upon the sod. And Nada turned and went unto the way of the road unto the house of Nadab.

And when she had gone, lo, Panda and Abraham took up the rug, and it lay heavy between them, and they bore it unto the without. And the Rome's man, who watched at the gate's-way, turned his back unto them that he see not. And Panda spake to Abraham:

" See! this man is indeed of Rome; for look, he turneth his eyes from wickedness and deemeth he knoweth not of such."

And when they had gone upon the way unto the hut of Joel, the ass stopped and made that it move not. And Panda stood and looked unto its ears that lay flatted upon its neck, and spake:

" See thou, Abraham, the folly of an ass may set the best of wisdoms awry."

And Abraham spake: " Thou hast spoken truth, man. Yea, and this brother ass of me hath done this thing at the gate's arch and shewn the withining unto the gate's man, when lo, did he to on amid the hosts no man might see! "

And he lay blows upon the ass's rump and made words that no man spake within the temple walls. And Panda watched and waited him and spake that blows fetched no ass at the on, yea, but the tickle of eat might set his wisdoms at work.

And Abraham said that he then would seek not that he work wisdoms upon the ass but tether him and set upon the way. And they did this thing and went upon the way.

And Abraham oped up his lips unto Panda and told of his days, and asked that Panda tell of what set him upon this path at the bear

of such a pack. And Panda told that this pack held one that had died
at the sup of waters of the street's pool in Jerusalem, and this was his
land they sought, and he did this thing that this one might rest him upon
his own lands.

And Abraham woed that he had bid that the tongue of Panda speak
of sorries. And Panda told of the babe, Indra, and that Lucius watched
the flock. And this was at the time that they had come upon the spot
where the hut of Joel stood, and upon the high place showed the white
of the sheep. And Panda cupped his hand and sent the note unto Lucius,
who lay upon his back and waited his coming. And Lucius stood upon
his feet and waved his hands unto Panda afar and shouted that Panda
hear. And he came forth from o'er the slopes, and the sheep stayed them
upon the high place.

And lo, afar from whence the form of Lucius shewed, there sounded
amid the thicks the answer note of him. And he came him up unto
where Panda stood and looked unto the eyes of Panda and then unto the
eyes of Abraham, and then unto the rug's-pack. And he made words,
saying:

"Lo, Panda, night hath brought naughts, and Lucius hath filled
upon stars!"

And Panda spake: "Lo, 'tis not an ass who plucketh his feed from
off the sky's arch."

And Lucius laughed and looked word unto Panda that asked what
had brought forth Abraham. And Panda said that Abraham was this
man's name and he had come from the without of Jerusalem. And 'twas
upon the woe of him Panda had worked follies upon Rome's man. And
they spake one unto the other of what had been, and Abraham made that
he lend of his hand unto the works of the laying of Joel.

And this thing was done and at the finishing, lo, Panda sent Abraham
upon his way speaking of the days that followed that they should seek
out one the other and make known unto the other of his hours.

And Lucius stood and watched the form of Abraham seek unto the
thicks and up the far rise unto the ass that stood tethered, and lo, he
threw o'er the ass his leg and onned upon his way.

And Panda heaved his breast and spake: "Yon man goeth unto the
inn of Jerusalem with packs of withered greens, but fresh words for
peddle unto the men he meeteth."

And they sat them there at the hut of Joel, and Lucius spake no
word but cast of pebbles unto the road's-way and waited the word of
Panda. And Panda spake:

"The babe had sorry, at the eve's hour, of the lone of the flocks."

And Lucius looked unto the eyes of Panda and then unto the far hill and pointed unto a lamb that e'en then made unto the spot, and spake:

" This lamb hath sought out the staff that it lay it down at the side of me through the night's hours."

And lo, the sheep, though they lay them down upon the field's green, had set their bleating upon the airs, and lo, he had made of the note the babe had spoken and they had set them silent. And Panda spake:

" Lucius, word of note and days of babes fill up a man's rests and weary hours. Yea, but the time hath come when thou and Panda shall do naught save that that be for the hands of men."

And he spake of the bin of Joel within the market's place, and shewed unto Lucius of the sheep that eat upon the hill's side and said that this was the all of the store of Joel, save the babe Indra. And Lucius shook of his head, yea, yea, yea. And Panda spake that Jerusalem knew o'ermuch of the days of Panda, for lo, the days of Panda stood cloak unto the days of Hatte, and it was not meet that Jerusalem know of this cloak save of the out of it, and not of the 'neath of it. And he spake that no man cared that Lucius should set him within the bin of Joel, and this thing should be. And lo, he would bring forth Hatte unto the hills, for the sheep were unto his days as the sweet dreams of the dreamer's nights.

And Lucius looked unto the eyes of Panda and his lips spread of smiles and he spake:

" What, Panda, thou dost deal Lucius unto the market's place, next the bins of Jacob? Woe! Woe! For hath Jacob not e'en now drunk of drops and shed no mites from out his purse's place? "

And Panda spake: " Lo, Lucius, thy days are even now full of the woes of the Jews, and thou knowest that that setteth full the Jew's cup that he pay thee well for the full."

And Lucius said: " Yea, Panda, but Lucius ne'er did tilt of the water's jug without the Jew shewed his hand well up his mantle's sleeve! "

And they laughed and made words unto the full of wisdoms of what the days that followed should shew. And when this thing was o'er, lo, they arose and Panda went unto the hut and looked him within and spake that the morn should find the days of Panda walled within the hut of Joel.

And Lucius said that this thing was well, but suredly Jerusalem should love not that he should set him within the market's place; for how then might a one who knew of naught save waters deal of wares?

And Panda stood and looked unto the spot where stones lay o'er the place where Joel lay, and held his hand high and spake the words of his land. And when this thing was done, lo, he took up the hand of Lucius and bid that they should seek out the ass and on unto the house of Nadab, where the lone waited them.

And they came unto the ass's tether, and lo, Panda spake:

"See, Lucius, Panda hath filled upon the days that come and hath forgot that Abraham hath ridden him hence, e'en though his eyes took this in!"

And Lucius shook his head and spake: "Panda, thy lips speak much wisdom, and yet e'en thou dost folly!"

And Panda said: "Woe is the man who follieth ne'er."

And they sought the way unto the sheep's gate; for Panda spake: "Lo, when a man knoweth o'ermuch, Lucius, 'tis the lips of him that itch that they spill. Yea, and doth the day to offer not that he tell, lo, the wet of wisdom dryeth!"

CHAPTER XXII

AND they went them within the sheep's gate and gave unto Rome that they in. And sought out the narrowed places, and Panda looked not upon the men upon the street's-way but sought the house of Nadab.

And lo, Nada stood looked unto the road's-way that she see and upped of her hand that she set a sign that the eyes of her saw the coming of Panda. And Panda, whose arm lay about the shoulders of Lucius, made sign unto her, and they went them up unto the spot, and Nada spake in soft voice: "Is the thing o'er?" And her cheeks showed scarlet and her bosom heaved. And Panda spake:

"Yea, yea, Nada, o'er; and yet Panda hath brought Joel back unto the house of Nadab; for the heart of Panda is full of him."

And Nada said: "Long, long, the day's hours did drag. Yea, Nadab hath slept, and Caleb rowed, and the babes, Hatte and Mary, set them at the soothe of Indra, who wept."

And Panda touched the arm of Nada, and Lucius hung without the door's ope as they went within. And he upped of his shoulders and held his hands oped and made that he lift them after the manner of Jews.

. And Panda, seeing this thing, stopped and bade that Lucius come within, and Lucius spake:

"Doth then a man's eyes take in the fulling of a house and see there be no room within for him, 'tis folly that he set foot unto the door's ope!"

And Panda reached him and smote Lucius upon his side and laughed, and the cheek of Nada burned.

And they went within, and Panda's arm lay about the shoulders of Lucius, and Nada held within the hand of her one of the hands of Lucius.

And Panda asked of Caleb, and of Aaron, and Nada shewed unto him, from out the ope at the east wall of the hut, Aaron and Hatte and Mary and Indra, and o'er the cheek of Indra showed dark stains of dusts, wetted amid tears. And lo, Hatte sat him upon the sod that shewed it amid the sunk flags, and Mary lay her beside him, and Indra sat, wide-eyed, and listed unto the word that Hatte made. And lo, his lips sounded through the follied laugh of Aaron, who tossed of wooden bits and laughed much.

And Panda stopped and made the sign of silence unto Lucius and Nada, and they listed, and Hatte went on with the wording and the words sounded out, saying:

"Lo, within the temple place hath Hatte of a sire. Yea, and he holdeth of the treasures of Jerusalem. Yea, and there shall come a day when he shall stand him upon the temple step and cry aloud the name of her—Theia!

"And they shall bear her forth from out the city's people and set her upon the high place, and he shall take of the treasures and deck her o'er, and lo, the locks of her shall gleam as sunshine and her eyes as sapphires. Yea, and the people shall fall upon their faces and speak out her name.

"And the brother of the flesh of Hatte who hath spoken within the hill's place shall step Him unto the high place and confound the priests with wisdoms. Yea, for He hath spoken He, too, is of the sire of Hatte.

"Yea, and He, the brother of Hatte, shall be called the Elder, for lo, Theia hath spoken that there shall come a day when this man of the East shall shew Himself. Yea, and this brother of the flesh of Hatte hath known of his sire e'en before the days of Hatte knew of him. So then shall He be called the Elder. Yea, so hath He the right that He be kinged. Yea, the thing is right. Be this not a truth, Mary?"

And Mary spake: "Yea, the elder brother standeth unto the throne's step."

And Hatte spake: "Yea, yea, and Hatte shall look upon this Theia who sitteth decked, and shall step him, drinking within his eyes the lovely of her. Yea, and lo, shall she ope up her arms, and Hatte shall go within them, and no man shall say nay.

"Yea, and Hatte shall look upon his brother crowned. Yea, and no man of earth shall envy of this crown, yea, save Hatte."

And he stood him up unto his full height and swayed and ran swift unto the dark of the in of the hut crying out:

"The slaying! The slaying! Nada! Nadab!"

And he fell, and Panda swift went unto him as he lay and took him unto his breast and spake: "The lamb of Panda! Smitten, smitten sore!"

And the head of Hatte lay upon his breast, and tears fell unto his locks from out the eyes of Panda. And Nada looked her afar and not upon the tears of Panda, and Lucius looked him down unto the flags. And Panda's lips made words of the dreaming of Hatte. And he spake that these dreams stood as the dreams of Theia; for Theia had dreamed so; but woe had dulled of the hurt of dreams. And he shook his head and spake:

"Ah, the woe of the dulling for Hatte!"

And Nada stepped unto them and made that she soothe with the hand of her o'er the brow of Hatte. And Panda told of the hut of Joel, and of the sheep, and said that 'twas well that they should seek out this spot and dwell not within Jerusalem.

And Nada spake no word. And Panda said that he had of moneys that the hand of Samuel had dealt for hides, and unto Nadab should he offer of this. And Nada held her hand o'er her lips and shook her "nay." And Panda spake more:

"Lo, within thy walls doth Caleb and Mary dwell. And Nadab steppeth him not upon the earth without. And thou, Nada, shalt know that Panda might then offer unto Caleb that he go without the walls and unto this hut with him; for lo, doth a man wield of an oar, 'tis well that he doth use of it for his onning. As the shepherd's crook shall the oar be."

And Nada said this thing was wisdom, but though her lips spake her eyes told not that that the lips told. And Hatte still lay upon the breast of Panda, and he waked and listed, and Panda went on with the words of what should be at the come of the morrow. And he spake of the sheep once more, and told that there was the fold that shewed full and was worth much price. And Hatte spake:

"Panda, Panda, what is the thing that setteth fear unto the heart of Hatte?"

And Panda spake: "Hatte, thou hast dreams. Then take thou dreams as naught save the fancies weave."

And Hatte cried: "Nay! Nay! Panda, this blood floweth!"

And Hatte looked deep unto the eyes of Panda, and Panda spake of the hills without and the herds that stood waited that Hatte take up the staff. And Hatte sprung from the arms of Panda and stretched forth his body unto its high. And he oped up his arms and cried aloud:

"O, ye hills! O, ye hills! Ope up thy breasts and leave Hatte unto their fullsome * curve! Leave Hatte that he seek thee at the heat's burn and know thy cools. Yea, hide thee amid thy depths the lambs, that they suffer not the heats."

And he turned unto Panda and held forth his hand and spake: "Panda, as thou lovest me, lead thou me unto thy sheep."

And Panda said: "Hatte, Hatte, art thou strong? Art thou strong

* Used in its obsolete sense of "abundant." Frequently so used in this work.

like unto Caanthus of Rome's day? Canst thou bind thy heart? Canst thou shut within its binded walls, Theia?"

And Hatte's hand shook, and his eyes misted o'er, and he made answering: "Panda, 'tis the key unto this heart of Hatte, the love of Theia. And he hath locked it. Yea, yea, and yet Panda, what then is this thing that offereth unto Hatte new paths that ne'er do end within the arms of her?"

And Panda took him within his arms and whispered slow: "The God is wise. She hath spoken it so."

And Hatte made answering: "Panda, e'en though Hatte hath locked his heart with this key, 'tis the slender arms of Theia that beat and beat upon its walls. Yea, unto the streets of Jerusalem looketh Hatte and he would for to ope up his lips and shout aloud unto the townsmen and tribesmen: 'Theia! Theia! Thy nobled queen and the love of Hatte!' Panda, doth this day hold the sire who hath turned from the day of Hatte? And doth this sun beat upon him? Doth this heated air be the air he doth breathe? Doth his eyes look upon yon sky? Then Hatte hateth o' the day!

"Then, doth he abide in the temple place, wrapped of the regal robes of the kingly? Doth he shut up his eyes unto his flesh? Panda, Panda, Hatte telleth thee e'en though thou knowest He of the hill's said the sire of Him and me abideth within the temple place—yea, Hatte speaketh loud!—yon temple place is empty! Empty! Empty! Yea, save for the curling smokes of incense. He abideth not there! Nay, thrice, when thou knewest not of, Hatte hath sought and He answered not, e'en though Hatte cried aloud that He ope."

And Panda looked and his eyes stood filled of drops and he spake: "Nay, nay, Hatte, thou hast called with but thy lips."

And Hatte made answering: "Nay, Panda, though the lips of Hatte cried out, his heart run crimson drops that cried louder than lips!"

And Panda spake: "But she sayeth He is wise!"

"Yea, and Panda, hark! dost thou hear, e'en as the eve's breeze that beareth unto the hill's place from out the towns, the murmur of the eve? Hark! Hark! He shall come! He shall come! She hath spoke it so!"

And Panda lay upon the head of Hatte the gentle hand of him, and it shook.

And the time had set unto the dimming of the day, and gold hung 'bout the low of the skies and cast o'er the airs of Jerusalem a yellowed light.

And the babes, Mary and Indra, came up unto the wall's ope and peered them within and stood to hark. And lo, the laugh of Aaron sounded empty, yet full of mirth. And he arose and dragged of his nets unto the ope and made signs within it to Panda that he come without. And Panda shook him " nay " and made that Aaron come within. And they did this thing. And Indra sought out the side of Panda and asked of the flocks, and Panda spake:

" Morn, morn, Indra, bringeth light, and light setteth thee and Panda and Hatte and Caleb, and e'en Mary, upon the out-way."

And Hatte stood from the arms of Panda and made word in a loud voice: " And doth Aaron abide him within the walls of Nadab? Hath not this out-place airs for him? "

And Panda smiled slow, like unto his tribesmen. And Nada stirred and went unto Nadab, whose smite sounded within, and lo, Caleb had sought the side of Nadab and spake of broken days, and Nadab made answering and smiled that he mend of the breaks.

And it was the sup's time, and Nada stepped slow, and her lips shut, and her eyes dropped. And she went unto Nadab, and he sat and put upon his shoulders the hands of her, and she looked long unto the eyes of him. And Nadab looked, with his bright eyes burned, unto her and smiled and shook him " yea," and spake:

" Thine eyes have spoken. What needest thou of lips? "

And Nada made the sign unto the East, and she went unto the rug's cast and took of one, and spread it upon the stones of the floor, and set bowls and cast of loaf upon the rug, and brought forth meats, the flesh of sheep. And the loaf was of the black grain and shewed not fruit. And Panda came within the seeing of this thing and spake that the day shewed upon the board of Nadab as a day of fasting. And Nada's cheek burned and her lips made answer:

" May then not a one who sorroweth take of the manners of these Jews that he shew? "

And Nadab laughed much. And they sat them upon the rug's side; some as the men of the far lands and some as them of Rome. And Hatte looked upon Caleb, who lay after the manner of Rome, and then unto Panda and spake soft unto the ear of him:

" Panda, see! how is this that Caleb doth lie that he eat? "

And Panda made answer: " This is the manner of Rome at the feast."

And Hatte laughed and spake: " Bread that sheweth not fruited and meat that be not salt? Feast, Panda, feast? "

And he laughed and laid him long, even after the manner of Rome.

And Panda looked not upon this, but his eye followed the slip of Nada even as the shadow followeth the traveler upon a sunny day.

And when they had upped, lo, Nada sat her and took of bread and supped of vinegar and spake not. And the time wore unto the late. And the babes filled their words of the out-place and the journey at the day's-break, and emptied them of words unto the droop, and thence unto the naught, to sleep.

And it was so that Lucius had supped within the house of Nadab, and when the babes had sunk unto their rests, Nadab had brought forth of the water bowls and set within them berries that smoked, and offered unto Panda and Lucius and Caleb. And they lay them upon the floor's stones and took of the off-come of smoke.

And Panda told of all that had been of the day's hours and of their going at the dawn. And spake of the household of Nadab and of the love that dealt unto the road's cast from out his heart. And Nadab smiled the flash-smile of his land, when the lips flash and the eyes sober much. And his voice raised and he spake:

" Panda, man—thou hast spoken his name Lucius, Panda?—see! the house of Nadab is as the trees of the hills. Whatsoe'er the gods send unto them that doth home therein."

And Panda spake: " Yea, but the gods send of waters and light, and thou hast shut up thine eyes unto the moneys of Panda! "

And Nadab bent swift unto Panda and spake in the honeyed voice of his tribe, musicked, and his eyes looked afar:

" Such an rug! Such weavings! Such dreams Nadab shall set at the morrow! A new racksfull! Yea, and he shall dip of wools unto the glints of the every scarlet, from the sick pale unto the fire's glow, and so unto the fulling of this dream. And there shall be at the border, hills and sheep, and a dark one shall walk him o'er the sheen, bended and straight. And there shall be a one, a lad, and there shall be a one, a maid, whose locks shew black, and they shall follow one the other through this weave. And o'er the all, lo, hark thou, hark! there shall gleam the gold, the gold's bright, the locks of her the babe Hatte loveth. And no man shall know what this thing is but shall look upon this rug and shake his head and speak: ' Lo, this man hath coaxed the sun to kiss his wool! ' And whoe'er shall step upon its soft shall thrice warm of love! Yea, and the face of this dark one, lo, shall Nadab stain of the locks of Nada mixed of the wools."

And Nada stood her high and flashed of her eyes and went within. And Lucius stood forth and laughed loud, and spake that he should go that he make ready that he set upon the way at the dawn so that this might be that the ass bear of the burdens. And he spake that his household should know of the going of him unto the market's bin and told unto Panda of the babe, the sister of his flesh, and spake her name Paulia.

And of her he spake much, and Nada listed her and asked of the years of this maid; for the ears of her took in the words of Lucius and she harked within, to bring forth of light and stand that she hark more. And Lucius spake:

"At the fulling of her maidenhood, and her hair gleameth as the red sun of the morn."

And Nada looked unto Panda and spake not. And Nadab made the sounds of laughter, soft, and spake: "A babe, Nada, a babe!"

And Lucius went without, and his laugh sounded after his steps fell not upon the ear.

And Nada stood and looked upon the floor, and Panda stood and looked upon the floor, and lo, Nadab nodded him thrice and slept. And Panda's lips moved but made no sound and his hands pressed hard unto the whiting of the flash. And the cloth of the head of Nada had fallen, for lo, she stood not amid the days of Jerusalem as the sisters of her land who clothed of their faces o'er. And she took up the cloth and hid her face. And Panda sat at the side of the babes, Mary and Hatte, and Indra had slept upon the nets of Aaron. And Aaron rested him upon the seat of Nadab at the side, his head upon the rugs. And Caleb had gone within. And Panda looked unto Nada and spake:

"'Tis eve. The palms rattle o'erhead. The sweet scent clingeth o'er thy land and mine, and o'er the crescent upon the temple's place the moon's white resteth it."

And Nada made answer e'en as a chant:

"The walls stand black. The sands smell damp and the sky glittereth e'er as the sands beneath the sun. 'Tis eve! 'Tis night! Ah, Panda, the moon hath gone!"

And Panda answered:

"Yea, the moon hath gone, but returneth at the eve. Nada, the moon bringeth in the waves for their rest after the day's weary. Yea, her soft gleam, her pale smile, is but the sign her work hath been done. Panda's hands stand full of chaff. What, Nada! thinkest thou, within this chaff there may be grain? Should Panda then cast the chaff? Or should Panda tread it free and take therefrom the grain?"

And Nada looked afar and made answer: "Panda, thou art wise, but wisdom hath folly-feet, methinks."

And Panda said: "See! look thou upon Panda! Panda hath

strength. Yea, Panda's hands itch for the workings that offer unto
them! Yea, Nada, but lands are empty until man planteth them with
loving."

And Nada murmured: "The moon sinketh!"

And Panda spake: "Yea, to rise at the eve's hour of the morrow!"

And he took of her hand and led her unto the without and pointed
unto where the moon stood gleaming and spake:

"Ever hath she risen so, e'en though man seeth not."

And Nada spake: "Panda, thou knowest the moon doth hide!"

And Panda said: "Yea, but she strayeth not; for ever doth she shew
at the waiting."

And Nada turned unto the East and bowed and raised her hand in
sign. And Panda led her within, and they sought their couches out.
And Nada lay upon the rug within the in-place that shewed of the stores
of Nadab. And she sought the ope of the east wall and looked unto
the moon's climb and spake:

"Thou dost sink!"

And Panda stood and harked, and naught sounded unto him, and
he went unto the without and held high his hand unto the East and spake
unto the white moon:

"Thou shalt rise!"

And he went within and stood o'er the body of Hatte and stooped
and took him within his arms and sought the rugs. And Hatte stirred
and whispered:

"Panda! Panda! He is wise. Hatte seeth the hills, the hills of
Bethlehem."

And Panda made answer: "Yea, yea."

And Hatte's voice sunk unto but breath, and he whispered:

"He shall come!"

CHAPTER XXIII

AND they slept. And the moon spread out her white and crept o'er Jerusalem. And filth hid in her pure. And night stood still to wait the dawn. And holy white bathed the temples o'er, alike of Rome and of Jerusalem.

And o'er the Rome's hall hung sleep. E'en the hands of the wicked uncurled to rest, unbladed before the might of one white moon's ray's gleam. Sleep undoeth the mighty and prospereth him who hath naught. White gleamed o'er the pillar's curve and along the stoned base. The still hung close, close as a robe. The dark opes beneath the base shewed black. And sudden sounded:

" Jehovah! Jehovah! Why tarriest thou?"

And the words sounded out loud and sunk long upon the airs, until they died, soft, soft, still making of the question. And the moon looked on and smiled.

And Theia crept up unto the ope, and looked without and up upon her sad white, and spake:

" Thou hast risen since time and time, and thou dost wait, yea, wait for Him of the East who shall fade thy silver. So waiteth Theia. The God is wise. He shall come!"

And Jerusalem knew not of the words nor yet of the moon's sad. And night shewed whited until her climb unto the high, and darker until the sink.

And this was at the time that the cocks crew. And the babes within the walls wailed and the mothers hushed them.

And the house of Nadab shewed dead, sunk within the filth of Jerusalem, wrapped of the days of Jerusalem yet filled of the fruits of the far lands.

And the wearied night had hid, and the morn sped swift-footed upon the stilled Jerusalem.

The light bore mists and day darkened as she sped. The drops fell swift unto the earth and washed the stained walls o'er. And waters bathed the stones and onned to set unto the trickled way unto the wells.

And waking tarried within the walls. And fowls shrieked loud upon the airs. The asses huddled unto the wall's hug, and tight unto their flesh the hides shewed sleek. The house of Nadab wept of drops, and day awakened them within. Panda spake loud unto Nada, who sought the ope unto the out. And Hatte wailed that day shewed wet. Nadab's racks sounded out their thud and taper flickered at the wall's side.

" 'Tis the gods' weep, Nada, yea, yea, so!"

And Nada made answering: "Panda, speak not! The moon sinketh!"

And Panda laughed and took up the rug whereon he lay and rolled it unto the pack and cast it unto the rug's-cast at the wall's side. And Hatte's voice arose and he wept amid his words:

"Panda, the hills shall show sorrowed. Yea, the sheep, Hatte can see e'en now, packed one unto the other's sides. Ah, Panda, see! Did Hatte not speak unto thee at the yester's-eve that ever did paths ope unto him that led not unto her arms? Yea, and it seemeth, Panda, this path, like unto its brothers, leadeth not unto light."

And Panda took up one of the oars of Caleb and put unto the hand of Hate and spake:

"Set thee unto the work of putting unto the packs that that belongeth unto thee and me, and that of Mary and yet of Caleb, and yet the nets of Aaron. And the hand of Indra seek thou and take within thine own; for Lucius cometh and unto the ass of him shall Panda bind this pack that it bear it unto the out-place."

And Hatte's eyes dried and he spake: "Then, Panda, shall this path lead from out the east wall?"

And Panda's lips smiled slow and he made answering:

"Nay. He who hath sought and hath found should seek not the spot that he find more. See! we go then from out the sheep's gate and 'bout the walls unto the East. Yea, he who hath seen woe seeketh not more, Hatte."

And Hatte questioned: "At this gate, Panda, this sheep's gate, will the man of Rome still stand?"

And Panda answered: "Though Jerusalem belongeth unto the Jews and is the lands of the Jew, lo, still doth Rome stand at her doors."

And Hatte spake: "But this thing is not right, Panda. Who then hath spoken unto Rome that she seek and be the door's-reaper of moneys of Jerusalem?"

And Panda answered: "Hark, Hatte! no man hath spoken unto Rome this thing. Nay, there strideth upon earth a one who hath hunger past the fill. Yea, and man calleth this one ' Glut.' Like unto the death-hunt birds of the deserts strideth this one, and where'er gold sheweth, lo, there he whispereth."

And Hatte spake: " Panda, as then we pass this gate wilt thou give unto the hand of Hatte of the moneys that we cast unto Rome? "

And he swayed and his voice sounded far and he cried:

" Lo, lo, afar cometh a host! Yea, they shew as mighty hosts. Their swords' blades flame! Their mantles blood! Yea! Yea! And they sweep like unto flies o'er the market's place, o'er Rome! And lo, lo, o'er Rome they tread, laying her low!

" Yea, yea, and Hatte speaketh out. He seeth more. Up upon a high place, amid this Rome, there springeth of a tree. Yea, and the fruit of this tree sheweth as thorns. Yea, more, more! Rome shall take up one of these thorns and lay ope the heart of all the earth through ages! 'Tis come, Panda! 'Tis come! The dark and the slaying! "

And Hatte sought the arms of Panda. And Nada, seeing this thing, came unto him and spake: " Panda, thou goest? "

And Panda made answer: " Yea."

And Nada's eyes wetted.

And Panda spake: " Nada, go thou and bring forth the wares of Panda—Aaron, Mary, Indra, yea, and Caleb."

And without there sounded the pat-pat of asses' hoofs upon wetted stones, and Lucius called unto the within, and Panda made answering and bade that he come within. And this thing was done, and Panda lay his arm about the shoulders of Lucius and looked deep within his eyes and spake:

" Lucius, it hath ever been that he who hath supped the cup of Panda hath supped woe."

And Lucius said: " Lo, Panda, Lucius hath fed since his first wail upon woes. Then thine shall be as the sweet unto his soured wine."

And Panda raised his arm and swept the airs 'bout the room and spake:

" Lucius within this wall hath the grape been pressed that hath bled the sweetest wine that Panda hath e'er supped, and yet Panda goeth and suppeth not."

And Nada came forth and before her stepped Aaron who laughed, and Indra whose eyes stood wide and feared, and Hatte who led his lamb, and Mary who held unto the hand of Caleb, who turned his empty eyes unto a naught.

And Panda went unto Nada and took up her hand, and they turned unto the East and sunk upon their knees, and their voices raised in the chant of their lands. And when this was finished, lo, they arose and Panda led her unto the side of Nadab, who was within the in-chamber, and with them stepped the band of Panda, and Lucius. And Panda oped his lips and spake:

"Nadab, morn hath brought the oping of the path for Panda and his. Thy walls have housed his wastes. Thy heart hath given of its store and Panda would offer unto thee all of the all he possesseth. Yea, but Nadab, this at this hour is naught save wastes. Yea, but Panda speaketh loud, that amid wastes upon the sands stand the greened places and this is the thing that Panda goeth that he doeth. Yea, amid the waste shall he grow grains. Upon the shelter hills stand flocks that seek shepherd. Yea, unto them shall Panda minister. Yea, and set his hand unto the lands. E'en as thou hast put thy trust shall Panda fulfil it."

And he spake more: "Nadab, thou hast of a vineyard, and amid its vines a one that standeth past its sister-vines. And Panda would take of this vine, but 'tis not meet that Panda should offer that he take until he putteth of the full price. Then, Nadab, take thou the care of the dust of thy tribes."

And Nadab spake: "Yea, yea, Panda, thy lips speak not that that Nadab knoweth not. Waste thee not of words. Even as Nadab setteth his head unto this stone at the kneeling, so setteth his days upon this vine."

And Panda looked not upon Nada but turned, and before him went the "wastes." And Lucius took up the pack and said:

"Panda, Lucius hath word he maketh unto thee, and hath upon his ass goods that he beareth thee; but this time hath come not."

And Panda made no word but shook him "yea." And they went without. And the voice of Nadab called out words of the land of Panda, and they made witchery upon his days that the gods be pleased and Allah send mercy. And Nada tarried, and when the house stood empty save of Nadab and Nada, she went unto the rug's cast and counted out unto the five and one, and made of them a pack and went unto the without and spake loud: "Panda! Panda!"

And Panda, hearing, came forth, and she held forth the pack and spake: "Upon the dreams of Nadab sleep thou and thine!"

And she raised her hand unto the East.

And it shewed dark, and rains swept and wetted her locks and her head-cloth, and her voice shook and she murmured: "The moon sinketh, Panda!"

And Panda looked unto her eyes and spake: "Nay, she cometh! She cometh! She suredly shall rise!"

And still the voice of Nadab shouted and Panda sat upon the ass, upon the binded pack, Hatte and Mary and Indra, and they hung close, one unto the other, and o'er them Panda cast a hide, and about him and about Lucius he wrapped of hides, and beneath his own took he Caleb; for there was not more of hides. And Aaron followed, and o'er his head spread of his nets.

And Lucius made the call unto the ass, and it stamped its hind hoof and backed its ears and moved not. And Lucius spake:

"Lo, Panda, what fool loveth folly more than ass loveth lash?"

And he snapped his skin's-lash and lay it upon the ass's hide and it went on, still swinging of tail.

And they turned at the way unto the sheep's gate and Hatte spake: "Panda, the moneys thou hast said Hatte may cast!"

And Panda reached unto his mantle and brought forth a coin and gave unto the hand of Hatte, and Hatte took it and held within his shut hand. And when they had come near unto the gate's arch, lo, Hatte spake:

"Panda, within the heart of Hatte no sorrow setteth at the leaving of Jerusalem. Panda, the hills! The hills! Look! Nada spake that the lad of the hills had hid and they, the Sire and His mother who is called Mary, had sought and sought far, and all of the market's people had heard of His going, and Panda, what think'st thou? Nada sayeth He had gone unto the temple place. See! He hath gone unto His sire and mine. Yea, and His sire and mine, Panda, hath let Him in, and Hatte hath He denied. What man hath turned the earth 'gainst Hatte? Panda, wrapped ever is Hatte within woe."

And they had come unto the gate and Hatte called unto the Rome's man: "Awake, Rome, and take thy price!"

And he spat upon the coin and cast it unto the Roman. And the Rome's man laughed, and Panda made no word, but the voice of Hatte raised loud and he cried out:

"Laugh! Laugh! This coin shall bear but one drop of the blood that thou shalt sup!"

And the Rome's man laughed, and Hatte spake:

"Panda, see! Rome laugheth. Yea, yea, and yet Rome hath hurt her. Hatte shall freeze this laugh! Hatte shall be as a Jew. Yea, Hatte shall know naught save her. Theia, and the hurt of her, and that Rome hath done this thing. Yea, look thou! Look, Panda! e'en now Rome hath done this thing! Yea, look thou! Look, Panda; e'en now within the wet walls creepeth them who bear unto Rome's purse. Yea, look! and they scarce have that that hides their naked! He of the East, He that Theia waiteth, He the sire of Hatte, shall, shall, shall undo Rome!"

And they went them on and the hills shewed; and they followed the walls about Jerusalem. And Hatte made more words, speaking out:

"See! See! Jerusalem lieth walled and yet within her walls hath she walled her undoing."

And he looked unto the hills and oped up his arms and let the rains to wash him o'er, and cried out: "The sheep! The sheep! See, Mary, see!"

And he turned unto Panda, crying out: "The lamb, Panda, the lamb of Hatte!"

And Panda pointed to Lucius, who held it beneath his hide. And they came unto the hut of Joel, and went within, and Panda oped the wet pack, and his tears fell upon the rugs of Nadab. And he took out loaves that Nada had rolled within, and Lucius made that he set them married, and Panda took up a bowl and spake:

"Lucius, wilt thou bring forth a she-goat that she offer of milch that these babes sup?"

And Lucius did this thing, and they sat them down that they take of bread, and Panda's voice spake that they make thanks unto Allah. And Hatte said: "Theia hath spoken not his name so."

And Panda spake: "Yea, yea. Jehovah, Allah, he the God o'er gods whate'er thou speakest, Hatte."

And Hatte said: "Panda, dost thou speak that Hatte should make thanks? Nay! Where is she? Let Him bring her forth! Rome hath taken golds, yea, golds, metals, Panda, but none so precious as Theia's locks. Ah, Panda, look!"

And he oped his mantle and took forth a strand and spake:

"She smote her flesh, Panda, she smote her flesh, and Hatte tore this loose."

And Lucius questioned: "He speaketh of her that Rome hath?"

And Panda made the sign of silence. And Hatte sprung forth and cried: "Rome hath her? Rome, Panda?"

And Panda soothed him with wise words, and Lucius spake soft:

"She has left of her within the bin of Joel. Lo, when the men of Rome laid hold of her raiment she had cast off the skins, and was clothed within a whited mantle like unto the Jew's men; and this skin and a pack stood beneath the wares of Joel, and the market's men said that when the Rome's men went that they seek her she cast this therein."

And Lucius went without and brought forth the skin and pack, and there showed jades, armlets, ankle rings, neck metals and the sandals woven of golden strands. And Hatte took this up and looked long upon it and spake:

"Panda, what is this thing?"

And Panda answered: "Theia, Theia, Hatte, hath stepped upon the court's floors with this."

And Panda took up a whited thing and lo, this was the wool's robe. And Panda sunk his face within its soft, and Hatte touched it and spake: "And this?"

And Panda answered: "This, Hatte, is the robe of mists."

And Hatte sprung forth and cast his arms about its folds and wept, and his voice spake:

"Yea, yea, as a cloud she boundeth, yea, soft as the clouds that fleet o'er the skies of Bethlehem, Panda. Yea, and her feet gleamed within the golden sandals as the sun's glist through the cloud, and the locks streamed as his rays. See, see, Panda, the skies have oped! See, the sun! The sun! Look! Look! The hills! The sheep arise and scatter. See, Panda, see! Ah, Caleb, that thou mightest take this thing in!"

And Caleb made answering in broken words. And Hatte took up the hand of Indra and spake:

"Unto the hills shall we go! Yea, and Mary shall lead Caleb, and the lamb shall follow, that it know the fold."

And they went without. And Panda looked upon the pack and then unto the bounding form of Hatte, and he said:

"Lucius, wisdom sayeth wait, but Panda's heart burneth that he ope the Rome's hall and lead her forth. Yea, but she sayeth He is wise. So then it shall be."

And Lucius spake of the market's place, and they made words of his going forth. And Panda told unto Lucius that he should seek the hut at the every day but home among his own.

"Yea, since thou shalt sup Panda's cup, then doth Panda give unto thee the half of all his."

And Lucius spake: "Panda, thou art my brother."

And he departed, strided upon the ass.

And the day wore on; the hills dried; the sheep shewed whiter and Hatte tarried among them. Upon his back lay he, weaving of rugs even as Nadab had told unto him. And he wove of the clouds, of the trees and of the stones, and of the sheep, and of Theia and Panda. And the hour came unto the eve and they sought the hut, and Panda stood loned, waiting them. And he led Caleb within, and spake words unto Hatte and the babes that sounded as the light heart, when lo, dark hung, and they supped once more upon the bread of Nadab, and Hatte fell silent. And at a later time he spake:

"Panda, the hills fill not Hatte's breast! Panda, hark! Nadab's racks would sound and Nada sung and the bowls that smoked and the wicks that Nada made! Panda! Panda! Jerusalem holdeth all!"

And Panda answered: "Yea, all."

And Hatte took up the white mist's robe and the sandals and went without. And Panda followed, and the babes, Mary and Indra, sat at the knee of Caleb and made words.

And Hatte stood and looked through the deep sun's red that bathed all and cried:

"Panda, Panda," and his tears flowed, "thou art loned even as Hatte! Why hast thou left her? The love of Hatte earth claims, but thou hast her!"

And Panda answered: "Lo, Hatte, see! the sun sinketh him. Then shalt thou and Panda lay them down and wait the moon's come."

And they did this thing, and between the time when the sun sunk and the moon's come, dark hung, and Hatte wept.

And there sounded out upon the road's-way the voices of men who prodded asses and bidded camels on; and locusts sung; and Panda sat silent; and Hatte whispered:

"Lo, the without of Jerusalem hath swallowed all the lone of earth!"

And lo, upon the dark, the rim of silvered gold crept, slow, slow. And Panda pointed unto it and spake:

"She hath risen. Yea, she cometh. Look! ever 'twas so."

And Hatte said: "Take thou me unto the hut, Panda."

And Panda spake: "Wouldst thou leave thy Panda?"

And Hatte arose and ran unto his side and wrapped him in his arms and cried out: "Ne'er, ne'er! Panda, thou hast Hatte. Yea, but Hatte filleth not thee."

And he still held close the robe and sandals of her.

And lo, there sounded forth a call, and this was the voice of a one, a woman, and it called forth:

"Panda! Panda! See! the moon hath risen!"

And she rode upon the ass of Lucius, and lo, she bore packs, and she spake soft. And Panda stood straight, and his breast heaved, and he oped his arms and went forth that he take her from off the ass. And he spake: "Nada, thou hast left Nadab?"

And Nada answered: "Yea, yea, yea, Panda, this is right, yea, meet and right. Nadab spake it so. Yea, he said that Jerusalem held no dreaming for his rugs; that he should seek the out-places and come even unto thy hut. Panda, this breast of Nada hath ached for the lone of Hatte. Speak thou! Speak thou! The moon doth rise. See!"

And Panda murmured: "Yea, yea, He then is indeed wise!"

And he sunk; and Nada wrapped him in her arms. And Hatte looked not upon this, but put upon his feet the sandals of Theia, and spread o'er his head the mist's robe, and spread it wide and bounded up and cast it freed upon the airs beneath the moon's paled gold. And he cried loud:

"Thou hast sunk unto sorrow that she spread thee not and shewed thee not the wonder of her bounded feet. Look, look! I pledge thee that Hatte seeketh her! Yea, within the sandals of her feet Hatte steppeth in sign."

And he stood clothed of the robe of Theia, and his bright locks gleamed e'en as hers. And he stopped and cried aloud unto Panda:

"See, Panda! at the west there standeth cloud that cometh on, and at the east, lo, naught save one star. Drowned within the moon's bright, her sisters!"

And he spread his arms and cried out:

"Oh, thou of the East! Why tarriest thou?"

And amid the clouds the lightnings flashed and the storm came on. And Hatte stood tall, and shewed dark upon the light that flashed. And the moon hid, and quiet filled the airs, save for the rumble of the lightning's voice. And Hatte turned, and Panda and Nada passed within the dark.

And the moon shone bright 'neath the cloud, and lo, it shone upon a one who held within his hands bright bits, and his laugh chattered upon the still.

And Hatte stood and knew not of what stood within Jerusalem nor yet that that hung within and 'bout the hut.

And the storm broke, and lo, it flashed and darked, and the winds arose and the flash shewed the robe of Theia spread upon the wind's wings.

And Hatte's voice rung clear upon the airs:

"I am strong! Strong like unto Caanthus! Yea, I am him. Yea, strong!"

And he threw his arms wide and bounded upon the storm's rage, and sped unto the dark. And the winds roared and swallowed the voice of him and the flash shewed not his form.

And the storm spent, and quiet came soft-footed on upon the night. And the hut of Joel shewed dark and still.

And one star gleamed, and the clouds shewed unto the west. And beneath the light there lay a shape like unto a sheep, white-swathed.

And it stood upon its feet, and waters dropped from the mantle. And it raised its arms and cried aloud:

"Oh, ye hills! Oh, ye hills! Wherein hast thou hidden her? Oh, thou of the East! What sand's waste tarrieth thy caravan? Hatte's lips speak hate of his sire, and lo, his heart droppeth blood's drops! Oh, ye hills! Comfort thou me!"

And he raised him higher unto his utmost and strained unto the heavens and cried out:

"He shall come! He shall come! She hath spoke it so."

And he swayed, and his lips spake soft:

"Yea, yea, Theia. Hatte cometh suredly, e'en so as doth He."

And he turned and fled, crying out:

"The slaying! The slaying!"

And he swept up unto the hut and the door's-way swallowed him.

And the one star gleamed.

And the clouds banked at the west.

BOOK II

HATTE

CHAPTER I

AND behold, there shone from the east the white light of the early dawn. And this was at the fulling of the days unto the tides and the tides unto the many.*

And Jerusalem stood upon the down-turn of the hill's-bowls. And the road's-way unto her walls stood as the strands of a web.

And lo, there rode, upon a camel's pack, a one upon the in-road unto her, and this shewed within the white light. And the sun came up and lo, reds crept and golds glinted, and upon the young sun's redded ball the camel man shewed black and the camel sunk and rose upon his loose legs. And the one cried out: " E-e-e-o-e! E-e-e-o-e! " And the beast stealth-slipped on.

The packs glisted of sands. And the one plucked sands from his binded head and shook his raiment, the whited mantle that hung loose at the arms. And he reached within his mantle sleeve and brought forth sands. And within the cloth that bound of his loins, the many colored cloth, he slipped his slim fingers and brought forth metal dusts and weighted them within his palms and slipped unto a sheepskin sack. And he oped up his lips and cried out unto his beast: " E-e-e-o-he! " And the beast onned slow unto the gate's arch.

And this was the oping time. And the one cast unto the gate's man the sack of metal dust, and he who watched at the gate's-way questioned: " Whither and whence? "

And the one answered: " From the sands of the Shur." †

And the gate's man spake: " This meaneth naught unto Rome! "

And the one said: " Yea, yea, so! But Rome shall know of what bindeth within this pack."

And the gate's man questioned more: " Whither goest thou? "

And the one made answering: " Up unto the palace places; for lo, he, the mighty, seeketh rugs afar."

And he spake the name " Tiberius." And this was the shutting of the lips of the gate's man.

* There is a lapse of about seven years between the ending of the first volume and the beginning of this, the second. In this interval Augustus has died and Tiberius has become the Roman emperor.

† A desert upon the eastern border of Egypt.

And the one plucked forth dates from the pack and eat thereof, and drained of the date's wine. And the camel sagged him on. The Jerusalem's men looked one unto the other as this thing shewed and spake them of the coming within of this one; for lo, upon his camel's cloths shewed the sign of him who stood King o'er kings.*

And the one went him up unto the market's place, and the camel knelt that he slip the packs. And lo, he called unto the water's man that he bring forth of his wares and give unto the camel's thirst. And he loosed the packs and stood silent that he wait the beast's rest.

And within the market's place sat a one whose beard shewed white. And he came out and his mantle shewed it long at the fore and less at the bended back's hem. And he swung his beard. And he went up unto the camel and looked unto the one who stood beside and raised up his hands and cried:

"Awoe! Awoe! A dark-skin cometh unto the market's place! Woe! Woe! Woe!"

And he went unto the bin and cast of cloths o'er his wares and sat him down beside, wailing loud.

And he who rode sat upon his folded legs at the camel's side and unbinded his head and shook sands from out the cloth's folds. And he loosed his sandals and shook loose the sand within and cast of drops o'er their soles. And spread forth his bared feet within the shade of the market's place, and set drops likewise o'er their skins. And he damped his headcloth and binded 'bout his heated brow, and took up a cloth and wetted it and bathed o'er his arms and breast.

And the men of the market's place cast their eyes upon this thing and spake one unto the other, saying:

"Look thee! Look thee! He who hath come from without the walls hath upon his camel's cloths the sign of the great one!"

And they came without the market's place and offered fruits that he buy. And he looked not upon them, but lay him beside the camel upon a camel's cloth and eat of dates.

And he who wailed looked upon this and swung his beard and wailed loud unto a one who abided with him within the bin's place; and spake:

"Seest thou? Samuel, my son, thy sire hath spoken unto thee, saying no good cometh from out the far lands unto Jerusalem. Look ye! he beareth not unto the Jews of his coin!"

And he laid his hand upon the arm of his son and made soft words unto him:

"Go thou unto this one, and shew of thy wares and offer unto him

* Caesar.

that he give but one rug of his pack in return. And doth he speak thee nay, say thou unto him: 'Rome is far. Who hath Rome's ears or yet Rome's eyes?' For a man's purse hath no tongue!'"

And Samuel went unto this one and bore his wares and spake even as Jacob had willed. And lo, no word sunk within the ears of him who ate of the fruits of other lands. And even amid the words of Samuel he rose and " hei-o-e-ed " unto the beast of the sand, and it shut up its eyes and stretched forth its neck and lifted its back upon its bended knees. And the binded strands of palms rattled where the loosing had been.

And the one cast of the stones of the fruit unto the street's-way, and took up the loosed ends of the strands and binded the pack unto the beast's back, and looked not upon the market's men, nor asked the road's-way unto the where he set unto.

And Jacob set up a wailing unto his brethren:

"Look ye! Look ye! Unto Jerusalem cometh the tongues of all lands! Yea, Gentiles, and yet the Romans; for look ye! these be of Rome, these men who have set even within the synagogue, the holy place of the Jews. Yea, unto the temples hath Rome come and laid ope her raiment, when lo, no Jew would do this thing! Nay, for even so holy doth the Jew set this place as the body of his bearer! Jehovah! Jehovah! E'en do they abide within the holy walls! Their holy blood, their king's blood even, be not fit for the holied place, and yet this thing hath been!'"

And they raised up their voices and spake: "Yea, yea, yea."

And Jacob cried aloud unto them, saying: "What manner of Jews stand them and leave these beasts of the pit to enter unto their holied?'"

And they spake loud: "Yea, yea, yea."

And there stood amid them a one who looked upon this thing and laughed. And the market's men, seeing this, spake unto him and bid that he tell unto them what set him at laugh o'er his brother's word. And he spake in answering:

"Lo, a one deep in age, whose locks shew white; yea, and whose hand beareth not e'en a blade, setteth him at the war of words. Yea, he setteth him up and swingeth his beard and setteth men low beneath words! Ha, ha, ha!'"

And they shook them " yea " and raised their voices against Jacob. And the one who laughed spake more, saying:

"Look ye! no blade setteth Jacob e'en so low as doth the loss of one mite."

And they bid him tell unto them of this one who had ridden unto the market's place upon a camel who bore the sign of Tiberius. And he held his hands high and spake:

"What! hath one ridden unto Jerusalem and emptied not his purse and yet not his tongue's full? Woe! Woe!"

And there came up unto the market's side a youth who bore a slain lamb, and this he offered unto Jacob that he buy. And lo, the men hushed their tongues and looked unto the buy and sell. And the lad shewed unto Jacob of the white fat within the lamb's flesh and the blood that he bore within a skin sack. And this was a sign that the lamb had been slain at the hand of a rabbi, for this sack was one that all knew as the sign. And Jacob took up the lamb's flesh between his fingers' grasp and smelled at their damp, and shook him nay, nay, nay, and spake of a blight that had fallen upon the young lambs, a smite upon the ear wherefrom sores sprung, and asked of the lad had the flocks of his sire shewed of this thing. And the lad spake "nay" and shewed the skin, that had been packed wet upon a stripped branch and lay upon his shoulder.

And Jacob took the blood's sack and looked within it, and spread forth his wares and spake not. And lo, the lad looked upon the litter of the shammed golds, and hung o'er their bright. And Jacob dipped his fingers within the blood sack and smeared upon the lamb's side and upon this spread filth. And lo, there shewed thereon, upon the slain lamb, a sore. And this was beneath the pit of the fore leg. And he set up a loud wail and shewed unto the market's men and spake that even among the Jews thieves stood.

And he shook the lad and cast unto him a sack of small bits of metals and cried loud that he should off and ne'er shew him unto the eyes of Jacob, or woe upon him!

And the lad started up and set upon the way that followed the camel man. And lo, the lad came upon this one, and looked unto the camel that strode him slow. And the one spake soft of words of a tongue the lad knew not. And the lad harked. And the one, hearing the thud of the bared feet turned and looked unto the lad, and his lips smiled and he reached forth his hand and spake in the tongue of the Jews, for he saw the lad was of the Jews.

"Hast thou then loosed thy tongue unto the Jew who waileth him? For lo, hast thou done this thing, thou shouldst know that such a Jew would pull at the teats of a she-goat until she gave forth blood! What hath he dealt unto thee?"

And the lad oped up his lips and spake: "Thou art from the far; why, then, should a young Jew speak unto thee his woes?"

And the one answered: " Jerusalem holdeth not wise ones that thou shouldst ope unto; for lo, Jew setteth against Jew. Yea, one sayeth that his brother liveth e'en though he die * and another speaketh this is folly! Yea, and Rome cometh unto the ministering and setteth up a warring wherein the three blades clatter! Yea, and when one brother loveth the other, or yet when Rome shutteth up her eyes unto the Jews, lo, there starteth up then a warring among the men one against the other o'er sheep, or yet gods, or yet their flesh! They dream dreams, and sleep sleeps and game days, and war them 'mid all the doing! Jerusalem! Ha, ha, ha! Where in Jerusalem doth a wise man dwell? "

And the lad spake: " There abideth amid Jerusalem no man who hath wisdom, but without the wall doth Panda bide, and Jerusalem seeketh his hills, whereon he setteth him at watch of sheep, even as she doth seek the wells for cool drink. Yea, and unto Panda doth Paul seek! Yea! " And he raised clenched hands unto the market's-way. " And yet before the sun sinketh behind the city's walls shall Panda cause Jacob to give forth the full for the sheep's price, e'en though he pluck it from out his beard! "

And the one who rode spake: " Sayest thou the man's name is Panda? Whence cometh he unto Jerusalem? "

And Paul made answer: " From the out-ways and far."

And the one spake: " U—m! And thou knowest him? "

And the lad cried: " Know Panda? All men know Panda. Yea, he draweth wisdom as from out a well's deep."

" And she? "

And the lad looked unto him and asked:

" She? Whom dost thou then know of Panda's women? "

And the one's lips shewed thin, and he spake: " She whose hair gleameth."

And Paul made answer: " Yea! Yea! Black as the crow's wing! "

And the one spake " nay." And Paul said: " There abideth not a one among the women who hath bright locks."

And the one spake: " Knowest thou among thy men a one who weaveth and whose name is called Nadab? "

And the lad made answering: " Amid the hill's place whereon Panda watcheth lieth Nadab."

And the one spake: " So? And where then hath the wares of Nadab abided them? "

And Paul answered: " Lo, hast thou ne'er heard of the rugs of Nadab? At the eve's hour they speak unto the dreams of folk."

* The Sadducees and Pharisees.

And they had come unto the wall's ope and the lad spake:

"Out upon the way doth Paul seek. The peace of Jehovah rest thee."

And he cast of a metal unto the gate's man and set him on.

And the camel went it upon its way unto the mighty one's palace. And Jerusalem had shut upon him who rode.

CHAPTER II

THE day whined on, and the streets lay tired beneath the trod of men. The doves upon the paves panted and spread their wings to droop, and dogs dropped froths from their oped jaws, and asses sweat, and men sweat, and the sun beat, and Jerusalem lay glistened of heats.

The sun hung long and crept slow, slow, o'er her walls to slip unto their o'erbase. For lo, he who knew Jerusalem knew not the sun's sink nor yet his rise save from up and o'er the wall unto the down and o'er.

And when the time had come unto the dark, lo, Jerusalem was loth to sleep. Without, the roadways shewed dark and creeped o'er of dark things that fled from out the heats within the walls unto the hill's places.

Amid the dark, at the ope of the east wall, shewed afar a taper's glow, and this was the taper within the hut of Joel. And a one sat upon the floor within upon a golded rug. And the taper shed gold upon its sheen, and lo, at the side of the one there stood a babe. And the soft voice of the one spake:

"Yea, hark thee! Seest thou this yellowed gold? Nadab, thy loved and mine, did coax the sun to set his wools, and this that gleameth is the strand of her whom Jerusalem hath swallowed up. And this, ah, this the dark, is the strand of thy mother, Nada. And this, seest thou? this chained thing, is the net of Aaron, lest he lone, Nadab sayeth. And this, this, seest thou? this whited thing, is the moon. See! sunk unto the half. And this, this, Panda loved, is the moon, risen! And this, seest thou? the whited dove, is thee, ahover 'bout the hut, long before thy coming!

"Go thou out from the door's ope and call and call thee loud, 'Nadab! Nadab!' and shew unto him the door standeth oped, that he come within. Shew unto him this thing, loved, and he shall see."

And the dark babe went unto the door's ope and cried unto the dark: "Nadab! Nadab!" And oped up his arms and shewed of the light. And Nada made the sign of silence, and they hung silent and listed. And the winds arose and sounded, and it sounded as the thudding of the racks and Nada spake: "Yea! Yea! He hath heard!"

And Nada pointed unto the stilled racks and smiled: "Yea, he setteth cross-legged and laugheth unto thee and me!"

And without there sounded the feet of them that sought, and the door oped and Paul came him within and hung unto the hand of Panda, whose beard hung and whose eyes deeped, and whose lips had prisoned of a smile, chained amid the seaming of his cheek.

And Nada looked wet-eyed unto him and spake: "From out Jerusalem hath woe sought thee, Panda?"

And Panda made answer: "Should Panda loose his woe, lo, would Panda be as one whose shadow had forsaken him! This, Nada love, is not woe. Nay, but the barting of Jacob, and thou knowest Jacob hath ne'er a measure rod for his brother's wares!

"Paul shall abide within this wall unto the morrow and Panda shall seek Jacob and the market's place and pluck out his beard one hair, then its brother, until he giveth full the measure. Yea, e'en now, Nada, Jacob knoweth this and woeth. Yet the tickle of gain shall ease his sleep unto the morrow. Bring forth sup, Nada."

And Panda oped up his arms and took within them the babe and sat upon the rug of Nadab and asked of the day. And Nada answered:

"Unto Jerusalem hath Hatte gone and hath ne'er returned, and Aaron even so. And Indra thou mayest hear at the grind of grain."

And Panda spake: "Where thinkest thou Hatte hath sought?"

"Panda, the lad sorroweth since the going of Caleb and Mary. Yea, and he seeketh the streets of Jerusalem and maketh words with Jews, and seeketh the Jew's words of their scripts, and knoweth the temple's priests. Yea, he sweareth unto the Jews he is of them and hath their blood."

And Panda spake: "Youth, Nada, youth hath sorrow as his pack. Yea, but joy he knoweth not."

And Nada held ope her arms unto the babe, Panda, that she take him from the arms of Panda, and smiled, to flash whited teeth and spake her:

"Panda, youth truly hath sorrow as his pack, but Nada dreameth dreams that she shall fill unto the pack of thy loved and mine."

And Panda smiled and spake: "Nay, nay, Nada. He who hath ne'er packed sorrow knoweth not the freeing of the weight; and this be joy. Upon this loved of thee and me Panda wisheth full weight of sorrow, lest the joy be lessened."

And he turned unto Paul, who waited sup, and Nada left unto his arms the babe and arose and brought forth that they eat. And Panda spake unto Paul, saying:

"Hast thou seen among the men of Jerusalem a one that speaketh unto the multitudes and calleth of his name John?"

And Paul spake: " Yea."

And Panda made words unto Paul and spake of the Jews and the coming of this one unto Jerusalem that he tell of the workings of a Jehovah that Jews list. And Paul told of the going of the market's men and the land's men * unto the still places within the hills that they hark. And Panda listed and spake:

" Lo, this man hath sought Jews that he fill them up of wisdoms, for he is a godly one, and lo, the Jews turn, e'en amid his words, and laugh them loud. Yea, e'en hath the hands of the Jews lain hold of him and set him upon the roads, e'en though he would stop that he tell unto the men of the city words of wisdom."

And Paul spake slow: " Panda, there cometh word from out Nazareth of a one who worketh Him 'mid woods and speaketh words that no man knoweth.† Yea, at the market's place, e'en this morn's hour, a one rode him upon a camel from out this land and spoke of this one and told of ones of Nazareth who had sought Him out and e'en though He shewed as a lad of young years the aged scribes sought Him and bade that He speak unto them."

And Panda spake: " What then doth Nazareth speak as the name that He beareth? "

And Paul answered: " Jesus," and told of the word among the people of visions and wisdoms. And Panda looked unto Paul and spake: " And thou hast spoken His name Jesus? "

And Paul made answering: " Yea," and told more; that among the Nazarenes who sought the one, abided many who knew the words He spoke and brought them forth unto Jerusalem, and these ones said that this Jesus spake not as the temple's men, but of sands and leaves, and made mighty walls of sand's grains, and forests deep of leaves.

And he told that among these men were two brothers who had of a flock, each one the half. And lo, smite‡ fell upon the one half of the flocks and the brothers fell wrathed one against the other that the half that shewed smite should be set unto the half and that the half that shewed whole be set unto the half. For lo, the one spake that the sick half was that of his brother and the whole his own. And they set each upon the other's flesh.§

And Nazareth saw this thing and bade that they seek this Jesus and tell Him of this.

And they sought Him out and lo, He stood at the stripping of

---

* Men of the land—farmers and gardeners.
† Beyond their understanding.
‡ Sickness.
§ Came to blows.

barks from off the woods. And they spake unto Him, and lo, He lifted not His eyes. And they cried out unto Him:

"What! listeth thou not unto thy brother's woe?"

And He made answering: "Yea, mine ear harketh, yet followeth this hand the Father's bidding."

And they told unto Him of the flocks and raised their voices one 'gainst the other. And He looked not upon them but left their words that they mingle in wrathing.

And they cried aloud, and He harkened but turned not.

And the brothers wearied of their wrath and spake one unto the other of the whole ones of the flocks, and shewed one unto the other that these scattered upon the fields e'en as they warred.

And they spake soft and sought more of the words of Jesus, and lo, He stopped and lay the woods by.

And they told that the airs spread forth His locks and His mantle blew and wrapped Him 'bout. And He raised up His hands and looked unto the fields and spake:

"Call thee unto thy sheep."

And they raised their voices and cried out the sheep's call, and lo, the sheep came unto them and hung 'bout their limbs. And Jesus oped up His arms and shewed this thing unto them and spake:

"Seest thou? Sheep know not one brother from the other. Go thou and do likewise; for lo, doth the sheep's lead go unto the rutted places, even so the flock.

"Alike them, thou sons of man, seek thee the fields and know ye one sheep be like unto another; even so men."

And they looked upon Him and He took up a lamb and held it unto Him and spake:

"Even as lambs come unto the fold and the shepherd ministereth unto them, so cometh woe unto thy brothers. Do thou then but turn the shepherd's staff unto the days of man, for lo, thy brother needeth not more of thy ministering than one of these, doest thou this in loving."

And they raised up their voices and spake: "Tell unto us of the wisdom, and where in the fields and the days of Nazareth a man may find wisdom and know wisdom."

And lo, He took up a bit of stone and dropped this within the pool, and spake:

"When man knoweth the all of this, man hath wisdom. Yea, for wisdom, like unto this stone's path, swalloweth up even its own course."

And Paul looked unto Panda and made questioning: "Panda, is this wisdom, or empty word?"

And Panda looked him far and spake: "Wisdom! Wisdom! Deep as a well's pit!"

And Paul said that John Baptiste * spake even as this, and when they of Jerusalem had with one accord spoken out crying "Messiah" unto him, he had said "Nay! Nay!" and made promising to them of the coming. And his words held unto the Jew's men what had been told that this coming was near upon them. But these Jews harkened not with emptied hearts but held them full of temple's words. And Panda spake:

"Yea, the fatted temples have filled up the Jews with fatted words that shrinketh their hearts e'en as the fasting shrinketh flesh. Paul, Jerusalem's temples fill ye not, nor yet Panda. Sit ye, that we break bread."

And they sat them there, and Nada brought forth that they eat more.

And it was the late hour and dark sheltered them, and the eve hung long, and they spoke among them of their days; of flocks, of greens, of Jews, of Rome, and of the land of Panda. And night fell, and they bided within the walls and slept.

* "See that ye speak it Bap-teest," directed Patience.

CHAPTER III

And the days sped unto a score and one, and Jerusalem made it ready for the Passover. And among them Rome stood.

The bins of the market's place shewed empty of fruits or yet meats, but Jews brought forth wares that no man might eat.

And it was at the morn, and Jacob sat upon his folded legs and counted of metal's coin from out a sack, and rubbed of them upon his palm's flesh.

And there came unto him a one not of the Jews, and this one bore of a pack and spake words unto Jacob, saying:

" Thou Jew, within thy wares hast thou one armlet or one ankle ring that be of pured copper or yet gold? "

And Jacob set his eyes up unto the white and spake that no man might know, so wrought were the wares of Jacob.

And the one stood close unto the ear of Jacob and spake:

" What wouldst thou give unto Rome for the pure gold? "

And Jacob wailed that Jerusalem dealt unto the purse of Jacob less than the grain's buy for breads.

And up unto the market's side came a one who looked upon this Rome's man and listed unto the bart, and he stood tall and his arms gleamed.

And Jacob spake: " What hast Rome that she would offer unto Jerusalem? For lo, doth Rome ever take from out the Jew's very mouth and give not unto his belly! "

And the one of Rome took up the pack. And the one who watched looked upon this thing. And the one oped the pack and shewed the gleam of pure gold. And Jacob raised up his hands and wailed and wept, and reached forth.

And lo, the one who watched raised up his arm, swift, and the blade gleamed and fell upon the one of Rome, and he lay him low.

And the one who watched took up the pack and sped out, and on, and past the multitudes wherein he melted unto a naught.

And the blade shewed not within the wound of the smitten one, but drops shewed upon the speeder's way. And the long limbs sped out and past the temple's place and up unto the east way. And the one who sped cast unto the gate's man and sped without.

And lo, he stopped within the thicks and reached within the pack and brought forth the gold, and it hung soft and swayed. And the one spake:

"Rome, thou hast paid! Theia, Hatte knoweth thy gold!"

And he sunk, and lay the locks up unto his face, and brought forth the blade and wiped the blood upon the locks. And his hands shook and he spake:

"Of this shall Hatte weave a scourge, knotted of gold. Yea, Hatte shall seek the fields and hark unto John, who telleth of gods!"

And his lips spread thin, and he set unto the weaving, and he spake:

"Yea, Hatte shall lay upon him the scourge! Gods! Rome hath eaten the gods of earth! Yea, and John's tongue hath beset of devils! Let Rome deal and Hatte shall cut Rome with this gold! The flesh of woman hath set of hell, for lo, hath Rome's women set this gold free!"

And he brought his fingers shut unto the cut of the nails and spake:

"Even as he holdeth tight the gold, Hatte shall bind this 'bout the neck of Rome's woman unto the cutting off of the breath!"

And he sat long lone and looked him far, and he breathed out the words amid the laugh of hate:

"He of the hills told unto Hatte of the sire within the temple, and called Him the brother of His flesh. Ha, ha! Lies! Lies!"

And he spake the name "Mary," and looked upon the gold locks, and his lips spake more:

"Caleb, the broken, hath put of the bits one unto the other, so, and Rome called his name Flavius, and swallowed her."

And his lips spake a curse, and this was in the tongue of the Hebrews. And he spake loud these words and sought him up on the hill's-way.

And the fields lay stilled, and the sheep crept their curves, and Hatte looked upon this and still his fingers wove of strands.

And he went up unto the high place whereon, upon a stone's flat, lay Aaron, asleep. And Hatte touched his flesh, and Aaron sprung up and cast about his neck his arms and embraced him, and laughed of joy.

And Hatte's eyes shewed sorrowing. And Aaron, seeing this, cast his net and brought forth leaves and stones, and laughed and bore them unto him. And Hatte's smile crept slow, and he spake unto dulled ears:

"Unto Hatte, stones. 'Tis fitting!" And he stretched forth his hands unto Aaron and took the stones therefrom and smiled. And Aaron sunk, and he lay him down at the side of him. And out from the dumbed drank he of comforting.

And he spake words unto the ears that heard not, and told the all aloud. And Aaron laughed, and Hatte looked unto the empty of Aaron and spake:

"Unto Panda Hatte goeth and findeth the full well. Unto Aaron Hatte cometh and he may weep the rains unto his filling."

And he arose and took up the sheep's staff and the hand of Aaron and they went them unto the hill's curve and sent the sheep's call, and they came forth from the by-wayed places unto the fold.

And the hour hung late, and the red sun set the greened hills browned, and the sheep's wool gleamed red-tipped, and they swept before them as they came slow. And they came unto a watered place, and the sheep stood within this, and they waited them.

And Aaron's laugh stained the still. And Hatte's eyes looked far, and the scourge hung knotted within his hand, and he reached forth unto a thorn's bush and broke therefrom a branch and upon this binded the golded scourge. And he cut the airs about and his laugh bit in hating.

And Aaron looked unto the strands bounded upon the thorn's branch and smiled up unto Hatte and shewed unto him the bright that gleamed as the sun's rays glinted them. And he reached within his mantle and took therefrom bits of bright metals.

And Hatte looked unto this thing and shewed unto Aaron his wrath, and took within his hands the bits and cut Aaron o'er the flesh at the shoulder. And Aaron stopped and his breath came hard, and his bosom heaved and he looked unto Hatte and waited him long. And lo, unto the eyes of Hatte he looked and his lips broke unto a smile, and his laugh sounded out, and he held forth his arms and came unto the side of Hatte and laid them about him. And he took up his nets and offered unto him, and Hatte took him within his arms and held him close and spake:

"Emptied nets earth offereth! 'Tis well."

And the sheep had drunk and crept scattered o'er the up of the far hill; and Hatte pointed unto this thing and made that they set upon their ways.

And lo, the eve hung late, and late had crept unto the dimming of the earth, and behold, upon the east sky the eve's star gleamed. And the clouds arose at the west way, and Hatte looked unto the star's beard that streamed the sky.

And he turned unto the west and looked him unto the clouds that rose, and stood long, and long looked so. And within his one hand he held the scourge, and within the other the shepherd's staff. And he looked unto the one and then unto the other and long looked he so. And behold, he gave unto the hand of Aaron the shepherd's staff, saying:

"Unto the fool the earth giveth power; unto the wise the scourge. 'Tis well."

And he set upon his way. And Aaron chided the sheep and dragged within his free hand the nets. And afar the scent of the burned dusts of far lands scented faint unto there, and within the deep gray shone a taper's glow. And they went unto this thing. And Aaron laughed upon his way, and Hatte stepped slow, his lips shut.

And they came unto the water's place wherefrom the hut of Joel took of waters, and beside the welled place stood Indra.

And lo, she stood beside the well's place and upon her head the water skin, and she waited the coming of Hatte unto the side of the well. And Hatte came slow and the scourge hung at his side. And Indra saw this thing, and spake unto Hatte, saying:

"Eve hath hung. Scentest thou the myrrh's dusts? Nada hath set upon the rugs, and the babe hath called unto the dark that Nadab hear."

And Hatte spake: "Indra, who is this Allah? What hath beset Panda, or yet Nada, that they set smokes that he seeth the hut and come unto it? Indra, Jerusalem hath beset its street's-ways of gods, and all men who enter of the walls bear upon their backs their gods!"

And Indra said: "Panda, Hatte, hath wisdom. Hast thou then ne'er learned this thing, that ye know that Panda knoweth a god who harketh and calleth his name Allah?"

And she took from off her head the water's skin and set it at the well's side, and leaned her 'gainst the stones and looked far and spake more:

"This morn's hour, Hatte, Panda and thy Indra sought the market's place and there sounded therein much word. And they told of one who had been smitten at the bin of Jacob, and they called this one Caelius. And a one came him from out the Rome's hall * and asked of the market's men who had lain upon this one the smite. And no man knew. Jacob had wept o'er the golds and set his eyes dimmed.

"And this one who had come from out the Rome's place knew not thy Panda nor yet thine Indra, but spake loud so that their ears took within the words.

"And they told that Caelius had within the Rome's walls given of himself unto a one, a woman, who lieth within the pits. The Rome's men who set them o'er the pitted ones, told, within their cups, of this

* The palace.

thing, and this word hath gone out unto Jerusalem that the woman had set free her locks from off her head and given unto the hand of Caelius and bid that he seek Jacob and offer unto him. And they spake words saying that the Rome's men believe of Caelius that he had lended of his hand unto the freeing of this woman, and set that he sell unto Jacob these locks and bear back the barting of it."

And Hatte lay his hand upon the flesh of Indra and looked him unto the deep of her eyes and spake upon breath that came panted:

"Indra speakest thou this man's name 'Caelius,' and sayest thou he lended of his hand unto the woman of the pit? What name did these men speak that this woman beareth?"

And Indra spake her: "Hatte, they spake no name, but spake of 'her of the pits.' Yea, Indra telleth unto thee this truly."

And Hatte took up the scourge and flung it wide upon the airs and smote of his own flesh and cried:

"Hatte, Hatte, hath lain smite upon one who hath lended of his love unto Theia!"

And he sunk him upon the sod, and Indra set her low o'er him and lay her hand upon his locks and spake:

"Hatte, Hatte, come thou unto Panda; for lo, Panda lendeth unto the emptied, ever."

And they arose and looked them unto the flocks that had hung about the water's place, and Aaron sat laughing and casting within the well's deep the nets. And Hatte arose, and Indra took up the skin sack and set it upon her head. And lo, it was dark, and the taper glowed within the hut of Joel. And Indra held unto the hand of Hatte, and they went upon their ways. And the sheep followed e'en through the dark.

And they came up unto the door's ope of the hut of Joel, and lo, Panda came him unto the ope and bade that they come within. And Nada had set the sup that they might eat. And Hatte stooped, and Nada took from the hand of Indra the water sack and went within. And Hatte sunk him, his lips shut, unto the rug's-cast, and looked him not unto the sup. And Aaron came within and bore of a young lamb and lay it beside him and sat that he eat.

And behold, the eyes of Panda looked unto Hatte and saw that that shewed within his eyes. And he went unto him and sat beside the place where he had sunk and lay his hand upon the scourge, and took it up, and spake not. And Hatte's hand stole unto the hand of Panda, and he looked unto Panda's eyes and oped up his lips and spake:

"Panda, woe is upon us! for Hatte's hand hath smitten and felled his own sheep!"

And Panda spake: " Hatte, thou speakest not that that thy Panda knoweth."

And Hatte spake: " No more, Panda, doth Hatte know; for lo, this hand doth that that biddeth and he knoweth not the why."

And he spread forth his hands and, lo, the scourge fell. And Panda took it up from whence it had fallen and his eyes pierced the eyes of Hatte, and Hatte hid his face. And Panda spake:

" Hatte, he who hath emptied his water sack may then fill it up of the fresh drops."

And Hatte spake: " Panda, 'tis not meet that Nada hark, nor yet Indra know."

And Panda said: " Wait thou then their sleeping."

And he went unto the sup. And Hatte held within his hand the scourge, and his eyes shed drops, and he spake not. And Indra, e'en though her hands shewed busied and her head turned not unto Hatte, still the long lashes hung o'er eyes that gleamed and knew of all.

And when they had eaten of that that had been set, lo, Nada arose and bore the sleeping babe within unto the sleep-rugs. And Indra tarried within the shadows. And Aaron wearied and slept, the lamb within his arms.

And Panda saw that this was the time wherein he should seek Hatte and minister unto him. And he went up unto the lad's side and oped up his arms and lay them about him and said:

" Hatte, long hast thou forgot the arms of Panda! Come thou unto them. Art thou strong? "

And Hatte stood tall and his cheeks burned and he spake: " Panda, play hath stripped from off Hatte even as his loin's-cloth hath given place unto a mantle."

And he took up the scourge and held it forth.

" Look thou upon this, Panda! Rome hath done this thing! "

And Panda knew not that that Hatte spake and bade that he tell of all. And Hatte oped up his heart and told of the market's place and what had been. And Panda spake:

" Hatte, no man may wrest from Rome's breasts the torn flesh, nor yet the sacrifices Rome holdeth that she feed unto them. Nay, nay. Man, then, shall play of a game with Rome. Lo, shall he wait; for Rome, like unto her fair-fleshed sons and daughters, knoweth not what the waiting meaneth.

" Thou shalt know, Hatte, that the tides hold all wisdom, and man then hath naught to do save wait that he read the full of wisdom from the oping tides.

"Yea, and Rome's beasts ne'er destroy the all; for lo, when they eat the flesh, the bone remaineth. So, then, the bone shall be for any man who claimeth it. Wait thee! Wait thee, and Rome shall give forth. For lo, this beast that holdeth her careth naught for bones, but eateth flesh, full and fair. Wait thee! Wait thee!"

And Indra came forth from the dark place and went unto Panda and Hatte and oped her lips, saying:

"Whom hath Rome claimed? This pit's woman sicketh. The market's men told this thing. Yea and more, it seemeth that she hath that that Rome would have. And one Phaeton, who hath offered of his hand unto Flavius and made that Rome take him unto her, knoweth of this that she hath."

And Hatte held unto the flesh of Panda and Indra spake more, saying:

"This one of Rome hath told unto the filling of the ears of Rome's men, and this man, Caelius, told unto ones at the market's place, e'en as they bore him unto the within that the sun beat not upon him, that these of Rome bade this pit's woman that she come unto them and set words unto her that she tell of this that she hath, that they might take of it. And more; that e'en though sick hath set her limbs weakened, lo, she boundeth up and danceth and laugheth unto them, and they deem that she hath been beset of an evil one, and spake that she knoweth not that that sheweth unto her.

"And these men spake a name unto her, and this name soundeth much as the mighty's name. And lo, she looketh with eyes that see not, and harketh with ears that hear not, and crieth out of the palms and the sands and spices. And the men laugh."

And Hatte sprung him unto the throat of Indra and cried aloud: "Stop thou, lest this hand stop thee ever!"

And he threw Indra upon the flags and took up the scourge and sped through the ope of the hut unto the dark. And lo, his voice cried out in wailing, and the dark covered him.

And Panda set his hand unto Indra and his eyes shewed sorrowing, and he spake:

"Indra, thy lips set wounds even as a steeled blade. Go thou!"

And Panda turned, and his head hung. And he set the sign unto the East and went without, and his voice cried out unto the dark. For lo, the moon still hung beneath the earth and no sound made answering, save afar the bleat of a lamb, or the barking of the dogs within the walls of Jerusalem.

And Panda sought till wearied and set upon the way unto the hut, and lo, he came unto it and Nada stood without awaiting him. And he came unto her and Nada spake:

"Woes, Panda, more of woes?"

And Panda answered: "Yea, for lo, the ewe who sought the stoned place, brought forth, and lo, the shepherd sought within the dark that he find this lamb. And lo, he took it up and behold, the ewe is lost and the lamb wandereth! And the shepherd staff the days of man have snapped, and still unto the shepherd's heart the lamb is the lamb of the loved ewe, and he heareth the lamb's call within the dark! Nada, unto the days of the she-lion and the days of the lion hath this god sent a lamb for to bed with beasts!"

And Nada spake: "Come then within, Panda, and call thou unto Nadab that he send a dream."

And within the night set they upon the dream-rug, and unto the new day dreamed on.

CHAPTER IV

THE light shewed wets, and rains swept that chilled. And the market's places crept with men, even as an ant's hill when waters beset it.

And Ezra, who sat within his fruit bin, looked unto the daughter of his flesh, Reba, who sat, casting of palms upon the damped airs that flies swarm not. And without stood the men of Rome, and they laughed among them and made words that the Jews hear, and spake:

"Lo, these Jews await a King! Yea, no Jew hath precious stuff but that he waiteth that he give unto this one!"

And they laughed loud and spake of John who set the ears of Jews full of promising. And they spread forth their hands unto the Jew's places and laughed:

"Look! Look! Within this shall a king be brought forth!"

And they spake more, and laughed o'er the words that had come from out Bethlehem, and said that this was indeed a truth; for lo, a Jew had been brought forth within the asses' bed. And they smote one the other and bended o'er of laughter and cried out:

"A king o'er asses!"

And Reba's hands shook, and she spake unto Ezra, saying: "Ezra, thy daughter's ears take in the bite of Rome's words."

And Ezra said: "Harken not, O thou my flesh! Behold, the prophets wrote that that all Jews know. Rome's people eat of swine, and he who eateth swine eateth that that filtheth them."

And his beard hung low upon his breast, and he spake unto the Rome's men: "The peace of Jehovah be upon thee!"

And they spat upon his fruits, and made loud words, saying:

"Behold, Jerusalem hath been beset of locusts and desert's fleas! And Jerusalem's men fill upon this!"

And they laughed, and went them unto the temple's steps and stood upon their wet, and cried out of the king born of asses, and cast stones up unto the temple's doors.

And behold, from out the market's places swept Jews, and beneath beards gleamed steels, and blades cut the air. And the Rome's men bared their blades, and the airs rocked with cries of mock prayers from Rome's lips.

And Ezra swept up upon a Rome's man and raised his blade and cried: " He who blasphemeth the temple payeth with his tongue! "

And he took the Rome's man's head within his bared hands and bended it back unto the very snapping of the neck, and behold, the hands of the Rome's man fell limp, and Ezra took his blade and oped the lips of the Rome's man and cut out his tongue.

And the Rome's men lay their hands upon him and tore his beard. And he held the tongue high and laughed and spake:

" Even as this man hath given up his tongue, so shall Rome's tongue be stilled! "

And they bore him unto the earth, and one among them sped unto the market's place and brought forth the flesh of him, Reba. And behold they shewed this unto him. And one among them sped his blade and she fell. And from off her face he tore the cloth, and took up her hair and cut it with the blade of him, and bore it unto Ezra and shewed it unto him and bore the body of the smitten one unto him that he see this. And lo, Ezra cried out, and they stopped his words with his own blood.

And one among the Rome's men, seeing a Jew lad of young years, took him up and cut ope his bowels, and tore them loose and cast unto the paves that men trod upon them.

And among the Rome's men there stood one, tall and strong o'er his brothers, and this one bore a babe that had lain within its mother's arms within the cool of the temple's shade; for lo, the sun had crept o'er the wets and set them heated and slimed. And he took this babe within his hands and raised it high and cast it unto the stones.

And behold, from out the Jews sped a one whose long limbs shone, and he sprung upon the neck of this one and sunk within its curve a thin blade. And the one fell. And the men of Rome cried out: " Phethon! " And he turned the blade within the wound. And they laid hold of him, and one among them laid his cheek ope and he fell; and they laughed.

And behold, the temple's steps shone red-stained, and the pools shewed red, and limp lay the flesh that had been of the Jews, and limp the flesh that had been of Rome, and neither knew his brother.

And the Jews scattered unto the dark of the street's wind. And Rome stood o'er.

And long the time hung unto the creep of dark, and no man shewed within the market's place. No man offered of wares save him who had forsaken not his bin, nor did the hand of Jerusalem take up its dead. And Rome looked not upon them, but took up the flesh of Rome.

And when the time had come and Rome had turned from the temple's place and looked not upon the temple but unto the place of Rome, behold, a one stirred and arose slow, and like unto a young kid this one bounded o'er the steps and down the winded ways of Jerusalem. And lo, his path shewed his going, marked of red. And within a narrowed place he came upon a pool that had lain within the shadow, and he stopped and leaned him o'er and bathed of his wound. And his swelled lips laughed.

"And they spake his name Phethon! Ha, ha, ha! The God of Theia hath sped this hand!"

And at the deep of the water pool, lo, his hand came unto that which he brought forth, and this was a blade, such as the Rome's men shewed unto Jerusalem. And Hatte slipped his fingers o'er its steel and knew this thing, and spat upon it, and set it beneath his mantle and spake aloud:

"Rome turneth her blade unto her own breast, even in the hand of Hatte."

And he swayed, and his eyes looked unto the dark and he cried aloud: "Jehovah! Jehovah! The slaying!"

And at the east way, lo, the Rome's man knew not his going therefrom. Like unto a shadow shape crept he swift, and sped and sped and sped, unto the way unto the hills. And his voice sounded within the dark: "Not unto Panda! Nay, unto the hills and the sheep!"

And he came unto the folds and sunk upon the sod and beat his hands upon the stones. And lo, a calm came upon him, and he turned his eyes unto the way unto Bethlehem, and behold, one star shewed.

And he arose and took forth the Rome's blade and raised it high and cried:

"He shall come! Theia, where in thy words of promising hath the fulfilment hid?"

And behold, at the late hour, when dark came heavy upon the lands, there sounded upon the hill's place the step of a one, and the sound of the drag of cloths upon the earth. And there came from out the dark one who laughed upon his way. And he came unto the spot where Hatte lay, and Hatte sprung up swift and lay hands upon this one, and lo, the one laughed and set his arms 'bout the flesh of Hatte. And Hatte cried out and flung wide his arms and took the one within them, and sobbed and cried out amid his tears:

"Lo, there cometh an empty one unto Hatte that he cast his woes thereon. Yea, and Hatte sayeth him so shall earth be empty, empty of mercies unto Hatte's woes."

And Aaron looked unto Hatte's woeing and spake out sounds that made naughts, and pointed him unto the taper's light that gleamed afar. And Hatte looked unto this and shook him "nay." And Aaron laughed and took within his arms the body of Hatte and bore him swift unto the light's glow. And the voice of Hatte cried out against this thing, but the ears of Aaron took this not in. And behold, the door shewed oped, and the lights streamed far into the dark, and within the ope shewed the form of Panda. And behold, he held his hands high and cried him loud:

"Unto thee, Hatte, Panda calleth him! Yea, that thine ears hark; for lo, hath Panda sung his sheep's call unto the hills, and no sheep heard thereof!"

And Aaron sped within and cast the form of Hatte upon the rug's-cast, and shewed unto Panda his woeing. And lo, Hatte hid his face within the dark and looked not unto the eyes of Panda.

And Hatte's lips oped and he stood him up and raised his eyes unto the sorried face of Panda, and held ope his arms and cried out:

"Panda, Hatte, Hatte hath loosed his hand at his heart's bidding and knoweth not the whyfore! Yea, Panda, look unto this hand, for lo, it hath sunk within the flesh of Rome the blade of a Jew! Panda, where in this heart doth this bidding dwell? For like unto a mighty voice speaketh the bidding unto it! Like unto a mighty voice dinneth this ear, and like unto a stream of the king's robe's dye staineth o'er these eyes! For lo, Hatte seeth not, yet his hand doeth!"

And Indra stepped from within and harked, and Hatte turned unto her coming and spake:

"Panda, shut thy household unto all save Aaron, who harketh not, and thee who harketh but stoppeth word."

And Panda spake unto Indra: "Indra, thy tongue hath set woe and thou hast oped wounds that still run red. Set thou away. Yea, seek thou Nada and the babe and wait the bidding of Panda."

And Indra did this thing.

And behold, Hatte loosed his tongue and cried out unto Panda's listing: "Panda, the earth runneth red. Yea, Jerusalem hath shed her blood. Yea, and Rome hath shed her blood. Yea, and ones of far lands did shed their blood. Yea, and this, Panda, o'er gods! gods! gods! And Theia spaketh there be but One, a God o'er gods. And He leaveth this thing to be!"

And Panda looked unto the glistened eye of Hatte and took the fevered hand and laid it within his cooled grasp and spake soft.

"Hatte, Hatte, look thou unto the city's wall. Look thou unto the

city's builded walls within. Look thou unto the flags that mark the
road's-ways. Look thou unto this. This is the setting of man. Yea,
look thou unto the temple. This is the setting of man. Look unto
the slaying of the sacrifices. This is the setting of man. Yea, but
wait thee the rising of the morrow's sun. This, Hatte, is the setting of
one God!"

And Hatte stood silent and looked afar, e'en through the hut's walls.
And Panda's voice soothed on:

"Look thou, Hatte, unto this sign. Past the touch of man, fitting
sign for such a God."

And Hatte stood, still silenced, and Panda stopped his word and
waited him. And Hatte sunk unto the rug's-cast and cast his head upon
his clasped hands. And Panda waited him, and the eve sped on and lo,
amid the waiting, Aaron laughed. And the laugh lay e'en as a lash
upon Hatte, and he started up and cried aloud:

"Panda, this breast shall burst ope! This heart shall leap forth
streamed of this body's blood for man to trod upon! These hands
shall split ope Rome! For Rome holdeth her, Theia! Panda, hath
no man yet an ear that he hark unto this, the cry of the loned? For e'en
when the night wrappeth Jerusalem and the out-wall vanisheth and no
man sheweth upon the earth's paths without, or yet within the city,
when the God hath emptied earth, Hatte heareth, clear, yea, like unto a
steeled blade, the voice of her cry out: ' Hatte! Hatte! He shall come!'
Yea, and the night's hours are filled with dreams, dreams that come
like unto mighty hosts, and behold, upon these dream-fields and roadways the mighty stalk!

"Yea, e'en he who setteth o'er Jerusalem and milcheth the she-
goats that Rome be fed; he that shutteth his eyes unto the house of
Jad, wherein, e'en though a Jew abideth, still this Jew holdeth a
trued blade unto Rome. Yea, he shutteth up his eyes and taketh from
out this Jew's household his fairest flower, the daughter of his flesh.
He whom Hatte knoweth not * save in dreaming. Yea, he setteth him
upon a high place, and behold, beneath the high place there sheweth unto
the eyes of Hatte the naked flesh of men, wherein the blades of Rome
have sunk! Simeon limpeth and looketh unto him, and behold, from
the oped bosoms of the naked ones streameth scarlet, and the royal
diadem sheweth clothed of its scarlet. And behold, this one's mouth
openeth and from out the lips there creepeth a serpent, and it archeth
out and spreadeth forth its tongue and striketh, and lo, it smiteth the
one o'er the heart!

* Tiberius.

"And behold, within his hands gleameth the mighty scepter, the ball, and upon his brow gleameth the circlet, wound of laurels. And the ball shrinketh unto a rotted fig, and the circlet gleameth hot of fires, and the laurels sear and the dusts fall within the one's eyes and he standeth blinded!

"And behold, before him, then, there seemeth a one to stand—and, Panda, this one is Hatte! And within his hand a scourge of gold! And then, and then—the slaying! the slaying!"

And he sped without. And Aaron took up his nets and sped after.

CHAPTER V

AND it came to pass that the nights swept o'er the lands unto the one and four, and Jerusalem had wept bloods and dried them up. And the market's men spake in whisperings of what set their land. And in the night's hours, within the Jew's walls, sacrifices were made, and within the temples peace offerings offered up.

Yet the blade of hate hid beneath the Jew's mantles and Rome stalked white-legged o'er Jerusalem.

And within the Rome's places Rome made words for the confounding of the Jews, and behold, within the Jew's walls the Jews set at the untying of the nets of confoundment.

And the priests within the temple hid e'en the inner vestments, that Rome know not the sanctuary. And within the inner place at the night's hours, lo, the priests stripped save of the holied vestments and lay beside the ark,* that no man defile. And that no man sleep, lo, one chanted him loud.

And Jerusalem knew the temple tottered, and feared the bursting of the walls and the freeing of her god from out the temple place.

And Rome sat and smiled, for lo, Rome had gods for the tipping of their every blade! For Rome looked unto the heaven's father, Jupiter, for the up-going of the sun and the swing of the moon, and knew not of a god o'er Jews.

And among the men of Rome at the Rome's place, wherein the mighty-seat stood upon the stones of the Jews, behold, there spake one unto another. The one shewed sick and his brother spake his name ' Caelius.' And Caelius called his brother's name ' Phaeton.' And they spake of what Rome dealt unto the Jews. And Caelius shewed unto Phaeton the wound wherein a blade had sunk and spake of the hate of Jews. And Phaeton looked upon this thing, and lo, the voice of Caelius worded on:

" Phaeton, thou knowest, thou knowest where in this flesh Rome hath sunk a blade that smiteth sorer than this the Jew hath sped."

And Phaeton shook him " yea," and bade that Caelius tell unto him of this wound. And Caelius oped his lips and spake:

* This reference is explained in a later passage.

" Thou knowest, Phaeton, the silent one of the pits. What man of Rome, or yet of any land, hath gain by this thing? "

And Phaeton looked unto the inner places and bowed and set his voice low and spake:

" Much word do Rome's men speak of this thing. Yea, and one rode from out Rome who hath oped the ears of the Rome's ones within Jerusalem at what he beareth."

And Caelius looked him frighted and waited the word of Phaeton. And he spake more, saying:

" This one, Ahmud Hassan, bore rugs from out the lands of Tiberius, and his lips oped not save unto the ear of the mighty. Yea, but eunuch's ears take in! "

And Caelius spake: " Yea, yea."

And Phaeton told of what had come from out the slaves' places and told of a Jew, Paul, who had told of a wise man called Panda who lived without the walls.

And behold, this Ahmud Hassan spake that the woman of this man, Panda, shewed black-locked, and he spake unto the mighty one a name, but this one knew not of such. And behold, there came unto the ears of this one, who rode from out Rome's place with the bidding of Rome's mighty, words that told of a woman who had slain the flesh of Alexis. And they told that her locks hung long, and this one sought out the mighty one and spake of this thing, and behold, the mighty one knew not of such a one and wearied of the word and said:

" Within the pits there sheweth the offcast of Jerusalem, and the intake of Rome beneath the hands of Rome's men, but not of this hand. So, then, should a man sleep not o'er his brother's doing? "

And this one, Ahmud, told unto the mighty's ear that he who sat Rome and rode upon her back, even as the men of the citadel rode upon the pack ass, sought word of such a one, for lo, the hand of this woman held a blade that Rome would wrest therefrom. And the mighty one spake:

" Then shall Rome's pits belch forth their filling that thou mayest look upon the filth and take therefrom."

And the mighty one asked: " Hath this maid much of beauty? "

And he rubbed his hands one upon the other.

And Ahmud Hassan shook: " Yea. Yea. Youth and beauty."

And Phaeton looked unto the strained eyes of Caelius and he spake: " At this day's high sun the pit's ope! "

And Caelius looked unto the sky's arch, and behold, the sun stood at the hang o'er the city, and ones of Rome set up a beat upon the

metals of shields. And Phaeton stood him up and Caelius took up his
blade and they set them step unto step. And at the stoned step of the
walled place, lo, their brothers came unto them, and Caelius took up the
lead and went unto the pit's opes.

And behold, the sun gleamed, and they threw ope the pits and
called within. And the wailing of the sick broke upon the airs. And one
came from within, bended much, and behold, his skin gleamed sores and
the beard hung matted and the hair grown unto it. And he fell upon
his face at the blind of the sun's light. And there came forth a one who
tore at the airs and shrieked out a name * that knew no flesh. And the
flesh hung even as a camel's skin, haired and filthed.

And they came forth unto the score. And a one came who flung ope
his mantle and shewed the white flesh, the fall flesh.† And behold,
the Rome's men upped the blade and slew him. And among them
shewed not a one who looked even as a woman.

And they laughed upon this, and the men cast word one unto the
other that e'en the pit's beasts should fall short of feed.

And these they swept before the mighty-seat. And Caelius stepped
him beside a one who bended, whose locks shewed matted, whose arms
gleamed naught save bone; and the lips drew them o'er the arched teeth,
and the eyes shewed o'erbright, and the cheek sunk deep, deep, drawn
in lines that spelled waiting.

And Caelius moved his lips and soft words fell, and he shewed his
hands empty. And the voice of this one cracked like unto the dried
parched crackling of branch against branch at dry season, and spake
hollowed:

"Not e'en a Jew to buy gold? And no man shewed unto thee? Did
no man look upon this?"

And Caelius shewed the wound and told of the Jew who smote.
And the eyes started and the lips smiled and the voice crackled laugh.
And Caelius wept, and took from out his mantle metals and laid within
the thinned hand and spake: "The fill of Rome's men ‡ for their emptying."

And Theia, for this was Theia, cast the metals unto the stones and
wiped upon the filthed mantle, crying out:

"Metals! Metals! Of such doth Rome build up her gods!"

And she spat upon the bits and whispered: "Who setteth o'er
Rome?"

And Caelius spake slow: "Tiberius."

---

* The name of one dead.   † The leprosy.
‡ A soldier's pay for a soldier's work.

And lo, she fell even as one dead. And the Rome's men laughed. And Caelius looked unto them, and his eyes pierced unto Phaeton, and behold, Phaeton came him forth and they bore her up. And the pit's ones wailed on, and Caelius spake:

" E'en though this breast burn as fires, no man shall know. Phaeton, as thou lovest me, cast this one unto the stones, that they laugh and know not."

And Phaeton took the weaked one and went within among the wailing ones.

And Ahmud Hassan sat at the right hand of the mighty one, and behold, they brought them up before the mighty-seat the one the other and on.* And the mighty one laughed and smote upon the back of Ahmud, and amid his laugh cried out:

" Thinkest thou that Rome casteth that that holdeth worth unto the pits? Nay, Rome filleth empty with empty! "

And the eyes of Ahmud Hassan looked upon the score of the pit's ones and rested them not upon a one. And behold, Phaeton stood and bore up the form of Theia, and he looked upon this and started. And Phaeton cast her upon the stones. And Ahmud Hassan arose and went unto the spot and kicked the flesh and spake: " Jew flesh sheweth white! "

And he looked upon the face of Theia, and the locks hung matted o'er the brow, and filthed. And Ahmud Hassan looked long and spake unto the one who lay:

" Ope up, thou aged! What hath Rome dealt thee? "

And the one turned eyes that saw not and laughed, laughed, laughed. And she looked unto Ahmud Hassan and spake:

" What hast thou of Jews? See! See! " and she tore out the locks and cast unto him. " Take thou this! 'Tis all! all! all! "

And Ahmud Hassan, at the wording of her tongue, looked unto the mighty one and spake: " This one knoweth Rome! "

And he went up unto the mighty-seat and spake soft unto the listing of the mighty one, and behold, the sick ones sunk, one, then the other, and they that stood wailed and looked empty-eyed unto the mighty one, who looked not their filling. And Theia sat, her matted locks hung o'er the thin face and claw hands locked within their mat. And the eyes shot e'en as the lightnings of the young spring, that flasheth and stoppeth not but setteth here and setteth there and yon. And Caelius looked not upon this but upon the stones, and Phaeton laughed and shook of her bended body.

* One after another.

And Ahmud Hassan came forth unto her and spake: "What land hast thou?"

And the tongue of Theia made no answering, and he spake once more: "What land hast thou?" And behold, Theia raised her up and stood, even as a bended bow, and laughed and laughed and shewed of the filth upon her flesh and upon the mantle and spake:

"Land? Land? But dust of Jerusalem hath Rome dealt unto me!"

And she turned unto the mighty one and spake:

"Bid thou, O mighty sire, that slaves bring forth waters that Rome wash this clean; for Rome hungereth e'en for the dusts!"

And she swept up unto the mighty-seat and kneeled her beside the feet of the mighty one, and laughed, and touched the jeweled sandals that bound his feet.

And they spake: "This one is mad!"

And Ahmud Hassan looked him far and spake: "Nay; Rome hath no measure for madness like unto this."

And he spake, slow, the name "Tiberius."

And she stood listed, and laughed on, and spake e'en as the echoing of it:

"Tiberius! Tiberius! Ha, ha, ha, ha! Yea! Yea! The swine-herder without the walls! Yea! Yea! Yea!"

And mid her laughs, lo, she stepped her unto one of the Rome's men who bore a broad-blade, and touched upon its metal, and set the thinned fingers o'er the sharp, and lay her cheek up against the chill of the metal's smooth and took it within her grasp and spake soft:

"So, thou art of Rome! Yea, he who setteth o'er Rome reacheth forth his hand and thou smitest!"

And her voice cried out like unto the wailing of the tempest's gale, shrieked, peal upon peal, and behold, she let fall the blade and it clattered upon the stones. And she cried out:

"Look! Look! E'en as thy point toucheth upon the stones, behold, a crimson fount springeth! See, sire! See thou! Up and flee! Even unto thy mighty-seat it creepeth slow, yea, heavy slow, even as the chilled blood! O-o-he! O-o-he-o! See! thy feet shew crimsoned o'er. Yea, e'en as thou steppest thy step sheweth upon the earth stained of it! Ha, ha, ha! And look! thy breast hath oped, and behold, within thy vitals sheweth thy belly's sack, filled of it! Yea, hung unto it upon one strand is thy heart, yea, and it sheweth of stone!"

And she swayed and chanted of the name: "Tiberius! Tiberius! Ha, ha, ha! Yea, the swine-herd! And thou the swine!"

And the mighty one bade that they set upon her and cast her forth.

And lo, she stood e'en as a she-lion, the breath hot as fire's burn, eyes blazed even as fire's leap, hands shaking, breast panting, feet pawing even as the thudded lion's paw. And she laughed, and the laugh froze them that heard. And behold, she tore ope the mantle that hung as rag and shewed unto them the breast, and upon this gleamed white and scarlet, streaked even as the fires that bite the hill's sod at the dry tides. And she cried out:

"Look! Look! Thou hast slain one of these! Come forth and lay this chaff of Rome low! Yea, cast this dust that be all of all of the plaything Rome hath cast! Come thou! Yea, set low such! Yea, cast forth the dusts of her who danceth and I speak unto thee——"

And they lay smite * upon her. And she cried out, but made words, saying:

"This dust shall leave upon Rome that that shall unbuild her! Yea, unto the swine shall Rome's nobled blood be cast, even by Rome's own hand!"

And they looked them one unto the other and murmured that this woman shewed filled of devils.

And Ahmud Hassan stood silent and bowed, and lo, he stepped unto the mighty one and spake: "Out from this a wise man may drink wisdom."

And he turned unto Theia and looked upon her, and lo, even though the smites shewed upon the flesh, she shewed no tear. And Ahmud Hassan looked upon this thing and spake loud, even so the ears of Theia should hark, and told unto the mighty one of Paul, the lad he said the roads had shewed unto him at the coming within the city's walls. And he set his eyes unto Theia, and told that Paul sought a wise one he called of the name "Panda," who lived without upon the hill's places.

And lo, this sunk within the ears of Theia, and the cheek burned even as one who supped wine. And behold, she swayed and pointed afar, and the mists of the see-woman spread her eyes. And they stood silent before this thing, and she chanted her:

"Behold! Behold! The sands gleam white, yea, and the East hath oped, and lo, He sheweth not! Wait thou! Wait thou! Yea! Yea! O'er the sweet curve of the damp sands, at the morn's hour, when the red of young day cometh, behold, He cometh! Yea, upon the whited camel! Yea, yet shall this thing be!"

And she turned unto the pit's ones and cried out:

* Struck her.

"Arise ye, brothers! Come forth, thou who hast suffered! Look! Look! The palms nod. Yea, yea, He cometh!"

And Ahmud Hassan's eyes leapt, and behold, he leaned far and listed, and his white teeth gleamed.

And she swayed and swayed and caught at the airs, and swayed, and knelt, and rose, and cried out: "Jehovah, this thing shall be!"— and fell!

And the hand of Ahmud Hassan reached unto the sign of the mighty one * that hung about his neck, and his eyes shut, and his lips thinned, and behold, he turned the sign unto him that no man look upon it. And he spake unto the mighty one:

"Mad! Mad! Mad! Yea, look! wouldst thou give unto this hand the ridding of such from out Jerusalem?"

And the mighty one spake: "He who offendeth Rome, payeth."

And Ahmud Hassan turned the mighty-sign. And the mighty one looked upon this thing and spake: "So be it."

And behold, the cheek of Caelius burned and his hand fell upon his blade, and Phaeton started and reached forth. And Ahmud Hassan looked upon this thing and saw within eyes that blazed that that sheweth within the she-lion's for the cub. And his lips spake unto the Rome's men:

"The mighty one shall deal the dealing unto this one. Take thou him without and leave that he seek the day; for lo, there shall climb but a sun and a sun and a sun, and lo, his ever-night falleth."

And Caelius sped up unto the fallen one and Phaeton reached forth, and behold, Caelius bowed him low before Ahmud Hassan and made the sign of obeisance unto the thrice. And Phaeton bore up the fallen one. And the lips of Caelius oped and no word came. And Ahmud Hassan spake, saying: "Rome listeth."

And Caelius spake: "Hath the pit given this one up? Doth Rome loose the Rome's doors? Shall Jerusalem ask naught?"

And Ahmud Hassan shook him "yea," and made the sign that he on upon the way.

And behold, the mighty one sat and supped, and fondled o'er a slave's flesh.

And Caelius kissed his blade and took up the burden.

And the pit's ones wailed, and Rome set her men unto the driving them, like unto chaff, back unto the waiting.

---

* The sign of Caesar; an emblem of delegated authority. "It be," said Patience, "the head a-laureled—the Mighty (Tiberius) a-laureled." That is to say, the head of Tiberius crowned with laurel.

And Ahmud Hassan stood and looked after, and his lips spake:
"Rome, thou hast builded up a mighty undoing. Even amid thy
hosts no noble sheweth who hath might like unto him who stood here
beneath thy lash. Thou hast offered the cup of bitter aloes, and behold,
even as the potioned sup hath froze the blood he standeth up upon the
hope of the east sun and draineth the last drop.

"'The palms nod!' Yea! Panda without the wall! Panda
without the wall! Yea, and at the east way. Then morrow findeth this
one sought."

And Ahmud Hassan turned, and behold, his hand raised unto the
east, and his lips oped, and his eyes turned about the mighty Herod's
court.* And the wailing of them of the pits sunk unto naught like unto
the whimper of the babe at the chastisement's end.

And Ahmud Hassan looked upon the mighty-seat, and behold, no
man sat upon it, but one fly held mighty sway! And Ahmud Hassan
looked upon this, and his lips spread in smile, and he reached forth his
hand and wafted therefrom the mighty one.

And Ahmud Hassan shut up one eye and sunk his beard upon his
breast, and his shoulders heaved, and his lips spake:
"This, and the mighty-sign hid!"

* But wherein was no Herod.

CHAPTER VI

AND without sunk the forms of Caelius and Phaeton, who bore Theia hence. And they made soft words and no sound reached within the mighty place. And Ahmud Hassan looked upon this and stopped that he watch their going without. And behold, he stood long. And when they had sunk unto the naught, lo, he turned and went within.

And Caelius held Theia within his arm's grasp, and Phaeton looked upon her as she lay, smitten of hunger's fill.* And Caelius spake soft:

" Phaeton, Rome's ones shelter not Jews, nor yet slaves, nor yet chaffs. Whither to? "

And Phaeton spake: " Rome shutteth unto Jews, but Jews ope unto Rome, and unto chaffs. Among Jews be shepherds, yea, and men whose hearts shew deep as well's pits. Unto Levi, the herder. Unto Levi, whose daughter, Sherah, the night-eyed Sherah, shall minister."

And Caelius shook: " Nay; this woman hateth Jews."

And Phaeton spake: " Caelius, men hate not the Jews, but man's word of Jews. Behold, Jerusalem hath nested the gods of all earth, and Rome filleth up the nest unto the full; and the far lands that house within Jerusalem's walls find no room within the nest for their gods. Jerusalem is the she-bird and her own nest she hath builded. Then 'tis meet that she bring forth but that that she hath lain within it. Caelius, no man hath right for to blaspheme Jews."

And Caelius spake: " But within Jerusalem a Jew hath dealt wrongly unto this one's flesh. Yea, the flesh of one who hath driven forth this one's flesh setteth the market's places, and behold, is the brother of one of Bethlehem who drove it forth even young like unto a ewe's lamb. Yea, this one, Theia, hath sworn unto Jehovah, the Jew's God, but eateth not Jew's flesh."

And Phaeton said: " Caelius, doth a man shew his brother's mantle's filth unto a brother, behold, he doeth wrong. But sheweth he the filth and stoppeth that he wash it cleansed, then hath he dealt wisely. Then, unto this one wash the mantle of the Jews! "

And Caelius looked upon the face of her he bore, and behold, it shewed whited unto the white of the summer's cloud, and the sun's rays

* Starvation.

248

had left no touch upon the cheek. And his eyes glistened, and drops fell, and he spake unto Phaeton:

"Unto yon well, that water bring forth the withered vine."

And they went unto the stoned place wherefrom drops flowed, and he dipped within the drops and bathed o'er the white brow. And behold, like unto the white moon, shewed her face, and the shadows within the moon, her eyes. And she murmured:

"The sands! The palms!"

And her eyes looked upon Jerusalem, and her lips oped, and the eyes gleamed, and words came and she spread forth her hands and cried out:

"Lo, the gods play! Look!"

And she sunk. And Caelius took her up, and Phaeton bade that he follow swift; for lo, did Levi dwell within the shadow of the tomb * of the mighty-seed. And they set upon the way. And ones upon the street's-way looked after, and some spread laughs o'er their faces and shrugged, and men wagged and onned at their bartings.

And behold, they went them unto the house of Levi, and Caelius smote upon the door unto it. And Levi came forth, and lo, his hand was raised after the sign of the greeting, and his lips spake:

"Peace, peace be upon thee."

And Caelius spake him, "Amen." And Phaeton bowed his head in sign thereof. And the eyes of Theia oped upon the household of Levi, and they flashed, for she knew this was the house of a Jew. And Caelius saw this thing and he spake unto her listed ear that lay next his cheek:

"He whom Rome casteth forth looketh unto men in vain that they succor; for lo, he whom Rome hath cast forth hath naught save ones that Rome holdeth rein o'er that may deal unto his needs. Therefore, Rome's offcast be cast unto Jews."

And Theia's lips oped but they spake not, but shewed dry and parched. And behold, her eyes drooped shut and she made no word in answering.

And Levi looked upon her, and unto Caelius, and raised his hands and cast his eyes unto the heavensward, and cried out:

"Sherah! Sherah! Behold, unto thy hand hath Caelius brought forth one that hath need."

And there came forth a one, black-locked, and lo, the locks hung even as the ripples of the sea's waves, and metaled bands held the waved strands close unto the brow, and the cheeks gleamed scarlet, and the lips shewed wet of youth's damp, and the lash o'er her eyes glisted dark,

* The tomb of David, at that time within the walls of Jerusalem.

and the breast shewed soft and curved, and the arms gleamed white from beneath the mantle that hung loose and girdled 'bout at the hips with a metal girdle. And at the lips' break unto smile, behold, there gleamed like unto the dimple that flasheth within the pool at the meeting of the rain's-drop. And the hands reached forth, and behold, she looked upon the smitten Theia, and tears wet the lashes o'er, and the hand, pink-palmed and soft, slipped o'er the heated brow, and she lay the soft cheek of her 'gainst the sunk one of Theia.

And Levi looked unto Caelius and then looked he unto Phaeton and shewed this thing unto them. And Caelius spake unto Levi, saying:

"Levi, unto thy hand hath Caelius dealt that that be of more worth then even the high sign, the mighty-sign of office. Yea, she who hath been brought forth lieth beneath Rome's heel."

And Levi looked on high and spake:

"Jehovah's mercy flow even as honeys from out the pierced comb. Jerusalem, Caelius, lieth 'neath Rome's heel. Yea, even though a Jew walk upon his land and call the city of David his own, even so his heart's blood standeth within Rome's bowl, that Rome cast forth or drink!"

And Caelius spake: "This one is no Jew."

And Levi said: "Even so, Jerusalem hath woven her days of broken palm's strands. What, then, careth a Jew that wastes be cast unto his hands that he weave thereof? This is the will of Jehovah. Behold, then, Levi shall go unto the temple and bring forth a peace offering that he purge him of e'en the thought 'gainst his brothers."

And even as they spake Sherah had brought forth waters and set her fingers 'mid the matted locks and set them straight, and bathed o'er the flesh of the shrunk cheeks.

And Theia waked, and behold, the sweet voice of Sherah crooned even as a mother o'er her babe, and she oped her arms and took her within. And Caelius looked him after and spake:

"Levi, if this God, Jehovah, doth this thing——"

And he brought forth his blade and kissed it. And he sat him upon the rug within the oped door place, and Phaeton sat him beside, and he told unto the listing of Levi of Theia and what had been; but told not of him who had swung the sling that cast the stone a-whirred o'er seas and lands from out Rome's place unto Jerusalem.

And when the ears of Levi had taken in all, behold, Caelius brought forth a shekel and gave unto the hand of Levi. And Levi shook him "nay" and oped up his palms and lay them at up and spake:

"Even so, this is the Jew's sign of the giving of all. So be it."

And Phaeton looked upon this, and Caelius turned unto him and spake:

"Seest thou this? Thinkest thou Rome and Gentiles hold all of men that bear of deal unto their brothers?"

And Phaeton spake: "Caelius, thy words sound unto these ears, and behold, even at the high sun thou knowest thou didst speak that this woman loved not Jews. And behold, did I not speak unto thee of the cleansing of the Jews' mantles unto her?"

And Phaeton lay his arm 'bout the neck of Caelius and smiled unto his eyes the smile of loving. And Levi looked upon them and spake:

"Even as Jews take within the temple's place that that no man knoweth of, and bringeth not out of the temple's place that that they take therein, even so hast thou brought unto the hand of Levi a sacrifice of Rome."

And Caelius spake in answering: "The morrow, the morrow, Levi, and Caelius cometh forth."

And Levi spake: "So be it."

And they went their ways. And Levi looked unto the within of his household, and his lips smiled and he spake:

"Behold, woman's tears balm. Yea, their salt healeth."

And he turned and sought without, and there sounded the sandal's slips as he went his way.

CHAPTER VII

AND within the house of Levi Theia lay, upon a rug's-cast. And beside her knelt Sherah. And Sherah's lips moved, and she cleansed the filth and cast the rags unto the heap, and brought forth cloths and waters and a mantle of one piece, and sandals, and their cords. And behold, she looked upon the locks and set her at their straightening, and bathed them, and dried them upon a soft cloth.

And Theia lay, her eyes stared unto the naught, and lips oped and dry. And Sherah, when the cleansing had been, brought forth wine and poured it within a bowl and set unto the lips. And Theia's eyes looked upon its red and spake:

"Blood! Blood!"

And she cast it forth and shrieked. And behold, it streamed o'er her mantle and stained upon the white cloth of the mantle of Sherah. And Theia cried out:

"Seest thou? Seest thou? Dost thou minister unto Theia, behold, thou woundest Rome, and Rome bleedeth! Look! even upon thy mantle sheweth the stain!"

And Sherah knelt at the feet of Theia and cried out: "What wouldst thou of thy sister?" And kissed the thin hand.

And Theia looked upon this, and upon the spot the lips had pressed, and her eyes started forth, and she lay mute, and her breast heaved, and behold, she cried out and threw her unto the arms of Sherah even as the babe seeketh the breast of its mother.

And Sherah's lips pressed upon the damp locks and she said: "What hath smitten thee?"

And Theia answered not, but wept. And Sherah's lips spake more: "Shed thou thy tears even unto the stream. Yea, for upon the stream of tears floweth thither woe."

And Theia oped up her lips and spake: "Bread!"

And Sherah arose and sped and brought forth loaf. And this was of fine flour, meals of the full grain, that none save the Jew who possessed much fed upon. And Theia's hands sought the loaf, even as the hands seek amid the dark that they stray not upon wrong paths, and she set upon the loaf even as a wolf upon a young kid. And she spake: "Sup! The milch of goats."

And Sherah went forth and brought back sup. And Theia ate of the loaf and drunk of the milch. And Sherah looked wide-eyed upon this, and her eyes took in the sunk cheeks, and her hands touched the thin arms even as Theia supped, and she spake:

"Hast thou set upon the travelway long and long? And from what land, yea, whither from?"

And Theia answered: "Long and long, from out Rome. And whither to, thou askest? Yea, Theia asketh thee, whither to?"

And Sherah took this not in, but bade that she speak more, and asked of the men of her. And Theia's eyes gleamed, and she cried:

"Behold, the man * of this flesh,—ha, ha, ha!—herdeth swine, yea, and the flesh of him hath he cast unto their pit. Yea, look unto the raiment thou hast stripped herefrom. Look! is not this a royal robe?"

And she lay weak. And Sherah looked upon her and spake: "Thy words hold bitter."

And she held Theia close and murmured: "Ope up thy wound that it bleed. What then shall these hands do that thou shalt know thy sister loveth thee?"

And Theia caught at the hand of Sherah and spake:

"List! upon the street's-way of Jerusalem, behold, thy sister hath lost a precious thing! Yea, a jeweled cup! Even of sapphire, yea, and filled of precious stones, even as them that deck the priests' beards. Yea, yea, and Jerusalem knoweth not that she holdeth so precious a thing.

"Yea and hark! what doth day then speak that thou knowest she loveth thee?"

And Sherah spake her name "Sherah." And Theia whispered it:

"Sherah! Sherah! Sherah! Thy sister hath offered gold that she buy word of Jerusalem of this precious thing, and no man made buy of it. See! See! Yea, thy sister hath shorn her of all."

And she reached unto her locks and shewed unto Sherah that they were shorn. Even so they did stand thick about the shoulders, and their drying had let the glints to gleam.

"Sherah! Sherah! Thou art of Jew's flesh. Hast thou, then, the ears of Jerusalem?"

And Sherah spake: "Yea."

And Theia looked unto the deep-darked eyes of Sherah and spake more:

"Sherah, hath thy breast e'er known of smite, deep, deep, deep unto the pit of thy heart's warm?"

And Sherah threw high her hands and cried out:

* The mate.

"Yea! Yea! The mother of this flesh hath gone. And behold, Levi, the sire, slumbereth not but setteth upon the housetop and looketh unto the sky's arch, and Sherah knoweth Jerusalem is empty unto him. Yea, Levi's eyes look upon the mighty-seat and—but Sherah telleth far o'er what is right nor yet meet that a woman speak."

And Theia spake: "Doth he, then, look unto the East?"

And Sherah took from out her breast a script and shewed unto Theia. And thereon shewed the Jew's scribe. And this told naught save the sign of Rome and o'er it gleamed, in the blood of sacrifice, the sign of Jerusalem, the mighty-sign of the house of David.

And Theia's eyes took this thing in and she spake soft, even as the hollowed breath:

"He waiteth one who shall set the high place within his lands?"

And Sherah trembled. And Theia spake:

"He dwelleth even within the walls! Yea, thy sister telleth thee this, Sherah! Yea, and his step is as the young deer, yea, and his eyes look unto the morrow's morrow's morrow's morrow!

"Yea! Yea! His blood is nobled. Yea, and he hath purged in sacrifice. Behold these hands! Behold these limbs that bear not this form! Even as morrow dawneth goeth Theia unto the road's-way and beggeth of Jews that she seek, seek, seek, and find this one."

And Sherah spake: "Unto Levi shall Sherah tell all."

And Theia cried out: "Nay! Nay! Ope not up thy lips, nor yet shew of this script; for thou, Sherah, knowest not Rome's bite!"

And Sherah hid the script within her bosom and sunk at the feet of Theia who lay, and she looked unto her and spake:

"And thy lips have spoken thy name 'Theia.' Theia! It floweth upon the tongue! Theia! Yea, it floweth on, on, on, and it seemeth for to empty unto naught! What hath emptied thine eyes?"

And Theia answered: "The looking unto the East."

And Sherah spake: "What lookest thou unto the East that ye seek?"

And Theia answered naught. And Sherah questioned more: "Dost thou wait the sun's coming?"

And Theia's eyes looked far and far, and she spake slow: "Yea."

And Sherah spake: "Hath thy flesh forsaken thee?"

And Theia made answering: "Nay. Look! even as Rome hath stripped the flesh from off these arms, so hath Rome stripped the day of Theia's flesh. O-h-e-e! O-h-e-e!"

And Sherah cried aloud: "Ah, sister, thy wails cut, even deep!"

And Theia wailed her more, "O-h-e-e!" And Sherah looked unto her and cried:

"Tell, tell thou unto Sherah! Empty of all unto her heart. Sherah hath dreamed dreams of far lands where sands shew and mighty temples stand, and one who would ride from out and find, within Jerusalem, Sherah. What, what is love?"

And Theia caught at the hand of Sherah and spake:

"Lo, love is the honey-sweet of the locust flower. Yea, and deep within it the sting lieth, like unto the bee that nests within the locust's gold and taketh within its cup its sting. So love. Love is the galley that floateth the sea, and the heart throbs the galley's slaves. Love? Love? Love is the tender morn, split asunder of storm's wrath. Love? Love? Love is the ever-spend—the give of all and take of naught. Love? Love? Love? Ah, love is fleshed even as a lovely maid. Yea, and spelleth flesh-joy. But lo, like unto the dim star of morn that day hideth, so this maid falleth shrunkened, and behold, up from out her flesh floateth, as incense smokes, love, love, stripped of flesh! Love? Love? Love may turn from out the anguished tears dews of gentleness. Love may touch earth's weary, and behold, they slumber. Love? Love——"

And she arose and held forth her hands, and her eyes looked empty, and she turned and looked unto Sherah, and her lips murmured:

"Where hath it flown and left Theia? Sherah, where, where?"

And Sherah looked long unto her and spake:

"See thou, sister, Sherah's hand lendeth to thee. Yea, thou and Sherah shall seek out the lost one. Then shall the path lead among the high places or yet the lowly?"

And Theia said: "He is youthed, yea, and wisdomed, yea, and strong. Yea, the God, thy Jehovah, hath set him upon a high place. Yea, and Theia knoweth him nobled."

And Sherah questioned: "Within this land, then, was this flesh brought forth?"

And Theia answered: "Bethlehem."

And Sherah cried: "Jesus? The Nazarene? Ah, Theia, Rome hath spat upon this! Behold, the Jews oped up their arms unto His coming, and the priests said He was the seed of David. Yea, and calleth Him Messiah. Behold, Rome hath spoke: 'How may flesh be brought forth of woman when man knoweth her as a wanton, and be called holy?' And yet, Theia, hast thou looked upon her?"

And Sherah spake more: "The eyes of her shew soft as the temple's doves. Yea, and chastity clingeth her even as a mantle. Behold, Theia, her eyelids shew weighted of holy, and deeped, deeped, e'en as though they held the know* of all men. And He! His lips did confound the priests, yea, and He plucked out their words until they shewed as the stripped bones! Yea, and from out Nazareth cometh word that He speaketh unto the hill's people and they drink up His words, and He sheweth unto them bright days that gleam far fairer than earth's ones. What thinkest thou?"

And Theia said: "What speakest thou? What wanton? What man knoweth? Jesus? Nay. This is not the precious one."

And Sherah spake: "Mary!" And Theia swayed and cried: "Mary! Mary! Thou still upon this path? And He thou hast borne still claimeth crown? Mary! Mary! Thou shalt know Theia, and Theia, Theia shall see His crowning! Yea, yea, and the flesh of her crowned, too!

"Sherah! Sherah! Theia seeth more. Yea, long and long, the path! And hosts, hosts upon its way. And behold, there standeth at their lead a lad and a lad. And one beareth of a bowl, and behold, it sheweth fulled of red. And behold, the other beareth of a bowl and it sheweth red. And the multitudes look upon this, and behold, this red floweth into the bowls from the oped sides of them. And behold, more! more! the multitudes take of one and call it wine. And behold, turn them away that they look not upon the other, and cry out: Blood! Blood! Blood!

"Jehovah! 'Tis gone! Gone the seeing and I know me not which be he!

"Wait! Wait thee, Sherah! Sherah! The see cometh. Yea, look! look! The heavens opé and gold streameth, and behold, from out the bowl leapeth forth the red and mingleth, and floweth as one stream, up! up! up! Yea, one the sign of flesh and one the sign of Jehovah!

"Sherah! who is he who standeth with a golded scourge and cutteth at the heavens?"

And Sherah stood and looked upon this thing and her eyes shewed fright, for Theia swayed and her eyes misted o'er. And Sherah reached forth that she lay hold upon Theia and spake soft, and her voice shook: "Who? Who? Yea, and what seest thou?"

And Theia waked from out the dream-see and answered:

"Naught! Naught! for why should a one fill his succor upon such?"

And Sherah spake: "Knowest thou men within Jerusalem?"

And Theia looked swift, even as a wolf, unto her and said: "Nay."

* The knowledge.

And Sherah said: "What set thee wearied sore? Levi hath told naught that might set thy sister that she know. Art thou of Rome?"

And Theia answered: "Rome? Rome? What speakest thou? Nay; within the land of me * gods rove the pathways. Yea, and the hands of my people take up e'en the earth and fashion out beauties. Yea, and upon the stringed music-branch smite they, or deal out trumpet's sweet blasts. Yea, and the maids sway even as the young tree, and their feet bound in joy."

And Sherah cried: "Is this, then, the Promise-land?"

And Theia answered: "Nay! Nay! Nay! For Theia sayeth the Promise-land hath floors of silvered sands and lieth shaded o'er of palms."

And Sherah spake: "Within thy land doth youth shew the men fair?"

And Theia smiled slow: "Youth! Youth! How ye do fret that love slay ye! Sherah, love is the thief! Yea," and she touched the crimsoned cheek, "yea, he coveteth ye these! Yea, he setteth upon thy red lips and plucketh out the crimson. Behold thy sister! He hath of her within his coffers. And she—and she—and she—is glad!"

And Sherah sunk and looked upon her and cried: "Glad?"

And Theia spake: "This land, this land of me, behold, she sheweth as a lovely maid who beareth of a lamp, yea, and garlands. And behold, her feet sheweth sandaled. But hark! She danceth—and then, and then—whither goeth she? For her lamp be lost and the garlands fall! But behold, yet shall earth take up the lamp, and know the garland! Yea, alike unto the east-sun sheweth she, the beacon of the day."

And Sherah wept and looked unto Theia and spake:

"Look thou upon Sherah, thy sister. Behold her land! Weeping, sore, weary—and the King tarrieth!"

And Theia stood tall and spake: "Nay, the time is at hand! Yet, sayeth Theia, she seeth thy land, her black locks hanging long, long and black, like unto the death's sign! Yea, and her robe sheweth red, red, red! And Rome holdeth the goblet that hath thrown the red thereon!

"And yet—ah, the tears! the tears! the scourges! the scourges! yea, the racks! the racks! yea, the flesh torn! the flesh torn through time and time! and Jerusalem layeth low, smitten! smitten! and then—He cometh! Yea, from out the East and all men shew a-clean!

"Ah, Sherah, hark and comfort thee! For thy people shall take up

* Greece.

their tears and sing them! Yea, e'en upon the racks, from out the hearts
and through the lips of thy flesh, shall joy flow. For hark! out of the
mighty pressing of the King's press, shall honeyed wines flow. Yea,
and even when scourge hath ceased and the hands that wielded it are
dusts, behold, within the hearts of thy people of that day shall the song,
the tears shed, well out, and men shall know the sorrows of Jerusalem.

"For behold, within the lowly flesh of Jews shall He set the sign.
Yea, and even though earth hath oppressed them sore, and they but set
the share unto the lands, lo, shall the hand of them smite musics and
their voice be lifted, and no man know the answering!

"And this shall be a day not thine, Sherah, not yet Theia's, and
men shall have forgotten Jerusalem and her woe, and remembered but her
sinning. And they shall list unto some one of these and hear the echo of
this day well up and pour forth!

"For He loveth Jerusalem. Yea! Yea! Yea! And her freeing is
at hand! But she, loth, even smitten past the bearing, shall look in
fearing upon this freeing. Yea, and He, lest earth forget, shall tune the
Jew's song of woe, ever, ever, ever! Yea, even though Jerusalem and the
Jews stand full-fleshed and free, yea, and forget her woe and the woer,
behold, her lips shall ope and her song be tuned of woe, and this shall
rebuke earth!"

And Sherah wept more and spake: "Levi hath sacrificed like unto
the Jew's laws, and looked, and looked, and yet He tarrieth!"

And Theia said: "At morrow, morrow, Sherah, thou shalt seek
within Jerusalem this King, with Theia. Weary, weary hath lagged
this frame. Sherah, dry thy tears; for yet shall love offer thee goblets
full that ye quaff, for him."

And Levi came him back, and asked not Sherah of her who abided
within his walls save: "Hath sup been offered?"

And Sherah sunk her upon her knees and spake:

"Yea, sire. Yea, sup and water's cleanse, and ah, sire, that thou
mightest hear of her lands, wherein youth sheweth fair! Yea, and she
telleth of the Ki—. What hath day within the market's place, and
yet the temple?"

And Levi spake: "The brethren went up unto the temple and bore
of peace offering—doves; yea, and sacrifice was made. But Sherah, what
doth sacrificial flesh buy that hath been squeezed dry of blood by Rome?
Levi's eyes have looked upon men from lands and lands and lands, and
behold, upon their shoulders shewed the white hand of Rome! He
tarrieth!"

And he touched within his bosom. And Sherah sat as youth, and looked far and dreamed dreams of one who came, and harked not unto Levi.

And he went up unto the parapet and oped up his arms and looked unto the East. And o'er Bethlehem's way the star hung, but he saw not.

And night fell, and Jerusalem's woes sought dreams, and lo, dwelt therein unto the morn.

CHAPTER VIII

AND when the morn had come the stoned ways rattled even as chains. Jerusalem set at the bear of burdens for all lands, and all men knew the Jews and the Jew knew no man save his brother. And no man save the priests saw within the temple's sacred place, wherein the sacrificial feasts were held. Nor yet unto the inner place, upon the table that bore horns and shewed like unto the ark,* save the loosing of the hover. For even at the bearing hence, still held they unto the sign thereof, and guarded there threefold.

Rome walked without and Jews stood kinged within. And they went them in and out, and at the early hour, behold, the priests came forth, and one among them washed and dried upon soft cloth and took up a taper and went within and set the glow of candles lighted.

And Rome cared not. And the markets whined and swarmed, and the kinged ones stayed the hill.

And Jacob sat asleep even at the early tide, and Samuel made word unto one he called of the name Lucius. And Samuel spake of word abroad that Rome had sent forth a one who rode upon a camel.

" And thou knowest, Lucius," spake he, " no camel opeth up his lips! And behold, he who rode looked not upon Jerusalem. Yea, Jacob telleth unto Samuel he eat of fruits of far lands. And behold, he shewed his packs not, but out from the Rome's place cometh word that he hath caused the pit's ope and cometh him bidded that he seek one, a woman, and that Rome had loosed one among the pits at the bidding of him."

And Lucius said: " This, Samuel, bringeth not unto thee nor yet unto Lucius, for he who cometh from out the pits beareth naughts."

And there came forth a one bended and filthed and sored, and cried unto Samuel for fruit's rot, and whined and shewed sores. And Samuel looked not upon him, but Lucius looked and smiled and said:

" Not e'en the rot, Samuel? Look thou! this one hath sores. Cast thou unto him."

And Samuel spake: " Feed such an one that he filth the day? "

---

* The original ark disappears from history with the destruction of Solomon's temple. This ark, the text asserts, was a symbol of the original and constructed in imitation of it but without " the hover," the cherubim.

And Lucius reached unto his fruit's store and dealt unto the hand of this one, and he sat beside the shade and eat thereof.

And Jerusalem passed upon its way and the beggar sat and slept, and waked and plucked forth fruits that no eye saw.

And behold, at the high sun, came forth a one who dragged nets and laughed upon his way. And he came up unto the side of the bin of Jacob, and Jacob waked and cried out:

"Woe! Woe cometh! Yea, look thou, Samuel, the empty one who filleth ever!"

And Samuel spake: "Even as the stranger upon the hill's side scattereth the sheep, so scattereth this one Jacob's dreams!"

And Lucius laughed: "Samuel, this lad hath naughts to deal but empty smiles."

And he held forth his hand and took that of Aaron's, and Aaron made sounds and shewed his catch within the nets. And this was stones and wood-bits. And he made that he bart of them. And Lucius made wide eyes and offered of fruits, and took from the hand of Aaron the wood-bits and stones as price. And Aaron sat and eat. And the women came and looked pities unto this one, and spake unto the babes and shewed unto them his empty. And Aaron laughed up unto their day.

And Jacob cried out: "Set this one awhither upon his way lest he up and lay hold the flesh of Jacob!"

And Samuel spake: "Nay, he eateth and harketh not."

And at the mid of the aft-hour came forth Hatte. And he slunk, even as a sheep's dog at his master's chide; his limbs loose and crouched, the locks tawned, the breast narrow and arms strong. The limbs of him shewed naked, and cloth was bound 'bout his loins and skins hung o'er and he carried the scourge and a sling.

And he came up unto the spot where Aaron sat, and Lucius cried out in greet. And Hatte made the sign of silence. And he went him up unto the bin of Jacob, and looked unto the fruits of Lucius that lay upon the outbin, hung of cloths. And behold, at the side of him sat the beggar and looked unto him, and his eyes took not in this thing, but his lips oped and he asked of Aaron.

And Jacob held high his hands and cried aloud:

"Behold he cometh and shouteth out the name of the empty one, and behold he sleepeth! And what then, Lucius? For doth Jacob know that his nets be emptied of his wares? Nay. Within his oped mantle, at this tide e'en, may be the choicest of Jacob's wares."

And Hatte spake not in answering but looked upon Aaron, who slept beside the market's place. And behold, flies swarmed o'er his flesh; and his lips hung oped, and his face looked empty, and e'en his lips showed they ne'er spake word; and his eyes, shut, shewed that they looked upon naughts and knew their all.

And Hatte went up unto the side of him who slept and lay his hand upon the flesh of him and wafted therefrom the flies and sat him upon a skin of grain, and looked not upon the market's place but far, far, e'en o'er the temple's walls.

And behold, the market's men spake one unto the other, and he harked not, but looked him still afar. And camels came unto the market's place, and asses, and yet goats and sheep, and the sheep's dogs and the shepherds and greens men.* And he looked not but sat, and still his eyes turned upwards unto the far, and within the hand that shewed not upon the flesh of Aaron hung the scourge, and the sling shewed within his loins-fold. And the beggar squatted beside the bin and watched the come and go of the out and in of Jerusalem. And Hatte's breast rose and fell even as one who had set upon the way packed, and the fingers that grasped of the scourge oped and shut.

And the Rome's men mingled 'mong the Jews, and the eyes of Hatte looked not upon them, but at their fall, did they to rest upon one of Rome, he shut them and bowed his head.

And the beggar came up unto the side of him and looked upon the scourge and touched it, and spake no word but looked unto the face of Hatte and held forth a hand and whined. And lo, the eyes of Hatte fell upon this one and saw that he touched of the scourge, and behold, he stood him up and raised the lash and lay it upon the beggar's palm. And the one whined and begged more, and Hatte looked upon him and spake:

"Hath Rome fed thee not, that thou seekest an out one who weareth but a skin's covering? Knowest thou not that he of the hills hath naught of metals, but scattereth sheep upon the market's men? Lo, unto one a sheep and taketh grain, lo, unto another a sheep and taketh greens, or yet fruits and cloths?"

And he who begged whined out: "Thinkest thou that a hungered one may fill of metals?"

And Hatte laughed, and sat him down upon the skin's sack from whence he had stood him up, and spake low: "This thou shalt unravel."

And he sank his eyes'-look unto the stones of the street's-way and sat mute, and wickeds flitted from 'neath his lids. And the beggar still squatted near and spake unto the ears that listed not. And behold,

* Gardeners.

the eyes of Hatte looked upon Aaron and the wickeds melted them unto a smile.

And the beggar looked upon the face of Aaron and spake unto Hatte, saying: " Is this thy brother? "

And Hatte let fall his hand upon the mighty hand of Aaron, weak in sleep, and spake: " Yea. Yea. Yea."

And the beggar said: " This lad is past thy days."

And Hatte spake: " Yea, for he doth know naughts, and he who liveth days and days knoweth not this thing. Then his wisdom is o'er the days of me."

And the beggar spake: " Thy tongue speaketh word and behold they be e'en as a cup that holdeth not drops."

And Hatte looked him far and cried: " How then may the cup that Rome hath emptied be filled? "

And the beggar answered: " Thou hast spoken truth, for lo, Rome doth empty."

And Hatte's hand took up the scourge, and he looked upon its gold and drops stood in his eyes. And the beggar looked upon this thing and asked of the gold within the scourge, and Hatte made answering:

" This gold hath grown out of the heart of love."

And the one who begged asked of Hatte: " Is this, the scourge thou holdest, thine? "

And Hatte spake: " Yea, from out the flesh that hath borne of this gold hath this flesh sprung."

And the one spake more, saying: " And dwellest thou within Jerusalem? "

And Hatte spake: " Nay. Nay. For Jerusalem holdeth her, and walls bind off the look unto her. Yea, these walls be e'en as irons that chafe. Yea, the hours within Jerusalem torture this flesh even as the racks. Nay, out, out, far, far, among the hills, yea, 'mong sheep, sheep, for they ne'er did set hurt unto her. And doth Hatte see not the look within the ewe's eyes he doth forget and wickeds mount up within his heart, and behold, doth he to seek the ewe and look unto it, he remembereth."

And the beggar spake the name, " Hatte." And lo, the eyes of Hatte looked far, and he waked Aaron and looked not upon the beggar but took up the scourge and held unto the hand of Aaron and went upon the way.

And at the going, behold, there came forth Ahmud Hassan, and he went up unto the beggar and asked of what had been. And the beggar arose and went upon the way beside Ahmud Hassan. And they made

words and the beggar told of what had been and spake the name
" Hatte." And Ahmud Hassan spake it o'er:

" Hatte? This is not of Rome nor yet of Jew."

And when they had come unto the shadow of the temple's wall they
came upon women who rested within the cool, upon their ways from
bringing forth waters. And among these shewed the forms of two who
shewed unto the day the swathed cloth o'er the face and eyes gleaming
from out the ope.

And one looked upon Ahmud Hassan, and her eyes sunk, and the
lashes lay dark upon the white of the cloth. And Ahmud Hassan looked
unto this one and passed upon the way.

And the one spake unto her sister: " Didst thou see the eyes of
night's dark? Ah, sister, Sherah's heart hath leapt. He hath come
from out the far, and out the sands; but behold, he sheweth not youthed.
Nay, and he whom Sherah hath looked upon steppeth long-limbed, and
his locks gleam as copper's sheen, and his eyes look far. He hath come
from out the walls unto Jerusalem and passeth the house of Levi."

And Sherah pressed her hand unto the heart of her, and behold,
her eyes gleamed and she caught at the mantle of Theia and spake soft:

" Look! Look! 'Tis he and the empty one! "

And Theia stopped, stilled, and murmured: " The son of Peter!
Hate! "

And Sherah spake: " Nay, nay; thou hast spoken that thou hast
known love. This one is love, ne'er hate! "

And behold, beside sat a one, dark-skinned, whose eyes flashed and
whose breast heaved, as she harked unto this. And the women called her
name Indra. And they looked not upon her, but the eyes of them followed the steps of Hatte. And behold, the eyes of one looked loving
unto the fullness, and the eyes of the other looked loving that was but
waked.

And the lips of Theia whispered soft: " Hatte! Hatte! Hatte! "
And stopped at the voicing of the word, so: " Hat-te! "

And Sherah looked unto Theia and spake: " Dost thou know this
one, and of his days? "

And Theia reached forth her arms and took Sherah therein and
pressed her lips upon the white brow of her and whispered:

" Sherah, Sherah, love hath offered a bittered cup! "

And Sherah's lips broke in smile, and the fresh of her laughter
spilled 'mid the sorrowed words, and she spake:

" Ah, thou knowest not! Thy lips have spoken words of sorrowing,
and behold, e'en now thou mayest look upon the gleam of his locks. And

thinkest thou that love should crown him of such gold and yet offer sorrows that he drink?"

And Theia's eyes looked far and she spake: "Love looketh not upon the crown; nay, but dealeth, dealeth ever, bitters 'mid her sweetest cup."

And Indra listed. And behold, the street's-way swarmed of men and market's wares. And Sherah looked upon this, and shewed unto Theia, and asked of her did not wisdom speak it that they should off unto the house of Levi. And Theia made answering: "Yea, unto the house of Levi; for unto Theia all paths offer naughts."

And they went upon their ways even in the steps of Hatte. And Sherah's cheeks burned red, and she watched the youthed Hatte step among men. And Aaron lagged and stopped that he pluck up from the stones of the street's-ways fruits, skins, bones that dogs had stripped, bits of cloth, broken bits of water jugs; and laughed and put within the nets.

And Theia took this thing in and went up unto where he stood and touched his flesh. And Aaron looked unto her, empty-eyed. And she took from out the mantle's fold a copper ring, whereon shewed the sign of Augustus. And Sherah looked upon this wide-eyed, and Theia spake:

"This is the all, the last of all; for within the strands of Theia was this thing bound."

And Sherah cried: "'Tis the sign of a mighty one."

And Theia spake: "Sherah, e'en a fool may take within his mouth the name of the mighty."

And she took up the hand of Aaron and put within its grasp the ring, and pointed him unto Hatte. And Aaron looked upon the dull metal and laughed, and behold, he took it up within his grasp and made that he threw it from him. And Theia cried out, and Hatte turned at the sound and came up unto the spot and looked upon Sherah and then unto Theia, and his eyes looked as dead fires.

And Theia held unto the hand of Aaron wherein the copper ring shewed, and Hatte looked upon this and he shook "nay" unto Aaron, and spake:

"Hath this one, then, taken this of thee?"

And Theia answered: "Nay."

And Aaron oped his mantle and looked unto the way unto the bin of Jacob and shook nays and nays. And Hatte took up the ring and gave unto the hand of Theia and spake:

"This is but for a one nobled and sheweth worth much."

And Theia said: "Yea, yea, he who gave this unto the hand that shewed it unto the day took price, much price!"

And Hatte looked upon the sign and spake: "Rome? Yea, the price was full!"

And the hand of Theia shook, and her eyes started forth, for out of the lips of Hatte sounded not the bitters that shewed within his eyes. And Hatte looked upon Aaron and plucked at his mantle, and took up the nets and turned and looked not upon Theia nor yet Sherah. And behold, the sun shone upon the scourge and it gleamed, and Theia's eyes rested thereon, and she caught at the heart of her, and she reached out her arms, but spake naught. And Sherah said:

"What hath smitten thee? Dost thou know this one? Ah, his eyes! His locks! But didst thou see the scar, the wound upon the cheek? It seemeth like unto a wicked; for behold, the one cheek gleameth youthed and soft, yea, and love-curved; and the smitten one looketh wicked. Yea, his lips smile, and the smile melteth the heart to flow wines within thy veins. Yea, and his eyes frighten, for wickeds bideth in them."

And Theia spake: "Yea, yea, at the breast of Jerusalem hath this babe of Rome nurtured. Yea, and Jerusalem hath been fed rots by the hand of Rome. Therefrom Rome's own suppeth from out the breast of Jerusalem the food of Rome!"

CHAPTER IX

AND they went upon their ways unto the house of Levi. And behold, at their coming thereto, Caelius and Phaeton had come forth and sat within the walls. And Levi, seeing their coming, went forth in greeting and spake unto Sherah:

"Go thou within and leave this one unto the hand of Caelius and thy sire; for behold, the day hath much for the righting."

And Sherah went within, and Theia came unto the place where Caelius sat, and Phaeton rested him upon the rugs. And she sunk beside the form of Caelius and her breath came fast, for weary had set upon her. And Caelius looked upon her and spake:

"Then hast thou trod the streets of Jerusalem even at the one day after the pit's oping?"

And Theia pressed unto her heart and murmured: "The hunger! The hunger biteth! The cup, the jeweled cup, the precious thing, Theia seeketh!"

And Caelius asked of her had the eyes of her looked upon this thing. And Theia answered, "Yea."

And Caelius spake: "Theia, e'en though the pits did ope, Caelius feareth Rome hath yet shut unto herself a thing she hath ne'er shewed. This one, this Ahmud Hassan, he looketh even as a flesh-eat * bird."

And Theia shook her "nay." But Caelius spake more.

"Unto him hath he called the ones who beg and spake words within their ears. And Phaeton knoweth, and Caelius hath taken this in."

And Theia swayed and beat her hands one upon the other and cried: "The cup! The cup! E'en though it be empty, 'tis Rome that would take it from out the hand of Theia!"

And Caelius spake: "Thou, Theia, then shouldst shut thy lips. Yea, ope not e'en unto Sherah their tell of all. Levi knoweth, but Levi's mouth is ever as a sealed pit."

And even as they spake, and Levi listed, there came ones of Rome unto the spot and bade that they come forth. And they lay hands

* A vulture.

267

upon Caelius and Phaeton and cried out words that these had turned their blades 'gainst the power of Rome, and taken of Rome and dealt treasons.

And Caelius stood, a Rome's one at either side, and his head bended low, and he spake:

"Rome! then thou wouldst take thy lover unto thee, to slay for treason he who but drunk the wines of loving for thee!"

And Phaeton raised his blade and smote, and behold, struck the flesh of one who came up unto Theia.

And the one ran him through! And Caelius sunk upon his knees. And Theia sat as one of stone, and behold, her eyes raised, and her stiffed lips moved, and the words came soft:

"Jehovah! Jehovah! Why tarriest thou?"

And they lay hands upon Levi, and called his name, and spake of the moneys of him, and bade that he give of his store lest they spill his cup.

And Theia sat her still. And the form of Phaeton stirred, and he turned, even as the red gushed, and he reached forth his hand unto Caelius and spake, amid the panted breath:

"'Tis well, Ca—e—lius! Take thou the blade of Phaeton for Rome, e'en though Rome hath drunk his wine."

And he sunk. And the Rome's ones took up his body, and he was gone therefrom. And they spake: "This putteth one up unto his claim of honors."

And they said that they should bear him unto the mighty-seat and shew this unto the mighty one and tell of the turning of his blade 'gainst Rome.

And Levi stood, his eyes flashed, his black beard hung long upon the white mantle of him, and his eyes looked unto the within of the household. And Theia turned her eyes thereto.

And the men of Rome laughed and said they should look unto the whole of the household. And Theia stood her up, and behold, her strength scarce bore her, and she went up unto Caelius and spake:

"What thou hast spoken is true; Rome hath ne'er left the empty of her pits."

And Caelius said: "The morrow hath oped unto thee, Theia, and Caelius hath but the shutting of the day."

And the Rome's ones spake the name: "Theia!"

And Caelius started, and Theia stood still and spake:

"Start thou not, Caelius. Rome hath worn the flesh of Theia unto the thickness of an oxen's skin. She feareth not! The cup! The cup!

Rome knoweth not the cup! And Theia, ah, Theia careth not for her own flesh."

And the men laughed at the words they spake and bore the body forth, and took Caelius bound upon the way, and cried out 'gainst Levi that days yet should tell the all of him.

And when they had gone, behold, Theia stepped slow unto the stain that lay upon the floor and stood and looked upon it, and spake unto Levi:

"Ah, sire, this is the cast of Rome upon thy mantle of her red wines! Set thou me to flee! Bid that I seek the hills! Offer unto me of rags, yea, bring forth the tatters Rome bedecked me of! For woe cometh upon thee!"

And Levi spake: "Jehovah hath spoken unto His son and He hath ne'er spoken that one who cometh for succor be sent hence! Levi's household is thine, even unto the spilling of Levi's cup!"

And Theia looked unto the within of the house and stretched forth her hand and spake unto Levi, saying: "She, sire, thy flesh, Sherah!"

And Levi raised his hands up even unto the utmost unto the heavens and spake:

"Sherah is of the flesh of Levi, and the flesh of Levi suffereth; for how may a man sever him from his flesh? Yea, and thou art of the flesh that hath builded man. So thou art the sister of the flesh of Sherah. Jehovah shall lend unto thy hand and mine."

And Theia sunk, and her eyes looked far and she murmured:

"He tarrieth! He tarrieth! Long! Long! Levi, Theia hath danced upon the stones of Rome and the dance hath led unto Jerusalem and sorrow. Theia hath looked upon the gods of Greece, yea, and the gods of Rome, and unto the gods of the casts of all people. And Theia speaketh true, these gods be dumb! Speak, sire, hath Jehovah a tongue?"

And Levi stood long, and dropped his arms from on high, and made answering:

"Yea, o'er the babel of Jerusalem, o'er the roars of wicked tongues, Levi heareth the tongue of Jehovah! Yea, and Levi speaketh unto thee trued, that when Jerusalem hath been crushed and earth sheweth naughts, and man hath dipped the well of wisdom dry and died of thirst, and all men lie low and the earth standeth stark; behold, then shall the tongue of Jehovah sing on and on, even as the singing of the mother unto her babe. Yea, and when man's wisdom hath ceased, then shall the tongue of Jehovah speak unto man the first law."

And Theia arose and leaned far unto Levi and listed, and her eyes flashed and her bosom rose and fell and her feet stepped, and she swayed and spake: "Yea, yea, unto Theia He singeth!"

And her form swayed as a lily upon the tendered stem, and her lips chanted:

"Yea, yea, even though Sherah suppeth the cup of Theia, 'tis right; for Jehovah hath sent it."

And behold, as she danced and Levi stood bowed, there shewed through the door's ope, Rome's men, and beside them a beggar. And behold, they stood 'bout a one, and after followed an empty one who laughed and dragged nets. And Theia took this thing in, and stood stilled, and pointed this thing unto Levi, and her lips could bear not words, yet they came as breath:

"Ah, sire, look! The cup! He hath waited unto the last hour! He hath tarried too long!"

And Levi touched her flesh and spake:

"Levi hath that of Rome that shall wrest from out her hands this cup! E'en though they tear out the limbs of Levi, this thing shall be! But hark! Levi speaketh true, Jehovah seeth!"

And behold, the Rome's men parted, and there shewed the lad, Hatte. And his eyes looked even as a hawk's, and his body curved of strength, and his naked skin gleamed, and the skins 'bout his loins lay dark against the white, and the young hair o'er his breast gleamed gold, and his locks shewed glistened. And beside him the Rome's ones looked even as oxen unto the deer. And there hung at his loins the scourge, and his hand clutched at this thing. And the Rome's ones cried out:

"This, then, is the flesh Rome seeketh! And doth Ahmud Hassan turn the sign then Rome's mighty one layeth it low."

And they spake unto Hatte, saying: "Who is thy sire?"

And Hatte made answering: "Thou hast spoken it."

And they murmured: "This one should follow John; for he speaketh naughts, like unto him."

And Hatte's lips sneered. And they spake: "What woman bore thee?"

And Hatte plucked forth the scourge and answered: "Hatte hath sprung from out this!"

And they laughed, and behold, through the ope came, soft, a chanting:

"Yea! Yea! from out the East He shall come, upon the whited camel! This thing shall be."

And Hatte stood still and listed, and behold, his hand upped and the scourge cut at the flesh of one of Rome. Yet he spake not, and his lips whited, and his brow glisted of the freeze-sweat.

And they swept him on. And upon the way they came upon a camel, packed, and upon it sat Ahmud Hassan. And he looked upon this. And he drew the camel unto its knees and spake unto the Rome's ones and asked what this thing led unto.

"Who hath sent thee upon this one?"

And they spake the name of the one of Rome within the walls of Jerusalem. And Ahmud Hassan smiled slow, and he spake:

"Ahmud Hassan hath wafted from off the mighty-seat the mighty fly; still he buzzeth ever back!"

And he shut up one eye and spake unto his camel:

"Back! Back unto the Rome's place, that we stir him off! Within Jerusalem a one of Rome playeth with Rome's blade, and Ahmud Hassan feareth he shall cut him upon it."

And the camel sagged upon the way. And there followed the Rome's ones, and Hatte, and Aaron, laughing. And they went up unto the place wherein Rome's ones abided, and before the mighty-seat stood Caelius, bound.

And they brought forth Hatte. And they had bid that Aaron wait without; for what might Rome drink from out an empty cup? And Aaron stood and looked, and his laugh stopped, and he sped on unto the east way gate.

And within the walls they made words, and told unto the mighty one of the blades of Caelius and Phaeton that turned 'gainst Rome.

And Ahmud Hassan shewed not, but sat without upon his camel. And Caelius stood and spake not. And they shewed the body of Phaeton, red-dyed. And Hatte looked upon Caelius and his eyes spake unto him, and Caelius spake back unto him from out his eyes.

And they told unto the mighty one of the woman that Ahmud Hassan had loosed, and said that Phaeton and Caelius had borne her unto the house of Levi. And the mighty one listed, even as though he had ne'er set the beggars upon the list and knew not of this woman.

And they brought forth Hatte, and asked of him was this woman of his flesh. And Hatte made answering:

"Nay; all of the flesh of me is this." And he held the scourge forth.

And they asked of Caelius the name of this woman, and Caelius spake it not, but the Rome's ones cried out: "Theia."

And they asked of Caelius was this lad of her. And Caelius looked unto him and spake: "Nay, this lad is of Jew's flesh. Yea, the hand of him hath raised 'gainst Caelius within the market's place among the Jews."

And they asked of Hatte was this thing true, and he spake: "Yea, Jerusalem is the land of me, and the name of her who hath said she bore me forth is Rhea, and the sire, Ezekiel."

And they asked where in Jerusalem he abided, and he spake: "Within the household of Lucius; for Rhea and Ezekiel abide within the hills of Bethlehem."

And they laughed, laughed long and loud, and cried: "Behold, again from out Bethlehem cometh a king!"

And Hatte stood silent, and within his hand hung the scourge. And Caelius looked upon him and unto his eyes, and there shewed much from out the eyes of one unto the other. And the Rome's ones still laughed, and they cried out, even so that the mighty one's ear take in:

"The king of asses came from out Bethlehem! Yea, and hither cometh from out Bethlehem a King of Jews who hath white skin and looketh as a one of Rome. Then hath the hand of Rome reached unto Bethlehem and caused flesh to spring and grow?"

And Hatte's cheek stained dark and he said: "Nay; the hand of Rome plucketh, but ne'er putteth the share nor yet the seed."

And the mighty one leaned him from out the mighty-seat that he look upon this lad who spake words that wearied the intaking. And they saw this thing, and shewed unto the mighty one the scourge, and bid that he set the lips of Hatte oped. And the mighty one spake: "So be it."

And Hatte stood tall, and the gold scourge hung and swung 'bout his limbs, and his voice sounded clear:

"This is folly! For behold, the son of Rome knoweth her lash, but should Rome smite Jew's flesh? Behold, sire, I am a Jew!"

And they looked upon him, and Caelius cried out: "Yea, this thing is true. Thou mayest seek his sire within Bethlehem!"

And the arch sounded the sandal's slip of a one, and behold, Ahmud Hassan stepped unto the place, and his hand hung o'er the mighty-sign. And the mighty one looked upon this and spake:

"Seest thou? 'Tis chaff, blown from off the street's-ways of Jerusalem."

And he made the sign that they loose Caelius and Hatte. And Ahmud Hassan looked upon this and spake not, but his shoulders raised. And he turned unto the body of Phaeton and raised his brows and upped his hands and set his lips unto the round, and spake:

"So? So? A mighty wind hath risen that bloweth such within!"

And his hand fell unto the sign, and Hatte stood loosed. And

Caelius sunk upon his knee even before Ahmud Hassan. And Ahmud Hassan made the sign that he arise, and bowed him low unto the mighty one and spake:

"Unto the mighty one go thou and bow obeisance. Yea, and lift thine eyes in gratitude."

And Caelius went unto the spot and made obeisance. And the mighty one arose and spake that Caelius should stand at the lead of the in-guards. And Ahmud Hassan looked on high. And Caelius arose and took the broad-blade Rome had stripped him of. And still the Rome's men stood about Hatte. And Ahmud Hassan came up unto him and spake:

"Lad, should woe befall a one, then should his tongue speak the all of truth, even though the truth build up his yoke."

And Hatte said: "Sire, Jerusalem ne'er sheweth such learning."

And Ahmud Hassan spake slow: "Yea, but Jerusalem hath a learning, of her kind."

And he looked upon Hatte close and spake: "Knowest thou the one o'er all the lands?"

And Hatte said: "Nay."

And Ahmud Hassan questioned: "What thinkest thou of a one who reigneth o'er all?"

And Hatte made answering: "Sire, his seat is builded of live coals. Yea, and he drinketh fire."

And Ahmud Hassan spake: "What! thou dealest not e'en of a drop unto his cup?"

And Hatte answered: "The draft his cup holdeth stinketh. Yea, for 'tis rotted blood!"

And his eyes shewed as the hawk's, and his breast curved. And Ahmud Hassan looked close, and Hatte spake more:

"Yea, sire, from out this cup this scent shall arise and sicken the earth."

And Ahmud Hassan shook his head and spake soft: "Thou lovest deep thy nobled sire!"

And he questioned more, saying: "Then thou art a Jew?"

And Hatte looked keen unto the black eyes of Ahmud Hassan, and made answer: "Even though these lips speak, thine eyes read out the truth. Yea, but the eyes of this one," and Hatte looked at the mighty-seat and whispered, "be e'en as dead fishes' eyes!"

And Ahmud Hassan shut up one eye, and his lips spake: "Hast thou e'er suffered the eat * for seeking far?"

* The desire.

And Hatte answered: "Nay, sire."

And Ahmud Hassan spake: "Youth, then, abideth even as the aged upon the land that brought it forth!"

And Hatte spake: "Yea, sire."

And Ahmud Hassan looked upon him and said: "How then is this thing?"

And Hatte spake, and his eyes fell upon the scourge: "Jerusalem hath taught that man should hold within his mouth, shut by his lips, what lieth close unto here." And he touched o'er his heart.

And Amud Hassan spake: "She who lieth there! Hath her eye youth or hath age set upon it?"

And Hatte's lips smiled, and he looked far, and his eyes melted soft, and he spake: "Age? Age? Nay, sire; within them gleameth the fount of ever-youth."

And Ahmud Hassan questioned: "And her locks? Shew they long and black? Or doth the wind arise and send them danced upon the air like unto the tendril of the grape?"

And Hatte caught at the scourge and cried: "Her locks? Her locks? Sire, amid them Jehovah hath hid His stores."

And Ahmud Hassan's eyes gleamed, and his teeth flashed, and he looked close, close, and spake: "Jehovah should mind lest the store be lost—severed, say."

And Hatte laughed and spake: "Nay, unto the hand of her loved hath Jehovah delivered it!"

And Ahmud Hassan said: "And this, thou sayest, this scourge— from whence?"

And Hatte's eyes eviled, and he spake hissed: "Sire, a man may un-belly unto his brother, but unheart, nay, save unto his flesh!"

And Ahmud Hassan spake: "This unto thine elder?" But his lips smiled.

And the Rome's one who sat the mighty-seat went him without. And Caelius took up step unto his brothers even as on the fore-days. And Ahmud Hassan looked upon this and said:

"Should the Rome's ones set thee upon thy way, which path should be thine?"

And Hatte answered: "This flesh is Rome's, be it 'neath Rome's hand, but the steps of Hatte be his."

And Ahmud Hassan spake: "What wouldst thou? Should the blade be dealt thee that thee slay and thou shouldst find the ewe mourns o'er her wounded lamb, wouldst thee then strike?"

And Hatte looked unto Ahmud Hassan and said: "What sheep

man would slay his ewe when her lamb sheweth wound? What sheep man sendeth out a one, a server of him, unto the fold that he slay? For a sheep man knoweth his sheep, and his lambs and his ewes are his heart's throbs. Sire, this blade is thine and thy sheep man dwelleth not the out-hills, else he bid ye not."

And Ahmud Hassan spake: " Knowest thou a one the earth calleth Panda?"

And Hatte answered: " Yea, all Jerusalem knoweth Panda."

" He dwelleth where?"

" Without the walls. For no wall sheweth high nor wide enough that it holdeth Panda."

" At the west wall?"

" Nay, for the east sun riseth and the west wall shutteth it away."

And Ahmud Hassan smiled and spake: " Go thou! Go thou unto the without! Yea, the without of the walls unto the wide opes. For thou art a son of Panda, verily."

And he made the sign that Hatte go without. And the Rome's ones had gone, and Hatte strode him loose-limbed out, slow, like unto one who wore regal robes. And Ahmud Hassan looked after, and when the form of Hatte had gone from out his sight Ahmud Hassan sat him down upon the stone steps, and he spake soft:

" Rome, thou art at the stripping of the vine of leaf and branch, when behold, the full fruits have fallen!"

And he sat long and spake more: " He sayeth the east sun riseth and the west wall shutteth it away. Then Ahmud Hassan seeketh the east way."

And the steps of Hatte led him on and he mingled amid men upon the way. And the hour shewed late and he sped on and out the wall, but stopped that he cast to Rome.

CHAPTER X

AND lo, within the walls, with sped feet, stepped Panda. And after, chattering, followed Aaron. And Aaron's chatter mocked the even's still. And they swept on and down the way unto the house of Levi. And when they had come unto it, behold no light shewed within, nor did the eyes of Panda fall thereon. And he swept on, and they came unto the market's way, and men walked and bore of brazen torches, filled of soaked wools. And the burn of oils smoked the air and within the light sped Panda on, and Aaron, still chattering and laughing.

And behold, Panda, in his speeding, came upon a one, and they ran each unto the other's arms 'mid the dark. And the lights blazed up at the wind's rising and fell upon the face of Theia. And Panda looked upon it and cried out, and Theia's lips made sound, but no word. But her hand pointed up unto the Rome's place, and Panda spake:

"Yea! Yea! Yea!"

And Theia looked unto Panda's eyes, and behold, they streamed, and she threw her hands high and cast her upon the bosom of Panda.

And they stood still, pressed one unto the other. And Panda sunk down, down unto his knees, even before Theia.

And Theia spake: "Panda! Panda! Panda! Panda! Ah, 'tis music! Panda, this is Jerusalem, and Rome hath slaves. But here Rome hath forgot her dealing. Arise!"

And Panda said: "Rome dealeth not slavedom, nay, nay. He thou seekest dealeth, and Panda giveth what is but thine."

And Theia spake fast and soft: "Panda, Panda, Hatte, Hatte—he is there!"

And Panda looked unto Theia and spake: "And thou, and thou art here!"

And Theia said: "Yea, yea! Rome playeth with the stripped bones!"

And the dark shewed darkened, for the light that men bore had gone. And the stars came forth pale and the sky, within the walls, seemed higher. And ones came upon the way, for steps sounded, and behold, about the temple's wall and up through the pale dark sagged a camel. And Panda looked upon this and spake:

" Theia, who rideth upon a camel even at the night's watch save one who hath the sign of Rome? "

And the voice of him who rode cried out: " O-o-e-hu! O-o-e-e-hu! "

And Panda raised up his head and spake: " This is a camel and yet he who calleth so should stride upon a fleet-foot, one whose mane floweth as summer's clouds, one whose forelock streameth long like unto a banner and is wrapped of scarlet cord."

And Panda made the call and there sounded back the answering, and the camel sagged up unto the spot. And it was white star's light. And the one upon the camel spake:

" Where setteth the east way wherefrom the sun riseth? "

And Panda answered: " Yea, the east way, where the moon tarrieth at the young day. Where, from out the deep, Allah's light flameth and tippeth the crescent upon the temple's place."

And the one made more of words: " Yea, wherefrom the sun riseth and opeth the mouths of the priests."

And Panda spake: " What hath the east sun of priests? For behold, Jerusalem babbleth at the sun's arising and the priests call forth; and within the temple's place whereon the crescents stand, behold, men bear forth of Allah each his own tongue." *

And Ahmud Hassan's smile flashed even in the dark's hush and he spake: " Then thou art of Allah's land, and ne'er a one of him a-robed within Jew's mantle."

And he made question: " Knowest thou of one, Panda? "

And Panda answered: " Yea, yea, and little be for the know! "

And Ahmud Hassan spake: " Where to unto him? "

And Panda cried: " Behold! Ope up thine eye and behold! "

And Ahmud Hassan's eyes looked unto Theia, who shewed not clear, save as a woman, and he spake: " What! sendest thou upon the way, and with woman's flesh? "

And Panda said: " She hath lost that of her upon the ways of Jerusalem."

And Ahmud Hassan questioned: " A cup? A jeweled cup? "

And Theia's lips cried out: " Yea."

And Panda made that he silence her. And Ahmud Hassan spake:

" Behold, Rome did hold this cup that she drink therefrom, and behold, the hand of Ahmud Hassan did dash this cup from out her hand.

---

* Indicating the absence of ritualistic religion among the Arabs of the time. Each man worshiped Allah, this seems to assert, without priestly direction, interpreting his god in his own way, in marked contrast to the Jews.

Yea, it lieth without Rome's walls, and behold, it hath sprung legs and walketh unto the east way."

And he swung from off the camel and climbed down the rush-thongs, and spake unto the camel:

"Down! Down upon thy knee, even before Ahmud Hassan! Seest thou not the mighty-sign?"

And the camel folded up and drew down, but stopped not its chew. And Ahmud Hassan looked upon this, even within the dim light, and spake:

"Look thou! this one is of Rome; for behold, he cheweth not at the 'bout and 'bout, but rubbeth o'er and o'er and grindeth, grindeth, grindeth. Ha, ha, ha!"

And he turned unto Panda and said: "Leave her whom weary hath set that she seat upon this rocked vessel, and we shall go upon the way unto the east wall, for he who hath sprung legs goeth thereto."

And Theia cried out, and the voice of her sounded loud amid the still that hung o'er the street's-way:

"Nay! Not unto the out-walls! Nay! Unto the house of Levi, that Theia sound out her voice in calling unto him and bid that he come forth and know that she seeketh without; for Sherah, Sherah waiteth. Yea, and hath sought upon the street's-way. Yea, she hath stepped the stones of Jew's ways that she seek this cup, and Theia goeth thereto."

And Panda spake: "Then, upon the way unto the house of Levi."

And Ahmud Hassan leaned far unto the camel—for the beast had su ik upon its knees at the pull upon the palm strands—and spake unto its listed ear:

"Unto the house of Levi! hearest thou?"

And Theia spake loud, and Panda harked unto her word. And Ahmud Hassan smiled; for behold, she cried out:

"Hath the cup gone unto the out-wall? Hath Hatte sought the paths unto the hills? Hath Rome loosed the flesh of Theia? Hath this thing been truly done? Away! Away, Panda, upon the way!"

And Ahmud Hassan lended of his hand unto her that she arise and set her upon the kneeled camel. And this thing was done. And still the lips of Theia spake:

"Behold, the feet of Theia itch that they go unto the hill's places; that they bathe within the damped roots and grasses blades; that she speed them o'er the moon-bathed path; for look! yonder o'er the city's walls cometh light, white light; yea, the moon cometh!"

And Panda looked unto Ahmud Hassan, and Ahmud Hassan made

the sound unto the camel that the sand's men know, and the beast coughed and stretched its neck long, and arose.

And Ahmud Hassan and Panda followed upon the way. And Theia sat upon the camel's back, and lo, her hands she beat one upon the other. And Panda spake unto Ahmud Hassan:

"Unto the house of Levi; she hath spoken it."

And Ahmud Hassan spake unto the camel:

"List thou! list thou! he speaketh of the house of Levi unto one who knoweth not Jerusalem!"

And they went upon the way. And Jerusalem lay bathed of pale star's-light. And the moon rose slow, and whited o'er the walls and street's-way like unto the fallen wood's ash. And behold, when they had come unto the street's-way that led unto the house of Levi, Panda went up unto the door's ope and set his lips close that no man wake who listed save them within, and called: "Levi! Levi!" And no sound made answering. And Panda called him louder: "Levi! Levi!" And lo, from out the shadows came forth Sherah, and the white light shewed her face as the white of marble, and her eyes looked bright within the white. And Theia spake:

"Sherah! Sherah! Theia goeth that she find the cup."

And Sherah raised her hand unto her brow and swept it o'er, for weary hung her 'bout, and her voice sounded dull, and she said:

"Nay. Nay. Nay. Thy words have set sore, Theia, sore within this heart!"

And Theia cried out: "Levi! Levi! Where, Sherah, hath Levi gone?"

And Sherah spake: "Levi feareth no man. Less feareth he Rome's ones."

And Theia questioned: "Hath Rome gone and left thee and Levi in peace?"

And Sherah made answer: "Theia, doth Rome know the path unto the lair, behold, she seeketh. Ever she hath taste, yea, hunger, that she seek, seek, seek, and take unto herself! Levi sayeth the stem of Levi's goblet is e'en so thin as one hair, and Rome may snap it at the drink, e'en at the morrow."

And Theia spake: "Nay, nay! This one, this one who hath oped the pits unto Theia, he shall speak it true; Levi shall go him unmolested!"

And Sherah shook her head slow and spake: "No man may speak for Rome."

And Theia questioned more: "Sherah, hath thy heart sore at the woes of Levi?"

And Sherah spake her: "Nay, nay, for long and long hath Sherah sat and dreamed of the glinting of his locks."

And Theia leaned far o'er the camel's back and reached forth her hands unto Sherah and murmured:

"Sorrow thee not, Sherah; sorrow thee not! The light of the moon hath risen. 'Tis the young night, and young day followeth and beareth hope. Await thee the gleam of the morn's sun! Await thee, and know that joy shall come unto Theia at the dawn; for she hath found the cup!"

And Sherah spake "yea," and turned and went within.

And Theia beat her hands one upon the other and flung wide her arms and cried:

"Out! Out! Unto the hills! Unto the lands without a wall!"

And Panda looked unto Ahmud Hassan, and behold, the hand of Panda sought within his mantle and he brought forth a blade and held it unto the hand of Ahmud Hassan and spake:

"If thou art of the lands that know Panda as its son, if thou art the brother of Panda, leave this within his hand; but oh, thou who hast ridden unto this day, if thou art what thy lips tell not, and thine eyes speak not, then take thou this and smite her and Panda!"

And Ahmud Hassan looked unto the camel, and unto the woman who beat her hands one upon the other, and stood long and waited. And the camel listed for the call. And Ahmud Hassan raised his hands high and faced unto the east way. And Panda sunk upon his knees. And Ahmud Hassan let fall his hands upon the shoulders of Panda and made that he arise, and took the blade from out his hand and went up unto the camel and spake:

"Is this thing thy wishing, O mighty one?"

And the camel coughed, and Ahmud Hassan fell low in obeisance. And Panda looked upon this and laughed, and Theia shook back her locks, and behold, her lips broke in smile, and faint laughs spilled.

And Ahmud Hassan arose and they sought the way thence.

And Jerusalem slept and dreamed dreams, and Rome mingled 'mid the dreaming of Jerusalem. And the ways shewed dark, but bright o'erhead. And the path led unto the east gate, and Ahmud Hassan spake but one word, "Tiberius," unto the gate's man, and the gate's one fell upon his face, and Jerusalem's walls gave up of Rome.

And without the skies spread, unblacked of walls, and the stars shewed many, and the sky shook in glistening, and the moon hung, and the hills shewed dark, and silence stood, save for the camel's pads, slipped o'er the stones and dry earth.

And afar upon the way shewed the silver of the hill's sands, and this they went unto. And behold, up unto the place of Panda where, upon the hill's side, shewed the white sheep sleeping. And the hut shewed dark and still.

And up unto this the camel strode, and Ahmud Hassan followed and Panda came upon the way. And Theia leaned far out and her eyes shot ever here, there and yon. And Panda spake:

"Theia, this, this is the store of Panda."

And Theia cried out: "Panda! Panda! Thinkest thou he hath come unto this place?"

And Panda answered: "Panda knoweth Jerusalem, but Panda knoweth not Rome's flesh, nor the flesh of Greece that Jerusalem hath fed."

And Ahmud Hassan pulled upon the palm strands and the camel knelt. And Panda took therefrom Theia and went up unto the hut and called aloud: "Nada! Nada! Ope!"

And from out the shadow came forth a dark one who stepped soft, and Panda cried aloud:

"Indra, call thou unto Nada."

And Indra spake: "Nada sleepeth."

And Panda said: "Then Nada waketh."

And he looked upon her and asked: "Hath Hatte come from without the walls of Jerusalem, out unto the hills?"

And Indra spake: "How, Panda, should Indra know this thing?"

And Panda called loud: "Nada! Nada!"

And Nada came forth, and Panda spake unto her and told of what had been, and called the name of Ahmud Hassan unto her. And she knew the words had come from out her land, and cried out in greeting, and looked unto Theia, and Panda spake:

"This one is she of the gold locks."

And Nada sunk upon her knees. And Theia looked upon her and reached forth her hand and spake:

"Unto thy sister, come thou!"

And Nada arose and took the hand of Theia and made that they go within, and behold, they did this thing. And when they had come unto the within of the hut, Nada went unto the in-place and brought forth lamp's wicks of skins, soaked of oil, and she set this aglow. And behold, Theia sunk upon the rugs, and Panda sat, and Ahmud Hassan stood and looked upon the within of the hut. And Aaron's nets lay upon the floors. And Ahmud Hassan went up unto them and touched them, and spake:

" Nets? Upon dry land? "

And Panda smiled slow and said:

" Brother, Jerusalem hath follies within her. Yea, men of Jerusalem fish even upon dry lands, but shew not their nets."

And Ahmud Hassan cried: " Man, did the mighty one know of what Jerusalem held, he should die of tickle 'mid his dreams! "

And Panda said: " Rome's one should die of laughs. Yea, for his dreamings, ah, they should shew even as the dreams of babes! "

And Ahmud Hassan spake: " Allah's fear upon thee! "

And Theia watched the form of Nada, for Nada brought forth the spices of her land, and the brass bowls and the rug, the golden rug of Nadab, and spread it forth. And Ahmud Hassan let his head bow, and Theia spake:

" Panda, is the sacrifice unto thy god? "

And Panda bowed and answered: " Yea."

And Theia spake: " Upon this dost thou bow? And this, is this the fire of sacrifice unto him, this Allah? "

And Panda said: " Yea."

And Theia spake: " Then Theia boweth unto Him, for He doth come from out the East."

And Panda and Ahmud Hassan fell upon their faces and made obeisance unto the East, and Theia did this thing. And behold, even as they made the chants, there sounded out the step of one who sought, and Panda made the sign of silence. And without the moon had gone, for clouds had arisen, but the stars still warred to shew. And Panda spake soft: " Hatte! "

And Theia arose and bounded unto the door's ope, and Panda stepped unto it and held ope his arms and cried out: " Hatte! Hatte! Come thou, for she hath come—Theia! "

And behold, the lad stood still, and the lamp shewed his white face, and he threw his hands high, and his voice pealed forth in loud note, and he fled, and his voice sounded upon the speeding: " O-o-he! O-o-he! O-o-he! "

And Theia stood as one dead-smitten! And Panda let fall his arms and spake: " The lash Rome cut hath left his flesh sore. Panda goeth out upon the hills and seeketh his lamb."

And Theia stood still, and the sunk cheeks burned, and her eyes leapt fires, and her hands oped and shut and she spake even as the hiss of the serpent:

" Rome hath taken price of Theia's flesh and spent her store. Ah! ah! ah! Rome, thou hast slain! The blade's point up unto the half lieth here!"—and she touched her heart o'er—"and thou wouldst more? Jehovah, hast thou oped the storehouse of Theia unto Rome? Nay! Nay! It shall be! He shall come!"

And Nada came forth and took within her arms the form of Theia and spake:

"Wait thou! Wait thou! Panda shall seek."

And they looked unto Panda, and he went without unto the dark. And they sat, and Ahmud Hassan's lips shewed thin, and he went up unto Theia and spake:

"Ahmud Hassan hath spoken follies. Yea, but Ahmud Hassan seeth the wound and sorroweth."

And Theia beat her hands, and Nada soothed her with soft words.

And they waited, and behold Aaron waked and his laugh sounded, and Theia shook. And Nada murmured: "He knoweth naught."

And Theia spake: "Yea, his laugh telleth."

And Nada came forth with bread and gave unto the hand of Aaron. And Aaron took this from the hand of Nada and sat that he eat. And his eyes looked upon Theia. And Theia hid her face. And behold he arose and took from out the nets of their store, and of his bread, and offered unto her hand. And Theia looked upon this and unto Ahmud Hassan and Nada and spake: "Is this the son of Peter?" And Nada answered, "Yea." And Theia oped her arms and took him within. And Aaron laughed, and sat him down and babbled naughts, and shewed of his nets. And Theia looked upon him and waited.

And without sounded steps, and Panda came, hung unto the hand of Hatte. And Hatte stood, his arm o'er his eyes. And Theia oped her lips and cried: "Hatte!" And Hatte tore loose from the hand of Panda and shut out the sound from his ears. And Theia touched him and he shrunk and cried out:

"Jehovah! Jehovah! 'Tis o'ermuch! Touch thou not the flesh of Hatte! Nay! Nay! Speak not, for Hatte feareth the day hath ended doth this thing be!"

And Theia spake his name and her lips stopped upon it: "Hat-te! Hat-te! Hat-te!"

And he sunk and hid his face.

And Theia stood o'er, and her hands beat one upon the other. And she spake soft: "Unto Theia's arms, Hat-te!"

And he cried out: "Nay! Nay! Hatte would see the racks! Even so would the arms of Theia torture his flesh! The hills, the hills have given up their dreams! Theia, Theia is within the trees! Yea, her step soundeth within the waters! Yea, her voice cometh within the winds; the still stars smile her smile; the white moon sheddeth her love, and thou, and thou, thou art stripped!"

And he oped his eyes and looked upon her, and his eyes started forth, and he took up the scourge that hung within his loin's-cloth and looked upon it and held it forth and spake:

"This is Theia! And thou, thou,—where hath Hatte seen thee? Wait! Wait! Yea," and he swayed, "Hatte knoweth. He hath seen the mighty-seat that setteth o'er all and he * who setteth upon it. And beneath his feet, thou! And thou art empty as the skin of the lion that lieth o'er his couch! And Hatte seeth this one laugh. And Hatte seeth more; this scourge cutteth the air and smiteth him, and he knoweth not 'tis the smite of Theia!"

And Theia swayed, swayed, and chanted: "Yea, yea, and the sands gleam and the palms nod, and the camel sheweth white! Look! Look! Hatte, what seest thou?"

And Hatte spake: "Nay, nay, no more!" And he arose from the leaning-far, and Theia cried out:

"The hunger! The hunger! And Rome hath eaten the bread!"

And Panda spake soft unto Ahmud Hassan: "Seest thou? Thy brother offered thee the blade for this thing."

And Ahmud Hassan spake: "Ahmud shall set the spice's smoke that it rise and blind the nobled."

And Hatte stepped out the door's ope, and behold, he stood and turned unto the way unto Bethlehem. And Theia came forth after him and took him unto her, and he looked afar, and behold, o'er the hill's-way gleamed one star!

And they stood them before the sign, and Theia's eyes looked unto the way unto the land that had brought forth Hate.

And Hatte stood silent. And Theia touched him, and he made that he put her away. And the moon came forth and they shewed white within her light. And Theia bended her unto the face of Hatte and looked close unto it and she beat her hands, and her feet stepped swift, and she reached unto her locks and set them freed. And Hatte cried out in anguish.

And behold, she sunk unto her knees, and her voice cried out in the chant of prayer:

"Jehovah! Jehovah!"—and she raised her arms in supplication— "Jehovah! Jehovah! Jehovah! Hark! Jehovah! Jehovah! Jehovah! Hark! Thou hast tarried long, long, long."

* Tiberius Caesar.

And she beat her head unto earth. And Hatte stood and looked unto this thing, and Theia looked not upon him, but cried aloud:

"Where in the Emptiness, where in the Silence, where in the Waiting, hidest thou? Jehovah! Jehovah! Jehovah!"—and her voice broke upon the word in tears—"thine own awaiteth thee! She looketh unto thy day. Why tarriest thou? Hath the desert's sands gleamed fires, and hath thy caravan stopped for sup within some wooded place? Why tarriest thou? Behold this cup! Behold, its wine hath spilled! Stream thou! Stream thou even as a mighty sun's-beam unto this loved of thine!"

And she harked, and no sound made answer. And she cried out: "Within this silence hast thou spoken?"

And no sound made answering. And she stood up and lay her hand unto her ear that she hark, and still no sound came forth. And she sunk and cried louder: "Jehovah! Jehovah! Jehovah! Hark!"

And she swayed, and her lips smiled, and she spread forth her hands and swayed in dance, and spake:

"The whited camel cometh! Even now hath he arisen from the pool's side!"

And Hatte cried out, and flung him within her arms and cried aloud, and she looked upon him, and he sunk upon his knees and kissed her feet. And Theia stood even as one nobled. And Hatte wept and cried:

"The hills gave up the dreams and they died within the heart of Hatte that thou mightest live therein!"

And Theia shrunk and spake:

"Dreams flit like moths, golded within the sun and silvered within the moon. They shew unto thee and thou, ah, thou canst know them even though they flit thee ever. Dreams! Dreams shew, and precious stuffs fall as dusts before their lovely! And dost thou reach forth and prison the moth, it sheweth but the moth! Hatte, thy mother would bear thee garlands. She would weave thee a cloak of gold. She would mail thine armor of her smiles. She would sandal thee with the skins of young lambs and sew thy sandals with her locks. She would lay low the mighty for thee. But look! look! the pits have emptied her!"

And Hatte cried: "Nay! Nay! From out the heart of Hatte shall she pluck forth the dead dreams and cloak the moth. He shall see the gold locks gleam and spread the airs, and see the feet, like unto the young fawn, bound upon the sweet-herbed earth. He shall see the hill's places, and Simeon who limped, and Peter who spake wisdom and lay his thumb upon his nose, and Mary whom Rome hath taken.

And look! look! Seest thou the white clouds that shew within the light? Upon the hill's side hath Caanthus lain and looked unto these clouds and dreamed of thee. 'Caanthus, art thou strong?'"

And he took forth the scourge and cut the airs and spake: "Yea, yea, yea, for her!"

And Theia looked her unto the hills at Bethlehem's way and spake soft:

"Simeon! Simeon! The white mist Theia waiteth thee!"

And Hatte listed and sat him down, and Theia stood long, and the time sped. And Ahmud Hassan and Panda and Nada waited within, but came not forth.

And Hatte spake: "Theia, mother."

And Theia murmured: "Yea, speak thou this; 'tis music."

And Hatte spake slow: "Theia, mother, what setteth Rome like unto the wolf upon thee and Hatte?"

And Theia cried: "What! Hath Rome set thy path?"

And Hatte answered: "Nay, but Rome lieth like unto a shadow unto all men of Jerusalem. Rome croucheth ever, and Hatte hath fear that Rome shall undo him."

And Theia shook, and her lips spake:

"Hatte, Theia's lips are shut. She shall speak not that that should ne'er be spoken. Thy mother hath drunk from out the goblet of Rome and knoweth the bitters, and would offer thee not the cup."

And Hatte said: "Thou didst smite the flesh of Hatte, even at the time that they took thee forth."

And Theia spake: "Yea, that thou shouldst know not the bitters."

And Hatte questioned: "Who, Theia, is Panda? Ever Hatte would seek that he tell unto him who be the sire of his flesh, and Panda hath told unto Hatte of thee and thine and that he stood as thy slave, and yet his lips shut at this thing. Who is this nobled one that hath forsaken thee?"

And Theia spake not. And Hatte asked of her: "Who is this one?" And Theia's lips still shewed shut. And Hatte spake:

"Theia, mother, Hatte seeth his days, e'en the days of Bethlehem, within the house of Ezekiel. He feeleth the wet earth upon his feet and seeketh upon the paths unto the hills where he found but lone * and sheep; and the paths he sought amid the ways of Bethlehem wherein he found men, and lone; and the paths of Jerusalem, wherein he found but lone and lone and lone. E'en when the breast of Rhea lended unto him, there seemed unto Hatte within him—lone. And Panda

* Loneliness.

filled this lone up of words and binded up his wounds. And the words
shrunk with the passing of tides, unto the time when the wounds shewed
bare; and out of the filling of words hath grown—lone. Thou art
of the flesh of Hatte, and thou hast spoken it, and yet the blade of
Rome hovereth at thy breast. Yea, and this one hath forsaken thee.
This one who hath packed thee of woe with the flesh of Hatte. In the
filling of thee of woe he hath emptied thy day. He held unto thy lips
the cup of loving wherein man springeth root, and set the vineyards of
bitterness upon the hills of hope and left thee that thou pluck the grape
and sup the bittered wine—lone."

And Hatte sunk upon his knees at the feet of Theia and flung wide
his arms and cried out, and his breast heaved:

"Theia, mother, speak! This cup thou didst sup that set the roots
of the living flesh of Hatte that they spring; this cup that hath drowned
thy words"—and his voice sounded as the breath amid the husks—
"was this cup drunk in loving, or in hate?"

And Theia shewed white and still, and spake: "Hatte, no cup that
hath been supped, e'en in folly, but cometh unto thee at the dawn of
some new day. Ask thou not of me this thing!"

And Hatte cried, and his voice sounded clear:

"Speak! Love or hate?"

And Theia beat her hands upon her bosom, and her lips pressed
close and shewed shut. And Hatte arose and took up the lash, the
gold scourge, and raised it high and cried out:

"Love or hate?"

And Theia wailed: "Theia's own locks! Theia's own flesh! 'Tis
o'ermuch, Rome, o'ermuch!"

And Hatte again cried out:

"Love or hate? Speak! Speak! Speak!"

And Theia crouched, even as a she-lion, and her eyes shone, and she
laughed and spake:

"Out of the cup of hate drank Theia love."

And Hatte said: "Nay, the cup of hate holdeth not the wine of
love!"

And Theia held her hands high unto the heavens and cried:

"Yea, yea, Hatte, the hand of Jehovah doeth this thing!"

And Hatte spake: "Hate! Hate! And this thou hast spoken even
at the first breath of Hatte. Hate! Hate! The earth's day is but
lands of woe swept through by the waters of hate!"

And Theia leaned far, and touched the flesh of Hatte and her voice
sounded as the temple's doves. "Hatte, Hatte, this thing is true;

but the airs, the skies, dreams, dreams, yea, out from thee and Theia shall come forth dreams * that shall set the waters of hate to dry and the lands of woe to send forth spurts of young green that spelleth hope!"

And she swayed. "The east way sheweth, and the west wind hath brought forth a seed,† and it hath fallen and sprung root, and its roots sink deep even unto the foundation stones of the temples; and the temples shake even at this root's touch. And behold, the young green sheweth even at this time, and no man knoweth but that this is the first blade of the grain's stalk that feedeth Jerusalem. Yea, but hark, Hatte! upon this stalk there shall show a golden sheaf, and from out this grain shall the bread of earth be fashioned. And they shall feed, feed and feed, and thank not. And the golden grain shall still shew, and they shall eat, and eat, and eat and thank not. And still shall the golden grain shew, and the earth shall know not the whyfore of this thing. And they shall plant them new fields, and grow new grains and fashion new breads, and still the golden grain shall show. For Jehovah hath spoken unto the listing ear, and e'en though they hark not and stop His whispers with blood, still shall He whisper on!"

And Hatte swayed and chanted him:

"Yea, yea! Hatte seeth this grain's stalk and golden sheaf, and it noddeth to him and speaketh, 'I am thy Brother,' and the sweet lips stop and laugh, and the word cometh amid a laugh, 'Hate! Hate! Hate!' And Hatte turneth unto the east way, and behold, the sun cometh and his tongues speak out, 'Hate! Hate!' And the temple's stones echo it, and the airs sing as the birds of the trees, 'Hate! Hate! Hate!' And Hatte taketh up this golden scourge and presseth it unto his parched lips and smileth and speaketh love—and his hands shew scarlet, and the scarlet drippeth upon the earth even at his feet, and within the dripping they fall and spell: 'Hate'! Yea, Hatte seeth him upon the path, and he would slay his very self. And he layeth stones upon his own flesh, and setteth blade unto it, and it fleeth as a phantom, on and out his reach, and laugheth back, 'Hate! Hate! Hate!'"

And he threw his hands high and cried out: "The slaying! The slaying!" And ran unto the dark.

And Theia stood shaken, and her limbs gave under her, and she arose even upon their last strength and held her hands high and cried:

"Jehovah, this hand is thine, but this, ah, this shall cut the throat of Rome for this thing!"

And there sounded out the laugh of Aaron, who sought.

---

* Another reference to the present.　　　　　　† Christ.

And Theia harked, and her lips spake soft: "Jehovah, is this the answering?"

And she arose and went unto the hut, wherein the light still shewed, and behold, upon her knees Nada shewed, and her lips made prayers. And Panda sat bowed, and Ahmud Hassan's arm lay about his shoulder. And Indra sat, her eyes like unto the wolf's, hungered for fill.

And they looked not upon Theia, even though she came unto them, but waited her word.

And Theia looked upon Nada and touched her and spake: "Call thou loud! The god slumbereth."

And Nada's lips moved, and she threw her hands o'er her head and made obeisance thrice and thrice and thrice, in fearing.

And Theia drew up unto her utmost and spake: "Then dost thy god lash thee unto fearing? Jehovah speaketh in silence!"

And she sunk and murmured: "No more of words."

And Panda waited, and Ahmud Hassan waited, and Nada chanted low, and Indra listed and looked.

And when they had waited long and the lips of Theia had ceased their quiver, she spake, and the words shook:

"He——hath——gone."

And Panda spake: "Yea, Theia, like unto the hawk, he seeketh the lones that he may cry out his tongue."

And Theia came up unto Ahmud Hassan and said: "Sire, thou knowest, thou knowest much of Rome. Thou hast brought forth of her. Thou hast heard the name, Theia. Thou hast loosed the pits. Thou knowest him, and thou dost wear his sign even upon thy breast. Speak! what hast thou within thy mantle sleeve?"

And Ahmud Hassan answered: "Woman, thy cup runneth o'er. What then, that thou shouldst seek more of Rome's wine?"

And Theia spake: "Look! As thou lovest Rome, as thou hast sworn thee unto the mighty one, speak! Is thy hand at this breast, or dost thou seek Hatte!"

And Ahmud Hassan oped his lips and made the sign unto the East, and spake: "Unto Allah speaketh Ahmud Hassan. Unto Allah hath he kissed his blade, even though the shield of him be of Rome."

And Theia cried, and her thin cheeks burned: "Tiberius! Tiberius! Hath he spoken unto thee?"

And Ahmud Hassan answered: "Yea."

And Theia questioned: "Knoweth he of Theia's fruit?"

And Ahmud Hassan spake him: "Yea."

And Theia spake: "The fruit of Theia is but the market's wares unto him, and why seekest he out of Rome unto Jerusalem for such fruits?"

And Ahmud Hassan answered: "Tiberius! Tiberius!"—and he whispered low—"Tiberius! his wine is glut, its bead vanities, its dregs blood! Yea, and his drunken dreams lead unto paths wherein he yet may slay."

And Theia shut her harking o'er with her hands. And Ahmud Hassan looked upon her, and she sunk to list, and he spake:

"This man suppeth locust wine, the honey-sup, and spatteth forth blood."

And Theia whispered: "The courts—the slaves—the women—the eunuchs—all grapes from which he presseth his wine!"

And Ahmud Hassan spake: "What didst thou that offended him? Supped out the chalice with some noble and brought upon thee his wrath?"

And Theia answered: "Nay."

And Ahmud Hassan questioned: "What then?"

And Theia made answering: "Didst thou ride from out Rome that ye bear word unto Jerusalem?"

And Ahmud Hassan answered: "Yea. Tiberius fell drunk, and whined at the music's note, and shut up his eyes unto the slaves, and wrathed upon his household; and called forth Ahmud Hassan and gave rugs unto his hand, and said that within Jerusalem dwelled one who danced, who danced, and danced. And he laughed and laughed and spake: 'Danced unto her falling, and Tiberius would set and see this one dance, dance, dance!' And he swayed him 'bout and made that his steps bound. Yea, he made that he dance and said that this one had of fruits of which he would eat!"

And Theia sat as one of stone, and she looked unto Ahmud Hassan and spake: "What would he of the fruit of Theia?"

And Ahmud Hassan answered: "Vanity beareth not even a shadow."

And Theia laughed, and the bitter of her laugh cut, and she spake: "He hath builded up a shadow that shall show through ages."

And the hour was late. The day e'en then did raise the night's robe that earth dance. And the airs burst musics for her stepping. And they stopped their words that they rest when Jerusalem had waked. And the sun arose from out the East's arms, and it was new day.

CHAPTER XI

AND when the light had come unto the hill's depths, behold, it shone upon a one who slept among the sheep. And the one stirred at the touch of light and spread forth his arms, and lo, this one was Hatte. And he stood, and looked unto the way unto Jerusalem, and unto the way unto the hut of Panda, and his lips spake:

"Even hath the dream of Hatte emptied; for he seeth her stripped, stripped!"

And he laughed and let fall his hands, and knelt beside a lamb and spake more:

"Thou dost slumber. Thou art young, young and tender, and yet the ewe, e'en while thou dost slumber, may be offered up in sacrifice. So hath Hatte lain and slumbered and she hath been offered up. She spake the name 'Jehovah,' and He hath let this thing that it be! Hatte's head splitteth at the taking-in of this thing. Who is he who hath ridden here? Who is he who hath the mighty-sign and setteth the one of Rome within Jerusalem that his words be naught, and opeth up the pits? Who is he? Jerusalem hath asked this thing, Who? Who? Who? Is this then he? Hatte knoweth not his sire and the words of Jerusalem speak out 'who'!"

And he touched the lamb and it waked and he took it unto him.

And behold, there shone the wings of a bird of the high airs. And Hatte looked unto this and made that he put the lamb from him, and took up a stone and cried out:

"Thou! Thou mayest sail thee high above Jerusalem, aye, and Rome, and the wickeds of man, and thou art but a winged one! Jehovah, this thing is not meet nor right that dost thou lend not unto man thou shouldst give in full unto his lesser kind."

And he sped the stone, and behold, there fell from out the sky the winged one, even at the feet of Hatte. And he laughed and took it up and looked upon it, even upon its glisted feather, and he spake:

"This, then, is the work of Jehovah. Thou dost spread thy wings and skim the skies, and the throw of Hatte stoppeth thee. Yea, yea, and yet the work of Him is past the work of Hatte, for thou lookest even as a noble in his mighty robe."

And he held the bird within his hands, and sudden his eyes leaped and he whispered:

"Hatte, Hatte, what hast thou done? Knowest thou that e'en now within the hill's places his mate's note calleth? A dream touched and 'tis but a moth."

And he knelt and lay the bird upon the sod and wept, and went forth unto the waters and washed him and spake:

"Hatte, thy blade hath behind its point, who?"

And he went forth unto the hut of Panda, and they still slumbered, and Hatte made way upon the road's-way unto Jerusalem.

And upon the way his head hung, and behold, when he had come unto the near of the wall, Paul came forth and made the sign of greeting. And Hatte looked upon him and spake slow: "Hath Jacob drunk thy waters and left them dry?"

And Paul made answering: "Nay. Nay." And he looked upon Hatte. "Hath Jerusalem's woe fallen upon thee?"

And Hatte answered: "Yea."

And Paul made words that they should seek the shadows that he speak much, for behold, he had come forth filled of words.

And Hatte said: "This thing shall be, for Hatte hath emptied and would that he hark!"

And Paul spake: "There soundeth word within Jerusalem, Hatte, that a noble hath sent forth one to bring unto him his flesh. Yea, Jacob hath told this unto all the emptied ears that come unto him. He hath wailed and spoken that ne'er did a dark-skin come unto Jerusalem but that woe befell him."

And Hatte listed and spake: "This noble—what man knoweth him?"

And Paul told that Jacob had listed unto the Rome's men and this had been their word. And Paul said:

"Hatte, this noble abideth at Nazareth."

And Hatte spake: "What setteth thy tongue to speak this thing?"

And Paul told that men who had come from out Nazareth had brought forth word that this nobled one had gone thereto and that his sire had taken him unto Bethlehem that the scripts be fulfilled. And Hatte spake: "Is this one of Rome?"

And Paul spake: "Nay, no man who shall stand as the King o'er the Jews may be born of Rome's flesh."

And Hatte said: "Yet flesh of Rome sitteth o'er."

And Paul spake soft: "Yea, yea, but Jerusalem is even now upon her knees and the time shall come when she shall stand forth."

And Hatte said: "Yea, yet Jerusalem shall kneel long and long. Who, then, is the sire of this one's flesh!"

And Paul made answering: "Jerusalem speaketh this so: 'Who?'"

And Hatte touched the flesh of Paul and spake: "Thou speakest his sire's name 'who?' Then he is the brother of Hatte."

And Paul said: "Nay, this one is of the Jews."

And Hatte said: "Even so Hatte."

And Paul spake: "Jacob hath told that thou hast been up unto the Rome's place. Yea, that Rome had even her hand upon thee and thou wert set free."

And Hatte said: "Yea."

And Paul looked upon him and asked: "Didst thou fear?"

And Hatte spake: "Nay."

And Paul told of this one of Nazareth, and said that even within Jerusalem words crept from one man unto the other and spake this one's name; for behold, even though the priests had known of His coming, no man had taken this unto him as law. And behold, like unto the murmur of the market's place, the words of Him would not out. And men took up His words and bore them like grains unto the days of Jerusalem. And within the hills men knew of them, and the Jews, the scribes and men of the Jews, spake His name and even shook their beards that the King had come.

"But Hatte," Paul cried him loud, "Rome laugheth, laugheth, and speaketh this king is king o'er asses!"

And Hatte touched the hand of Paul and spake:

"Hatte hath heard this thing. Yea, look!" and he touched the red scar that lay his cheek; "this telleth thee that Hatte hath heard."

And Paul asked: "Dost thou go unto Jerusalem this morn's tide, Hatte?"

And Hatte made answering: "Hatte's heart leadeth unto where he knoweth not, yet Hatte's feet lag and set his heart hungered that he await and look upon her who hath been stripped."

And Paul spake: "What dost thou set upon thy tongue?"

And Hatte looked afar and made word, saying: "Paul, man should keep within his cup one sup that is for him, one sup that he leaveth hid from men. Panda hath spoken this thing."

And Paul looked unto the hut's-way and spake: "Panda hath wisdom."

And Hatte said: "Yea, wisdom, and he hath milched out the milch of wisdom from the dried breasts of earth. Paul, this one, this one of Nazareth, knowest thou more of Him? Is He one who went unto the temple and spake unto the priests and came unto them with word that, Jerusalem speaketh, hath set wisdom ope even unto its vitals? Is this one He?"

And Paul spake: "Yea, and e'en though He is of the seed of David, for men know this thing, thou knowest upon Him is the scourge of red."

And Hatte spake: "Who—what man speaketh this thing? Hast thou looked upon this woman?"

And Paul made answering: "Nay, but men of the market's place laugh, and yet the wise ones speak that His words shew them clothed of regal robes and will not out. Even though they fall within Nazareth they spring fruit upon the roads'-ways that lead out, and come even unto Jerusalem. Yea, men take them unto the priests and speak them out and the priests shake them, 'yea, yea, wisdom.'"

And Hatte swayed and spake in the see-chant:

"Rome! Rome! Jerusalem! Even within an ass's skin hath Jehovah sent thee the King. Yea, the hills, the hills, the sweet damp of the morning tide! The dark, the step, and He cometh and speaketh, 'I am thy brother, even as thou art mine!' And the woman, Mary, whose smile drowned sorrow. Within her sorrow's tears, yea, within their very pool, shall earth wash clean. The feet of Hatte itch that they seek thee! Yea, he shall set upon the way that he know his Brother."

And Paul cried: "Hatte! Hatte! Wake! Dreamest thou with wide eyes?"

And Hatte started and spake: "Nay, Hatte dreameth not. His heart streameth streams and he swimmeth them. Behold, this thing is the work of Jehovah. Speak thou more, Paul, of Him."

And Paul stood long and looked upon Hatte, whose eyes shewed the look that leadeth on, and he spake:

"There sheweth little, Hatte, of Him save in words, for He cometh not unto Jerusalem, and when the men of Nazareth seek the teacher, behold, He goeth unto the fields and unto the streams and setteth Him down and leaveth the waters that they flow o'er His feet, and speaketh that within the waters is wisdom that man may not drink. And the men say that this is folly."

And Hatte laughed and spake: "Paul, from man's lips this word 'folly' falleth far easier than any word."

And Paul said: "Then thou seest wisdom in one who batheth His feet that He take of wisdom."

And Hatte spake: "Yea, for this one would that His holied step ne'er mar the golden path of wisdom, and washeth that He be clean."

And Paul questioned: " And thou goest unto such an one? "

And Hatte answered: " Nay, not at this tide, for Jerusalem shall hold Hatte until the going of her. Come thou, Paul, the light hath waked the flocks and they unshepherded, for Panda slumbereth. Come! "

And they set upon the way. And Hatte turned unto the hill's path and spake:

" Not at the light! Nay, nay, Hatte still hath shadow 'pon his dream."

And Paul made no questioning, but followed; for youth forgetteth sorrow in youth. And the hills took them in.

CHAPTER XII

AND the light had come unto the past of high, and the house of Panda waked.

And Ahmud Hassan sought out the camel that lay within the sun, and flies swarmed it 'bout, and it shook its head that it free it of them. And Ahmud Hassan's lips shewed shut and the teeth gleamed not. And Panda followed him unto the without and brought forth grain and dried grass that they give unto the camel.

And behold, Indra came forth and bore of a skin filled of goat's milch, and this she hung unto the branch of a fig tree, and beat * upon it, and wheys dripped unto the earth from out the leg's tie, and flies clustered within it. And she spake unto Panda:

" Panda, the milch sheweth thick. The goats feed upon the hills and bring forth their filling, yea, but the filling sheweth short."

And Panda made answering: " Yea, 'tis time for this thing."

And Ahmud Hassan looked upon Indra and unto her eyes and spake: " Sheweth she right, that she hath come from out † the far? "

And Panda answered: " Yea."

And Ahmud Hassan went up unto her and spake words and asked of that that shewed bound 'bout her neck. And Indra laughed and spake: " Panda knoweth the all of this thing."

And Ahmud Hassan spake: " Nay, nay. Panda may be wise, but this thing knoweth he not."

And Indra looked unto Ahmud Hassan and asked that his lips speak clear. And Ahmud Hassan spake: " Leave thou this within the hand of Ahmud Hassan."

And Indra did this thing, and he looked upon it and spake: " Yea, yea, the eyes gleam green. Unto thy hand who hath delivered this thing? "

And Indra answered: " Indra knoweth not save that when the time had come unto the full when her lips spake words and her ears took the words of men in, a one spake of this unto her and shewed it unto her and told of far lands wherein scents hung sweet and men stalked

---

* A primitive churn.
† From a distant land. Indra's mother was a Hindu.

296

them robed royal in flaming color. And this one, sire, Indra knoweth not more of. Joel knew the all and bound this unto Indra and spake naught unto her of what the sign it bore."

And Ahmud Hassan spake: " This one, her face? "

And Indra answered: " Nay, sire, Indra knoweth not even this, nor yet was this one a woman. But word remaineth. But Joel had within his cloth, his pack, that that had been given unto his hand as the goods of Indra."

And Ahmud Hassan questioned: " And this thing is thine at this time? "

And Indra answered: " Unto the hand of Panda hath Indra delivered it."

And Ahmud Hassan asked more: " Hast thou looked upon this? "

And Indra spake: " Nay, for Joel's lips had said that Indra's eyes should not take this thing in."

And Ahmud Hassan looked unto Panda. " Hast thou this? " he questioned.

And Panda let his hand sweep unto the hut's-way and bade that they come unto the within. And they did this thing, and behold, the babe Panda played upon the floors and poured sands from one bowl of brass unto its brother, and his eyes gleamed wide and black and his teeth shewed white. And Indra stepped her unto him and took him up, for Nada had set that they drink of milch, and Nada spake:

" Hast thou brought forth the beaten milch, Indra? "

And Indra smiled slow and said: " Nay, Nada, nay; for this one, this Ahmud Hassan, hath much that hath set Indra's heart hungered that she know and her hands that they fall."

And Theia waked, and called unto them, and Nada spake: " Thou hast waked? Come thou, that we sup."

And she brought forth ripe figs and lay them before Theia.

And Panda spake: " Nay, Nada, not the sup, for Ahmud Hassan would look upon the goods that Joel hath left unto the hand of Panda."

And he brought forth a skin, and it was bound of strands, and they sat that they ope it. And behold, Panda let the latchets loosed and cloth fell it free, and within the cloth shewed metals. And the cloths gleamed, for they held spun gold; and the wools that shewed gleamed rare colors. And there was bound unto the cloth, with silver thread, discs of metal, and they sounded at the touch as the metal song of the stream driven forth before winds. And within this there shewed sandals, and these were not as them of this land; and within them strands of gold, long, that bound the limbs up even unto the knee. And a thing like unto that that hung unto the neck of Indra shewed, and this was carved of alabaster. And still within there shewed a feather, and this gleamed royal, for it was one from out the peafowl. And at its base, bound thereto with metal, a hand's grasp,* carved of ivory.

And Ahmud Hassan's eyes gleamed, and he touched the precious stuff and spake: "The price! Ahmud Hassan knoweth the one who hath done this thing!"

And he touched the feather and said: "Yea, Ahmud Hassan lended of his hand that this be fashioned."

And he touched the metal. And Indra started and cried: "Speak! Speak! Tell thou all, for Indra's heart would leap within Jerusalem, yet it reacheth out and she falleth feared lest in so doing her heart would bathe of filths and not 'mong her tribe."

And Ahmud Hassan spake: "Nay, Indra, feed thee not upon this, for here endeth the dream. Before thee sheweth the price Rome lended that thy mother be bought."

And Indra's eyes shut unto the very tight and she cried out: "Speak! Speak! What meanest thou?"

And Ahmud Hassan made answering:

"Unto Rome cometh all lands. Yea, and Rome taketh in all men who bear unto her. Yea, and Rome shutteth up her eyes unto women and fawneth upon men. Man she bladeth and woman she unbladeth. Ahmud Hassan hath oped his lips and yet he may not speak the all. Await thou!"

And Theia came unto the spot and looked upon the goods of Indra and touched the feather and spake: "Where hath Theia looked upon this thing?"

And Ahmud Hassan smiled the smile of knowing unto her. And Theia touched it o'er and waited and spake:

"Yea! Augustus Caesar! This thing belongeth to him."

And Ahmud Hassan shook him: "Yea," and touched the sandals.

And Theia looked upon them and cried: "Theia's!"

And Ahmud Hassan smiled slow. And Theia took up the god of alabaster and looked upon it, and unto Ahmud Hassan, and unto that that hung 'bout the neck of Indra, and her eyes oped wide and she touched the cloth and spake: "Theia's!"

And Ahmud Hassan said: "Yea. This stoppeth the tongue of Ahmud Hassan, for he who hath that that belongeth not unto him hath but one name."

* A handle.

And Indra made of a sound like unto a serpent, and cast the stuffs unto the floors. And Theia spake:

"Indra, do thou not this thing; for no man knoweth what hand delivered this unto thine nor yet unto them that delivered."

And Indra cried: "Thou! Thou white-skin! Thou and thine! No good cometh of the brothering of dark-skins unto the white."

And Theia shrunk, and Indra cried out more: "Thou! Thou, an emptied one! One whom man hath finished of! And he whom thou hast borne, the offcast of the feast!"

And Theia stood regal and spake: "Thy lips have oped upon Theia. Yea, and Theia wearieth of such word unto the wearying that she e'en would not stop thy tongue."

And Panda spake: "Indra, without!"

And Indra cast the babe unto the floors, and it wailed, and she laughed and went without.

And Theia looked unto Panda and her eyes shewed tears.

And Nada spake: "Panda, Nada would wrath upon Indra, but the wound she hath dealt unto Nada smarteth not as the wound she dealt unto Theia!"

And Theia said: "Nada, Theia feareth woman. Yea, for the tongue of woman lasheth even as the scourge of man; for behind the lash the knowing bideth! One woman knoweth well her sister, and knoweth the hurt that hurteth past all hurts."

And Panda oped not his lips, and Ahmud Hassan spake: "Panda, thou art of the sands; for thine ears take in naught save thy camel's pads, even though the fowls of the air scream loud."

And Panda said: "This, Ahmud Hassan, is but one strand that shall bind the pack of Panda closer unto him."

And Theia questioned: "Who, sire, hath brought forth word of Theia from out Jerusalem?"

And Ahmud Hassan answered: "There hath come forth words from out the offices whereto Jerusalem hath whispered, but this reached not the mighty ear."

And Theia asked of him: "Who, then, hath loosed his tongue?"

And Ahmud Hassan spake: "A one who hath come from out Jerusalem, but the lips of Ahmud Hassan may speak not a name his ear hath ne'er taken in."

And Theia said: "This, this sandal dipped of dye, whose sole is thrice thick—this Theia stepped upon, even at the time when Rome drove her forth."

"Ursus! Ursus! thou didst hold the blade. Ursus! Ursus! and

thou didst hold within thee a sheep's heart. Theia priced thee with
cloth and golded latchets. And Alexis! Theia's smile led him forth,
even unto his journey's end; for he sought Jerusalem. Alexis, who
looked upon Theia, who bore of a king, as a she-goat that he might
milch and bring forth gold of kings. Ursus, whom Rome hath forgot!
Ursus, who drank naughts but vanities from out the day!"

And Ahmud Hassan listed, and Panda spake him no word.

And behold a shadow showed, for Indra listed. And Theia pointed
unto this thing and looked unto Panda, and Panda spake:

"No hill but hath a cloud. Indra, come thou within."

And she came forth and her eyes gleamed wickeds, and she spake:
"So! the nobled set thee even as a rug that they wipe their feet upon
thee."

And she spat upon Theia. And the hand of Ahmud Hassan fell
upon Indra and smote her, and she spake a word that in the tongue of
the Jews stood as a curse.

And Panda commanded: "Go thou unto the out and seek thee
Hatte and bring him forth."

And Indra spake: "Thou mayest seek; for he sheweth not his
face, but goeth unto Jerusalem and seeketh a dark maid, yea, a Jew.
And Indra shall seek this one and tell her that Hatte is no Jew!"

And she raised her up unto her utmost and sped forth from out the
hut, nor tarried that she wait word of them within.

And Panda said: "What is this thing, Nada, that setteth Indra that
she speak wickeds?"

And Nada leaned her close and spake: "Indra hath the sting of
loving. Yea, the worm hath eat at the heart of her, for her eyes look
upon the hill's-ways that they meet Hatte."

And Panda shrugged and smiled slow, and turned unto Ahmud
Hassan. And Ahmud Hassan spake: "The sting hath waked the evil
one within her. Look! her feet speed, and fires flash from their trod,
verily!"

And Panda looked after the fleeing Indra and said: "Yea, but the
waters of love swell as torrents at the wet tide, and dry them speedy;
for the heats of love sear the drops."

And Ahmud Hassan looked unto Theia, and Theia sat clasped of
the goods of Indra. The sandals hung upon their golded latchets
unto her arms, and the feather wafted slow. And her eyes raised like
the waked babe's and her lips spake soft:

"Panda, the gods cast back the golded wastes of the play. E'en
of this have they finished!"

And she took up the sandals and spake unto them:

"Behold thou, Theia! Thou hast sped her, and at this tide her heart weigheth past thy bearing. Yea, thou art bound of golded latchets, and she, bound, bound, and the latchets tied, yea, and the hand of Rome holdeth them!

"The pits have oped. Yea, yea, and Theia may step forth. Yea, even unto her hands hath Rome delivered her cloth, her goods. Yea, Rome is good. Yea, Rome is kind. Yea, Rome feedeth well the beast that Rome's food be rich and full. Theia may step forth free, free, free! Hark ye, sires! Hark ye, Theia is free! Ah, thou without —the green afar, the blue o'erhead, the sands that glint, the dusts that speed the airs—hark ye, Theia is free! She may step forth, her breast torn ope, and cast the crimson of her drops o'er the dusts of Rome, that they arise not and cause the mighty one to sneeze!

"Behold the mock that lieth upon the lips of Rome! Theia seeth her lips to curl and the eyes of her to shut unto the bare oping, and the glance to speed from out the very corners, that they be sharp and hurt. Behold, behold, that thou shalt know, that thou shalt know the fullness of this mocking, behold!"

And she held forth the cloth and the sandals and the feather, and took up the metaled cloth. And Panda started forth and cried:

"Enough, woman! Enough! Do thou not this thing!"

And Theia laughed, laughed, and held forth the metaled rings that shewed as armlets, and put these upon her arms, and they fell upon the upraised arm even unto the shoulder, for no flesh held them. And she stooped and put the sandals upon her feet, and brought the latchets unto the shut and the flesh filled not their opings. And the cloth she spread forth o'er her shrunk form and it hung in billows. And the metaled cloth she spread forth behind upon the flags and spake:

"Look thou! This did Caesar bid fashioned that Theia should dance, dance. Yea, and the mighty halls were lined of waving fans of peafowl's flaunts. Yea, and Theia was the bird—the sign of vanity! Yea, and she eat of fruits, and he who caught of one the tooth of her had sunk within cried out in joy.

"And Caesar had set oped the hall, the mighty hall, and the walls were hung of the royal scarlet, and the purple of the mighty one, and the feathers of the vanity.

"And the floors of the halls were strewn of purple lilies and white locusts that sent up sweet at the trodding. And the pool within belched forth waters, and upon the stream flowers rose and fell, and slaves poured sweet oils upon the waters.

" And the slaves, robed, one rank of white, one of purple, one of scarlet, one naked and draped of grape leaves and purple fruits. And the virgins wore wool's fleece caught upon their shoulders with trailed vines, and their heads shewed bound of blooms, and their feet bared and saffroned upon their toes. And the metals of their anklets beat like golden treasures at their stepping.

" And behold, youths stroked upon golden lyres, and their limbs shewed bared and their brows wound of laurels. And others blew upon trumpets.

" And the black ones gleamed as ebon, oiled, and their loins wrapped of leopards' skins and white goats.

" And behold, they, the women of the court, came them forth robed, and their flesh gleamed rosed, and their locks shewed of gold dusts, and their necks were bound of flashed gems, and their breasts were guarded with gold discs set with jewels.

" And babes of young youth bore fruits and flowers, yea, and cups and chalices. And the men of Rome drank not from these, but begged that they might sup from out this "—and she held forth her curled hand—" and drink the laugh of Theia amid their sup. Yea, Rome was good! Yea, Rome was kind."

And the tears sped o'er the thin cheeks. And Panda shrunk as 'neath the lash, and cried out: " Enough! Enough! "

And Theia smiled and spake: " Nay, Rome would on with the play! "

" Behold thou! Behold thou! Then did the trumpet blast sound even as the cry of the peafowl, and the feast was called. And they lay beside the feasting place, and each took unto himself that that he coveted that he eat, be this flesh or fruit.

" And this was the time—this. For slaves came forth and bore a golden salver, and upon this the royal bird shewed. And they sat that they eat, and behold, the bird stood up. And this was Theia! This was Theia! This!

" And upon the feasting place she stepped and swayed. And this did she pluck from out her locks—this! "

And she held aloft the feather and laughed upon it and stroked it and spake her on: " Yea, Rome's nobled did she tickle with this."

And her throat swelled, and she reached unto her heart and swayed, and her eyes stood out, and she spake:

" And he was there—Tiberius! Yea, he was there. And Rome knew much * her smiling lips held behind their smile. And the bird

* A reference to the amours of Julia, wife of Tiberius.

of vanity bowed before her sire, and honeyed words dripped from off a wine-sweet tongue.

"The day had oped unto Theia. Yea, the voices of the multitude called her name, 'Theia! Theia! Theia! Theia!' And it sounded as music. And she tripped her, spreading forth her flaunts and preening her that she eat from out the noble hand. And knew not, knew not, that the hand of Caesar should cause her slaying!"

And Ahmud Hassan's eyes gleamed wicked, and Theia looked unto him and spake:

"But even though the bird had danced, the feast sped on. Yea, fruits lay sweet-spilled upon the floors, and wine-shook hands turned ever-spilling founts of wines. But Theia was drunk, drunk, upon words and glances.

"And behold, they had drunk unto the flaming of fires, and they set unto the building up of a mighty cup that each should add unto. And they brought forth a golden bowl whose lips gleamed of sapphires, and a cup fashioned out from one gleaming jade. And this they gave unto the hand of Theia.

"And she set unto the building up of the cup. Upon the honey-locusts poured she wines, and they sunk therein pomegranates and spiced grapes and leaves of the cinnamon and barks of it. And ripe figs therein they emptied, and they brought forth flower wines that smelled as the spring's wake, and poured unto it. And it gleamed and shewed the taint of the sweet of the pomegranate and the scents of flowers and the bite of the spices. Yea, and this was the cup that should send the dream-god unto the merry-make.

"And behold, slaves came forth and brought them lilies bound 'bout of sweet grass, and these were cups. Yea, these they called lotus lilies, and they dipped these unto the stems o'er and ate of the cup. And behold, they slept amid the feast's leave, like flies swarmed and stilled o'er filth.

"And Theia saw this thing, and waked and shook and knew the night of Rome mocked her day! This, then, was Caesar's household without the slaves' place! Theia knew the pits, the games, the dance— but this! Behind this smile, what lay?

"And he, Tiberius, had drunk not his filling but spake word that Theia knew not and feared.

"And Panda looked upon this. Didst thou not, Panda?

"And he was kind, Tiberius, he was good, like Rome. And he promised a new day. And Theia spread her wings and strutted even as the vain-cock, and listed."

And her weak form stepped, and she strutted, and behold, she looked upon herself and burst forth laughs, peal upon peal. And amid her laugh she spake:

" They slept, but one waked and then the other. And his noble mightiness slept heavy. And wine had heated of them o'er, and they cried out for game, for laugh, for merry-make. And Theia now watched afar.

" And they bid that coals of fire be brought forth, and this thing was done. And they laughed and drank and sang, and the coals glowed. And they bade that a black slave, a young one, be brought forth, and this thing was done, and they lay a scourge upon her and caused that she dance upon the coals. And the smell of seared flesh scented o'er the sweet. And she fell, and they lashed upon her flesh and she danced. And they laughed and cast their wines upon the coals that they flame. And the slave sunk and rose not more.

" And Theia knew what hid behind the smile, and feared, and fled up unto where her sister lay—Eunice, who knew not yet Rome's nights.

" Even though at the morn he, Tiberius, had come upon Eunice and Theia dancing amid the garden's place, and looked upon them, still the sear had touched not Eunice.

" And the morn brought fear, and within Theia had sprung up a mighty Why? Within whose hand stood this stone that pressed upon her? And Rome answered not upon that day.

" And the time came that Tiberius should go forth, and behold, the slaves' place oped and women came forth and took Theia out unto the hall's place. And they called forth Panda and bade that he go and bring forth the goods that Caesar had given unto the hand of Theia. And Caesar gave unto Theia this "—and she brought forth the seal *—" and this, thou canst see, showeth the copper, yea, the gleaming green and sapphire of the vanity-cock. This he put upon the thumb of Theia, that Tiberius might look upon it and know his kindness, his goodness! " And she laughed!

" Then, then, Theia, the vain one, drank honeyed words and ate of first-fruits and went forth sorrowed, but waiting the new day of promise.

" And it came, too soon! Theia knew the vat's dregs. Knew that grape and worm maketh wine. Afar, afar, she learned this thing, and Rome smiled not.

" And sick came upon her, and no word comforted—no word. And Theia knew how full days might be as empty as skulls of deserts' dead.

* The copper ring bearing the signet of Augustus, previously mentioned.

"And then, and then, Theia knew not what was upon her. And this she poured unto the empty founts of Panda's ears. And Panda spake of Rome, and the times of the games, and of Ajax, and Theia remembered, and knew that the pits had held her heart even while she played with it as with a pebble that she caught and cast.

"Theia knew that Ajax, at the stepping upon her rose, had crushed her heart within the pit's sand. Yea, Theia knew this and sicked sorer, for the golden discs fell from off her eyes and left but crystal tears to hide the real day.

"And yet, and yet, Theia hated not. Nay, hate had not yet been born unto her.

"And then came forth the word unto Tiberius, and he spake not of the fullness of it unto Theia, but at a time later he called her unto him, and with his kiss delivered her unto Rome's hand that held a blade! And unto a babed heart hate crept and slept close, waiting and waking.

"'Unto Rome,' spake he, 'unto Rome that thou dost wait!'

"And the sands, and the wastes, then Rome. And Rome smiled not, but laughed in scorn! And Theia knew!

"Yea, Theia knew! Rome's laugh shewed empty. Yea, emptier far than Rome's smile. Unto Theia's listed ears Rome spake not what she held for the dealing. Yea, and Simeon—Ajax—Rome had emptied her of him. Nor did Rome leave the tongue of Theia that she spill unto Rome's ones. Nay, e'en her sister Eunice, Rome had shut away. A slave whose feet had stilled stood as naught unto Rome. And then, should a noble eat when he had eat his fill? Nay, ne'er unto the nobled was that offered that he had eat of once, nor would Augustus eat of his kinsman's leave.

"Augustus! Augustus, who dealt slave's flesh unto his own flesh's * flesh! Yea, what though a man had wifed, slaves should minister unto him. Slaves! Slaves! Ah, slaves are but the feed for swine!

"Lone, lone, Theia waited, and unto the hand of Ursus, who fawned but held Rome's blade, was she delivered. Ursus, the flesh of the grister † whose legs sped him unto Rome's games. Yea, and who had drunk Rome's pomp out of Rome's words of praise, and who, like unto a dog, licked the feet of the mighty!"

And behold, there sounded the step of one who came, and Panda made the sign of silence, and stepped him unto the door's ope and called at the seeing: "Lucius! Lucius!"

And Lucius came within, and bore of fruits and grain's-grind, and

* Tiberius, the husband of his daughter.　　† The son of the miller.

his smile broke forth. And he looked upon Theia and the goods of Indra and spake:

"What speedeth Indra unto Jerusalem? For, Panda, Lucius came upon her upon the ways thereto and she looked not upon him, but sped, sped her on."

And Panda answered not, but smiled slow. And Nada made answering unto the words of Lucius: "She hath sped her feet upon wicked words."

And Lucius looked unto Theia and stood still. And Panda spake: "Lucius, this goods is of Joel, the goods he hath bidden for the hands of Indra for to receive. Knowest thou of this thing?"

And Lucius answered: "Yea and nay. What wouldst thou?"

And Panda spake: "Knowest thou who delivered this unto the hand of Joel?"

And Lucius looked upon the goods and touched them o'er and said: "Yea, Joel's flesh knoweth Rome, for the brother of Joel, Ursus, was of Rome. This is goods of Rome."

And Panda let fall his eyes unto the floors, and Lucius spake more: "Yea, the market's men said that Ursus fell 'neath Rome's blade, yea, that he had drunk from out Rome's noble hands and returned not the cup."

And Panda listed unto the words of Lucius, and Theia leaned her far that she list. And Nada stood with the babe Panda pressed at her side, and they harked. And Lucius spake him on, that Joel had come unto Jerusalem even at the slaying of Ursus.

"For Rome would not of the blood of Ursus, e'en though the sire of his flesh ground of meal of grains that Rome eat thereof. For behold, what would Rome of one who ground, for Rome, doth she need, reacheth forth and taketh unto her that that she needeth. Yea, and the grister raised his hand 'gainst the slaying. So, at the raising of his hand Rome's hand raised, bladed, and fell.

"Ursus had taken unto him a one of the far land and this one was young, yea, and gold-skinned. And unto her hands Ursus delivered the goods of Rome, and her head lifted in pride and she came, even before Rome, clothed therein. And this one fruited and died, and unto the hand of Joel fell her fruit."

And Lucius turned unto Panda and spake: "Panda, thou knowest the lips of Jerusalem's own flesh ope not that they speak loud. Yea, and thou knowest that he who hath come unto Jerusalem as the wind's casts, stoppeth his lips; for Jerusalem's stones speak. So, Joel's lips told naughts."

And Theia said: "So, the stopping of the blade of Ursus that it fall not upon Theia but tarried it. Yea, it fell upon Ursus and spilled his vanity."

And Ahmud Hassan came forth, even up unto Theia, and made words, saying: "This, then, is the full weave of the cloth Rome still holdeth. Hark! Ahmud Hassan, with his own hands, fashioned out this, the golden ball that decketh this, thy folly-feather. Yea, Ahmud Hassan knew not the nobled, but hath bought favor by the bart of wit, yea, and the weigh of words."

And Theia spake: "Didst thou know Theia?"

And Ahmud Hassan answered: "Yea, as one who danced, but ne'er as a woman."

And Theia breathed long and spake: "Yea, thou hast spoken true. Rome knoweth slaves not as women but as vassals. Yea, a slaved heart, unto Rome, is but a fowl that she filleth of rots."

And Ahmud Hassan asked of her: "What is this thing thou didst that left thee unto Rome's walls * even within Jerusalem? This thing oped Rome's ear."

And Theia spake: "Yea, yea, sire. Theia shall empty all; for within thine eye she readeth that that lieth within the eye of Panda."

And Ahmud Hassan spake: "Yea, a man's eyes may look them unto all ways; yea, unto the east, yet unto the west, yet unto the four corners, and still there sheweth from out them, be it there, the look that ever findeth his brother. Thou hast oped the script of Ahmud Hassan."

And Theia held forth her hands and they shook; and the robe fell as the withered petals of some purple lily languished late unto the second sun. And the armlets shook metal's music, and she spake:

"Theia telleth thee all. Out of thy well of wisdom then, thou, Ahmud Hassan, shalt draw forth sup that she know what and whither.

"Hark! Unto lands, unto sands, then unto waters, Ursus sped with Theia. And Theia knew that beneath the soft paw of this beast lay the claw, and she feared. And one of her goods she offered for one day, and yet one, that she know of one more.† Yea, and this she did with honeyed words, and spake of Tiberius, who yet should step unto the mighty-place. And she put upon her tongue the tale of his powers, and yet the tale of his love for Theia. And bright she shewed this thing. Yea, and ever turned the ear of Ursus that it hark unto the promising, that, did he this thing 'gainst Augustus, Tiberius should hold forth full price.

---

* What had she done that caused her imprisonment in Jerusalem?
† Stayed his hand from day to day by bribes.

"For Rome's ones smelled the rots that lay even at the mighty-seat. Even at this time Rome knew, and Ursus knew Rome's whisper. Yea, Ursus had taken sweets even out the hand of the flesh that belonged unto Tiberius! Yea, Ursus knew that the seat of Augustus leaned far unto the tilt, even far unto the spilling; and this leaning fell toward Tiberius.

"Behold, the mighty one casts forth his hand and scattereth the women of the courts even as flies. The hand of Augustus wafted the men of Rome from off the sweets of Theia that his flesh might eat thereof. This is Rome! Yea, Rome! kind Rome! good Rome!

"So, Ursus knew these things, and Ursus thought within him, doth Tiberius cast me up and catch not, behold, his flesh shall hold forth her hand and catch. Yea, Ursus was but a ball for the casting.

"And Theia knew this thing, and knew more; that his hands itched that he put within his belly its fill, that he take back unto Rome and vomit forth and its sour wake the mighty! Theia, the coin, would he spend. It mattered not be she no more, but that she be not unto Rome. And more; Ursus was of Rome, good and kind, and blood soileth!

"And at the waters, behold they came upon Alexis, and Alexis— ah, Alexis hungered that he play with Rome's nobled plaything! Yea, Alexis could drink waters of filth from out a noble's track and smack full o'er it.

"Yea, and more; Alexis filled of himself unto the wine's heat. Yea, and he felt the tickle of joy that he lend a hand unto Theia, whom the men of Rome spake much of, that he might sit him among Romans and look afar and speak: 'Theia? Theia? Yea, Theia hath been the flesh of Alexis, but a man wearieth!'

"So Theia spent smiles, one for one day, and it fevered him. Yea, Theia smiled, smiled joyfully for Rome's goodness, and her heart swelled until her ribs put bars upon it!

"And Alexis lended his hand. Yea, for Alexis saw and knew a rot of Rome and would eat of it for the unbellying 'mong the men.

"The pits know the within of beasts and the pits feed thereon, but Rome's men feed upon the within * of women! Like vultures they pick and tear that they know all that filleth women. This is the fill of the nobles' mouths. This they eat even among their feasts.

"Hark! Theia knoweth of one, a woman who oped her lips o'er-wide and Rome caused hot irons to be run through her, living, from throat unto the middle! This is Rome's play, that her lips find cause for smiling.

* Reputations.

" More Theia knoweth of one, a Jew, who gave unto his utmost, of flesh, of goods, even of his son's blood. And Rome had finished of him. And he was but a Jew, and he hungered, and took of Rome's. And Rome caused that his head's skin be laid ope, and tied unto a tree a hungered vulture, close, so that he who was bound should feed from out his skull's cup the vulture's hunger! And this was Rome's play!

" And Alexis took of smiles and filled his eyes. And Theia went unto the way unto Jerusalem, for Alexis sought out the Rome's place therein. And Theia knew not the road's-ways and the sea's-ways that led thereto, but ever smiled, smiled, smiled. And Panda slept but at Theia's waking,* and waited, waited, waited.

" And when they had come far, and far, Alexis spake unto Theia, saying: ' Thou shalt go not unto Jerusalem, for Alexis feareth.'

" E'en though he had from the lips of Theia the promise that she follow him. And Theia knew, at these words, that Alexis had no blood from the god Mars.

" Yea, and Theia's heart chilled; for the sick was upon her. But within the pack she bore still was the gold's dusts and metals and that that she might turn unto bread.

" And upon a time night fell, and the men of Alexis, and Theia and Panda, had set upon this way upon camels, and when the dark tide shewed deep, Alexis caused that they stop. And behold, he spake not, but his men laid hands upon Theia, and unpacked her from the camel's back, and cast her forth with Panda upon the hill's path. And this was upon the way unto Bethlehem. And Alexis turned, for he had gone from out his road's-way that he cast Panda and Theia forth that they seek not upon his path.

" Ah, then the hate bloomed! Yea, from out the deep rooting sprung the living hate and bloomed!

" Unto the silent sky's dark, unto the weary hill's-way, unto the sharp stones, unto the lone, Theia was commended!

" Ah, sire, Theia may not tell with word the bitters that lay within her cup. She may not tell unto thee the dealing Rome dealt unto her; for no man's eyes might look upon her suffering; for it lay upon the Theia Rome knew not.

" With the quickening of hate this Theia was born. Jehovah touched her, Theia, and within her she waked! And the smile dropped from Rome's face and Rome's arms shewed but rot-ragged flesh! Yea, and her lips, at the stir of her smile, stank as the carcasses plucked by

* Slept only when Theia was awake.

birds upon the deserts. Theia knew, knew, knew! and the knowing hurt, hurt sore.

"And behold, Theia waked within the shadow of Bethlehem, and bore a thing of Rome that nurtured at her breast! Jehovah! Jehovah! 'Twas o'ermuch! And still Rome tortured; for this thing reached deep and fastened unto Theia's heart's chords!

"Behold thou Theia! Behold her, sire! Ridden of Love upon the back of Hate! Behold thou Theia!

"Hatte! The cup! Thou knowest him, sire. Hark! Come thou unto Theia that she fill thine ear." And Ahmud Hassan came forth close and Theia whispered: "The son of Tiberius!"

And Ahmud Hassan spake: "Thy path hath led long, but Ahmud Hassan knew this thing even at the coming within the walls of Jerusalem. Behold!"

And he drew forth a script of goat's skin and shewed unto the eyes of Theia. And they looked one unto the other, and Theia spake:

"Then Rome hath put the blade within thy hand?"

And Ahmud Hassan answered: "Yea, but Rome wove the cloth within which she clothed the tale. Behold, unto the ears of Ahmud Hassan poured the song that Theia hungered for riches, yea, and sought the mighty one with threats and held her son as the blade against his breast. And it was the pleasure of Tiberius that she be brought forth at the slaying of this flesh of her, and be caused to dance."

And Ahmud Hassan's teeth bit upon his lips, and he said: "Ahmud Hassan may speak lies unto Rome, for truth would sour Rome's vitals."

And Panda spake: "A stream of lies may float truth unto the lands of refuge. Lie, lie, yea, lie, brother!"

And Ahmud Hassan's eyes took in the hunger of Theia's, and his lips flashed smile, and he cried:

"Panda, await thou! Ahmud Hassan goeth without that he seek his humped one."

And he did this thing and returned, solemn, like unto a priest, and spake:

"Yea, he even now is packed of lies! Jerusalem shall know not this legged cup as the cup of Rome."

And Theia murmured: "Yea, yea, but thou, thou hast yet to seek Rome, and Rome awaiteth word."

And Ahmud Hassan spake: "Thou shalt return. Yea, and loose thy feet; for thy heart shall ne'er weight them down."

And Theia stood and looked upon the mantle and unto the sandals, and touched her locks and looked upon her arms, and sunk and sobbed. And she wept, and Nada came forth unto her and spake:

"Thou shalt wait. Yea, Nada shall bathe thy locks of precious oils. Yea, and bathe thee of sweet oils, and thou shalt return."

And Theia wailed: "Theia's steps then lead back unto Rome! Simeon, hearest thou this?"

And Panda spake: "Shall the hand of Panda lend unto thee?"

And Theia answered: "Nay! Nay! Thou art free, and Theia goeth, yea, goeth."

And Lucius listed unto what had been and spake not word, for his days had followed Panda. And Panda spake:

"Lucius, thine ear hath not a bottom, and hath left flow all that went therein."

And Lucius said: "Yea, yea, the sheep show blight of the sun's scorch, for the fields burn."

And Panda looked deep unto the eyes of Lucius. And Lucius took up the skin that shewed filled of grain's meal and set unto the hand of Nada. And Ahmud Hassan sat him long and looked unto the eyes of Theia, and upon the thin form of her, and his eyes shewed glisted of drops.

And Theia stood decked in the drooped robes, and looked upon her thus, and sunk upon the rug's-cast and laughed and laughed and laughed. And behold, she reached unto the armlets and plucked them from off her arms and cast them unto the flags and laughed amid the metal's stroke of musicked notes. And her feet she put forth and reached that she untie the latchets, and behold, they slipped from off them even though the latchets were tied. And Ahmud Hassan spake no word, but watched. And Theia started up and spake:

"Where hath he gone? Unto the hills, or yet unto Jerusalem, where Jews await that they drink from out him his blood?"

And Ahmud Hassan said: "Await thou! Panda shall seek."

And Panda sat him afar, even at the door's ope, and turned that he look upon Theia and spake:

"Nay, nay. Panda seeketh not. Nay, for hark! when a man of the land of Panda smiteth his horse's flesh unto the sore and it fleeth him, well he knoweth the horse shall ne'er come as the young maids at the eve's hour unto the casements that they know the even's cool and make them love's tuned notes. Nay, the horse, smitten, ne'er whinnieth of loving. And this lad hath felt the smite, and Panda hath not that that healeth it."

And they waited that Panda speak him more, but no word came, and he shook his head, " nay, nay."

And Lucius looked upon the out-way and it was speeding on unto the mid light of the eve, and he spake:

" Panda, thy tongue hath spoken wisdom unto Lucius, and dealt comfort's full unto Jerusalem's woed. Hark! Lucius hath learned much. Behold, the light fadeth slow and assuredly cometh night, and even so assuredly cometh the morn's sun. Yea, and the new morn's sun holdeth balms past man's word. Await, await the morrow's sun."

And Lucius cast the emptied skins o'er his back and smiled him unto the woed and went him upon his way speaking: " The morrow's sun cometh. Yea, wait!"

And Theia looked unto Panda and spake: " Panda, this man hath spoken truth, but this truth is for the balming of flesh, ne'er of the heart's smite, for no morrow washeth away the smite of woe that sinketh deep within the heart. Nay, the bosom shutteth the heart away, dark, dark. Panda, thy words shadow the sun's light. Where hath he gone?"

And Panda spake: " I know not; but Theia, the hills have drunk his woes these days and days. Yea, and the sheep he hath shepherded took up woes even so heavy that Panda wondereth that man who hath eat of them hath not woed!"

And Theia spake unto Ahmud Hassan: " Seest thou, sire? This is the shadow of Rome that falleth upon her own."

And Ahmud Hassan said: " Thy words have oped the eyes of Ahmud Hassan. Yea, and he hath drunk the fullness of thy bitters and knoweth well the sting that hath sunk within thy heart. Yet sayeth he, thou shalt return, that thou mayest hold the chalice for the drinking of Rome, lest the wine be drunk o'erfast."

And Theia threw wide her arms and cried: " Look thou, look thou unto Theia! Doth Rome then mock her more? Behold, Rome hath sunk her cheeks, hath eaten her heart, hath shorn her locks, hath stripped her flesh, and yet would Rome have more of her?"

And Ahmud Hassan spake: " Ahmud Hassan hath spoken and hath spoken in wisdom, woman."

And he turned unto Panda and said: " Ahmud Hassan would that he might even slay himself before he step upon the road's-way unto Rome and bear this woman, but Ahmud Hassan's dying would but spill the wine."

And Theia asked him: " When shall this thing be?"

And Ahmud Hassan answered: " At the morrow's waking; for

within Jerusalem is one that hath the eat of envy, and writheth even as a serpent beneath the heel of Ahmud Hassan. Yea, at the morrow's wake."

And Theia spake: "But he hath gone, and Theia would that her eyes fall upon him!"

And her eyes shewed the softing, even as the young deer's, and she murmured: "Ah, his limbs are strong! Yea, his arms shew man's strength. Yea, his eyes hold the look of the birds of the high air. Yea, he hath within him, locked, the gold of love, and Theia, Theia would that she might ope this treasure up."

And she stood regal and said: "He sunk, yea, he kissed the feet of Theia. Yea, and Theia shall go unto Rome and her feet shall speed upon his kisses! Yea, yea, sire, this thing is right and meet."

And she sunk upon her knees and looked unto the high and spake: "Jehovah, whoe'er thou art, where'er thou art, do hark! Theia awaiteth thee. Yea, she awaiteth thy coming. Yea, and this, then, is thy will? Even though Theia's eyes are blind unto the wisdom, she danceth unto the path thou hast willed.

"Theia hath known the touch of evil, the rot that falleth flesh, that emptieth—the fall flesh. Theia hath known the scourge. Theia hath known hate. Theia hath known the pits. Theia hath known the turning of blades unto the emptying of evils. Yea, Theia knoweth well. She hath learned well! Oh, thou Jehovah, well! But hark! hark! hark!"—and she raised her voice unto the utmost—"hark, hark, hark! But ope thy heavens one whit that she may see if thy lips do smile, and what thou holdest for him! Then, oh, thou Jehovah, 'tis enough! Cast thou Theia as dusts. Yea, smite her low if this be thy pleasure!"

And behold, from without came forth one sheep, even unto the in of the hut. And Theia looked upon it and cried:

"Be this the sign of sacrifice?"

And she shut up her eyes. And the sheep started at the words she spake and fled without.

CHAPTER XIII

AND eve came upon the land. And it was known unto Theia that the morrow would ope the roadway unto Rome, and she waited that the night give forth Hatte.

And within Jerusalem Indra had sought out the house of Levi, and behold, Sherah had not been within its walls. And Levi sat among his brethren, and spake the Jew's laws, and emptied him of his hopes and fears unto his brothers' ears. And they did this even so unto Levi.

And Indra sought the street's-way, but found not Sherah upon this way.

And the eve had come unto the darking, and the moon had shewn.

And Indra wearied of the seeking, and weary lagged her wickeds, and lo, she sought the way unto the without of Jerusalem and stepped her upon the roadway, and looked unto the hills and spake soft:

" He hath gone thereto. Then Indra shall seek him out."

And she set upon the way, and came upon Aaron, who dragged his nets and made sounds within his throat and sought Hatte. And Indra looked upon him and unto the thicks that shewed dark, and made signs that they should seek these paths together.

And they did this thing. And the thicks led up the hill's sides, and the heights shewed stoned and the thicks thinned unto the bareing.

And when they had sought long, behold, they came upon the flocks, and they had laid them down. And upon one stone that stood high above the earth, there shewed a one against the pale sky, and he sorrowed, for his head was bowed and his shepherd's staff fallen and his hands shut upon a scourge of gold.

The moon shone pure upon the sorrow, and the stirring of the sheep waked the one from out his dreams, for the sheep arose at the sounding of the steps of Indra and Aaron and sped them out their ways. And Hatte arose and cried aloud: " Who art thou? Who art thou? "

And Indra made answering: " Aaron and Indra."

And Hatte's voice broke in anguished sounds: " Begone! Begone! Wouldst thou trod upon this heart? "

And Indra spake: " Theia, the woman, is within the walls of Panda and waiteth thee."

314

And Hatte spake: "Begone! Leave Hatte but the dead ears that he speak his sorrows! Go, thou, that he weep salts and put upon his wounds that they heal!"

And he came forth and took within his hands the hands of Aaron and lay his arms about the mighty shoulders of his brother, and his voice cut unto the ears of Indra: "Go! go! By the pure of yon moon, go!"

And Indra saw the bidding within his eyes and went upon her way, and her steps sounded long upon the stones.

And Hatte went up unto the stone wherefrom he had risen and took Aaron unto him. And Aaron brought forth his nets and took from out them the wastes he had plucked from the day, and babbled naughts, and offered these unto Hatte there beneath the moon's quiet.

And Hatte spake unto the dead ears: "Aaron, brother, thy lips, when Hatte knew thee within the hills of Bethlehem, babbled few words yet they spake of a brother whom thou hadst lost within the hills. And now, now they stop and speak no words. Is then Hatte he thou didst seek?"

And he looked up unto the stars that came and spake more:

"Hatte, Hatte, who art thou? A stone about which the waters of Rome wash. A stone that lieth within Jerusalem, yet Rome's stream seeketh thee. Who art thou?

"This one whom Bethlehem knoweth, whose breath came forth within an ass's bed—who is this one? For Jerusalem's king slayeth flesh that he cut off this one. Who then is He? Rome, thou art sore wicked, sore wicked; for even so as this slaying was done, thou hast shut up thine eyes unto it, even though thou wilt war o'er words. What be flesh of Jews unto thee?"

And behold, the moon hung and shed its light. And the light paled and still did Hatte sit and look unto the emptiness. And he turned his eyes unto Aaron and looked upon him, and lo, Aaron had sat him down and spread forth his nets and made that he tie up the strands that shewed broken. And his eyes raised them up that they look upon Hatte.

And Hatte stepped unto the side of Aaron and laid his hands upon his shoulders and sunk upon the earth whereon Aaron sat. And his eyes narrowed, and his arms lay loosed about the shoulders of the empty one, and he spake:

"Jerusalem, within thy mightiest ranks standeth not a one even so mighty as he who sitteth here. For behold, thy mighty ones deal of their mightiness through smite, through lusts, through pilfer. Yea, and they know not their brothers; and he, ah, he holdeth the mightiest blade that man e'er wielded—silence. Yea, silence he offereth as balm unto the day.

"Yea, and Jerusalem, Hatte speaketh unto thee, thou shalt fall. Thou shalt seek thee a brother that may deal silence, yea soothe, and stop thy dins. Thy street's-ways run red of bloods, thy men drink their brothers' bloods, yea, no brother knoweth but his own kind; and I speak me, a one shall come," and Hatte looked the far-look of the seeing, and swayed and spake:

"Yea, a one shall come, yea, and His scepter shall be a lily, yea, and His armor shall be a smile. Yea, and His left hand shall hold of a staff, a gentle shepherd's staff. And His feet shall know thee, yea, and His eyes shall look upon thee, and thou shalt turn therefrom, yea, and strip His hands of the scepter. Yea, and put within the grasp of Him thorns.

"Yea, and thou shalt strip Him even of armor and leave Him naked. Yea, and spill His blood even within the street's pools. Yea, and they shall drop from out His wounds even upon the flags, and each drop shall hold a thousand tongues that shall cry through the ages. And even though thou shalt strip Him of the scepter, I speak me that this hand shall hold of a lash that shall fall upon the Jews and scourge them for time and time.

"Yea, and more, Hatte seeth Him to stand at the scourging. Yea, and for every wound He shall shed tears, tears, tears!

"Wait! Wait! Hatte seeth the Path—long! long! dark! dark! And this one standeth Him bearing a cup, and this cup is filled of His tears, and they glitter even as the ruby, yea, or as the young dew. And He offereth this unto Hatte that he drink——"

And lo, Hatte threw his hands high and cried aloud:

"The slaying! The slaying!"

And he sped unto the dark. And Aaron looked upon this and took up his nets and laughed, laughed, laughed, and went that he follow.

And the clouds arose and banked and bellowed up. And the moon hid and the clouds played o'er her face. And the winds arose and whined and moaned afar. And the dusts started up and they sped upon the road's-way, and shewed like unto smokes when the moon stole forth from 'neath the cloud's war. And the night birds cried, and the storks flew up and spread their white wings beneath the light that shewed and then darked.

And the night crept black, and the lightnings flashed, and the clouds rifted them that they let loose the bolts. And the heavens cried out in anguish, and the sheep huddled them one unto the other. And behold, afar the voice of Hatte made the sheep's cry, and there sounded the laugh of Aaron upon the winds.

And out from the hill's place shewed the hut of Panda, and the winds cried about. And behold, when the rains had stilled, out through the heavy wet of clouds and the lightnings' flash, there shewed a one who crept forth from the hut's ope. And this one was robed of purple and the vanities, and she sought the out-places whereon the sod shewed smooth, and she spread forth her locks and turned her back unto the winds and raised up her arms and let the winds to blow her upon her way.

And her feet raised up high even as a charger's, and her steps sped, and the winds caught the thick locks and blew them close o'er her very face. And she bended her back even unto the bowing upon the winds and cried out and made sounds like the night birds' screaming.

And the lightnings flashed and she bounded up and fled and cast her unto the east and unto the west, and sunk and rose, and ever did she keep the wind that it blow her upon the way.

Yea, she bended unto its blowing, and when the lightnings had split ope the heavens, behold, she leapt her high, even as though she would arise and go up even unto the oping.

And the storm shrieked and wailed and beat and sobbed, and she flitted like a moth amid the angers. And of a sudden she stopped and swayed and sunk, and moved not. And the storm broke o'er her and swept rains o'er her fallen form.

And the night sped on unto the spending of the wrath of the heavens. And the dark hung close, for the moon had gone and few stars gleamed between the clouds that still sped or banked and hung o'er the moon's-way and shut her from the night. And the hush-calm of the storm's death fell upon the lands, and the cool kiss of rains lay upon the hills. And the clouds fled, and the moon shewed her silver hung within the morn's sky. And the sun crept gold-sandaled o'er the east and spread his rosed robe, wove of star's dust, o'er the earth's curve.

And the hut of Panda shewed silent within the first light, and when the sun had come up unto the shewing, behold, the door's-way oped and Panda came without and sought. And his eyes fell upon the fallen one, and he sped up unto her and cried loud:

"Nada! Nada! Come thou without! She hath wandered. She hath sought out the fold."

And Ahmud Hassan and Nada came forth, and Indra shewed at the ope but came not forth. And Nada came up unto where Theia lay

and oped her arms and took her in, even unto her bosom. And lo,
Theia shewed wet, and her locks hung close unto the thin cheeks, and
her mantle of purple clung unto her arms and legs, and upon her feet
hung the sandals of scarlet, the royal-dyed sandals—their golden latchets
had slipped and they scarce stayed upon the feet. And Panda spake
soft:

"Theia! Theia!"

And Theia murmured: "Ah, wake me not! The hills did I seek
and sent up my voice that he hear. Yea, upon the path of lightnings
Theia danced and would that the winds blow her unto him. Panda,
where hath he gone? Theia would that she might hold him unto her
breast. Panda, Panda, what o'ertaketh Theia? Jerusalem slippeth
away! Even thou and thou, Nada, art dim, dim."

And she sunk. And Ahmud Hassan spake unto Panda: "This
thing Rome hath done is far more the slaying than the feeding of
flesh unto beasts."

And he leaned far and spake unto the listing of Panda that a one
had ridden unto Jerusalem (and this had come unto his ears even at
the yester's-day) and the one had spoken that the mighty one chafed
and had set a blade even unto the hand of him who rode. And he said:

"The feed of flesh unto the mighty one shall stop the blade. And
Ahmud Hassan shall pack his caravan of lies."

And more he spake: "Should the one seek out Panda and ask him of
the spot wherein this flesh of Theia had lain, Panda should shew unto
him the abiding place of the body of Joel."

And Panda bowed him low, and Nada bid that they bear Theia
unto the hut. And they did this thing, and when it was done Panda and
Ahmud Hassan came forth and builded up a rack of woods that should
fit upon the camel's back and bear Theia.

And it was young day, and they spake soft one unto the other.
And when the rack had been finished, lo, they went them within and
Nada had brought forth breads and the thick milk, and they supped.

And Nada had made Theia dry. And Theia supped little and
watched unto the door's-way, and listed and spake her: "Panda, thinkest thou that he shall come?"

And Panda answered: "Theia, Panda knoweth not. Nay, Panda
knoweth not."

And the time had come that they set them on. And Nada made a
pack of breads and a skin of vinegar and yet one of sweet wine. And
brought forth rugs and rough mantles and the goods of Indra, for she
spake: "Unto the hands that hold the right, deliver that that be theirs."

And she brought forth the fire-jug and spread about it the grain's meal, wetted that it bake. And they looked them upon this and waited, for this was the meal cake that Theia and Ahmud Hassan should take upon the ways.

And when the finish of the drying had been, Nada took it from off the jug and broke it up unto bits. And the eyes of Panda followed the brown hands of Nada as swift they moved. And he held unto his bosom the babe, Panda, and he sorrowed within him but spake no word.

And Nada stopped and went up unto Theia and sunk upon her knees and spake: " Thy sister knoweth. Yea, she would that she might know thy sorrow's deep, for should the day take her babe from out her bosom——"

And Nada started up and sped unto the side of Panda and tore from out his arms the babe, and kissed him o'er and wept. And Theia's lips trembled smile, a sick smile, and her weak hands lay still, and she spake:

" 'Tis well. 'Tis well, Panda. Theia is ready that she shall look not upon Hatte. Nay, this thing may not be, and Theia knoweth 'tis well. One drop unto the deep-thirsted one, and then the parch killeth! "

Steps sounded without the hut. And this was Lucius, and he came him with asses, one that should pack and one that Ahmud Hassan should ride upon. And they bore Theia without and set her upon the camel. And Panda looked upon her, and Nada wept. And it was so that Indra had shewed not her face but hid within the in-place of the hut.

And when they had finished and it was the time that they should go them hence, Panda turned unto the east way and made a chant, and Nada did her likewise. And this thing done, Panda spake:

" Ahmud Hassan, brother of the tribe of Panda, Panda hath delivered unto thy hand his treasure. This thou shalt keep even within thine own heart. Yea, do thou this thing."

And Ahmud Hassan spake not, but raised his palms unto the East and bowed his head low. And Panda spake:

" Panda goeth upon the way. Yea, up unto the high place yonder. Panda taketh his lamb unto the hills lest it lone."

And he took up his staff and stepped after, close up unto the camel. And they set upon the way. And Theia turned her face unto Jerusalem and then unto the way unto Bethlehem, and her throat shook as a singing bird's. And she held forth her weak hands and spake:

" Jerusalem, even though hates abide thee, Theia hath lost her hate upon thy street's-way. Yea, and this hate hath turned unto love and

walketh o'er thee. Yea, Bethlehem, Bethlehem, the leaven of love;
for hate, born within thy shadow, hath taken of love. Yea, and what
hath come from out thee shall leaven the earth with love!"

And she turned her eyes unto Panda, and behold, her thin lips
smiled, smiled, even though the tears slipped within the smiling, and
she made words unto Panda, saying:

"Panda, seest thou? The gods did lead Theia even out of Rome
and o'er lands, yea, o'er seas and unto Jerusalem. Yea, and Jerusalem oped her arms at Rome's bidding and took Theia unto her
breast, and even though her ribs were iron and seared the flesh of Theia,
Jerusalem held her close, close. Yea, and Theia showed hate unto
Jerusalem, but the gods have won! Theia, Theia looseth her heart, for
behold, she taketh it out of the walls of Jerusalem, wherein it lay upon
stones, unto Rome. And Panda, Rome hath hunger; but 'tis well, for
Theia's heart shall feed her hunger. And Hatte, Hatte hath Jerusalem
and thou, Panda."

And Panda looked unto her, and they had come unto the high place,
and Panda touched the camel's neck and bade that it stop upon the
way, and spake:

"Theia, Panda shall look not upon thee. Nay, thou shalt go upon
the day's path and Panda shall know not the drops that still remain
that thou shalt shed. Panda hath dreamed thine eyes were wells, ne'er-
emptying wells, that shall ever stream. And he would not see, for his
hand holdeth not their drying."

And Theia reached down and touched the staff of Panda and spake
in the prayer chant:

"Theia sendeth her voice up unto the skies. Yea, Theia would
that Jehovah hark; that He shall bend down from out His vasts and
touch this staff of Panda, that whene'er his sheep stray they shall come
up unto the staff, even though the voice of Panda calleth not. Panda,
Panda, even though thy flocks are full-tided and readied that man shall
eat, thou hast one that shall ever be a lamb."

And Panda turned unto the hut's-way and murmured: "Yea,
yea."

And Theia spake: "Panda, when the camel hath sunk that thou
mayest not see, wilt thou call thy sheep? Yea, when the days shew
dark, Panda, wilt thou speak unto Hatte, Hatte, so? 'He shall come.
He shall come! Yea, at some morn when the earth is golden bathed,
the sweet tide of the young day shall show the royal caravan, the white
camel whose ankles shall ring of golden bells and whose eyes shall
gleam like rubies.' And this thing shall be, Panda! And Theia shall

unwind her mantle and dance to meet His coming. Yea, she shall bear her warm heart fresh plucked from out her bosom in her bared hands, up unto this mighty one who rides. It shall be! It shall be!"

And they went their ways and the voice of Theia sunk unto naught. And Panda sunk upon his knees and murmured:

"It shall be! She hath spoken it so."

And he waited long, and sent up his voice in the sheep's call. And there came back soft: "O-he-e-e! O-he-e-e!"

And Panda threw high his hands and sobbed, and shut out the sound that he might not hear.

And he sought the way unto the hut, and behold, there shewed upon the path's-ways out the hills, Hatte, and Aaron who followed. And they came swift, and Panda awaited them. And Hatte cried out:

"Panda, hath she slept? Hath she awaited the coming of Hatte? Behold, the night hath soothed the woes, and Hatte hungereth that he kiss the sorrowed lips, that he light the fires that lie dead within her eyes. See! Hatte hath come, yea, and upon the way hath he plucked blooms and woven of a crown."

And Panda stopped his coming with the upraising of his hand, and spake:

"She hath gone."

And Hatte started, and his eyes flashed, and he plucked the crown unto naughts and took up a stone and spat upon it and spake like unto a serpent's hiss:

"This would Hatte cast deep even unto the heart of Jehovah, for she loveth Him. She came stripped unto Hatte, and she sleepeth and decketh beauteous at the young hour and goeth that she meet Jehovah. Her lips spake His name and honeys drip from off it.

"Aig-h-h! She sayeth 'tis Jehovah, but 'tis ne'er a truth. This word cloaketh her love! Yea, she hath gone even unto this man 'Who.'"

And he threw his hands high and cried aloud: "O ye gods of Rome! O ye gods of the East! Yea, ye gods of the West, even of the South, and yet the god that hath upon his crown the North star, hark! hark! hark! Thy son is borne down! He may not cast forth this pack of woes and straighten him in his strength and pluck his bowstring that it whirr free! He is old, old in sorrow! The founts of the wisdoms of Panda have dried. The stones of Jerusalem, even, may not take in the tears of Hatte, for they are full, sodden of her men's blood.

"Behold thou thy son, even upon bended knee! Behold thou him! Within the earth's day liveth Rome. Yea, some breeze even now doth cool his brow. Mayhap his palms itch that they touch her, Theia, and she is Hatte's. Doth ne'er within him—this man whose name be naught save the laugh of scorning spoken in one word, Who—doth ne'er within him stir an eat that hurteth, that telleth him of his flesh that would pour forth his loving? E'en now these hands would take up his blade. Yea, and keep its bright gleaming. Yea, this head should ne'er bow save that it received the crown."

And he stopped and cried: "Hatte, crowned! Jehovah, Hatte hateth, hateth, hateth, hateth thee!"

And Panda touched him and spake soft words. And Hatte shrunk.

"Panda, thy words are gentle rains, and Hatte is the desert—dry, dry, hungered dry, for torrents!"

And Panda spake low and sweet: "Yea, Hatte, but even the gentle rains upon the deserts cool the creeping mites, and Panda hath naught save words, even though he would give even unto the all of his goods unto thee who art the flesh of her whom Panda knoweth as his mistress."

And Hatte spake: "Panda, Paul hath told unto Hatte of a Nazarene who hath wisdoms that no man knoweth the deep of. Yea, Paul hath told that He setteth Him beside the stream and leaveth that the waters bathe His feet and speaketh that the waters have wisdoms that no man knoweth.

"Such is the wisdom Hatte seeketh. Hatte seeketh this one called Jesus, the Nazarene. Men know not the all of His coming. Yea, e'en within Jerusalem hath Hatte seen Jews that made wise signs when the name was spoken. His sire is who? He hath spoken unto Hatte that He knoweth His sire, and the words were empty, for did not Hatte seek the temple wherein He had told His sire abided, and He was not there?"

And Panda spake: "Much word cometh of this one. Hatte, what wouldst thou that Panda should tell unto thee?"

And he cried out: "Panda, the walls of Jerusalem lay like unto scourge unto Hatte. The hills shew empty, for the dreams of her abide not there. Hatte shall push sorrow away. He shall seek yon, yon, yon, even unto the fartherest cap of yon hill through the wildernesses. Yea, for they are empty and Hatte may fill them. Thou shalt lend unto Hatte but of breads and, Panda, Aaron. For Aaron is like unto the shadow of Hatte and would sorrow should he ne'er follow. Thou knowest his lips did once prate of the brother upon the hills. And he found Hatte, and his lips then spake no words. Yea, thou shalt leave Aaron unto Hatte. His empty cup catcheth Hatte's tears."

And Panda spake: "This thing is so. Hatte, thou shouldst tarry not within Jerusalem. Ahmud Hassan hath spoken it."

And Hatte cried: "This is not a bidding that setteth Hatte upon the ways! But, Panda, he shall burst like a bubble upon the sea's wave doth he not away!"

And Panda reached forth his arms and took Hatte within them and made sign unto Aaron that they seek the hut.

And the day crept slow upon the earth and set the shadows long, and at the eve's come set them shorted unto the naughts.

And the come of eve shewed Hatte and Aaron upon the way.

CHAPTER XIV

And the tides swept unto the thrice of full moon's, and thence unto the fullings unto the tide of four fulls of grain's ripes and sowings.*

And Jerusalem shewed gaunt.

And locusts had stripped the herbs close unto their roots and eat the figs and scarred the pomegranates and e'en had they stripped the young barks. And the kine lay, legs up unto the sun, and the heavy of flesh rot clung the airs. And the dogs lay within the streets, dead, shrunk, flatted.

And women, shaking, bore babes that moved not. And their voices shook like grains within an emptied jug.

And the serpents came up unto the wells and stretched and died. And the flies fatted upon carrion. And sheep lay rotted. And behold, the weak airs bore the heavy scent that arose from off the carcasses at the vulture's pluck.

And the walls of Jerusalem sounded out the wailing of men. And the sacrifices were burnt at the hours ne'er set for their offering. And the camel's men offered but their wetted hands unto their beasts. And the birds of the air fell. And the grain stalks rattled, and the stones laughed in glisting, and the air looked even as whited bubbles.

And men cried out unto their brothers for aid. And Rome's alike, fell beneath the smite. And lo, without the walls shewed the hill's white and the burn of grass, like mock gold; and the roads smoked dusts.

And beggars tore ope their head-bands and frothed, and sent forth their tongues, and their bellies fell in and they died. And women wailed and wept, and thirsted babes drunk their tears. Yea, e'en them that suckled drank of their own milch. And behold, within the walls men came forth and sought of sheep's flesh that had been new smitten that they eat. And stones they let down unto the well's shallow waters and left therein unto the wetting, and unto their lips pressed they this.

And upon the hills without, at the hut of Joel, stood Panda, his eyes shewed narrow. And the valleys were dotted of the white of his fallen sheep. And Nada came forth with an emptied jug and offered unto the hand of Panda and spake:

* Indicating the passing of four years and three months.

324

"Panda, his lips shew dry and his eyes dry."

And Panda looked afar, and drops sprung his eyes and fell, to dry upon the jug. And Nada wrapped her hands within her mantle and cast it o'er her head and wailed, and raised her hands unto Panda and cried:

"Panda, Panda, Panda, the sky must give up one drop!"

And Panda spake, and his throat sounded dry: "Yea, yea, Panda shall split ope a stone but that he bring a drop!"

And he went forth, his head bowed. And he sought the valleys and the stream's flow. And the stones rattled laugh. And Panda spake low: "And she hath said the God is wise!"

And he sought the up-hills and even the sheep's tracks, and turned unto the way unto Jerusalem, and spake:

"Panda, folly is thy brother. Jerusalem knoweth but her own thirst."

And he spake more: "Lucius! Lucius! His cup hath dried and he hath gone. Yea, and Levi"—and he stopped and murmured: "Unto Levi."

And he went upon the way. And behold, the wall's ope of Jerusalem, at a later time, shewed him come forth speeded. And he bore of a skin and it rattled; for there was within but the supping for one. And Panda ran swift, and his sandals slipped, and the stones cut, and his feet left red upon them.

And he came unto the hut's place, and Nada came forth, her eyes soft, like night, and she spake:

"The young swallow * hath flown."

And Panda stopped and oped his lips, but no word would come. And he let fall the skin, and Nada started forth and took it up and lay her head upon the breast of Panda. And he threw wide his arms and crushed her to him. And he swayed and spake:

"The Far Land shewed sweet, cool sweet. He hath hovered but to sweet the garden with his note, and his wings did chafe that they speed."

And he spread forth his hands and spake more:

"The day was young and the sands soft and damp. Yea, he hath sought the land that lieth beyond the sands."

And Nada listed but her ears heard not, and her hands clutched one unto the other. And Panda's eyes glisted, and his lips shewed the sad smile, and he spake in the voice he had wooed the babes:

* It is said to have been a belief of the ancient Arabs that the departing soul took the form of a bird.

"Nada, the caravan did come. Yea, o'er the gold sands they came, and they were white babe camels and their packs dripped sweet waters."

And Nada looked unto the grief-heavy eyes of Panda and spake: "Thou dost thirst?"

And Panda answered: "Nay."

And Nada said: "Nor doth Nada. Panda, see! there be but few drops. Leave these unto Nada's hands that she shut his eyes. They look unto wheres. And his lips, Panda, parch."

And she turned unto the hut. And they went unto the spot, and Panda stopped at the door's ope and spake: "Nada, go thou and do thou this thing."

And Nada said: "Panda, ne'er Nada, but thou and Nada."

And they went within. And the babe lay quiet, still. And Panda sat him down and wept. And Nada went unto the in-place and brought forth the golded rug and spake:

"Panda, this, that his dreams be golden."

And they knelt upon the rug's-cast and made the chants and brought forth spices and burned and anointed the body of sweet oils and scented the rug's folds of spice. And Panda wrapped the babe in a young sheep's skin and put within his hand a staff.

And they wrapped him within the rug, and Panda said: "Upon the breast of Joel shall he lie."

And Nada murmured: "Panda," and her voice sounded afar, "thinkest thou the moon shall rise?"

And Panda spake: "Yea. Yea, she shall come borne upon the young swallow's wings."

And they went up unto the body of the babe and Nada wailed:

"But until the eve, Panda, but until the eve. Wait thou, the sun is hot."

And Panda spake: "Yea, Nada, we shall wrap him within moon's silver."

And they waited silent, and eat of dried fruit that they thirst not. And the night came, and the moon, even so surely. And they did the thing that waited.

And behold, even as they arose, drops fell!

CHAPTER XV

And lo, the road's-ways swept up in dusts. And the rains fell. And the sheep arose weak and ran weak. And kine stretched forth their necks and sent forth their bellows low. And the stones hissed.

Jerusalem stirred, and the door's-ways of the households oped, even as hot pits, and they within came forth to stretch and turn their faces up. And men called them one unto the other:

"Water! Water! Jehovah, water falleth!"

And they brought forth jugs and bowls and held them up unto the heavens. And behold, upon the temple steps the priests came forth and called the tribes that they come and give of the chants and a sacrifice in thanks.

And the waters mocked the dry earth and swept the dusts unto sticky clays. And the stones of the walls at the meet of drops sent up a heat-mist. And within the market's place no man had shewed, for the sun's heats had driven them forth even as a lash. What! should man offer that his brother buy of hides when his feet shewed burned unto the thick of sandal's skin, and his throat parched for waters and no man would sell of this thing?

And they made words within the households that the time was still unto the tide * that rain might cause seed to spring.

And within the house of Levi, Sherah stood o'er the couch where Levi lay smitten. And Sherah spake soft:

"Sire, water hath come! Hark! the sound filleth up the ears."

And she sped unto the door's ope and let the rains wet her hands, and sped her back and held them forth unto Levi, saying:

"See! See, sire! 'Tis water, water, and it falleth!"

And Levi looked him far, and Sherah spake: "Sire, he who came unto thee spake that his babe lay low. Panda, then, hath felt the smite of Jehovah. Sire, didst thou deal unto him?"

And Levi answered: "Yea, the one half of all Levi's is his brother's."

* Not yet too late for planting.

And Sherah spake: " Sire, thou knowest the abode of Panda is filled of his babe, and the hearts of Nada and Panda know no filling save the loving of its flesh. Thinkest thou the drops fell at the time that should stop the speeding caravan of death? Sire, speak! Sherah's heart droppeth drops. Yea, and Sherah would seek the out-way and go unto them that do for all men that know of them."

And Levi said: " The rains sweet, and, Sherah, beasts shall come forth from out their lairs. Thou mayest not go unto the out-ways. And hark! Levi would that thou shouldst lend unto him thy hand that he seek the door's ope and know the wash of waters."

And Sherah lended of her hand that this thing be done. And the light fell upon the face of her and the eyes shewed them sorrowed. And Levi looked deep within them and spake:

" Sherah, thy heart is sealed and thou hast within it a bee that stingeth."

And Sherah looked down, and Levi said more:

" Panda hath told unto thee of the going of Theia, and thou hast heard that the son of her hath sought the Nazarene, the Promised One; for this man is He. For Sherah, flesh of the flesh of Levi, Sherah, the green sprig of the dead tree, out from Nazareth way cometh words that creep, even though men would stop them. Yea, out upon the road's-way this man speaketh and men go unto Him and take their tides, be they of good or yet of woe, and His words buy of the good and soothe of their woe.

" One hath told that a man whose back had bent unto a bow would seek of Him, and behold, His words would straight the back. Yea, and unto the hands of this one cometh all men that come e'en within the echo of His words. This is the Promised One, and Levi would that he might see the tribes call His name Blessed."

And Sherah murmured: " Hatte hath sought Him, and Levi, no word hath come forth from his path."

And Levi questioned: " And thy heart hangeth upon the path that led him forth?"

And Sherah spake: " Sire, this thing is not that that eateth. She, Indra, who hath gone unto Rome's halls, hath spoken that that hath smitten sore. She hath told unto the ear of Sherah that Hatte is not of Jew's flesh, that he knoweth not his sire. And sire, thou knowest unto Sherah that is the wall that sealeth up the pit. And Indra speaketh that words sound among the Rome's men that tell that he hath been laid low. Thinkest thou this thing is true?"

And Levi looked unto Sherah and smiled.

"Within the eyes of Panda Levi hath seen not one flame. This telleth."

And Sherah spake: "Panda sayeth he seeketh the Nazarene, but this he hath spoken but unto the ear of Sherah. And Indra speaketh that Rome embers o'er this lad and that the men of the Halls speak the name of him who sitteth the mighty-seat of Rome, and hide their lips and whisper.

"What thinkest thou, sire? Doth Rome know that that should send forth her hand unto Jerusalem for Hatte? Panda hath spoken that Sherah should lock her lips save unto thy ears."

And Levi spake: "Theia holdeth within her purse a coin of Rome. Levi knoweth this, even though he hath spoken it not. And Caelius and Phaeton—dost thou remember? Thinkest thou that Rome would do this thing save that she would stop for reason, heavy reason, the tides that bear her rotted-laden crafts?"

And Sherah said: "Sire, there are men among the market's place and even among the land's men, who speak that this lad is he whom the Jews await. Else what set Rome upon the path?"

And Levi spake: "Time, yea, the sweep of tides, bloweth ope all doors that be shut."

And Sherah said: "Panda, thou knowest, telleth, yea, his tongue speaketh words and they be wisdoms, but sire, they tell naught that man may weave unto cloth that he may sit upon."

And Levi said: "A wise man's words are like unto the fisher's nets, and fools are the small fish that slip them through."

And Sherah spake: "This thing is true, but sire, Samuel of the market's-way milcheth the men of the road's-way as she-goats for words that might tell of Hatte. And men speak that Jacob knoweth o'er his full."

And Levi smiled soft and spake: "Yea, Jacob is like the bowl that catcheth whate'er the day offereth unto it."

And Sherah said: "Sire, sire, within the heart of Sherah sorrow creepeth. She would that thou wouldst leave her that she go unto Nada."

And Levi spake: "Thou shalt go up unto the spot where the household of Paul sheweth and thou shalt say unto him, 'Paul, go thou with Sherah unto the household of Panda.' And dost thou then seek the way with the hand of Paul this thing shall be."

And Sherah looked unto the without, and lo, the rains washed them o'er the stone flags and swept them down from the high city and on out the gateways and out Jerusalem.

And Sherah spake her: "Sire, waters wash, and yet there is a deep eat within the heart of Sherah, and Sherah would that she seek Nada."

And Levi said: " That thing shouldst thou do dost thy heart eat. 'Tis the sign of Jehovah. Yea, Sherah, e'en though the waters wash, go thou; for the eyes of Panda spake fires that lay them within his breast and his lips spake soft the name of Nada, and he cried: ' Levi, water, water, for her eyes flow salts that sting. Yea, and the babe's lips shew swelled and dark, dark, like unto the flesh that hath lain beneath the sun for two watches.' "

And Sherah spake: " And thou didst minister unto him of thy store? "

And Levi answered: " Yea, for within the pit, beneath the floor's place, there still remaineth one skin of water. And this had slipped its binding and the waters had gone from out, save one bowl's fill, but the stopping of one thirst, and this thirst should be not the thirst of a man, but thirst of a babe, lest it fall short of the quenching.

" So, Sherah, Levi looked upon this and spake unto him deep within him, ' Levi is full tided, yea, and Sherah, his flesh, and a babe thirsteth. So, then, the babe shall drink and the drop be delivered unto the hands of Panda.'

" See! this thing was right, yea, right and meet, for Jehovah hath sent the waters."

And Sherah took up the hand of Levi and led him unto the within place, and brought forth a bowl and took up water that had fallen into the bowls that set without that they catch the downfall of drops from off the wall's drip. And this she offered unto the lips of Levi. And he took sup and held his hand in the sign that she should go her forth.

And Sherah brought forth skins and wrapped her in them, and put upon her feet sandals of thick skin, and took of fine meal and wine and still of the store of dried fruits and even of fishes, and this she took within a pack upon the way, and she went her forth, even unto the house of Paul. And she made known by the smiting upon the door's place that one would come within.

And behold, Paul came him forth, and Sherah spake:

" Paul, without the walls Panda and his household lie smitten. Panda hath been within the walls and came unto the household of Levi and begged of waters, and he hath spoken that Nada weepeth o'er the babe, Panda, that lieth low, yea, that his lips stopped in stiffing."

And Paul spake no word, but lended of his hand unto Sherah that she come within, and even as she spake took up a skin filled of vinegar and put it o'er his shoulder and he took of herbs, lest the hand of Nada fall not upon that that should lend soothe. And his lips moved and he murmured him:

"Panda and Nada lie beneath the sear of the sun! What hath betided thee? Paul hath sought not the hill unto them. Paul hath lended not his hand, and lo, Panda hath ever lended unto the hand of Paul."

And he held forth his hand unto Sherah and oped the door's-way and they stepped them out upon the rain-swept way. And the winds beat the mantles of them, and the skins ran waters and their locks dripped and the limbs of them shewed beneath the cloth.

And the opes within the walls shewed white faces, but the limbs of them had weaked past the bearing out. And behold, they passed, upon the way, women who came them forth with babes that lay stilled forever, and held them unto the drops and made prayer. And Sherah shut up her eyes unto this thing.

And they came them unto the gate's-way, and behold, the Rome's men stood watch even under water's smite and heat's sear. And they made the price for the withouting, and Sherah speeded her upon the way of Panda. And Paul spake:

"'Tis but gray wet. Yea, look thou, Sherah, unto the way. Seest thou through the rain's sweep one sign of Nada or yet Panda?"

And Sherah looked her even amid the rain's silver, and the hills shewed not save the path but one furlong beyond. And they went them on even up unto the spot wherein the body of Joel had been laid. And Sherah's eyes looked upon this, and she touched the flesh of Paul and pointed unto what shewed and she spake soft, and her cheeks flamed:

"Look thou! Look thou! The earth hath been torn ope! The caravan hath come even before thee and Sherah."

And Paul looked upon the spot and spake: "Yea, Sherah, the caravan hath been and hath gone it hence."

And Sherah clasped close the pack and ran swift, even up unto the hut's place. And the door's-way stood ope, and she stepped her unto the ope, and the water ran from off her and her locks dripped, their long strands hung close and wetted upon her bosom and o'er her shoulders. And she looked her within, and lo, Nada sat, and her eyes shewed no knowing, and she swayed her arms and rocked. And at her feet lay the brass bowls of sand that had been the love of the babe that he pour one unto the other. And Panda sat him bowed. And Sherah cried:

"Nada! Nada! Nada!"

And Nada looked not unto her. And Sherah went up unto her and touched her flesh and murmured: "Nada, thy sister hath come."

And Nada spake soft, even like unto an echo: "Didst thou see the young swallow winging it hence?"

And she arose and went unto the door's ope and strained her that she see within the skies, and murmured: "Nay, nay, his wings shew not."

And Panda looked him sorrowed and came forth and took her unto him, and his eyes spake unto Sherah, and Sherah said:

"Nada, Nada, list! What meanest thou?"

And Nada spake: "He hath gone. Hark! the young lambs call. Yea, they wait his small staff. They wait. Look! Look! Seest thou the small speck yonder? Look! Look! He wingeth him away!"

And she pointed unto the skies. And Sherah wept. And Panda looked unto Paul, and delivered Nada unto the arms of Sherah. And Paul came forth, and he shewed him tall, and he lay his hands upon the shoulders of Panda and spake: "Brother, thy brother hath come."

And Panda said: "Paul, Panda knoweth thee as his brother. Canst thou but tell unto him what from out the day he may pluck that he may offer unto Nada as balm?"

And Paul answered: "Nay."

And Panda looked unto Sherah, who had wrapped her arms about Nada and taken her unto her bosom. And Nada wept and clung even as a babe. And Sherah spake soft:

"Unloose thy tears. Yea, unloose them, for Sherah shall dry them with her loving."

And Nada wailed: "His lips parched!"

And Sherah sounded a sob of sorrow.

And Nada spake, and her eyes flowed drops:

"He called, called the name 'Nada, Nada, mother,' and 'water, water.' And, Sherah, Jehovah's heart was stone, and Allah but a stone god. And the skies seemed dry vasts, and the sun a well of fire that fed streams of flame!

"And Nada cried aloud, and even did she seek her unto the sheep for milch, and the goats had dried, and the sheep had sickened and Nada feared that she deal of their milch. And Panda hath sought, sought through heats and gone unto Jerusalem with all the store, that he offer one, then the other, unto the time that there was but dried fruit, and little, little e'en of this store, save that Nada eat and Panda fast and eat and fast and fast and eat and fast and fast and fast and eat and fast and fast, and there then should be not enough."

And Sherah cried: "Hath Panda drunk?"

And Nada answered: "Nay, he mocked of drops and would not sup of them."

And Sherah arose and oped the skin of vinegar and spake: "Panda, sup! Sup, in the love of Allah, sup! Eat! See! Sherah hath brought forth meal and fruits. Yea, and fishes. Take thou this! Levi would that thou shouldst share. Sup!"

And Panda spake: "Nay," and his lips shewed dry. And Nada stopped her and spake:

"Behold, Panda, the swallow cometh, and about his neck hangeth a golded cup. This is the sign."

And Panda leaned forth and took up the skin and drunk therefrom. And when he had supped him long and Nada had stood that she take in his drinking, he put unto the hand of Nada the jug of vinegar and spake: "Drink! Drink! Even vinegar may free the founts of Allah within thee."

And Nada drank deep, and sat her down and looked afar. And Sherah sat her down even at the side of Nada. And Paul stood within the door's ope and watched the fall of drops. And Nada reached forth her hand and took up the wet locks of Sherah and kissed them, and Panda looked upon this and smiled and lay his hand upon the dark head of Nada and whispered: "Allah hath waked thee."

And Sherah spake: "The hill's-ways are beat of rains. Yea, winds sweep and torrents wash, and Panda, thou knowest the wildernesses. What! should one dear unto thee tread the wildernesses? Ah, woe, woe!"

And Panda said: "No loved of mine or thine troddeth the wildernesses. Cast thee not thy woeing, Sherah, for they be waste."

And Sherah spake: "Yea, but shouldst there be one dear within them, woe! woe! Or yet within some lone land wherein no heart answered unto him, woe!"

And Panda said: "But new lands deal new joys, Sherah."

And Sherah stood up and looked her unto the floors and spake: "Yet, Panda, it seemeth me that the heart loveth old robes. Yea, e'en a tattered mantle."

And Panda said: "The heart of youth putteth patch of new loves upon old mantles."

And Sherah said: "Panda, a man knoweth his own blade and its sharp, and one knoweth her own love and his depth."

And Panda came him up unto the side of Sherah and murmured: "Thou art indeed fitting."

And Sherah spake: "But Panda, he hath looked not upon Sherah. Nay. E'en though Sherah did strand her locks of scarlet and trod the street's-way. A-ayea, and a circlet of shell did she bind o'er her locks, and he saw not! Panda, thinkest thou that a youth of any land did have within the skies one whit so much for the seeing as he did there?"

And Panda spake: "Sherah, thy tongue doth loose upon his name. Fear ye! Fear ye, lest it lead Rome unto him!"

And Sherah said: "Sherah hath a heart locked e'en so tight that Rome's blade might not loose!"

And Paul listed and came forth and spake: "Panda, the heats oped the out-gate, and one came within from out Bethany, and this one is of them that trod the dark ways and shew not to the days; a plucker of sheep from out the flocks of men. Yea, and a plucker of vineyards and greens that grow them beneath his brother's hands.

"Unto the house of Jacob this one sought and Paulia had gone thereto that she buy of fruits. And Paulia's ears took in that this one dwelled within the hill's shelter out upon the way unto Nazareth. And the heats had loosed his tongue, and he told of them that abided within this shelter and called a name Abner and spake of one, a Rome's one, called Caanthus, and a fool. Thinkest thou this is Hatte, and the fool Aaron?"

And Panda spake: "Yea. Did the tongue of the dark one speak more?"

And Paul answered: "Yea. Jacob drank up the tale, and Paulia knew the evil of his eyes. Yea, she said that even as he listed his hands fondled his purse.

"And the dark one spake that these had come not unto him, but that the heats had driven them, even as the beasts, unto the hill's-ways seeking shadows. And the fool bore of this one, Caanthus, who had sunk, and the leg of him had broken. And he said that the fool had wound him with a net such as them the fishers cast, and offered the nets unto him, but his lips could tell naughts. And the one said that this was naught that man might take as wondrous save that the man Caanthus had within his goods a golden sandal and one robe of fleece. And these were such as Rome dealt unto her nobled.

"And it sunk within the ear of Jacob. Panda, Paulia hath spoken it. And e'en at this morrow, within the heats, Jacob sought out the Rome's place, and Paul sought after the steps of Jacob, fearing lest he betray with word thy loved, Panda.

"And Jacob came forth with men of Rome, them that wear blades, and his beard swung and his feet scarce bore him up, and his mantle hung long before even as the nobled women leave fall their raiment behind!"

And Nada listed and spake: "Panda, Nada knoweth the empty that eat Theia. She is far, far, and yet her heart hideth within a nest as a young bird and the nest be the breast of her son."

And Panda said: "Yea, Nada, yea, and Hatte lieth close, close, deep, deep, within the heart of Panda. Panda hath ministered unto him, hath watched his limbs grow strong, watched his eyes light with knowing, and even so surely hath Panda seen the shadow hang him about as the mantle of mourning. And Nada, his going hath hurt sore."

And Nada said to him: "Panda, thy lands have been stripped and shew as the plucked bones of the dead, and the sheep—look thou, few, few! And the store—gone! Yea, the dreams of Nadab * brought but bread's-meal. And yet, Panda, even when the empty of the hut hurt at the yester-eve, even as the drops fell, Nada dreamed she heard the thudding of his racks."

And Panda smiled slow and spake: "Yea, even so Panda."

And Nada said: "Thinkest thou that we should seek this lost sheep?"

And Panda answered: "Nay."

And Nada looked unto Sherah, who listed, her lips hanging oped and red. And Sherah spake: "But Panda, the ways are full of wolves. Think thou!"

And Panda looked unto Nada and then unto Sherah and said: "How long, oh, how many days, shall a man-child abide babed within the heart of woman? Ever, ever, ever! Sherah, Hatte standeth tall and strong."

And Nada spake: "Panda, this one, this one of the Jews, this Jesus—thinkest thou He hath wisdom that He might deal that I bind me up this heart?"

And Panda answered: "Nada, thy tribes and mine know but one god, Allah."

And Nada spake: "Yea, Panda, yet each man who cometh within thy household speaketh him a new god. This seemeth folly; for all men know but one throb that meaneth Him within their hearts."

And Sherah said: "Levi sayest this one is the Promised One, but no Jew dareth that he ope this unto Rome. Even beneath the earth,

* The rugs that had been sold for bread.

within pits, the men of the high places among the Jews have caused counsels and spoken this one is He. Even though He hath come from out Bethlehem, and no man knoweth the all, so say the wise ones. This is the will of Jehovah that man know not his rooting.

"But Rome, Rome mocketh, and even hath her men spoken that Hatte was the Promised One. They fear a young youth and look upon one that be o'erwise with greater fear. Even hath word gone out that this one, this Promised One, is not of Jew's flesh; that Mary, His mother, hath been taken as the flesh of one of Rome and this one not of the tribe of David. Yea, they have even spoken her a wanton, and their lips laugh that a king should come forth within an ass's track."

And Panda spake: "When Rome laugheth 'tis that she cover rots. 'Tis wise Rome. Yea, wise. She feareth a youthed king and sheweth unto men two youths that men play at catch and fall."

And Nada spake: "Panda, leave thy sheep unto the hand of Paul and come thou with Nada that we seek this one."

And Panda questioned: "Canst thou leave yon spot?" And he pointed unto the rain's wash o'er the fresh earth.

And Nada spake: "Behold, Sherah, he sheweth clays unto Nada, when the young swallow fleeth upon swift wings! Panda, Nada would know the words of this one. Yea, and Hatte hath gone upon the way that he seek. Come thou!"

And Sherah spake: "Yea, Panda, go upon the way. Sherah shall look unto thy hut by day and Paul shall ope thy lands and shall set seed, for Levi shall give of his store for seed, and thou shalt go and seek sup of wisdom. Levi waiteth that he hear words come from fresh off this one's lips."

CHAPTER XVI

AND the days sped unto the time when the asses stood packed, and it was so that Levi lended unto them of his—his ass's flesh and one that should follow, and a youth that should go upon the way. And this youth was called David.

And behold, the earth had waxed soothed, and even the seeds had sprung like young hair upon the head of a babe.

And Jerusalem's walls gave them up, for they sought them through the city unto the way from the house of Levi. And behold, when they had gone, Sherah stood even at the side of Levi and spake:

"Sire, word shall come straight from out Nazareth unto the Jews, held e'en so close as Panda's own breath, and when they shall return the Jews shall rejoice."

And the day wore unto the closing when the men of the out-ways came them weary unto their abodes; for the without held the field whereon they tilled. And lo, the roads shewed still wet; for rains had swept even o'ermuch.

And at this time the way from out the Rome's hall shewed Jacob and two of Rome's men upon the way unto the house of Levi. And they sought it out and smote upon the door's ope, and Sherah made answering. And when she had spoken in greeting, they came them within and Jacob's voice shook as he spake:

"This household holdeth the all of the telling."

And Levi came forth and looked upon Jacob and said: "Thou a Jew! and even beneath the temple's shadow deliver thy brother unto Rome!"

And Jacob shook his hand and swung his beard and spake: "The Jews feed off Rome! Yea, doth Rome not ope her coin's place and leave flow? Even at this morrow did not ones of Rome buy of Jacob?"

And Levi answered: "Yea, yea, Jacob, yea, Rome hath bought of thee."

And he turned unto the Rome's men and said: "What wouldst thou?"

And they spake unto him and told that it had gone out within Jerusalem that Levi stirred treasons against Rome; that within pits he spake of things and even sat him upon his housetop and looked unto a far land for the King's coming. And more, that he even knew the flesh and had laid his hand upon this one he called King.

And they spake that he should ope his lips and tell unto their ears this one's name, that he be brought forth unto the mighty-seat and bade that he shew his kingship.

And Levi spake not. And they shewed a script that had the seal of the mighty one, and Levi looked upon it and spake:

"Mightiness moveth men, but mightiness may not move a man that he betray his brother. Levi is within thy hands, but his tongue is his."

And they turned unto Sherah and lay hands upon her and bade that she speak by what path this one should be sought. And she stood mute. And they spake unto her more and told her that the flesh of Levi should suffer should her lips shut. And she spake: "This one should be sought upon a path that no man may trod whose lips have spoken 'gainst his tribesmen."

And they said that this was not the telling. And she answered: "Levi hath sealed lips, and Sherah, his flesh, hath suffered so. Behold, her lips lock and she shutteth them up and would ope them not."

And they spake among them that this was the end; that they should seek with these Jews unto the place wherein Rome held the lash.

And the thing was done. And when they had come unto the spot it was eve and dark, and they shut them within the pits unto the morn for such time as the mighty one should wake and please.

And when it was still and Jerusalem slept, Levi spake soft: "Sherah, even though thy tongue be torn loose, remember thou art a Jew and the flesh of Levi. Thou knowest the prophets have spoken no blessing for him who betrayeth his brother.

"Who, then, is thy brother? Jew is the flesh of the Jew, the sign of brother. Sherah, thy sire is of the tribe of Jacob and knoweth but the Jew's laws, and yet within all men seeth he his brother."

And Sherah leaned her far unto the ear of Levi and spake her soft: "Sire, sire, Sherah seeth within the smarting that lieth upon the Jews at the scourge of Rome's lash the loosing of the cleave of one brother unto the other. Yea, Jews shall hold but unto Jew's flesh and shrink them from the eyes of their brothers that be not of their flesh. And this thing sheweth even now, for look ye! among the market's men even, the Jews cleave one unto the other, and the Jews' eyes look from out their shutted slant unto the brothers of other tribes that come thereto that they buy.

"Yea, the mockery of Rome! And Jews suffer deep, deep, sire. And look ye unto the Promised One who cometh; there are among Jews them who take unto their hearts Him who was born within Bethlehem, and yet there are them, Indra hath spoken it, who look unto Hatte and point the finger of scorning and speak: ' He even hath a sire—Who, Who, Who; and He who was born in Bethlehem hath a sire—Who, Who, Who.' And behold they take not even Him of Bethlehem nor yet Hatte. Sire, thinkest thou Hatte is He? Sherah feeleth deep within her that the Jews have come unto a temple place where they do stand even before the holy of holies, and it is laid upon them that they bend their knees if they shall choose, or yet uncrown, their King. Yea, Jerusalem is a stone within the sling of Jehovah, and Rome the winds that shall bear the stone from out its course. Sire, Sherah's lips stand locked."

And Levi spake: " Sherah, thou knowest not the hand of Rome, thou knowest not, thou knowest not. The out-walls of this very hall's place shall shew unto thee the sunlight, yea, the young day's wine, the street's-way, living, living, living. And thou, Sherah, shalt look without and shut thine eyes and thy lips shall shut even though their oping buy for thee the day."

And Sherah said: " Sherah is the flesh of Levi, of the tribe of Jacob, and the day, sullied of her brother's blood, is ne'er a day that is fitting that Sherah lift her hand therein."

And Levi took within his arms the form of Sherah, and even up unto his bosom pressed her, and upon the brow, whereon the black locks parted and white gleamed, pressed he his lips, and he spake slow and soft: " Jehovah, lend thou thy mantle unto this one of thee! "

And he raised his hands high and brought them down upon the head of Sherah, and she kneeled at his feet and kissed his mantle hem. And Levi bade that she arise and delivered her unto the dark. And she went thereto and sunk her upon the flag's bits and earth and rag, and thereon she slept.

And Levi sat long and long, and the night wore it heavy-slow. And the morrow brought grays, and heavy-laden clouds arose and banked and swept upon Jerusalem and set the waters coursed upon the street's-ways.

And within the walls of the Rome's place at the early tide, there came forth men of Rome, they that hold of blades for Rome's fend, and they waked them that abided within the walls, and the hall stood busied of the fall of feet.

And the time had come unto the mid sun, and the clouds still hung, and the mantles even of them within shewed damp. And behold, there came forth a one who shewed of the sign of Tiberius, and he bade that he hold ear of the mighty one and spake the name of Jacob. And lo, at a later tide came there forth Jacob and Samuel, even unto the hall's place, and they were brought forth even before the one from out the land of Tiberius. And he spake unto them, and Jacob shook his beard and beat the airs with his palms. And the men of Rome who stood them about spake one unto the other:

"What hath Rome that eateth her heart that she send a one who remaineth even through seasons at the mighty-seat, and speaketh unto beggars and even unto sheep's men, and hath sought the bypaths? Is this man a one who seeketh this Jew of Bethlehem? And what hath Rome that she fear a Jew's King? And yet, who is he who abideth without the walls that the tongues of men call Hate? And what hath caused the hand of Rome that it lay Hate low, for hath not the word gone forth that he was slain? And yet moneys creep up the sleeve of the Jew's mantle yonder and the Jew honeyeth his words and smileth o'ermuch. Yea, and opeth up his mouth's pit unto the emptying unto the men of the out-roads."

And they leaned far and whispered: "Tiberius quaketh. Tiberius hath spent the noble coin upon the women of the land. Yea, even upon slaves."

And yet they feared that they ope their lips aloud of this thing. And when the one of Rome, that had been called Aurelius by them of the halls, had spoken long unto Jacob and Samuel, behold he called that the mighty one hark. And this was taken unto his listing and he came forth and they held audience.

And Aurelius spake unto the mighty one even so that the ears of them who waited heard not. And he listed, and they spake the name of Levi. And the mighty one spake unto Aurelius, saying that Levi had been under the eyes of Rome, for the lips of the Rome's men brought forth word that Levi held treason within his breast, and that among the Jews stood a tribe that held one unto the other, and these were they that had taken unto them the Nazarene as the King. And they put unto the fires more, that it burn, and it was well that this man be brought forth that he ope and the fill of Jews' knowing be let free from out of him. And Aurelius said:

"The road's-way unto Rome shall see not the going of Aurelius until the hills'-ways have given up their very tracks. Thinkest thou that Aurelius shall take as truth the words of far tribesmen, Jews, and the slave's flesh freed of Rome? This one who abideth within the land of Nazareth the Jews speak of as King, and yet Aurelius feeleth this is not the thing that should set fear within Rome's mighty one."

And he laughed loud and spake: "The Jew's word speaketh that the Nazarene hath a cloak of sweet smiles and a voice like unto a stream of honey. Ha, ha, ha! This is not of Tiberius! And this one who hath gone unto the wheres; his blade leapeth and he runneth anger even as torrents run the hill's-way at wet season. Even among the market's men soundeth the tale that he sought the temple and bade that they leave him in and said that his sire abided within."

And Jacob spake and his voice whined: "Levi knoweth! Yea, and Sherah is the locust that tempteth this bee of Rome. Empty Levi! Empty Levi!"

And Samuel spake: "Yea, and Sherah! for Sherah's lips have asked all men who trod the out-paths whom they have met upon the way."

And Aurelius said: "This Jew speaketh rightly."

And they bade that they bring forth Levi and Sherah. And when they who had come that they bring them forth had come unto the pits, Levi took up the hand of Sherah and spake: "Sherah, unto thy hand Levi delivereth him this."

And he put with the hand of Sherah a skin sack and spake more: "Sherah, shouldst thou fail, look, look deep within the eyes of Levi and thou shalt find sup. Thou art a Jew. Thou art of the tribe of Jacob and thou knowest the words of the prophets, and thou knowest thy sire and his pledge unto his brothers. Dost thou ope thy lips and leave words of the Nazarene to flow, thou dost ope the pits unto Him. And dost thou ope thy lips of him who hath gone, thou knowest this is the undoing of Panda, and yet Theia. And more: the loosing of words that shall weave the net that shall bring the Jews like fishes unto Rome's feast."

And Sherah spake: "Sire, a dry well is a dry well. How may a man draw forth waters when there be none?"

And they stood and waited them that they be led forth. And the men of Rome lay hands upon them and bore them forth even unto the spot where Theia had stood.

And the mighty one sat and plucked at his teeth. And Aurelius sat him at the right hand. And behold, Levi and Sherah were brought forth even unto the feet of them, and they stood awaited. And Levi's eyes looked unto Jacob, who stood at the side of the men of Rome who waited at the fend of the mighty-seat.

And Samuel plucked at his mantle, and the hands of Jacob slid them up and o'er his arms beneath his mantle sleeve and out, and rubbed one upon the other.

And Aurelius spake: "Is this man Levi?"

And the hand of Jacob shot forth and his thin finger-point shook and his voice cried out: "This man is Levi and he is filled, filled of treasons against Jews and Rome!"

And Aurelius questioned: "Knowest thou of one who abided without the walls within the hut of a man called of the name Panda?"

And Levi's lips moved not. And Aurelius asked again: "Knowest thou this man, Panda?"

And Levi answered: "Who hath called a man 'Panda,' and what tribe doth he know as his brothers?"

And Aurelius said: "Panda was called 'Panda' by Rome. Yea, he was of the slave's flesh of Rome. Caesar was called that he look upon a boy who spake naughts, and his skin shewed as the skin of a panda.* And Caesar looked upon him and called his name Panda, for Caesar had had brought unto his hand the skin of this beast. And the lad oped not his lips nor spake the name his tribe had called him, but took of the name Rome dealt."

And Levi shook his head and spake: "That Levi knoweth Panda, the herder, meaneth naught."

And Aurelius said: "Yea, but dost thou know Panda, the herder, thou knowest his sheep, this one Jerusalem calleth Hate?"

And Levi spake: "Thou hast heard this one is gone, yea, lain low. The lips of Panda hath told thee this thing."

And Aurelius said: "Yea, but the lips of man may honey even a lie; yea, and doth a lie stick, a man may pour thereon oil that it slip through."

And Levi spake: "A Jew who lieth hath broken the law of the prophet."

And Aurelius cried: "Ha, ha, ha! The prophet's laws lie broken unto bits upon the streets of Jerusalem."

And he turned him unto Levi and spake: "Knowest thou of this Nazarene, Jesus?"

And Levi answered: "All Jews know of this one who struck fear unto Herod."

And Aurelius looked him keen and spake: "What knowest thou of Him?"

* The panda is a small carnivorous animal found in the Himalaya region. It has a reddish brown fur.

And Levi made answering: "But what all men know who have lain 'neath the might of Herods and yet of Rome's ones."

And Aurelius questioned more: "Dost thou then know that this young Jew hath spoken words that the men of Judea know and deliver as breads unto their brothers?"

And Levi said: "Yea, e'en the market's men know this thing."

And Aurelius spake: "Among the Jews, then, dost thou know there are men who speak this man as King, the Promised One, for whom the Jews have waited?"

And Levi answered: "What hath Rome that she fear a King who hath been brought out even from the lowly? A king, or yet one mightier than a king, weigheth man's goods and taketh therefrom what be his right. Then, O sire, may not a king, or yet a one mightier, take from out a man's words, be they rich, unto them as their store and profit therefrom? This is the bart of the lowly, for they drink but out their brother's cup of wisdom, else who ministereth unto them?"

And Aurelius spake: "Yea, but out from Nazareth there cometh word that the men of the city take not this one unto them, for they say, 'Who is He who hath sought the laws and speaketh them and speaketh more unto them, even as the prophets spake?' E'en do they say this man is a Jew and yet His walls He buildeth not about the words of the prophets, but buildeth He wider walls."

And Levi shook him "yea" and spake: "And Rome keepeth her watch upon such a lowly foot and the paths it seeketh? Sire, look thou upon Jerusalem. Doth the King's hand reach forth in succor unto her men? Dareth one Jew for to cry him out lest Rome shut his crying? And this one, this young Jew of Nazareth, shall Rome shut His words? For lo, word cometh that He hath spoken that His words be like the waters of earth, sent of the God, free unto all men as living sup. And He taketh not of Rome a price, nor yet of Jews, nor yet of Gentiles."

And Aurelius said: "A man who laboreth and taketh not full price is one whom the eye should look upon ever, yea, watch and know the why. This is not of the Jews that they give free!"

And Levi spake: "Sire, most noble sire, thou speakest of them that bart o'er skins and flesh. For behold, the Jews have set to flow free their very blood. Yea, they bear unto the full measure unto the temples that they give unto Jehovah the fullness of their vineyards and yet their precious stuffs.

"Yea, and Jerusalem hath set her blood to flow that ones of Rome be spared, and this thing was free, free given. Behold thou! have not even the priests stood against the wrath of Rome? And Jerusalem is thine, and thy heels trod upon her, and no Jew asketh the price."

And Aurelius said: "Nay, for reason, heavy reason—the wrath of Rome."

And Levi spake: "Woe upon Levi that thou knowest not his brothers, for when a man's belly is split how may he eat? How may a Jew break bread with Rome when Rome hath eaten full and cast not e'en a crumb unto the feet of her where she hath cast Jerusalem even as a dog. Sire, Levi shaketh. Yea, for hark! the dog shall arise and lick the hand that hath cast it down. Yea, and Rome shall lay smitten of sores, and the dog shall lick her wounds. For that that hath been cast down shall surely be assembled together and set up.

"Ye grow fat upon the lands of the Jew, and the Jew shrinketh and hungereth. Yea, and Levi sayeth long shall the dusts of Levi and his tribesmen lay, long and long, and Rome's shall mingle with them, and sire, the tides shall sweep, and from out thy dust and the dusts of the tribes of Levi shall spring a new man, and He shall be called a name not of the Jews nor yet of Rome,* and yet out from His hand's labor shall the smitten Rome deck and the Jew be remantled.

"Yea, and He shall know not the Gentile nor yet the Jew, but shall feed upon the freed waters of the cup. And His heart shall sore that His brother shall suffer, and behold, He shall raise the wrecked walls builded by the tribes of Levi; yea, and wash the temple's face; yea, and cause the stones to spring olives and leave whited doves to nest whereon the blood hath flowed.

"And Rome! He shall raise her fallen head upon His breast and kiss her wry-fallen lips to smile. Behold thou, sire, thou puttest value upon words. Hark! the bow that shall lay Rome low is strung of words. Yea, and the hand that shall set the bow to quiver and speed the arrow's point is raised in loving.

"Yea, yea, and more, sire. The Jews bow in shame and burdened low of their brother's hate. But the blood that dripped from out this wound shall wash the hate unto love, and yet Jerusalem may raise her weary head and smile! Thou mayest cast her down. Thou mayest eat her breads. Thou mayest play Rome's treasons upon her. Yet thou shalt drink her blood. Yea, and the earth shall wash clean within the blood of the Jews. Jehovah smileth; for He will not that one brother be o'er his brother's flesh. Yea, and He offereth the cup of blood's sacrifice out of the Jew's flesh. How then, sire, mayest thou sup and feed thereout if thou hatest?"

* Christ, a Greek name.

And Aurelius listed, and the mighty one shook unto him yeas, and their look one unto the other told much. And Aurelius spake:

" Then thou art of them that look unto Nazareth and Bethlehem and whisper."

And Levi answered: " Yea."

And Aurelius started: " Who, then, are thy brothers? "

And Levi spake: " I am not my brother."

And they pointed unto Sherah and said: " Since thou dost speak not their names, unloosing the lips of thy flesh shall loose thine."

And Levi spake: " Sire, this but telleth Levi that thou knowest not a Jew."

And they turned unto Sherah and questioned: " Knowest thou this man of Nazareth? "

And Sherah answered: " Nay, the eyes of Sherah have ne'er beheld Him, but His voice cometh as a song that soundeth afar."

And they spake: " Hast thou the knowing of them within Jerusalem who look unto Him? "

And Sherah spake not, but pointed unto Levi and then unto her own bosom. And they asked her of the knowing of Hatte, whom they called Hate, as this came from out Bethlehem. And Sherah answered not.

And they asked again: " Hath thine eyes beheld this one? "

And she smiled, and her eyes shone, and she spake: " Yea."

And they spake: " Where on the hills'-way steppeth he? "

And she said: " I know not."

And they made question: " Hath his lips spoken unto thee? "

And she answered: " Nay, no word."

And they looked one unto the other and shrugged and asked of her: " And thou lookest afar at the speaking of his name and thy cheeks glow? "

And she spake: " Yea, for doth not the pool blush at the sun's morn-kiss? Sire, Jehovah setteth the itch within the breast and man may not bid it thence. Sherah knoweth not the stirring, nor knoweth she him who stirreth it, save as the far stars know the moon, yet forsake they not her."

And they made words unto Sherah, and bade that she tell of what had been before the going of Hatte. And she said:

" Rome knoweth the all. Sherah hath but offered sup unto them that Rome had made hunger. Rome knoweth, sire, the blade that lay Caelius low and why. Yea, and Phaeton. Sherah knoweth but that

Caelius sought the house of Levi and said the morrow would he seek, and he came not."

And they spake unto her: "Thou knowest the tribe that holdeth treasons?"

And Sherah answered "yea," and they said: "Then unloose thy knowing."

And she swayed and spake: "Nay."

And they cried: "Knowest thou that Rome hath within her hand a thing that is a great teacher?"

And Sherah looked unto them and answered "yea," and her lips scarce moved.

And they spake: "Dost thou know that thou art now at the feet of Rome?"

And Sherah answered: "Yea, sire."

And they spake: "And thou fearest not?"

And she answered: "Nay, sire."

And she looked deep within the eyes of Levi, and his lips shewed shut thin, and his white beard hung long, and his hands shewed white, and his hair long and white, but his eyes young and lit of fire. And they waited that she speak, and no word came, and they said:

"Thinkest thou the smiting of him yonder might loose thee that thou speak?"

And she caught one hand unto the other and answered. "Nay, for did the lips of Sherah ope, thy smite could cut not even one-half so deep within him. Doest thou this thing, Sherah shall seal her eyes and stop her ears, even though she look upon it and hark."

And they said: "This Jew is of high estate, and she eateth of fine flour, and look! her raiment sheweth her of fullsome store."

And the mighty one spake: "Yea, yet he is but a Jew! What though his hide hath thick hair!"

And they said: "Wouldst thou that thou shalt be slaved?"

And she smiled and spake: "And thou speakest this unto a Jew? Thy mirth is dull, sire."

And they waited, for they sought that the words they spake might weave the net. And Aurelius said:

"Hassan hath gone out of thy lands and his words sealed not the tomb unto Rome. And she who hath gone, the woman Theia, danceth her like unto one drunk in joy. And they shut her eyes unto the seeking and she danceth, that her footfall bear Rome off the path."

And Sherah looked and spake: "Sire, then hath Rome sent o'er seas and lands unto Jerusalem for one lad who weareth but a sheep's skin and was born of Bethlehem?"

And Aurelius said: "Bethlehem hath brought forth o'ermany."

And Jacob came up unto the side of Aurelius and spake soft, and Samuel followed and spake word when Jacob had silenced. And Aurelius listed and spake word unto the mighty one, and the mighty one spake unto him even so that the ears of Sherah or Levi might not take in that that was spoken. And when this had been Aurelius turned unto Sherah and said:

"Then thou knowest not that this man, Hate, is within the hand of Rome?"

And Sherah answered not, and Levi shewed not by any sign that he had taken in the words. And Aurelius said: "Word of thine might stay the hand of Rome. Shouldst thou speak the names of them who treason, Rome might smile."

And Sherah spake not, and Aurelius looked close unto her and asked of her: "Knowest thou this thing?"

And Sherah answered: "Sire, Panda is a shepherd, and no lamb of his might fall unto the wolf, save that the eye of Panda see and he know."

And Aurelius said: "Thou knowest this man, Panda, hath spoken that the man, Hate, is lain low, slain; and hath shewn even the spot where his body lieth?"

And Sherah spake: "Yea."

And Aurelius turned unto Levi and said: "Knowest thou that this one is lain low?"

And Levi spake not. And Aurelius wrathed and cried:

"Thinkest thou, thou Jew, that Rome shall play thee such a gaming? This is no cast of discus! Speak, or the flesh of thine shall be delivered as slaves' flesh!"

And Levi spake not, and Aurelius wrathed hotter and called forth that they bid this man be lain beneath the waters until the time when the flesh be o'ertender and then the lash be lain.

And Sherah moved not, and Levi raised his hand and spake: "Sire, Rome's folly rideth thee. The lash of Rome—ah, sire, Levi's eyes look even unto the first dawning of the Promised Land, and the lash shall be but leaps and bounds unto it."

And they were angered sore and led him forth. And Sherah stood, and the flesh o'er her brow gleamed white, and her lips paled, and the black locks hung long o'er the mantle that hung her o'er. And they spake unto her that that Jacob told of the tongue of Levi speaking out that he held of a coin that he should spend for Rome's undoing, and they told that Jacob had brought men within the market's place that digged a pit beneath the earth even unto the house of Levi, that he take in that that was within the walls. And Samuel told of one that the heats had driven forth and that within the hill's place where this one abided, this man, Hate, lived. And the lips of Sherah smiled.

And they said that they should send forth and bring him even unto Jerusalem where he should be dealt unto. And Sherah spake:

"What hath this man done that Rome seeketh him?"

And Jacob cried aloud: "Jerusalem knoweth this one is the flesh of the mighty——"

And Aurelius stopped his words. And Sherah spake soft: "Mighty! Yea, even among the market's place walked he regal. The pit hath sealed against thee, Sherah. Jehovah hath mocked thee, for Jew's flesh, then, loveth Rome!"

And she turned unto Aurelius and said: "How then is this thing? Thou sayest Rome hath him within her hands and yet he abideth afar."

And Jacob wrathed him hot and his beard swung and he looked upon Sherah and turned unto Aurelius and spake:

"What then! thou leavest the tongue of the Jews that they speak out words past the prayers of the temple place? She knoweth, and he thou hast sent hither holdeth the full of the word!"

And Aurelius said: "Thou shalt speak, woman, or woe filleth!"

And Sherah raised her hands and let them fall and spake: "So be it."

And they brought forth slaves who bore lashes and shewed unto her, and her eyes looked upon them, and lo, she raised her hands and loosed her mantle o'er the white of her shoulders and bowed. And Aurelius smiled and spake:

"Thou art dull! Rome shall deal unto thy sire, for he hath age and thou knowest one suffereth thrice through the suffering of his loved."

And Sherah stood white and shaken. And they sent forth and bade that Levi be brought unto the spot. And Sherah stood and her eyes strained that they see his face, and behold, the door's ope shewed them bearing him within.

And his face gleamed even as one of marble, white and lumined of the sun, and his lips smiled. And they brought him forth and loosed his mantle.

And Sherah thrust her hand deep within her bosom and, behold, it stained red and she fell! And even as she sank, her voice cried:

"This is the first blood shed for Him of Nazareth, and him of the hills!"

And Levi sprung forth and leaned o'er her, and her face lit of sweet smile. And he cried out:

"Jehovah, take thou this lamb of sacrifice!"

And the hand of Sherah raised and shook and fell and Levi sunk. And Rome stood mute o'er that that Jehovah had willed.

And Jacob's voice raised in awful fearing. And the Rome's men waked from out their smite of wonder and stepped them unto the fallen ones and, behold, they took up the body of Levi and turned the face that they look upon it and it smiled unto them.

And the form of Sherah stirred and she murmured: "Levi! Sire!"

And no word came, and she sighed her long, and slept.

And behold, there came within, slave women who bore of sup unto them that waited within the halls, and one stepped up unto the spot whereon Sherah lay, and laughed.

And this was Indra. And Jacob went unto her and gave her a skin of metal. And Aurelius spake:

"Rome hath ridden her flesh o'erlong."

And he turned unto Jacob and said: "Thou sayest that this man, Hate, abideth upon the road unto Nazareth, within a place within the hills that lieth upon the bank of Jordan?"

And Jacob spake: "Yea, this one who hath come hath come out of Bethany, wherein his kinsmen abide, and he herdeth within these hills of Jordan's way."

And Aurelius said: "Then Rome shall send upon the way with this one a one who shall find the full knowing."

And Aurelius put within the hand of Jacob price for his brother's blood. And they went them out the walls.

And the word of what had been, by the even's tide, had swept Jerusalem and come unto the ears of Paul. And Paul sought out Jacob and spake unto him, saying: "What hath Rome done? Where hath she taken the flesh that belongeth unto Jerusalem?"

And Jacob answered: "Rome hath dealt but wisely, and Jacob knoweth not where the filth lieth."

And Paul spake: "Thou shalt go unto this man of Rome, and thou shalt speak unto him that he deliver these unto the hand of Paul, or, by the evil one, Paul shall ope thy throat and fill thy mouth of the filth of the streets!"

And Jacob spake: "But Levi hath sinned against the temple and against priests."

And Paul said: " Unto a swine the grape is swill! "

And Samuel listed, and Paul spat upon him. And Samuel wrathed, and they came one unto the other and Paul bore him down and, even as he lay, spat upon him. And Jacob wrung his hands and cried out that he then would do the thing bidden.

And at the eve's deep Paul went unto the Rome's place with a litter and an ass and bore what was Jerusalem's unto the out of Rome's walls and spake soft:

" Panda hath gone, but the land of Panda welcometh."

And the night shewed the spot still, and peace-bathed of pale star's-light. And this had Jerusalem suffered.

CHAPTER XVII

AND within Nazareth morn broke.

The hills lay wrapped of rose; the sky's mantle shewed decked of stars and hung of white fleece; the vineyards glisted of gems and the sweet airs stirred the deep-grown fields; and the sheep lay not yet waked.

And behold, a one came Him forth and trod the hill's path even so that the sun that came forth o'er the brow shewed Him radiant.

And He stretched forth His hands and called soft, and the sheep arose and came unto Him.

And He sat Him down and looked Him far, even o'er the ways that shewed from the high summit. And the lights shewed Him smiling unto the far.

And His feet were bared, and His mantle wet of young dew, and His eyes deep, deep blue, even as the sky, the sign of the might of God. And His locks flamed within the light and hung long and o'er His stooped shoulders. And the brow gleamed stained of the sun's heat, and His thin beard hid not the sweet that clung His lips. And lo, when He raised His hand, it was even as the soft skimming of a swallow's wing.

And the sun kissed the bended back whereon earth's woes should rest; and the grasses lay soft 'gainst His feet and even clung.

And He stretched forth His hands and looked upon them, and behold, upon the flesh shewed the stain of the staff. And He looked upon this and smiled, and took up a staff of broken wood that lay, and spake:

"The Son of Man shall fashion out His staff,* that they know."

And He arose and sought the valley; and the sheep followed, and the road's-ways swallowed their going.

And out along Jordan, within the hills' places, smoke arose, and this was a fire whereon flesh of sheep lay that it sear. And one stooped him o'er and lay coals unto the 'neath of the pit whereon it lay. And this was but the flesh of a sheep and not of the whole.

* The Son of Man shall so shape His life that the world shall understand its purpose.

351

And he who stood o'er called unto one who sat within the shadows of the stones and spake a name " Nada," and she came forth.

And this was at the sweep of four * tides.

And Panda spake: " Nada, come thou and eat of this. See! Panda hath given of his metals, e'en though they be little, that we sup."

And Nada spake in answering: " Panda, thinkest thou the way shall shew the ass weary o'er his bearing? And thou, Panda, thou hast fasted even so that thou hast not yet taken on thy full flesh."

And Panda said: " Man knoweth not his flesh, Nada, when his eyes look o'er his foot's trodding."

And Nada spake: " Yea, but Panda, the way hath been long, sore long. Thinkest thou that we shall come upon Hatte? Word hath sounded upon the way that telleth not of him but all men know of Aaron."

And Panda said: " Yea, for any man may know a fool."

And Nada spake: " Nay, Panda, Aaron's days shew folly, but his loving knoweth not the fool's smile."

And they sat that they sup. And they eat of the loaves ministered by the hand of Levi. And Nada spake her:

" Panda, thinkest thou that Nazareth shall take from her heart and give unto thee and me? Jerusalem's breast let grains slip through, e'en though she did not this in loving."

And Panda answered: " Nada, thou and Panda seek not grains; nay, but balms. And Levi hath told of this one within Nazareth unto thee, and thou hast listed. Behold, we have sought the path and he who rideth the sands rideth but unto the blue afar and knoweth not but the blue until the time when the lands without the sands appear."

And Nada spake: " Yea, Panda, but thou knowest not the empty of days, nor yet the empty of nights. E'en when Nada looketh up unto the great moon she seeth within her the swallow's wings. Yea, and the stars wing them ever upon golden pinions, and Nada shutteth out the sight, and behold the leaves wing. Yea, and the clouds, like white doves, ever, ever, ever fleeting, fleeting! "

And Panda said: " Nada, this telleth thy empty, but Panda seeketh not in dreams the hills whereon a young shepherd tendeth. Nay, the sheep flee before his dream; for they know not the shepherd who tended within the dreams of Panda."

And Nada spake: " 'Tis spoken that He of Nazareth knoweth wisdom's wisdom."

* Four days.

And Panda said: " Nada, wisdom is a thick cloak for thy brother, but 'neath it thou mayest fall smitten of cold."

And Nada said: " Yea, Panda, man weaveth wisdoms beauteous like unto the spider's spin, but the winds of day tear them to tatters."

And Panda leaned far and spake: " Nada, this Nazarene, Levi hath spoken, wrappeth His wisdom in rags. Yea, the laws of the prophets hath He taken forth out of their holy sepulcher and stripped them of their winding cloths, and He held them forth clothed of rag. Yea, wisdom He strippeth, and the dust's grains He magnifieth."

And Nada looked her far and started up and cried: " Look thou, Panda! See! yonder sheweth sheep! "

And Panda spake: " Yea, then man abideth him close."

And they arose and made clean and put of the seared flesh within the asses' pack and set them upon the way unto the spot whereon the sheep shewed. And behold, this was upon a high place, stoned, and waters flowed them near, and upon the hill's side there shewed a pit * hung of skins. And they went them up even unto the pit's place, and Panda called unto the ope, and no sound came forth. And Panda turned unto the sheep and called the sheep's call and they came them forth. And one who watched arose and came forth, and this one dragged of nets. And his eyes looked upon Panda, and he threw his nets high and ran and fell upon his neck, and his lips gave forth sounds that shewed his full of happiness.

And Nada came unto him and lay her arms about him, and lo, he stood and laughed and waited.

And Panda pointed unto the pit, and Aaron laughed and went forth, and behold, he went within and there came forth a one whose beard hung young, and he leaned upon a staff, for he was smitten. And Panda threw his hands high and cried:

" Hatte! Caanthus! "

And the one stood still and spake: " Nay, I am not strong."

And Panda looked sorrowed upon the smitten form of Hatte. And behold, Nada stood wide-eyed and stepped even up unto his side and laid her hand upon the smitten limb. And Panda's lips spake:

" Caanthus, thou art Caanthus of Rome? Come, lad, speak thou art him! "

And Hatte let fall his head upon his bosom and sighed and spake: " Nay, nay, Panda. Hatte hath sought new lands, and thou knowest a grain falleth upon new land and doth for to spring or waste. And man may know this grain hath sprung and grown by the plucking of

* A cave.

its grains' sheaves. Yea, but doth there be no plucking he knoweth 'tis waste, waste! Panda, hast thou heard within the market's place of Hatte, or the growing of his grain?"

And Panda shook him " nay." And Hatte spake, and his cheeks burned, and his lips sneered, and he pointed unto Nazareth's way and spake: " But He, He, the Jews do secret love. Ah, His grains spring even though Rome would trod them down, yea, and Jews break their stalks. Yea, they grow, they grow!"

And he sneered dark. And Panda spake him soft: " Hatte, Hatte, hath the sun and the sear burned thy heart?"

And Hatte cried: " Heart, Panda, heart? The heart of Hatte is within the hand of Rome, and Rome doth press it dry even of its blood!"

And he turned and shewed unto them the pit's ope and spake: " Come thou! come thou! Hatte is nobled. This thou knowest. Yea, his kingdom, behold thou, and his throne!"

And he laughed bitter, and he leaned upon his staff and dragged of his limb after as he went upon the way. And Panda went unto him and spake: " Hatte, is this smite new?"

And Hatte answered: " New, ever. Who is he who hath done this thing? He of Nazareth telleth of soft words. He knoweth not Rome, nay nor the stone's cut. He smileth—Hatte hath seen this thing—and these Jews smile them back even as young flowers unto the sun. Yea, He smileth!"

And he laughed and spake: " His sire, ' Who,' hath found Him not, even though He hath called Joseph his flesh. This man was no noble. Nay, and even Nazareth nor his kinsmen wept at his going. Hatte sought Him out and He spake He was the brother of all men and not of the flesh of Hatte. Panda, He hath lied!"

And Panda raised his hands in the sign of silence and spake: " Hatte, a man taketh within his ears the mold that shapeth the words that flow within them."

And Hatte questioned: " Hast thou heard from out the hills or the road's-ways of her—Theia?"

And Panda answered: " Naught but that she speedeth her feet."

And Hatte sunk him slow upon a skin's-cast o'er a stoned place within the pit's ope, and spake: " Thy words are wine, Panda. Is this the sup that maketh a man? Earth taketh all the sweets from out the vintage she offereth unto Hatte, and Hatte may weak for one sup of a noble's wine."

And Panda turned unto the spot where Aaron stood, his lips spread in empty smile and the long arms clasped of his nets. And Panda spake: "Hatte, hath Aaron e'er wearied thee or wearied him upon the path?"

And Hatte's eyes leapt bright, and his lips smiled and he spake: "Panda, Aaron is the wine that ever sheweth sweet sup. Yea, his hands hold naught, but Hatte drinketh from out his empty cup a draft sweet, sweet, for his cup holdeth but the grape, yea, the juice that Hatte presseth unto it."

And Panda asked of him: "Hast thou abided within Nazareth?"

And Hatte spake: "Yea. These hands, look upon them, for they are cut of thong; for Hatte hath fashioned out skin jugs for the marketing. But Panda, Rome knoweth the pathways unto Nazareth. She seeketh, she seeketh; Panda, I know not, but 'tis He whom Nazareth knoweth as Jesus or else, Panda, Hatte."

"Yea, and this man Jesus, whom they call Christus, groweth, Panda, past the hold of Nazareth, for the priests have heard of His tongue. Yea, and His hands spread o'er the multitudes, and sweets flow from out them even unto their very faces, for they fall beneath His words. Their eyes glist, their lips smile, their breath hangeth, their ears list; they stand them hunger-thirsted; and when Hatte sought, they drew aside their mantles, yea, and they stepped from him.

"Earth hath armored against me, Panda. Look! these arms are strong, these legs were strong, but they wither and these arms raise in vain. No fashioning of these hands stand. The sheep blight. They seek me not. The hills scorch. The fields grow bare. Words sour, even as wine vats. Hatte hath sought, sought, and he knoweth, knoweth the waters draw them close, close. They sweep him on, on. And one noble hand might stay the tide and it reacheth not forth. Neither doth this God of Theia, nor the Father of this Christus, who, He speaketh, holdeth dominion o'er all, lend an aid."

And Nada listed. And there came unto the spot one who bore a slain sheep, and they started. And Hatte spake: "'Tis Ezra. Sit ye! His heart is like unto this stone and he knoweth no man and careth not that man shall know of him."

And Ezra came on unto the pit. And his jaws hung ope, and his eyes shewed like lightnings that flash hither, thither, yon and on. And his hands clutched the sheep and shewed red of blood, and blood streamed o'er his mantle.

And Hatte looked not upon him, but he came on and up unto the spot. And he spake naught, but pointed unto Panda. And Hatte spake naught unto his listing, but shewed unto the eyes of him a skin's sack with but few metals therein. And Ezra made of the sound like unto a swine and turned and went unto the thicks and bore the sheep. And Hatte spake:

"The hand of Hatte is nobled but to thieves. Look ye! at the bidding he goeth, for he knoweth the full is his and no word hath told this."

And Panda smiled and said: "Yea, Hatte, but the stretching forth of the hand doeth not this thing. Nay, 'tis the shewing of metals."

And Hatte spake, and laughed: "Nor is the hand of the noble the thing that moveth men. Nay, 'tis the casting of his golden dust!"

And Panda said: "Hatte, thy days are hands that fashion out thy measure. Yea, but thou dost fashion thy measure not that it measure man rightly, but that it measure out the days for thee. What sought thou within Nazareth?"

And Hatte answered: "Did not the lips of this Nazarene, Jesus, speak that He was the brother of Hatte? Then the brother is of the flesh and sired of the same sire. And Hatte seeketh Him out and findeth that His words have no meat; that He speaketh naughts that shew as meat, but that that be but the shadow of it.

"His sire, He hath spoken, is the sire of all men. Ha, ha, ha! Look upon His workings! He hath sired thee and Nada and Aaron yonder. What a mighty work! And He hath sired this man, Jesus Christus, and shed riches upon Him, for earth loveth Him. Yea, I speak it out they even now fear that His honey shall drown the noble fly!

"Yea, and He, this great sire, hath sired Hatte, the he-wolf that earth houndeth, out of Rome, out of Jerusalem, out of Bethlehem, out upon the hill's-way, unto the tide when he is empty, empty and withered, and yet he may not rest!"

And Panda spake: "What hath this man, Jesus? For word cometh even unto Jerusalem of this one, and Nada hungereth that she seek and fill the empty, for, Hatte, the babe, the young swallow, hath winged hence."

And Hatte stood and laughed, and spake: "This, then, is the work of this mighty sire. Thou hast asked of Him, the Nazarene, Jesus, what hath He? I know not, but it chafeth Hatte. He smileth upon man. Is this folly? I do ask ye. He speaketh sweets to the wicked, yea, unto the bitter feedeth He honey. Is this folly? Yet hath He no grain nor yet sup that He might feed unto the hunger here," and he touched his heart o'er. "He turneth woods within His hands and they fall righted, yea, unto that which He fashioneth, and no man may speak against His handiwork. Yea, His sheep tendeth He and no man hath sheep like unto His.

"Yet He knoweth not hate, and knoweth He not hate, how may He then minister unto it? Nay, Panda, this man would soothe the wounds of all men with one herb. And His sweets smart the cuts upon Hatte. The evil one might sear the wounds and fall short in hurting as the sweets sear!

"He speaketh 'His Sire,' and smileth sweet, sweet, and His eyes soft, and Hatte harketh—then, then, Theia danceth within the very airs o'er the blue skies, and Hatte hateth!

"Is Hatte then the footcloth He troddeth that He be crowned? Shall Hatte smile upon His sweet mantle when blood creepeth him o'er? There are men, Panda, who blind them in a cloak of loving, but those men know not the seed of hate! Ah, if the feet of Hatte shall trod the sharped stones and bleed thereon, they shall cry out hate! hate! hate!"

And Panda spake: "Hatte, thou art plunged within the sea of self. Yea, and thine only succor is the broken beam of thy brother, that thou shalt cling unto it and let it bear thee up. For know thee, within the sea of self floateth naught but broken beams, for one who swimmeth it knoweth not his brother save as one broken. Yea, but dost thou reach and shut thine eyes, behold, the beam shall be strong, and thou shalt speak, 'Brother! Brother!' And dost thou search for one who is whole, then thou sinkest." [12]

And Hatte rose him high and cried: "Panda, thy words sound like unto His, the Nazarene. Stop! Stop! Hatte shall pin himself unto an arrow; yea, and Time shall be the bow, and Hatte shall speed through the earth's heart unto the ages. And the blood that floweth at the pinning shall cry out through time, Hate! Not even within the hearts of men may Hatte rest. Nay, and all men who have been born within the red mantle of hate shall be called of his name, Hate!"

And Panda spake: "But all men may wash them white from out the red mantle by the tears of sorrow."

And Hatte said: "Panda, sorrow is like song. No man sorroweth like unto his brother nor singeth his brother's song. Love is but hate gone follied. Yea, hate is the deep note of love's song. And love is the flame that burneth and outeth, and what hast thou, Panda? But charr, waste, hate! Yea, hark! then hate is the substance that feedeth love!"

And Panda held high his hand and spake: "Nay. Nay. Nay. Hate is the ash of love that falleth but that new blooms arise!"

And Hatte leaned and hissed: "Yea, and the bloom shall be scarlet!"

And Panda lay his hand soft upon Hatte, who shook of angers, and spake: "Bear thou, then, thy bowl of hate—bear it! But thou shalt drink loving out of it. Bear it, Hatte, but at the every dawning watch, watch! The wine within it shall shew less and thy hand weaker, weaker, weaker. And when thou hast sunk and do thirst heavy, there shall be no drop within it and thou shalt weep tears of sorrow, and drink them."

And Hatte arose and sprung and smote the cheek of Panda. And Panda stood dark, dark, and reached forth his hand and cried:

"Weep! Weep! Weep!"

And the form of Hatte sunk in sob. And Panda stood and smiled. And Hatte stretched forth his hands and looked unto the eyes of Panda and murmured: "Panda, look! these hands speed and Hatte knoweth not the bidding! Shew thou me the path!"

And Panda spake: "Hatte, the hand of Panda hath set thee not upon thy path. Nay, but his hand is thine."

And Hatte said: "But the path windeth and stoppeth, and when Hatte hath found a rest, behold, he is driven forth."

And Panda leaned far and said soft unto him: "Hatte, when she whom thou lovest, Theia, thy flesh, thy mother, felt the smite of the bright spot, lo, she sought the hills where such men abided, and binded upon her back a cross of wood in sign that she bowed beneath the hand of Jehovah. She hath spoken this unto Panda. And she knew not the great Sire who had ministered this unto her.

"Arise! Bind thou the cross upon thee and walk ye the rough path, and look, at the day's tide, but unto the sun, and at the night but unto the moon."

And Hatte arose and spake: "Bind thou the cross upon this back in sign? Panda, thou knowest that Rome hath done this thing unto them she despised. Yea, the flesh of men she binded of the cross and set that they labor so binded. Upon the white flesh the scarlet of its chafing burned. Yea, Hatte hath heard this thing and knoweth a man who abideth in Nazareth who hath such a sign seared within his back's flesh. Even of thorned branch did Rome build up these signs. And this Sire, this goodly one, knoweth this!

"Panda, Hatte would that his every atom would build up one mighty voice that would cry, why? why? why? O Sire, why? Did not Hatte seek this Jesus and tell unto Him these things, these wickeds, and His lips smiled?

"Yea, and His hands did pluck green herbs, the living leaf of a fig tree, and did hold forth unto Hatte and speak that the words of the prophets were writ upon them. Is this folly?

"Yea, He spake that the ears of Hatte harked unto earth for the Sire's voice. Yea, and He spake that man should pin him unto a star and hark unto the heavens, even though his feet trod mires.

"Behold thou here within the breast of Hatte!"

And he oped his mantle and took therefrom a skin's-sack, and his lips spake: "How may the fig's leaves bear the words of the prophets? For the words of the prophets are everlasting and the leaves wither."

And he oped the sack and took forth the leaves—and they shewed green, fresh green! And Hatte let fall the leaves and stood white, and his lips stiffened, and he spake in whisper:

"Panda, who is this man? He said unto Hatte that his words were false; that the prophet's words were not everlasting save by the loving of man."

And Panda's eyes looked long upon the greened leaves and he spake soft: "And this man hath done this thing?"

And Hatte answered: "Yea, yea. Panda, ope not thy lips, for they will stone Him."

And Panda took up the leaves and let his lips that they press thereon and his cheeks burned like unto one who had supped wine.

And Hatte sprung up and cried: "Thou wouldst kiss this man's handiwork? He hath lied! His sweets are sick-deal!"

And he caught unto the hand of Panda and took therefrom the leaves. And behold they shrunk—brown, even as dust, and floated thither upon the airs!

And Nada started up and came unto the side of Panda and pointed unto Nazareth way and spake: "On, on, Panda! this man hath balms."

And Hatte cried: "What! seekest thou unto Nazareth? Hath Hatte not hung as the mantle's hem unto this man? Thou shalt fall short in thy seeking."

And Panda spake: "Hatte, within Nazareth, among her people, what word speak they of this man? How hath wisdoms come unto Him?"

And Hatte answered: "Nazareth holdeth a wise man, yea, one who knoweth the Jew's laws, who hath fellowed with the priests and who knoweth the far land's laws. And this one hath oped his wisdoms unto this Nazarene. He hath brought forth youths of young years and filled their ears. Yea, but his wisdoms o'erfill the shallow of the youth's ears.

But this one, Jesus, is like unto a sand's stone within waters. He taketh in His fill and drieth it within Him and soaketh up more. Yea, Panda, and at the eve's hours, even at His young years, did He bring forth the youths and speak the heavy wisdoms of the teachers and the wisdoms shrunk unto that that all youths knew.* Yea, within the pebbles shewed he the mighty stone's weight."

And Panda cried out: " Hatte, a wise man! A wise man! For none but a wise man may pack his goods that it be the pack of one ass doth he possess o'er the carry of one ass! "

And Hatte questioned: " Then thou seekest this one? "

And Panda answered: " Yea, Hatte, at the pass of the sun o'er the high."

And Hatte looked afar and spake: " Wouldst thou that we seek? Shall Hatte, then, leave thee that thou shew unto him the path? "

And Panda answered: " Hatte, goest thou burdened of hate no man shall make price and buy it from thee? "

And Hatte spake: " Panda, thinkest thou the sun touched not the leaves and they remained them fresh? "

And Panda said: " Nay, Hatte, nay. This thing is a wisdom's work."

And Hatte spake: " Panda, Hatte feareth this man."

And Panda said: " Nay, Hatte, the way is ope."

And Nada said: " Yea, yea, Hatte, bring forth thy bowl that we shall seek."

And Hatte pointed unto Aaron, who sat at the plucking of leaves from off a branch. And these he took forth from out the nets and made known that these were fish from which he plucked scales. And Hatte spake: " Panda, Aaron shall follow and we shall seek; for Hatte would that he be within Nazareth when this noble one claimeth His own."

And Panda touched the flesh of Hatte and said: " Nay. Stay thou within this spot, if this be thy bidding."

And Hatte said: " Nay. Wait thou! Hatte shall seek yon thick and deal the metals unto him who waiteth, and the high sun shall pass and we shall seek."

And he went unto the spot wherein was kept flesh and breads, and offered unto the hands of Panda and Nada and spake: " Set ye and sup, and wait."

And he went from out the pit's place and on unto the thick.

And Nada sat her long and broke the bread slow, and looked unto Panda and spake: " Panda, thinkest thou that he who set upon the

* He put their teachings into simple words within the understanding of youth.

path with thee and Nada * hath gone unto Jerusalem's walls at this time?"

And Panda answered her, saying: "Yea, this morrow should find his feet upon the threshold of the house of Levi."

And lo, the road's-ways shewed a one who rode, and this one was upon the back of a camel. And he raised his hand in greeting, and Panda started up and went without. And this man was called Saul, and he spake:

"Art thou called of the name Panda, and hast thou come from out Jerusalem?"

And Panda answered: "Yea."

And the one who rode said: "Then thou shalt stay thee here within this spot; for one cometh by the name of Paul and hath bidden all men he hath met upon the ways that they seek thee."

And Panda spake: "Then thou sayest that Paul is upon this way?"

And the one made answering: "Yea, he hath sought upon all paths save this."

And Panda said: "Where upon the path is he?"

And the one Saul made answering: "But at the first bend of Jordan."

And Panda asked: "Did his lips speak aught else unto thee?"

And Saul answered: "Nay."

And Panda said: "Whither goest thou?" .

And Saul made answering: "Unto Nazareth way, that mine ears fill."

And Panda said: "Goest thou that thou dost hark unto Him?"

And Saul answered: "Yea, the son of Mary, and thou knowest no builder suppeth from out his woods and barks such wisdoms as these."

And Panda spake not. And Saul leaned him far and said: "Art thou a Jew?"

And Panda answered: "Nay, but the Jew is the brother of Panda."

And Saul said: "Knowest thou that this woman was fruited green? Out of Rome creepeth the word that they seek such a man's fruit."

And Panda spake: "Yea, Rome hath such a tale."

And Saul leaned close and spake: "Thinkest thou this man is the fruit?"

And Panda answered: "Thou knowest Rome. Rome's hand plucketh all fruit, be it ripe or yet green. But within Nazareth men ply

* The boy, David, who had started from Jerusalem with them and had been sent back.

woods unto the fires and the smokes e'en now smart the eyes of the nobles."

And Saul said: "Knowest thou John? He hath spoken this man is the one awaited. And the Jews hide their hands beneath their beards and make signs one unto the other."

And Panda answered: "Shouldst thou seek thou shalt find; for His words are honey."

And Saul touched his camel and it stretched forth its neck, and he spake: "The sun is still high. Saul setteth the road's-way, for he hath within his pack but bread enough to fill his days unto Nazareth. Await thou, for Paul seeketh."

And he rode him hence. And Panda returned unto Nada who waited within, and spake: "Nada, Paul seeketh thee and me upon the way."

And Nada said: "Thinkest thou that evils have befallen them within Jerusalem that hold thy love and mine?"

And Panda spake: "Nada, no new thing befalleth within the walls of Jerusalem; for bloods and curse be rife. Steel thy heart. Theia hath spoken that he who ministered unto her should suffer."

And Nada said: "But Sherah, Panda, Sherah, whose eyes are stars of early dawn, whose locks are midhour's blacks, whose brow is moon's white! Sherah! Panda, no evil might befall Sherah?"

And Panda spake: "Nada, Rome careth not what stuffs have fashioned the bowl in which she dealeth filths."

And Nada said: "Thinkest thou, Panda, that Paul shall shew upon the way at this eve's hour?"

And Panda answered: "Yea, even at the pass of the midsun."

And they looked unto the thicks wherein Hatte had sunk, and behold, he shewed him coming. And Aaron followed, and he carried upon a wood staff a sheep skin, packed, and came even up unto them. And they told unto Hatte's listing of what had been, and told unto Hatte of Sherah, whose eyes shone at the speaking of his name; and of Levi, who had ministered unto Theia, and of the famine's scorch, and all that had been. And Nada spake:

"Hatte, this maid, Sherah, thou hast seen within the market's-way."

And Hatte said: "Yea, the eyes of Hatte have taken in of her."

And Nada spake: "Hatte, Sherah hath spoken unto Theia that she held within her heart a gladsomeness at the beholding of thee."

And Hatte cried: "But look, Nada! the cheek of Hatte sheweth scarred of a stone of Rome, and his limb hath withered in strength."

And Nada said: "But Hatte, what if eyes blind them in this mantle of loving thou hast spoken of?"

And Hatte spake: "Nay, this is not of a maiden that she do this thing."

And Nada said: "But they have sought that she speak thy name. Yea, Hatte, this is true. Jerusalem seeketh thee! Her street's-ways are sought by Rome's ones who see even within the dark. And Sherah hath sworn unto her God her lips shall lock."

"And she doeth this thing for Hatte and Hatte holdeth not loving?"

And Nada said: "Hatte, thou hast sworn that thou lovest the moon's white and the star's cool and the night's deep. Sherah is all of these and the scarlet of the summer's blooms."

And Hatte spake: "Yea, Nada, the maid is fair, and Hatte hath passed upon the way and looked him high when he saw him low. Theia was the morning fair, and she the eve."

And behold, upon the road's-way shewed the form of Paul, who smote upon an ass. And Panda went forth that he meet him and they stopped them even upon the spot, and this was scarce a score of leg spans from the pit's place. And Paul spake soft words unto Panda, and Nada waited in anguish. And Hatte stood, and behold, his hand fell upon his hip, whereat hung the scourge of gold.

And Paul leaned close o'er the ass's back and Panda leaned upon the back of the beast. And Paul spake: "Panda, woe hath fallen! Rome hath smitten Levi and gutted his household. Yea, and felled his daughter's flesh. Sherah hath bended her head unto Rome and is no more, and yet Levi."

And Panda cried: "Paul! Paul! Say thou not this thing! Levi stripped, and Sherah no more? For what wicked?"

And Paul said: "The locking of Levi's lips and Sherah's, that they betray not the faithed ones, the Christus sayers."

And Panda stood him tall and made words, saying: "Paul, no chain of metal's weld is like unto the weight of Rome! A man may free him of his grains, or yet his mantle, or e'en his flesh, but ne'er of Rome! All men are dipped within her pool of greed and washed to naught. Panda standeth freed, yet Panda's hands are bound! Yea, and Rome's cross is upon him!"

And Nada came forth, and Hatte followed upon the way. And Paul told what had been, and Hatte spake fevered:

"This maid hath sunk?—is no more?"

And Paul said: "Yea, and within the hall's places the tongue of Indra hath spoken that that Sherah spake when Rome smote."

And Hatte hissed: "Indra, the serpent of the slimed places, who hath sold herself for a pack of cloth! What did the tongue of Sherah speak?"

And Paul spake: "She smote her breast and told unto them that listed that this was the first blood shed for Him of Nazareth and him of the hills. And the one of the hills had been called Hate unto her."

And Panda spake: "Thou sayest that Sherah hath let flow her blood that she said be for Him of Nazareth and him of the hills?"

And Paul spake him in answering: "Yea, for she showed the flushed cheek, the men of Rome said, at the name of Hatte, and still her eyes drooped and her lips broke in smiling at the speaking of the Nazarene."

And Panda cried: "And Rome let the hand of Sherah that it empty her breast?"

And Paul held high his hand and spake: "What would sto a Jew that he empty? Nay, Rome would aid his hand."

And Panda said: "But thou sayest they sought word!"

And Paul spake: "Yea, yea, Panda, yet Sherah's hand held cunning o'er Rome. From out the breast plucked she the blade, and this was lended by the hand of Levi."

And Hatte turned unto Panda and held forth his hands and said: "Panda, look! art thou not filled of pride at this work of thy God?"

And Panda spake, and his eyes looked deep unto the flashed eyes of Hatte: "Yea, Panda is proud, for the cup of this God's folly would drown man's wisdom with its least dreg of wisdom. Yea, Hatte, the earth's tears He smileth o'er and they blow them dry within His warmth. Thou hast supped the bitters. Awake, thou, and cease thy folly!"

And Paul turned and looked unto the smitten Hatte and flung wide his arms and cried out: "Hatte! Hatte! Is this, is this thee?"

And Hatte looked not upon him, but answered: "Nay, he thou didst know is lain low. Yea, his legs fail—his heart is no more—he is empty."

And Paul touched his flesh and made word, saying: "But thou didst seek thee the Nazarene and word cometh that He hath let this mantle fall upon Nazareth until all sheep be warm and no beasts seek them."

And Hatte laughed and spake: "He weaveth a mantle of words and they hold not one unto the other, and Hatte hath clothed him within His word and is frozen."

And Paul smiled and looked unto Panda and spake: "Panda, hast thou not left him one fire's glow from out thy heart's warmth?"

And Panda answered: "A man's wrath swalloweth the coals and setteth them aflame, and flames ne'er warm but scorch."

And Nada came forth and held her headcloth that the sun not beat, and came up unto the side of Panda and touched his mantle and spake: "Panda, dost thou not know that fires burn? Even though thou dost throw drops upon it it hisseth and flameth high. Even the heat's mists from heated drops * burneth. Knowest thou not this?"

And Hatte spake: "Yea, Panda, Nada hath spoken it."

And he turned unto Paul and said: "Paul, what hath set thee that thou dost seek Panda and Nada upon the Jordan's way unto Nazareth?"

And Paul spake: "Hatte, thou hast sought far. Hath ne'er the eat of lone set thee upon the way unto Jerusalem?"

And Hatte laughed and answered him, saying: "Nay, Jerusalem hath no more of loving for Hatte than she hath for the dogs that lie her streets."

And Paul touched him and spake: "But Panda hath stayed without the walls, and all men know Panda's wisdom, and yet Panda suffered the famine's drouth. And thou—hast thou suffered?"

And Hatte answered: "Nay, what is thirst to heart's eat? Aaron and Hatte sought that they go them unto the first city's place unto the west way, and behold, the waters shewed not upon the way, and the stones slipped."

And he touched his leg and smiled bitter and spake: "The Great Sire, the Great Sire, slipped the stone that it snap the leg. Ha, ha, ha!"

And he spat upon his withered leg and turned unto Panda and cried: "Thou'rt His workings. Ants, yea, maggots of His earth!"

And Panda spake: "Come thou, Paul, that thou dost rest; for the time hath come that Nada and Panda shall seek them unto Nazareth. Since the hills hold bitters, then Nazareth holdeth sweets."

And Hatte laughed bitter, and his lips curled and he went forth and held his hand unto the pit's-way and pointed unto the within and sped him limped thereto. And he came forth bearing of a skin jug and held it unto the hand of Panda and 'mid his bitter laugh spake: "Bear thou back this man's sweetness, His honeys, and this shall be thine."

And he shewed metals. And Panda harked not nor reached forth, and spake: "Paul, where goest thou?"

And Paul shewed within his bosom the sign of the Christ ones,

* Steam.

and said: "Unto Nazareth, bidden by the word of Levi, left with his brothers."

And Panda spake: "Come thou then, brother, come!"

And they brought forth the asses. And Nada sat upon one and Panda followed with the other that shewed packed of packs. And Paul turned not nor spake he unto Hatte.

And Hatte stood mute, and Aaron laughed at his net's dragging. And they set upon the way.

And Hatte stood long, until their going from out his seeing. And behold, when they had gone, Hatte arose unto his height and looked upon his smitten leg, and went him up unto Aaron and made signs that he should follow. And went him unto the pit's place and came him forth packed.

And the hour had come unto near the sun's sink, and red bathed the hills, and behold, Hatte took up a staff and limped upon the road-way unto Nazareth. And Aaron followed him, laughing.

CHAPTER XVIII

AND the nights followed days unto the time when the road's-ways shewed Panda and Nada seeking with Paul a city's place. And behold, they came them up unto a one who spake his name Jared. And they asked of him the way. And Jared spake unto them, saying:

"Thou shalt seek thee upon the straight way up and o'er the hills unto the oping wherein is sunk the mighty's sea." *

And Panda asked if this stood upon the way unto Nazareth. And Jared made answering: "Nay; thou hast the right tree but the wrong branch."

And Panda spake that their bread had gone less, and waters then they should seek, for about the waters suredly men rested them. And Jared spake:

"Yea. Art thou a Jew?"

And Panda answered: "Nay," and he made the sign of the East and touched his brow with his hand's back. And Jared spake:

"The lands of the Jew be like ants' rests trod of swine."

And Panda listed not but asked who within this sea's place would minister for moneys. And Jared laughed and shrugged.

"Nathaniel. Nathaniel shall give unto thee for metals. Yea, doth Nathaniel fall short, he then shall deal thee shorter."

And they went upon the way and behold the hills raised higher and they came unto an oping that lay smooth, and within the oping shewed the far stretch of waters. And the waters shewed cool in the morning's gray, and the green about shewed dark, and the pale gold of morn stole soft o'er the sky close unto the earth's rim. And fishers called one unto the other, and they shewed busy that they set them gone, and no man looked upon them.

And Panda called unto ones that went unto the waters and offered of moneys for fish and bread, and these did to minister unto them.

And Panda spake the name of Nathaniel and they said that Nathaniel had gone at the early tide unto the sea's-way with them that fished.

And behold, they went up unto the sea's side whereon the sands shewed and sat that they eat of the breads. And the flesh of the fish

* Sea of Tiberius.

they ate, dipped of salt. And when this had been they took up their packs and went unto the shades that they rest. And the mid's-hour shewed them upon the way.

And time swept unto the morrow when, at the late of eve, they came unto Nazareth. And the stars shewed and Nazareth lay quiet 'neath the gray, jeweled skies. And they sought out the city's place and made known unto ones therein they sought that they eat and sleep.

And the asses had wearied and they shewed hollow and their breath came heavy. And Panda was stained of the road's-way and Nada wept of weariness. And Paul spake:

"No tears, Nada; this is the fount's head."

And Nada said: "Paul, see thou, how lone the quiet of the households! Thinkest thou the steps of thee and me have led unto naught?"

And Paul answered: "Nay; this sign within burneth, Nada."

And he touched the sign of the Christus ones. And Nada wept soft.

And Panda made words unto a man who dwelled within one of the houseways. And this man was called Hezekiah, after the tribe's name. And his hands he held forth in sign that they should seek his household within. And they led the asses unto a stabled place. And Nada waited, and Panda came forth and took her hand and led her within, and Paul followed.

And Hezekiah spake the name Balaam, and a lad of young years came forth, and the lad was sent that he bring forth sup. And lo, he came back bearing bowls of milch and wheat's cake. And flies shewed within the milch, and Hezekiah took up the bowl and spake words of the days of Nazareth while he sunk his thumb and finger unto the bowl and brought forth the flies.

And Nada looked upon this and turned unto Panda, who spake on and took the bowl from out the hand of Hezekiah and drunk deep.

And words mingled of the city's day, and Rome's day, of Jew's burdens, of the lands afar and near. And Hezekiah asked what had brought them forth. And Panda spake naught, but Paul raised his hand in a sign, and the lips of Hezekiah whispered, "Jesus Christus," and he oped his arms and drew them close and spake soft:

"Rome hath men within Nazareth who seek Him. It is told that they follow the sheep's-ways and yet the market's places and look upon His day at the morn and night, and even the midday. And there hath been word that the mighty Tiberius hath offered much that this man be, like a light of night's hour, shut out. They came them and asked of one called King of the Jews, and called his name Hate."

And Panda started, and Nada cried out: " This man Jesus Christus is not——" and Panda stopped her words.

And Hezekiah spake: " No man knoweth deeper wisdom than this Jesus. Yea, His cunning hath turned the words of the prophets and He hath drunk the old wines from out new cups.

" Out from Egypt hath come ones who have sought that they see this one who hath caused the shaking of Herod * upon his throne; for even though Herod knoweth not, and the blood of Herod knoweth not, this young Jew is that that hath caused the throne's quaking. And these men are wise ones who know the prophets of all ages, and this lad suppeth their wine-skins dry. Yea, their words He speaketh, their scripts He knoweth, their wisdoms He sheareth as sheep and keepeth the wools. And one among them hath lended unto Him all his knowing, and behold, He hath taken not the lending but the keeping of it. And no man asketh He of an aid. Even when famine hath set He feareth not. When all men cry out He smiles."

And Panda spake: " Then this one, thou dost believe, is He whom the Jews awaited? "

And Hezekiah made the sign of silence and said: " Man, thou shouldst know no man should set his camels upon a journey until his packs stand ready."

And Panda spake: " But thou shouldst not then leave them that they stand long readied, for man shall know."

And they spake of the day's travel. And it was the time when they should seek the couch of rugs, and this thing they did. And behold, when the household was dark, Nada touched the flesh of Panda and spake: " Arise! Come forth! "

And he followed her, and they sought the without, and lo, the moon shewed pale silver and full, and upon her white face the swallow's wings shewed. And Panda took her unto him and they went within. And night set Nazareth and they slept.

And at the morn, from out the household of one Isicher, came forth two brothers, and their robes shewed them of Rome. And they sought the hill's-ways and the sheep's places, and came upon the shepherds at their tending and spake words unto them and asked if the hands of this Jew, Jesus, had wrought witcheries. And the shepherds said that this was against the prophet's word. And the Rome's ones spake:

" Yea, but word goeth forth that He hath done this thing."

And they sought them on. And behold, they came upon Him,

* Herod Antipas, tetrarch of Galilee.

Jesus, the sheep's tender. And His sheep stood within the valley while
He sat Him high, bowed o'er a script of skin.

And His ears took not in their coming. And they came up unto
Him and spake words, saying: "Art thou Jesus?"

And He spake Him "yea," and His eyes shewed unto them the
depth of peace. And they said:

"'Tis spoken that thou art the Son of God, the King of Promise
unto the Jews."

And He called unto his sheep and spake not. And they made more
of words, saying: "If this saying is true, cast thee down, for thy Sire
shall take thee up."

And He looked not upon them but spake of sheep. And they shewed
unto Him gold and rare stuffs, and said: "Shouldst thou cast thee
down, this is thine."

And He spake not.

And they said: "If this is thine, thy brothers shall fall down and
worship thee."

And He held His hands high unto the coming sun and spake:

"It is written that no man shall worship save one God."

And they said: "But thou shouldst be a man among men."

And He spake: "Nay, nay, but a shepherd among sheep."

And they pointed unto lands and leaned close and whispered: "The
mighty one could minister unto thee even a kingdom."

And His lips smiled the smile of a father's sorrow o'er youth's
folly. And He stretched forth His arms unto their utmost and
spake:

"Behold thou the sky! Behold thou the lands! Behold thou the
kingdoms of earth, and all men! These are the heritage of the Son
of Man and the goods of my Father."

And they laughed in mockery and spake words of scorning and
made them more of words, telling of that that should fall unto His day
should He cast Him down and know not the Jews as His brothers.
And He spake: "Get thee behind me, evil ones! I will not of thee!"

And He took up His staff and walked unto His sheep and spake
no word more, even though they followed Him on the way.

And it was so that they passed upon the way. And the sheep of
Jesus followed the street's-way of Nazareth through unto the field's-
ways upon the hills at the other side. And the sheep fluttered their
feet among the dusts, and the dusts arose before Him as He followed.
And the Rome's men spake one unto the other:

"This man is a fool. He is ridden of Jews and deemeth His kingdom waiteth."

And Panda sought the ways without with Nada even at this time. And Panda's ears took in what the Rome's men had spoken, and his eyes looked upon the youth-wearied one who followed His sheep's sweep and his lips smiled sorry and he spake:

"Nada, this man is He. Look! Rome hath told Panda this; for Rome's ones follow Him. Behold, His nobleness! A king, a promised king o'er Jews trodding of dusts and sceptered with a staff! Yea, His very crown, the dust's-fall! And Rome envieth!"

And Nada started and cried out His name: "Jesus Christus!"

And behold, He harked and stopped Him and waited. And Nada shrunk, and He turned unto the spot and waited. And she went forth, and Panda followed, but they spake no word. And He oped His lips and said:

"What! hast thou lost thy sheep?"

And Panda's eyes misted and he spake: "Nay, nay, but the young shepherd."

And Jesus said unto them: "Return thou! for even as thou hast spoken he is given unto thee; for no thing is lost, neither forgotten."

And He touched the bowed head of Nada and spake unto her as she sunk unto her knees:

"Arise! I have spoken it. Thou shalt see the sign upon the moon's face."

And Nada cried out and looked frighted unto Panda, and Panda spake low: "This is He!"

And they bowed them down within the dusts, and the Rome's ones looked upon it. And Jesus turned upon His way. And Nada arose and spake:

"Panda, the vulture that hath plucked at this heart hath flown."

And Panda said: "No man hath wisdom whose robe traileth the skies and draweth down the stars upon its hem; but this man hath wisdom not of man but of the Thing that setteth up the winds."

And Nada spake: "Yea, yea." And they looked after His going upon the way. And Panda turned unto Nada and said:

"Behold His few words, yet thou hast eaten full, and Panda even so."

And it was at the mid of the eve's sun that the road's-ways gave forth Hatte and Aaron, and behold, they sought the valley way unto

Nazareth. And they came upon Jesus upon the return way unto Nazareth and He spake:

"What seekest thou?"

And Hatte answered, bittered: "Hate."

And the eyes of Jesus smiled sorry, and He said:

"Seek not; thou hast found it."

And He spake more, saying: "Give thou unto me the cloth of hate for the full measure of loving."

And Hatte laughed and said: "That thou shalt deck within it and I shake of colds within thy tattered cloth? For earth hath torn at the cloth of love since time."

And Jesus spake: "Yea, but its rents are precious, yea, jeweled. Yea, it flameth scarlet, broidered of earth's day's rending. Love is woven upon the loom of earth, and hate is the shadow beneath the loom."

And Hatte laughed, and Aaron echoed it, and he limped him on upon the way, and Aaron, weary, dragged his nets after.

CHAPTER XIX

AND it was true that the Rome's men within Nazareth spake them among the people, even unto them who would believe:

"This one, this Christus, filius nullius. Yea, filius terrae." *

And they who mocked spake it o'er and shook them, "yea."

And at a later tide they sought out Jesus and made words that He should seek Jerusalem even with them. And they took Him upon word's path unto the temple's place, and whispered unto Him that even on the topmost pinnacle of the temple would Tiberius lift Him up for His casting down.

And this was spoken within the people, and the Jews shook them that Tiberius waxed him fearful of even a Jew's trodding. And they said that Augustus had spoken that should a man speed his steeds o'er their speeding † his chariot should be folly. But Tiberius setteth his chariot before his steeds and smiteth his chariot's wheels that his steeds do on. For even though he cast down this Jew, what then?—for the Jews would lift Him up.

Even these words came unto the ears of Panda, who had set his hand at the weaving of nets for fishes within Nazareth, that they await the wisdoms of Jesus. And Panda shook him nay unto this, for he spake that even though the Jews did lift up this one at His casting down, Rome would break the Jews. Yea, snap them like dry twigs before Rome's steel.

And the days shewed them filled of busy for the hands of Panda. And it was true that, within the household of Hezekiah, the babe of his flesh had sicked, and this babe was of youthed years. And his mother sorrowed o'er his flesh's shrink. And unto her breast took Nada this one, and behold, out of his shrinking drank she comforting; for his eyes looked the full of loving unto her and his flesh fatted at her touching. And they marveled them that the words of the Christus had come even unto them.

And among the men of Nazareth at the market's place stepped the

* A nobody; of unknown origin.   † Beyond their strength.

373

smitten Hatte and Aaron, who followed even as the shadow of bright
day. And no man knew the words of Hatte, yet he drank deep of all
men's words and out of them supped the words of Jesus.

And at the night's hours, behold, the market's places shewed dark
and no man knew them, and Hatte lay him down within the shadow
and eat of that that fell as waste. And Aaron's net brought forth
much that they fed upon. And they shewed them not unto Panda, for
Hatte had wrapped him of hate and feared naught but sweetness and
wisdom and gentleness.

And the time swept unto the fortnight, and Panda had bought of
stuffs and fashioned unto nets. And they stood ready for the casting
of men. And they said unto him that he should seek Galilee and offer
these unto them who fished. And Nada wept not but bade that he go
upon the way, for her heart fed.

And Paul and Panda made ready the nets upon the asses' backs
and sought them the road's-way unto Galilee. And they journeyed
them unto the time when the city shewed, and they sought the sea.
And lo, the crafts came in and they smelled of fish and waters. And the
sea's smooth was roughed, for their coming set the waves danced, and
the eve's sun set it gold like molten metal.

And there came a craft unto the shallow. sea, and they within
sprung them out, even within the waters, and brought forth the craft
even unto the sands. And the craft shewed it full of fish, and they
gleamed as metals with the sun's gold upon their silver, and they
sprung up and their wet sounded at their falling.

And the men came them out upon the sands and the sands clung
unto their bared feet. And they were clothed but of loin's-cloths of
coarse stuffs.

And it was so that Panda and Paul came up at this time, and
they called unto these who had come from out the sea. And Panda
spake unto them, saying: " Wouldst thou of nets? "

And they made answering: " Nay, nay, but yon craft hath lost its
net, and it is the craft of Peter."

And Panda sought out the craft they shewed unto him and Paul
led forth the ass. And Peter sat within his craft, bowed, and no fish
shewed therein.

And Panda brought forth Paul and cried out unto Peter: " Wouldst
thou of nets? "

And Peter spake not nor listed, but sat him lost within his dream.
And Panda went up even unto the water's lap upon the sand, and out

unto the craft, and touched the flesh of Peter and spake: "Art thou a fisher, and wouldst thou of nets?"

And Peter turned unto him and spake: "Who art thou, and whither from?"

And Panda answered: "No man of thy lands, but one who brothereth with all men."

And Peter looked unto him and said: "Knowest thou that these are the words of the Nazarene?"

And Panda spake: "Nay, but in so much as all men's words that are dealt in loving are of one sire."

And Peter looked unto the nets that shewed them packed upon the ass, and shook his head and spake: "What doth thy brothers speak as thy name?"

And Panda answered him: "Panda."

And Peter said: "I am Peter and know the seas."

And Panda smiled and spake: "I am Panda and know the lands. And thou knowest that he who knoweth the lands knoweth far o'er him who knoweth the seas; for each leg's span of land is teeming full of woe, and he who is acquainted with woe knoweth wisdom's fulling."

And Peter looked him o'er the sea and said: "Yea, thou hast spoken it. The sea is empty. Peter would that he cast his nets among men."

And Panda looked unto Peter and spake: "Wouldst thou of nets?"

And Peter answered: "Yea, for the men of earth shall hunger and Peter shall minister unto them."

And Panda oped the nets and Peter took them from out his hands and spread them forth unto their fullness, and looked upon them and spake:

"Thou hast dealt fairly, for the nets are of full size, and the knots tied by the master hand, that knoweth the cunning."

And Panda said: "It is right that he who offereth price offer the full for it."

And they barted, and it was so that Peter took from Panda the nets. And the night shewed Panda and Paul upon the asses upon the way unto Nazareth.

CHAPTER XX

AND within Nazareth the market's men sat at the high hour and spake one unto the other of things that beset Jerusalem, and of the thing that abided within Nazareth that should be the undoing of the o'erriding of their brothers.

And Hatte walked about the outskirts of them and listed, and went up unto them that made words, and spake little, but listed. And they turned unto him and asked was the deeping of Jerusalem's sorrow sore upon him even as upon them. And Hatte laughed and spake:

" Nay; even though Jerusalem hath lain beneath the lash of Rome, and Rome's ones look them for the King, their steps lead unto follies, for they look them unto the lowly blood, and I speak unto thee, a noble walketh among ye."

And they raised their brows and shrugged and spake: " Point thou unto him."

And Hatte said: " Nay. 'Tis the great Sire's will that man fall o'er his own folly, and the Jews are they He hath chosen as they that shall fall o'er the greatest folly of earth."

And one among them spake: " How may a man know a noble, save this nobleness show within his words? "

And Hatte said: " Thou art indeed a fool; for look ye! the noble's slaves he dusteth o'er of gold dusts, and they speak wisdoms, and he smileth him, fatted of self, and dealeth these words unto his people as the words of him."

And they said unto him: " Thou hast a tongue of cunning! What wisdom's dealer hast thou sought? "

And Hatte looked unto them, and his lips curled, and he spake: " Ne'er thy King, the dealer of honeys, for no man may feed upon honey but that he fall sick."

And they looked at his mocking and spake: " This man thou sayest dealeth honeys, Jesus Christus, dwelleth upon the rise of yon hill's side, even beyond the thick of the households of Nazareth, within but a hut's place. Yea, and He is acquainted with famine's bite, yea, and mockery. And lo, He goeth at the eve's hour and drinketh from out His mother's eyes the honeys that sweet His bitters, for all Nazareth knoweth the peace that abideth within her eyes, that, e'en though they weep not, seem that they float like blue lilies upon teared waters."

And Hatte spake hissed: "And He hath His mother's bosom! Jehovah, 'tis o'ermuch!"

And he spread his arms wide and fled. And they cried out unto him, and even did they speed after and laid hands upon him. And he shewed gaunt, and his eyes sunken, and his cheeks thinned, and his ribs arched in tracery, and his leg fell heavy.

And they brought him back unto the spot. And Aaron watched their speaking one unto the other, and his lips smiled like the wan smile of summer through the winter's thick of cloud. And they said:

" What hath set thee that thou shouldst flee at the naming of Mary? "

And he answered not, but his eyes flamed and his cheeks paled, then crimsoned o'er. And they spake more: " What wouldst thou seek that thou dost flee? "

And Hatte spake: " Jesus Christus, that I slay His tongue!"

And they cried: " What! Wouldst thou seek to slay His tongue when thou shouldst know that Nazareth drinketh His very word?"

And Hatte spake not, and they said more: " He is nobled. He is the one the Jews await. Yea, the Jews e'en now blade them and all men know the sign."

And Hatte spake: " What! thou then wouldst array this man in fine linen? From out the hut's place wouldst thou pluck a whelp and call him nobled? "

And they said this man had wickeds within him and they spake: " Unto Jesus Christus shall we bear him forth."

And Hatte murmured: " Theia! Theia! Is this thy flesh's heritage? "

And he made unto Aaron the sign that Aaron knew. And Aaron arose and let fly his arms, and behold, the men fell back and Hatte sprung even as a smitten deer and fled. And Aaron's voice sounded as the swine's grunting. And they spake: " This one is mad."

And they let him go free, nor followed they Hatte.

And behold, they sat them down unto their wording, and spake much of this man who blasphemed the God and mocked the Nazarene.

And lo, the eve shewed Nazareth weary 'neath the sun, and the late hour brought forth cool airs to soothe. And the skies were thick of coming storm about the west way, and the sun shone beneath the clouding red. And the pale stars gleamed within the softing gray o'er the arch whereon no cloud shewed.

And when the eve's quiet had hung o'er Nazareth, there sounded upon the road's-way unto an out-hill the steps of men who sought, and the pale light shewed Hatte and Aaron. And they sought out the hut of Jesus. And the lightnings sprung up and flashed and died, and they set the thunders roared, and behold from out the cloud sprung flamed tongues that licked the billowed cloud.

And Hatte sought, and lo, a hut's door oped and one came her forth and strained her that she look upon the hill's-way. And Hatte shrunk that he wait the light's flash that he take in this one. And Aaron plucked dry leaves upon the way far behind.

And the woman of the hut's place looked upon the shadow and spake in the voice of loving: "Hast thou come?"

And Hatte shook and his voice chattered: "Yea."

And the woman oped her arms, and behold, Hatte arose slow and crept unto their ope. And she lay her cheek upon his head's bend. And lo, he started up, and his laugh cut the airs, and he sped unto the dark ways. And his form slunk as that of a dog that knoweth the lash. And he threw him upon the sod and plucked up grasses and bit upon the sods, and cried:

"Ne'er a woman's arms for Hatte, for the sea that drowneth him lieth there! Nay! Nay!" And he cried him aloud: "Who, who, who hath the word that untieth this binded script?"

And it was true that a man came him upon the way, and this man was Jesus. And Hatte heard His footfall and came up unto Him and spake:

"Who dwelleth within yonder hut?"

And Jesus made answering: "Mary, the mother of this flesh."

And He touched His bosom. And Hatte spake not but went upon his way unto the seeking of Aaron. And when no sound came unto him, he stopped and murmured:

"Mary! Of the hills! And the seeker, the lad who said His sire was mine! Theia, where art thou? Hast thou forgot? Thy lips did speak me 'Hate,' yea, and thou didst bring this flesh forth from out a cup of hate. Theia, what man setteth this task; what man or god?"

And he reached within his loin's-cloth and plucked forth the golden scourge, and beat his legs unto his crying out. And he fell and sobbed loud, and his shoulders heaved and his throat swelled and he wept, and amid his tears he spake:

"Dost thou still look unto the East?"

And behold, Aaron came up and took him unto his breast and laughed. And the storm broke and winds swept, and the rains came them riding forth upon the winds. And Hatte reached up and lay his arms about Aaron and they arose. And Hatte stood and let the storm beat upon him. And the rains fell unto the blinding even of the lightning's flash, and he stood and cried out:

"This! This is but the merry-make! The flesh rejoiceth in its smarting, for it easeth that within."

And Aaron was frightened, and Hatte spake aloud: "The fool feareth his flesh's hurt, and the wise man the hurt of his spirit. Yet unto the fool the flesh is his spirit, and to the wise man the spirit is his flesh. Yea, but unto flesh or yet unto spirit, this God dealeth the hurt!"

And he raised his hands unto the skies, and the rains swept him o'er and ran from off his hands, and he cried out:

"Hell might unbelly and waste its fires, but the sweet words of Him—" and he shook his shut fingers unto the way unto the hut,— "ah, their flowing is the consuming of hell's fire! They leap like tongues of flame, His smiles the feeding of the flames, His eyes their darting and His words the burning."

And he stopped and his arms fell heavy, and his eyes turned within the dark unto all ways, and he stood as one lost, and spake:

"Where? Where? Where? No man welcometh me. Panda? Ah, for the sup from out the bowl! And it is empty and Hatte's hand is weak."

And he wept. And Aaron stood waited, and Hatte bade that they seek the way back unto Nazareth, for he touched the flesh of Aaron and pointed him unto the road's-way. And Hatte's lips spake soft:

"No drop falleth. The star standeth high o'er the hills. The clouds shew not, and she is there within the trees. At the morn's hour Hatte seeth a young tree, slender, tall, and it swayeth and danceth, and it is Theia."

And his feet he speeded, and even did he try that he dance, and his word sounded soft: "When the morn cometh the sky shall gleam rosed like her limbs, and the morn shall shew draped of white fleece-clouds o'er the rose, like the wool mantle o'er her, the mist's robe. Yea! Yea! It is there! It is there, Theia, there!"

And he sped limped. And Aaron followed, and his lips smiled. And they came unto the forsaken market's place. And the rains still swept, and they crept unto a sheltered niche o'erhung of skins wherein men shewed fruits. And Hatte stood him high and spread forth his arms and drew them up, and murmured:

"I am strong, strong like Caanthus of Rome!"

And he sat him down, and so sat unto the tide when the sun shewed

through the break of cloud. And his eyes took not in that the rain had
ceased nor yet that the light had come. And Aaron slept.

And the market's men came forth and brought out their wares, and
wiped dry the bin's places. And they looked upon him and said: " This
is he who spake wickeds and sped."

And a one of them spake: " Nay, he is but a beggar, and his dog
knoweth naught."

And they offered of rotted fruit unto his hand. And he waked him
from out the far-dreaming and took it from out their hands, and his
eyes looked empty and he spake not, but eat the fruit.

And they said: " Art thou then still seeking this Jesus that thou
shalt slay His tongue? "

And he smiled weary and said: " Nay, His kingdom is His, and
Hatte may not buy it."

And they cried: " Thou sayest His kingdom is His? "

And he bit the fruit and ate more and spake weary: " Yea."

And they came unto him and asked what had stopped his wrathing.
And he answered not, but sat him long. And they spake one unto the
other: " Hearest thou? He hath given out the word that the kingdom
is His."

And Hatte smiled and said: " Yea, and Hatte shall wait and sit,
even as a beggar at the feast, unto His crowning. It is written upon
the sky, and no man, nor Hatte, may wipe it out. His heritage is not
flesh nor—" and he stopped long—" hate."

And they laughed and spake: " This one, too, is mad."

And Hatte smiled and said: " Yea, hate is madness." And he
touched the scourge, tender, and spake:

" Theia, thy son is unbladed! Where to shall he seek for that to
war with earth? "

And he unloosed the golden strands from off the thorn's staff and
tied them 'bout his neck and whispered:

" Theia, where is thy God? Where? Shew me the path. Even
o'er blood shall Hatte seek Him."

And even though the day of Nazareth had waked and the people came
them forth upon the street's-ways, he raised him not, but sat and drank
in with smiling lips the wording of them that came unto the spot.

And Aaron sat, when he had waked, tying of his nets. And Hatte
offered unto him the fruit, and he ate and waited the going of Hatte.

CHAPTER XXI

AND Nazareth set upon its day. Men came unto the market place
with rain-beaten greens. And the beasts that came packed still shewed
wet, and their legs were wet of earth's wet, and the road's-ways at their
stepping sent up pools within the spot wherein they trod.

And a man came from out the hill's-way where the winds had
havocked, and spake of the wastes and told that the hands of a man
called "Panda" had set them at the setting up of a hut within the thick
growth, and the winds had laid it low. And he told that this man had
little and was no Jew, but had wisdoms that e'en Nazareth had listed
unto. And he said that this man's woman, whom he called of the name
"Nada," wept, and sought the spot and even lended unto the upbuilding
of that that had fallen. And he told that Hezekiah had woed o'er the
woe of Panda and had sent his son Balaam unto his aid, but Balaam
tarried and there labored within the hill's place but the woman, Nada,
and the man, Panda.

And Hatte harked, and behold, his empty face lighted, and he
stretched forth his arms and brought them up and spake soft:

"Thou shalt spend not upon wrathing, but upon building."

And he touched the bended back of Aaron who ate upon the fruit's
middle wherein the seed clung. And his fingers brought forth the
seeds and he lay them within his palm and touched them o'er and
laughed, and made sounds and laughed again. And Aaron started up,
and Hatte made the sign that he should follow, and they went unto the
one who spake, and Hatte asked whereto should he seek that he find
this man Panda. And the man shewed unto him the spot far upon the
hill's-way.

And they set forth, and the eyes of Hatte raised not but watched
the wets that lay upon the way, and he sought even through the deep of
earth's wet.

And when they had come unto the spot, lo, Panda had stripped him
save for a loin's-skin and Nada bended under heavy stone and wood
beams. And Panda looked up at the sound of the coming of Hatte but
his eyes shewed no welcoming, nor his lips oped.

And Hatte came forth silent and held his hands oped in sign that he offered aid. And Panda shook him "nay" and said: "No man may fashion his household in hate."

And Hatte looked deep within the flashed eyes of Panda and pointed unto the hill's-way whereon the hut of Jesus stood, and spake: "Look thou! Hatte hath left his hate there."

And Panda said: "But a man may not leave his hate. Nay, doth he build of hate and even cast the beams a-whither, the dusts of hate cling thereto. Nay; a man must wash him clean. And thou knowest Panda hast spoken that no man may wash clean, robed in the mantle of hate, save through tear's wash."

And Hatte's head sunk, and his arms hung limp, and he raised his eyes unto Panda's, saying:

"Panda, the thirst came upon me and I did weep in sorrow, and have drunk, and know these hands are weak."

And Panda took up a beam and spake: "Brother, lend thou unto me thy aid."

And they spake not but builded; nor did Panda's lips ope in rebuking or yet in comforting. And when they had labored long, Panda spake: "Hatte, what dost thou seek, and whereto dost thou abide?"

And Hatte answered him: "Panda, thy brother is like unto a hawk and may not rest. He hath found a high spot and but waiteth that he seek him higher."

And lo, upon the wet way there came forth a sheep's herd that trod the sod, and one followed upon the way, and this one was Jesus. And Panda stopped and watched His going up unto the high place whereon the sun would first dry. And Hatte hung his head low, nor looked he upon this.

And the eve shewed wild clouds arisen, and the roars afar told that winds would seek. And it grew dark, and no thing shewed within the valley's place. And Panda speeded with Nada unto the city and he begged that Hatte follow, and they went them amid the dark down the hill's-way o'er the wets.

And the airs sounded as frightened birds that wailed amid the dark. And the blasts that swept bended the trees' tops down even unto the earth. And the markets' bins were swept like bits of dry woods on, to rattle deep within the dark.

And Aaron clung unto Hatte. And Panda had speeded him before with Nada and had found shelter within the house of Hezekiah. And Hatte stood within the wind's cut and his eyes flashed wide, and his arms lay about Aaron who hid his head upon his bosom.

And lo, there sounded the wail of a woman, and she sought amid the winds. And this was Mary. And she spake in shaken tones unto the airs, and no man shewed upon the street's-ways. And she came up unto the spot whereon Hatte stood and spake:

" He is there within the high places and His sheep have scattered! "

And Hatte looked upon her within the dark, and her face shewed white and the dark hid her form, but the face shewed as one illumined. And Hatte leaned close and held Aaron unto his breast, and Mary spake:

" He is there! There! And no man aideth, and it is dark! "

And Hatte's breast rose and fell in fullness of what lay within his heart, and he cried:

" Go thou back unto thy household! Go! Rest thou, for hate shall go upon the path of loving and succor it! Hark, ye winds! Hark! it shall be! Hate hath been called! His sheep shall he bring together, yea, and His falling shall he lift up! And then, and then, give unto His hand the staff, and leave. Yea, leave, lest His mantle be touched of mires."

And Mary listed and spake: " Unto thee doth His mother commend the tending. Yea, and she knoweth the morn's sun shall tell the trust hath been done."

And Hatte leaned unto her and said: " Speak not these words! Nay, for I am he who would take His crown."

And she touched his bared arm, and he shrunk even within the dark and her voice came soft: " Nay; for all men hath there been crowns set up."

And Hatte leaned him closer, and his hot breath burned upon the cheek of Mary.

" Even for him who hateth and smiteth sore? "

And Mary whispered: " Yea; doth a man lift his head out the dark of hate, 'tis his! "

And Hatte spake him louder, for the winds roared: " May a man take it with the blade of hate? "

And Mary's voice came back, as an echo from afar:

" Nay! Nay! Ye may not war love save with love."

And behold, the lightnings split ope the heavens and shewed her even within a golden light, for the space of but one eye's shut and ope. And Hatte fell him down before her and kissed her mantle, and flung the form of Aaron forth unto the fallen woods of the market's place and sped the ways, o'er stones and wet earth and fallen beams, unto the high, high, high place!

And naught sounded unto his ears, for his feet speeded with loving.

And behold, he fell o'er a young tree that had uprooted, and his lips spake curse and he spat upon the fallen tree. And the lightnings flamed the sky unto the light of day, and the thunders spake in the voice of a mightiness that befitteth God. And Hatte cried:

"Oh, thou feet of me, thou dost stumble! And thou, the tongue of me, even so."

And he murmured: "Hatte seeketh Him the Jews await as King. The blade of Hatte might stop their word. But the god buildeth up wisely—this God of Theia. Even should the blade of Hatte do this thing, it might ne'er cut His words from out the earth's heart. Hatte knoweth! Hatte knoweth! For he hath found him with a blade and no man aided. But this man, this Jew-noble, hath no blade, yet the very airs about Him seem drawn, bared, blade-points that fend Him. How may a man war the hosts of an unseen hand?"

And he stumbled on upon the way, and stopped sudden, and swayed, and spake:

"Hatte seeth a sea wrathed of mighty waves, and out of the sea's wrathing standeth high a stone, and this stone is mighty, yea,—and what sheweth upon it? A babe-town!—the hills—Bethlehem! And he who standeth high o'er the stone's summit is a shepherd. It is He! And His hands spread forth, and lo, the seas calm and the young sun riseth unto a fair day.

"And Hatte! Hatte—where hath he gone? For he shewed at His side, and now,—ah, Hatte is the staff within His hand!"

And there sounded the bleat of sheep within the storm's roaring, and Hatte harked and stopped and he spake:

"Yea, a man may take his hate and set it that it do the work of love." And he cried as he sped: "Theia, thy son is uncrowned; yet so near, so near he feeleth his crowning that he joyeth!"

And he fell, blown upon the path's-way. And the lightnings shewed the sheep of Jesus, swept, even fallen, and crying out. And the shepherd lay within the lightning's light, smitten! And the rains swept down upon the winds so that the feet of Hatte could scarce step, yet he sought the fallen one, and lo, he came up unto Him and bright lights shewed forth from the heavens, and Hatte leaned o'er Him and murmured: "Hatte, what tarrieth thy hand?"

And he leaned far o'er the fallen one, and the lights shewed the face white and rain-swept, so that the cheeks were as one who wept, yet the sweet lips smiled.

And the sheep wailed, and a few of them had come up unto the fallen one and hung about. And there were twelve. And one had seen the coming of Hatte and ran that he meet him, and Hatte lay his hand upon this one and brought it up unto its shepherd.

And there seemed the heaven's emptying, and Hatte sunk upon his knees and took up the King unto him. And when he had pressed Him close, behold, his eyes wept and he heaved of sobbing. And lo, the cheek of the King was washed with the tears of hate, and they mingled with the drops of rain thereon unto one stream.

And Hatte took up one hand of Him and it shewed torn, even so that blood dripped, and the blood stained the flesh of Hatte. And Hatte cried out:

" The tears drink one the other, yea, and the blood shall drink one the other! Unto one stream, the flesh; but the spirit, where to? "

And he cried amid the storm: " The slaying! The slaying! "

Yet he sped not, but clung unto the form of the fallen one.

And his weeping voice called the sheep's call, and they came unto him. And he set upon the way, bearing Him.

Unto the arms of Hate was commended the earth's cleansing flesh!

And he sought on, bowed of the burden; and the sheep followed in faith of his shepherding. And the tears of Hatte ceased and his head raised, even so that the rains swept his face, and his lips smiled.

And he came unto a shelter place and lay his burden down, and waited the sheep's coming, and drove them unto the shelter, and stood him without and waited.

And the light came, and the rain ceased, and it was young day. And the fallen one roused and started up, and behold, Hatte held forth the staff and fled.

And it was true that the shepherd went Him unto the city's place and drove His sheep before Him, and His lips smiled soft, sweet, and His hand held the staff.

And unto the staff there hung a golden strand!

And Hatte stood him upon a high spot and watched, and murmured: " His mantle sheweth no mire."

And he followed slow the steps of the path of Jesus.

And when Jesus had come unto the city's place, behold, He looked upon the unbuilding of the work of the hands of the city's people, and speeded His steps. And lo, Mary came her forth and took Him unto her breast.

But no man looked upon the coming of Hatte. And he sought Aaron, and the men who were setting their hands at the building up of the unbuilded said that he had been taken by Mary. And Hatte stopped and spake:

"Wilt thou then go up unto the hut of Jesus and speak unto Aaron that his brother waiteth and that thou wilt bring him forth?"

And they did this thing, and Aaron came, dragging his nets o'er the wets, and laughed at the meeting of Hatte.

And Hatte asked of them that had sought the market's place, where Panda had abided while the storm raged, and they said: "Within the house of Hezekiah."

And he sought the spot they shewed unto him, and Hatte stood that he make known his coming, but stopped and shook his head and spake: "Nay, the hawk must seek, seek, seek."

And he turned and sought that he give aid unto them that made right the market's place.

And there came thereto the two of Rome, who followed upon the path of Jesus, and they looked upon Hatte and spake one unto the other: "This is he. This is the man who calleth his name Hatte."

And within the market's place Hatte set him at the upbuilding, and lended his hand unto the aid of Reuben. And Aaron ate of that that the winds had havocked.

And the men of Rome came them up unto the spot and spake unto Hatte: "Wherefrom unto Nazareth hast thou come?"

And Hatte looked not up but pointed unto the hill's-way and spake: "Like unto a wolf was this flesh brought forth within a cave's place yon."

And they asked of him: "What doth Nazareth know thee by?"

And Hatte answered: "By the sheep's staff."

And they said: "Then where is thy flock?"

And Hatte spake him: "High upon yon hill's-way."

And they looked upon him and their eyes took in that he had been within the storm's wrath, for his legs were stained of waters and wet earth, and his locks still hung wet and the skin that bound his loins shewed wet. And Aaron was wetted o'er and his mantle hung close unto his legs and his breast was bared and the nets shewed thick of wet earth.

CHAPTER XXII

AND the Rome's men sat down to watch the workings of the men, and spake of other things even though their eyes took in all that Hatte set unto. And Hatte labored fevered unto the time when the bin of Reuben was righted. And Reuben brought forth skins that he offer unto the men of Nazareth, for they were beaten skins, soft and cleansed.

And Hatte sat him down that he rest, and Aaron plucked up bits of woods and fruits and wastes of the market's-ways, and made sounds like unto the swine. And the Rome's men looked upon him and questioned: " Is this man thy brother? "

And Hatte spake him: " Yea."

And they said: " Doth Nazareth know thee by the name ' Hatte '? "

And Hatte made answering: " Yea."

And they raised their brows and looked one to the other and spake: " Knowest thou this man ' Panda '? "

And Hatte answered: " Nay; this man hath come from out the Jerusalem ways unto Nazareth and is no Nazarene."

And they said: " And thou, art thou a Jew? "

And Hatte spake him: " Yea."

And they asked of him: " Knowest thou this man, Jesus Christus? "

And Hatte's cheeks burned, and he spake: " All Nazareth and e'en Jerusalem knoweth this man."

And they leaned unto him and asked: " Dost thou then believe that He is the coming King? "

And Hatte spake him: " Hast thou, then, dwelled within Nazareth and drunk of Jew's waters, and know not be they bitter or yet sweet? "

And they looked one to the other and said: " A wise tongue for a sheep's man! "

And Hatte spake: " Then thou dost measure wisdom? Thou art follied, for man may drink wisdom from out a sheep's track."

And they spake soft unto but their own listing: " This man's wisdom is not the wisdom of Jews."

And Hatte said: " But Nazareth is as a net within the sea; for she catcheth all that the road's-ways send unto her; and from out their wisdoms within the market's-ways a man may drink."

And they laughed and spake: " Jerusalem holdeth market's-ways, and men sleep within them and walk within them, but sleeped or waked they are not wise! This Nazareth market's place doth suredly hold wisdoms that man may drink; for look! this Jesus Christus hath tickled the ears of the lands afar. And this man——"

And they laughed. And they spake unto Hatte more; that without the city's place, at the east way, they had sheep and they would that he look upon them, and they said: " Wouldst thou come unto the spot? "

And Hatte made readied that he seek upon the way; for he took in from out these Rome's men that that they knew not and he hungered that he know more. And they looked unto Aaron, and Hatte smiled and shook his head and spake:

" Yea, he goeth upon the way, for he is the shadow of the day of me."

And they set upon the way. And when they had come unto the spot whereon sheep stood, they reached forth their hands and shewed them unto Hatte and said: " These are they."

And Hatte looked upon them and spake: " These sheep are the sheep of the Jews of Nazareth; for lo, they hold their wools, and no Rome's sheep might shew his wool."

And they looked unto him and one of them shut up one eye and spake: " He knoweth Rome! "

And they said: " What knowest thou of this Jesus Christus? "

And Hatte spake him: " Naught that thou knowest not; for the Jews are full of Him and Rome hath eaten full and sickeneth unto the time when she should spat Him forth."

And they said unto him: " Hast thou heard that 'tis abroad that this Jesus Christus awaiteth the hands of the Jews to pluck Him forth and set Him up o'er them? Yea, that e'en now they band them together that they make of a mighty blade that they shall slay the great one o'er all, Tiberius? "

And Hatte spake low: " Slay Tiberius? Tiberius the great? He is dead and rotteth, and knoweth it not! His wisdoms walk upon the legs of other men. His greatness is held within the hands of his war's men. Yea, and his crown of laurels resteth upon a rotted brow! Slay Tiberius? No Jew would sully him so."

And they cried: " Dost thou then know thy words are 'gainst the mighty one? "

And Hatte smiled sweet and spake: " Nay, these words are honeys. Thou shouldst know the bitters this tongue might flow."

And they looked upon him and said: " ' 'Tis abroad that there is a man called Hate that holdeth a coin 'gainst Rome. Knowest thou this man?"

And Hatte smiled and spake: "Thou speakest this man Hate hath a coin 'gainst Rome? How, by what wisdom, did he wrest it from out Rome's grasp?"

And they answered: "By no wisdom, but by folly."

And Hatte said: "Then his folly is wiser than Rome's wisdom."

And they spake: "Nay, he did not buy the coin."

And Hatte said: "Who then wrested it that it fall within his hand?"

And they answered: "His flesh; for his mother brought him forth in folly."

And Hatte said: "Thou speakest wisely! How dost thou know this thing?"

And they answered: "This woman hideth within her breast that that Rome would know of her; for she danceth within Rome's courts, even though youth doth not set her."

And they saw not the leaping of the blood unto the cheek of Hatte. And Hatte spake: "What woman danceth?"

And they answered: "The Greek."

And Hatte spake: "What! her land is Greece?"

And they said: "Yea."

And he spake: "And Rome calleth her?"—and he stopped and listed. And they said: "Theia, the dance woman."

And he spake: "And Rome waketh from out her sleep and seeketh the paths o'er the folly of one who danceth—a woman of other lands— a slave?"

And they answered: "Yea, for she hath drunk from out a noble cup."

And Hatte's breast panted and he cried: "What noble? Who?"

And they shrugged and spake one to the other and laughed: "Who! Who!"

And Hatte leaned far, and took from off his breast the gold strands, and held them forth that they look upon them, and spake:

"See thou! A one came forth from Jerusalem and brought this, and it hath fallen within these hands."

And they looked upon the strands and spake: "This is but a woman's hair or yet a young youth, but no Jew."

And Hatte cried: "But look upon the flame of this!"

And they looked and he hissed: "This, this is gold that Rome hath bought and Rome hath paid no price; but Rome shall fall to dusts and this shall be the price she shall pay for such workings."

And the men of Rome looked one unto the other and spake: "This word of a sheep's man against Rome telleth what?"

And they turned unto Hatte and asked of him: "What hath Rome done unto thee, and why shouldst thou demand price of Rome for the thing she hath dealt unto him who hath lost his locks?"

And Hatte stood but spake not, and his eyes flashed. And they leaned unto him and spake:

"It meaneth that thou hast much within thee 'gainst Rome. It hath come to our listing that thou art him whom the Jews know as Hate, of Rome's flesh, even though thou speakest that thou art a Jew."

And Hatte spake: "Nay, I am not of Rome." And he spake aloud even as though they listed not: "Of Rome? This meaneth that a man is of Rome's flesh. Of Rome? To hold Rome as one's land? What then is a man's land? Be hills, be street's-ways, be walls, be temples, be wondrous towers or tombs his land? Shall he worship the dusts of his land? Shall he bow to the mighty ones within her? Shall he love them that deal woes unto her people, because they be of his land? Of Rome?"—and he turned unto the two that listed close and spake: "Of Rome? Brought forth from out her womb? Then he who is brought forth from out such a harlot is ridden of rots! Yea, he cometh forth leprous of sin. Yea, I speak more; Rome shall fall short of bearing sons, for her womb shall rot!"

And they that listed spake: "Thou shouldst shake; for thou hast treasoned!"

And Hatte laughed unto them and cried: "Treason upon a harlot who buyeth her bread in treasons?"

And they spake: "But he who sitteth o'er Rome, Tiberius, would shut thy speeching."

And Hatte laughed him in mocking: "Tiberius! This is Nazareth. This is Jew's land. This is not Rome!"

And they said: "Yea, but he, Tiberius, hath sway o'er this land."

And Hatte spake: "Of Rome? What, then, is a man's land but the hearts that till her? No man is o'er the kingdom of hearts! This kingdom is unkinged! But wait thee! wait! This king shall arise! And the metal crowns of fools shall fall and rust, and leave the fools' brows naked, yea, as oped scripts that earth shall read! One shall fall, then another, yea, and on and on, unto the tide when earth shall know no King save Him who sitteth o'er the Kingdom of Hearts. Yea, yea, the walls of His kingdom no man may destroy. Nay, I speak it loud—hark! no man may sully it nor unbuild; for Love is everlasting, and of this stuff shall His kingdom be walled."

And they listed, and watched the thin face of Hatte, that flamed red within the cheeks, and the eyes of him that blazed even as fires. And upon one cheek gleamed the white scar that Rome's stone had writ upon it. And he flung his arms ope and spake unto them that listed:

"Ask thou me be Rome my land, and I speak me: within Rome if there be two hearts that beat in loving, Yea! Ask me if Jerusalem be my land, and if there be hearts therein that love, I speak me, Yea! Yea, ask thou me if Nazareth be the land of me, and I speak me, Yea, if there be therein hearts that love. Yea, yea!

"But hark! Even so, these hearts lend not unto me. I would be of them, yet they will not of me. I have brought forth a blade and bared it, and tried that I carve ope the earth and set this heel unto it and spake unto it: 'Love thou me! Give unto me that that be mine!' And the wound the blade hath caused hath felled love. And now hark! Hatte shall war earth with a shepherd's crook!"

And they spake: "Thou dost lie! No shepherd speakest as thou. Thou knowest nobles, or thou hast fellowed nobles' slaves. No Jew hath drunk hate for Rome and knoweth what is within Rome."

And Hatte stood silent, and they said: "Thou knowest that Rome searcheth for a one, youthed, who causeth sore fearing for the mighty seat?"

And Hatte raised his hands unto his brow and pressed thereon and spake: "Go thou! Go! For this head will take not in Rome's workings! She maketh mighty word o'er a Greek slave woman and searcheth o'er lands and seas and taketh her back. Thou hast spoken it."

And they cried: "Then thou knowest that this woman was cast out of Rome?"

And Hatte answered not; and they spake: "What knowest thou?"

And Hatte said: "Naught."

And they spake: "This woman was follied. Yea, she was wrapped within folly's robe, for she drunk the noble's wine."

And Hatte said: "Thou shouldst know that Rome bendeth the knee and pryeth ope the lips that she make man or woman drink that that she offereth."

And they shook them "yea," and one spake: "But hark! This man, Hate, should fear, for this Nazarene seeketh that He lay claim unto the noble birthright of him."

And Hatte looked with pity upon them, and spake: " Neither Rome nor any man may take this Nazarene's crown. Rome hath not the crown to take nor yet to give."

And they said: " Should this man ' Hate ' cast him down, Rome might give unto him. And should he not, then Rome might empty him even of his blood."

And Hatte said: " What thinkest thou that thy words should be unto me? I am not him ye seek."

And they spake: " Who then is He? "

And Hatte laughed and cried: " Who? Who? Who? I bart ye Who for Who."

And they feared, but said: " Knowest thou that this Nazarene worketh witcheries? "

And Hatte answered: " Yea. Yea, even so. He taketh His sheep unto the high and feedeth them, and they fat. This is witchery. Yea, He opeth His lips and speaketh wisdoms, and unto Rome's fools this is witchery. I speak me that Rome holdeth not sway o'er wisdom, for it be like unto love, everlasting and for all men."

And they said: " Thou speakest of love, yet thy words reek of hate! "

And Hatte spake: " Yea, this is the right Rome hath dealt."

And they questioned: " Wilt thou go unto the spot whereon thou dost abide and shew unto us that thou art of Nazareth? "

And Hatte spake: " Thou knowest not the sheep's men, then, for look ye! a sink within the earth is his bed, and the sky his household's covering."

And they said: " But hark! 'tis told that this man ' Hate,' whom Rome seeketh, hath a fool as his shadow. Who, then, is this man yonder who waiteth filled with naughts? "

And Hatte spake him: " Ask thou him, Who? who? who? "

And they said: " Then thou wouldst do no thing to save her? "

And Hatte spake not but listed, and they said more: " This man ' Hate ' holdeth the blade that may save the woman, the Greek; for 'tis told that Tiberius hath set the time that the road's-ways shall give up her flesh or else she fall. This Nazarene, or the man Hate, is her flesh." And they brought forth their blades and shewed unto him and cried: " Which man is he? "

And Hatte laughed: " Thou hast offered wine unto a camel. Yea, fed the ass upon swill. Thou seekest upon the wrong roadway. I am not he, nor yet is this young Jew Jesus."

And they spake: " But this man, Jesus Christus, doeth things that set the tongues of the people full of Him. And thou, if thou art Hate, even so; for all men within Jerusalem know the lad that abided with Panda, the dark-skin, and his hate."

And Hatte said: "Take thou me and him yonder unto this man, Panda, and thou shalt see he knoweth me not nor him."

And they said this should be, and that the man Panda labored within the hills. And it was so that they sought the spot. And when they had come unto the hut's place that the hands of Panda had set up, they called, and Panda came him forth. And his eyes saw that these men were them that had followed Jesus upon the way. And they spake unto Panda, saying: "Who is this man?" And they shewed unto him Hatte.

And Panda spake: "I know not."

And they cried: "Thou dost lie!"

And Panda said: "That be thy word; and all men weigh their words within their own measure. Yea, and they weigh 'gainst them their brother's words. And I speak unto thee that Panda deemeth thy words are heavier with lie than his."

And they said: "This man's wisdom savoreth of this youth's." And unto Panda they spake: "Shouldst thou lie, then we shall slay this one."

And Panda's eyes shut narrowed, and he went unto them and spake with shut teeth: "Doest thou this, Panda shall unbelly what is within him, and the Jews will arise like a mighty, wicked sea! And thou shalt fear, not alone for thy skins but even for Rome! Panda knoweth that thou art the shadow of Jesus Christus. Thinkest thou the Jews would list unto this? This Jesus Christus smileth and speaketh not, but Panda—" and he stopped—"hath no thong that seweth up his belly, nor yet his tongue. Thou art not within Rome!"

And these men listed, and Hatte stood silent, and they spake: "This fool; who is he?"

And Panda answered: "Then thou weighest what man be wise and what man be fool? Look upon him. He is empty, yet he followeth them he loveth for loving. And thou art full, and follow them thou hatest, for filling. What man is the fool?"

And Panda went up unto the side of one of these men of Rome and looked deep within his eyes and spake him even as the law's word:

"Panda is no slave of Rome. The day hath known Panda ever as the slave. Youthed, he served Rome as slave's flesh, and Rome cast him forth with flesh she would be rid of. And Panda was ridden of slave's pack for the flesh of this one. And it seemed that earth's day dealt more and more unto him that he set beneath the slave's task. Yea, and from out the dulled mantle of slave's cloth did he weave of a cloth in

which he did mantle, and take within its folds his loved. Yea, and the
day dealt fullsome unto Panda; for his love brought forth fruit and
shewed the fullness of free days unto him. And now, the day hath lost
this fruit, and Panda and the love of Panda seek but that they find the
path that hath led him hence.

"And Panda is free! Free! Hear ye, Rome's men, free! But
yon, within the walls afar that did know Panda as the slave, abideth a
one, a woman, and Panda is a slave unto her heart.

"Rome, then, seeketh Panda and his path, and the flesh of this
woman? Hark! E'er Rome shall touch this one Panda shall split his
flesh unto shreds and cast the bits unto the rot birds.* Yea, and set
and watch unto the time that each bit be eat. And no hand of Rome
may stop him. Be this loud and clear? Or shall the blade of Panda
ope thee and put the word within the ope?"

And they stood silent. And one brought forth a sack heavy of
gold's dusts, and oped its latchet and shewed the dusts, and spake:

"Then thy words weigh heavy. Couldst thou speak † their weighing?"

And Panda looked unto the skies, and thereon floated a white cloud,
scarce the hand's span. And Panda pointed unto it and spake:

"The word of Panda may be bought by the weighing unto the bal-
ance by yon cloud."

And they laughed, and Panda said: "Thy laugh is e'en so empty
as thy wisdom, and thy purse heavy. Then deal unto thyselves of thy
purse's heavy that ye be heavied of wisdom."

And they marveled at this man and spake: "And thou sayest thou
wert a slave?"

And Panda answered: "Yea."

And they spake: "But slaves that labor have not the full of wisdoms. But the women of the courts, and them that make-merry,‡ know
wisdom."

And Panda smiled slow and said: "Thy wisdom hath rusted; for
know ye, the legs of slaves carry the wise heads that deal labors for the
mighty, and their hands bear the cups out of which the women and the
merry-makers sup their wisdoms."

And he laughed and spake more: "Panda hath spoken a wisdom
clothed in but loin's-skin, a child of his wisdom, brought forth naked
and clothed but in words that Panda knew, and lo, at some time later,
he hath heard a one within the court utter his words robed in linens and
fine stuffs. If wisdom were a stuff that a land might empty a man of,

---

* The vultures.　　　　† Name their price.　　　　‡ The nobles.

then Rome would have emptied Panda. But," and he turned unto Hatte who listed, " the taking out of wisdom from a man but buildeth up more. From the side of Allah floweth wisdom, and it floweth ever, and man hath but to do the holding of his cup. But holdeth he his cup not unto the stream, but seeketh him, he is empty."

And they waxed wrathed at these words of Panda that spake 'gainst Rome, and told naught. And one spake:

" Thy words scatter as grains that catch the winds. I speak, is this man Hate, and yon fool his shadow? "

And Panda reached within his loin's-cloth and brought forth his blade, and felt upon its sharp, and spake unto Hatte: " Hark! the sheep call yon upon the highways. Away and seek! "

And Hatte spake not, but took up a wood staff and made the sign unto Aaron that he set upon the way. And Panda spake unto the Rome's ones soft:

" Panda is within the household of a Jew whose hand itcheth that he touch the blade and shew unto his brothers Rome's wrongs upon them. Thou shalt seek thee upon the out-ways from Nazareth! The suns are hot and the days long within Nazareth. Seek ye, then, a pleasanter land. Go ye upon the way and take unto Rome the word that without the walls of all lands there abideth a people, within the land of no man, bounded not of walls. And these people have found the wisdom's stream, and Rome may not stop their lands nor stand o'er them.

" Say unto Rome, her sons love her not, but the mothers that brought them forth.

" Say unto Rome, that at the head of these people without walls a Shepherd stands. Tell her this.

" Say unto Rome, her king knoweth the lowly; that he hath eat leper's bread; that he hath known Rome's blade; that she hath cast him forth stripped of his laurel, empty-handed. And he hath worn weary with hating and hath set upon the way that leadeth unto no mighty-seat. That within his hand no blade of honor flasheth, but a crook of thorn wood!

" Say this unto Rome, that her noble son suckled at a slave's breast; a slave whose land called her noble. This hath Rome done! Tell her this!

" And more! Tell her that her slave, Panda, speaketh unto her mighty one that Rome shall not bend her knee unto her noble son. Nay, that earth shall stone him. Tell her this!

" Yea, but hark! out of the shame of his land shall he arise at some tide and cast his mantle and claim his own! And Rome shall know not; for Rome shall be but dust! This Panda knoweth, for Allah casteth not down save that he pluck up."

And they looked upon Panda, and the one who had shown the golded dust made that he hide the thing. And they spake:

" This man then is not Hate? "

And Panda answered: " Thou hast spoken it. But hark! mind ye that thy tongues speak but what thy wisdom's cup holdeth."

And they spake: " But thou didst chide him that he seek sheep, and thou didst speak that thou didst know not the man."

And Panda shook his head and said: " All Nazareth hath seen this man and his sheep."

And they turned and set upon their ways. And Panda sat him down upon a stone and sunk his head upon his folded hands and looked afar. And when they had sunk unto a naught, the paths shewed Hatte speeding unto Panda. And he called soft: " Panda! Panda! "

And Panda arose and went unto him and lay his arms about him and spake:

" Panda would that he might hide thy woes within his bosom, but man's woes do grow them. As youths grow unto men their woes grow even so. And Panda may not know thy full sorrow save that he know thy heart's depths."

And Hatte looked unto the eyes of Panda and said: " Panda, these men have told that Theia is within Rome; that she danceth; that Tiberius, the great one, hath spoken that her flesh shall come unto Rome or she fall. Tiberius! Tiberius! Tiberius! Panda, Tiberius! And they spake that Hatte was the fruit of folly. Did Theia, then, e'er know folly?—Theia, whose wisdom fills Hatte unto this day?—Theia, whose feet fell like swallow's wings? Folly? Panda, hath Rome a crown that belongeth unto this head? "

And Panda pressed his dark hand upon the scarred cheek of Hatte and spake: " Chafe ye not, Hatte. Earth holdeth a crown for all men, and they may not take it, but build it."

And Hatte said: " Yea, this is for the people; but unto him that hath a crown that waiteth, may he not take it? "

And Panda spake: " Then, Hatte, thy wisdom shrinketh? Wouldst thou fill thy days at the dinning of the metal of thy crown? Would its music fill thee? "

And Hatte's eyes flashed and he said: " But the earth is beauteous and the day filled of richness. Yea, and there are men that e'en ne'er * walk! "

* Who may always ride.

And he looked him o'er his naked limbs and to his coarse loin's-cloth and spake:

"Panda, this hurteth. Fools walk the days and move and slay, and the people bow down. Think! Think thee, Panda! Think, if Hatte might set him o'er and they bow down, Hatte hath wisdom and might raise up his land. If Rome be his, his hands itch that he pluck blooms and hide her rots; that he speak unto his sire his folly, and set her high. Theia's step telleth she trod not but that they bore her.

"Tiberius! Tiberius! Panda, it is not Tiberius? Speak it out! Speak! Ah, nay! His blood would burn Hatte unto a living flame of hate!

"And he setteth o'er! His hands do wrongs and no man crieth out. They fear him as a he-wolf; but Hatte, did he know Tiberius was Who, would split him ope and smear his throne with his rotted blood unto the sicking of all men, that no man would e'er sit upon it! Yea, Hatte would stand and watch the maggots eat him and laugh at their havoc! Panda, say it is not Tiberius! In some far land some kingdom awaiteth a king who mourneth her. Say it is so!"

And Panda shrunk and murmured: "Nay, Hatte, not within some small kingdom, but within a mighty land, the king mourneth her."

And Hatte spake: "Who, Panda, who?"

And Panda answered: "Youth hath for to learn the waiting, Hatte; for haste hurteth ever. The rugs of Nadab were wove in waiting. He knew not who would trod them, nor asked he Who? who?"

And Hatte spake: "But Nadab was old and his legs withered, and I, Panda, am smitten, but youth speedeth me."

And Panda said: "The sign, Hatte. Thou hast speeded o'ermuch and Allah smote."

And Hatte listed not but spake on: "I shall seek Rome even upon my smitten leg! Yea, I shall seek and speak loud within her walls that all men hear!"

And Panda laid his hand upon him and said: "Nay; wait! Out of the waters of Nazareth drink thee wisdom, and wait. Hatte, thou wouldst be thrown forth as a beggar and cast unto dusts within Rome. Wait thee! Thou didst speak that thou hadst lost thy hate. Where then didst thou find it?"

And Hatte sunk upon the sod, and Aaron even so, and offered unto Hatte of broken twigs, and laughed. And Panda spake not, but waited. And Hatte raised his hands unto Aaron and touched him and said:

"Brother, the waiting is long. Wilt thou upon the way?"

And Aaron laughed. And Panda turned that he set unto the building up of the hut's place, and lo, Nada came unto the spot bearing forth loaf and bread of fruit, and an earthen vessel of milch. And Panda oped his arms at her coming, and she went unto them. And they spake words of loving one unto the other. And Panda turned unto Hatte and said:

"Come thou! Eat of Panda's bread. 'Tis little, but it is thine."

And Hatte asked of Paul, and Panda said that Paul had sought him back unto Jerusalem, unto where he bore a sign unto the brothers of Levi, that they know. And Hatte said: "Bore he the sign of the Nazarene, Jesus?"

And Panda spake: "Yea."

And Hatte said: "What is this sign?"

And Panda spake: "Within Nazareth is a man who scribeth, and upon skins he hath writ the wisdoms of this one, and these the brothers bear one unto the other, and the lands marvel; for they that read thereof fall beneath the words. And among men that war there falleth a peace. And no man knoweth why; for His words are but words."

And Hatte spake: "Thinkest thou this one is he that Rome seeketh? For these Rome's men's tongues drip lies."

And Panda answered: "Nay, this one is not of Rome."

And Hatte said: "Panda, within the storm's wrath the woman, Mary, sought aid, even upon the streets; for her son was upon the highways. And the storm broke o'er the hills and swept down, and Aaron and Hatte stood forsaken; for thou hadst sought within unto the household of Hezekiah. And Mary came upon Hatte and told her woe unto his listing. And Hatte listed and when she had told the words unto him that spoke that Jesus was within the hills and suffered His flocks that they be beat whither, and he was lone, Hatte sought!

"Panda, is this thing not strange? He is ever upon the heights, and Hatte seeking. He is not a god. He is flesh; for Hatte hath borne Him within his arms unto a shelter place. He is flesh. Hatte's blade might have stopped Him, but His word—Panda, this Thing hangeth upon His word and clingeth Him about, and the eye seeth it not but it is there suredly!

"It has come unto the ears of Hatte that He hath cried out unto them that prayed aloud for aid for their smitten sheep: 'Cry ye not aloud, save that thy hand be busied!' And when His sheep had suffered smite and He ministered unto them, even after the manner of shepherds, men came upon Him so and spake: 'If thou art Him, make thy sheep whole.' And He answered them: 'No man may make whole that that be broken save that he do this with his hands. Behold ye, sheep are like unto flesh of man and is broken, nor may ye set it whole. But I speak unto thee, within ye is that that no man may break nor yet minister unto. And this thing shall I make whole. The tabernacle is builded by man but the inner place is filled with the spirit.'

"Thinkest thou, Panda, that His wisdom be of pured metal?"

And Panda spake: "Yea, Hatte, for His words did heal Nada's wound within her breast, and Panda stayeth him within Nazareth e'en though his feet would seek Jerusalem. His heart abideth here. Levi is gone—Paul hath spoken it—and Sherah, his flesh. And no man remaineth within Jerusalem that Panda would seek. Lucius fell beneath the famine's bite. What then doth Jerusalem hold that Panda would take of?

"Paul hath told that Jacob did betray his brother Levi unto the hands of Rome; that upon Jacob rested the mantle of blame. Panda would seek Jacob, but since he hath heard the words of this Nazarene he would not that he touch Jacob."

And Hatte spake: "Panda, all things leave Hatte. And thou, Panda, even thou, art left. Peter and the ones of Bethlehem, they unto Jerusalem and even they within her walls, have forsaken us. What is this thing, Panda, that strippeth Hatte and e'en thee? Is the stripping that Hatte shall be new mantled royal? And thou, Panda, dost thou then stand stripped that wisdoms shall weave thee a royal robe?"

And Panda said: "Nay, Hatte, thou art looking unto earth. Look in the day's hours but unto the sun, and at the night's tides but unto the moon. List! these men of Rome have within them much that may turn their hands 'gainst thee and me. Thou, then, shouldst seek thee not within Nazareth unto the time when they have gone. Stay thou amid the hills, and come thou at the eve's hours to this spot, and Nada shall minister unto thee and Aaron unto the time when the hut is builded up and fit that we house within it. Nets shall Panda weave, busy, for Galilee's land, and sheep shall he buy of the moneys therefrom, and thou shalt lend thy hand that thy word be true that thou art a sheep's man."

And Hatte spake: "Panda, Hatte may not do this thing. Nay; his wings would he spread and seek, seek, seek. Yet he would know which man hath claim unto this crown, e'er he goeth."

And Panda said: "Hatte, thy seeking of this thing but leadeth thee unto woe."

And Hatte asked: "Thinkest thou that this man Tiberius would slay her?"

And Panda answered: "Nay! Panda deemeth this the blade these men of Rome would pierce thee with."

And Hatte sat long and looked afar. And Nada brought forth bread and they offered it and Hatte eat thereof. And Aaron lay upon the earth's breast and slept.

CHAPTER XXIII

And lo, at a later tide, came forth Balaam, who brought word unto Panda that within Nazareth the Jews, at a hidden place, would hold forth and speak within a council and set unto the hands of their brothers the signs that they be borne forth.

And Panda said: "Thou speakest this unto a dark-skin, no Jew?"

And Balaam spake: "Yea, but Hezekiah sayeth that thou hast been within Nazareth with a young Jew, and Nazareth knoweth not this Jew, but he hath spoken with the Nazarene and Hezekiah sayeth that this man is one of them."

And Panda looked unto Hatte and spake: "Who is this Jew?"

And Hatte answered: "Hate. Panda, I go and seek, seek, seek."

And Panda spake: "Then thou dost speak thee a Jew?"

And Hatte shook him: "Yea."

And Panda said: "'Tis well. Go."

And Hatte looked unto Balaam and spake: "Will this Jesus Christus be among ye?"

And Balaam answered: "Nay, the Jews tell not unto His ears that His wisdoms tell much unto them, lest He hark and cease His giving forth."

And Hatte spake: "Say unto the man, Hezekiah, that the young Jew will seek."

And Balaam went upon the way back unto Nazareth. And when he had gone Hatte turned unto Panda and said:

"Panda, Hatte shall go unto this council and list and fill him up upon what hath filled them, so that he know which of these men shall wait the crowning."

And Panda went unto his building up of his hut, and spake: "Go then upon thy ways; for wisdom may not chide thee from sorrow's path. Then go."

And Hatte touched 'Aaron and awoke him and took up his staff and went unto the hill's-ways, nor looked he back unto Panda or Nada.

And when he had sunk within the high places, Nada spake her: "Panda, this lad seeketh bitter waters."

And Panda looked unto Nada and came up unto her and said: " Yea, Nada; if a man be brought forth in hate then his wisdom is but hate's woof and warp. Hate measureth wisdom in hate's cup, and love, doth her cup fall short of the holding, buildeth unto it."

And Nada said: " Panda, Nada loveth Hatte and would minister unto him. Yet Nada shrinketh even under his glance. He looketh unto Nada even as one looketh unto his slave, and e'en, Panda, he standeth o'er thee. What thing may set him upon the path that be right? "

And Panda smiled sorried and answered: " Naught save that his feet learn the stones. He hath no fear of stone's sharp, nor hate, and hath learned not the green fields nor yet the shadowed places. And he who knoweth not the quiet of the shadow, but seeketh ever the sunbeat paths, wearieth at his young youth."

And they set them at the building. And the eve came upon them, and when they had labored even unto the darking, the moon arose. And within her light they sought the paths unto Nazareth. And when they had come unto the city they went unto the market's place that Panda seek one who would give unto his hands that that he might weave unto nets.

And behold, while they spake unto this one, a man who had ridden forth from Jerusalem stood that he bart his wares for the morning's market offer. And he told of the day of Jerusalem and spake the names of men who trod the street's-way, and he spake him:

" Within Jerusalem there hath come forth a Roman called Flavius, a one whose days have been scattered unto him."

And he told that Flavius had dwelled within a kingdom dealt unto one whom the mighty one had set up for his service. For the man Flavius had within him that that might ope the eyes of the mighty one unto a thing he sought. Rome had taken this man unto her even after he had been broken for this thing. And he spake that Jerusalem had known this man as one who saw not, but that did a man not see, Rome could yet take out of him that which she coveted. And the market's men listed and spake:

" Then this man, Flavius, is one that hath been sent forth for this man that the mighty Tiberius seeketh, too? "

And the man who had ridden unto them said:

" Yea. What thinkest thou? Is this man that is known by His wisdoms as Jesus Christus He? Or is this man who seemeth like unto a wolf and dwelleth not among men and whose glances are dark and whose tongue streameth wickeds, and whom the Jews call Hatte, he? For hark! there is a crown that belongeth unto Who? Who? "

And this man spake more: " Among the Romans there is word that the mighty one, Tiberius, lusteth and glutteth, and Pontius hath spoken among them that should the roadways give up this flesh that Rome seeketh, they should cause an upheaval like unto an earth's quaking, and hold up the folly of Tiberius unto his people that they be fed.

" Tiberius knoweth this thing and sendeth him afar that he find. The Rome's ones speak a woman's name, and within the court of Tiberius is one man, Julius,* whose knowing holdeth Tiberius fearful that he rid him of this woman; for this one Julius is of the blood, and Tiberius knoweth and feareth. This is the word that filleth the mouths of Romans within Jerusalem, and within the very royal halls is Flavius housed, for he knoweth not that they would betray him. His day is scattered and he dealeth his words unwisely."

And the market's men spake: " And Jerusalem knoweth this? "

And the one said: " Yea, and the men have looked upon the flesh of Flavius, called Mary. And she is youthed and sheweth as a tall lily, and Rome hath robed her in purple."

And they listed unto the words this one dealt. And unto the market's place came forth Hatte, and Aaron followed. And this was the time that this one who had ridden was speaking unto the market's man, and they spake:

" Rome hath robed her of purple? "

And he answered: " Yea."

And Hatte came up unto them and listed, and they turned and spake: " This man hath ridden forth from Jerusalem and telleth much of the coming of a man called Flavius."

And Hatte started, and his eyes shot fires, and he cried: " Flavius? "

And they said: " Yea."

And Hatte asked: " Where from hath he come, for his eyes see no path and his hands ply oars."

And they spake: " What! thou knowest Flavius? "

And Hatte answered: " Nay."

And they looked unto him and said: " But thou hast spoken that his eyes see not! "

And Hatte stood straight and said: " Nazareth hath within her even another who worketh witchery, for I speak unto thee this man, Flavius, hath a daughter of his flesh, called of the name Mary."

And they made word among them: " This word hath much of Rome's days. What are Rome's days unto a Jew? "

*Possibly a reference to Julius Marinus, who was with Tiberius in his exile.

And they spake not more of Flavius. And Hatte listed long, and when they spake of other things, lo, he sought the one and spake:

"This woman, Mary, thou sayest is within the Rome's place within Jerusalem?"

And the one answered: "Yea, slaved."

And Hatte raised his hand high and smote the one who spoke. And there arose a loud wail among the men, and Hatte stood him hot of angers. And lo, this reached unto the ears of Panda and Nada, and they came thereto, and when the eyes of Panda fell upon Hatte in his anger, he came forth and spake:

"Thou didst say, Hatte, that thou wouldst seek the hill's high."

And Hatte spake: "I am come unto the council."

And they told unto Panda what had been and Panda spake unto them: "Leave thou this man that he go, for thou knowest not what sore cut thou hast dealt."

And they fell back and Panda sought the side of Hatte and said: "Come thou."

And Nada followed, and Aaron. And when they had come unto a spot wherein no man shewed, Panda spake:

"Hatte, the day hath come that thou shalt try thy strength. Thou art strong in hate; make thee even so strong in love that thou be a full bowl."

And Hatte listed not, but his lips spake: "Rome then hath taken her—Mary. Is it not o'ermuch, Panda? Is it not? For Rome plucketh all the blooms and leaveth Hatte but chaffs and hate that eat him. Panda, at this thing, hate hath rooted anew!"

And Panda said: "Hatte, take thou the chaff. Fill thy days of loving. Yea, fill up the empty with love."

And Hatte spake him: "But Panda, whom shall Hatte give his love unto, for he holdeth but one love and it is Theia's?"

And Panda spake: "Hatte, if thou hast no man for to love, look, list! Panda hath told thee; look unto the moon and love her, and unto the sun and love him. Yea, even love thou the field's-ways. Yea, and hark! love thy hate and it will sick and die."

And Hatte stood him high and spake: "Panda, Hatte is no great man. No man but he who is great and mighty may love hate."

And Panda cried: "And thou seekest a crown! Thou art not noble, for the noblest upon earth is he who weareth the crown of hate, and smileth."

And Hatte spake: "Yea, thou askest this of Hatte, that he shew him noble, and hark! this Nazarene, Jesus Christus, He knoweth not hate nor wears the crown, and He is called noble by the Jews."

And Panda smiled and said: "'Tis one thing, Hatte, to be born crowned, and another thing to be crowned at the hand of man. Hate may crown thee by thy right, or be dealt unto thee. This Nazarene, thou sayest, knoweth not hate. Yet Panda speaketh He is a full man and shall know hate. Yea, doth He know her not, earth shall minister her unto Him. For hate is the bottom of the pit of man's days. Yea, think ye, Hatte, should man know but love and love be all, how might man drink it?

"And hate is the cup! Man buildeth his cup upon earth that he drink the full of loving, and he should set him at the task even in his hate. Of the metal of hate should he bring forth a perfect cup, for this is the time that he setteth his hand unto its fashioning."

And Hatte spake him: "Panda, thy wisdom hath the sound of the temples, but hark! 'tis like unto them, for a man may hunger within the temple's walls; even so within thy wisdom."

And Panda spake: "Hatte, Panda hath taken thee unto his breast, tides and tides, and he would to do this thing now, but thou wilt not. Go! Go upon thy path, but hark! doth the path seem long, look thee unto the sky. Promise! Promise, Hatte!"

And Hatte answered not but lay his hand upon the flesh of Aaron, and turned unto Nada and spake:

"Nada, Hatte loveth Panda, but he would that Hatte drink his wisdom when Hatte is pressing from out the day's vineyards new wines."

And Nada came up unto him and raised her night-dark eyes so that the moon shewed their peace, and spake:

"But Hatte, new wine is not fit that thou shouldst drink it!"

And Hatte spake not but went his way.

AND Panda and Nada sought the household of Hezekiah, and when they had gone within, behold, the Jews came forth and sought a pit's place, lit of oil's lamps. And the light still shone white unto the mid-hour. And when the Jews were assembled together, behold, they shut the pit of stones.

And this was upon the hill's up-way. And when they had shut the pit, there shewed Hatte seeking unto the spot, and Aaron who followed him. And lo, when the sound from within told they worded much, Hatte listed that he hear, beside the stone's sealing of the pit. And a voice came unto him that asked:

" Is this man a Jew? There is word among the brethren that he is of Rome and no Jew."

And one among them answered: " Yea, this hath come unto mine listing. But if this thing were not true, even then would I deny him, for he is a fool and his hands do no good work. His wisdoms have bottoms even as jugs."

And Hatte's lips sneered and he listed not more, but sped him, and dragged Aaron after and went unto the hills and lay him down upon the earth beneath a tree, and spread the nets of Aaron and made the sign that he rest beside him. And when they had lain them long he spake aloud:

" So, even the men of Nazareth do judge me. I am no Roman, nor yet a man of Jerusalem nor Nazareth. Nay, no man claimeth me as brother, but Him."

And he turned unto Aaron and Aaron smiled not, for he slept. And Hatte touched him, and he struck at his hand in his sleeping. And Hatte shrunk. And he arose and looked unto the east-way, and called:

" Theia! Theia! Theia! "

And behold, o'er the far line hung a star. And unto the west clouds arose. And lo, deep within the valley sounded a voice that called unto sheep, and this was the voice of Jesus. And Hatte threw his hands high and stopped his ears.

And the night came on, deep dark, save for the stars' light, and they shewed pale. And the voice of the shepherd sounded far and far and far, unto its sinking unto naught.

And Hatte took from off his ears his hands and stopped that he list. And no sound came unto him save the braying of an ass.

And he sunk, and dark wrapped him, and there sounded but the breath of Aaron. And through the night's hours Hatte sat him waked and watched unto the East. And lo, at the fore hour of morn, the silver of the stars' glow shed unto the earth's rim and shewed the day the path. And the sun followed and shewed pale the gold of his ray. And he tipped the hill's crests and touched the night's robe that clung the trees. And the birds awoke to spread their wings and circle o'er the golden arch.

And when the light had come unto the spot where Hatte waited him, behold, he arose and stretched his limbs and looked unto all ways, and turned his eyes unto the sun. And Aaron slept, and he looked upon him and thence unto Nazareth's way, and spake even unto his own listing:

"Then Rome's noble is unto Nazareth a fool; for they seek a Jew, and a man's tongue may not claim his land, for his blood springeth out of her. Hatte shall seek this Jesus and speak unto Him. Yea, he shall empty Him that he know the fullness of what the words of Nazareth hold.

"They speak Him nobled, yet He is not of the flesh of the man Joseph, and there be men among them that have spoken this one is the son of no man. And Mary is no slave, but of the blood, and no man may point unto the man who hath taken her.

"Who hath set this witchery upon Nazareth, that a man who hath naught, who tendeth sheep, who asketh ever whys of the teacher, who doth take from out their mouths their words and set their wisdoms upon new legs; a man who clotheth Him of coarse stuffs, whose feet shew the wet earths of His land and know the stone's sharp; a man whose eyes look upon the lowliest and calleth them brothers; who would touch a beggar's sore and leave thereon a tear to fall, and felloweth with the filthed; whose smile is like the new sun at each day's coming—for behold, doth the sky torrent, His lips smile quiet, and doth the day shine, behold, His smile sheweth dazzled of bright; that a man who goeth among the hungered and maketh them full of His words; that a man who, doth a one take unto Him sorrow, giveth it back unto him washed; that, doth a man take unto Him hate, giveth it back unto him made new within a robe of loving words; that a man who seeketh not nor raiseth His hands to claim His crown, should witch them, should slave them unto the bending of their knees and their lips speaking King! King! King!

"Hatte speaketh that the man lacketh the back of him who warreth; that His arms fall short of strength; that His shoulders stand not proud, but bended as of age; that He careth not for His flesh, but leaveth it clothed but of that that falleth unto Him; nor seeketh fine raiment; that His words are like o'ersweet wine and lend no strength unto him who would war."

And he sat him down beside Aaron and looked upon him and spake:

"Aaron, brother, thy smiled lips, thy broken voice, thy empty eyes and thy full heart, are wine. And yet, where shall Hatte seek that he find a one who will touch his wisdom's flesh and speak, ' Morn, brother, morn!' "

And he waked the sleep 'of Aaron, and Aaron stood him up and shook the clinged bits that hung him o'er. And Hatte took up the nets and gave unto the hand of Aaron and made that they seek the far side of Nazareth; for Hatte knew that Jesus had fed His sheep upon the hills at the eve's hour of the yester's night, and would seek new fields at the morn.

And he walked him slow down the valley's-way and plucked the green leaves as he stepped, and tore them unto bits and cast them down. And Aaron came after and plucked up that that he cast down and put into the nets.

And they came unto the city's place and sought the street's-way, and Hatte went him not the way that led unto the household of Hezekiah, but 'long the path that passed the hill's-way whereon the hut of Jesus stood.

And at his coming, behold, Mary came forth, and held within her hands a bowl of grains, and stones, that she grind. And Hatte stood him afar and looked unto her and watched long the bruising of the grain. And when he had stood long, lo, he sought the spot. And Mary started, and looked unto him and her lips smiled sweet, and her eyes lighted up, but Hatte looked not the look of a fellow unto her.

And she spake her word of greeting and called his name, "Neighbor." And Hatte smiled not. And she spake his name, "Lad." And he smiled not. And she spake his name, "Son." And Hatte sneered and spake:

"Son? Son? No man calleth this flesh son."

And she said: "Nay, but one woman doeth this thing."

And Hatte spake: "Yea, but the sire hath forsaken her."

And Mary bruised the grain and spake not. And Hatte said:

"Thou hast spoken ' son.' I tell thee no man calleth this flesh son, and no man speaketh welcome."

And Mary's lips hung of smile and she spake: "That that a man dealeth unto his wine flavoreth it; but his hand maketh good wine or bad."

And Hatte said: "But this hand hath ne'er dealt unto the wine. Nay, for 'tis pressed and offered unto these lips e'en though they hate the sup."

And Mary spake: "Doth a man not love the taste of his neighbor's wine, let him go and pluck new grapes."

And Hatte spake: "But a man who laboreth lone, save for a fool, may make little wine."

And Mary said: "The tongue of man may not speak 'fool'; for 'tis wise that men be emptied of wisdom that their hands be fulled of labor; and his hands, then, be his wisdom. Yea, and the earth's walls be builded up by such men. And who knoweth whose hands build the Promised Land's walls? Think ye, man, this thing might be; that these that men call fools do build it."

And Hatte spake him: "Wouldst thou then speak it unto me that the beggars who pluck naught but their sores build?"

And Mary answered: "Yea, of precious stuff—pity. For their brothers look pity upon them and their hands build it up in waiting."

And Hatte spake: "Thy words chafe."

And Mary said: "Thou art worn smarted beneath thy hate, and no man may soothe."

And Hatte spake him: "Thy flesh, thy son, hath spoken that His sire had forsaken not Him; that he abideth within the temple place, and I am of his flesh. And I have sought Him out, and His words are like unto questions unto me. How may a man answer his brother by questioning? If this man is His sire and mine, why then doth he forsake his flesh? Is he of Rome?"

And Mary answered: "Yea."

And Hatte asked: "Is he then come unto Nazareth?"

And Mary spake her: "Yea, even so."

And Hatte cried him out: "Shew him unto me that I may make him naked unto all men!"

And Mary arose and her eyes looked unto the far, and she spake: "Nay. Nay. He *is* naked unto all men and they will not see."

And Hatte cried out: "Hath he forsaken thee?"

And Mary pointed unto her lips whereon smiles hung and spake: "Read thou thereon thy answer."

And Hatte looked upon her smiling and said: "Thou too dost hold his name unto thee. Theia will ne'er empty her of it, and thou, then, art true unto him, even though he hath forsaken thee and Theia."

And Mary spake her: "Within woman abideth the earth's rooting place of trust."

And Hatte said: "Thou too dost speak thee in answerless word! Knowest thou that the Jews would set thy son crowned?"

And Mary looked unto the grain's bruising and smiled and waited long e'er she spake in answering: "He will not of it."

And Hatte said: "But thou knowest He is noble. Why then hold thy speech and speak not the sire and claim not His right?"

And Mary spake: "This thing shall be answered not unto thee. But the days that shall dawn when thou art gone and Jerusalem hath lain her down, spent, and the lands passed unto naught, shall read the answering from out the writ words of man and know that that earth shall list not unto."

And Hatte said: "Theia, even as thou, doth keep her faith in the faithless sire. Where hath thy son gone?"

And Mary answered: "Unto the household of Silas."

And Hatte spake him: "But Silas is filled of woe, and his household but a pit o'erspread of skins. What hath led Him unto the household of Silas?"

And Mary answered: "That He eat until full."

And Hatte spake: "But Silas hath naught for to feed unto his sick ones, and all of Nazareth giveth unto him."

And Mary said: "Yea, this thing is true, and He hath gone unto Silas that He speak unto him and hear his wisdoms; for he hath the full wisdom of waiting. Yea, and faith."

And Hatte spake him: "Then a man may eat full of such a thing?"

And Mary answered: "Yea, and fatten."

And Hatte shrugged. "Thy words lead a man's wits unto follied lands. Theia cloaketh her word, but thou dost wind them within winding sheets!"

And he turned and walked unto the street's-ways of Nazareth. And when he had come unto the market's-way, lo, he came upon ones who spake of the days of the lands without.

And one among them told unto the Jews of a certain man who had sought Rome and taken thereto a sign of the Nazarene, Jesus. And when this had reached the ears of the noble one,* he harked unto it and spake unto them of his court who listed unto the wisdom of the lands,

* Tiberius.

and shewed unto them the skin whereon was writ the wisdom. And they looked upon it and spake them:

"Out from Nazareth cometh the land's undoing."

And the mighty one had caused this Jew to be brought unto him, even unto his feet, and had made questioning that might bring forth from out this Jew the answer of what man the Jews held as o'er them. And he called this man to read from off the scripts unto them that listed, and the words spake that there stood not a noble seat * but that its shadow fell upon the people. Yea, and the hands of man that builded up the seat unto a higher point but builded more of shadow.

And the noble one had spoken that this was against the mighty-seat, and they bade that the Jew speak the name of him who had writ, and he would do not this thing. And they said that he then should taste the wine of Rome, and caused that a vessel be brought forth. And it was done, and they gave unto the hand of the Jew a cup and bade that he hold it that it be filled. And from out the vessel they had caused hot metal, even heated unto the flowing, to pour, and he was caused to drink and had fallen. But no man had found his lips spilling that they speak the name of him who writ.

And Hatte listed and they spake them more. And Aaron came thereto and stood, his lips hanged ope and his hands busy at the nets. And they told that the thing that set fear unto Tiberius was that he had within walls he knew not flesh † that was his.

And Hatte started and listed and they spake them more, saying:

"No man knoweth why he reacheth not forth and plucketh this flesh from out the lands; for he feareth it, and he hath sent afar ones to bring forth word that told where the woman had hid that had brought it forth. And it had been that they had brought forth a dance woman called Theia. But Rome feared not this woman's flesh, but he who had wisdom past his brothers, for how might mighty wisdom be, save sired by the mighty one?"

And Hatte spake him even unto the loud: "Theia hath goods of Rome and Mary naught!"

And he listed and they spake: "Should the mighty one find his flesh, 'twould be but to slay; for he glutteth, and no man may dare that he speak wisdoms that his ears take not in and he full understand but woe fall upon him."

And he listed and moved not and they said: "He hath within him a living flame that seemeth it consumeth him. Even they that serve

* Throne.   † A son.

doth he slay, and smile upon their going. Within him is a heart that is black."

And Hatte spake: "Yea, they speak them true—black! black! How may a man whose heart is black know pure and free him of the stain? Tiberius! So, thou art him! Tiberius! Tiberius!" And he shut his teeth and hissed forth the word: "Thou hast begat the evil one! Thou hast unloosed thy filth unto thy flesh's blood! This, then, is the bidding, the drop of thy blood that defileth hers!"

And he cried aloud and ran unto the market's place and called unto them:

"Behold thou me! Behold thou me! I am him, the flesh of the mighty one whose might is filth and whose riches lusts! I am the flesh!"

And he beat his bosom and called aloud: "Behold these legs, bared! Behold this head, crowned but of the sun's rays!"

And he wept amid his words, and his teeth chattered like one smitten of death's cold. And they mocked him and cried: "He is mad! mad! mad!"

And they drew them away and left him that he cry alone.

And he turned unto them as they went their ways and cried out: "Look! Look! Look thou unto me! I am him!"

And they laughed. And he stood long, as one that had been beneath a heavy smite and who knew not that the day sped on. And Aaron stood and laughed up unto him. And he cried out:

"The son of a noble is the brother of a fool. This is not strange; for the crown resteth upon a fool. Yea, worse, a fool who is the evil one. It is true! It is true! This evil one setteth upon the mighty-seat that he hold forth the cymbals of gold and rattle them unto the weak, his follied kingdom. And Theia, thou didst dance unto his cymbals! Thou, then, didst do this thing?"

And he walked as an aged one, and his leg dragged slow, unto the household of Hezekiah. And he made the sound unto them within that he waited without. And Balaam came forth, and he called the name Panda. And behold, Panda came forth. And Hatte oped his lips, but no word would come. And he tried him thrice, and his lips were mute. And he whispered:

"Panda, behold the son of Tiberius!"

And his knees gave way and he sunk, weary. And his throat swelled and shut tight and choked. And Panda cried out loud and wailed:

"Thou hast taken wisdom, Hatte, and I did blind thee that thou shouldst see not! Come! Come!"

And he kneeled beside the fallen one. And Aaron chattered and laughed and offered his net's stores. And Panda made the sign unto him that he follow, and took up Hatte within his arms and bore him within.

And they spread rugs and laid him upon them, and his eyes shone bright and looked far, far, and he spake no word.

And Panda called his name, " Hatte," and he answered not. And Panda touched his fevered hands and spake him, " Hatte," and he answered not. And Panda whispered, " Caanthus," and he murmured, " I am strong."

And Panda smiled and bowed his head and made a chant low, and he brought wet cloth and lay 'bout the heated brow of Hatte. And his lips shewed dry and his eyes shone brighter, and he reached within his loin's-cloth with trembled hands and brought forth the golden strands and lay them upon his brow and smiled and spake:

" Crowned of gold! "

And Panda spake unto him, and his words sounded low: " Who hath spoken unto thee? "

And Hatte answered: " Ever hath this thing lain upon me—within Bethlehem, within Jerusalem, but no man but one from out Rome might speak the truth. This is fitting Rome. Panda, list! Hatte knoweth the depth of thy silence, and knoweth thy silence is not e'en so deep as thy wisdom, for in folly wisdom's sup sicketh and thou wouldst have shut mine eyes unto this to save the laugh of folly. Panda, they laughed and mocked the son of Tiberius! They laughed! They laughed! Ah, a man may war hate, but his blade falleth short upon mockery! "

And Panda listed, and sat him beside the rug's-cast whereon Hatte lay, and held unto his hand and stroked upon it, and he said:

" Mockery, Hatte, is but the echo of hate's laugh."

And Hatte spake him: " Yea, Panda, but they laughed, laughed! I did speak me out unto them and said that I was the son of the mighty one, and they laughed! "

And Hatte sat him up and cast the hand of Panda aside, and tried that he stand. And he swayed and stood swayed long, and his lips moved and no sound came, and he sunk upon his knees and sobbed. And Panda leaned over and spake no word, but lay the hand of soothing upon him. And Hatte's eyes shut and he swayed upon his knees' bend and spake:

" Hatte seeth a mighty-seat. Yea, this is the thing he saw long agone. And upon this seat—ah, 'tis he! And Hatte dreamed 'twas Hatte! For he looked so like!"

And he bowed him low, his brow even upon the earth and cried out: "Hail! Hail! O sire, hail, hail!"

And he bowed him thrice. And he rose and stood like a young tree, proud, and stretched forth his arms and cried in firm tones:

"Hail! I am him thou dost await. Behold the strength! Behold!"

And he drew up his arms that he shew the billowed strength, and he touched the golden strands that fell like loving vines about his head.

"Behold! I am the prince of thy lands, crowned at her hands. Oh, sire, lead forth thy loved, that these eyes may look upon her. Bring forth sweet musics that she may dance the joy within her. See! she hath dreamed these feet that they speed."

And he stepped faltered, and sunk, for his leg sunk in the smite. And he arose, and e'en though his strength failed, stood proud and hid the smitten sag. And his lips made more of words:

"Yea, sire, yea, I am thine. See! the mighty-sign of Rome is upon this cheek."

And he touched the scar. And he turned him dull-eyed, yea, vacant-eyed, unto Panda, who leaned close and felt the flesh that burned fevered. And Hatte laughed, laughed long, the empty laugh, and spake 'mid his laughter:

"Panda, he is wise, yea, and noble! And—ha, ha, ha! he would merry with his flesh; for he sleepeth!"

And he took up a rug and tore at its cloth and bit upon it; and took up bowls and broke them, and the thunder of his havoc sounded 'mid his pealed laughter. And Panda stood striving that he stop his madness. And Nada fell feared, and the household of Hezekiah came forth and stood them awestruck.

And Hatte took from out his loin's-folds a thin blade and held it high and his eyes burned as fires and his lips shewed white and shaken, and he cried:

"Down! Down before thy king! Down!"

And he flashed the blade before Panda's breast, and Panda sunk upon his knees and his lips spake soft:

"Even so, thou art a king!"

And Nada sunk her beside Panda, and the household of Hezekiah sunk in fearing. And Aaron looked upon this and moved him not and busied at his nets. And Hatte looked upon him and cried:

"Ah, sire, thy son knew not that thou wert here."

And Aaron laughed and Hatte echoed it, and he flashed the blade o'er the breast of Aaron. And Aaron stood him up and towered mighty and made the sound of the swine, and took up the body of Hatte and cast it upon the rugs. And Panda sped unto the spot, for the hands of the fool would to slay Hatte. And he cast him off and took up the spent form of Hatte unto him and spake:

"Come thou, come thou, Hatte!"

And he made the sign unto them that stood within the place that they go. And he smoothed the brow and took from off it the strands and lifted them unto his lips. And he put them within the loin's-cloth of Hatte, and he spake:

"Come! Come, Hatte! 'Tis early morn. Within the thicks the dews still cling. The sun cometh. Dost thou hear the sheep? Upon some height where Panda knoweth not, his lamb hath strayed. Where? Where, Hatte?"

And Hatte answered not, but his brow smoothed, and Panda leaned unto him and spake: "Where? Where?"

And Hatte answered: "He hath followed a sun's-beam that he find the sun, and he is lost. But he is lame and smitten, yea, and his bleating leadeth off the fold. Nay, Panda, seek him not. Ah, I saw him at the early morn follow off a fleece-cloud that beckoned him and danced."

And Panda spake: "But the fold loneth, and Panda heareth his lamb call, and 'tis dark, dark. Knoweth he not his shepherd?"

And Hatte smiled. "Ah, Panda, his shepherd is a woman, a maid whose locks spread as the sun's-beams, whose feet trod the grasses and disturb not the dews."

And he threw back his head and pealed laughs and laughs and cried: "Seest thou not the crown?"

And Panda sat long, even through the day's hours and unto the coming of night, and he spake words that led the straying one unto him, but to lose him. And lo, at a later hour, silence came unto the lips of Hatte. And Aaron slept at his feet.

And Panda was sore wearied and feared that he move and set Hatte waked. And behold, Nada came forth, soft-footed, and bore a taper's light, and held her slim hand that it shew not upon Hatte. And she looked upon Panda, and the light fell upon her face and her eyes shewed glisted. And Panda spake him soft:

"Wait thou, Nada! The lamb hath strayed and Panda seeketh. Wait!"

And she set the lamp that it be shadowed and slipped her soft without and but turned to flash her white teeth in smiling. And Panda murmured him:

"Nada! the silver soothing moon of Panda's night!"

And he sat him upon the floor's flags, and his eyes rested upon the sleeping Hatte, whose lips sneered in sleep. And the place was dark, and the lamp cast a glow within the ceil, and the shadows winged about the walls like bats. And Panda sat him silent.

CHAPTER XXV

And it was true that the days sped unto a fortnight, and Nazareth waked upon a day when the Jews made feasts. And they that abided about Nazareth came thereto for the feasting, and among them mingled Rome's ones. And market's places were filled to fullsome of fruits and that that made the feastings.

And within the out-places they digged pits and set therein whole sheep and bullocks, and the bullocks were filled of young fleshed fowls, and this was bittered.* And the men of market's places brought forth their wares that men buy, and the women followed them unto the feasting, and the babes even so.

And there shewed upon the road's-way a one who held within his hand a thorn branch, and upon his head shewed a crown of green stuffs. And he cried unto the ones that trod his path: " Where to? Where to? "

And they spake: " What manner of man is this that asketh ' where to ' when he seeth the feasting? "

And the one cried out: " Which roadway leadeth unto Rome? "

And they laughed and answered: " All ways unto Rome; for her men creep the earth like lice upon a beggar."

And behold, one ran up unto the spot and laughed, and this was Aaron. And Hatte laughed in answering. And the road's men backed their thumbs and shrugged, and said: " Mad! Mad and follied—follied! "

And Hatte listed and spake him: " Thou dost speak follied? I am him, the son of the mighty one. This is the land of me; for I may stretch forth my hand and all men shall bow."

And they came them and crowded about him and laughed and tipped his crown, and his lips laughed back unto them. And Aaron laughed. And behold, they sat him down at the feasting and called him king. And he held sway over them, and bade that they rise, and set, and that they bear him feasts, and bring sups. And they did this thing in mocking, and brought forth a sheep's skin and clothed him within it. And one among them brought forth an ass's skin and spread this o'er so that the ears fell limp o'er his head. And he supped and laughed and held his sway.

* Flavored with herbs.

And when they had finished their feasting they made ranks and waved bones that they had stripped at the feasting, and made that they lead him forth royal. And when they had come unto the roadway, they pointed thereto and spake:

" This way unto Rome! "

And Hatte walked him proud down the path's-way, and Aaron came him after, dragging his nets. And they that had set them upon the way looked after and beat one upon the other and laughed unto an uproar, and watched until they had sunk from out their seeing.

And behold, Hatte sought the street's-ways as one who knew not the paths. And men came forth that spake the man Panda sought this one. And Panda shewed speeding and anxious-eyed upon the way, and he cried out: " Hatte! Hatte! "

And Hatte spake him: " Look, brother, this man Hatte sought yon path and is gone. Rome hath eaten him. Yea, Rome hath eaten him; for these eyes did see the feasting yon, yon."

And he pointed unto the out-ways whereon the smokes arose. And Panda turned him unto the men who stood within the market's-ways and spake, saying: " Hark ye not. Hark ye not. For a man who taketh in folly taketh in folly's sinning. For he who listeth unto folly listeth unto folly's wisdom, and this be naught."

And they spake unto Panda, saying: " This man is he who hath rested in the shadow of the market's place and hath been known unto Nazareth as Hatte. Yea, the Rome's men have followed him even as Jesus Christus."

And Panda raised his hand in the sign of silence and spake: " As thou lovest thy brother, shut thou thine eyes unto his infirmities."

And the eyes of Panda looked in loving upon Hatte, and took in the ass's skin that hung o'er his head, and his eyes shot fires and his breast heaved and his lips hissed. And he pointed his finger unto them that listed and it shook, and he spake in wrath-clothed word:

" Behold, the fool calleth his brother an ass. Even so, the fool may ne'er clothe empty ones of asses' hides and make of them asses; for the hand of Him o'er all filleth the hide of beast or yet man, and He hath made them fools and emptied the ass's skin."

And he tore the thing from off the head of Hatte and the hands of Hatte clutched unto it and he cried aloud: " Nay! Nay! Strip me not of the crowning! Thou, too, dost seek the crown! "

And Panda stood before him and looked sorrowed at the empty eyes, and listed unto the follied words and spake: " Thou art right, Hatte. If this thing be the will then Panda's hands may not undo it."

And Hatte spake: "All the earth seeketh the crown. Look! within Jerusalem they seek. Yea, the morn's paths are filled within the shadowed places of them that seek, and the night's hours—ah, they creep within all paths and seek, seek, seek! Yea," and he pointed his thin fingers unto Aaron, "and he seeketh it, too!"

And the market's men and them of the street's-ways came about and listed, and Hatte put upon his head the ass's skin, and the ears hung and the legs clung 'bout his shoulders. And he took up a staff of rotted wood that had fallen, and held it as a scepter, and cried:

"Thou Jews! Thou, the kine of the fields, yea, and swine of the filthed! On! On upon thy seeking! For thou art follied. Behold, I am him, robed of fine hairs of precious skins! Behold, Rome hath done this! Yea, she hath lifted her son up before thee, robed fitting! Rome glutteth that she give unto her son all!

"Hath thy heart emptied? Rome hath given it unto her son. Hath thy hope fled, fled at each morrow? Didst thou arise at the young hour for to detain thy hope, but to see it flee like unto an evil bird? Rome hath given this unto her son.

"List! shouldst thou fall short of merry-make, speak unto thy sire and say unto him to bring forth thy mother's flesh and throw it unto the mires that thou mayest dance thee merry o'er it. This hath Rome given unto her son. For a king must possess riches— riches!

"Behold my sire! Did his throne shew the stuff it was builded of it would beat, living; for 'tis builded of living hearts! Aye, and when his mightiness doth weary of merry-making and the slaying palleth —ha, ha, ha!—he counteth the beats within his throne!"

And he stopped, and his eyes ceased their flashing and he looked empty, even as though he saw no man. And he stretched forth his hands and clasped them on high and cried out:

"Oh, my sire! Oh, my sire! I do love thee! Oh, my sire! Oh, my sire! Why turnest thou away? Oh, my sire! Oh, my sire! If thou wilt not of me, oh, my sire, give thou her unto my heart!"

And they that listed sent up shouts of laughter and cried out: "Fool! Fool! Mad! Mad! Mad!"

And Hatte shrunk and sent up his voice loud and cried out: "O thou, my sire! Hearest thou not? They mock the son of Tiberius!"

And they made louder their mocking, and the voice of Hatte arose, fevered thin:

"This will Hatte do for thee! This shall he suffer for thee, O sire, for thee, and love!"

And his voice broke and his knees sunk and he sobbed as a little babe. And Panda took his form unto him and made way among the men that mocked and railed, and they cast stones at them as they went their way.

And the sobs of Hatte sounded long upon the path. And they listed. And one turned unto the other and spake " Madness," and others among them spake " Fool."

And when silence had come, behold, there sounded out a wail, a piercing wail from far down the path's-way, and the words came back: " Theia! Theia! Theia!"

And upon the way Panda sped, his arms about the weak form of Hatte, and his lips spake soft words of soothing. And Hatte's voice cut, edged of fevers, and he licked his lips and beat his hands.

And it had come unto the gray of eve, and the eyes of Hatte looked unto the sky, and behold, one star gleamed white, steady white, yea, heavy silver. And he looked upon it and pointed and spake: " Panda, look! Look! The star! The star! The star! Bethlehem is yon! Come! Come!"

And Panda murmured: " Yea, Hatte, yea. Panda will seek with thee."

And Hatte smiled like the young youth of the hills, Caanthus of yore. And he spake, honey sweet: " Come! Hatte shall shew thee her stepping. She abideth there. We shall seek, seek some wooded thick. Yea, wherein the grasses shew. We shall seek the shades; yea, and the heights, for she hath hid. Panda, thinkest thou she doth abide in yon star?"

And Panda answered: " Yea. Look, Hatte; the star's pure is her, and she beameth unto thee. 'Tis she! 'Tis she!"

And Hatte turned within the gray light and. looked unto Panda and lay his arms about him and rested his head, weary, upon his breast, and he spake: " Panda, tell thou me. What besetteth my day?"

And Panda answered: " O'ermuch dreaming, Hatte."

And he turned his dark face up unto the star and spake: " The madness consumeth and leaveth unto Panda the babe. Allah, Allah be praised. For man taketh in folly from out his days, and weaveth cloths and robeth him within them, and through the fires of sorrow must he tread that he burn him naked, naked of cloth and naked of folly."

And Hatte's steps slowed, and Panda's even so, and they stood once more, and Hatte spake: " I am weary, weary, weary."

And Panda said: "But few more spans unto the house of Hezekiah, and at morn thou shalt seek the hut of Panda. Within this thou art within thine own walls."

And Hatte spake: "List! list!" And he took from out his breast the hair of Theia and shewed it and said:

"This is Hatte's gold, and he shall sack it and go unto Rome and buy the Empire. It is worth, worth, Panda; for 'twas grown from out the blood of Theia. But she is empty. Yea," and he shut his eyes and cried out, "yea, she came, and her arms were bone and famine's shadow clung her face! Yea, yea, she is empty! Her teeth shewed yellow, long, like camel's. She is gone, gone! Ah, Panda, what besetteth me? Not unto the household of Hezekiah. Nay, not among these that look upon me as mad. Nay, Panda, unto thy hut. Unto the hills, that I may wrap within their shadows and rest."

And lo, they heard the fall of sheep's feet and from out the depths came forth Jesus, and His sweet voice chided soft, soft, soft. And Hatte harked and shut his ears with his hand's cup. And Jesus drew on unto them, and Hatte looked upon His shadow, dark, that shewed clear, clear, clearer, unto the seeing within the veil of eve's gray, and Hatte spake:

"'Tis He! 'Tis He, Panda, the Nazarene! Wait thou! Wait thou!"

And he sped up unto Jesus, and the sheep parted that he come unto Him. And he cried out:

"Thou hast wisdom. Give unto me the sign, the blade with which a man may war the earth."

And Jesus spake no word, but His lips spread in smile.

And Hatte cried: "Thou speakest no word!"

And he looked close within the dim light unto the face of Jesus and looked upon the smiling, and he stopped his words and turned and sped unto Panda and spake:

"He smileth! Panda, thinkest thou these lips might smile?"

And Panda caught unto his heart. And Hatte stood long and his lips drew thin, and he smiled. And when he had done this thing he flung up his arms and cried aloud:

"Oh thou, my sire! Thy son smileth! 'Tis done!"

And he laughed and laughed and laughed, until his body shewed weak, nor could he stay the streams of laughter.

And Jesus went His way smiling. And it was darker, and when the flocks had gone down the way, behold, they scattered unto the by-paths, and the voice of Jesus called the shepherd's call. But they scattered

more, for Aaron came speeded upon the way in following. And he
came unto Panda and Hatte.

And dark sunk and Panda spake unto Hatte, saying:

" Come thou! the eve hath come unto the hills and the birds have
ceased their singing. Yea, the beasts have lain them down. Come! "

And they sought the up-hills and came unto the hut where Nada
waited. And the moon had come and hung o'er the hut's-way and
Nada came forth arm-oped in greeting. And they went within and
supped. And Hatte lay him wide-eyed through the eve and spake not.
And Nada busied at the task of sup.

And when Aaron had ceased his chatter and rested, and Hatte
slept, Nada came unto Panda and spake:

" Panda, ope thou the hut's ope and set the taper that Nadab see.
Hark! unto Nada it hath seemed that his rack thudded and some night-
bird laughed. Panda, Jerusalem's walls have called. The Nazarene
hath put peace within me. Panda, see! Hatte hath come, and Aaron—
the wastes. This is as Nadab would have it."

And Panda said: " Nada, Panda hath heard from out Jerusalem
that Hassan hath come thereto."

And Nada spake: " Thinkest thou he hath proven false? "

And Panda pointed unto the moon and answered: " Nay, Hassan
is true, yea, as true as yon moon."

And Nada spake: " But what seeketh he? "

And Panda answered: " Panda. Even though he jest with Jerusalem and seek for slaying, he seeketh in truth, Panda, for to deal
succor."

And Nada said: " Then shall we seek Jerusalem? "

And Panda looked far and spake: " Nay, Nada, for Panda's hands
have fallen short of bringing forth worth that may buy the way. And
Levi is gone and may lend no aid. Rome hath driven thee and me
unto Nazareth, and no hand aideth."

And Nada spake: " What then? "

And Panda answered: " Hassan shall hear that Levi hath fallen,
for he knoweth him, and he shall hear that Panda is within Nazareth,
for men of Jerusalem know this thing. And Hassan shall bow unto
his camel and speak, ' Do we then seek? ', and make the camel's answering, ' yea.' And at some morn the camel shall come laughing unto
Nazareth."

And Nada spake her: " Hassan, of thy land and mine! He knoweth
the smell of sands and palms and morns and eves; for morn hath a
youth-sweet smell and eve is full of day's scents. Hassan! Panda,

thinkest thou he might lend an aid? Ah, Nada loneth for the spot whereon the young swallow hath fallen."

And Panda said: " Nada, days speed waiting, and waiting is sweet. 'Tis the sweetest of all tides. Rememberest thou when Nadab's hands wove within the golden rug the swallow with the green branch within her bill? Thou, Nada, and the green of hope—waiting! Waiting!"

And Nada went within and brought forth a soft rug, one of the weavings of Nadab, and wrapped her and Panda about with it. And she answered: " Yea. Yea. Wait for Hassan and the laughing camel."

And they went them within. And Nazareth was wrapped within moon's-light. And the night's beetles sung, and the sounds of silence crept the hills. And the heavy silver star still gleamed, steady, steady, steady!

CHAPTER XXVI

And lo, when the night had ceased and the morn waked, at an early hour there came forth, from out the hut's ope, Hatte and Aaron. And Hatte clung unto the hand of Aaron, and Aaron led him unto the road's-way. And Aaron's lips made sounds that builded not words, save among the sounding one that sounded as " brother," " brother."

And they sought the pathway that Aaron pointed out, and behold, Aaron wearied that he seek upon one path and sought a spot and sat him down and took up his nets and shewed unto the eyes of Hatte. And lo, the hands of Hatte set at their mending, and they laughed one unto the other.

And it was true that Balaam sought the hut of Panda, and the eyes of Hatte saw his coming and he called unto Balaam, speaking out:
" Behold thou! Behold thou! The son of Tiberius! Hast thou then been sent forth that thou should bear back Hatte? "

And Balaam spoke not but went him on. And Hatte arose, and Aaron even so, and they sought the way unto Nazareth.

And when they had come unto the city's place, behold, the men had stirred and the market's wares were upon asses' legs seeking the bins. And Hatte sought out a spot that shewed between the bin of one who sold of skins and one who offered lamps and metal stuffs. And he sat down, and his lips' spake ever soft words:
" Theia. Hatte. Tiberius. Panda. Where hath Nadab sought? Ah, he hath gone that he find Hatte. What tarrieth Hatte? Ah, they did eat him. Yea, o'er the pit they did sear his flesh. Nay, they stripped him of his skin and decked the king in it."

And they that made readied their wares shook their heads and spake:
" Mad! Mad! Mad! "

And Aaron sat at the feet of Hatte and looked unto him and seemed that he knew his words. And it was true that the bin man who offered of metal stuffs brought forth a bowl of brass. And this was one that had been wrought by the smite of a man's hand,* and upon it shewed the signs of the mighty one. And this the bin's man set brighted and lay that the sun might shew its glowing. And the eyes of

* Hammered brass.

424

Hatte looked upon this thing and behold, they strayed not, but set upon it. And his lips still moved and words slipped through that hung not one unto the other. And lo, within the market's-way a dog came forth, and even so the dog of one of them that held a bin close by. And this was the tide that the wares were bought. And it was true that the dogs set one upon the other and the men ran them forth that they look upon them.

And within the market's place Hatte stood up, and his eyes lighted and his hands itched, for he rubbed one unto the other, and his eyes took in that no man looked upon him. And behold, he went forth unto the bin's place and took therefrom the bowl of brass, and looked upon it and laughed and took up the hand of Aaron and sped, even from out the spot. And no man saw, and his feet sought the hut of Panda. And Aaron laughed him loud and touched the brass that shone, and he chattered, and Hatte let his laughter mingle within the laughter of Aaron.

And they sought on unto the household of Panda. And it was true that Panda stood without, ready that he seek the high places with the few sheep that his hands had brought together with that he had taken from out Nazareth and Galilee for his net's weaving. And he turned at the sounding out of the coming of Hatte and Aaron upon the ways, and he leaned far that he take in what set them speeded. And behold, the hands of Hatte held forth the bowl of brass and he cried out:

"Panda! Panda! Thou hast spoken that a man fashioneth his cup out of hate. Within Nazareth a man hath found the cup of Hatte and he is gone. His sire hath taken him. Take thou this and deliver it unto him."

And he stepped before the eyes of Panda and spake: "What road-way sought he?"

And he stood long and Panda smiled, but spake not. And he sent forth his empty laugh and spake:

"Nay! Nay! I am Hate! Hate! They speak mad, mad! Hate is madness. Theia held her cup of love and Rome filled it of hate. Tiberius—Panda, is it right and meet that he should hold her? She is noble, and Hatte, Hatte, no man welcometh him, and he hath gone that he seek welcome. Panda, thou hast sought this man, Hatte. Thou knowest where he is hid. Where, Panda, where? They say that Tiberius is his sire. Nay; he is begat by the evil one."

And Panda took up his staff and lay it within the hand of Hatte and spake in sweet tones:

"Hatte loveth the hills. He hath sought there. Go thou and

find him. Call within the thicks and list. He will answer thee from off the hill's-way that lieth near."

And Hatte listed, and he spake: "Yea, yea. Within the hills, upon the heights he is lost."

And he set upon the way unto the higher hills, and Aaron followed. And when he had come unto a high spot and no man shewed, he called:

"Hatte! Hatte!"

And there came back: "Hatte! Hatte!"

And he listed and started unto the way wherefrom the sound had come. And he sought a thick spot and called him:

"Hatte! Hatte!"

And the leaves made the sound: "She-e-e! She-e-e! She-e-e!"

And he stopped and spake: "Yea, yea. Thou dost fear that the call wake him."

And he stepped soft o'er the sods and made the sign unto Aaron that he make no sound. And he sought afar, and when he had wearied, he stood and looked unto all ways, and his eyes shewed empty, and he called:

"Hatte! Hatte! Hatte!"

And there came back faint: "Hatte! Hatte! Hatte!"

And he sped unto the way the sound came out, and Aaron wearied and wept of sore weariness. And the legs of Hatte were scratched by the twigs, and his feet bruised by stones, and his eyes sunk with weary. And still he sped, and when he had come unto the spot from out which had come the call, he looked unto all ways and his bosom heaved and his eyes wept, and he spake him:

"Where? Where?" And he sent up his voice: "Hatte! Hatte! Hatte!"

And lo, out from the spot wherefrom he had come came back the sound: "Hatte! Hatte! Hatte!"

And he stood and cried: "Thou mockest me! I am come from the spot from out which thou criest!"

And he laughed, and the laugh mocked him back. And he cursed, and the curses came back. And he feared, and he turned and ran him swift from out the hill's-way, like unto some beast that feared a stone.

And Aaron, weeping, came after. And Hatte wept, and his lips dried, and he swallowed hard. And when he had come unto the paths that led unto the out-ways of Nazareth, behold, he came upon one who rode. And he stopped and called loud, and the one came unto him, and he spake unto the one, saying:

"Hark! call thee unto yon hill, for a man hath lost him therein."

And the one sent up a call, " O-o-h-o-e," and the echoing spake it back, " O-o-h-o-e." And Hatte spake:

" This man is lost and no man may find him, for dost thou seek he is yon, and when thou art yon he is hither, and when thou art hither, behold, he is hence. This man is called of the name Hatte and belongeth within this skin," and he beat his bosom. And he spake him: " Knowest thou Tiberius? "

And the one threw high his hand and cried: " Thou art a fool."

And Hatte stopped and said: " Fool? Fool? Fool? What fool? A fool is one who hath lost him within the hills."

And he looked trouble-eyed unto the one.

" This head is a brass bowl. All men are bowls. Do they loose their wines from out their bowls naught filleth them. Yea, naught be the calling that hath no answering. A fool is one who calleth and listeth and may hear not the answering. A man must hear his answer. And doth his answer stride the hills and come not unto him, they speak him fool. Fool! Fool! I am the bowl and Hatte is the wine that filled me, and he hath gone."

And he turned unto the one who listed in fright and spake:

" A man within yon hut hath a bowl. Come thou and these hands shall shew thee. Thou mightest touch it."

And the one spake: " Then thou art the one that hath taken the bowl from out the market's place. They seek thee."

And Hatte said: " Should they find me wilt thou speak it unto me? Tell them that I have sought yon hill's-ways and called. Tell them this."

And the one spake: " Come! Shew unto me the bowl."

And he turned that they seek the hut of Panda. And when they had come up unto it, they called and Panda came forth. And he held a sheep that he plucked wools off. And he looked unto them, and the one spake:

" This man hath spoken that thou hast a bowl and this bowl belongeth unto one within the market's place."

And Panda said: " Yea."

And the one spake: " Give thou the bowl unto my keeping and I shall bear it back."

And Panda said: " Nay. Shew thou unto Panda the man who hath claim unto the bowl and Panda shall deliver it unto his hands."

And the one said: " This man is a thief."

And Panda spake him: " Nay; a man who knoweth not his brother's goods may not be such a thing."

And he turned unto Hatte and said: "Go thou within."

And Hatte cried: "Thou speakest so unto the son of Tiberius?"

And Panda spake him: "Go!"

And Hatte stepped feared, for the eyes of Panda shewed fires. And Panda said unto the one who sought:

"Come thou, and our feet shall seek the way unto Nazareth that we bear the bowl unto the market's place."

And they set upon the way. And when they had come unto the spot, Panda spake:

"Shew unto these eyes the man whose claim may speak this bowl his."

And the one who had ridden forth with Panda pointed unto the bin's places and shewed unto him the Jew who had shewed the bowl for barting and spake: "This man is he who hath lost his bowl."

And Panda walked up unto the bin's place and brought forth from out his mantle the bowl and shewed it unto the bin's man, and the bin's man wailed that this bowl was lost and had come unto him. And he called unto his brothers, shewing unto them that this thing had been. And when they had come unto the spot they spake that the bowl had gone from out the bin and no man had seen the going. And Panda smiled and said:

"Yea, folly brought it from out the bin, and no man may see folly. Folly hath light feet and leaveth no tracking, yet a man cometh upon his workings and knoweth him. No man would speak aloud saying, 'Within me hath folly taken up household.' Nay, he speaketh that folly hath passed him by and housed with his brother. Even so, no man saw folly bear the bowl hence, yet they find his workings."

And they spake them: "Much word this that telleth naught that may lead a man that he know the offender."

And Panda said: "'Tis enough. The bowl is thine."

And he gave the bowl unto the bin's man's hands and lay within it a coin. And the bin's man spake him:

"'Tis enough, enough, but a man should know one who taketh the goods of his brother that he tell unto all men. How then hath this bowl come unto thee?"

And Panda answered: "Thinkest thou that a man would take of goods and bear them back unto thee, even within it a coin, if he would of thine?"

And they spake: "But thou hast spoken folly bore it hence; then may it not be that folly hath borne it thence?"

And even as they worded, within the market's place there sounded a voice calling: "Hatte! Hatte! Hatte!"

And they turned and spake: "This is the voice of the man who is mad. Hark, and thou shalt suredly hear his shadow's laugh."

And Panda said: "Thou sayest this man is mad? Look upon him. His hands bore the bowl from out thy bin."

And they shook their heads, saying: "Then no man may rest beneath the blame."

And Hatte came unto the market's-way, and Aaron followed. And Hatte spake unto them he met upon the way:

"Knowest thou the road's-way unto Rome?"

And they laughed, and some among them pointed wry ways. And he turned, for he listed not e'en unto their answering, but sought, sought, sought. And he went up unto one man and spake him:

"Wilt thou call him? Wilt thou call him? He sleepeth. Theia hath spoken he shall come, and he sleepeth. Awake him. Dost thou know Theia?—Theia, the deer-footed, the ewe-eyed, the sun-locked? Hark, he hath eaten her! Yea, Tiberius hath feasted upon her white flesh. And I am the bone of her, stripped dry. Dost thou know Tiberius? Men bow down unto him. He is nobled. His men are maggots that eat the Jews. And he is the blowfly that nesteth them amid filth and bringeth them forth. Hark, ye Jews! He hath within his hand, even now, a sling that will bruise thee through ages with its stone. Hark, ye Jews! His own hand shall slay his flesh and put within thine the blade. Thou askest how this thing be known unto Hatte? He knoweth not. He knoweth not. But it sheweth unto him. I am him, Hatte."

And he stopped and turned unto Panda, where he stood listing, and spake:

"Nay! Nay! Look! Look! Hatte goeth yon. Yea, call unto him and stay his going. He hath lost his wine."

And the market's men spake: "This man's tongue speaketh wisely, but yet his words hold not one unto the other."

And the Jews spake among them: "Tiberius glutteth. His women be the things that no Jew would call a name. The mothers of his men be not true unto their flesh. They spend their laughter and buy more of rotted flesh. Rome is beset for more men. Yea, even their slave's flesh make new Rome's men. Maggots? Yea, this mad one hath spoken true, true."

And they clutched their hands and made the sign one unto the other that told hope. And Panda spake:

"List! Panda is not of thee. His heart lieth beneath the sands afar; for a man's heart is rooted within his land. But list! This mad one speaketh true. Rome hath come even unto Nazareth, and even so surely unto Jerusalem and all lands whereon Jews tread, that she may buy. Care thou that she do not buy the Jew's very birthright. Fellow not with Rome, oh thou Jews, for he who felloweth with wickeds falleth beneath the lash of wicked's punishment. The evil one tarrieth not at the scourging. This is thine. He is full kind and would that thou have the full of thy folly."

And Hatte listed, his lips hung ope, but he took not in Panda's words in their fullness, but swayed and chanted:

"Hatte seeth vasts, vasts, vasts, that seem them endless! And a chariot whose wheels speed slow through ages! And the chariot is filled with blood, for it drippeth drops through ages! And within the chariot a he-one standeth mighty, a one mantled royal! Yea, and his eyes' opes be hollow, and his hands but bone beneath the robes! And he speedeth his steeds, and they are many, many, for they go before the chariot as hosts—and they are Jews! And within the he-one's hand is a lash that drippeth blood—and this is a cross! Wait—wait thou! The chariot shall stop, for look! look! look! The Jews sink upon their knees and cry out: 'Brother! Brother! Brother!' and make the sign unto him whom Rome hath slain. And he steppeth before them, and smileth sorry upon their folly and holdeth his staff in loving. And this one is—ah, Christus! Christus! Christus!'"

"And the he-one—ah, ah, ah, Tiberius! Might! Might! Yea, and within his hand, slaying—slaying! And within the hand of Christus, naught but succor! Yet succor lifteth up, and slaying casteth down!"

And he swayed even unto the falling upon his knees, crying out: "Blood blindeth! The slaying! The slaying!"

And Panda threw his hands high and cried unto the market's ones: "Touch not his flesh; for no man may succor save in loving. He hath spoken it true."

And he bended down unto Hatte's falling and took him upon his breast and spake: "Go thou and bring forth wine that he wake."

And the white face he turned upon his bosom, and his dark hands smoothed the matted locks that blew about his brow. And the lips of Hatte shook even though he knew not, and sweats dripped from off his flesh. And o'er them stood Aaron, fumbling at his nets and chattering, chattering laughs.

And one among the market's men brought forth wine such as the

land's men supped, sour; but stale grape's filling. And they filled a
cup and brought it unto the hand of Panda. And Panda reached forth
that he take it, and his hand shook and his lips spake soft:

"Theia, thou hast spoken the gods do win. Panda feareth, feareth,
even though he would believe."

And the men asked: "What besetteth this one?"

And Panda looked unto them even as he ministered sup and spake:

"He eateth earth's bread, hate. For man ever eateth the bread
of hate from out the day. Yea, and there shall yet be a sign that bread
feedeth, but sup reviveth.* Bread, then, shall be the sign of hate, and
sup shall be the sign of cleansing—one of the flesh and one of the
spirit."

And they spake: "Thou speakest o'erwise for one who shepherdeth
and weaveth nets. Fellowest thou with Jesus Christus?"

And Panda answered: "I am no Jew."

And they spake: "Yea, this thou mayest say, but this man, Jesus,
knoweth men from out His tribes as His brothers. This thing eateth
among us; for if He is the Promised One, He is but for the Jews."

And Panda smiled and stroked the cold cheek of Hatte, and he
spake: "The Jews shall unlearn the prophets' words, for the prophets
are gone. Yea, their bones rotted and a New Man hath come. He
walketh in Nazareth, yea, and His footfalls have e'en now writ them
forever upon earth."

And they said: "His wisdoms shew Him o'er men, but He casteth
Him among the lowly, the filthed, the scourged, the wicked. Yea,
them of much He leaveth lone, that they seek, and them of little He
seeketh."

And Panda spake: "And thou sayest this is unworthy of the
Promised One? Hark! unto him who would walk upon the heavens,
Panda speaketh, wisdom sayeth that he shall first know the sand's
motes. Ye Jews measure Him within a bottomless bowl. He buildeth
well, and hath a bottom unto His building. Ye would have One who
abideth even so high o'er thee that thou mightest ne'er look upon Him.
Nay, this is not worthy of the Promised One. He will of thee, even
though thou wilt not of Him."

And they spake: "Yea, but prophets have arisen and have spoken,
and been proven false."

And Panda answered: "Yea."

And they spake: "But this one is born of Mary and was not of the
flesh of Joseph, even though a man knoweth no man may be brought

* The Sacrament.

forth save he be sired. They would that we take in this one among us, a fallen star, rooted within flesh at no man's touch."

And Panda said: "This, this is worthy of the Promised One!"

And they spake: "How mayest thou speak this unto the Jews?"

And Panda answered: "Thou wouldst that the heavens ope and that the Promised One ride Him forth within a light that will strike thee blind; but this would be folly's working, fitting the in-take of a man's fancy, but not worthy of a god. He hath brought forth from out slime a lotus,—and thou doubtest. He opeth the earth's eyes and shutteth them,—and thou doubtest. He sheweth day and night and sendeth the seasons; from out dead fields He springeth herbs,—and thou doubtest! Thou! Thou! O ye men of all men whom He hath sought and set His very self within thy blood's building—the flesh of Jews!—thou dost doubt! Thou wouldst set thee that ye judge! Hark! The fruit of thy woes, thy persecution, is Him!"

And they cried them: "Stop thy words; for shame o'ercometh. 'Tis within us. Hark! We build the foundation of His throne even now. But what may a sicked swallow do beneath the hawk's eye?"

And Panda spake: "Bear her seed unto her young and leave the hawk to feast."

And the Jews looked one unto the other and made the sign.

And Hatte stirred, and Aaron strayed unto a fruit's bin and took therefrom and eat. And Panda spake soft: "He waketh. Speak not! Go thou and leave to his waking but that that he knoweth."

And Hatte stirred more, and they went them from the spot. And when the eyes of Hatte oped, Panda smoothed his brow and spake soft:

"Hast thou waked, and didst thou dream? Did dreams trouble thee, Caanthus?"

And Hatte smiled like a weary babe and answered: "Yea." And he put forth his shaking hand and lay it upon Panda and spake:

"Panda, art thou there?"

And Panda said: "Yea; ever, Hatte, ever."

And Hatte murmured: "I am weary. Hosts trod my skull's arch."

And Panda lifted him up and spake: "Didst thou bear the sheep unto the high places even as Panda chided thee?"

And Hatte spake him: "Nay, there was but one sheep and he gamed mockery. Panda, Hatte lost him."

And he put within his loin's-skin his hand and whispered: "Rome hath bought me. See! she hath sent forth a chain." And he brought forth the locks of Theia.

And Panda spake: "Nay, nay, Caanthus. Rome hath ne'er chained thee with this; but the God of Theia."

And Hatte's lips flashed smile, and he spake: "Thou speakest He hath done this? Panda, thinkest thou He will awake my sleeping sire?"

And Panda spake slow: "Yea, at some time."

And Hatte gave unto the hand of Panda his hand and said: "Panda, lead thou me unto the high hills, to some shadowed spot. I am weary, weary."

And Panda spake: "Yea, this shall be. But lean thou upon Panda."

And Hatte stepped, but his legs sagged, and he laughed soft and said: "What eateth my strength, Panda? What felled me? Some mighty hand reacheth forth and smiteth me, that I see not the all. Panda, this hand is the Thing Hatte feareth."

And Panda spake: "Nay, nay, Hatte, the hand smiteth in loving. Remember thou! Remember thou!"

And he made the sign unto Aaron that they set upon the way. And Hatte's legs sunk, and Panda took him up within his arms and murmured: "Rememberest thou the journey unto Jerusalem?"

And Hatte spake: "Yea, but where is the young lamb, the sheep that clung? Panda, Aaron followeth and his laugh falleth like unto a lash upon me! Ah, Panda, I am Caanthus, the youth who burst of strength. Look upon me. I have fed the strength unto hate, and it made no wine. Panda, the bowl of hate is empty—thou didst say it—and I thirst."

And Panda waxed hot beneath the pack, but wearied not, and bore the limp form of Hatte unto a shadowed spot within the hill's-ways and lay him down and set beside him, and spake:

"Tell thou all that eateth thee, unto Panda."

And the hands of Hatte plucked up grasses and his eyes fevered and he piled the grasses unto a deep soft and spake:

"Thinkest thou her bosom would be so soft and cool? Ah, Panda, that Hatte might rest his head thereon! Speak, Panda! hath she loved unwise, and am I the fruit? Did Hatte, in his loving, sully her? Am I her shame? Hath she lost her for the price of me—such an empty price? See! I would arise and shew me noble for her. Yea, Panda, even for him, loveth she him. Panda, thou deemest not that the man, Jesus, is the son of Tiberius?"

And Panda answered: "Nay, thrice nay."

And Hatte caught his hand and kissed it and spake: "Panda, I am his flesh. I am noble. I am his flesh, and he is o'er all lands. He may have his lands, his might; but Panda, Theia, Theia is mine, and I am o'er him!"

And Panda spake him in clear tones: "Thou hast spoken it, Hatte! Ah, thou hast spoken it!"

And Hatte arose and looked him troubled and spake: "But Panda, her eyes have sunk, her flesh is fallen, the young winds have ceased to speed her feet. Hatte seeth her dancing, but weighted down with his dead body. Hatte heareth mockery, laughter, yea, feasting—glutted ones, and a faded one that danceth, danceth—and laugheth! Like unto a dead man's lips, her smile! They feast, ah!"—and he cried out in moaning—" and cast plucked bones unto her, and laugh, laugh, laugh! Panda, I split ope! 'Tis the laugh! The laugh! The laugh! Ah, Theia, I do come unto thee and bear thee out of this and split ope Rome!"

And he swayed, and his eyes emptied and he touched his withered leg like a babe some new thing, and spake: "But I am empty! The wine hath flown out of my bowl!"

And he laughed and cried out from his cupped hands: "Hatte! Hatte! Hatte!" And the echo came it back: "Hatte! Hatte! Hatte!"

And he laughed, and the laugh sunk within the far hill like some evil thing, to hide. And Panda sunk upon his knees and bowed low, even his brow unto the sod, unto the east-way, and he cried:

"If, within Thy wisdom, Thou mayest hark, list, list unto him! But if this is Thy will, so be it."

And he held forth his hands in sign they were offered. And Hatte looked afar and spake:

"Sup, Panda, sup. I hunger. My bowl hath an ope. I may not fill it."

And Panda spake no word but led them forth—Aaron the empty, and Hatte the emptied.

And they went unto the hut's place and Nada ministered unto them. And Hatte seemed him soothed, for he smiled the smile that youth had shewn, and spake of the coming days, and the sheep they should bring together, and the land he should till. And Panda listed and spake soft unto Nada of what had been and he said: "He hath forgot. He is soothed."

And when the hour had come unto the late, still the moon shewed. And they made them ready that they sleep, and Hatte spake:

"Panda, come! Hatte would see the moon. Think thou! she shineth upon Bethlehem—yon, yon, far yon."

And Panda said: "Yea, come and look upon her. Leave her beams to wind thee like silver webs, to dream. For moon's webs weave sweet dreams."

And they went without, and Hatte stood long and looked unto the moon's peaceful white. And it was still. And he smiled and turned unto Panda and pointed unto the moon and spake:

"List! List, Panda! She whispereth. Yea, hark! the moon speaketh. Hearest thou?"

And he kissed his hand and held it up unto the moon, and murmured:

"Hark! Hark! The words! 'He shall come! He shall come!' Suredly, suredly! Ah, Panda, I am weary."

And they went them within.

CHAPTER XXVII

AND the night wrapped the woes within her dark shadows, that they rest. And at the young hour the sun arose upon the hill's heights and waked the day's first sound. And Panda arose and came forth and looked upon the path's-ways unto the hills and called:

" Hatte! Hatte! "

And behold, from out a thick the voice of Hatte rang free:

" Yea, Panda, yea! Hatte is here. Behold, the day hath come. See! Here Hatte hath vinegar and loaf and Mary waiteth yon."

And he spake soft: " List! We shall seek the hills, for she hath called therein amid the dark. Panda, Hatte hath heard her calling, calling."

And he came forth and shewed stripped, even as when youth was his, and his loins were wrapped of a skin, and his locks hung matted, long, and filled of leaves' bits. And his cheeks shewed them sunk, and his eyes happy, happy. And he came unto Panda speaking soft:

" Panda, list, list! Wilt thou take Hatte unto Jerusalem that he seek the temple and knock? Hark! Peter calleth! Yea, he seeketh thee and me. Nay! Peter? Where hath Peter gone? Call him and deliver Aaron unto him and say that Aaron is broken and fit not for to hold wine."

And Panda said: " Come thou, Hatte! Come thou unto Panda!"

And he held forth his hands, and Hatte came forth and Panda looked unto his eyes and spake: " What lightest thine eyes?"

And Hatte whispered soft: " Hatte hath gone. Hatte is gone. Caanthus saw his going at the first light's break."

And he turned and spake: " Panda, tell thou of her. She is like unto the young season when the buds spurt; like the living waters of the wells, ever pure, ever sweet. She is like the birds of the air; for her step leaveth no tracking. Tell thou! Tell thou!"

And Panda spake him: " List! List! Caanthus, wouldst thou leave Nazareth and seek new lands?"

And Hatte laughed. " What! Wouldst thou leave Bethlehem? See yon spot?"—and he pointed unto the hut's place—" This is the spot that she rested upon. The stars hang still o'er the spot at the night. See thou the hills? They are Bethlehem's hills. Bethlehem's! Bethlehem's! Panda, list! Hearest thou her voice? 'Tis upon the winds and musics cling 'bout it. Hark! Hark!"

And Panda touched his brow and spake: "Nay, this is not Bethlehem but Nazareth."

And Hatte laughed: "Panda, thou art follied. Thou hast followed of hate. Seek not thy lamb. Seek him not; for he hath found some green spot whereon he feedeth; fear ye not."

And Panda spake: "Come unto the market's place that Panda bear his goods. Wake thou Aaron and bid that he lend his aid."

And Hatte cried him: "Thou wouldst that the son of Tiberius lend unto market's toils?"

And Panda answered: "Yea, yea. Hearest thou? Yea!"

And Hatte laughed and spake: "Panda, Caanthus is but dreaming. See! his dreams float the skies. Look! yon golden cloud is a chariot. See the steeds, the chargers, speed unto the East! Look upon the mantle of him who lendeth his hands unto the steeds' speeding. It clingeth of stars. Look! Look!"

And he pointed unto the cloud's-way where they shewed speeded o'er the arch. And Panda spake not but took up thongs of dry skins and binded the nets unto packs, and upon the bended back of Hatte binded he the pack, even as unto Aaron when he had waked. And he took up a one binded unto his staff and they set upon the way, even without sup or the waking of Nada.

And the ways shewed no men, for the day was young. And they sought Nazareth and went within her stilled streets, and when they had come unto the market's spot, behold, there sounded out loud words. And within the bins Jews stirred and brought forth their cloths and stuffs, and the voices that spake loud came unto the listing of Panda, and the words sounded out:

"Who art thou, that thou shouldst bind up silence? Speak! Who art thou that thou mayest eat of stuffs and tarry that thou put price? Who art thou that thou mayest come unto the market's place and spread forth thy pack even within the shades, and no man know thee as brother? Off! Off!"

And there came no answering. And the voice arose and called unto the brother market's men:

"Come thou and look unto this one! Look upon him! He hath eaten seven figs and threescore sups of camel's milch, and nay price!"

And Panda went unto the spot, and behold, there lay upon the stones, neck longed in rest, a camel, and beside it a one who laughed and eat and spake not. And lo, he arose and bended low even before the camel and spake:

"Hearest thou, oh wised one? Hearest thou? This Jew would of thy master. Shall this thing be?"

And he went up unto the camel's side and leaned down unto his very mouth and listed long, and arose and spake:

"He hath spoken it. When a man's belly is filled, behold, his purse opeth."

And Panda looked upon this thing and cried out: "Hassan! Hassan!"

And Hassan turned and looked upon Panda but spake not. And Panda cried out: "Hassan! Hassan!"

And Hassan turned unto the camel and spake: "Knowest thou this one?"

And the camel shook him and Hassan spake: "So thou knowest him? Then is he a Jew?"

And Panda ran up unto the side of Hassan and lay his hands upon him, and he turned and said: "Brother, Panda, I am come!"

And Panda looked him long unto the eyes of Hassan and spake: "Hassan, thou knowest not how sore the need."

And Hassan whispered unto the ear of Panda: "Wait thou! Wait thou! The walls hold ears!"

And Panda spake: "So be it."

And Hassan questioned: "Whither abidest thou?"

And Panda answered: "Within a pit's place; a hut without upon the hills."

And Hassan looked unto the market's men who stood, mouths oped, and spake: "Look!" And he oped his purse's sack and cast them forth metals for that he had eaten. And his eyes turned and looked upon Hatte who stood and spake not, and he said unto Panda:

"Who is this man?"

And Hatte cried out: "I am the son of Tiberius!"

And Hassan held his hand in the sign of silence. And Panda spake: "Nay, brother, thou mayest not stay his tongue; for he hath not within him that that thou mayest tell."

And Hassan held within his hand a coin, and upon it shewed a sign, and this was the head of the mighty one,* laureled. And he held it up and looked unto it and then unto the face of Hatte, and he bit at his lips and drops sprung his eyes. And he held it forth that Panda look upon it. And Panda did this and hung his head low.

* Tiberius.

And the hands of Hassan made fast the packs upon his camel and made it arise. And Panda spake:

"Go thou without and wait thou, for Panda hath nets that must bring forth metals."

And Hassan spake: "Nay," and he took from the hand of Panda his pack, even so the packs of Aaron and Hatte, and binded them upon the camel, and spake:

"Come thou! shew thou the way unto thine abode."

And they made way out of Nazareth and unto the spot whereon Panda abided. And when they had come unto the hut's place, behold, Nada sat and looked unto the way unto Jerusalem, and saw not their coming.

And upon the way Hatte had spoken no word, and Aaron had followed him silent. And Panda had told unto the listing of Hassan of the going of his babe and what had been within Jerusalem. And Hassan had spoken that within Jerusalem his ears had taken in that Levi had fallen beneath Rome, and even so his daughter Sherah, and more, that within Nazareth there had arisen a murmuring from out the Jews, and it was told among the Romans that there was within the Jews a power that even at the every day grew mightier; that even within Jerusalem men of the Jews waited but that they smite. And Hassan spake:

"Knowest thou this Nazarene they would pluck forth and raise unto power?"

And Panda answered: "Yea; He is called Jesus Christus by the Romans."

And Hassan spake: "Rome hath cause to shake."

And Panda said: "But they seek the lad, Hatte, and follow this Nazarene like unto a shadow."

And Hassan spake him: "Yea; doth Rome hunger, she would not of one fish, but would pluck forth all fish."

And he turned that he look upon Hatte and spake: "But what hath set upon this lad?"

And Panda answered: "Thou didst hear him speak that he knew his sire. This thing hath undone him."

And Nada heard their voices as they sought the spot, and turned and looked upon their coming. And she threw her hands high and cried out:

"Hassan! Hassan! And the laughing camel!"

And she sped unto them and fell upon her face even before Hassan and spake unto Panda, saying:

"He hath come! He hath come! Thou didst speak it that he should come, and this thing is."

And Hassan offered unto Nada his hand that she arise, and she threw her hands high unto the camel's side and lay her head upon it and wept. And Hassan looked unto Panda and spake:

"Brother, then thou didst know that desert's men know one the other as brothers."

And Panda said: "But word came that thou didst suffer for the thing thou didst not do; that Rome held thee not in favor."

And Hassan laughed, and his teeth gleamed, and he let fall his hand upon the shoulder of Panda and spake unto him, saying:

"Then thou art not wise, for doth a man's wisdom not weave for him a cloak within which he may hide, then 'tis follied wisdom. Hassan's tongue might not be stopped, even though Rome should stop him. Ah, Hassan is a pack of seeds, and Rome's men fertile soil."

And Nada said: "Come thou within! Come!"

And they went within the hut's place, and Hatte followed, even so Aaron. And they sat them down and Nada brought forth bowls of sup. And they ate of that that she offered and spake on. And Panda looked unto Hassan close and turned his eyes slow unto Hatte, and he shook his head. And Hassan spake: "I am come from her."

And Panda said: "Is the day, then, well with her?"

And Hassan looked sorrowed and answered: "Nay. She hath sent Hassan; for thou didst hear thee rightly—Hassan is not within Rome's favor. But his cunning plucketh from out the packs of men wondrous stuffs—rugs, metals wrought in cunning, jewels, yea, and Hassan needeth naught of Rome. Hassan hath come forth once at the bidding of Rome, but Rome's hands shewed red, and they came them near, sore near, to leaving stains within the mantle folds of Hassan. But he hath washed him clean and will not minister Rome's wickeds. Hassan hath come forth from her at the bidding of her.

"She hath bidden that I speak unto thee that Rome dealt bitters, bitters, even the bitter dregs of hate's wine; that she hath danced for Rome, not that they look upon her and cry out 'Theia! Theia! The fleet foot!' but that they wallow in mockery. She hath bidden that Hassan speak unto thee this, and more: that the cut of mockery may not reach within the armor of love; that when they laugh and she steppeth, her steps lag not, for they tell out her loving.

"And more: she sayeth they have spoken that they would stop her steps doth not the road's-ways give up her flesh, and she feareth. Yet she sayeth ye should fear not, for doth Rome find her flesh and lay hands upon him, even though she be smitten sore and falleth, she shall come."

And Panda spake: "Yea, yea, these are the words of Theia."

And he pointed unto Hatte, who listed as a babe unto some words he took not in, and spake: "Hassan, brother, look upon him!"

And Hassan said: "'Tis well, for Rome would not have an emptied one."

And Panda laughed bittered and spake: "Rome refuseth not e'en carrion, doth she hunger."

And Hatte listed and spake not; and Hassan leaned unto Panda and said:

"She spake: 'Hassan, Hassan, speak unto him "Theia." Look unto his eyes and see doth their depths leap. Yea, lean thou unto him and speak his name, "Hate," and look close unto him and see doth he shew bitter sorry; for his eyes seem fires that burn me through the dark.' How may this thing be?"

And Panda answered: "Speak it not unto her that he is gone; that he is even as one dead unto the day. Nay, nay; tell her not that hate hath consumed him. Ah, nay!"

And Hassan spake: "Nay, nay; this thing shall not be. But Panda, look upon him and that that Rome hath done that hath filled him with hate's wine. Hate is sore heavy and a man may ne'er fill upon it save that it break him."

And Panda questioned: "Within Jerusalem hath word spoken his name as him that Rome seeketh?"

And Hassan answered: "Yea; but the Jews fear for this Christus and they fear that Rome seeketh Him. Panda, dost thou remember a man within the markets, one Jacob? There is the sting of the serpent that shall set up sore!"

And Panda spake him: "Yea, yea."

And Hassan said: "It hath come unto the listing of Hassan that Jacob's words delivered his brother Levi unto the Rome's ones, and even now his words tell much of his townsmen unto them that would deliver them up."

And Panda spake: "Jacob's tongue, then, is the lash unto his brothers that driveth them unto their enemy. Woe unto the man whose tongue is his brother's hang-thong!"

And Hassan said: "But this man, Jacob, glutteth; for Rome shelleth her grain into his sacks."

And they sat them long, and Nada listed, and she oped her lips and spake:

"Didst thou pass, upon thy way, the hut of Panda, and look upon the spot where the young shepherd hath lain him down?"

And Hassan smiled and said: "Yea, and young grass had greened the spot."

And Nada spake: "Ah, Nada sought Nazareth that she find balm, and she hath it, but the nights seem dark and the moon's-beams are white arms that beckon, beckon unto Jerusalem. And Hassan, Nada would that she seek the house wherein Nadab wove. The racks seem but echoes within Nazareth, and Nada seemeth for to see him sitting, weaving, weaving, and waiting, yon within Jerusalem. Hassan, brother, we seek new gods when He abideth within them that be near! The eyes of Jesus Christus seemed the eyes of Nadab, and Nada hath seen within her babe's eyes His eyes. The God is old, old, older far than Nadab; yet young, ever young. Nada knoweth; she hath seen this within the eyes of Jesus. She is ready that she seek Jerusalem, and know her God within all men, and seek not, but remember. Hassan, within thee canst thou find it right and meet that thou shouldst lend thine aid that we seek Jerusalem?"

And Hassan said: "Yea, but the time is not now. Hassan knoweth that Jerusalem careth little for Nazareth, and the lad should wrap him within Nazareth's mantle."

And Panda spake: "Thinkest thou they would lay him low?"

And Hassan touched his binded loins and drew forth his blade and spake as he pressed his lips upon it:

"Nay. Rome shall find her brother, Hassan, hath struck first. Theia hath spoken this: 'Slay him in loving, that Rome slay him not in hate. This doth Rome seek, and doth Rome take him, Hassan, leave not his eyes that they see the mocking of his mother.'"

And Panda arose and went up unto the side of Hassan and gave unto his hand his own. And he turned and spake:

"Look upon the work of a noble! Look!"

And Hassan said: "Yea, Tiberius, thy handiwork is what thou wouldst have it. Broken! Broken! And a vessel of a noble that is broken is not one whit more than that of a beggar."

And Panda spake: "Yea, this thing is true; yet there be some brothers that lack a bowl that shall drink from out the broken pieces, and revive. Oh, thou son of Tiberius! out of thee shall earth drink when she thirsteth sore, and lift her head, cooled of thy sup! Begat of evils, rooted in hate, thou shalt bloom forth a fair flower of love to lay upon the tomb of earth's woe.

"Hassan, brother, this vessel is within thy keeping and mine. She hath spoken the God is wise. 'Tis enough."

And he turned and took up the hand of Nada and spake: "What doeth she within Rome?"

And Hassan made answering: "Handmaid to harlots. She danceth unto laughter. White, white she sheweth, but her lips smile, smile, and her feet!—ah, speeded upon the desert's flesh's hoofs! Hassan hath seen this, and at the night hath he seen her, like some shadow, glide soft out of the sounding of Rome's din unto some thick-grown spot, and sink and leave loose her locks and kiss them and speak soft: 'Hatte! Hatte! I love thee!' Or turn her unto the moon's white face and arise and speak: 'It shall be!'"

And Panda spake him: "Hassan, she sayeth then that e'en though Rome hath done this unto her and hers, the God is wise?"

And Hassan answered: "Yea; each morn seemeth for to bring new wine upon which she suppeth and reneweth her faith. And Panda, brother, she spake unto Hassan that he should tell unto the ears of Hatte that she shewed fair and had become his love, his dream within the hills; that her locks shewed long and beauteous; that her hand stroked them that they wax bright and fair for him."

And Panda spake him: "Panda knoweth not that that might make a man so full upon faith."

And Nada looked her down and spake soft: "Nay; thou hast ne'er brought forth flesh, Panda. This thing doeth more than the hand of any man might do."

And Panda lay his arm about the form of Nada and murmured: "Yea, thou hast spoken it."

And Hassan spake: "Panda, should the tongue of Hassan speak unto him, the lad yon, would his ears take in that that the words held?"

And Panda shook him nay, but spake: "Speak thou unto him; for who knoweth what may set him upon the path's-way whole? Hassan, this is not within the knowing of Panda. Thou hast spoken Theia's words. Then there might be upon them the power to chide him. Speak!"

And Hassan turned him and went up unto the side of Hatte and spake: "What wouldst thou of thy brother?"

And Hatte looked unto him, and pointed unto Aaron who plucked up bits that lay upon the floor's flags, and said:

"Yon is a fitting brother for the son of Tiberius."

And Hassan spake him: "Nay; speak thou! What wouldst thou that thy brother should do? Speak it, and it shall be done."

And Hatte arose and his eyes looked far and he spake in the tones of one who commanded.

"Go thou and bring forth Theia! Go! Set up musics. Yea, knock thee the musics from out dry woods. Bring her forth! Go thou! Hearest thou the son of Tiberius?"

And Hassan answered: "This may not be."

And Hatte cried in loud tones: "What! then thou dost deny me? Thou wouldst say that the noble's flesh may bid thee that that he would of thee and thou then dost refuse?"

And Hassan spake: "List! Thou speakest as one who knew not. Awake! Awake!"

And he struck upon the flesh of Hatte. And Hatte smiled the whither smile and spake:

"Call thou! Call thou! 'Tis well; for Rome hath put her son beneath the stones and he heareth not."

And Hassan went from him and spake: "Nay, Panda, 'tis vain. Ah, that Hassan might lead this man, this young youth, yet man, up before Rome and shew him. Yea, hold him up; for he looketh so like unto his sire that one forgetteth him and remembereth his sire. Hassan would lead him forth, and speak unto the multitudes saying: 'Behold!' and Hassan would point unto the mighty-seat, 'Behold thou thy noble! He is not that he would have thee believe him, but look thou! This is what his hand hath done; not unto thee that thou mayest look upon his workings, but upon thee, when thou mightest not see, he hath betrayed his flesh and made thy noble empty.' Panda, list! men shall hold up Tiberius as a stone and hurl him down and he shall break even unto dusts and shew he is but clay."

And Panda spake: "Yea, and his clay is not fit that it be molded unto a bowl. Hassan, what is the roadway Panda should seek, and what shall his hands do? For look! yon nets and yon sheep that are few be all that Panda hath, save faith."

And Hassan spake him: "Nay. This is not true. List! Thou hast a rug, a golden one. Thou didst speak it. Where is this thing?" And he laughed and said: "Hassan may spread forth this rug and smooth it o'er and whine, and some Jew shall vomit forth gold, metals, dusts of precious stuff. Panda, bring it forth."

And Panda looked unto Nada and spake: "This thing may not be, Hassan. The rug, the golden one, hath bought dreams of gold, and robed the young shepherd. Nadab's dreams sleep that they shall become dusts and be fashioned unto bowls for other lips. When some noble shall take up a cup at some time, long hence, and make that he sup, behold, the cup shall bloom about its brim living buds that send sweet scents that stifle him within golden dreams. And o'er the brim he shall look unto the lands of pure, the lands wherein dreams abide, and meet Nadab. There is a land where the sun is ever young, Hassan, and the dews ne'er dry, and the sweet, soft breezes ne'er become winds. And within this ever-morn-land there steppeth within the golden light a young shepherd; in his hands a small staff and about him hangeth the golden dreams of Nadab. And he clingeth unto the hand of a one whose legs shew not shrunked, but who steppeth the path's-ways with him."

And Nada threw high her hands and wailed aloud: "Ah then, Panda, is it right that we should wait?"

And Panda shook him: "Yea." And he spake:

"Hassan, there is within Nazareth this Jesus Christus, the man they speak God."

And Hassan spake him: "Panda, dost thou believe?"

And Panda answered: "Yea; for no man falleth within His words but that his heart awake. No man might sway the scepter o'er a man's spirit. A man's spirit is his and his God's."

And Hassan spake: "Then Panda, Hassan believeth, if thou sayest this is true. List! within Jerusalem Hassan's ears took in that Samuel, the son of Jacob, and the aged one, Jacob, would seek Nazareth that they sup carrions that they fill Rome. This, they spake, would be but few sun's rises and sets after the passing of Hassan."

And Panda said: "Then, Hassan, we shall hide."

And Hassan spake: "Nay; for they look them for hidden things, and that their eyes take in that all men may see, be not worth price."

And at this time Aaron had sought without and set upon the hill's paths, and Hatte followed and called his name: "Hatte! Hatte!" and harked, unto the time when his calling had sunk unto a naught.

And the hands of Hassan and the household of Panda set at the unpacking of the camel's packs. And they ministered unto the camel. And Hassan brought forth his goods that they look upon them. And the night came, and Hatte and Aaron sought the hut, and they supped and rested.

CHAPTER XXVIII

And the nights waked unto days unto the passing of the moon from the full unto the half. And Hassan's camel stood packed without, awaiting the hands of Hassan that they drive it unto the market's-way of Nazareth; for a camel knoweth not the market's-ways of Jerusalem, neither Nazareth. And Panda and Hassan came forth and they walked them, and the camel drove they before. And when they had come unto Nazareth, behold, within the city shewed a coming forth of men. And asses, packed, passed them upon the way, one and one and one, and upon the asses the packs shewed light. And when they had gone they heard the men upon the way speaking: " He who belongeth the asses hath gone before."

And Panda laughed and spake: " Where is he unto whom the asses belong? "

And they pointed to the market's-way, and they looked thereto, and behold, Jacob and his son, Samuel, had come down from the asses' backs, and Jacob rubbed his bended legs and wailed. And Hassan touched the flesh of Panda and whispered:

" Jacob! Seest thou? The vulture! "

And Panda answered: " Yea."

And the men of the market's place came forth and bowed them down, for they had taken out of the market's word that Jacob was a man o'er them, one who had much and made rich price. And behold, Jacob looked upon that they offered him of their goods and threw his hands high and cried:

" Is it not enough that a man buy within Jerusalem, or dost thou then look unto him that he buy of thee? "

And he took out of his breast's folds his own goods and set up a wailing that they buy. And his hands took up goods like unto that he offered and held his own 'gainst it and shewed unto their eyes that the goods of Nazareth fell short. And the market's men went from him. And he sought sup, and no man offered that he sell. And they spake:

" This man is no Jew but a thief."

And the eyes of Panda and Hassan looked from afar upon this. And it was true that Jacob spake unto ones within the road's-way saying:

" Canst thou shew this Jesus Christus unto the eyes of a one of Jerusalem? "

And they spake them: " All eyes may look upon Him."

And Jacob questioned: " At which roadway? "

And they spake: " Await thou! for it is near the tide when He seeketh the shadowed sides upon the hills and will pass among us."

And Jacob awaited him, and bought of sup, and Samuel sat him that he await. And their asses they grained from out the packs.

And when the sun was high, Panda and Hassan still awaited afar that they see what should be. And the road's-way gave up Jesus. His sheep sought slow before Him. And they came them down and past the market's-way. And the market's men spake unto Jacob, for he slept:

" Awake thou! Awake! He cometh. This is Christus—Jesus, the Nazarene."

And Jacob awaked and rubbed his eyes, and he arose and rubbed his hands one upon the other and swung his beard. And his weak eyes strained that he look upon Him, and he saw that He shewed but a shepherd and clothed of the stuffs that shepherds robe of. And Jacob raised his hand and his fingers shook, and he cried out:

" And thou callest this man a god! "

And he laughed. And behold, Jesus had come up, and His eyes rested upon Jacob, and the tongue of Jacob was stopped; nor could he utter one sound; for he was stricken dumb. And he choked and reached his hands unto his thin neck, and his hands clenched at his beard and his eyes started forth, but no word would come.

And Hassan ran forth, for the men gathered them about the smitten Jacob, and Samuel fell, shrunk and frightened. And the men spake soft:

" Didst thou see this thing? The hand of Something smiteth for Him."

And Panda followed Hassan, and when they had taken in what had been, Hassan looked unto Panda and spake:

" Hassan believeth."

And he took forth his blade and kissed it and spake:

" The God hath stopped the tongue of the serpent that it smite not."

And Panda looked unto Hassan and made the sign of them who banded within Nazareth and among the Jews. And the sheep of Jesus swept on and past the market's-way, and He turned not nor saw what had been. And the market's men came close unto Jacob, who sunk smitten, and they spake them:

"What is this Thing? It abideth about this Nazarene, Jesus Christus, and fendeth Him. Look upon this Jew who denyeth Him; he lieth low!"

And they feared among them. And when the eyes of Hassan had looked upon Jesus, and Panda had come forth, behold, Jacob's eyes looked unto Panda and he pointed unto him and tried that he speak out but no word came forth. And Panda spake unto Hassan:

"Come thou, even before the lips of Samuel ope, for it be not wise that he know that Panda abideth herein; nor yet the lad, Hatte; for the words of Samuel will step them upon many legs and creep the path's-ways even unto Rome."

And Hassan made answering: "'Tis true. Come thou!"

And they turned upon the way and sought the house of Panda.

And within the market's place words ran among the men and they spake that this thing, the smiting of Jacob, was the sign. And the Jews stood them and made the sign of the banded ones one unto the other. And some among them sought out Jesus who had gone to the far side of Nazareth unto the west.

And it was true that His sheep had gone unto the greensward, and He plucked up woods and broke them and made of a pack. And they came unto Him and spake:

"What! thou art Him, the wise one, whom the teachers fear, and thou dost pluck up woods and minister unto sheep, when thy wisdom might pluck the jewels from out the noble's crown!"

And He stood long and looked upon them and spread His hands forth free from the plucking, and spake unto them, saying:

"A noble's crown is jeweled but of the goods of my Father."

And they looked one unto the other and spake:

"This man hath no glut for crowns nor yet riches."

And He spake not but went upon His way unto the thicks wherein He plucked woods. And when He had finished they still stood and watched that He come forth. And He came, bowed beneath the pack of woods, and called unto His sheep, and they came unto Him and He walked back through Nazareth and left them that had come watching His going.

And within the market's-way and upon the street's-way men still stood. And they had taken up the smitten Jacob and borne him within a bin's place. And Samuel stood o'er and cried him loud.

And it was true that the street's-way shewed the coming of Hatte and Aaron, and they sought the spot wherefrom the sounds of the voice of Samuel arose and sounded out. And Hatte went up unto the spot and Aaron followed, and when the eyes of Aaron fell upon Jacob, behold, he laughed and made noises and shouted. And Hatte looked upon Samuel and Jacob and spake slow:

"Know ye not the son of Tiberius? I am he."

And Samuel turned unto the men of the market's place and spake: "Who is this man? Is he not the lad belonging to a man called Panda, a dark-skin who wreaketh woe to all men? Behold my sire, smitten! What man among ye will go unto a one who will bring him forth? For his lips are stopped and he is smitten sore."

And the men of the market's place said: "Nay, nay. Not one among us shall lift his hands; for the evil one hath let him down."

And Samuel cried out: "What! among thee is there no man who will minister even for world's goods?"

And they spake: "There is that that world's goods may not purchase."

And Hatte went up unto Samuel and spake: "Come thou unto the house of my father. Come thou unto the hills where Panda abideth. Eat of Panda's bread; for it filleth all empties. Call thou Jesus of the hills and He will minister unto Jacob."

And Samuel spake him: "This man speaketh wisely."

And the market's men said: "Nay; he is empty. His words hold them not one unto the other."

And Samuel said: "But if a man is empty, then one may fill him up with that that he poureth within him. 'Tis well."

And he called unto the market's-ways and bade that some man among them lend aid that he put the fallen Jacob upon the back of an ass that he take him unto the hut of Panda. And no man came forth. And they looked them unto the earth and made that they saw not the fallen Jacob nor heard the words of Samuel.

And Hatte arose unto his full height and stretched forth his hands and spake:

"Arise thou! Arise and come forth! The son of Tiberius biddeth thee!"

And they laughed and mocked him, and he spake unto them even though they looked not upon him:

"Knowest thou this one is beset of evils? His sire is the mighty one, Tiberius."

And Samuel spake him: "What! thou speakest this? Look upon him. He is a fool."

And they made answer: "Thou hast spoken it, but a fool may be of the noble blood."

And Samuel said: "Yea, but this thing is not true. 'Tis gone before from out Nazareth that this Jew is the flesh of the noble."

And the Jews laughed and spake: "List! List! Tiberius would pluck out a Jew whose wisdom sheweth bright and call him his flesh!"

And Samuel cried: "Make ye not words but come forth."

And no man would aid, e'en though they spake unto him, but busied them at their bin's wares.

And Hatte went him up unto Samuel and spake: "Didst thou come from Rome? Ye bear word from Theia that she would speak it out that her son should seek his noble sire?"

And Samuel said: "Cease thy words and leave thy hands to aid."

And Hatte stood him o'er the fallen Jacob and made that he take him up; when sudden he rose and his eyes shut close and his lips chanted, for he swam within the sea of seeing. And he cried out amid the chant:

"Lo, Hatte seeth a Jew! A Jew! A Jew! And behold, a maid, and her breast is ope and streaming fresh blood, and there sheweth a one, a white one, aged, that pointeth unto the Jew. And—wait! wait! wait thee! his lips ope and call this Jew Jacob! And the Jew would that he answered when, sudden, a bolt from the heavens smiteth him."

And Hatte swayed and cried out: "Nay! Nay! Fear hath seized me!"

And Aaron, hearing the crying out of Hatte amid his empty, believed that Hatte wailed o'er the fallen Jacob, and he took Jacob up unto him and sped out the road's-way.

And the market's men looked unto the going of Aaron and cried out: "Seest thou what hath been?"

And Aaron speeded fast unto the hill's-ways, and Hatte turned that he look upon his going and cried out:

"This is right and meet, for he taketh Jacob that he eat the bread of Panda and feed upon wisdom. Jacob is empty. Yea, like unto Hatte, he is empty. He hath emptied unto Rome."

And he laughed him loud: "What! thou standeth so and lookest upon this thing and laugh not? Hark! Hark! Yon goeth Jacob unto the hands of Panda whom he hateth. It is well."

And Samuel, seeing what had been, cried out: "Thou Jews! Thou lendest not thy hands unto thy smitten brother and leavest this fool to bear him unto his undoers!"

And he sped after the form of Aaron that fled. And Hatte followed.

And the market's men cried out and speeded them after and laid hands upon Aaron and took from out his arms the form of Jacob. And they spake unto Hatte, saying:

"Knowest thou this fool dost do a thing that no man shall leave be? Look! the son of this man cometh and wreaketh angers upon thee. Wait thou!"

And Samuel came up unto the spot and cast him upon Hatte and made that he smite him. And Hatte looked upon Samuel and spake:

"So, thou dost seek the son of Tiberius? List thou! He shall be lifted up and the Jews shall be cast down. Yea, and thy dusts shall be but bits upon the winds when he shall arise out of the ages and cleanse him within the new days. And earth shall lift her head and look upon him and call out: 'Tiberius! Tiberius! Thy son hath arisen that he venge him 'gainst thee!' And thou, thou, thou Jew, thou shalt cast the stone that shall fell him and shew him naked unto his brothers. Nor shall thy hand lend it unto him; but thy tongue shall rot for this thing, even as thy sire's hath stopped!"

And Samuel looked upon Hatte and feared his madness, and behold, he cried out unto the Nazarenes who had come forth:

"Look ye! Look ye unto him! He babbleth follies and thou standest listed unto him. And he hath plucked from out the mantle of Jacob. Look thou within his hands!"

And behold, they looked unto Hatte and within his hands shewed bright stuffs. And this was but that that had fallen from out the mantle of Jacob when the hands of Aaron had plucked him up and sped him hence. And they laid their hands upon Hatte and took from his grasp the stuffs. And these were armlets. And they shewed them one unto the other and spake them:

"This man is a thief indeed. Did he not pluck forth the brass bowl? And his hands hath done this thing. Look upon him. He is a thief."

And the hands of Hatte shut and oped and his breast heaved. And he looked upon them and sprung unto the one who held the armlets and took them within his grasp, and cried out:

"They speak the son of Tiberius a thief! This is fitting; for the blood of Tiberius holdeth all things. Yea, all evils. And Tiberius needeth not that he thieve, but his son shall do this thing that the blood fall short not one whit of wickeds.

"They speak the son of Tiberius a thief! Ha, ha, ha, ha! 'Tis assuredly right that this thing should be. Hath he not trod upon the paths that were grown thick of blooms? Hath he not supped e'en since his birth, sweets, honeys, yea, his mother's blood, his mother's shame?

Ha, ha, ha! What! Thinkest thou that the son of Tiberius should fall short, or that he should be thief, thief? Yea!"

And he cast the armlets unto the face of Samuel even so that they cut within the flesh, and spat upon him.

And Aaron stood him making the sounds of the swine, and his shoulders heaved and his breath came like unto hot winds and his eyes shewed wicked. And behold he sprung upon Samuel and laid him low and took up of a stone and smote him upon the head, and made loud noises. And the men of Nazareth drew them away, for they feared.

And Hatte stood o'er, and behold, he took of a stone within his hand and stood o'er the men and shewed that he would draw near. And they feared, for they saw that madness was o'er wisdom, and madness draweth from the fires of the evil one that it feed its strength unto the follied.

And the market's men spake words that they caused the ears of Hatte to take in, and bade that he stop the hand of Aaron. And behold, Aaron ceased, and Hatte stopped and looked him empty, and made no words unto them that he might shew unto them that he knew what had been, but turned even as though there had been no thing that had claimed him.

And he sought the path and called his name: "Hatte! Hatte! Hatte!" unto all ways. And Aaron let fall the stones and sped after Hatte.

And the market's men looked upon Jacob, who feared but might make no words; and upon Samuel who rubbed upon the stone's smites. And the market's men looked upon what had been and cried out:

"Look upon this. How may a man weigh a thief 'gainst madness? For madness tippeth all beams."

And they left the spot and left Samuel wailing and looking upon Hatte, who went his way unto the highways.

And behold, the voice of Hatte sounded long calling, calling: "Hatte! Hatte! Hatte!"

And they that went them back unto the markets spake:

"Hark unto his madness, and look upon this one, this Jew of Jerusalem, who hath brought forth moneys and deemeth that he may buy his brothers even though his sire's lips spake them 'gainst the one, the Promised One, and calleth Him not a god."

And it was true that a one came from off the hill's-ways and drove an ass. And Samuel offered unto him of his stuffs that he bear Jacob unto a shelter place, and the thing was done. And no man looked unto the ass as it went through Nazareth packed of the drooped form of

Jacob, nor upon Samuel who sought after. And the one who rode took them unto his household, which was but a hut within the thick of the city's place.

And the eve sped and it came unto the gray hours and thence unto the moon's coming, and behold, within the moon's light, within the high places, shewed the dark speeding of Hatte who sought, sought, sought. And he had wearied, and yet his voice called: " Hatte! Hatte! Hatte! " And lo, he fell upon his face, and his hands plucked up sods and he bit upon them. And Aaron sought him out and would that he lend his soothing, even though his lips spake no words.

And Hatte turned empty-eyed unto Aaron, and they burned bright, and his cheeks shewed flamed, and the red shewed as shadows within the white light. And he raised his hands, in which shewed sods clutched, unto Aaron, and his shaken voice spake:

" Brother, brother, if thou lovest me, shew me the way he hath gone! Brother, unlock thy lips and tell thou what lieth behind their still. Speak! Speak! Speak! Where hath he gone? "

And he called, " Hatte! Hatte! " and his voice broke, and he sobbed. And lo, he stopped amid his crying out and sobbing, and his face lifted within the light and shewed radiant, happy. And he arose, and his leg dragged, and he stepped and spake:

" Theia! Theia, mother, 'tis thou! Ah, flee me not! Dance thou not away! Thou seemest for to flit mine arms. Tarry! Tarry! Leave these lips to cool upon thy flesh! Leave thy son's weary, weary head to rest upon thy bosom! Theia, Theia, I am weary, weary! Look! I shall lay me down and rest. Come thou, and leave me thine arms, thy bosom! See! I am weary, weary! "

And he sunk upon the earth, and his eyes hung heavy, and he murmured: " Weary! Weary! "

And Aaron kneeled him down and took him unto him, and he lay his head upon the breast of Aaron murmuring, " Theia! Theia! "

BOOK III
JESUS

CHAPTER I

It was night within Jerusalem, and the street's-ways shewed white and rimmed of deep dark. But few men walked the ways, and their shadows followed, stealthed. And dogs bayed, and the hours sounded out cock's crowing. And there sounded the kicking of the asses within their shelter places, and the shaking of their ears. And the temple place sounded the whirring of the doves that nested there, as they sought the depths. And afar sounded the piping of some shepherd who loned.

The Rome's hall * stretched it 'neath the light and told not of what wickeds hid within. And behold, within an ope shewed a maid who lay within the light, and one who rested near. And the maid came unto the ope and looked unto the moon and spake unto the one who still lay:

"Look! Dost thou remember the moon within Bethlehem?"

And Indra answered her, for 'twas Indra who rested: "Nay, Mary, Indra knoweth not Bethlehem."

And she arose and came unto the ope, even where Mary stood, and stretched forth her hands and looked upon them within the light and spake:

"Indra would forget Bethlehem; for look! Bethlehem hath held the thing that hath told Indra of her own, that she would know not."

And Mary spake her: "But thou knowest the moon's white of Bethlehem?"

And Indra said: "The moon's light within Bethlehem is even as the moon's light within Jerusalem or any land."

And Mary spake: "Nay, Indra, the sky is higher there and the moon—ah, Mary hath clasped her hands and circled her arms and the moon was even larger far. And the hills held scenes that no land holdeth."

And Indra spake her: "I am sick of this thing! The lad, Hatte, chanted this, and all of ye within the house of Panda. I am sick. Give unto Indra this," and she shook her robes and fingered o'er her armlets and touched her anklets o'er whereon jewels flashed. And Mary turned her eyes upwards unto the moon's pure and spake:

* The palace.

457

"I am sick of this! Rome hath bought me for my father's breaking, bought me out of the hands of loving that have no thing for to stop them. Indra, he knoweth not his flesh's shame. Thinkest thou that they shall find Hatte? Thinkest thou this, Indra? Speak! My nights are filled of him, and my days filled of burning blushes. Indra, Mary but liveth Jerusalem's days that she await him."

And Indra looked upon Mary, and her eyes narrowed, and she spake: "Yea, this doth thy sister know, but thou hast but to await, for thou art fair. Thy skin is white; thy locks"—and Indra touched the soft golden strands—"are gold, even as his mother's. He will take thee unto him and ask thee not of thy yester's-day."

And Mary said: "Nay, Indra, this is the thing that eateth me here," and she touched her heart o'er. "Even though the day giveth him unto Mary, she may not go unto him; for she is robed of scarlet, and hath known Rome's days. She is not the hill's bloom that knoweth naught save the sun's kiss and the wind's arms. Mary is Rome's and knoweth slaves' days."

And she shuddered and murmured: "Ah, moon, bathe thou me clean!"

And Indra's lips curled, and she laughed soft but spake honeyed words: "Thou mightest have a love even out Rome's men. Behold, the opes of this hall take in men from without."

And Mary arose and cried: "Say thou not this thing! Mary may sup bitter aloes from Rome's hand for the love of her sire and his breaking, but Mary is whole within. Indra, Mary hath looked upon her within the bath's clear crystal and sought that she see that she looked as his mother, Theia. The days are filled of her. My locks are as hers. Yea, and I am of her land, for my mother was her sister of Greece. Rome hath taken her from him, and Rome standeth with Mary clutched within her arms and laugheth mocking unto him doth he come."

And Indra leaned unto Mary and lay her arm about her and said: "Word hath come that he abideth in Nazareth and is lame. Thou wouldst not of a smitten man?"

And Mary cried: "He is lame? Then the hand of Mary shall lead him."

And Indra laughed. "A royal slave to lead a beggared one!"

And Mary spake her: "Nay, Rome's royal slave is not so clean as the beggar."

And Indra said: "Word hath come that he is mad. Even hath it come that Jacob hath sought that he find him, or that he bring this Nazarene unto Rome's hands."

And Mary spake: "Indra, thou wilt not betray him do they bring him forth?"

And Indra spread her hands and raised them, palms up, and spake: "What! Indra lie? Nay!"

And Mary said: "Then Mary shall lie her thrice and prove then that thou dost lie!"

And Indra's eyes narrowed and she said: "But there are men within Jerusalem that shall point him out."

And Mary spake: "Then shall Mary fall deeper within the scarlet; for she shall sell her unto a one who coveteth her, that she free him; for Mary would fall even unto death that she see him stand o'er men, even though he look not upon her and cry her shame aloud.

"I am of Greece, my mother's land, who hangeth her blade with flowers, yet warreth she. Her sons would sup honey from out the blossom's cup, but even so gladly lie beneath them. I am of Greece—her daughter. Yea, and doth the day call that I shall war, I shall cover my blade, the blade that slayeth me, with love's smiles, the blossoms of my spirit. Do I sink, and he look upon me even in scorning, Mary shall die happy.

"Oh, my brother, whose feet sped the hill's paths, who danced upon the wind's skirts, whose voice burst the airs ope with happiness—what hath smitten thee? Wilt thou bathe within this heart and rest?"

And she looked unto the moon and cried: "Hatte! Hatte! Thy sister calleth!"

And lo, upon the high hills within Nazareth, Hatte stirred and smiled.

And it was true that Mary lay her waked even through the night's hours, and Indra slumbered.

And when the morn's hours had come, behold, there came forth handmaids unto them, and they brought bowls of scented waters and sweet oils, and Indra wetted her locks of oils. But Mary touched not the oil but spread her locks that they gleam, and loosed them o'er her spread fingers. And the handmaids bathed their flesh, and robed Mary, and brought forth fresh robes for Indra who spake cutting words unto them. And the handmaid of Mary whispered:

"It hath been spoken unto thy handmaid that thy sire biddeth that thou dost seek Arminius."

And Mary spake her: "Say not this thing. Go unto my sire and speak unto him, saying, 'Mary would keep her chamber and not seek Arminius.'"

And the handmaid went unto the sire of Mary and spake unto him, and returned unto Mary bearing words that her sire would take not her nay, but bade that she seek. And Mary arose, and her eyes stood filled of tears, and she bound her locks close beneath a cloth and fastened it of a metal circlet, and her mantle drew she close and girdled even so that she shew not that that lay beneath. And the handmaid spake unto her:

"What! thou goest unto the side of Arminius and bedecketh thee not, when thy tongue might call forth the treasures of Rome that thou mightest deck within them!"

And Mary spake, even as though the ears of the handmaid heard not: "Oh, that I but had a cloak of pitch!"

And she pointed unto the way and stepped her unto the couch of Indra and spake:

"Art thou waked? Flavius hath bidden that I seek the side of Arminius."

And Indra's eyes flashed and she bared her teeth.

"Go thou and spend of thy love, that thou shalt fall short thy measure unto thy Hate!"

And Mary looked unto Indra.

"Indra, even though thy sister would love thee, thy words cut deep, and she falleth unto wondering dost thou return her love."

And Indra spake: "Seek thou Arminius! He shall teach thee new tricks of loving."

And Mary covered her cheeks, that burned crimson, with her cool palms, and sought the courts without. And behold, she came upon Flavius, who stood him decked within the cloth that covereth Rome's men who bear blades. And the men who stood them guard laughed upon him. And he looked not with seeing eyes, and called them brothers, and stood him proud, his hands grasped of his blade. And Mary came her unto him and threw wide her arms and cried aloud:

"Sire! Sire! Hast thou bidden Mary seek the side of Arminius?"

And Flavius answered: "Yea, this thing is well. Rome hath spoken it. Thy sire standeth high of office and it is fitting that one nobled should woo thee."

And Mary spake her: "Sire, sire, thy flesh is not nobled but slaved."

And the ones who stood them guard came them unto them and spake: "She hath spoken falsely. Behold, touch her brow. Thereon resteth a circlet. This be the noble-sign."

And they sounded out the dinning upon shields that called the blade's men one unto the other. And lo, the hands of Flavius sought theirs and they bore him away. And his ears they filled of his high office, and his hands grasped theirs in full trust.

And Mary let fall her hands heavy, and her head sunk. And her feet stepped slow unto an inner chamber wherein pots stood that smoked and a couch was spread.

And behold, a one waited her, and he shewed him young and beauteous, but his eyes held heavy lusts. And he came forth unto her, and his breath sounded heavy, and he called her name, Mary. And she stood swaying, her eyes closed, and held her hand forth in sign that he draw not near. And she spake in hoarse whisper:

"Wouldst thou touch the wings of Psyche? Wouldst thou defile the goddess of beauty, yea, and love? Behold, her wings enwrap me, and doth a mortal touch them he falleth smitten."

And Arminius looked upon her and laughed and spake: "Thou dost cloak within a borrowed cloth."

And Mary said: "Yea, I have come beggared unto thee."

And Arminius spake: "Speak! What wouldst thou?"

And Mary leaned her close unto him and looked deep unto his eyes and said: "Thou lovest me?"

And Arminius answered: "Yea, yea; love consumeth me, even as the sun eateth the lotus from her white unto the burn of ash!"

And Mary held her hand high and cried: "Swear it!"

And he cast him down unto his knees and touched her mantle unto his lips and spake: "By all that is within me, I am thine."

And Mary said: "Say that thou lovest me."

And he spake it: "I love thee."

And she looked unto him and said: "Thou then wouldst do the thing that would please thy love o'er all?"

And he made answer: "Even unto the oping of this breast."

And Mary spake her: "Swear it!"

And Arminius said: "This shall I swear, dost thou say thou lovest me."

And Mary said: "Speak it, and these lips shall speak the words in truth."

And he swore him, and Mary spake: "List! it hath come unto mine ears that Rome coveteth the flesh of a one who, unto Mary, is dearer even than her sire."

And Arminius asked: "Is this one a lover?"

And Mary answered: "List! dost thou know within thee the sweet that clingeth unto a fresh-oped lily? Even so pure is this love. And thou hast it within thy hands."

And Arminius said: "Then these hands shall defend it, even unto their falling stilled."

And she spake: "Rome shall bring a one forth and he is broken. Rome hath broken him, and within his breaking he knoweth not that they would slay him. Wilt thou, should the day shew him within these walls, lend thy hand, lend thy heart, lend even thy life?"

And Arminius answered: "Yea; but Mary, the price, the price!"

And Mary threw her arms wide and spake soft: "Look upon thy price, doth this thing be."

And Arminius made that he crush her unto him, and she stayed him, saying: "Nay, nay, it is o'ermuch! Mary is but a thing with which Rome's men play in folly, not in loving. Touch her not; it hurteth. Like some bowl given unto the hands of a babe that he marreth in his wisdomless glee, is Mary. She may stand beneath this thing, but that one who hath wisdom and love should touch is o'ermuch. Mary is like unto the goods of Jacob, she sheweth what she is not."

And Arminius spake: "All this shall be if thou art the price, Mary. Come! leave the hand of Arminius to lead thee forth that thou shalt be his flesh and not beneath Rome."

And Mary spake: "Nay, nay, leave me to empty, that I shall be emptied in full and suffer not when I shall fall."

And Arminius said: "But these hands may go unto Rome's ones and offer price and take thee."

And Mary looked unto him and spake her: "But the flesh! Wouldst thou the empty casket? Await thee, and Mary shall come at the finishing of this thing and thou mayest claim her even without price.

"Arminius, what is the thing that besetteth men? Behold, they take the flesh of woman and mar it of their touching and know them not they have rotted their own foundation. For woman is the foundation of man. It seemeth that the women of this tide stand fair, fair, sweet, pure; but rooted within the rot of man's doing. Behold, out of woman springeth new bloom for earth, else earth dieth, or lieth stripped, a wilderness.

"Oh, my sisters! Woe is upon us! No hand aideth! yet the mothers of this day shall bear ones, e'en out the rots, that shall lift earth out of the din of hate unto new days of peace. It is true! E'en now the sons of my sisters fall, fall, fall, but stones upon the path's-ways for new hosts to come. Ah, that I might spread my wings as a whited dove and flee; but the hosts must feed that they strengthen, even though it be upon dove's flesh.

"Arminius! Arminius! Should one grain of my dust speed some

new blade, upon some distant day, that it carve out some mighty truth unto which these eyes are blind, 'tis not in vain!

"Arminius, look upon the slaves, the women; their empty laughs, their follied feet, their weak lusts, their hunger for that that sicketh! Look upon this, and turn unto Rome's men. They have made them but empty! empty! empty! And through the empty of their women they shall fall!"

And Arminius looked unto Mary and spake: "Mary! Mary! Cease thy words! Fling thy sorrow from thee. Sorrow weaveth dull clouds that dim thine eyes. Fling thy sorrow from thee, for sorrow eateth thy white flesh. Fling thy sorrow forth. Look!"

And he held forth his arms that he take her unto him, and stepped unto her. And Mary cried aloud:

"Arminius, step thou not one step nearer, for doest thou this thing Psyche shall fell thee! Mary sweareth!"

And he laughed and took her unto him, and she gleamed white within her mantle. And his arms closed about her, and Mary spake one word, and this thing stopped him. And he harked, and let her from him. And Mary shrunk and covered her face and spake:

"Is this thy words of swearing? Thou, then, art even as Rome's men. Thy words build cups that have not bottoms, and they flow them whither, neither doth the cup hold them."

And Arminius stood him, head bowed, and spake him: "Go! Go! Go! For how may flesh war spirit?"

CHAPTER II

AND Mary turned and went slow through the hall's-ways, and her mantle flowed o'er the stones behind her and swept soft in sound. And she went unto the slaves' place, and behold, the slaves had waked, and they lay toying with golden discs and anklets, even polished metal they held unto them that they look upon their flesh. And they saffroned their fingers' tips and even put saffron upon their lips. And Mary stepped unto the side of Indra, who had slept even while her sister slaves toyed with Rome's empty stores. And she touched the flesh of Indra and spake:

"Sister, awake and come forth from out the din and list unto Mary, for Mary sorroweth."

And Indra said: "Go, and leave Indra that she dream new dreams of greater gifts and deeper Rome's days that flame crimson of joys."

And Mary said: "Indra, awake thou, and come from out Rome's crimson days unto the cool without, within some shadow that hath known no touch of man. Come, that thy sister Mary speak with thee."

And Indra arose from off the skin where, on the stone, she lay, and stretched her limbs and spake wearied:

"Make then thy sorry-song! Indra listeth, but sing thee not of Hatte but of some new love."

And Mary spake her: "Indra, list! A love that hath worn unto tatters is dearer than thy kinfolks' dusts. Yea, Indra, thou knowest that within thee thou dost remember some night wherein the moon hung, stranded unto the sky with silver webs; wherein the night's songs whispered them, the breezes coming soft, soft, and echoes clinging unto them of other days, some soft scent of spice that hath come—where from? Mayhap from out some winding sheet of Egypt's daughter; mayhap some dust that hath blown from out the skull of a noble that hath fallen. Love, aged, is riper, yea, and sweeter. Indra, thou art all that Mary may speak unto. Lend thou me thine ears; lend thee thine arms unto thy sister. She is weary of the day. Yea, Rome would have her play, but weary setteth her limbs. Yea, Rome biddeth her women play, play, dance and play, and she weareth them unto death at play, play, play. Ha, ha, ha, ha! Rome, thou art wise, for thou dost offer gauds and play, for life, life, life!"

'And Indra shook her robes and spake: " Rome, this is well. What wouldst thee of thy daughter? See! she danceth."

And Indra stepped her steps and laughed into the face of Mary. And Mary said: " Cease thou, Indra, and come! "

And Indra stopped and followed the steps of Mary unto the without. And when they had come unto the great hall, behold, the men had set them that they await the coming of the mighty one. And they looked upon the maidens, and Indra cast her eyes down and made slow smiles and raised her eyes unto them that looked. And Mary looked upon the stones. And one among the men cried out: " Come thou unto this spot."

And Indra took up the hand of Mary and drew her thereto, and the men touched their flesh and made words unto them and made that they should tarry and make follies. And Indra spake her:

" Look upon this one. She is sick of love, when Rome is teeming o'er of love."

And Mary looked not upon them, but stood bowed.

And Indra spake more: " Touch her! Look! she is like unto the marble that hath stood the sign of gods carved out by men. She is e'en so cold. And thou mayest look upon her like unto some distant star, and even though thou dost touch her, she is even so distant."

And Mary stood proud and drew her mantle close about her, and said no word but shrunk within her. And they spake among them:

" This woman is of the flesh of Flavius and thou knowest he is of high office. Yea, he hath been among Rome's nobles. Then Rome hath seen fit that he cast his flesh unto Rome's men that they drink therefrom."

And Mary spake not, and Indra said: " Yea, but the men do tarry that they sup."

And she held fast unto the hand of Mary and drew her up even unto her and cast the cloth from off her head, and the metal circlet rung clear upon the stones. And Indra loosed the locks of Mary, and they hung as a veil about her and she hid within them. And Indra spake amid her laughter:

" She treasureth all her beauties for one of whom she singeth in the nights. Yea, she raiseth her face unto the moon and singeth sorrysongs. Yea, and her lips smile but unto the way unto Nazareth. Hast thou then heard of the mad one—this one who is lame that they seek? He is a thief. It hath come unto the ears even within these walls."

And the men spake yeas and nays among them. And Mary's bosom rose and fell fast, and her lips she pressed unto the whiting.

And Indra cried: "He is a beggar! Look upon a woman who might take unto her arms any man, who yet would seek a beggar and lead a mad one! Look upon her! She looketh as the white of early dawn; yea, her cheeks the fleece of the clouds, and her lips the crimson of the young sun!"

And the men had made merry among them and circled about Indra and Mary, their hands clasped, and plucked at their mantles, and e'en they made that they draw them unto them. And Mary's eyes blazed hot angers, and she cried aloud one word and held her hands high:

"Unclean!"

And they stood them awestruck, and looked them one unto the other and spake:

"What! Thou abidest within the wall of Rome and house thee unclean?"

And Mary answered: "Yea, for the filth is Rome's! Laugh! Laugh! Laugh! It is merry-make. Yea, Rome hath sore smitten one who is but a slave."

And she laughed loud. And Indra stood stricken and cried out:

"Mary, hast thou done this thing? Is this thing true? Art thou smitten of filth? Hast thou even touched the flesh of Indra? Knowest thou not"—and Indra hissed her words—"if thy lips speak this aloud then Indra loseth favor and shall be cast forth?"

And Mary answered: "I have spoken it. Mary is unclean. Her heart hath rotted; her flesh is defiled; her lips tainted of filth, the drivel of lusts. Unclean! Unclean! Unclean!"

And she flung her hands high and ran from out the hall, crying aloud, and sobs and laughs mingled one unto the other. And she sped unto a spot where no man shewed nor step sounded. And her locks hung thick o'er her bended head and she flung her upon the stones and knelt, and of a sudden she stopped her sobbing and turned her eyes upwards and her lips moved:

"Oh thou, the quiet cool, the pure of the hill's shadows! art thou still there within the hills of Bethlehem? Oh thou, the he-star that arose bright, heavy bright, at the late season, hast thou forgot Mary? Mary longeth that she read thy beams; for at the youth-tides Hatte pointed him unto the morn star, weak, and called it her; and when the eve's star came, his voice called it 'him.'"

And she sunk, sobbing sore.

And without Indra stood, smitten dumb. And her eyes narrowed, and her teeth shut close, and her hands shewed clinched even unto the cutting of nails unto the flesh. And the men looked upon her and spake:

"Knowest thou not that filthed flesh is cast unto the out-ways?"

And Indra tore ope her mantle and shewed unto them her bared breasts and cried out: "Look upon this flesh! 'Tis clean!"

And they stopped their laughter and drew near, and Indra laughed unto them and asked: "What wouldst thou that Indra be thine?"

And one among them said: "This," and held forth a sack of golden dusts. And Indra laughed unto him and cried:

"What! Thou wouldst woo decked within the sagum?* Behold Indra would rest upon the soft folds of the toga."

And they mocked the one. And the men cast lots, and behold, one among them offered unto Indra his thumb ring and even a sacred beetle and a chain of copper upon which it hung. And Indra looked upon that that they had lain down and she took up this and spake:

"Away! Rome would that her daughter know the depths of her days."

And the one who had offered these took her unto him and bore her out the hall's-ways and through the court unto the chamber places.

And they came upon Mary kneeling. And Indra laughed, follied-drunk, unto her. And Mary sunk deeper within her locks and hid, and her hands shook, and her face gleamed white. And behold, men followed, and one came upon Mary and offered that he take her unto him, and Mary started up and cried:

"Nay! Nay! Touch thou not Mary, for Mary goeth unto the chamber of Arminius!"

And they mocked her and spake: "What! thou hast set the lions within the honey-singer that they leave him no rest? Thou hast spoken folly. Come thou! we shall bear thee unto him."

And they lended their hands that Mary arise, and they bore her unto the chamber-way of Arminius. And they smote upon the door's-way, and Arminius came forth. And Mary spake soft unto him:

"They seek me, and I have spoken it that Mary would abide with thee."

And Arminius held his hands forth unto her and bade that they go. And they went them whither. And when they had gone Mary sunk unto the stones upon her knees and bended low before Arminius and spake:

"I am come a beggar. What doest thou?"

And Arminius came unto her and aided that she arise, and spake:

"Without! The sun is yet young. Go! seek the shades and rest. Arminius would war the gods fair. Mary, their tongues touch thee

* A soldier's coat.

not. Arminius shall offer price for thee and take thee and thou mayest be thee and Arminius be Arminius. Seest thou?"

And Mary lifted up her face unto him. And it gleamed scarlet through the thick locks and her eyes were swelled of tear's bite. And she arose and murmured: "Arminius, wouldst thou but speak thy words o'er?"

And Arminius said: "I would weary thee not, but have thee rest within the words; for the cup that holdeth them is bottomed and holdeth fast."

And Mary spake: "They do believe that I abide with thee. 'Tis well that I should tarry. Wouldst thou that Mary rest herein?"

And Arminius answered: "Yea, cast thee there," and he pointed unto the couch, " and Arminius shall sit at thy feet."

And Mary sunk and spake: "Arminius, look! I am Rome's, and e'en less unto her than a pence that she casteth the beggar; for Rome clingeth to her pence, but her slaves—" and Mary shrugged and looked down, and she tarried her words, and her fingers smoothed o'er the skin that lay the couch. And her hair fell bright about her and her arms gleamed beneath it. And she turned and spake her:

" What hath bidden thee and stayed thee?"

And Arminius answered: " I know not, Mary, but long, long, at the early youth days, Arminius hath dreamed dreams. He hath gone unto the arena's side and looked upon the wrestling and dreamed that the flesh of them that wrestled was filled up of men that would do no thing less than win. Arminius hath rested his eyes, even when his lips scarce spake words clear, upon a one called Ajax; one who wrestled but whose eyes sung songs; whose hands smote but whose eyes soothed the smiting. Mary, Rome broke him. Arminius saw him broken. And within something stirred that had ne'er lived before. Thine eyes set it stirred, even as his, as thine looked unto me. Ajax wrestled Arminius and won."

And Mary cried: "Ajax! Ajax!"—and her eyes oped wide— " was this man called Caanthus?"

And Arminius spake him: "Yea."

And Mary arose and her voice sounded sweet: "Caanthus! Caanthus! Thou, then, art the warring one that hath lended aid! Thou who hast been the wine of strength unto Hatte! Caanthus! Caanthus!" And she sung the word.

And Arminius questioned: "Knowest thou Caanthus?"

And Mary answered: "Yea. Upon a high spot, upon a hill of Bethlehem, lieth he. And she bore leaves and blooms and danced o'er the spot. Hatte hath spoken it. Ajax, Rome called his name; but unto her he was called Caanthus. He hath wrestled even there, Arminius, wrestled and fell!"

And Arminius spake him: "Nay, speak it not so; for thou mayest not know the look he turned when he fell. Up unto the vast throngs he turned his bared soul."

And Mary said: "Yea, Mary knoweth. He fell within Bethlehem's hills, smiling, for he fell warring for love, beneath—Arminius, list!—beneath the leprous fever."

And Arminius cried: "Ajax suffered more of smite?"

And Mary told unto him all that had been that she had known from the lips of Panda and Hatte, and even what the days of Bethlehem had told unto her. And when she had finished, Arminius stood him high and spake:

"Thou sayest no hand might aid, in fearing that they should fall beneath his fever? Arminius sayeth they might touch in fearing that they defile such a one."

And Mary said: "He spake unto the woman, saying, If this thing was her rose his hand should pluck it. Hatte spake it. Panda told it unto him."

And Arminius touched the locks of Mary even unto his lips and said:

"Mary, Rome's days are heavy-hung of leprous fever. Behold, that that thou dost suffer even so shall Arminius."

And even as they worded one unto the other there sounded out a smiting upon the door's-way and the voices of them that sought. And Arminius went unto the without and behold, there had come unto his chamber's place Theodamus and Indra, for he was the Rome's man that had borne her hence. And he spake unto Arminius, saying:

"This woman who abideth with thee hath the filth smite * upon her flesh."

And Arminius spake him: "Nay, thou hast spoken folly."

And Theodamus pointed unto Indra and said: "Indra, tell unto the listing of Arminius the thing thou hast spoken."

And Indra told unto Arminius what had been within the hall's place. And Arminius spake him: "What wouldst thou that should be done?"

And Theodamus answered him that the woman be brought forth unto the hall's place and be made that she shew unto them within that she be clean.

And Arminius said: "Nay! thou hast spoken that that shall ne'er be."

* The leprosy.

And Indra's eyes narrowed and she flashed her teeth and spake: "Arminius, thou speakest words and thou dost deem them the ending of this thing, but Indra hath sought the mighty one and hath told unto his ears the lips of Mary have spoken that she be not clean, and he hath bidden that she be brought forth."

And Mary came unto the spot, and her hands she pressed unto her bosom, and her eyes she turned unto Arminius and her lips moved, and she spake:

"Doth Rome seek, there is no end of the seeking. She hath bidden Mary forth. Arminius, thinkest thou they shall cast Mary forth? Ah, speak it! For Mary would seek even the beggars and bed upon the shadows and eat but the off-falling of the market's bins, far, far gladder than these days of Rome she abideth."

And Arminius said: "Wait thou, Mary, wait!"

And they that had sought laughed among them and spake: "Come! they await thee within the hall's place."

And Mary feared, and Arminius spake no word but his cheek paled. And they stepped unto the hall's place, and behold, the mighty one sat the mighty-seat, but eat of fruits and looked not upon them. And Indra drew near unto the mighty-seat and held unto the hand of Theodamus. And Theodamus made word unto the mighty one, saying that the woman was set of filths and that the flesh of them beneath the same wall lay ope unto her contamination. And he spake long and Indra goaded him that he set his words hot. And behold, there had come within the hall all them that had heard the words that had set up, and they shewed many. And the mighty one looked not upon Mary who stood clinging unto Arminius.

And the mighty one listed unto the words of Theodamus, and when he had harked long, behold, he shrugged and spake:

"That all men see that her flesh be clean, bring forth slaves and strip her!"

And Mary cried aloud. And Arminius flamed crimson upon his cheeks and his hands shewed whited upon his blade's hilt.

And there came forth the slaves and the men, and the slaves crowded them about that they look upon Mary. And they tore her from out the arms of Arminius and lay hands upon her mantle, and behold, they oped it up and lay her shoulders bare and stripped her bosom. And her locks hung thick as a veil, and her eyes streamed tears, and her lips shook. And she clasped her hands o'er her bared breasts and spake no word, for shame had sealed her lips. And they made that they bare her flesh, and she cried aloud. And no man harked, but their lips spread in smiles and they looked one unto the other. And Indra's lips spread in full laughter, and her hand fell upon the shoulder of Theodamus and they laughed one with the other. And Arminius stood even as one who was smitten and had been carved out of stone. And behold, Mary stood clutching at her mantle folds, and the slaves made that they take them from her and she tore it unto shreds. And behold, she sunk, sunk unto her knees, and tore her locks that they fall o'er her. And they took from her her raiment and Mary knelt before them, clad but in her locks, her flesh gleaming white, her face scarlet and her eyes weeping, weeping!

And she cried out unto them that stood: " Behold, Mary hath but a cloak of thy pity! Wilt thou leave it her? "

And she turned unto them her sorrowed face. And they stood silent. And one man among them turned unto her his back, then the other, unto the all of them! And the women hung their heads and looked not upon her. And her voice sung sweet:

" Oh, thou goddess Psyche, thy wings are armor! Oh, mighty sire, bid not that Mary arise! "

And Arminius stood, his eyes upon the stones. And his hands tore ope his toga and he stood him naked unto his waist, and this he cast o'er her.

And the mighty one spake no word, but sat that he eat the fruits. And they that gathered within the hall's place went upon their ways. And Arminius waited their going and bended him low o'er Mary and took her up unto him and bore her unto the slaves' place. And he looked not upon her, but whispered through his teeth:

" Go thou and robe! Arminius seeketh Theodamus; for the blade of Arminius thirsteth, yea, it rusteth for whetting! "

And Mary went within.

And Arminius sought through the hall's-ways unto the chamber places, and lo, he came upon Indra, who stood decking her within the copper chain and sacred beetle. And Arminius stepped him unto her and drew him up, and behold, his hand spread forth and smote her full upon the flesh of her cheek. And his lips made words, saying:

" 'Tis such as thou that needeth no hand of man to defile."

And Indra spake a word that was a curse, and spat upon the stones of the floor, and laughed unto him and spake:

" Rage mounteth high even as flames, but all flame dieth. Indra may live Rome's days and Mary *shall* live them."

And Arminius drew forth his blade, and behold, his breast was bared and but his loins binded, and his ribs rose and fell in strength, and he held the blade forth and spake him:

"This blade shall free Theodamus of what he hath eat!"

And Indra cried aloud, and fear started her eyes that they ope unto the full. And she sped up unto the side of Arminius and spake:

"Goest thou unto Theodamus?"

And Arminius turned and looked upon her, and her breath came short. And Arminius spake him: "Yea."

And Indra said: "Doest thou this thing Indra shall wreak woe upon Mary that shall have no bottoms."

And Arminius spake unto her: "Go thou unto the slaves' place! Thou art a slave, and the morrow shall see not Mary beneath Rome but beneath Arminius."

And Indra cried: "Thou mayest do not this thing; for Rome would of Flavius and Flavius shall stay beneath the hand of Rome lest they lose the thing they seek."

And Arminius spake him: "Indra, Arminius hath the ear of the mighty one, and thou shalt be cast forth dost thou speak e'en one word to undo Arminius."

And he turned and went him hence. And Indra stood within the halls of the chamber places, and her clenched hands she shook at the going of Arminius. And when he had sunk from out her view she turned and went unto the without where stood ones that watched them, and unto these men spake she:

"Seek thou Theodamus and bid that he come unto the slaves' place, unto Indra, and speed him, for Arminius seeketh him."

And even as she spake there arose loud noises from the court without, and the men ran unto the spot and Indra sped with them that sought. And they came unto a place where stood Theodamus, bladed, and angers bathed his cheeks with flame. And Arminius spake in loud tones:

"Thou dost bare a blade for Rome? Thou callest Rome thy maiden, when behold, thou wouldst defile her young maids and shew shame unto thy brothers? What manner of man art thou? Thou hast plucked from out the slaves the serpent and left the blooms, yea, and Arminius hath struck the serpent, but her bite falleth, she hath spoken."

And Theodamus drew forth his broad-blade, and Arminius laughed upon him, and cried:

"Nay, nay! Thou art a Roman and Arminius is Rome's son. Metals are of any land. Leave Rome's flesh war Rome's flesh. These hands shall ope thy throat! Cast thy blade and shew if thou art the son of Rome or falsely named her son!"

And Theodamus looked upon them that had come that they look upon what should befall, and they cried out: " So be it! So be it! "

For among them were men that had looked upon what had been within the hall's place. And Theodamus towered him tall o'er Arminius, like unto some mighty tree o'er a beauteous shrub. And he looked upon his bared hands and upon the form of Arminius and laughed. And he said unto them that watched:

" What wouldst thou that these hands should do unto this babe? "

And Arminius looked unto him and spake: " Waste thou not words but come! "

And behold, Theodamus bended him that he set upon Arminius, and they fell one unto the other, and the legs of Arminius bowed beneath the weight. And Theodamus sunk his hands within the flesh upon the arms of Arminius, and tore at them. And the face of Arminius whited but he stood beneath the hurt. And behold, Theodamus bended him even unto the earth, and Arminius turned upon his belly and shut him up. And it was true that he turned Theodamus upon the earth with one mighty heave, and he fell heavy. And Arminius stood up, his eyes dim with the hurt and his arms hung limp, even so that he stood long, even as one who forgot he had wrestled.

And Theodamus arose and sprung upon him, and behold, he flashed forth his blade and sunk it within the neck of Arminius. And Arminius turned, dull-eyed, and plucked from out the wound the blade and flung him upon Theodamus, and sank the blade within his belly, and slipped it upwards, even so that he shewed oped.

And they that stood about cried aloud: " Theodamus hath fallen! Theodamus is no more! "

And they laughed one unto the other, saying: " His words were o'er him. The babe hath fallen at the hand of Arminius! "

And Indra heard this thing, where she stood at the edge of them that had crowded about, and behold, she bit at them that stood and her hands tore at their raiment. And she made way unto the spot where Theodamus lay within a pool of blood. And Arminius stood him, head bowed, o'er the fallen Theodamus. Still dumb of hurt was he, and blood streamed o'er his back from out the wound that had been caused by the hand of Theodamus. And Indra flung her at the form of Theodamus. And behold, she looked upon what had been, and she arose shuddering and her face ashen and her teeth shaking, and she hid her eyes. And Arminius looked upon her and spake in weak whisper, and he held forth the blade with which he had slain Theodamus:

"Hang this unto thy coppered chain! The beetles shall feast upon this carrion."

And he kicked at the fallen Theodamus. And Indra shrunk from the blade and spake: "He is no more. Indra then shall seek new loves!"

And she sunk upon her knees and let her hands slip through the toga of Theodamus and brought forth his skin's-sack of stuffs and emptied it upon her palm. And behold, there shewed jewels and dusts. And Indra set them within the sack and put this within her breast, and arose and flung her arms wide and spake unto them that looked upon this: "Behold, the dead be dead. Indra is live! live! live!"

And she made that she lay her arms about Arminius, and he cast her from him. And she laughed unto the men that stood about and spake:

"Indra careth not, for if one wine is denied her she may sup another."

And she tore ope her mantle and from off it bits, and held unto Arminius, saying: "Take thou this that thou mayest stay thy drops."

And Arminius answered her: "Nay, nay! Arminius would that he flow free that he shed him of the filth of the blade of Theodamus."

And the blade had fallen upon the earth. And Indra looked upon it, and her eyes narrowed, and her lips thinned, and she plucked it up and held it within her palm and looked upon it and thence unto Arminius, and spake:

"Indra shall hang this upon her coppered chain. Yea, yea, and when it rusteth she shall whet it upon thee, or yet upon Mary, or the thing thou holdest dearest."

And she pressed the wet blade unto her lips, and behold, blood shewed upon her flesh and her hand was wet of it. And she wiped this upon her mantle, and took up the chain that lay upon her breast and hanged the blade upon it, and leaned her swaying unto Arminius, saying:

"See thou, Arminius! Indra's love dyeth at the dying of flesh. Behold, Mary is a moonless night, yea, and a sunless day; and Indra is the night besprinkled of stars and glowing of silver. Yea, the sunnied day, glinted of the fullsome lights. Behold her and awake! Look! she would leave thee not lone."

And Arminius answered not. And the men listed and spake no words. And Indra made more of words, saying:

"Without Jerusalem Mary hath left her heart to stray. She hath bought thee with the kid's eyes, and wooed thee with the golden strands of her locks. Yea, but—" and Indra spake it soft—"without, without these walls, within Nazareth, is Hatte, her love. Even would she buy thee with the price of her flesh that he live. Ha, ha, ha! And thou art sweet-sicked and spilling the blood of thy brothers. She would buy thee that he live!"

And Arminius drew him up, even though the spilling of his blood had weakened him, and spake: "Even so would Arminius be bought that he live."

And Indra said: "Then thou wouldst of the pale bloom of Mary, when thou mightest pluck a purple lily?"

And Arminius answered not, and Indra spake: "Indra hath of all men within this wall—golds, stuffs, skins; but of thee but thy scorn."

And Arminius answered: "Yea, for a man who is rich in slaves is beggared of love."

And he turned him unto the men that had come unto the spot, they that stood guard, and spake: "Lend thee aid—I sink!"

And behold, they lended him their aid. And no man looked upon Indra. And she followed their going unto the within. And they bore Arminius unto his chamber and called forth slaves that should minister unto him.

CHAPTER III

AND word spread among the hall's people of what had been. And Indra sought the slaves' place, and behold, Mary had cast her upon the floor and wept. And the slaves had come unto her and stood them round and spake words of soothing unto her. Indra, seeing this thing, cried out:

"Leave thou this woman that she drown in her tears; for Rome would be rid of her. What! shouldst thou wail unto her; for is she not of Rome? Then he who is of a land should live the days of his land."

And Mary spake her: "It may not be, Indra, Mary liveth within her, and the day of Rome is like unto the creep of worms about her. Is this the hand of Rome upon Mary, this hand that clutcheth her she may not free her of, that sendeth chill unto her very flesh and maketh her nights frightful vasts of folly-dancing, that wearieth her even so that the morn findeth her spent?"

And Mary looked upon Indra, and lo, her eyes fell upon the blood that stained her mantle and she pointed unto it and cried:

"What! What! Speak thou! What is this?"

And Indra shrugged and spake: "Indra supped Theodamus and Arminius sought that he, too, sup, and he spilled his wine. Theodamus is an empty cup. Indra seeketh a new vessel."

And she touched the blade that hung about her neck and laughed and shewed it unto Mary and said:

"Indra would loose the skull of Arminius and drink his blood out of it! But Indra is weary and waiteth a new day, for Arminius is lacked of blood that she sup in full."

And Mary looked upon the blade and spake: "Indra, Indra doth fear not quake thee? Indra, is this thing the blade that hath done the deed?"

And she reached forth her hand that she touch it and drew it back hasted. And Indra laughed.

"Look upon it! It is but a blade, and hath done its task. Blades loose bloods. So be it."

And Mary shook, and spake in fright: "Indra, hath Theodamus slain Arminius?"

476

And Indra smiled slow and answered: "Nay. Theodamus was a camel who would have kicked at an ass, but the ass felled him. Mary, what is the golden light that springeth up at the touching of some new love? Indra deemed Theodamus a man, but Theodamus, ah, Theodamus was an ass! With his legs drunk he warred the sober Arminius. A man may woo drunk but not war drunk. Ah! ah! and Indra had all but the golden armlet. The morrow, the troth, and 'twere hers; but he is no more. And Arminius! a man unto the eyes, but empty, empty."

And Mary stood, her face white of fear, and Indra laughed unto her. And Mary murmured: "Thou dost weep not, and Theodamus no more?"

And Indra spake her: "Tears may not build a man back. Look, Mary! Is not this beetle beauteous? And the blade? See! golds gleam upon it, and a sapphire set amid it. 'Tis beauteous, beauteous! A one might e'en be willing that he fall beneath so beauteous a thing."

And Indra turned unto the handmaids and spake: "Begone! Bring forth fresh raiment. For who would look upon blood? Bring thou forth the purple robes that sheweth stranded of silver, and the sandals of silver whose rims are set of jades. Indra would seek without; for why mourn? The day hath but one morning. Why then should one live all the hours as morning? Why mourn in the night when new eves shall bring new loves?"

And she stripped her of the stained mantle and cast it from her and spake: "Fare ye well, Theodamus! Rome, bring forth thy new days."

And Mary stood looking upon Indra even as the handmaids robed her. And Indra looked unto Mary and spake, and angers mounted her eyes:

"So thou! The young lamb! Snowy white! Weak, bleating weak! Thou, the dove at the temple! Thou, the pured dews! Thou mayest bid a man to slay! Thou mayest enchain him upon thy bleating! Make of a man a goat!"

And she stretched forth her hand and grasped the hand of Mary, and drew her unto her, and with her free hand pressed the locks from off her brow, and looked deep within her eyes, wherein fright shewed, and she spake:

"Ugh! Thou lookest as a man who hath vomited the night through. Pale! Pale! Ugh! How might a man of red blood beget thee?"

And the slaves stood them listing, and they laughed one unto the other. And Mary stood trembled, and held forth her hands unto Indra and cried:

"Indra! Indra! Do not this thing unto thy sister. Dost thou remember not the house of Nadab wherein we sought shelter? Hast thou forgot the hut of Joel? And Panda! hast thou forgot the wisdom of Panda?"

And Indra leaned unto Mary and cried: "Speak! What was the wisdom of Panda?"

And Mary waited her, and spake slow: "Mercy, clothed of gentleness and bladed of a smile."

And Indra said: "Yea, but Panda plied his wisdom upon sheep, and they know not wisdom."

And Mary spake her: "Indra, Indra, wouldst thou betray thy very own? What hath Mary done?"

And Indra said: "Stop thy bleating! Thou shouldst be within some fold. Indra is the falcon, robed of pinions that will not of the dull day, but soareth up, up, up. But should the pinions fail, Indra would creep, like some green serpent upon its belly, among that she coveteth and receive it. Mary, leave thine eyes that they shew that that is within thee. Bare thy flesh and walk thee proud and Rome will bend unto thee. Why shouldst thou seek the shadows and court thy pallor when Rome offereth unto thee her sunlight's warmth? Indra shall rest her but that she grow more beauteous, that she take out of Rome her fullest price."

And Mary spake her unto Indra, saying: "Indra, how is this thing that thou shouldst learn thy tongue that it speak out such words, when thou knowest that within thee thy heart sheweth not that that thy tongue doth speak? Mary knoweth that thine eyes may weep, for Mary hath seen drops within them. Mary knoweth that thy heart may sorrow, for Mary hath seen sorrow's cloud upon thy brow. Indra, speak that thou art not what the eyes of Mary hath seen of thee. Speak it out."

And Indra spake: "What! thou wouldst that Indra strip her of what thine eyes have taken in, and shew unto thee but Indra as Indra is beneath the skin? Mary, what hath set thee that thou shouldst mourn o'er Indra? Is not a woman's flesh pure e'en though she doth leave filth to touch it, if she batheth her? For what may cling unto Indra's spirit that she hath done unto her flesh?"

And Mary's eyes started, and she spake heated words unto Indra, saying: "Indra, the thing that befalleth thy flesh marreth thy spirit! Look! a man's spirit may be blinded by his flesh's smite. Indra, thou hast lost thy wings, for wings be made of pinions, and flesh may not fly."

And Indra spake: "Upon earth there be no thing a man's legs may not lead him unto. Thou hast spoken of the wisdom of Panda.' Panda hath not wisdom, for Panda's wisdoms build paths that have by-paths and lead unto some unknown land that no man may look upon or know. Indra knoweth a man, a man of Jerusalem, whose wisdom fitteth her day. Behold, a man loseth his leg and he seeketh this one for his wisdom's lend, and this one speaketh: 'Thank thee that it be but one leg. Pluck up a staff and step thy day legless. 'Tis well; thank, thank. Doth a man o'ereat and lose his eat, 'tis a thing to sorrow o'er.'"

And Mary looked upon Indra in fearing and spake her: "Indra, dost thy tongue speak truth that thou mournest not Theodamus?"

And Indra laughed, laughed long, and amid her laughter cried: "Ha, ha! Theodamus! Ha, ha! Theodamus! Ha, ha! Where hath Indra—ha, ha!—heard of such a one? Did he step Rome's day? Pray, Mary, tell."

And Mary shook her head and spake: "Indra, Mary knoweth thee not as her sister. Where is Arminius?"

And Indra said: "Within some pured air, dreaming dreams of white days and whiter hours. Mary, wash thy fleece, for Arminius might set him filthed of e'en thy pure."

And Indra flung her upon the skin's spread. And she robed of the purple-clothed mantle stranded of silver, and her bare feet were shod of the sandals rimmed of jade, and the latchets were of silver strung of sapphires, and her locks were bound of silver cord, and at her brows were binded purple blooms. And she looked upon her flesh, robed so, and spake:

"Mary, look upon Indra, and this," and she touched her mantle. "What careth the flesh for wisdom? Wisdom causeth warring, Mary. When a man becometh o'erfull of wisdom he emptieth it upon his brothers. Look! the wise ones of Rome war, and the fools love. Look! doth a man have wisdom o'er other men, then they beset them. Look upon this Jesus of Nazareth. Rome spreadeth her nets that she bring Him unto her. And Hatte, whose crooked wisdom besetteth the days; even him they seek."

And Indra looked close unto Mary and spake her: "Mary, wouldst thou know Hatte's face should thine eyes rest upon it?"

And Mary answered: "Yea! Yea! Like unto the days of Bethlehem 'tis graven upon mine eyes. His locks would gleam bright; his eyes like unto a hawk's, bright, bright and keen; his lips wreathed of smiles; his youthed limbs strong; his breast high; his arms gleaming, strong and white! Ah, Mary should know him! Indra, thinkest thou that they shall bring him forth? Speak!"

And Indra answered: "Suredly; for Rome doeth that that she setteth unto. And Tiberius—ah, such a man! His wickeds make the wickeds of other men seem grinning follies!"

And Mary said: "Indra, Mary would seek Arminius, but Mary feareth."

And Indra laughed. "Thou fearest the sharp cut of loving glances? Ah, Mary, what fool begot thee?"

And it was true that without, within the hall's place, men spake of what had been. They breathed the name of Mary and spake of Flavius, and bade one unto the other that no word be spoken unto Flavius that he take in the fullness of what had been.

And Arminius had called forth ones that would come unto him, and he bade that he be borne unto the place where the mighty one had rested him. And it was true that this thing was done, and e'en before the coming of the down-sun Arminius had within his hands Mary's days,* even though his office had been stripped from him. And Flavius knew not.

For 'twas true that the tongue of Arminius had spoken words that offended much the mighty one, and his hand had displeased the high one that it felled Theodamus, and lo, the word was spoken that bade that he rest him within the halls but unto the time when his wound should stop. And 'twas spoken that Mary should be cast forth, for Rome's halls might not house a one not held of Rome. And Mary's days were within the hands of Arminius. And behold, Arminius arose, even off the couch whereon they had borne him unto the mighty one. And, even though his strength failed, he had spoken out that Rome might minister unto her men, but Theodamus had suffered the minister of Rome's man. Even so, that did a land offer not succor unto her daughters then her sons should forget, forget that this land be his and seek succor with his sister.

And the mighty one had listed not, but taken of the full price for the flesh of Mary, and had spoken unto them that listed that even though the hand of Arminius led forth Mary, he might not lead forth Flavius, but Flavius should be kept within the Rome's wall that he be emptied in full. And Arminius stretched forth his hands and spake unto them that stood:

"Hark ye! a man who shall empty him of Rome shall fill him upon

* Had bought her release.

a choicer stuff. Arminius shall drink the pure of love and know not women and woman's folly, but shall know one woman and her wisdom. Behold, within Rome abideth much wisdom, but they that keep of it keep it within jugs of folly."

And the men of the hall's place looked upon Arminius and spake: "What! thou wouldst waste thy strength, yea, cast thy office like an out-worn cloak and follow the steps of a woman?"

And Arminius answered: "Yea. What is an empty office but an out-worn cloak? Rome's nobles wear the cloth, and the slaves the heads." And he drew him high and spake: "Arminius casteth his noble name unto the winds and seeketh wisdom's deep."

And they asked of him: "Whither goest thou?"

And Arminius answered: "Since Rome would of this Nazarene, these eyes would look upon Him. He is creeping upon Jerusalem like an awful storm; for His wisdom purgeth like rain's wash. Yea, and Rome should fear, for Rome walloweth in oils and sweet stuffs, but of waters Rome drinketh little and washeth her less."

And he turned and went unto the slaves' place, weak-stepped. And he made sounds upon the doors'-ways, and behold, Indra arose and came swaying, like unto some glided thing of night, unto the spot, and she stood within the door's ope, robed of the purple, and upon her breast hung the blade and beetle.

And Arminius spake: "Bid thee that Mary come forth."

And Indra said: "Mary courteth dreams and prayeth unto the moon that she become whiter." And she looked unto Arminius with narrowed eyes and spake:

"Come thou, and Indra shall minister unto thee! Come! for thou hast weaked beneath thy blood-flowing."

And Arminius said: "Call thou unto Mary!"

And Indra laughed and spake, even as she spread forth her hands, ringed much and glittered: "Indra is weary. Call thou unto Mary." And she laughed. "Art thou then afraid that thou shouldst be lain low shouldst thou enter the slaves' hall? Ah, Arminius, the in-ways bring unto the in from without. Rome careth not. The slaves' hall blusheth not. Enter!"

And Arminius called the name of a slave who played upon reeds, and she came unto him, and he called her "Ursa," and said that she should bring forth Mary. And Ursa cast her reeds unto the earth and knelt before him. And he spake him: "Go!"

And she went within and came forth leading Mary. And Arminius said: "Mary, 'tis done."

And Mary spake: "What meanest thou?—that thou hast slain Theodamus?"

And Arminius answered: "Yea, this is done, and thou art the flesh of Arminius."

And Mary stood still, and her eyes lighted bright and her lips shook and she threw her hands forth and cried:

"Mary may go from out these walls? Mary may know the fields whereon no jewel sheweth? Mary may pure her within the waters of the morning dews? Arminius, when may this thing be?"

And Arminius swayed, for he was weak, and answered: "Speak no word, Mary, but go and bring forth thy goods."

And Mary said: "Nay, Arminius, Mary hath but a mantle of coarse stuffs that is hers, and sandals of grass. These would she take, and leave Rome's cloth to cover Rome's."

And Arminius said: "Even so Arminius. He shall seek with thee."

And Indra listed and spake amid sneers: "Beggars! There be not enough but these would fellow with them."

And they listed not, but Arminius gave unto the hands of the men his blade and even so his girdle; and unto ones that had been unto him loved, his rings and armlets; and unto them also delivered he his togas and mantles and even his metals of office. And they offered that they bear him and Mary unto the spot they would seek. And Arminius said:

"We seek amid Jews. Unto the house of Isaac seek we."

And the Rome's men looked upon him and cried out: "What! then thou shalt fellow with Jews? Knowest thou not that no Jew holdeth within him love for them of Rome?"

And Arminius spake unto them saying: "Even so no man of Rome holdeth o'er his filling of love for a Jew. But this man, Isaac, hath lended unto Romans his wisdom and hath been e'en as a brother unto them, and Arminius knoweth him and his household. Yea, and Arminius would seek him and know the fullness of Rome's cunning 'gainst this Nazarene, and this one, this Hate, that all men know yet all men may see not, for Rome hath sought him out and ne'er hath a man lain hands upon him."

And they laughed at the words of Arminius and spake: "Knowest thou not that the flesh that Rome seeketh is the flesh of Tiberius? Tiberius feareth the flesh he hath brought forth amid his slave's flesh."

And Arminius spake not, but made him words unto them at the later time when he had stood lone and they had cried out unto him: "Dost thou go without the sorrow that befitteth a brother at the going?"

And Arminius spake slow: "Yea, for e'en though Rome will not of her son; e'en though Rome dealeth falsely unto her smitten ones that they fall sorer smitten, still Rome is fair and Rome is the land of her son. Yet Arminius, who loveth Rome and hath shed for her his blood, goeth, and Rome careth naught. Nay, nor yet doth Rome reach forth that she hide her daughter's shame. Look ye! was this woman, Mary, a Jew, Jews would stone her, for no woman who had shewn her naked before the host might be called clean amid the Jews. Yet Rome would leave this thing to be. Yea, Rome would care naught but laugh in merry-make unto the shame of her maiden."

And the men that stood them about spake: "Nay, Arminius, rememberest thou not that we amid the hall did hide us that we look not upon her, and there is not one among us that would not to hold thee o'er all among us for that thou didst deal thy mantle unto her. Go thou, Arminius, and though Rome remembereth thee not, thy brothers shall remember!"

And Arminius turned and held forth his hands in sign that he would be gone, and spake:

"Doth the brothers remember, then the land shall remember, too; for the brothers be the heart of the land."

And he turned that he seek out Mary and make them ready that they be gone.

CHAPTER IV

And 'twas the high sun, and Jerusalem's street's-ways shewed hot and bright-gleamed. And the men came them from out the shadow's-ways wherein they cooled, and behold, e'en before they had gone them seven score leg-spans they sweated unto the shining. And the dogs lay at the house walls, and their tongues dripped and their ears backed and their bellies heaved. And the packs made wet spots upon the sides of the asses. And the temple doves flew them unto the shade, and their wings hung and they oped their bills and panted. And the market's places smelled; the fruits' rots sent up scents and the fishes sweat unto the stinking. And the sheep that had been driven up unto the market's places sent up wool scents.

And within a bin sat a one who plucked wools and set into heaps. And his head was bald, and his beard hung long and whited of the wools. And within this spot there hung sacks of wools and dried fruits. And behold, a youth came up unto the bin-side and the bald one cried out unto him: " Isaac! "

And Isaac held within his hands a jug of milch, and the bald one brought forth fruits and weighed them within his hand that he deal unto Isaac for the sup of milch that his bowl would hold. And Isaac poured forth the milch, and he stood that he look upon the bald one sup it. And when the bald one had supped all of it he wiped his beard upon his hands and his hands upon the wools. And Isaac spake unto the bald one, saying:

" There hath been much that hath befallen within the Rome's halls. 'Tis told that one of the slaves was brought forth and stripped and the men within the hall's place looked not upon her but turned their backs and hid her shame from them."

And the bald one laughed and his shrunk form shook and he said: " This is no thing for to tempt wonder, for all Rome's ones are fools. Think thou what fools these men shewed them."

And Isaac shook his head and spake: " Thou art a fool, Abraham, and thy sire's sire a fool."

And Abraham said: " Fools beget fools, even as swine ever beget swine. 'Tis well, then, that Abraham be like his kind."

And Isaac spake: "But thou knowest Arminius, the nobled one?"

And Abraham answered him: "Yea, Arminius, who weareth a blade and covereth it with blossoms; who would war with honey and shoo the bees before him. Yea, like unto one who taketh all the sweets, nor would he e'en lend a rest unto the storer of the sweets. He taketh from out Rome the sweets and leaveth the war's men that they war while he dippeth his fruits within sticky honeys and eateth them. Yea, shooeth the bees before him."

And Isaac said: "But he hath stung him this day. Behold, he hath let the blood of Theodamus flow. Yea, he hath slain him o'er the slave, Mary."

And Abraham laughed. "'Tis well. E'en a drone may sting and die."

And Isaac spake him: "Yea, but Indra, the she-serpent, hath bitten him upon his heel, and he hath trod like unto a war's man this day, for he hath done with Rome and given forth his all within the Rome's halls. Yea, he hath e'en now left him and hath sought my sire's house-hold. Abraham, what meanest thou that Arminius is the one that shooeth the bees before him?"

And Abraham looked unto Isaac and spake: "What! thou, a young lad, dost deem that thy depth be deep enough that thou mightest take in the wisdom of Abraham? List thou! Look unto yon ass! his ears be long. Look thou unto yon camel! his neck be long. Look thou unto yon son of a Jew! his head is deep, and yon one, his head is shallow. This is wisdom, yet thou mayest not understand it."

And Isaac shook his head.

"Abraham, thou mayest be wise, and thy mantle of words sheweth wise, but thou hast a fool's cunning that no man may full understand thee."

And there came unto the bin's place a youth and his brother. And they had set them hot one unto the other o'er the meting * of their fruits. And behold, these fruits were grapes and ripe figs; and the figs were big and of a lusciousness. And the eyes of Abraham looked upon them.

And there were upon the tray three of figs and seven full twigs of grapes. And they shewed these unto Abraham and spake:

"How may this thing be done rightly? For look ye, my brother loveth not the fig and I care me but for grape. Yea, but my belly taketh in the figs e'en so well as his. How mayest this thing be done?"

And Abraham looked upon them, and rubbed upon his bald head

* Measuring; dividing.

and stroked his beard, and plucked forth a fig and eat of it and shut one eye up and spake: " This fig is blight-smitten."

And they looked upon him and said: " Yea, but the others shew them perfect."

And Abraham spake: " Yea, but how may a man know that this be true save that he eat of one? "

And he plucked forth another of the figs and eat of it slow and shut up one eye and spat, and spake: " It hath a worm at heart."

And they cried out: " But one remaineth! "

And Abraham spake: " 'Tis well."

And he broke ope the fig and offered unto Isaac the half, and said: " Taste thou this that thou mayest testify."

And he eat of the other half and spake: " 'Tis sour."

And Isaac's lips shewed smiled cunning, and he eat of his half and said: " Yea, 'tis sour."

And Abraham plucked up one of the grape twigs and ate therefrom. And the brothers cried: " But thou hast eat the figs and thou now hast plucked of the grapes. 'Tis enough! Dost thou then tell unto the listing of us that thou shalt mete out this ware? Where is thy wisdom? "

And Abraham looked unto them and spake: " When thou didst seek Abraham thou hadst of figs and grapes, and now," and he shrugged, " thou hast not figs, and less of grapes, and more of wisdom. For thou knowest thou hast lost. Go thou and mete the six remaining twigs. Abraham hungereth for one."

And he sat him down for to eat the seventh twig. And the brothers clamored them loud and spake words against his wisdoms and told that he had eat their wares when 'twas known that wisdoms should be free dealt. And Abraham laughed unto Isaac and spake:

" But a wise man whose wisdom taketh naught out of a fool is not a wise one. Thou hast to learn that thou mayest not sole a sandal with wisdom, nay, but with hides. Yea, and a wise man maketh the sole of the hide of a fool. And Abraham hath his sandals both soled, for thou art a twain of fools. Begone! "

And they went, still crying out 'gainst the dealings of Abraham. And Isaac said unto them as they went their ways: " Begone! One dealing of a follied wise man is enough."

And he turned him unto Abraham and spake: " Then this is thy manner of dealing. Thou art e'en so crooked as thy wisdom; for thy wisdoms mean naught."

And Abraham said: " Thou hast spoken that the wisdom of Abraham

meaneth naught? Paugh! Is not his belly full of figs, and yet a twig
of grapes remaineth? His wisdom hath meant this much."

And Abraham plucked one of the grapes and smacked upon it, and
then another, and shut his eyes and swallowed slow, and cast the skin
unto the street's-way, slow, and spake:

"It is right and meet that Abraham share his profit with the flies."

And he plucked one grape and looked upon it and spake unto it, saying: "Is it not well that thou shalt feed a wise man?" And he
swallowed it.

And Isaac watched him and said: "Thou wouldst share with the
flies, but not with thy brother Isaac."

And Abraham raised his shoulders and spread his hands, and within
hung the grape's twig, and he said:

"Nay; 'tis not well for a man, whose belly would take not in the
slaying, that he eat of the meats. Look ye! there be men who vomit at
the seeing of the lamb's slaying. Thou art one of these. Begone!
There remaineth but two grapes upon the twig and Abraham would not
have one lone for the other."

And he stopped his words and spake: "Come thou unto Abraham;
he thirsteth. Here!" And he plucked up some dried fruit and weighted
it out and offered unto Isaac that he sup more of milchs. And Isaac
dealt unto him. And Abraham took up the bowl's full and drank deep,
and sucked his beard and left the milk that it wash within his mouth at
the second supping, for he left it unto the fore of his cheeks, then unto the
back.

And Isaac spake, when he had watched long: "Abraham, 'tis not
only the slaying that sicketh a man."

And Abraham had supped the bowl unto the emptying, and he
fanned him with the bowl, and the flies swarmed o'er milch drops and
the fruits, and he wafted them thence.

And Isaac said: "Thou art like unto Jacob, one among the flies
that beset the market's place."

And Abraham cried: "Like unto Jacob? By the holy veil! By the
inner sacrament! By the flesh of my mother! By the lies that hold
my sire out of the Promised Land! By the slender hope that Abraham
holdeth that he ever see the spot! He speaketh that Abraham is like unto
Jacob! He hath spoken it. Do my ears hear aright? For Jacob is a
fool. He is pence wise, but Abraham, ah, Abraham weaveth a strand
strong to hang his brother, but he lendeth not his head for the hanging. By the horn of the sacred cow! Do ye hark? He hath spat upon
the spirit of Abraham!"

And he stopped and smiled and his eyes glinted and he spake: " See! Abraham would deal not unto thee as thou hast dealt. See! "

And he took up dried fruits and offered unto Isaac. And Isaac took them from out his hands and said:

" What! thou wouldst give unto Isaac of thy spiced dried fruits? "

And Abraham rose him up solemn and spake: " Yea; 'tis thine. Abraham would shew thee the besting of thee."

And Isaac sat him down and tasted of the fruits, and they tasted full well, and he looked not upon them but unto Abraham, and spake:

" Abraham, Isaac hath spoken with o'erspeeded words. He hath misjudged thee."

And Abraham spread his hands and drew his face long and shook his head in sorrow. And Isaac made more of words:

" Since, then, thou hast bested of the fools, 'tis thy right that thou shouldst fat o'er it."

And Abraham spake not but watched Isaac eat of the fruits, and when he had eaten all of them, Isaac arose and rubbed his belly and said:

" Abraham, a blessing shall befall thee, for Isaac thankest thee fully for what he hath eat. Thou mayest deal crooked wisdom, but thy fruit is good. What befell thee that thou didst give it unto the hand of Isaac? "

And Abraham plucked at his beard and rubbed his thin palms upon his knees, and looked afar and spake:

" 'Twere well to have it o'er. Yet a score of days and the worms would have eaten them, for they had bedded within them."

And Isaac cried out against such a dealing. And Abraham said:

" 'Tis well; for thou hast found thee that thy belly will take in worms e'en so well as it will take in the wisdoms of Abraham."

And Isaac spake him: " Abraham, this is merry-make. But list thee! Thou hearest the market's prattle. They have spoken that the Nazarene telleth He hath come that the Word be fulfilled. And Paul hath come from out Nazareth bearing word that Rome's men followed upon the path that the man, Panda, went, for they knew that he sought this Hate one, even though his words spake he sought the Nazarene. But Paul went by the way of Galilee, and the Rome's men heard among the Galileans that he would seeek not on; for they ate and slept them in rest upon the shore. And they told that Panda had spread words among the fishers that he might dwell there in Galilee and weave nets. And even before the Rome's men had sought them out they had fled. And they had followed unto Nazareth even, though Panda had thought that he blind them. But the lad that Paul sought was not with them at Galilee. This had come back unto the Rome's ones. And they came upon him they had claimed within the hill's-ways upon Jordan's way, but this man they found was lame and his face shewed scarred and he was one who besetteth the flocks that stray. And so these men of Rome deemed not 'twas the man they sought. And when they had worded with him he spake wickeds and when they spake more had shut him up and made no answering. And Paul told among the Jews that he had seen they were followed and he had spoken unto Panda: ' Bear unto the river way.' For they had stopped within the hills and had sought the lad even off the way that led unto Nazareth, for they had followed the word of them they met."

And Abraham listed and rubbed his knees and Isaac made on, saying: " Paul knoweth much, Abraham. He bore word for Levi and hath returned with much word from out Nazareth of this Jesus. He sayeth that within the synagogue He ariseth and readeth out the scripts and the words each seem a score and that that confoundeth cleareth as salted water. He hath spoken unto the people even within the streets. It is said that they follow Him and come unto Him with their woes and hopes. And unto them that speak out unto Him but believe not in their hearts He sayeth, ' Shew thou thyself unto the priests.'

" And they seek Him and tell unto His ears that there are some in Nazareth that would not of Him. And He sayeth unto them that a man might root within the land that bore him but He should branch upon the far places and blossom farther still.

" He troubleth not o'er that that troubleth men and woeth o'er that that woeth not man. When a man's flesh falleth fevered do they call upon His aid He goeth thereto and doth He find the fever cometh out of the o'erladen spirit—hath the man done wrongly and suffereth the hot of shame—'tis told that He ministereth unto him. And be it this thing, He freeth his spirit of the pack, and behold, the fever falleth low. But be it but flesh, He careth little.

" He hath spoken that there be two things that befalleth a man that setteth his flesh sick: he hath sinned, or his flesh hath worn it o'er labor or time's bite. He hath said that sinning setteth up flesh-rot * and is not of His Father's handiwork. The body, He hath told, is a vessel, and doth a man put within his vessel that that it be not fashioned for to hold, he suredly shall wear it or yet break it.

" Yea, and He hath told that did not sin write upon a man's flesh, and the writing hurt sore, he would fall short of his days; for his vessel

* Disease.

would ne'er hold. In these words hath He told that unto a man a bowl
is but a bowl, and a scar upon it but a scar and yet a break but a break;
for he may take him a new bowl. But his body crieth out at his own sinning. This is the chiding, for He speaketh that doth a man heed the
crying out, his vessel will last. And this is within the hand of man and
not the hand of His Father.

"Yet there be men that write upon their flesh so deep that it floweth
within the blood of their kind. And this man is an abomination and
shall be called that he wipe out the scripts he hath writ. Doth his flesh
come forth empty, as a fool, through his sinning, then he shall fill their
empty, even though 'tis within a new day.

"His Father's land, He hath told, Abraham, is a land where thou
art dealt fully unto. He that is empty shall be filled, for the empty ones
be the flowers of the full-dealt tree. Man is like unto a tree, and his
blood floweth out unto the last small bud, and even though this bud
leaf not, it holdeth that that maketh the leaf and shall burst unto a
leaf. He hath spoken this, Abraham. Is it not wisdom?

"And He hath spoken more: that the scripts upon earth are the
shadows of wisdom, yet man seeth wisdom within the scripts. Writ
words make no sound, yet loud noises. Out of the shadows which are
scripts man plucketh him a thing that is his. Nor doth he pluck it off
the scripts, for his brother may pluck, and his brother's brother, and
take unto them.

"Of such is the wisdom of heaven, He hath told, for it is the thing
that hangeth upon the scripts and maketh them bottomless pits of
wisdom."

And Abraham had let his jaw drop, and the flies crept upon his
hands, and he listed, and spake:

"This is like unto the waters of Jordan when the rain hath swept—
too thick that these eyes see the fish. Who is this Father He speaketh
of? A man might be glad o'er such a one. Scripts be shadows, Isaac,
when Abraham's eyes hath seen hands trace them? This young Jew
is weaving a strand and shall lend his head for the hanging. A dead
bud shall leaf? Hark thee," and he called unto a market's brother;
"do hark unto this man! He hath madded him!"

And Isaac spake: "Call not, Abraham—list! Thou knowest
Indra?"

And Abraham said: "What! thou pratest of wisdom and falleth
unto the pit of woman!" And he started and spake: "What hath this
wise Jew of Nazareth to speak upon woman? For no man is so tall that
he bend not unto some woman."

And Isaac said: " He loveth none, but His mother abideth with Him."

And Abraham smiled and spake: " 'Tis not enough that a man love not a woman but that she love him that he be saved; for woman will have of man. He, thou speakest, loveth not a woman? Then hark! a woman shall hang him."

And Isaac said: " Nay, Abraham, the Jews know Him even though thou, whose wisdoms lay like crossroads upon the temple's teachings, speakest 'gainst Him. He hath fastened upon the Jews. Abraham, Isaac loveth this one, His clean words; for what hath come hath washed the temple's teachings clean, and he findeth that the God may abide the day even out from behind the temple's walls. This is good, for a man loneth for his God and feareth, should the temple fall, where He would flee and where a man should seek Him."

And Abraham spake him unto Isaac, saying: " What hath this Nazarene done that a Jew should believe that out from the lowliest should spring forth a king? "

And Isaac answered him: " Abraham, thou settest and dealest thy wickeds and oilest thy words that they be swallowed with more ease, but this Jew, Jesus, hath words that shew a thousand shadows. Levi hath fallen in his faith that this man is the Promised One."

And Abraham stretched him unto his utmost and yawned in weariness and spake:

" Bring not forth Levi. Levi is dead, and a dead man is nothing to look upon. A dead Jew is but like unto a dead fly; for his wisdom is gone. And the fly is fit food for the birds that seek, and the Jew but good carrion. What should keep the eyes of Abraham that they sleep not so that he find a god? Hath not the Jews shut the God unto them; builded up walls about Him? Leave then the priests to set them that He flee not while Abraham sleepeth. Call thou yon man Isaac! Call thou! He hath palm's leaves and this God hath let the heat to burn. Call! "

And Isaac spake him: " Nay, Abraham, list! What doth Indra seek thee for? "

And Abraham answered: " For wisdom. Look! Indra hath learned Abraham's wisdom and hath turned her eyes and her lips, yea, and her fullsome flesh, unto gains. She hath brought word of this pale one, this Mary, a Greek, who leaveth her eyes to be lack-luster-dim of weeping, that Rome would have her play and be her daughter. This is woman, Isaac. When thou findest one that will thou shalt find twoscore that will and will not. Abraham will of no woman. Who is this man that Indra calleth Hate? "

And Isaac answered: " I know not save that Rome talketh among her men and they seek them one and it seemeth that this one is the Jew, Jesus, and yet some men speak his name Hate."

And Abraham spake: " Indra hath told that this man, Hate, is mad, and hath been smitten, and she would that Abraham send a messenger unto Nazareth to bring forth his where-abiding. And Abraham hath told unto Indra that it taketh much within his palm's weighting that shall send forth this one upon the path. Well? Abraham waiteth."

And Isaac had listed long unto the wisdom of Abraham and set him that he see the market's deal and take, and when he had heard this from Abraham's lips he started him up and spake:

" The milch doth sour, and behold, the skin leaketh. Isaac shall seek his father's house."

And he made way among the brothers of the market's-way, and they called unto him " Isaac! " and made the sign of greeting as he went. And the elders he passed head-bowed, and they spake: " God's peace upon thee," " Be thy days fruitful," and the words that meant the dealing of day's joys unto their brothers.

And Isaac shouldered him among the market's men and sought the street's-ways and set upon the path unto his father's household, and when he had come unto the spot, behold, the eve had come unto the dimming of day and within shewed the tapers lit and the smoke hung the air.

And his sire, Isaac, sat him cross-legged upon a sack of dried stuffs. And Arminius stood him up and spake words of what had been within the Rome's place. And Mary stood and listed. And it was true that they had emptied unto Isaac's sire, and Arminius had offered him unto the days of Jerusalem that he do work for bread. And Isaac had spoken unto him:

" Nay; this thing is not the thing that thou shouldst do. Hast thou aught within thy breast that is thine? "

And Arminius drew forth a sack and shewed his store and it was plenteous, but he spake: " How may this last doth not Arminius begin his labors? "

And he stretched his arms wide and drew them up and stood him unto his full height and looked unto Mary, and drew him a deep breath and spake clear:

" To be free! To wield thy strength for love! Oh, ye gods, what it meaneth! "

And Isaac spake: " And thou sayest thou wouldst seek the Nazarene, or this man Hate? "

And Arminius answered: "Yea; I seek the Nazarene; and Mary, Hate."

And Isaac spake: "Rome hath done with thee and Mary, but she may hunger and seek thee. Go thou unto a sheik and take his reins and seek ye out of Jerusalem unto Nazareth. They abide them there. Isaac knoweth. Go and bear thee this—" and he brought forth a white-skin such as they scribed upon, and spake: "See ye unto it that it be filled and returned. This is the sign of the Nazarene. And the Jews glut o'er the scripts, for they have woven Him a kingly robe."

And they worded long unto the night. And it was true that the morn found Arminius and Mary upon their ways. And Jerusalem had known them not among her men, and Rome had forgot that the flies had alighted upon her wares and flown.

CHAPTER V

AND the tides held hots and cools, and swept unto the full of seasons, and behold, it was young year, the bud tide, and the skies had wept the winters gray to blue.

And Rome shewed; her temples white, her pillared walls, her streets-ways, her garden places, her pools, her founts, rich robed of sun's gold. And the palace spread it wide, and flowers shewed grown unto its very wall's rims. And alabaster gods glinted white amid the green, and fountains flashed, to glisten 'neath the sun. And the chariots' wheels rumbled afar and even among the greens shewed they, and the flesh of the steeds shone and their trappings glinted rich of precious stuffs.

And lo, at a shadowed spot, knelt one at a fountain's side. And she loosed her locks and leaned far that she look upon her water-image, and her hands felt o'er her cheeks and slipped amid the shining strands, and she looked deep and deep, and arose and spread her locks forth and left them fall and the shining gold covered her. And her lips moved and she spake:

"He hath fled Theia. He knew her not. Ah, Venus, lend thou thy spell!"

And she stood her long, looking unto all ways slow, and raised her arms high and clasped her hands behind her head and spake even unto her own listing:

"The morning cometh and sayeth, wait; and noons come and speak, wait; and eves come and whisper, wait; and night sobbeth wait, wait, wait, wait, wait. Ah!" and she sobbed; "Theia hath waited, waited!" And she shut her lips thin and hissed: "It shall be!"

And she sat her down, spent, and looked upon her mantle that was fashioned of coarse stuffs, and her hands she busied at the putting away of her locks beneath cloth. And behold, when she had finished, her head was bound even as the men slaves binded of theirs. And she arose, and her feet shewed sandaled of grass, and her limbs bare.

And behold, a lad, black and shining, ran unto the spot and said unto her that Legia called. And Theia smiled and spake:

"Yea, tell unto her that I come."

And she followed the naked one through the thick growth and o'er the soft grasses and past the cool waters. And she looked upon the alabaster gods and her lips curled and she said:

"So, thou art gods, to stand ye gazing upon this!" And she covered her eyes and cried aloud: "What tarriest thee? Oh, Jehovah, strike them down!"

And she sped up and o'er the stoned steps and through the shadowed cool of the pillar's hollow. And her grass sandals sounded soft upon the stones. And men came and went and the slaves sped, and the noble's slaves shewed reclined upon soft couches within the chambers upon the way. And she went unto the spot where the chambers stood and she came unto one who lay sleeping. Dark her locks and glistened o'er of gold dusts and her white flesh gleamed and her eyelids lay their lashes long upon it. And her lips shewed full and her mantle had oped and her white breast shewed and it rose and fell soft. And within her hand was clasped a fan wove of feather and the hand was heavy of jewels.

And Theia stood o'er her and looked long and no eye saw. And she knelt and touched the soft arms with her slim fingers and raised the shining locks within her hands and looked on high and spake:

"Ah, for this! For this is youth."

And the maid waked, and her eyes shone dark, soft dark, and she looked upon Theia as she knelt and asked: "What meanest thou?"

And Theia answered not and the maiden asked her once more: "What meanest thou?"

And Theia spake: "Why should Theia tell thee, for youth may not take it in."

And Legia smiled and said: "Theia, that thou shouldst know all of the wisdoms thou dealest unto Legia, it seemeth thy head should burst. See! is not the day fair? Is not Legia loved? Is she not one among the slaves of the noble sire? Hath she not all of earth she would of? It is such a happy day!"

And Theia spake her: "This is true, Legia, true. Theia knoweth how true. But this day of Rome and the morrow of Rome and the morrows of many morrows shall be like butterflies that glint the day. Each day shall die even so, and not e'en its shadow linger. Thou shalt see, Legia. At some morn thou shalt look upon a gray sky and yon, yon, yon, afar, the gleaming wings of these days shall shew fleeting, fleeting from thee. Not e'en the tender dusts that cling shall be thine."

And Theia touched the jewels upon the flesh of Legia and spake: "Thinkest thou that these have hearts within them? Nay. And when thy heart is bruised, what soft comfort may they lend? Ah, Legia, wake and know the day!—not the folly-decked day but the stark day that beggeth thee."

And Legia said: "But Theia, look! Thou dost sorrow and thou knowest the stark day. Why wouldst thou then that Legia know this day? for Legia's eyes glisten of happiness."

And Theia answered: "Yea, Theia knoweth the stark day, and knoweth that happiness is but the cloud that beareth rain."

And Legia arose and sat upon the couch and wafted the fan and turned unto Theia and spake:

"Theia, it hath come unto Legia that thou hast a cloth that thou dost weave. What is this thing? It is spoken that it is even as mists and that thou art ever busy, busy."

And Theia sunk upon the floor and sat her at the feet of Legia and spake: "List! list! list! Look upon Theia, thy handmaid. See! she is but dusts, dull dusts. Yet Theia hath danced as yon bright beam that glinteth through the ope. Her feet sped upon happiness. Yea, happiness was spread as a cloth for her to trod. And Theia knew Rome. Even these walls had looked upon her youth, decked as thee. Theia—ah, dared she tell——"

And Legia looked upon the wet eyes of Theia and lay her arm about her and said:

"Speak! Speak! Slaves be slaves e'en though one be unto the noble and the other unto the palace. Theia, thy words strike fear here," and she touched her heart o'er. "Speak!"

And Theia wiped her eyes upon her mantle and spake: "Theia is little. Legia, the days were as thine save that thou art a woman of many, and Theia, Theia was but the prey of one. Yea, a noble gave unto Theia a jewel and he hath taken out of her the price sevenscore o'er and o'er."

And Legia questioned: "Who is he?"

And Theia answered: "I dare not e'en raise mine eyes lest this jewel be his."

And Legia spake: "Who is he? Speak! Legia shall slip his ribs with this," and she drew forth a thin blade.

And Theia spake her: "Nay. Nay. Theia held this thought within her. She deemed she might ope him, but there is one that stoppeth her, and He is Jehovah, or Him o'er all whoe'er He be. For knowing Him maketh a one o'er his day. His wisdom is the rein that, once within one's hands, he may drive his days o'er the gray ways, past the pits, up, up, up! And the very hate that lieth here for this one is rotted. Mine eyes look upon him and see—ah, Legia, 'tis mockery!—within his face the image of the one Theia loveth o'er all."

And Legia spake: "Wert thou then the love of some gamester or a bladesman? Didst thou see the backs of the discus casters heave and billow, and didst thou leave thy love to abide there?"

And Theia answered: "Nay."

And Legia spake: "What is the thing that causeth Tiberius to bid thee to dance? He looketh not upon thee and calleth thee the dead woman. And they mock thee; for thou art clothed as a woman's woman.* What merriment may this bring?"

And Theia said: "He calleth Theia the dead woman! He knoweth not that he is dead and that his grinning carcass still playeth, pitifully clinging unto days, when his spirit is rotten. He hath dealt from out his kingdom the most precious stuff his fool-rid day e'er held. He liveth. Yea, afar he liveth. And this is the only living worthy that earth record of him. Yet he would take——"

And she stopped. And Legia looked unto her, and her eyes started forth and she cried:

"What hast thou spoken? Is Tiberius he? Hath the mighty one cast thee unto this? Speak! Theia, is this the end?"

And she shrunk and cast her within the arms of Theia. And Theia spake:

"Legia, thou hast it; for Theia loveth thee. Even in serving thee hath she touched the flesh of youth, and her arms, entwined about thee, dreamed 'twas him afar. And Theia feareth, for Hassan hath gone long, long, and no word cometh. And Hassan is sure as the sun."

And Legia spake: "But this cloth, Theia; what is this cloth?"

And Theia murmured: "They have borne the jewel far, and Theia, serving here, is the door that defendeth him—shutteth him away. They have brought her forth and set threats, but Theia feareth not; for his legs are strong and he is beauteous. And some morn shall come and his deeds shall show him his blood's son, if not his sire's; for his sire is unworthy.

"And Theia hath naught, Legia, naught, and at this tide she shall be happy and would dance. At the dark hours she keepeth her feet light. Theia hath no robe. Nay, the mist robe is gone, and the vanities and the cloths have rotted; but look!"

And she oped her mantle and took forth a cloth like unto a spider's web, wove of her locks.

"This is Theia's, out of her very blood. Rome gave it not unto her! And each strand was plucked and caused pain, and the pain, joy. And the weaving hath spun hope."

* A woman's slave.

And Legia leaned unto it and touched the gleaming threads and spake: " But thou hast naught but this to deck thee? "

And Theia smiled and said: " Thou knowest not the dance of Theia."

And Legia spake her: " Dancing wearieth."

And Theia cried: " Nay! dancing maketh the sky seem nearer; maketh the moon many, and the stars many, many, many more. And it stirreth the dead heart."

And Legia asked: " Who is this one, this jewel? "

And Theia leaned close and spake: " Legia, thou art young. Thou knowest not what it meaneth to bring forth of thee. This one is mine. He is mine. He is mine; for upon him is the sign of hate. And he knoweth sorrow. He is his mother's son.

" Wait! Wait! " And Theia swayed. " Theia seeth Hassan and he listeth unto a young man. His eyes are full of love and he harketh close. And Panda harketh and a fair one, a maid. Hassan speaketh. Ah, it is Hatte! See! he is tall and hath his beard, and he is sweet-worded, and is before the multitude. He is his own man. Hark! what sayeth he? All men are my brothers! Wait! Nay, a one cometh who limpeth and hath a smitten face, and a fool followeth. And this one speaketh: ' Hatte! Hatte! He is gone. Where to? ' And the fool laugheth.

" What, what is this thing? For he is beauteous and strong and they list unto him. List! the smitten one speaketh: ' Nay man is my brother. I am empty.' Ah," and she cried out: " Look thou! Look! This is Theia! "

And she arose and swayed more and spake: " He turneth. His lips cease their music. He looketh! "

And she threw her arms wide and stopped, and her jews fell ope and she gasped and spake hollow:

" His eyes look and they shew flowing drops, yet smiling. And o'er him, what? A tree of thorns! Yea—wait! And he plucketh a branch and offereth it unto the smitten one. Wait! And the smitten one—ah, he hath kissed it!

" Stop! Stop! By the gods, stop that I see! It is gone! Hatte! Hatte! Hatte! "—and she beat her bosom—" Leave me not! Legia! " —and she stood, her eyes ablaze—" Legia, thou knowest not the aching of these arms. Oh, the nights fill them not, nor the days, nor the things of day. They are empty as yon sky and throb in aching. And yon, he who is dead still clingeth to his days. He hath emptied these arms, this heart, these days and the tides; but all of these are not so empty as he.

"And wait! A hand shall shut from him all that is his, the breath he breathes! He shall die, eyes oped, that he see his end! It is true. The gods shall forsake him. He hath caused new gods but they have not bellies that they fatten and shall die. With his hands hath he fashioned them and with their nothingness shall they repay him. He shall swallow his tongue. He shall die and no man shall aid. His tongue shall shoot forth and stop him. He shall lap at the airs as a dog lappeth waters.* It is written and shall be!"

And Theia sat her down upon the couch slow and her bosom heaved, and her eyes were shut, and she passed her hands weary o'er her brow. And lo, the cold of sweat had wet it, and she spake not. And Legia was frighted and arose and came unto her and spake:

"What is this thing? Thou hast slept and dreamed aloud. Awake! what phantom hath beset thee? Tell thou, is not all of this a dream?"

And Theia answered: "What mattereth this? If a man suffereth within his flesh amid his dream it is even so real as his suffering at waking, be his flesh already dead of suffering. Theia feeleth within her that Tiberius knoweth that them about him would hang him even with their glances; for his cunning is wicked and his wisdom bitter. He is a good judge, yet his acts o'erturn his judging. His days are, one filled of attainment, the other the attainment forgot; one filled of loving, the other the loving forgot. It is Tiberius. He is ice or water. He knoweth that Hassan hath told among his courtsmen much. He knoweth that Theia hath flesh afar. He knoweth that Hassan's sword wieldeth the plebeians, and he knoweth among them they would undo him. Hassan hath told among the people, the plebeians, the thing I have spoken, and they would cut the throat of Tiberius and raise up his flesh. Tiberius knoweth not that Hassan's smiling wisdom's-deal be a two-edged blade.

"It is written. It is written. Yea, in scarlet sign upon the skies. He shall spill a wine that he may ne'er stay, and it shall stain the whole earth and clothe him in the robe of shame. Legia, list! 'Tis written, and Theia seeth it. He may ne'er swim this sea of scarlet!"

And Legia clutched at the flesh of Theia and shook and cried:

"Stop! Stop! Sister, stop thy words. Din not these ears and set up fearing. What biddeth thee? Thy tongue is tipped of fires and thine eyes shoot forth sparks. Speak out! Why dost thou cast thy words even as coals upon the head of Tiberius? for thou dwellest within his walls! Theia, Hassan may turn but a hand's full of Rome's dusts."

* According to Suetonius, Tiberius was strangled by Caligula, his successor.

And Theia spake her: "Yea, this be truth, but among this hand's full be them that would do unto Tiberius. For out of their grains taketh he his full measure. Out of their stuffs taketh he, and they sweat but to sweat more and wax thinner. Ah, Legia, Tiberius would have the flesh of Theia, but he is growing strong afar. His feet are planted upon the mountains' tops and he shall drive the stars. But Hassan tarrieth and no word hath come. What is this? Theia hath been even as a shadow unto all who come from afar, if he would have drink or fruit or yet a palm, but that she drink their words. And they bring forth broken twigs, for they tell of a one afar who hath wisdoms and they speak him sireless. Yet Theia hath called her flesh Hate, and this one's wisdoms be sweet. Yea, his words sound upon the tongue like music and their sweetness creepeth upon thee as a lily's scent. Aye, and he loveth one man not o'er another. This Theia knoweth, for Tiberius laugheth at the words that come, and hath caused his angers to surge o'er the men's words that this one is building a kingdom. Yea, he hath even felled these."

And she sat her long and spake: "Theia feareth not. She shall wait, wait Hassan. He dareth not that he cut Theia down, for o'er him is a blade doeth he this. His lusts are weak and he glutteth that he be all. He shall know when the knowing will be too late; when he may not stop the thing he doeth.

"He shall raise up a staff, tall and straight, upon a hill, and the arm of the great God o'er all shall lay across it and it shall shew a cross. Wait! Theia seeth! Ah, wait! What! The skies o'er the cross pale in morning's light, clear, fresh as when the storm hath washed the heavens—blue, pale; and a face, sweet, sweet, the Woman of the Hills of Bethlehem! 'Tis hers! And the clouds veil it, and behold, her eyes stream, and sweet rains of her tears fall upon the earth, and behold, behold, behold, the fresh blossoms spurt the fields! Yea, for her tears fall o'er the birth of a New Day. Rome shall lie asleep and nations stop and rest in loving.

"Nay? This is Theia! See! The clouds her locks; for the sun hath turned them gold! Ah, Jehovah, betray thou me not! Shew me this clear! What is this thing? Theia's eyes stream and hosts whose eyes turn dumb empty, up, arise and stretch them full high and cry out: 'It raineth! Sup, brother, sup!' And behold, the locks of Theia fall from out the sky unto earth and the hosts climb unto the heights upon them!"

And Legia spake her: "Theia, thou dost fright thy sister. Arise! Go unto the pools and bathe that thou wakest."

And it was true that, even as they worded, a slave lad came forth and stopped before Legia and spake no word, but looked unto Theia and made that he speak, yet tarried.

And Theia said: " Come! what bid thee? "

And he answered not but pointed that she follow, and he sought without. And Theia made after, and when they had gone from out the presence of Legia, he spake unto her:

" A man hath come upon a camel, and he gave this unto these hands."

And he shewed a bright thing fashioned as an anklet. And Theia looked upon it and said: " This hath he given unto thee? "

And the lad answered: " Yea."

And she said: " Whither hath he come? "

And the lad spake: " He hath laughed long and spoken that his camel stinketh of Jerusalem."

And Theia started and asked: " Is this man Hassan, the trades-man? "

And the lad answered: " He hath spoken this word. And he said that the eve would fall and that shades held silence and that the shades were deep within the thicks yon," and he pointed unto the gar-den's-way, " and he spake: ' When the moon swings o'er the wing of yon wall, tell her she shall seek.' "

And Theia said: " Go thou unto Hassan and speak unto him, saying that Theia cometh. Yea, at the moon's climb shall she seek. Speak it so unto him and speak it so unto the thrice that he know."

And she turned and sought the path unto the inner-ways. And she came her unto the spot wherein Legia rested, and whispered:

" Legia, list! Hassan hath come. He hath come. He hath sent word unto Theia that the shadows hold silence. Yea, he hath spoken true—silence! silence! Theia knoweth silence even as she knoweth her shadow. And he who knoweth silence well knoweth the great God's tongue. Legia, list! list unto the morn when the earth is hushed! Then is the time when the great God speaketh unto thee; for a one must drive all of earth out of his heart that he hark unto His voice, this mighty one. List, Legia! Hassan hath come out of Jerusalem, out of the far lands. He hath seen him, the Hate! " and she drew her up and breathed her deep, even a singing sigh, and spake: " He hath seen him, Hatte, the flesh of Theia. Look, Legia! "

And she knelt before her and loosed her head's-cloth and shook loose her locks and spread them wide until they gleamed, and spake:

" Look! Look! This is Theia's. This is Theia's crown, and

Hatte loveth it. See, Legia! doth the lock of Theia gleam? See! is it not fair?"

And Legia leaned o'er Theia's bended head and touched the gleaming locks and answered: "Yea, they gleam bright, like gold."

And Theia spake: "Speak, Legia! is Theia beauteous?"

And Legia answered her: "Theia, thou art the Summer—late but still bloomed; but thy bloom hath faded. Yea, Time doth trick thee, for he is taking thy gold and returning silver."

And Theia rose and spake: "How may this thing be? For Theia's feet speed upon the wings of Spring, and even though her sorrows have riped and she hath harvested deep of her grain, still Theia remembereth the young green of Spring. Think thee, Legia, when the moon climbeth up, up o'er the wall yon, Theia shall seek and there shall Hassan wait her, and his lips shall smile and his teeth shall gleam and he shall tell him of Jerusalem and this far land that holdeth Hatte."

And Legia shook her head and said: "Theia, thy tongue carrieth thee like unto steeds, for thou dost become living-young when thou dost speak, and dead, dead as ash, when thou art silent." And she touched the flesh of Theia and spake more: "Come! Within the halls Tiberius lieth. He sleepeth and the air is hot. Come! Legia shall seek and waft o'er his sleeping a palm."

And Theia stooped and plucked up her head's-band and binded up her locks and spake: "Thou mayest seek. Theia will look not upon his sleeping, for his sleeping is unto Theia the sleep of the evil one, who sleepeth that he dream new dreams of fiery fury. Go thou and waft palms o'er his sleeping, for the days creep when the very palms that he hath looked upon shall dry as dust and the laurels he hath bounded upon his brow shall fall in dusts upon yon alabaster gods that he hath fashioned."

And Legia looked upon Theia and spake: "Thou hast waked. Thy dream is o'er. Leave Legia youth and days for to dream."

And Theia said: "Yea, for thy awakening is near upon thee."

And behold, Legia went unto the hall's place. And Theia sought the shadows and bore waters unto the court's-ways, unto them that thirsted and rested amid the cools, awaiting the eve's come.

CHAPTER VI

And lo, the sun tarried long, and red, and the light hung the earth unto the dimming of the moon's coming. And Theia waited, waited silent. And when the time had come when the moon stood upon the wing of the palace, she sought the thicks beside the pool wherein swam fowls of beauty. And the shadows hung the paths, and behold, damps fell, and Rome smelled sweet of eve. And Theia, like some night bird, flitted her way unto the deep of darks, and awaited. And she stood her long, listing. And it came to pass that there sounded the step of one that sought. And Theia's bosom panted, and she beat her hands one upon the other. And she oped her lips and made that she speak, but no word came. And the moon's light shewed green, and the shadows purpled deep, and the stars gleamed bright gold upon the greened sky.

And a shadow shewed upon the path's-way, and Theia fell upon her face and touched the shadow and cried out:

" Speak not, Hassan! Speak not unto Theia, for thy words would cut, cut. Wait, wait! Theia shall shut her eyes and wait unto the time when she may bear to look upon thee."

And the one who stood answered not. And Theia lay upon her face even as one who made obeisance, and raised not her eyes but spake:

" Ah, Hassan, he sent unto Theia a word, one word? He spake it and it sung sweet—' Mother—Theia.' Speak it! Speak it! "

And no word made answering. And she arose upon her knees and raised her shut eyes moon-ward.

" What! no word? No word from out Jerusalem's way? Hassan! Hassan! Thou hast the water and Theia is parched. Speak!

" Ah, Hassan! " And she let fall her hands like unto withered things, and her shoulders drooped and her head bended even unto the touching of the throat unto the breast, and she whispered: "Ah, what tarrieth thee? Theia would pluck forth her heart and crush it, but Hassan, it may not be crushed when e'en now 'tis dust. Theia would tear ope her throat and leave her blood to flow unto her emptying, but Hassan, Theia would lone for the aching. It is hers, this aching, like unto her heart of dust. Hassan," and her voice pleaded sweet, " Hassan—ah, he hath spoken unto thee! He hath forgot Theia, the spent one. He remembereth but her who danceth. Hassan, ah, woe is me! The airs stifle, the clouds even seem heavy upon this head; dins deafen and no word hast thou spoken! Where art thou? Leave thee but thy hand that Theia touch it e'er she looketh upon thy face. Ah, brother, Theia's lips would press it. Leave thy hand to touch her here," and she lay her hand upon her bosom. "See! the heart would leap from out this breast! Ah, he is there? Rome hath not eaten him? Hassan, speak!"

And she arose, and her limbs were stiffed and her breath panted. And she looked her swift unto the one who stood, and lo, her voice rang clear in shrieking:

"Tiberius!"

And she stooped and held her hands even in sign that his touch had defiled her. And her eyes shone and her teeth gleamed, and she spake no word but waited as a wild thing driven unto the end. And behold, the one spake:

"So! Even the dead speaketh! Even the silence of a tomb may spring a tongue! Rome spendeth her coin or her wisdom. Doth one not empty, the other lendeth unto the emptying. Jerusalem hath sent up stinking that reacheth like summer's heat upon all ways. Theia, what thou hast lost may be returned even unto thy hand should thy lips speak out. Where is thy son?"

And Theia laughed. "Might is thine, but thy blade may not split a dust grain. It is even mightier than the blades of hosts. See! I am a grain of the fashioning of the great God. Tiberius, turn Rome loose and destroy me!"

And Tiberius laughed and spake: "Rome shall split the grain ope. Where is thy son?"

And Theia answered: "In that spot wherein thine abideth! Theia hath done thee, Tiberius. Out of thee hath she begat dusts that shall shew thee as thou art, even at the passing of waters unto lands and lands unto waters and people unto peoples through ages' sweep! For thy flesh may not die but shall quiver in suffering through time by thy hand. Theia speaketh unto thee, loose Rome and all of Rome's! Ye may not undo flesh. Thy flesh is thy flesh. List! Thou mayest slay a fawn and wipe thy blade and turn to cut from off a slender stem a lily; but the lily may not pure thy blade even though its pure petals hide the stain. Even when thy hand is no more and some youngling of some tide, hence, hence, shall pluck up thy bones for a folly play, and cast thy noble brow's arch o'er some greened slope as waste, the blade that thou dost wield shall gleam in fire and write o'er the fallen one: 'The son of Tiberius. In his folly he begat his noblest work, the son of Tiberius!'

" The great God shall wreak a wonderwork. The shadows of thy days shall be the lights and the lights the shadows; and thereby shall earth know thee! Yea, and hark! Thy hand did reach forth and leave fall a curtain of black that should leave a shadow ever upon the days of Theia. And the hand that shall draw the curtain wide and leave the light to fall upon thy shadows shall be this! "—and she held her hand high. " Yea, e'en though the Land of Promise is but dust and Theia one grain, she shall roll her, damped of her tears, and gather unto her more of grains unto the tide when she is a great stone and shall fall upon thy dust! Where is thy might? Death unlocks thy treasures unto beggars! List! List! This hath not shaken thee? Then list! Afar is a one whose smile is thine, whose eyes are thine, whose lips are thine, who walketh as a noble, even as thy son. He is a Caesar, and thou, Tiberius. Upon an empty carcass hath the mantle fallen, and the real man, like a swift-winged hawk, hath sped and is yon. Thou art empty, sire, empty; for thy son is thy soul!

" I am but a Greek, a keen-edged blade, the battle's taking. Rome spent naught for the buying but the blood of her sons, and this is freer than meal in Rome. I am a Greek. List! Rome hath trodden down Greece; her beauties hath she crumbled, her sons felled, her sisters taken. Yea, yea, but Greece waiteth, sire, waiteth; for even out of dusts of ages shall her dead beauties arise. And Theia is one of these. Out the dusts of Greece an emperor was molded. A noble's flesh fell foot-cloth for a host who vanquished her land. Thou hast asked Theia wherein her son abideth and she answereth thee, where? "—and she laughed. " Yea, sire, unloose Rome! Cut this tongue from out its hollow and find thee the where! Bring forth the lash! 'Tis play; but tickle unto the seared flesh of Theia. Fetch forth thy musics and bid ' the dead woman ' dance! 'Tis but play; for she danceth upon thy heart and knoweth it! Set thee this skull ope and pour therein hot waters. 'Tis cooling drops unto the furies within Theia! "

And Tiberius had stood tall and his hand was pressed o'er his lips, and his eyes narrowed and he looked upon her close. And behold, she looked upon him and reached upwards with trembling hands and let free her head's-cloth. And behold, the locks fell o'er her, and she sunk even upon her knees before him, and murmured:

" Jehovah, love will not die! Slay it! "

And she shook as one who shook of colds. And Tiberius looked upon her and spake: " Thy folly is deep. Wherein doth he abide? "

And Theia looked keen unto his eyes and said: " But thou hast lied once. Theia would hate thee, but he is of thee. Ah, he is beauteous and he knoweth not he is thine. Why, then, loose this tongue? "

And Tiberius said: " And Hassan, then, is yon, and for thee— Hassan, whose camel laugheth? "

And Theia arose and cried: " Yea, and hath he come? Hath he come? "

And Tiberius answered her: " Nay. Wisdom led unto this, that Rome know."

And Theia spake: " Yea, and Theia knoweth this wisdom is the wisdom of a woman, thy woman. She knoweth much and envy is sharp-toothed. She knoweth and feareth and is wanton with her tongue among men. The bitter of her words send them searching, searching for what is thine. Theia will tell thee this: He is tall and hath his beard. He is gentle as morning. He is full of musics and his hands are even so lithe as the feet of Theia. He speaketh great wisdom and multitudes follow him. He is full his own man. Go ye and seek. The grain is thine; split it ope! "

And Tiberius pressed his lips o'er, for he mouthed as one whom sleep had smitten. And Theia walked her slow from out the shadow unto the full light and spread her head's-cloth and danced, and her laughter mocked the still.

And the dark followed the moon's going. And Legia lay her waiting within the slaves' chambers. And it was true that Theia stepped her weary-footed unto the spot, and Legia made that she look her like unto one who slept. And Theia came within and lighted of a lamp, and sat her down before its glowing and binded up her locks within the head's-cloth, and sat long, and her eye burned fires. And Legia stirred and she spake: " Theia, hath Hassan brought thee forth the word? "

And Theia said: " Nay. 'Twas Rome's fancy to dance within Hassan's mantle. Tiberius by smite could not bring forth that he would of Theia, so Tiberius stooped even unto the tying of a beggar's latchet and consorted with a slave. Legia, I am weary, I am hungered."

And Legia said: " Go thou and seek the hall's place and call forth Tomarus and bid that he bring forth bread."

And Theia stopped her and spake: " Hark! List unto Theia. It hath come from out Jerusalem and the lands afar that men of Rome went unto him and said: ' If thou art the son of the mighty one, make this unto bread.' And he, ah, he spake: ' Man may not live by bread alone, but by the words of God; for they fruit new at each new day and the hand of man may ne'er strip their branches. Begone, and seek ye wisdom's bread!' I am weary and hunger is new torture and pleasant. More hath come; for 'tis spoken that they sought him and brought wisdoms that men had made, and asked: 'Is this the wisdom of God?' And he spake: 'Smite it and if it break it is not the wisdom of God.' His hands he busieth. His work is well done. All this is come and they look unto him as o'er them. They know his nobleness."

And Legia waked her and stood and came unto the side of Theia and spake: "Then this one is he?"

And Theia answered: "Nay; he is but one that is o'er them. Theia speaketh nay, 'tis not he."

And Legia said: "But this one abideth with a woman."

And Theia spake: "Is she beauteous—young? Hath her feet sped in dancing and bewitched him? Doth he love her? Doth his eyes soft as the cloud-veiled moon? Speak!"

And Legia answered: "I know not save he abideth with a woman."

And Theia sunk and spake: "Woman! Woman! When thou art spent and dead, some new blossom bursteth. Woman! New days bring new women. Theia should have remembered this, but Theia would believe that one woman lived his days. Leave me rest, Legia."

And Legia lay her down upon the couch and Theia spread forth a cloth and stretched her upon the stones.

And it grew still and stiller still. And Theia arose within the dark and sought without and sunk upon her knees and lifted her hands high and spake:

"Jehovah, hark! Greece, my land! I am lone, thy daughter. These eyes may not look upon thee, but at some time Theia shall sit upon the sun and leave her locks to spread like beams o'er thee and it shall rain and the rain shall be Theia's tears. My land! My land! My land! Behold my love, and my heart thy throne! Jehovah, hark! Waiting! Waiting! Waiting! Send thee full. Theia waiteth."

And behold, within the East the morn star gleamed.

CHAPTER VII

AND heats had swept and cools followed, and winds had arisen and died, and Nazareth had set its days one as the other. And upon the hills shepherds watched their flocks and lay them dreaming naughts. And the land was lain weary 'neath the hot sun. The kine stretched their necks and shook them from side to side that they drive thither the flies, and the sheep had sought shades and waited the sun's fall that they eat; and their sides heaved.

And upon a high hill there stepped a shepherd, and he held unto a one's hand, and spake: " Yea, yea, he is gone; yet shall we find him."

And the one answered: " But the hill's-ways have these legs spanned and I have called, called, but he respondeth not."

And the shepherd's voice spake in the voice of Panda, and Panda's arm lay about the broken form, and he said:

" Come thou unto the cool and rest. Morn shall find thee fresh for the seeking."

And the one whom the lights shewed as Hatte spake: " There is no rest for the son of Tiberius. Panda, something speaketh unto Hatte that e'en his dusts may not rest, but be the blackening grime upon earth's face. Yea, they may not empty the son of Tiberius. And Panda, list! take thou Aaron and shut him within the walls; for Hatte feareth him and his laugh."

And Panda said: " Hatte, hast thou then fallen unto the hating of thy brother, Aaron? "

And Hatte spake him: " Panda, list! Hatte seemeth for to know that Aaron is like unto the hate that filleth Hatte. He shall live even after the going of Hatte and his laugh shall echo through eternities. Upon the earth he dwelleth, and Hatte's feet tread the paths, and yet he is a hawk, seeking, seeking, seeking."

And Panda made words of soothing unto Hatte. And they sought the hut of Panda. And the camel of Hassan was tethered beside it, and lo, Hassan made packs of nets and sang him in a note belonging to his tongue. And Panda came unto the spot and Hatte even so. And Hassan looked unto Hatte and shook his head sorrowed, and spake:

"Leave him that he seek within. Hassan would word with thee, Panda."

And Panda let free the hand of Hatte and bade that he seek Nada, and came unto the side of Hassan and asked: "What wouldst thou, brother?"

And Hassan looked deep within the eyes of Panda and stretched his arms wide and let them fall, and said:

"See! the mantle of Hassan is free of dust. Panda, these nostrils would smell sands. A desert's man is like unto one who boats; the sands leave the feet sink deep and the slipping is like unto the water's raise and fall. Hassan may walk sod but his feet itch for sands. See!" and he turned and pointed unto his camel, "See thou! his eyes weep, for waters drip them even o'er his hair. But how may Hassan seek? Panda, Hassan dreadeth not Rome but her. And Rome is upon Hatte even as upon this Nazarene, Jesus. Behold this man! He seeketh even afar for work that His hand shall do; for Nazareth may not give forth for His labors pence enough that He bread. His hands He setteth e'en at the turning of plough staffs. Yet His lips confound the wise men. These Jews know, Panda, know much; and mark ye, the words this Nazarene sendeth forth shall be like unto leaven and shall cause the arising of new days and greater strengths than Rome. Within the hands of the Jews is the mightiest sword that Rome e'er met.

"Nazareth is not running wisdom as the brook runneth waters. They know this man's wisdom, yet they understand Him not. List! even this man knoweth not the fullness of His day. It is abroad, Panda, within the mouths of all men, yet He hath not done this thing. It is even as a plague upon the land and speedeth even so suredly. He is but a trumpet and His words the blast. Yea, and Hassan sayeth unto thee, Panda, 'tis a mightier voice than the voice of a Nazarene that speaketh out of the trumpet's mouth. Rome feareth this blast; for unto Rome come these words of this man, running upon legs, hither, thither, yon. Tiberius knoweth that a man who may do this thing is one for fearing. Hassan knoweth they have cast up two pebbles and know not which be which. 'Tis well, Panda, 'tis well. For look ye! Tiberius is well pleased and the lad hath the fullness of man's dealing; for them that love him know his emptiness, and them that fear him, fear him whole and know not his breaking. Tiberius patteth his belly and glutteth that this wise son is his. Hassan shall bite upon his tongue and speak naughts, but should Rome vent upon this Nazarene, Hassan shall arise!"

And he let his fingers seek within his mantle and brought forth his blade and kissed it and spake: " Unto her, Panda, that Hate shall live unto the meeting of Rome, but that, when Rome shall bow and know him, he shall fall by this hand. Rome shall bow and know hate. Rome shall fall upon her knees and look unto the blind eyes of hate and plead for her children. Even this Nazarene knoweth this thing, for His justice waxeth hot at Rome's dealing. He hath spoken among men, here in Nazareth, that within Rome, when Rome hath fallen, shall arise a throne upon which shall sit one who serveth His Sire and earth's men shall call Him blessed. He speaketh that this shall be a mock unto Rome. Yea, He speaketh that even the street's-ways of Rome shall be filled of men that know Him and know His Father.

" And these Nazarenes laughed at this word when it was first spoken and spake among them: ' His father was who? Surely not the man Joseph! ' But Nazareth hath stopped this, Panda, and listed, for Nazareth knoweth that within her dry earth's crust hath sprung an everlasting spring of water. They come them thirsted and drink. Yea, and the crystal waters even find Rome and dry upon the stones. But Rome shall yet lay beneath its cool!

" Panda, Hassan knoweth the why of the tremble of his steed's ear. He knoweth the spreading of its nostrils. He knoweth the metal of its hard flesh's strength. But he knoweth not the deep black of its eye, nor what sheweth there, soft, hunger-soft. He knoweth not the why that this steed may track the deserts and find the paths, led by some unseen hand, even though, brother, thou hast heard among the tribes that the steeds are led by the ' maid of the east-wind,' or the ' king of the westward.' Thou knowest this meaneth but the thing this Nazarene meaneth when He telleth of His Sire."

And Panda spake: " Thou hast spoken truly, Hassan. They look upon this one and know Him not; for there cometh days that fall heavy upon Him and He seeketh the fields and leaveth His hands to idle, and they know them not the why. And He hath spoken among them that His labors are many and He falleth weary at such an time. Hassan, Panda feeleth fearful. This is a tide when fires glow buried. Panda hath eat the bread of the Jews. He hath taken of their goods. He knoweth them and they be even as brothers unto him. Levi—Hassan, no man hath e'er lived and died more true than Levi. And within Jerusalem there be many such as he. Jacob and his kind are few. Yet look ye, it taketh a few for to do a mighty thing that leadeth hosts. The Jew's tribes and their lands be but empty bowls for Rome to cast unto that which she would be rid of, even if they be Rome's own sinning. He who waxeth hottest be ever pointed unto as the brand that did the burn, and the Jews are hot and justly hot, Hassan. It hath come unto the ears of Panda that Levi told, even unto the Romans at his dying, of his brothers who had fallen and spilled their bloods that Rome's be spared; of the tribes that had been driven unto their falling and their stripping.

"Hassan, the waters are dark and storm-washed. 'Tis the tide when we shall look for the coming of a sun. Ne'er hath there been dark storm's-wrath but the sun cometh. Love might not be a thing save that it have a shadow; and the shadow of love is hate. And a shadow is a phantom of a soul. A dead man may not arise and shew his shadow; for his hate is dead even as his flesh. Hate is weak and may not raise a man up that hath fallen down. Love is an ever-speeding arrow and its mark the heart of the great God."

And Hassan touched the flesh of Panda and spake: "All this of nothing and the nets awaiting. How is the flesh of Hatte? Hath he healed so that he may hold him?"

And Panda turned and lifted up the nets and made that he bind them unto the camel's back, and spake:

"Hassan, Panda knoweth not the thing that hath beset Hatte. He is gone, this morn. Yet yester he knew and knew of his going. The nights seem troubled and the shadows set him feared. When the yester morn had come he arose and stretched him and spake: 'Panda, Hatte hath wearied and slept and awaked strong. Tell thou where he hath been, for it seemeth that the hills call, yet Hatte knoweth 'tis folly that calleth.' Hassan, he seemeth for to wake, yet within him he hath an hunger that he know this Jesus Christus, for yester, when he had waked and shewed like unto himself, he spake that he should follow this one and Aaron should follow, and he would seek the ways whereon this one ministereth."

And Hassan lended his hands that they fast the pack, and spake unto Panda, saying:

"Leave this for to be, Panda; 'tis well." And he stopped short and spake: "Leave Hatte that he seek himself within the words of this man. Make it known unto him that 'tis well; for Panda, the time hath come that thou and Nada and Hassan shall seek Jerusalem."

And Panda cried: "But Hatte is broken. It may not be."

And Hassan prodded the camel that he arise and spake: "Leave within the hands of Hatte enough that he may seek Jerusalem when he hath wearied."

And Panda said: "But Hassan, they will fall upon him and Rome shall seek him out."

And Hassan spake: " Nay. When thou art gone, and Hassan, they shall believe then that he is gone even so, and these who abide within Nazareth shall seek not after Jesus Christus, believing that where He is therefrom shall come His words and tell them. Yea, and Jerusalem knoweth not the smitten Hatte be he not at thy side.

" Panda," and Hassan followed the stepping camel, " Rome shall minister not unto this lad, nor the one she feareth, save within Jerusalem, before them that stand as Rome. Then thou and Hassan shall wait the rat at its hole."

And lo, they went them not within but sought Nazareth's markets that they sell unto them that in came. For Nazareth barted but small wares among her townsmen. And they sought the road's-ways, and scarlet blooms flecked the earth, and the blue of the skies shewed bluer for the flaming of the scarlet. And the camel swayed wry-necked and its legs sprawled o'er the road's ruts. And Hassan laughed at the beast's stumbling, and took up a hand's full of dust and cast unto the camel, and pulled its neck low even so that its nose sunk within his hands, and spread dusts o'er its lips and cast unto its eyes, and spake:

" So, thou art hungered even as thy master! " And he patted the beast's neck with his oped palm and spake: " Is this not a land of fools? "

And the beast shook its head. And Hassan spread his hands ope, palms up, and lifted them and shrugged and spake:

" See ye, Panda, he hath spoken! Ah, for a voice rooted within such a neck that it speak the belly's tongue! "

And Panda laughed, and turned his eyes o'er the hill's-ways and pointed unto a flock afar and said: " There, Hassan, is the flock of Jesus Christus."

And Hassan shook his head and spake him: " Panda, thy brother is filled of shame that thou shouldst speak this. Look! " and he swept his arms unto all ways; " behold, there is the flock of Jesus Christus! He is no man of one sheep nor of a small flock, for His voice reacheth the valleys even so well as the high places."

And they passed, upon the way, men who sought the greens with their beasts, and they made the sign of morning unto these. And behold, they looked unto Hassan, whose robe shewed him not of their land, and bended low, even unto their back's bendings. And it was true they came upon Hezekiah who sought the hut of Panda, and they worded with him at the road's side. And Hezekiah told of much that filled the days of Nazareth, for from out an ant's hill had arisen a tempest. And Hassan asked of Jesus Christus, and Hezekiah answered that He had been within Galilee, within the synagogues, and had spoken among their holy men, and had returned unto Nazareth and gone within the synagogue and spoken unto the people. Yea, He had oped the scripts and sought a spot prophet-tongued. And He had arisen up among them and spoken that the prophet's words were fulfilled, for He had come that He feed unto the earth the bread of God. And they had spoken unto Him, saying:

"Then call thee unto the rich men and bid that they come forth and give freely unto the poor, for we are hungered and Nazareth is filled of but poor. Since thou art come, do this thing."

And He had arisen, Hezekiah spake, unto a high place whereon the priests stood, and had spread His hands forth and looked Him unto the people and His eyes glisted of tears and He spake:

"I am come to make whole the broken, to bind up the broken-hearted, to soothe the bruised, to dry up weeping, to make of emptiness fullness. The bread of God shall I deliver unto them that hunger. I am come to minister unto the poor, be this the poor who have little of earth's wares or he whose spirit is barren. He that is full needeth me not. Thou wilt speak unto me: 'If thou art a healer, heal thine own sores. Physician, heal thyself.' And I shall answer thee: 'He who delivereth the bread of God unto His people is healed. Through each crumb is he purged. Look! among ye it is spoken, 'Is not this the son of Joseph?' I speak unto ye, a prophet may not be lifted up among his own people.*

"Look ye unto it. In the days of Israel, in the time when the heavens shut and famine came upon them, unto but one came there the sign. This is the sign. There may be but one who be the Father's Son; yet all of ye are His sons. Even so hath He begat me within His own love and brought me out of the earth a living sign unto man that He entereth all men."

And it had been true that the men had wrathed o'er this and spake that He set Him up o'er them and had spoken that He should go forth. Even with loud noises had they broken the worship. And it was true that Jesus had gone from their midst.

And Hezekiah told that He had gone down unto Capernaum and had preached among them and they had listed unto Him, but at one morn when He had gathered together a band that they worship beneath the sun, a man had arisen and spoken aloud unto Him:

"Who art thou that thou shouldst use the tongue of the priests? What have we to do with thee?"

* Luke 4.

And Jesus had spoken unto him, saying: "Thine evil is upon thy tongue and cometh forth."

And the man had spoken not, but stood and listed unto the words of Jesus unto the band of worshipers. And behold, this man had been known as one who was wicked and filled of the evil one. And when the words of Jesus Christus had ceased, behold, he fell upon his knees and cried out:

"I know thee. Thou art the Son of God!" And he had gone upon his way a new man.

And Hezekiah told that they that had seen this spake unto Jesus, saying: "Thou hast driven forth the devil within him; for this man hath bitten the airs in wickeds and made sounds even as the swine."

And it was true that Jesus had spoken that a man's evil might not be driven forth, but should the man sup of the living waters, behold, the evils might drown. "This is before thee and thou mayest speak it, but the days shall come when this shall rust and man know but the rust's crust. But the might of God shall touch the crumble of rust, and behold, the truth shall be upon thee!

"I am fulled and thou art empty, yet should I fill thee thou wouldst burst. Yet my words shall I pin unto the tongues of men through ages, that they shall speak His name."

And Hezekiah raised his hands up high and his eyes stood oped wide and he spake:

"What is upon us? The Jews, as men,* will not of this man, but as one man they love Him, each within himself. And hark! He breaketh down the walls of Judaism and taketh in all men. This thing the Jews fear. This is right, for thou knowest there is no man of far lands but who knoweth that his land hath cast a stone at the Jews. So they fear. Must the Jews, then, give from out their synagogues their God and lift up a one who teareth down the walls?"

And Panda spake him: "Hezekiah, a man may ne'er take unto him new lands save that he tear down the wall. The Jews are but waking."

And Hezekiah said: "Nay; there is among us, even as thou knowest, them that believe; yea, even know."

And Hezekiah took from out his breast some of the scripts that he had made ready that they be sent afar. And Hassan spake:

"Hezekiah, the Jews know not the mightiness of the blade that is within their hands. For a thing that hath done that that hath been done even now shall do far o'er this. The Jews may speak this man is not the Son of God, and the men of the market's-ways and other

* Collectively.

lands even so, but it remaineth that He hath done this thing: come from out a manger place and rose up o'er the backs of men unto a high place. Ye may not stop a man, nor his words, with nays. And be this man not, or be He, the Son of God, still He be. The stuff that hath made Him up meaneth naught, and the nays mean less."

And Hassan laughed loud and spake: "Panda, look ye unto it. 'Twas ever so, did an humbling rise up and set the seat of a wise one, behold, the wise one falleth unto the frenzies of folly and smiteth even as a lad in wrath! Ha, ha, ha, ha! Ah, to be an humbling and look upon the play! 'Tis well, Panda, eh? Well!"

And he smote Panda upon the back. And they spoke the parting unto Hezekiah and made them upon the way and spake o'er what had been said. And when they neared Nazareth, Hassan stopped the camel and stood within the road's-way and said:

"Panda, list! Hassan hath little. He is even unto the dusts of his skin's-sack." And he pressed his fingers' tips upon his brow and upon the brow of Panda. "Hast thou within thee a wisdom that would cause a beggar to belch gold? Nay, brother, even though Hassan loveth thee, he knoweth that the bread of thy wisdom would sour e'en a beggar's belly; it would shew heavy, heavy. Yea, Hassan knoweth it. Wait! Hassan shall bear a wisdom out of him that shall be bubbling as a spring's gush and tempt the beggar that he drink. Where in Nazareth may a man buy a thing with no gold for to buy, that he may sell for heavy price? Ah, it splitteth this head, Panda." And he shut one eye and spake: "Come!" And he spake unto the camel, saying: "Is thy master wise or a fool? Shake thee at up and down, be he wise, and at side to side, be he a fool."

And lo, the camel upped his head and cast it at the side, and Hassan oped wide his eyes and cried: "Look, Panda! he sayeth his master is both fool and wise man!"

And he made obeisance before the beast's path. And Panda, even though his eyes shewed burning of a thing that looked hunger, smiled.

And they sought the market's place, and it was true that Panda barted of roots, and Hassan left his side, and they came not one unto the other until the hour was late and the time come when they should seek the hut. And at this time Panda sought Hassan, who stood him at a bin's place wailing. And Panda found him not. And Hassan spake unto the bin's man:

"But this thing is but an underling for a camel's pack! Its stuffs dull! What man would make thee a full price for such an rug? See!" and he put through the rug's strands his fingers, " even hath it worn. It is not fit for a beggar's feet. Leave Hassan that he set upon it, for he knoweth the feel of a real weaving." And he spread it forth and set upon it and cried aloud: "Woe upon me! It is a thing fit for swine's beds. An ass would ne'er lay upon it! Here," and he plucked forth two small coins, "take this and thank thy days that it is o'er and done!"

And the bin's man arose and spake: "Thou art a liar! Even a thief! The thing is filthed but beauteous!"

And Hassan shrieked him loud: "Look upon such a man! He would rob his brother! See!"

And he spread the rug forth unto the eyes of them that watched and wept tears by the rubbing of his hand's back deep within his eyes. And even as he wept he made a pack of the rug and binded it within a cloth and made way unto the camel and came upon Panda who waited his coming beside the beast. And Hassan prodded the beast such a prod that it arose and shook and even speeded out of the market's place. And Hassan sped after, and Panda even so. And Hassan said, when they had gone well upon the way:

"The wisdom was born, Panda, and called its father's name. Hassan bowed before his bearing. See!" and he held forth the pack, "Hassan hath purchased with naught a thing of worth. Yea, and eat with the bin's man. Thou shalt see. Thou shalt see."

And they made way, wearied, unto the hut. And Nada waited, and her hands were busied at the making of grain's bread. And she shewed thin and weary, for the tides had been tides of heavy labor. And they came within, and Panda asked of Hatte.

And Nada spake: "He hath gone seeking, and Aaron followed."

And Hassan came him within and said: "Nada, list! the time hath come."

And Nada's knees sunk and her hands, white of meal, pressed unto her breast, and she fell down crying out: "The time is come, Panda?"

And Hassan said: "The morrow shall bring thee full price for the going, for look ye! Hassan's wisdom hath bought a thing of worth for naught. See!"

And he spread forth the worn rug. And Nada stepped unto it and sunk her, touching it, and her eyes raised unto Panda and she spake with stiffed lips:

"This is a dream of Nadab!"

And she touched the rug o'er and her tears fell upon it, and she murmured: "Nadab, Nadab, out of the days past thou hast spoken! Nada seeth thee cross-legged, even upon this rug. See!" and she touched the spot; "see! this is the broken bowl of earthenware that Nada let fall, and see! aside and about, the spots—these are the tears of Nada. Nada remembereth that she seeth Nadab laughing and heareth the racks. Panda, 'tis o'ermuch!"

And Panda came up unto the spot and let his arms fall about the bended form of Nada and spake: "Arise thee, Nada. Arise and smile. Panda would that Nadab see the smile."

And Nada arose and her stiff lips trembled, and she spake not, but smiled. And Panda smiled, and they turned unto the East and made the sign of the far tribes and sunk in chanting upon the rug of Nadab. And Hassan looked upon this thing and let his head to sink upon his breast and sunk upon his knees.

And behold, the eve had come and mists hung the valleys, and the sheep sounded afar, afar amid the mists, calling, calling. And Panda arose and took up his staff and spake:

"Nada, hark! They call, and the call of sheep is the same, be this within Nazareth or yet in Jerusalem."

And Hassan said: "Leave thou me, Panda, to follow that we fold them."

And Nada turned and took up a lamp and set it glowing, and behold, the light shewed her eyes glisting bright, and drops sprinkled upon her breast, and she looked unto Panda with star eyes and spake:

"Go thou and speak unto the night skies, that the time hath come. See, Panda, if the moon shall come forth from out the mists. See if the soft white silver of the mists shall wash the moon's face and shew her pale. And look, look, Panda, if the swallow's wings are spread. Speak unto Nada if this be true, for Nada dreameth that the swallow's wings do chafe to flee unto her breast."

And Panda went him unto the door's-way and looked unto the high, and spake: "The moon cometh, Nada, but it seemeth unto Panda that the swallow's wings are folded in comfort-rest. Wait, wait and Panda shall return unto thee, bearing the message of the moon."

And Hassan bowed his head and they stepped unto the out-way, and the mists swallowed their going.

And Nada stood long and looked unto the moon-whited mist, and her hands hung limp at her side. And she stepped unto the door's-way and flung wide her arms and called:

"Nadab! Nadab! Come! The light is for thee, and the ears of Nada would list unto the music of thy racks. Nadab! Nadab! Nazareth is far, far. Canst thou find Nada?"

And she turned slow and sought the rug's spread and sunk upon it. And behold, the winds started up and there sounded thudding, thudding. And Nada spake: " It is thee! Even though 'tis but a bared branch, thou didst speak! 'Tis thee! "

And it was true that Nada fell upon her knees and made chants, and from the road's-way her voice sounded musics unto him that passed. And it was night, and the mists hung them far deeper at the night's coming, even unto the dimming of the moon's light and the darking of the earth.

CHAPTER VIII

AND morn found the sods wet, and the trees dripped of drops. And within the market's places, behold, damps made the tongues of men wry one unto the other. And among the men little was spoken unto the time when there came forth a one who sought the bin of a brass-man. And he spake in soft words, saying:

"Look ye unto Nazareth sleeping. No man cometh forth with e'en one pence that a man might pluck out of him. Yea, Nazareth sleepeth even so unto that that is within her. See! Knowest thou that this man, Jesus Christus, sought out Capernaum and hath done wonders within the city's place? Word hath come that He hath called forth the men and plucked from among them a one who was beset of a devil. And He did call Him unto the evil one within him and bid that it come forth, and behold, it is spoken that from out the man came forth a thing that caused them that saw to shut up their eyes; for the sides of the evil thing that came forth from out the man were leprous, and its eyes hung upon thongs. 'Tis told that its tongue licked forth and flames sprang from out its throat's ope. Even had its head sprung branches even as a tree. Yea, and more, that it neither walked nor crawled, but rolled upon its belly."

And the brass-man spake: "Is this thing true? Thou hast spoken not the half that a brother told here in the market's place yester. What then? Didst thou see that that He hath done unto this thing?"

And the market's man answered: "The eyes of me have not taken in this, but he who hath given it unto me speaketh ever truly. It is true and he has spoken it, that this man spake with power even as a prophet, and the people fell feared, and the man from whom He had driven forth the evil one had fallen down and worshiped at His feet. And more, they spake, that this man, Jesus Christus, but stretched forth His hand, and behold, the thing was taken up unto the clouds. But hark ye! this thing doeth no good, for the Romans and the Gentiles of all sects shall harken unto it, and behold, they shall stone Him. It is not well that a prophet speak o'erloud."

And the brass-man answered him, saying: "Nor that them that harken unto His words shall blast them forth in loud trumpeting."

519

And the man went upon his way, nor answered his brother, for he wrathed at the rebuke. And the brass-man called unto a bin's man who dealt of hides, and spake: " Hast thou heard of the workings of this man, Jesus Christus? "

And his brother answered him: " Nay."

And the brass-man told of the man who had been filled of devils and said that Jesus Christus had spread forth His hands and all men had seen flames spurt from His fingers. And behold, the evil one had come forth out of the man as a stream of water and had quenched the flames.

And behold, the day was filled with devils, and at the eve's coming devils crept the road's-way out of Nazareth unto the far lands.

And at the morn's coming there shewed upon the out-roads Jesus Christus, and within His hands shewed a blade such as a wood's man * plied. And He sought the out-ways unto a city's place wherein He should wield this thing and bring forth bread. And behold, He came upon a man whose head was bowed and He spake Him, saying: " Whither goest thou? "

And the man made answering: " I seek Nazareth from out Gennesareth way. They that have sent me forth hunger that He come unto them, this man that dealeth the bread of words wherefrom men may eat. He is called Jesus Christus. They have sent unto Him of their goods," and the man drew forth a sack of moneys, " that He know they would of Him."

And lo, Jesus Christus touched not the skin's-sack and spake: " I go unto these who hunger, for I am Him, Jesus Christus. But no man hath goods that may purchase the bread of life. This do I minister freely, even as He that sent me ministereth rains, dews and sweet airs."

And the man sunk upon his knees and spake soft: " Master."

And Jesus said unto him: " Arise. I am but a shepherd and no man's master." And He spake: " I would seek, following thee, unto this spot where the hungered wait."

And behold, they set upon the road's-way, and from out the thicks shewed, following soft footed, Hatte and Aaron. And Hatte made sign unto Aaron that he make no sound. And behold, he followed afar, and the dusts that fell upon Him, the Shepherd, fell upon him of hate. Even did their feet trod the same path.

And when they had come unto the town's place, which was a babe town upon a shore's rise, behold, no man looked them welcome. And

* A carpenter.

he that had come unto Nazareth spake: " They that have sent me forth await yon."

And he pointed unto a thick of boats that loved the shore, and he said: " Within this spot there is no temple and the holy places would be shut unto thee. Master, we may but offer unto thee these that the people may hark," and he pointed unto the boats.

And Jesus Christus stood upon the shore and looked afar and spake: " It is well. Look ye! is not this a fitting holy spot? Boundless the sea's wave and the sky's arch. It is well. Come thou! We shall put the words within the boats that they float whither and seek new lands."

And they drew nigh where there stood upon the shore them that waited. And Jesus spake word of greeting unto them by the flashing of His sweet smile. And they cried aloud:

" We hunger! Thy words tear down the stone walls and leave us in."

And it was true that He stood among them and spake: " Busy thee at thy tasks, for the words I bring are for busied men."

And they whose boats stood sought them, and among them washed nets and made right for the going out. And amid the sweet notes of the voice that spake gentleness unto them sounded the lapping of the waters and the stirring of the waves about the boats by the washing of nets.

And upon the shore's-way rested them that would hark, and they spake unto Jesus Christus, saying:

" What may we offer thee? for look! there is no spot where thou mayest rest and thou hast trodden far. Even the dusts of the road cling to thee and weariness is thine."

And He made answer: " Draw thee yon boat up unto the water's edge and therein shall I rest and speak with thee, and ye shall sit even upon the shores and hark, so that when the words shall cease thou mayest hear the sea's wisdom."

And they brought forth the boat and made it to rest upon the shallow waters. And He walked Him unto it, and there followed, even within the waters, ones who would be near Him. And they spake:

" 'Tis spoken that thou hast the key that unlocketh the temples."

And He answered them, saying: " No key may unlock the temple, for within it abideth not the God. For man hath his God even as he hath his shadow. The prophets have spoken and told thee of the wraths. Behold, He hath sent a new tongue for to tell of mercies."

And they made silence before this thing and the hands busied at their tasks. And they that harked upon the shores sat them long waiting, and one who sat within the boat, even beside Him, spake:

"Master, tell unto us, for we are wicked. Yea, our deeds fall short and love abideth not among us."

And He spake Him, saying: "Behold, there may not be an earth save for love. The sky boweth down in loving unto the earth. The stars send reaching beams unto the earth. The moon leadeth the waters from one shore unto the other in loving. The sun sheddeth him o'er all things in loving. Behold, there be not e'en a flying bird whose shadow traileth him not. And this is the sign of love. Ye may not know the depth of love, save that thou lookest unto thine own shadow; for a man may not measure love save that he deal it, and looketh unto himself even so that he knoweth his shadow's tracking."

And they spake: "We know not thy words. Speak unto us within that * we know."

And He stood Him up within the boat and took up a net and left it hang within His hands, and said:

"Thou dost hark unto these things, and behold, the nets lie them idle."

And they spake: "But we have wearied, for the casting bringeth forth naught. Behold, look upon this morn's netting even at thy feet, scarce a score."

And He said: "Put thee off the shore and cast."

And they murmured: "Nay, 'tis vain; for the nets have been spread therein and brought forth naught. How then may we bring forth fish from out the shallow places?"

And He answered them, saying: "I speak unto thee in that thou knowest. Put thee off the shore and cast."

And upon the shore arose the voices, speaking out: "This man is wise! Do thou this thing!"

And the men whose boat He stood within made ready. And He stood even as the boat started off the shallows, and lights gleamed upon His locks, and His mantle of coarse stuffs hung soft unto Him, and His lips moved. And all who listed stood mute before the spell of the music of His voice.

And the boat slipped unto the waters off the shallows. And they watched, and behold, He bade that the nets be spread and let fall. And behold, Simon the fisher let down the nets but his words spake: "Why dost thou bid that we fish in the fished waters? It is vain."

* Within our capacity to understand.

And Jesus made answering: " Dost thou leave thy net down in no faith how may it find aught save thy folly? "

And He caused that Simon bring up the net. And Simon fell upon his face and cried out:

" I am a wicked man! Behold, before thee have I set my doubt. Aye, and how may a man's doubt become greater than his God, save that he put his doubt before his God? "

And Jesus said: " Thou hast acknowledged thy doubt and fallen down before it. Cast thou the nets! "

And Simon let fall the net unto the waters, and behold, the waters stirred and the boats swayed, even so that it seemed that storms lay beneath the water. And they made to draw forth the nets, and behold, the fish leaped high and the silver shewed glisted within the light. And within the boat the men were not enough that they draw forth the nets. And they that watched saw, and men sprang unto the waters and swam to the spot and lended aid that they bring forth the nets. And they marveled and said: " What is this man? " And they cried: " Master! Master! "

And behold, their voices arose unto a tumult as they brought the nets back unto the shores, and men swam with the boat and held unto the nets that they bring forth the catch. And when they had come unto the shore and the boat lay within the shallows Jesus called forth unto all of them and delivered the fish unto them. And they cried:

" This is wondrous! What is it? "

And Jesus made answer: " This is naught. For the netting of fish is little unto the bringing forth of men."

And Simon fell upon his face and spake unto Him of his wickedness. And Jesus said:

" Arise and put thy nets by; for thou shalt weave a net of thy love and bring forth men."

And they spake: " It shall be; for this man hath looked unto lands and even though his nets slipped the waters his dreaming was not there."

And they spake unto Him more, saying: " It hath come that thou hast lain low fever and hath cleansed and healed. What is that that is thine that is no man's? "

And He answered: " The time is not come that thou shalt know, but it is true that no man will hark save that a loud noise setteth up. Thou mayest not know, but within thy land the eyes shall ope and the ears hark, unto the eye's undoing and the confounding of the ears."

And behold, afar there sat Hatte. And Aaron found a boat that no man had looked upon, it being far from the multitude, and he busied at the nets, weaving his folly. And Hatte had looked upon the boats going out and coming in and had harked unto the words, and behold, he sat him watching, his lips curled, and he spake:

"Tiberius, thou art nobled yet the fishes come not at thy son's bidding."

And he arose and limped unto the shore's edge and stood that he hark unto the wonder that spread among the men. And one among them offered unto his hand a fish and spake:

"This is one that He brought forth, and look! there still remaineth many that no man may take, for there be o'ermuch for the dealing unto these."

And Hatte took from out his hand the fish and looked upon it and spake, and he laughed amid his words:

"He hath brought forth fish! Dumb things that may tell not whither from they have come! This is no wonderwork, for some wild storm hath troubled the waters and driven them shoreward. This is no wonder."

And the man who had delivered the fish unto him looked at the curled lips and harked unto the bittered tone, and spake:

"Thou art follied, for no storm nor yet troubled waters have driven them up that any man who cast might take them in."

And Hatte answered him, saying: "That thing has ne'er been done. Is not this the token that it can ne'er be done? Leave thou unto me thy boat and I shall take it forth and leave down the nets and bring them forth laden even as He hath done."

And the man made answering: "Do thou this thing. Yon is the boat thou mayest take." And the nets lay ready within it, and he called unto the people, saying: "Here is a man who would do even as Jesus Christus hath done."

And the words reached the ears of Jesus and He made no answering, but smiled. And they asked: "Is this thing true that he hath spoken?"

And He answered: "List unto his words and watch his works, and be they strong nets * fish shall come forth."

And they returned them unto Hatte and spake: "Jesus Christus hath told that a man may weave of his love a net and bring forth men, and this, the bringing forth of fish, be but the loud noise that all men be caused to list."

And Hatte laughed and answered: "A man may weave a net of his hate even as he may of his love. Yea, hate is e'en so strong as love."

---

* His words and his works.

And they brought these words unto Jesus and asked that He answer, and He looked unto them and spake:

"A man who speaketh out of hate is fevered. Hate may ne'er bring forth men but cast them from thee. Hate is a sling, and the man who wieldeth it useth his own heart as the stone."

And they returned unto Hatte bearing these words, and Hatte answered: "He hath lied, for Hatte hath no heart. This man buildeth up wisdoms that be a fitting path for His feet, but no man should tread a path save of his own building. He singeth a sweet song; but the days be not sweet and the dinning will not leave thee that thou mayest sing. Yea, His singing would be as a lash unto thee."

And they returned unto Jesus and told unto Him these things and He answered them, saying:

"A man may not build his own path, inasmuch as he may not build his own wisdom, for neither his path nor yet his wisdom is his but the Father's. All this is true, but a man may sing. Yea, he may cover up the stones of his path with the golden dust of loving and the dews of his singing."

And they wondered and spake among them: "His wisdom holdeth well; and this man's, who speaketh against Him, they sound as the heretic's." And they spake among them: "Let us then leave him go forth within the boat and see doth he bring forth fish."

And they did this thing, and even did they lend their hands unto the making ready the boat. And they asked: "Who art thou?"

And he made answer: "I am the son of the father; for inasmuch as yon man speaketh that He is noble, even so am I. My father might reach forth his hand and crush thee like unto a fly. Even the words of Him yonder might he shut."

And they asked of him: "Who is thy sire?"

And he answered: "Ask Him yon, and He will answer thee, 'who.' Even so, I answer thee, who."

And they spake: "Tell unto us in what thing abideth strength."

And Hatte answered: "Hate."

And they spake: "Go thou! Take the boat unto the shallows and bring forth a full haul."

And they raised him up upon their shoulders. And behold, his beard shewed thin, and his lips thin and pressed unto the whiting, and his eyes shifted as the flight of a hawk. And they bore him unto the boat and put him within, and they spake unto him, saying:

"Go, and return with such an net's full as did Jesus Christus."

And lo, the light of the sun was deep gold upon the waters. And the boat slipped slow unto the shallows. And Hatte stood him up within the boat and the light played upon him and he spake:

"Tiberius, thy son rideth unto his fall, but he rideth proud, and his wisdoms shall undo them. No man may rise o'er the son of Tiberius. No man may bow down and cry out save unto thy son."

And he went forth slow, and when the boat had come unto the spot where Jesus had cast, he let fall the nets and waited. And behold, no trouble shewed within the waters. And he drew forth the nets slow, and not e'en one small fish shewed within them, nor no thing save the wastes that beset the shallows. And they who watched saw what had been, and they swam out unto him and beset the boat and brought it up unto the shore. And they laughed and mocked him and cast stones and railed upon his wisdom. Even did they bring forth Aaron, who dragged his nets, and shewed unto him that even he had brought forth fish. And they set upon Hatte and bore him down.

And Jesus saw this thing and came unto the spot and made way, among them that bore him down, unto his side. And lo, he lay upon the earth at the feet of Jesus. And Jesus reached forth His hands and spake unto the men: "Be ye still!" and unto Hatte: "Arise!"

And Hatte turned upon his face and hid him and sobbed. And Jesus leaned o'er in pity, and spake: "Arise!"

And Hatte answered: "I may not arise. I am cast down. If thou art the Son make me whole. I am broken, yea, and wickeds abide with me."

And Jesus said: "It is easier far to say 'Thy sin is forgiven' than to say 'Arise and be whole.' Thy flesh is far more whole than the spirit within thee."

And Hatte said: "Yea, but I ne'er broke the spirit, nor may thy singing mend it."

And he arose and spat. And behold, Jesus stepped Him back that the spat fall not upon Him, and lo, where it fell He bended Him down and plucked up a white bloom. And He held it forth unto Hatte and spake:

"Look! even a man's hate may bloom. This is the folly of all men. And they shall yet know that they may not offend against the God; for their folly shall undo them. A man's hate mounteth up unto the pinnacle of heights, but to meet God. Man's path is upon a wheel. Even so is God upon the wheel and he shall come upon Him; for behold, the wheel is Him. Ye make much of wisdom, yet I say me that men are but babes that the tides shall wash unto naughts."

And Hatte stood him listing, and his lips curled. And behold,

Jesus put within his hand the bloom. And they that had seen this marveled and spake: " This man doeth things that setteth man's wonder running upon legs! "

And it was true that they left Hatte free, and he went upon his way, and Aaron followed. And they that sent forth for Jesus followed Him. And they sought their brothers that He might tell unto them the wisdom of peace.

And the even came and Jesus had wearied, and behold, they that had listed left Him lone that He seek rest. And the shores shewed within the light of the moon, and the waters shewed silvered and tremorous. And He sat at the water's edge and spread His arms ope and spake, and lo, the waters trembled in silver sheen, and the stars seemed to dance within the silver, and all things sounded the sounds of silence before Him. And the moon hung white, still, and her rays streamed like silver wings down unto the waters. And behold, upon the shore He sunk and bowed Him before His Father's gentleness.

And the bright light shewed the shadow of Hatte, seeking, seeking, and Aaron, slipping like a dark shadow after. And there sounded the shrill call of a nightbird, and the lips of Jesus smiled, and He spake: " I may not know thy heights."

And Hatte heard the call and started and shut the sound from out his ears and spake: " With one hand might I fell thee! "

And Jesus spake unto the night, even unto the bird: " Thy song hath no beginning nor no end, for it is of the Father."

And Hatte hissed unto it: " Thou singest, and at morrow's eve thy song may be stopped for aye."

And the bird called it on and on.

CHAPTER IX

AND it was true that there set the lands much of the fame of Jesus Christus. Men came them from afar to hark unto Him, and within Jerusalem market's men sold of wares and gave free of the telling of Him. And the days of Jerusalem set up loud noises of His fame and the Jews among them beat their bosoms and spake: "This is the Promised One!"

And the Rome's men took in all of this, and word crept the ways even unto Rome and set the tongues of the nobles speaking words that set Tiberius at unrest. And at this time, which was three score and ten days following the bringing forth of the fish, there shewed upon the way, Hassan, who, upon his camel, followed Nada and Panda upon asses. And the face of Nada was lighted up as by the meeting of joy, and she spake unto Panda, saying:

"Look, look, Panda! but yon hill and about it and then the spot."

And Panda answered not but raised his hand and pointed unto the hill and shook his head, "Yea."

And Nada spake: "Panda, dost thou remember that Levi sent thee and me unto Nazareth even out of his dealing unto us, for within Nada was unrest? Yea, Nada knew not the wisdom of rest and waiting. It seemed unto her that the swallow whirred yon, yon and yon, and she must follow. Yea, but Nada hath learned, for the Man of Nazareth hath wisdom that waiteth, even though thou and Nada do know He is more than man."

And she turned unto Hassan, and behold her face shewed thin and worn, and she cried out: "Hassan! Hassan! look! It is but about yon hill!"

And Hassan spake: "Tarry! Tarry long! For this is the sweetest time, the waiting."

And he drew up the camel so that he stepped slow. And Panda spake: "Yea, Nada, wait."

And Nada said: "Why should Nada wait now, for the waiting is ended. See! the flowers bloom the sods. See! scarlet and white and yellows sprinkle o'er the stones. Look! the earth is decked. Panda, it looketh like unto a dream of Nadab." And she touched a pack upon which she sat and spake: " Ah, Panda, think; this is the last, and it was not right that we might make price of it."

And Hassan spake: "It was true wisdom that took Hassan back unto the rug's man, for behold, he had bought these from the hand of Jacob. And Hassan thieved one and set small price for the other. When wisdom faileth then a man is right who thieves, for this one who held these rugs met a thief as brother. Hassan hath been an honest man, but the days of this land—ah, 'tis o'ermuch! They creep of tradesmen who bart, and doth the barting fall short then 'tis among them known that cunning warreth cunning. See! the gods forgive, for hath one rug not brought the price and yet another remaineth?"

And even though Hassan's words sounded on, Nada listed not, but her eyes eat the way. And behold, they came about the hill's curve and one came forth that he meet them, crying out: " Brother! Panda!"

And this one was Paul, and he hasted upon the way unto them, and when he had come unto the spot he spake: " Hast thou brought Hatte?"

And they answered " Nay," and Paul leaned close and said: " There is o'ermuch word within Jerusalem and his tongue speaketh o'ermuch and Paul feareth should he bring him forth."

And it was true that Nada drew up the ass and alighted her, and sped unto the hut's place and looked upon the spot, and sought the outspot whereon the babe lay. And behold, o'er the spot the grass stood thick, and the hands of Paul had brought forth a young tree of myrtle and it stood young green and bowed o'er the spot. And Nada knelt her upon the sod and held her arms as one who would receive a babe. And she turned unto Panda, and her eyes shone, and she spake:

" Panda, the time is long, and yet it seemeth he is but a babe. Nada seeth his great eyes and his golden skin and the black locks, and heareth him tell, in his babe's tongue, of the steed he yet should stride."

And Panda said: " Nay, nay, Nada. He is tall and slim and his legs speed like lightnings. Panda seeth him before a flock, yon."

And Paul came unto them and spake: " Trouble is upon the land. There is no time when there abideth much words within a land but that storms arise. Hassan, within the Rome's place abideth the she-one who telleth o'ermuch, and this is Indra. It hath come unto the ears of Paul through Isaac, who maketh much word with Abraham whose cunning is like unto a serpent's."

And Panda busied his hands at the unloosing of the packs. And Nada sped unto the hut and went her within and sought the grain's bowls and caught them unto her breast, and behold, she sought beneath a cloth's hang * and knelt her down and bowed her head upon the racks of Nadab. And Hassan brought down the camel and brought forth that it might feed. And they sought them within, where Nada had even then busied at the bruising of grain. And Panda looked sad-eyed unto her.

And she ran unto him and threw her arms about him and spake:

" Sorrow not, Panda. I have found him here. He is within the grain's bowls, within the walls, upon the floors. And see! even here standeth his bowls of brass waiting his hands. They know the wisdom of waiting. Nada shall keep the hut and wait. Yea, and wait. Yea, and be it well, wait her longer, longer, longer. For when the night cometh unto Nada he will come, and he still will be her babe. Yea, and Nada shall spread her wings and take him within her bosom, and they shall speed unto the moon, Panda, and wait the coming of the great bird, Panda."

And Paul brought forth waters and offered that they sup, and spake: " Panda, the few sheep have become many. Thou shalt take these and the days shall be well for thee, for Nada sheweth that the tides have dealt o'erheavy unto her."

And Panda spake: " But what is right shall be Panda's, and thou, Paul, shalt share."

And Hassan cast him upon the floors that he rest, and he turned unto Paul and looked keen unto his eyes and spake: " Within the Rome's places, then, a woman speaketh o'ermuch? "

And Paul answered: "Yea, and more; she hath caused slaying among the men and a man called Arminius hath fled with a woman slave from out the palace and sought this man of Nazareth that he be rid of her tongue."

And Hassan's eyes married, and he spake as he arose: " The beard of Hassan is black and his tongue is covered of slime. Yea, and Hassan hath a thing that may ope the Rome's places unto him. Look! dost thou not believe that Hassan might even lay a woman low? "

And Panda said: " Hassan, this is no time that we make merry."

And Hassan spake him: " Panda, doth Hassan then read thee right, surely thy wisdom must weight thee down, for it is heavy. Look! were the earth at the last day and all men sleeping, a woman might set them waked. There is no good that woman is not within, and little evil, Panda, little evil. Hassan knoweth that the sting hath set this woman, Indra, wrathed, and a woman wrathed—ah, Panda, a roused lion is tamer far! Hassan hath whetted his wisdom, yea, his wits, upon men's, but would a man possess a sharp, keen wisdom, he should ply it

* A curtain.

upon a woman that it edge. This woman knoweth o'ermuch. Like u. all women in this is she. This is the time that all men word, and she, like unto all women, would mix her words with the days."

And Panda spake: "Hassan, Indra hath truth but for her own flesh; and the truth within her hands at this time may be the sharpest blade that we may meet."

And Hassan said: "Panda, Hassan shall leave his camel that thou mayest seek it and look upon its smiling, dost thy wisdom o'erweight thee. Hassan would seek Jerusalem and walk among her men that he know what be, e'er he seek this woman Indra."

And the eve was come and they made ready that they rest, and spake words one unto the other of what lay upon them; for Panda held within him the knowing that Tiberius held such glut for power that no man might claim a people.* And it was true that when the dark had come, Nada lighted up the lamps and put them within the walls.† And lo, she uncovered the racks of Nadab and spread forth the rug and brought out the brass bowls and made the smokes. And when this was ready she oped the door and called. And they harked unto her calling, and Hassan spake:

"Thou callest Nadab, Nada. Is this thing a comfort unto thee? Knowest thou not that the nights be empty, that Nadab hath gone?"

And Nada held her hand up and spake: "Hassan, thy tongue jesteth. The nights are full. Yea, the dead live the nights, even as we who live, live the days. The night is the spirit of the day—white-pale, yet radiant. Look ye! is not the sun replaced by the moon, and the shadows renewed of softer stuffs? The day doth not die, neither he who liveth the day. The Nazarene knoweth. He taketh the heavens of the false prophets, wherein men toil in gaining, and setteth it full of the spirit of all things. Even the stream that hath dried, Hassan, floweth on there. All things hasten, hasten, Hassan, even as the young swallow, to know that land. This day is empty, He hath spoken, for a man's deeds be done and forgot; and he goeth on that he bring forth new deeds. For this is the time for labor and not for rest, Hassan. We begin the work here that ne'er endeth. We fashion from out our clays the stuffs that build up the eternities. The hands of to-day make new things of the ashes of yester's yesters. Even so is the Heaven. The Nazarene!—ah, the words of the prophets tell great things, greater than man's understanding, and His words tear their telling unto shreds and make them fit for the feeding of His flocks. As dry grain-stalks He offereth them unto the people, and they know the stalks, Hassan, though they know not the prophet's

* A nation.   † In niches.

hey may bed them upon the stalk's soft, and words be

said: " Nada, thou dost drink from out the Nazarene's
all men do not find."

pake: " But doth a man thirst after he suppeth such
cup, he is no man; for a man with no eyes may see the things He
offereth."

And Hassan smiled and said: " Then dost thou believe that Nadab
cometh, and is within the hut? "

And Nada sighed and answered: " Yea, even as thou and Panda."

And Hassan looked him about the lighted room and spake: " But no
eye may take this in. He is here, thou sayest, yet Hassan seeth he is
not."

And Nada shook her head and said: " Nay, Hassan, thy reasoning is
one-limbed; for thou hast for to learn that a man's flesh liveth only
within them that love him."

And Hassan spake: " But he speaketh no word. Did he come unto
thee bearing unto thee a thing thou mightest look upon and know, then
thou mightest say, ' 'Tis Nadab.' "

And Nada said: " There be men within Jerusalem who could do
this thing—bring forth words of Nadab and goods his hand hath
wrought. Even seers of dreams might tell unto Nada much. But Nada
would believe not, for she knoweth that he who hath gone upon the
river that spanneth twixt the Yon and Here, may not return save that
the waters that bore him o'er cling unto his raiment. For flesh is
washed. The Nazarene knoweth. He hath come to tell, yea, and for
to shew. Then did Nadab return, thinkest thou he would offer dreams
such as he wove within rugs? Thinkest thou he would prate of the
market places or the changing of moneys? Nay, he would bring forth
the stuff of another land. Man shall yet learn that he may not lay his
hands upon his God, neither bring the shadows to fill up a clay cup.
The silence of Nadab is the silence of God, yet Nadab speaketh through
every shade and shadow, yea, and light or darkness. Even so, God.
And this is right, for there is but one thing a one of the There might
bring forth, and this is the musics of heaven that shall blend unto the
riotous dinning of the days of earth and make of them melody. The
glory of the noon of earth fades before the new day's dawning. How
then, Hassan, may we sing of heavens? For when the last note of earth
is made, the highest of all, the deepest of all, there beginneth the
heavens. The words of man be cups, and we may not drink heaven's
fullness out of the cup of man."

And Hassan reached him over and lay his slim hand upon the head of Nada and smiled unto Panda, saying:

" Behold the small brown owl! Panda, know ye not thy wisdom is unfit for the feed of such an one? Forget these things, Nada, and live the day, not the dead nights."

And Nada shook her head and spake: " Nay. Nada would forget the things thou rememberest and remember the things thou forgettest."

And she arose and went unto a lamp and blew upon it and it darked. And she sought the other and stood her, holding it within her hand, and spake:

" Sleep, sleep, Hassan, and learn of the dead night's living things. Nadab forgiveth thee. I see his hands busied and his teeth flash. Is it not true, Panda, Nadab hath forgiven him? "

And Panda answered: " Yea, Hassan, thou shouldst become as one of the household. It is sweet to know that all things that be gone abide with thee, yea, even set at thy door's step and know thy board, yea, thy very bread; for that that thou takest from one of these is the bread he eateth. Sleep, Hassan, and in thy sleeping, wake; for when thou speakest so and be waked thou art sleeping.

" Nadab, set up the racks. The light shall burn beside it and we shall list to their music, and, lest we disturb thy dreaming, lo, we shall sleep and join thee."

And Paul rose and stretched him, and let his mouth ope in gaping, and spake: " All this of dead things, and, Panda, thou knowest the land is teeming full of life, and that life here in Jerusalem is like unto an evil day ever, for one man besetteth the other, yea, and one tribe oppresseth the other. Thou mayest dream thee then, but the day shall set thee well waked. Shall Hatte follow thee? "

And Panda answered him: " Nay, he abideth with Hezekiah and shall live the days of Nazareth."

And Paul said: " 'Tis well. 'Tis well. But this Hassan, this brother who hath given of himself unto thee that he deliver thee out of thy days of need and bring thee forth unto Jerusalem—Hassan, thou speakest him, he knoweth that dreaming doeth not the day's workings. Yea, he shall seek out the market's-way and go unto Abraham and make words at the morrow that he take in the fullness of that the tongue of Indra hath spoken."

And Panda spake: " Paul, 'tis night and the night is for dreaming. Begone unto thy rest and wait the day that it find thee at that thou wouldst do. Hassan, go thou and leave thy dreams to set thy wisdom keen."

And they looked upon Panda and Nada and smiled, and the light of the lamp streamed out unto the dark through the oped door. And behold, a night-bird beat its breast upon the door's-way, and Nada touched the arm of Panda and spake: "Look, look, Panda! Seest thou? 'Tis the swallow!"

And they turned, and Paul and Hassan sought the without, and Panda waited until their going, and behold, he stepped unto the door's-way and bowed his head and held his hand high. And Nada sought his side and they called: "Nadab! Nadab!" and went them within.

And Nada left the lamp that it burn aside the racks, and they sought the rugs. And lo, it was still within the room, and the lamp set the shadows creeping slow, like long-armed things, about the walls, and the smokes from the wick's tip curled slow and twisted unto a shape, and behold, the legs were withered! And the winds that came within swept it unto a naught, save a silver cloud that clung o'er the racks.

CHAPTER X

AND the morning came. And it had been that the young hours had been swept of rains, and the thunder had pealed and the lightnings had lit the skies, and when the light shewed, the earth lay fresh, cool, and the green stuffs hung of drops. And the vineyards' men were up and amid their fruits that they pluck them cool and cover of leaves and bring unto Jerusalem.

And Hassan had waked and called unto Paul, for they had worded long into the night. And Hassan had told unto Paul of what had been within Nazareth, and Paul had made full unto Hassan the things that had filled Jerusalem. And Hassan had spoken:

" Paul, Panda hath wisdom like unto a great stone and Panda would push this thing through the day. Yea, and this thing tarrieth his feet, and this is no time that a man may tarry. This thing thou hast spoken, that Indra hath driven forth a woman, a slave, with her tongue's lash and spilled out that that abided within her unto the ears of Rome, is a sorry thing. We shall seek out Abraham and find the things he knoweth. See! Hassan shall strip and deck but in a skin, and crook his hand so that he shew as a shepherd. Of the wisdom of Abraham shall Hassan drink."

And Paul spake him: " Brother, thou art wisdomed, and thy wisdom flasheth bright but hath not a sting. Abraham is a serpent. Watch ye unto it; he will empty thee and tell naught."

And Hassan raised his brows and rubbed his hands one upon the other and spake: " Hassan, seek thy camel! This shall be a day."

And he turned and took up an armful of dried stuffs that he bear unto the camel that lay, neck down upon the earth. And he cast the stuffs beside it and went before it and took its head within his hands and spake: " Smile, brother, smile! "

And the camel waked and made that it arise, and Hassan said: " Nay, brother, nay. Sleep, sleep! Panda sayeth it is well. In thy dreams hast thou found a she-one, white and glisted? Ah, that Hassan might dream a dream like unto thine! Aye, for Hassan knoweth thy dreams would be humped; for how might such a crooked beast dream a straight dream? Hark!—cease thy chewing!—hark! Thy master seeketh Abraham. Answer thou! is Abraham a fool? For thou hast spoken thy master is both wise and a fool. Speak! is Abraham a fool?"

And the camel looked sad-eyed and shook him nay. And Hassan laughed and spake: "Then woe is upon Hassan, but he woeth in joying."

And he cast the stuffs that the camel eat, and spake no word but turned and sought Paul, who stood readied. And he sought a skin cloth, a loin-bind, and went within, and came forth even as a shepherd.

And they sought the road's-way unto Jerusalem. And Paul shewed unto Hassan, as they went the way, the things that the seasons had brought to be. And the roads crept of them that sought the within of the gates. And when they had come unto the city and gone within, they sought the market's place and the bin of Abraham. And Paul touched Hassan, saying: "Yon is Abraham."

And Hassan looked unto him and his teeth flashed and he spake: "Behold, Hassan hath sought a lion and come upon a he-goat!"

And they stood and harked unto what was coming from out the bin's place, and the words sounded out saying: "By the prophets' beards! Hark unto such a man, who bringeth in a skin that hath been eat unto holes of sores, and would have full price!"

And there sounded the answering, and the voice of Abraham spake: "May the prophet curse thee, but Abraham will ne'er give full price for an holed skin."

And there came the voice of him who would of the price, saying: "Thou liest! for look ye, the wool is thick and the skin soft. This is a skin fit for a youth's robe!"

And Abraham wailed, and there sounded the beating of his hands one upon the other, and his voice cried out: "Look ye! Look ye, honest men, unto this one who would undo an aged man!"

And Hassan drew nigh and listed close unto the bin's side. And Abraham, seeing him, held forth the skin and shewed unto his eyes the holes, and wept tears o'er his cheeks that dripped unto his beard, and he cried out:

"Behold, brother! thou art not of the tribes. Look ye! this man would of full price for such a skin."

And Hassan smiled slow and reached forth that he take the skin within his hands and spake: "But a fool would buy such a skin."

And Abraham cried out: "Yet this fool would sell it!"

And Hassan spake: "Then hark! give unto him a coin for each hole therein."

And Abraham arose and held his hands up and they shook, and he said: " The brother hath spoken it. It is true and well spoken. Abraham would be the honest man and do that which is right unto his brother. By the word of Abraham, which is ne'er broken, he will do this thing."

And Hassan's hands slipped unto his bosom and his blade he brought forth, and he lay the skin into folds and slipped the blade through the all.

And Abraham arose and flung his arms wide and raised his eyes as though he worded prayer, and cried out:

" Not only is this man a thief, but an evil one, for he barteth his brother's bart. What doth a dark-skin know of barting? Oh, ye bones of the prophets, quake ye in rebuking! Set up a loud noise and call his name! He would that Abraham deal unto this man who beareth a skin filled of holes even so that it looketh unto a fisher's net."

And he made more of words, saying: " It shall be, for Abraham hath spoken out his word and the word of Abraham is ne'er broken."

And Hassan bended low o'er the earth and sought about the bin's place. And Abraham ceased his crying out and watched him and asked: " What doest thou, evil one? "

And Hassan looked him close unto Abraham and answered: " Seeking the broken bits of thy last word."

And Abraham spake. him: " If the words of Abraham be broken, Abraham will leave a brother to share his beard."

And Hassan laughed and said: " Thou didst say that thou wouldst deliver unto the hands of this man one coin unto the one hole, unto the full counting."

And Abraham wailed but shook him yea. And Hassan delivered unto the hand of the waiting one the skin and spake: " Offer thou thy skin, brother. Leave him that he count the holes."

And behold, the man spread forth the skin, and it shewed slitted. And the eyes of Abraham started forth, and the hand of Hassan sought his blade. And Abraham counted the holes unto the score, and his eyes took in that holes still remained, for the blade of Hassan had cut through the skin's folds thrice.

And Hassan spake: " The coins, bartman, the coins! "

And Abraham held his skin sack unto the whiting of his flesh. And Hassan watched him close, and Abraham laid him down ten coins. And Hassan spake: " More, brother, more! else thy beard's hairs rock within their pits."

And Abraham lay him down seven coins, and Hassan said: " Hark! thy beard cryeth out aloud! "

And Abraham spake him: "Nay, this is not an honest man's dealing."

And Hassan said: "Nay, thou art right, brother." And he whetted his blade upon a thong and reached unto the beard of Abraham. And behold, Abraham spread forth his hands in sign that he stop, and lay a coin beside its brother. And Hassan flashed the blade and cut free an half of the beard of Abraham. And Abraham cried out: "The swine hath defiled the flesh of Abraham!"

And he made loud noises unto the market's men, and they laughed among them. And Hassan spake: "The coin, brother, or the beard's * full!"

And Abraham cried: "There is no law that speaketh that Abraham should do this!"

And Hassan held high his blade unto the eyes of Abraham, saying: "No law save this!"

And Abraham emptied his sack upon the skin and spake: "'Tis done, and the word of Abraham is whole."

And Hassan said: "Yea, 'tis done, but the words of Abraham scarce held together."

And he handed unto the man who barted the coins and spake: "Go thou, and remember that this man is not as all Jews. If thou wouldst make full price come not unto a 'wise' man."

And the man departed. And Paul watched what had been and held his sides in laughter. And it was true that Abraham leaned far, and his hand covered his smitten beard, and he looked unto Hassan and spake:

"Thou art wise, for thy wisdom hath crooked legs that may follow crooked paths. What dost thou? For thou art not of the bartmen nor the market's feeders."

And Hassan answered: "Thou hast spoken that I am wise, yet thou wouldst the full of what a man doeth? No wise man telleth his feet's tracking."

And Abraham spake: "Couldst thou stand beside the bin's place and decry the wares, Abraham would deliver unto thee one-half the o'ertake." †

And Hassan answered him, saying: "Nay, thy tongue decrieth, and then wouldst thou have another man, a one who sought would leave and feel that he had been sunk into a pit."

And Abraham spake: "But think—the dealing! Ah, Abraham would make a fair price and thou mightest set up the undoing of the

* Or all of the beard. † The profit.

price and point out unto him who offered it that it be even less than a beggar's gift."

And Hassan said: " Nay; Hassan shall seek the courts of Rome. Yea, the very halls, for he hath goods for the women."

And Abraham spake: " Knowest thou the women therein? "

And Hassan answered: " Nay, but a man's eyes may speak and offend not."

And Abraham leaned close and said: " Yea, but should Abraham make thee known unto them that possess most among the women, wouldst thou make sharing of that thou dost deal? "

And Hassan answered: " Yea, a man might do this thing."

And Abraham spake: " What manner of goods hast thou? "

And Hassan answered: " Soft stuffs for mantling; silver threads and golden wires; gems of onyx, and ebon circlets; yea, discs of silver and more of such stuffs."

And Abraham spake: " Thou hast spoken that a man might share. Abraham knoweth that Indra would take of these much unto the many."

And Hassan asked: " Indra? What woman beareth such a name? "

And Abraham answered: " She is a she-thing of the courts."

And Hassan questioned: " Yea, but what land e'er named a woman so? "

And Abraham spake: " She abided with a man called Panda, a desert's man, who builded his hut yon, without the walls. And Abraham made her folly-wise, and she delivered her unto Rome for Rome's goods. Abraham hath made her wise, yet her tongue is follied, for she leaveth it to speed her angers, and it yet shall drive her e'en out the halls."

And Hassan said: " Yea, the word hath gone forth that such a woman drove a woman from out the Rome's halls with her tongue's lash."

And Abraham spake: " But Rome hath within her walls the sire of this woman, a man named Flavius. There are ones who have come straight from the mighty one, Tiberius, who would keep Indra and this man for what be within them, for they seek a one, a youth. Some say it is this Jesus Christus, and others among them that he is named Hate. Indra knoweth the full of this man Hate, for the woman she drove forth was called Mary and had been housed with Panda."

And Hassan said: " Cease thy wording! What doth Hassan care of the market's prattle? "

And Abraham spake: "But this woman, Indra, hath wisdom that shall bring her riches."

And Hassan said: "What a noble aim! Wisdom's weight for moneys! She hath much wisdom, indeed, Abraham. Where is she?"

And Abraham answered: "Within the Rome's hall. Go and speak unto her that Abraham hath sent thee and she will hark. Go and take unto her hands this,"—and he reached beneath the skins and brought forth a scourge of thorn and golden strands! And Hassan reached forth and took the scourge and spake no word, but his eyes narrowed.

And Abraham spake: "This will ope the ears of Indra. Begone!"

And Hassan said: "It is done." And he went upon his way, and Paul followed.

CHAPTER XI

And within the Rome's hall it was high hour. And within the bath Indra lay, and let the clear waters to drip crystal from her dark fingers' tips. And her locks shone wet of oils. And she was waited upon by a young slave who poured scents upon the waters and rubbed the flesh of Indra with myrrhed oil, and bruised buds o'er her locks. And Indra questioned: " Una, what is within the mouths without? "

And Una answered: " Little; but Una hath heard much word of the Nazarene. It hath come unto Jerusalem that multitudes follow Him and cry out, ' Lord! ' It is told that He hath not e'en held His hands forth that they bow, yet they cast them down unto their knees. And within the halls the men speak much of this, for His fame is creeping far. There are men among us who say His strength maketh the walls of Rome to tremble, and—Una feareth to speak, but she hath heard it is even spoken that this man is the son of Tiberius! "

And Indra laughed and spake: " Tiberius abided with a woman, and she a Jew! Nay, Una, nay! 'Tis not this game Tiberius playeth."

And Una said: " Yea, but 'tis spoken he hath a son, his very own, and not within the noble's rank, but of a slave, and she was called Theia."

And Indra stood up out of the waters, and drops ran like silver veils o'er her flesh, and her lips stood wide unto the white's gleaming, and she murmured:

" Theia! Theia! And Rome had thee? . . . Ah! So this is the why of the purple cloak! This, then, is the thing that putteth the legs of a deer upon Hatte! This then is the why! Indra, the gods smile. I feel thee fat. . . . Where, then, is the man of the camel? . . . They deem the Nazarene the son of Tiberius! . . . Ah, he is broken, he is mad. . . . So! Rome playeth a dull gaming! Theia hath gone— Indra knoweth this—unto Rome. Hatte is up Nazareth way. Yea; then Rome hath ne'er oped the lips of Theia. . . . What meaneth this? What doeth Rome with an aged woman as a slave? . . . Yet, how is this thing? for a one who hath come late from Rome said the woman, Theia, was handmaid unto a handmaid. Yet they say her son is the son of Tiberius! No thing would stop her from calling out this save

fear. And Theia was ne'er fearful. Then 'tis fearing o'er the son!
So, 'tis not Theia Rome would have, but the son. Then Indra filleth
up upon that she may that telleth of him; for hath Tiberius a sore and
the fly of jealousy besetteth it, he shall seek the fly. And the Nazarene
hath cause to have troubled dreams. The fox waiteth that the fowl fat.
Una, bring forth raiment. Helios waiteth."

And she robed her slow, making smooth her locks and resting that
Una fan her cool. And when she had done, behold, she sought the
without. And a slave came forth bringing word that a merchant man
sought the ear of Indra. And Indra spake: "What manner of goods
hath he?"

And the slave answered: "He shewed no goods but speaketh that
he hath much that thou shouldst know."

And Indra said: "Go thou unto him and say that he shall shew his
goods."

And the slave went from thence and returned, bearing the scourge,
and gave this unto the hands of Indra. And Indra looked unto it and
murmured: "Where hath Indra looked upon this?"

And she stood long, and her fingers slipped o'er the strands and she
said: "Hair! Ah, filthed, but hair!"

And she spake unto the slave: "Wait thou!" And she went within
the bath and dipped the scourge and made that she cleanse a part of
it. And it gleamed, and she arose and spake: "Hatte!"

And she returned swift unto the slave and said: "Go and bid the
man come!"

And the slave sped without and Indra waited, and her hands
clutched the strands upon the scourge, and she harked close that she
hear the coming of Hassan. And behold, the slave returned unto the
spot and Hassan followed but looked him not up unto Indra. And
Indra turned not but knew that he stood beside her. And when he had
stood long she turned and her eyes looked upon him and she said,
"Begone!" unto the slave, and the slave sped whither. And Hassan
waited, and when they were lone Indra looked unto him and spake:

"So thou bringest goods? What stuffs bearest thou save this?"

And she held forth the scourge. And Hassan answered naught, and
Indra asked: "What then? Wherefrom didst thou beget this?"

And Hassan answered: "'Twas but a waste within a swine's bed."

And Indra looked upon him and said: "Cast thou the skin's cloth.
Ope up thine eyes. Cast thy staff and be that that thou art, Hassan."

And Hassan said: "Unto thee, Indra, 'tis well, but beggars know
not men as brothers save that they be ragged and loused. Hassan would

fellow with the road's men and know their tongues' packs. List! thou hast wielded thy lash. Thy tongue hath cut deep amid Rome's. Thou hast done that that no woman save one whose flesh be rich might do; but hark! Hassan looketh upon thee as rotted carrion. Thou hast sold thy flesh, and what hast thou begotten? Hassan knoweth that he may turn Rome's beasts upon thee."

And Indra turned, and her eyes narrowed, and she answered: "Hassan, thou knowest not Indra. Indra feareth thee not, for look ye! Indra hath the coin that Rome's men bow unto, and Indra spendeth freely. And hark! 'tis come unto this hall that thou hast done not the thing thou wert sent unto. Nay; thy blade hath rusted and thou didst leave free the flesh of Rome. Yea, Indra knoweth Hatte is the flesh of Tiberius. Speak not! Thou mayest not deny it! Yea, and thou hast within Rome, Theia, the woman. She hath stopped their words; for Tiberius believeth that did his flesh live she would take it unto her. Tiberius knoweth not Theia. Yea, like unto this all men; for they know not one woman. Hassan, dost thou raise thy hand unto Rome against Indra, Indra shall spat up all of this! Theia, ah, Theia!—she then hath goods that be of the flesh of Indra's. She! Then she knew o'ermuch 'gainst the flesh of Indra. What and who knoweth but that, did she not shed her raiment and spend it unto the sire of Indra, Indra might not be of higher rank? Aye, Indra seeth her—a fearful thing—spent, empty, wracked like unto some dead thing crawled from out a burial pit—decked within Rome's splendor! Yea, and within Indra burned the flame that she would ne'er be set up o'er her kind. The woman, then, waiteth yon for her flesh, and Tiberius seeketh him. Hassan, thou art come for to do a thing, and Indra shall game thee. Which shall win?"

And Hassan stooped and touched his fingers' tips upon the stones, and behold, dusts shewed upon them; and he whiffed upon them and spake as one who had wearied:

"Indra, thou seemest for to have forgot that thou art but dust. Rome playeth with slaves as the winds with dust, and Hassan—ah, Hassan is not a noble, but one of his feet trod the nobles' path! Indra, dip thee within the bath. Thy wits are covered of dust, and Hassan shall blow a gale! Hassan shall warn thee that he playeth not fair. Nay, and shouldst thou be upon his path and what he coveted be beyond, then might his blade slip thy ribs and rest in peaceful, peaceful comfort. Indra, this is no sweet song that Hassan singeth but 'tis a true one. This is fair that he tell thee, and his fair fighting here endeth. Ope up thy lips. Tell unto the ear of Rome that Hatte be the flesh of Tiberius. Tell it loud. Speak of Theia as his mother. Tell this unto Rome.

Tell this. It is well." And Hassan slipped his thumb o'er his blade. "Some he-hawk that flieth high shall feast upon one of thy white breasts. It is well."

And Indra drew her up and spake: "Hassan, thy tongue is no steed, and there is a desert of sands that thou shalt cross before this thing be."

And Hassan reached forth his hand and plucked up the hairs upon his fore arm and spake: "Behold! this is a steed with flowing mane."

And Indra made a sound within her throat and said: "This is no merry-make, Hassan. Indra hath spoken she shall undo her tongue unto Rome, but at the time when Rome holdeth forth the first-fruit in full price."

And Indra looked upon Hassan and laughed, and Hassan turned slow and spake: "Behold, 'tis hot without. Methinks Hassan shall seek some cool shelter."

And Indra said: "Where didst thou find this thing?" and she held forth the scourge.

And Hassan answered: "I have told thee, Indra, within a swine's bed."

And Indra spake: "What man without upon the streets of Jerusalem told unto thee that Indra abided the hall?"

And Hassan answered: "A man who weareth half a beard."

And Indra spake: "What manner of Jew weareth half a beard?"

And Hassan said: "A Jew that is but half a Jew and half a rogue," and he shrugged. "But a man is more than whole since he be half rogue and half Jew and half beard. 'Tis then o'ermuch that we speak him Jew."

And Indra leaned her close and said: "Knowest thou Abraham?"

And Hassan answered: "Hassan knoweth a he-one who woeth o'er his brother's gain and sleepeth not that he feed his cunning. His wisdom is crooked and his words hold no truth. He would receive full measure for no price. Is Abraham such an one?"

And Indra said: "Thou hast spoken it. Abraham hath such a net of crooked wisdom that all men fall within it."

And Hassan raised his brows high and spake: "All men? Indra, nay; but follied women and fools."

And Indra said: "Hassan, hast thou stuffs for the selling?"

And Hassan answered: "Nay; thou, Indra, hast this thing. Hassan hath bought his goods with all that is within him, and they are his, shared not save with them who spend their loving."

And Indra spake: "Thy tongue speaketh as a Roman's in wine.

Look ye, Hassan! thou mightest step even upon the steps of the mightiest seat by unloosing of that that thou knowest. Deliver Theia up. Bring forth this man, Hatte. Who is he that thou shouldst leave him free? Look ye! Tiberius hath heard of the raising up of the hosts with Jesus Christus, and he glutteth. Yea, he deemeth that no man save one of the nobled blood might step o'er the purple. Speak, and stop the searching, for even here within these walls is Flavius, that Rome holdeth, fearing that he see the day aright and tell abroad that that he knoweth. And yet would they sup out of him that that he knoweth for Tiberius. Dost thou remember Mary, who dwelled with Panda and the woman, the child of Flavius?"

And Hassan's eyes narrowed and he spake: "Where is she? Bring her forth!"

And Indra answered: "She is gone from hence."

And Hassan cried: "Then she is the woman thy tongue lashed from out Rome's walls!"

And Indra said: "Hassan, look ye! Indra knoweth much, and thou art full of wisdom that Rome coveteth. Come! thou mightest but measure within the measure of Indra and behold, the fullsome gain! Hassan, art thou a fool? Knowest thou a woman? Look upon Indra."

And she stood her tall, her locks bright of oils, and her flesh gleamed golden. And Hassan answered:

"Nay, Indra, Hassan is not a fool, and he knoweth a woman. Thou hast the temple's pillars but not one beam to cover them nor yet a stone for the floors." And he smiled and spake: "Hassan hath shewed thee his goods. It is well. Thou mayest not buy, but thou hast looked upon them. It is enough."

And he turned and made that he seek without. And Indra stood long looking upon his going, unto the time when he shewed not. And when he had gone, a slave came forth bearing a cup unto her hand, and behold, she smote her. And when this had been she sought the slaves' place and tore ope her breast and clutched within her locks and spake:

"Indra, thou hast yet to weave the thong that hangeth Rome! Hassan! Hassan! The roads shall swallow thee. Yea, Indra shall seek the mighty ear and bid they lay hands upon thee."

And she lay her down and shut her eyes long and stroked her slim hands o'er her long locks slow. And lo, there came within the slaves' place a woman who had fatted at the hand of Rome, and she eat of sweet stuffs, honeyed fruits. And Indra oped her eyes and spake:

"Thou art, then, feeding. Ah, and thou knowest the sorrows of the night when the belly will not hold the fill."

And the one answered: "There is much within the halls among the men. They spake that one hath come out of Rome who seeketh a man who rideth upon a camel, and is called Hassan."

And Indra arose and clasped her hands upon her bosom and spake: "Indra, the sun hath come forth! Yet tarry! for doth the hawk fell the bird, why cast a stone?"

And she stood long and stretched her arms wide and spake no word, but sunk that she lay and slumber. And the Rome's men came and went within the halls.

CHAPTER XII

AND the paths shewed Hassan seeking unto the market's-way. And he came unto a well that he drink, and behold, within the well there hung a thong whereon was put a hollowed stone. And he sent it unto the waters and drew forth and drank. And there came unto the well's side a beggar whose back was bended and whose neck was sunk unto his shoulders,* and he made that he leave down the stone but his back was bended so that he might not do the thing. And Hassan spake:

"Wait thou, brother. Dost thirst? Leave me that I draw forth for thee."

And the beggar smiled, and behold, o'er his filthed face it flashed light like unto the sun that breaketh through the fleeced clouds of the young season. And he plucked at the sleeve of Hassan, the skin's leg that covered his shoulder, and said:

"Hassan, Hassan, what dost thou robed even as a shepherd?"

And Hassan answered: "What! thou? Ah! then Rome hath left thee forth?"

And the one answered: "Yea."

And Hassan spake: "The gods laugh. The nobles creep the high-ways." And he touched the bended back and asked: "How is this thing?"

And the beggar made answer: "Ah, Hassan, it is free! Even though bended, it is free; for it bendeth beneath a pack."

And Hassan laughed and spake: "Where hast thou thy pack that it sheweth not? The days offer unto all men's eyes that that men's eyes may not look upon. Where is thy pack?"

And the beggar answered: "Ah, that thou mightest know! Hassan, hast thou harked unto John?"

And Hassan spake him: "Nay; the words of John creep the high-ways, even as this Nazarene's."

And the one said: "Yea; knowest thou that the Nazarene taketh unto Him men He calleth His brothers, and they be laden of His words. James, even as John, knoweth His wisdom. Also the tongues of Simon

* A hunchback.

547

and Andrew. Hark ye, Hassan! this man hath a host, for they bear a thing that all men hunger for. Look ye unto the pack. It is the pack of love. How may I bend beneath it, for it lighteth my fear and sheweth new light unto mine eyes."

And Hassan shook his head and spake: " The Nazarene bewitcheth them that come beneath His spell. But hark! this Nazarene telleth of no new God, for the desert's men knew His God e'en before He saw the day."

And the one who sought the drops said unto Hassan: " Thou hast spoken truly, Hassan, yet what is a prophet save one who giveth the god a tongue that he speak unto man? Yea, and thou dost know that they sing not a new song, but tell one thing, be this voice that speaketh from out them God. The Nazarene speaketh in words that confound, yet His wisdom doth confound; for He speaketh words that hold a score of shadows. The Jews fear this man yet love Him; for behold, He eateth with the multitudes, breaketh bread with any man, be he Jew or yet one without the tribe's blood. He knoweth all men and opeth up the temples, yea, bringeth forth the priests' words like unto flesh, that men may eat. This is the thing, Hassan, that maketh the Jews to fear, for behold, have they not clung unto their blood and caused it to be an offense did a Jew spill his blood out his blood's tribes that they keep one stream? Even so they shut up their God within the temple, yet every man hath of Him, dealt by the priests. But this is not a full feeding. 'Tis but a substance fit to make him live and move, but not to fatten. Aye, this thing is true, but the Nazarene—ah, He bringeth the God down even upon thy path! He putteth the blade within thy hand and sayeth: ' He is thy Sire. I am thy brother. Go thou! this blade is thine, for Him. How knoweth thee but that thy blade is the thing that shall slay all that riseth 'gainst Him? Go thee forth, for Him, with Him, and lone not for Him.' And He hath spoken that the God followeth a man as his shadow, even far closer, for unto God there is no darkness that slayeth the shadow. It is a new day, Hassan! Look yon. Behold the sun, hanging o'er Jerusalem! It hath risen o'er Rome, and these eyes knew it not as the golden ball within the Sire's hands. Ah, Hassan, think ye! Look upon this back and think ye! I may raise up mine eyes and say, ' *My* Sire hath cast yon ball!' He is mine, and thine, and yon market man's, and even the God of the asses. But think, Hassan, think! O'er all He is mine! Think, Hassan, think! All men may take of Him, yet He is mine! Even *these* legs may walk proud! Even *this* head may lift up! For what be dusts, what be the curse of the market's places, what be the spat of Jew or Roman, what be a lash, what be earth, unto this, Hassan? He is *mine*—and the Nazarene is my Brother!"

And Hassan reached his hand forth and lay it upon the crooked back and spake: "Hassan knoweth not, but the Nazarene is wise. Suredly within this day, when no man may claim aught as his own but the cast of the hand that passeth him, it is well. Thou shouldst know that the sand's men knew this God even as thou; for beneath their steeds' hoofs the dusts spake Him, and the far line that rimmed the sands were His arms; while the sun was His gleaming head and the clouds His headcloths. The Nazarene is loosing much that shall set up woe among men, for Rome hath bended their backs and their heads even so, and He shall raise them up. It is well. But whither goest thou?"

And the one made answering: "Unto the bin of Abraham."

And Hassan laughed and spake: "What! take a god unto a godless one? He will not of a god save that the god hath goods. Aye, and did the god offer the goods Abraham would wail and loose his beard before he paid him full. Take thy God and on, for Hassan is full of woe and it is not his own."

And the beggar's eyes lighted bright and he spake: "Take thy woes unto the Nazarene."

And Hassan's lips thinned and he said: "Hassan feareth lest the woes be taken unto Him. Go, and may the God cling thee!"

And the beggar sped upon his way murmuring, and his face was bright, and his lips smiling.

And Hassan stood long, and sought not the bin of Abraham, but mingled among the men and listed and took in all their lips said of all that beset their days. And behold, at a spot he heard the voice of two that spake of the Nazarene; that He had plucked ears upon the Sabbath and eaten thereof; even had He bid His brothers that they do even so. And the Jews had rebuked Him, saying: "Look ye! thou dost eat with the men of the road's-ways, even of beggar's bread, and thy hands pluck grains and eat thereof upon the Sabbath. This thing is not right nor holy within the sight of God." And that the Nazarene had answered them that they spake falsely; for had not David eat the shew-bread out of the temple. Then a man should eat did he hunger. And they made much of this thing, saying that He broke down the prophets' laws and trod upon them. And He had listed not but eat, and even so His brothers.

And Hassan listed long, and behold, the two spake them, saying: "It is known that a one followeth Him and the Jews fear that he would do harm unto His flesh. This one is lame and knoweth not the full day, inasmuch as he is his own man one day and a chattering fool the other. It is spoken by many tongues that this lame one is a Jew, and by others that he is some Roman's blood. The multitudes speak his sire's name ' who,' even as the sire of the Nazarene; for what man believeth this man was brought forth save as all men? "

And they laughed among them, and Hassan's eyes took in that these men were of Rome and they spake with two Jews, and the Jews listed but laughed not, and made words, saying: " It is a fool who laugheth save that he know the depths wherefrom his laugh springeth. This man hath oped the eyes of all men. He hath done wonders. What god, even of the Jew, hath done this? Look! He hath healed sores and even hath the flesh become whole that had been born broken. Yet He doeth this not before the great ones that He take in power for His own day, but unto the humble and for no price."

And they told of the fishers, and the word that had come of the casting out of evil things from man's flesh, and spake: " What is this thing? Be He born of man or be He a god, be He a Jew or yet a Gentile, He is like unto no man; for all men that come beneath His words fall down. He is a man of full years, yet His eyes are the eyes of a babe."

And they wagged their beards and shook them yeas and nays. And Hassan listed long and took in all that was spoken, but no words came that told aught that might fat him.* And he sought out the ways where Paul waited. And this was within the market's places, and when he had come unto the spot, behold, it was beside the bin of Abraham. And Abraham wailed o'er grain that had been brought forth, and Hassan cried aloud unto the man who had offered: " Go ye yon, for thou hast brought thy grain unto a rogue! "

And Abraham turned and gnashed his teeth and tore at his beard, crying out: " By the sacred camel! By the bones of Egypt's kings! By the song of the serpent, yet by the bite of the dove! Look ye unto this man who hath done unto Abraham the defiling of his beard! "

And he lay his hand o'er his smitten beard. And Hassan laughed, and Abraham spake: " Whither hast thou gone? Hast thou then been within the halls of Rome and spoken with the woman, Indra? "

And Hassan laughed louder, and Abraham poured forth his words, saying: " Then hath she made thee price and taken of thy goods? Didst thou bear unto her the scourge? "

And Hassan laughed yet louder, and Abraham arose and spilled the grain o'er the earth, and he set up a full wailing, crying out:

* That might give him the information he sought.

"He bewitcheth me! for look ye, Abraham hath spilled the grain and e'en though it is rusted grain Abraham shall have to set a full price for the spilling!"

And Hassan still laughed, and Abraham looked unto him and his lips fell ope and his eyes started forth and he looked long, and spake: "What manner of braying ass is this? For in truth it is an ass that brayeth in glee o'er spilled grain!"

And Hassan held unto his sides his oped palms, flatted, and laughed and bended him low, laughing unto the shewing of water within his eyes. And Abraham cried out unto his market brothers:

"By all thy hopes that thou shalt come unto some pleasant realm at the losing of this day, lay hands upon this man! Bring him up; for his braying hath sicked him."

And he came from out his bin's place and went up unto Hassan and spake in loud tones: "Hark! Hark! Answer thou Abraham! Didst thou go unto the Rome's place? Hast thou looked upon the woman, Indra?"

And Hassan looked unto Abraham and stopped his laughing and stood long, and then burst forth in louder laughter. And Abraham spake:

"Stop thou, brother! Come! lend thy hand unto the plucking of wools. See! Abraham shall minister unto thee doest thou this thing."

And Hassan stopped and began that he wail, and he called unto the market's place:

"Behold thou this man, Abraham, who offereth price for the plucking of wools when these hands would set at labor for but the asking, and no price would he bid!"

And Abraham held his palms oped and spake: "Since thou speakest it, so it shall be. Come, brother, come!"

And Hassan cried aloud: "What! thou wouldst break thy precious word? Nay, thou shalt minister unto Hassan."

And it was true that they went unto the bin's place and Hassan sat him down at the plucking of wools. And Abraham spake of the days.*

And it came unto the eve's hours when the light was hot, the mid of eve, and still Abraham spake on. And Hassan plucked the wools, and Paul stood afar and watched, for he knew that Hassan emptied Abraham of what he would. And there had stood at the bin of a fellow merchant a one of young years who watched, and when it was late two came unto him who bore skins and they sought the bin of Abraham.

* Of current events.

And when they had come unto it they listed, and Abraham spake unto Hassan, saying:

"Thou dost know that thou art not of Rome even though thy feet trod Rome's paths. Thou art no Roman, nor is thy heart within Rome, for Abraham knoweth that a dark-skin knoweth no man as his brother save another dark-skin."

And Hassan raised his brows high and spake: "Abraham, did the lips of Hassan call thee brother? Dost thou then wish that thou mightest empty Hassan of his reason for seeking thee and knowing much of the days of Jerusalem thou hast set upon a stoned road's-way, for the camel of Hassan is long-legged and laugheth at the stones."

And the two who had sought offered their skins, and Abraham spake soft word unto them. And it was true that they stepped unto the spot where Hassan sat plucking wools and asked: "Art thou Hassan, the camel-man?"

And Hassan laughed and answered: "Any man knoweth Hassan be Hassan; even so Hassan sayeth Hassan be Hassan."

And they lay hands upon him and spake: "Come! for it is bidden. Out from Rome hath come forth ones who seek thee."

And Hassan raised him not up but sat plucking wool and spake slow: "Hassan, thou art fool and wise, eh? A crooked path leadeth unto a crooked man's bin and thou hast followed the crooked path, even unclothed, yet left any man to know thee; sought to play a crooked gaming and laid thee down a straight measure upon it. Ah, Hassan, thy folly hath o'ercome thy wisdom. But who would e'er believe that the fools knew thee? Thou hast sat at the plucking of wools and, behold, a Jew hath fleeced thee."

And he turned unto Abraham and bowed low and spake: "Abraham, thy beard is gone; but hark! thou hast cunning enough to pluck thy brothers, and set the hairs unto the pits. Thou hast undone Hassan."

And Abraham fingered gold and said: "Abraham knoweth that a man who telleth o'ermuch unto a woman hath wove his hang-thong."

And Hassan spake: "He who felloweth with a rogue taketh the rogue's mantle. 'Tis well. Come! Hath Hassan not enough wits or yet wisdoms for to undo one woman and one rogue then Hassan falleth short. Indra, Abraham, shall hang thee; for doth the thong bind her full throat she shall lend thy neck unto it. Await, Abraham! some fair morning thou shalt feel the squeeze of the thong. And Indra shall be within the bath, toying with some small token from some new love. Abraham, thou shouldst leave the hand of Hassan sever the half of thy beard that remaineth, for think!—should the thong catch upon it—think! to defile thee so! Leave thy neck free, Abraham, and delay not the hang-one's labor."

And the Rome's men bade that Hassan arise and come with them, and he did so. And Paul, who watched afar, took in what had been, and sped unto the hut of Panda, bearing word that Hassan had fallen into the hands of the Romans.

And night came upon Jerusalem, and unto Panda the knowing that Hassan was taken, that Jerusalem held o'ermuch of the knowing of Hatte, that the days were troubled, and that he too should seek "the house of Silas" for to learn the wisdom of waiting.

And within Rome much had come; that the Jew, Christus, had a host come unto Him, and that He followed the bypaths and that multitudes followed Him. And Tiberius was full of the power of this man; for not only did the Jews follow Him, but even the Gentiles and some of Rome and other lands. For lo, His words sounded upon all ways and flew as white-winged birds from one man's lips unto another.

And Tiberius had bidden that ones go forth and lay hold of Hassan and that when this was done Hassan should be caused to shew unto them the flesh * of Theia. And Theia knew naught of this thing, save the broken bits of words dropped about the palace places. And she waited, waited, and the days wore upon her even so that shadows darkened her eyes, and her temples sunk. And when it was night, lo, would she seek out quiet spots and sink upon her knees and cry out:

"O-o-o-h-e-e! O-o-o-h-e-e! O-o-o-h-e-e! Jehovah! Jehovah! Lend thou thy hand. Confound their steps. Make them blind unto what is, and let them see what is not. O-o-o-h-e-e! O-o-o-h-e-e! It is long, the morning's coming. Theia, weary not! Wait! Wait! Hassan will return unto thee. Thou shalt seek the long path unto the hill's bosoms that hold him. Wait! Wait!"

And her body would sway in weakness and she would arise and speak: "Theia, Theia, thy flesh hath lied. Look! thou canst dance!"

And she would pluck forth the golden cloth of her locks and weep, for much of silver glinted it, and she would cry: "Theia, Theia, arise! Wake, thou crumbling flesh! Arise! Ah, when shall the morning come? Tiberius, thou mayest make the night but thou mayest not bring the morning! The sands shall gleam, yea, and the palms wave, and o'er the glistening gold the caravan shall sweep, and at its lead a camel, white as goat's milk, whose eyes shall gleam as rubies. And Theia shall robe

* The son.

her within twined flowers and the golden cloth, and dance to meet the caravan. It shall be! Yea, and the golden glory of the morning's sun shall turn her silvered cloth to gold!"

And she turned unto the palace way and spake: "Tiberius, even now the tides have clutched thee and thou dost wither. Tiberius! Ah, Jehovah, hark! If Theia hath sinned, if Theia hath brought forth Hate from out sin, hark!"

And she bowed her down unto the touching of her brow unto the sod and looked her then up unto the heavens and cried: "Hark, and hark! Theia knew it not, for spite of the bitter, spite of all the tides, the smiting, the empty aching, the pits, the all, Theia loveth Tiberius! She may not die, save that she speak it loud and hear the words, for they have eat, eat, eat, in burning searing. Down deep beneath Theia's scorn the love lay laughing. She brought out of her love a fruit and called it Hate, and behold, the calling of it Hate mocked her, for he was the writ word, Love. Theia was cast away from out the arms of her love. Tiberius, thou dost not know the emptiness of the days that befell Theia then! Yea, and ah, the mockery! Even thy flesh * was denied me, for through thee Theia had ne'er held her own unto her. 'Tis not that thou art noble, Tiberius, nay, but that thou didst hold not a bowl full deep that Theia might give full her wine. Theia is nobled, yet this thou hast taken from her. O-o-h-e! Jehovah, this head splitteth! I would hate thee, Tiberius! Yea, but I shall save thee. Yea, even shall I live a dead woman for thee. Yea, even as Theia loveth thee shall she save thee. Thou shalt be uncrowned by them that hold thee dear. They that set upon the seats thou hast given them shall undo thee. It is written! Yet at the tide when thou hast done a thing that shall write thee down unto the ages, Theia shall be mute; yet shall she undo that that she hath done, even though she crumbleth unto dusts; for she might not rest beneath the searing stain!"

And the morn's sun oft found her sleeping upon the sod, spent.

* His son.

CHAPTER XIII

AND the tides swept unto the passing of the moon from the full unto the empty. And it was true that Panda had waxed fearful; for word came unto Jerusalem that a man who limped and who had as his fellow a fool, spake unto the multitudes and told unto them of the power of hate; that within the spot where Jesus Christus spake with the people, behold, he had gone and cried out against His teachings and the people had stoned him. And they had railed upon him, crying out against him.

And it was true that within a certain city multitudes had followed the footfalls of Jesus, and cried out unto Him that He fill them up. And He had come unto them with them that He had chosen for to be His brothers * and deal the living bread. And they wearied, for there was no spot whose walls were so wide that they might take in the multitudes. And these were beggars, publicans, sinners, aye, and Jews. Even them of other lands came unto Him that they hark. Thereby He wove of all men His footcloth.

And they that He called His brothers spake unto Him, saying: "Master, shew unto us how it is that the bread should be offered."

And He answered them, saying: "Yon, upon the mount, 'tis shaded. Come! bring forth them that would list, and seek the spot. Out of the city's places, away from all that that setteth din, come, and the bread shall be thine."

And they followed Him, but He spake: "Nay; go ye before! for the ages have preceded the Son of Man. Thereby He is even as the shepherd."

And they spake one unto the other, saying: "See ye, He putteth Him not up and o'er us. Behold, are we not the footcloths for all men? Do not our brothers trod upon us, and the priests hide the God?"

And they went up into the mount. And they waited the coming of Jesus. Even did they part unto the halving and leave Him through that He seek a high spot from where to speak unto them. And the brothers that He knew followed Him and spake: "Master, shew unto us the ministering of the bread." † And He made answer: "He may not feed a multitude. Nay, but break thou one bit for the feeding of one and another for the feeding of another."

* His disciples.   † The word.

And they said: " How then may we make words that we may feed every man? for suredly, do we cast the bread wide, some may fatten and others shall hunger."

And He spake: " He who ministereth shall touch that that he ministereth unto. The Father is with thee even as with me. Unto all men He is *the* God.* Unto one man He is *the* God. Unto all men He is the Father, but unto every man is He Sire."

And they said: " How dost thou speak this? We take it not in."

And He spake: " Bring forth thy brothers, one, then the other, that we feed."

And they brought forth a one whose body was covered not save of rag-cloth, deep-dyed of dusts, whose skin had shrunk and left his bones writ upon it. And they said:

" Master, behold, this man is a beggar. What manner of bread hast thou for him? "

And Jesus leaned unto him and took up his hand and spake: " Cast thy staff! thou needest it not, for thou hast bread. Blessed is he who hath not, for it shall be given unto him."

And He stood, holding the beggar's hand, and spake unto them: " Look ye; he hath not, but his day is thine, his water is thy sup, his breath is even as thine. The road's-ways that bear thee are his. His day is filled not of the changing and barting; thereby he is empty of goods of earth and may be filled up." And He said unto the beggar: " Even as thou art empty, even so shall it be given unto thee."

And lo, the beggar stood him up and cried out: " Master, it is true! Think ye! "—and he turned unto the multitude,—" my Sire cast yon ball! The bread is mine! Lo, out from Rome hath the noble blood † been cast within a crooked bowl,‡ for to be filled up of precious stuffs! "

And they looked upon the beggar and saw the light within his eyes and knew his words as truth.

And they brought forth another, and he fell upon his face and spake: " Lord, I am unworthy of such a God as thou bringest. I am lowly and not the son of one even so high as yon beggar. I am the dusts of the road's-way. I am unneedful unto the earth."

And Jesus bid that he arise, and He smiled and lay His arm about the one and spake, smiling: " Blessed are the meek, for inasmuch as they cast them down they shall be lifted up."

And He smiled unto the down-cast eye of the one who had come

* The italicized words in this and following utterances of Jesus are so emphasized at the direction of P. W.

† One of noble blood.

‡ A hunchback.

unto Him and took him unto His breast, and turned His peace-filled eyes unto the multitude and then unto His loved ones, His brothers, and smiled and whispered soft:

"Blessed are the meek, for they shall inherit the earth. All men shall list unto a brother who casteth him down. Yea, meekness buyeth love, and love hath the power for to buy the earth. Behold, a man whose raiment is beauteous, and filleth up the eye of his brother, o'er-cometh him. Yea, and the doors of the humble shall be closed unto him. But he who is clothed within the cloth of meekness, goeth into the door of the mansion or yet into the hut's place; thereby no door is shut unto him. The door's-way unto the house of meekness is oped wide, and shut unto no thing. Thereby he who abideth within it knoweth all men as his brothers. He becometh as the dust of the road's-way, even unfit within his own eye to claim of the Father. He is empty, save of his fullness of the greatness of his Sire. Thereby is he full. Meekness is not the cloak of the hypocrite, but the armor of a Son of Man. Meekness casteth its eyes down but unto the might of the Father. Blessed are the meek."

And the one, who stood looking deep into the sweet eyes, sunk upon the bosom of Him and wept. And He took him unto Him close and spake: "It is well. Thou hast eaten the bread."

And the one answered: "Yea, and I am full."

And the multitudes stood before Him and their eyes glisted, and they pressed them closer; even did some among them sink upon their knees and speak prayers. And He turned unto the loved ones and said:

"Bring forth thy brothers that they eat."

And afar the sounds of the city's day crept soft like an echo, and the trees that shaded, bended, swaying soft, and the ways spilled forth the singing of the winged hosts, and the bleating of sheep and the pipe of the shepherds came like the ghosts of some past day.

And His loved fell down before Him and murmured: "Lord!"

And He answered: "Arise! They hunger, and are not fed."

And they brought forth a one who came up unto the spot, crying out: "Behold, the days are empty! How may a man know the Sire, the Father? Behold, the sacrifices are but meat and feed us not. The bread that we eat within the temple hath not salt. Before the face of God they draw the holy veil. Yea, and fill up the temple with smoke, even so that no light may come unto us that we may see Him. The first-fruits are brought forth unto the priests, who eat it in His name. Thereby are they fed—and we hunger. This is not the Father thou tellest of, who would eat the grain of His son and respond not with His love. How may a man know the Father?"

And Jesus held forth His hand and took within it the hand of him who sought. And He turned unto the multitude and said:

"Behold, this man is one of ye, for he hath set upon his tongue the thing that hath bidden ye hence." And He spake, and His lips smiled: "Blessed are the hungered, for they shall be filled."

And the multitude cried out: "Lord! Lord! We would bow down unto thee, yea, and worship thee!"

And He held His hands high and spake: "Nay! a man's worship is His labor. It is true that no thing is done in His name by him whose hands are idle. Would ye then worship, be ye at His labors. How might ye love me, yea, or yet know me as thy brother in the Father, save that I be thy brother in the flesh? And do I bear thee words from the Father, then shall I come as thy brother, since thy Sire is mine. Nor shall the words pour forth like beauteous streams to flow about the hill's-ways of earth and be forgot; but as bread, that no crumb shall be lost, and fed unto thee with *these hands,* that ye know thy Father's bread was dealt by thy brother, in loving and in the knowledge of thy hunger."

And He turned unto His loved ones and spake: "Behold, these are the Father's hungered. Thou art delivered His bread that thou mayest minister it. Become as thy brother, not o'er him, save as thou mayest be fuller of the Father. Then hark ye! take out of thy fullness and lend unto thy brother."

And He chided them, saying: "Dost thou minister unto a beggar, make the bread beauteous, for his days are barren and he eateth crusts. And dost thou deal the bread unto him that is rich, strip ye it unto but the bread and minister it unto him, for it is well that he eat crusts. Bring ye the beggars that they kneel before the Father beside the rich. Robe them both in one cloth, the love of the Father. Take ye the rugs from out the temple that the beggars bed. Put ye not unto an altar His stuffs; for He hath builded the earth's day as His altar. Behold, the temple teems of gold; even do they bart upon her steps. The chalices of office * are of precious stuffs, filled with the blood of the first-fruits, when behold, the tears of babe's faces do dry upon the mother's breast and the mother hungereth, yea, looketh unto emptiness to find the Father of her day. The brightness that the Father looketh upon is not builded up of earth's precious stuff, but lieth within the heart of man. Thy riches are but the dusts of heaven. Blessed are the hun-

* The word "office" is used here in the religious ceremonial sense.

gered, for they are offered unto thee by the Father that thou mayest fill them. They are the golden chalices of office unto Him."

And they that harked marveled; for this spake against the temple. And He, looking upon them, perceived their marveling and smiled and said:

"Even though man doeth this folly, the Father forgiveth him; for in their blindness they build of that that earth offereth unto the eye; yet, in the storing unto the Father of earth's dross, they fall them short of their filling and leave the empty chalices of Him that they be broken against the day. Even so, all things proceed unto the heavens and no broken thing abideth it. And he who falleth short and leaveth the chalices that they break, behold, the breaking is within him, and the mending is his. Yea, and there is no light within the heavens save the Father's face, and woe unto thee at thy mending, for He shall not look upon thee."

And they were frightened, for within the multitude were them that feared the words would reach the priests and the high officials.

And Jesus perceived this and spake: "Fear not Truth, for she sootheth and healeth the wound she causeth."

And they said: "There are more that hunger."

And He held high His hand o'er the bended head of him that had come unto Him, and spake: "Nay; this one is not filled. He hath asked 'How may a man know the Father?' and I answer thee, know His works; for therein is He. No fashioning of man holdeth the breath of Him, save that he who builded it took out of Him. Ye may know the false from the true by this thing. No thing liveth without it is of Him."

And they harked unto these things and stood long looking upon Him. And He spake not, but delivered the one who sought that he know the Sire unto his brothers. And they pressed upon Him, crying out:

"Thou hast spoken that to know the great God, man must know His works. Whereon shall he look that he know them? Are the smokes of sacrifices His labor? The fasting and feasting, are these His works? What manner of labor doth He do?"

And Jesus answered them: "Thou hast looked upon the works of Him since thine eyes oped. Thou hast heard from the lips of the priests the words of the prophets, wherein it is written He hath builded up the earth. Look then upon all things, mean or yet little, great or yet mighty, and this is His. The sun writes Him upon the skies, yet the shadows of the leaves tell more of Him, for they are beneath thine eyes."

And they spake among them: "Look! yon standeth the mad one and the fool! Bring him up, for his wisdoms have mighty walls, even though he holdeth no thing within them."

And it was true that they went up unto the lame one, who was Hatte, and spake: "Take thy woes unto Jesus Christus, for He is ministering unto the multitudes."

And Hatte said: "Thinkest thou He might fill the empty cup from which the wine hath spilled? Hast thou seen Hatte? He is gone!" And he called: "Hatte! Hatte! Come forth! Bring thy bowl and this man may fill it!" And he turned his anguished face unto them and spake: "See ye! he will not answer nor come forth. Call him, brothers, call him!"

And they spake: "Thou art follied, for the men of this spot have called thee Hatte."

And he drew him up proud and said: "Nay! Nay! Hatte is but an humbling, and I am the son of Tiberius—Tiberius, who hath her. Knowest thou her? She is the young morn floating unto the day upon the night's breeze, and her feet twinkle as the stars. Her robe is the white morning's clouds tinted of the sun. Tiberius hath eaten her. Hatte seeth her bones to gleam."

And he cried out aloud. And Jesus harked and spake: "What is this thing?"

And they spake in answering: "This man is beset of a devil. An evil spirit abideth him."

And Jesus smiled and said: "Nay; his words are bottomless. They hold not."

And He sought the spot where Hatte looked unto the skies, and his face was lighted up, and he smiled and cried out: "Theia! Theia! Behold thy son! Look upon the multitude! They have come unto him for to bow down and call him noble!"

And Jesus touched him, and he drew him away, crying out: "Nay! Nay! Thy touch is like unto hers!" And he shrunk even unto the hiding of his face.

And Jesus spake: "Art thou hungered? See! there is bread."

And Hatte's face flamed, and he turned unto Jesus, and his great eyes burned, and he bit upon his lips and beat his hands one upon the other, and he spake: "Thou askest is Hatte hungered? Ah, is Hatte hungered? List! he hath ne'er eat. Where is the bread? These eyes see it not."

And Jesus spake: "Give unto me thy heart that I may feed upon it, and I shall give thee mine."

And Hatte drew him high and smote the cheek.

And behold, a beauteous light brightened the loved countenance, and He turned unto him the other.

And they that had seen this thing cried out: "What! thou dost offer the other cheek that he smite thee?"

And Jesus answered: "Yea, for a withered hand may not know that that it doeth."

And Hatte hissed: "Give thou me the bread! It is not thine, but *my* sire's."

And the multitude cried out: "Nay, cast him down! He hath defiled thee."

And Jesus answered: "Nay; inasmuch as he hungereth, it is his freely. That which a man giveth, he should give forth freely, nor look for the returning."

And Hatte cried out curses and gnashed his teeth and frenzied unto the shewing of his madness. And when he was spent, behold, he fell down before Jesus crying out: "The earth is shut unto me! My brothers know me not. All men cloak within hate before me. Look! even the multitudes draw them from me and would stone me." And he looked him troubled unto Jesus and spake: "As thou art a man, if thy words be true, why hath the Father that begat me and thee done this thing?"

And behold, Jesus raised His eyes, and His lips were hung of sweetness, and He touched Hatte's flesh. And Hatte cried: "Nay! Nay! Touch not this flesh! The touch seareth—'tis hers!"

And Jesus spake: "Hark!" and He pointed unto the westway wherefrom came forth clouds that told of rains. And behold the lightnings played the clouds. And Jesus said: "Look! yon is the storm. It shall pass o'er the valley's places and the fields, and rains shall sweep and winds rage. Yea, and lightnings flash. Even then the sun shall follow.

"Love is the sun, and the wrath of men the lightnings; the sighs of men the winds; the tears of men the waters of the rains. And the sun of love followeth them."

And they spake: "What sayest thou?"

And Jesus answered: "Behold, then when the fields stand clothed of the raiment of lilies and many blooms, what thing hath done it?— the sun, or yet the storm? That thou mayest know light thou shouldst know darkness."

And Hatte spake: "Yea, but how may he who ever troddeth darkness know light?"

And Jesus answered: "Each day that cometh lifteth the darksomeness. Like unto the scales of fishes the days shall fall. Man may not eat the flesh of the day, save that he live the hours, and no man eateth a fish who taketh not off the scales; even so, a man may not know his day until he hath taken off his scales of hours."

And Hatte looked unto Him and spake: "Thy words fill this head up and it falleth unto agonies. Behold, I hark, and within me crieth out: 'The Father hath done this thing, and thy brother loveth the Father, thereby would He make shadows o'er the Father's offending.' Thou didst lie unto me. Thou didst speak the Father abided within the temple. Thou didst speak that thou wouldst tell unto Him of Theia and her flesh. Yea, and I sought the temple and was mocked."

And Hatte swayed and his eyes misted and he spake him: "What is this thing?" And he cried out: "The slaying! The slaying!" and ran from the midst of the multitude that laughed in mocking upon his madness.

And Jesus Christus spake in words that cut the airs: "He who calleth his brother a fool is in danger of the Father's wrath, for the fool is His son! Rebuke not, for rebuking hath a ne'er dying echo, and shall come back unto thee!"

And the multitude marveled and cried out words one unto the other, saying: "What manner of man is this who speaketh gentleness unto him that smiteth and crieth out against Him?" And they turned unto Him, and one among them spake: "What! Thou hast left this man that he flee?"

And Jesus lifted up His head, and His eyes smiled sorrowed, and He said: "No man shall eat save that he look upon the bread; and how may a man, blinded of hate, see the bread?"

And they spake: "Thou didst minister unto him. Thou hast spoken wisdom, yet his ears take in not that that thou hast spoken."

And lo, Jesus said: "Thou hast seen not this thing. Behold, he is gone, yet the bread is living and shall be fit that he eat, even though he tarry."

And behold, afar there sounded the voices of many who railed against the one. And lo, a voice cut clear o'er all the dinning. And the multitudes looked and they spake: "The one hath sought yon, and crieth out unto his fellowmen. Come, that we hark!"

And the loved of Him said: "Nay, we would list." And they stopped their words. And lo, the voice of the one came unto them, and, amid pealing laughter, the words:

"Ha, ha, ha! He hath offered bread unto one who hath no bottom to his belly. This is folly. His bread is for men who labor not with hate as their fellow. No words He hath spoken mendeth e'en one wound. Yet they bow down unto Him and cry Him ' Master,' ' Lord.' Ha, ha, ha! They lift up a fool and call Him noble! "

And they that harked, when the words had ceased, spake unto Jesus, saying: " Didst thou take in this thing? "

And He raised up His hand and pointed afar unto the way of the storm's coming, and answered: " Man's day is even as the day of earth, and cloud shall come unto one even as unto another. And this have I spoken; that, even as thy brother in the flesh, shall the Son of Man know man's day, and even so the days of earth; that He shew unto them that He ministereth unto *thy* day, unto *thy* hunger, unto *thy* woe, in full knowledge of thy need."

And they spake: " Thou didst say that no broken thing abideth the heavens. How is this thing? Behold, yon man is filled of devils."

And Jesus answered: " The words upon thy tongue empty him not nor fill him. No thing that is broken abideth the heaven, for look ye, the heavens are not yet builded. He who is empty *shall* be filled. He that is broken *shall* be mended and brought together. It is written! For no thing He hath fashioned is broken save man. And this thing is true so that he who is set upon earth by the Father is set upon the building of heaven.

" In the Father's house are many mansions. Yea, and the Son of Man goeth before thee. Yea, proceedeth unto the Father that He prepare a place for thee. Look ye unto it. This is the labor of the mending, yea, the filling, yea, the building.

" Behold, the man that tarrieth, tarrieth heaven. He who breaketh a brother hath set the break unto heaven. This thing is true. And not until the building is taken up and set finished, and all men look upon their days as the building, shall the heaven be builded.

" Behold, men shall rise up and fall, thereby falling heaven. Men shall take up the broken and mend it, thereby mend the heavens."

And they spake: " Master, thy words confound us."

And He answered them: " Nay, not thee, but the earth's days that shall come, yea, and come. Yea."

And they marveled at the words He had spoken, and they said unto Him: " Tell unto us—tell unto us the filling of our hunger."

And He spake: " A man's tongue should speak not unto the seas of his brothers, but seek the small pools."

And they said: " Wilt thou then minister unto another? "

And He answered: " Bring him forth."

And they brought forth a one who cast him down and spake: "Master, I have given of my goods unto my brothers that they prosper, and no thing returneth unto me. Behold me! I am a man who loveth his flesh * and hateth his enemy."

And Jesus took him unto Him and spake: "He who giveth should not look for the shadow of his giving to come unto him in return, for there shall be no sun of thanksgiving. And he who loveth them that love him, what thanks hath he? for there be sinners who do this thing. Yea, and he who hateth his enemies, what thank hath he? for there be sinners among all men who do likewise. But a man should love them that love him, thereby building up love. Yea, a man should love them that hate him, even so that the persecutions offered unto him shall exalt him; for therein is the rod by which man is measured."

And they spake, answering His words: "But no man doeth this thing. A man is a fool who would love his enemy, for did he clothe him within his love, then should he know not only the blade's point of him but its broad part."

And Jesus smiled and answered: "Nay, this is not the manner of loving. Love him as thy teacher; for he sheweth thee thy measure."

And they cried: "This thing is whole, and holdeth!"

And it was true that the storm came upon them so that the grasses bended and swayed, and the fresh scent of new winds cooled the stoned ways and caused that the kine arise and stretch, and the sheep to seek one the other. And it was shadowed, and the green of the field's-ways and the trees deeped unto shaded ways wherein the dark of the storm's frowning shewed. And the multitudes made that they seek the city's places. And they sought the roads'-ways down from the hill's spots, and they came upon them that harked unto Hatte. And lo, Hatte stood upon a high spot upon a great stone and called his words loud in mocking. And they fell upon the ears of them that went their ways, and he called unto them:

"Bid the Nazarene come and make a wonderwork! How may a man know Him as one who hath come from the great God save that He doeth greater things than man? What are words? They scatter upon the coming storms and ride the winds, to be lost. Even this day shall sweep away and leave them not. Bid that He come forth and make a wonderwork! His words shall fall unto naught and no man shall e'en care."

And the multitudes looked unto Jesus and spake: "Look! the

* His kin.

storm cometh, and yet this man calleth out that thou shalt do a thing and shew thee mighty o'er him."

And Hatte called: "Thou hast lied unto Hatte! Thou hast failed for to make him whole. E'en though thou didst bring forth fishes, Hatte defieth thee! And he speaketh that hate is the undoing of love. What knowest thou of this thing? No man hath hated thee e'en when thou wert not. No woman brought thee forth from out hate. Thou art measuring wine that thou hast ne'er supped."

And the multitudes came them together and brought Jesus up unto the spot. And He looked upon Hatte and spake: "Thou art supping the wine of flesh, when within thee is the Father's wine. And the sup of the wine of flesh shall cause thee for to weak and thirst, and thou *shalt* know His, the Father's, wine."

And Hatte leaned him close, even up unto Jesus, and said: "Tell thy Father His son would not of His sup, be it one whit so bitter as that He hath poured within his day's cup. Make thou a sign, that I may see thee o'er me. Look! yon field is deep grown and no thing is thereon to aid thee. Go, and bring forth a wonderwork!"

And Jesus looked with pity eyes and spake: "A loud noise shall be set up."

And the multitudes followed unto the stone wall that bounded in the field's-way, and they let down the stones that Jesus go therein. And the storm's winds broke heavy, and it was dark. And lo, Hatte followed, limping close upon His steps unto the midfield. And when they had come unto the spot, lo, a calm fell upon the storm and all things waited the breaking.

And Jesus raised His hands high and made a call, soft. And behold, from out the deep growth there came forth, like unto startled things, a winged host. And they flew them up, and hung as a cloud o'er the heads of Jesus and Hatte.

And Jesus spake: "Behold my words!"

And the birds parted, and flew them unto the East and unto the West, yea, even unto the North and unto the South, and the byways of the ways.

And Jesus let fall His hands and spake: "Stop them!"

And the multitudes stood before this. And Jesus spake no word but sought the city's-way. And Hatte stood long, long, looking unto the storm's coming. And it lightninged and the thunder pealed and drops fell soft, then thicker, unto the coming down of torrents. And still he stood, dumb, looking unto the sky. And lo, o'er the stone way came Aaron.

CHAPTER XIV

AND when the morn had come, behold, Nazareth was filled of what had been the filling of the night; for lo, the hill's-ways had shown sheep felled, and their throats split ope with a blade, and goods of households were taken from out the shelter and made way of. And they of the market's places told of this, one unto the other, and spake that not only had wonders set the days but the nights; for whose hands had done these things? And lo, it was true that when the sun was come out from the cloud and the skies gleamed clear, the ways crept of the town's men. And up unto the market's place came forth Aaron and Hatte, and they made way unto a spot wherefrom they might make purchase of eat. And behold, the loin's-cloth of Hatte was stained of blood and the nets of Aaron shewed dark of that man might call blood. And they looked upon the coming of them and spake:

" Behold, this man hath blood upon him, and the fool even so. But look ye, this man is evil. All men know this is the mad one, and a devil abideth within him."

And some among them said: " Mad? Mad? 'Tis spoken he is not mad but wise and full of evil."

And they lay hands upon Hatte and took him unto the chiefs of the town's place. And behold, it came to pass that they did speak out that he might not abide within Nazareth, but be cast forth as unworthy. And they that bore them hence drove them out upon the road's-way and stoned their going. And when this had been Hatte stepped him limped, and Aaron followed, and when they had come long upon the way, behold, Hatte turned and spake: " Nazareth, thou too hast stoned me! "

And word was sent unto Hezekiah of what had been and he sent Balaam upon the way seeking, but he came not upon Hatte nor Aaron, and returned bearing no word of their going.

And it was true that Hatte sought him far up unto a hill's height, and Aaron followed, and they bedded them upon the sods and crept the ways unto the vineyards and eat of the fruits and herbs that grew free-grown and not by man's hands.

And the days sped and still they tarried, and hunger was upon them.

And Aaron wept much, and Hatte grew him whiter and his cheeks sunk and his lips shut. And the nights brought but the morn and stars or dark, and the days but sun or cloud, and no man. And at a tide later, lo, upon a morn, Hatte arose from the sod and cried out:

"Oh, thou God of Theia! Hatte hath sought thee and he hath left off of the searching. Find thou him!"

And it was true that the sheep of men were felled by night and found in the high hills; for hunger had set upon them. And lo, when the tide had come unto the seeking of the byways by the town's men that they bring forth him who had done this thing, behold, they fled and Nazareth knew not whereto.

And at a later tide, behold, within a certain city came Jesus Christus. And the fame of Him had swept like unto eating flames. All men knew His works. His words were like unto cooling cups unto the thirsted, and no man knew upon what road's-way he might come upon a cup.

And it was true that a certain man of office sent forth when he heard of His coming, saying:

"Go unto this man who doeth wonders and bid that He come unto me. I am o'er my brothers; for within my household are them that go when my lips speak 'go,' and come when my lips speak 'come.' The walls of mine abode are hung of rugs and my bread is of the whited grain's meal, yet am I unworthy that this man come unto me; for He hath that that causeth the riches of man to turn unto dusts. Speak unto Him and tell that my well-loved servant hath lain him down and is smitten, and cause that He come."

And they spake: "But how is this that thou knowest He will heal thy servant?"

And the one made answer: "He hath but to speak the words and it shall be done."

And they sought Jesus and told unto Him of this thing, and behold, He answered them, saying:

"Upon the footcloth of his faith shall I enter his household. The bread of faith shall lift up his servant and the wine of love shall succor him."

And He followed them that sought, and behold, when they had come unto the household of the man of office, he sent forth a servant who bore words that his master spake that He should tarry, for his master was unworthy that He come unto him.

And Jesus answered: "Return and say unto him, I am already

within him; for in loving I have ministered and he hath eaten the seed and grown his faith."

And they entered the place and the man cast him down before Jesus.

And Jesus spake unto him: "Arise and shew me thy servant."

And the man pointed unto the inner place where, on the rugs, lay his servant. And he called: "Arminius! The Nazarene hath come."

And behold, the head of Arminius raised up, and his eyes were misted o'er of the falling away of the spirit, and he shook but made that he arise and murmured:

"Jesus Christus, the Nazarene, whom she seeketh!"

And it was true that Jesus called that they bring forth water and with His own hands bathed the fevered brow. And His words flowed sweet as a mother's sound unto her babe.

And the fevered lips of Arminius spake: "But to lose the blade of Rome! The yoke of the oxen to fall upon a noble's back!"

And it was true that Jesus heard all that had been, and He spake words of comforting, and within the words of comforting shewed the light of promise. And He sat Him long, and His hands busied, and they who had brought Him forth watched, and behold, the head of Arminius sank upon His bosom, and he slept even as a babe tired of the day's hours.

And his sleep-heavy lips murmured: "Arminius, thou hast lost office but to find a Brother." And he smiled amid his dreaming.

And they that saw spake: "He shall awake refreshed, yea, renewed."

And they called the name of Jesus blessed. And the man of office spake words of thanks unto Him.

And He said: "This is not done save through thy faith; for upon the footcloth of thy faith have I come unto thy household."

And He departed upon His way, and taught the people within the city. And when the hour had grown late, a man sought Him out who was a Pharisee, and spake unto Him bidding Him come unto his board and eat of meat and break bread.

And the multitude said: "Look! He goeth then unto the household of a Pharisee! Is this thing right or meet?"

And He answered: "Behold, the bread I offer shall be eaten within any man's household who shall receive it. Even so there unto his board do I sit and break it."

And they shook their beards, but He followed and with Him His loved. And some among them that came unto the eating of bread questioned:

" How is this that thou feastest and the disciples of John fasted much nor supped? "

And Jesus Christus spake, and His lips smiled: " Thou dost rebuke John and his disciples that they fasted much and supped not. Yet thou speakest within thee, ' Here is he who cometh and glutteth upon flesh and bread, and suppeth much.' And I answer thee saying: ' That that proceedeth from out John fed not upon bread nor sup, yet liveth; even so that that proceedeth from out my lips hath not succor from bread nor wine.' "

And He broke a loaf and dipped it within the wine and eat therefrom; even did He take of the meat and offer unto them that sat with Him. And as they ate, behold, there came forth a woman whose head was binded up of cloth, and she bore an alabaster box. And her hand smote the door's-way and she spake words unto them within that they leave her look upon Jesus.

And they turned and spake: " Depart, woman! we see thee not."

And behold, she swept swift up unto the feet of Jesus and oped the box, and the scents of the ointment crept the airs. And she touched the bruised feet of Him with her hands and wept o'er the bruises, and her tears flowed unto the dropping upon His flesh. And she unbinded her head and left her locks fall and wiped them, and took up the ointment and soothed the bruises. And her eyes she lifted not, but her lips murmured:

" Thy words are like unto the stars that light the night, yet thy feet are bruised of stone."

And they that saw this spake: " This man is no prophet, for He would know what manner of woman was this." And they said: " This is a wanton, a she-one, not fit that she touch the flesh of one called clean. She is a magdalene called Mary,[18] the woman of the servant Arminius."

And behold, Mary fell upon her face and hid within her locks, and her lips moved and the words spake:

" Nay, nay, it is not true. I am free of Rome, and this," and she touched the alabaster box, " is the last of Rome's goods; the ointment of folly shall soothe the wounds of Him, thereby buying fullness for emptiness."

And they that looked upon this spake unto Him, saying: " Behold, this woman is unfit that she touch thy hem. Look upon her! she is a wanton and hath come unto the house of the righteous."

And Mary arose not, but let her face to hide within her locks. And lo, Jesus arose and spake unto them who harked, saying: " What man among ye hath come that he bear balm? Behold, her hands have come filled of ointment. Her locks hath she let down that she dry her tears that fell upon the bruising. What man among ye hath done this thing? A man's words may build paths, but behold, doth he set upon a way unto his labor, then his legs should trod the path. Even so a man speaketh righteously, yet his hands lie them idle. Let him that hath called her wanton shew his ointment. Let him that hath spoken her a magdalene call her name blessed, for behold, her hands have o'ercome her sinning."

And they marveled at His words and cried out against the woman, and spake that such a one should hide her face. And behold, Jesus said:

"Woman, arise and shew thy face!"

And Mary arose and parted her locks, even so that her pure face shewed. And the cheeks gleamed of drops, and her full lips trembled, and her bosom heaved, and she looked unto them that stood within the place. And Jesus spake unto them, saying:

"Behold, a man's sin is like unto a door. It turneth upon a thong and the thong is the thing that causeth it to ope and to shut. Thereby the thong is the door. What man herein knoweth the thong that hath oped the door unto this woman, or yet shut it?"

And Mary fell down unto the stoned floor before Him, crying out: "It hath come, the sun! It hath come to light the dark!"

And Jesus spake unto her, saying: "Arise! thy faith hath forgiven thee. Thy sin is overcome."

And they looked upon her, and some among them backed their thumbs and shrugged, and others oped eyes that saw new light. And Jesus spake: "Depart, and peace be unto thee."

And Mary lay the alabaster box upon the floor and oped its pit, and behold, tears fell within it, and she put unto it its cover and gave it unto the hands of Jesus. And He held it up before them that looked and spake:

"Her casket of jewels also hath her hands delivered. Behold, the herbs of Heaven shall be refreshed with these."

And they departed, and the morn found them that had harked, filled of wonder and fear; for no man might speak the forgiving of sin save that he make his sacrifices at the holy spots. And they were fearful among them.

CHAPTER XV

AND the Rome's hall within Jerusalem was yet not waked. Still the cocks crew and the wake-hour tarried. And within a pit's place sat Ahmud Hassan, and beside him lay a one whose beard hung long and half cut. And Ahmud Hassan sat him long looking unto a wall's ope, and his lips flashed a smile, and he roused him that lay, crying out:

"Awake ye, brother! Come up, Abraham—list! when a man hath found a pit he seeketh its bottom, but when he be within it it cometh unto him how may he find its top."

And Abraham spake unto him: "Thou son of the bones of the vulture, sleep! for what man would wake whose bin is stripped?"

And Ahmud answered him, saying: "Look ye, Abraham, unto yon hole."

And Abraham looked not upon it, but turned his face and spake: "Behold, Abraham would ne'er fall into a pit did he bart not o'er holes." And he wailed loud and cried: "But what man hath betrayed Abraham?"

And Ahmud thumbed within the ribs of Abraham and laughed loud and spake: "Behold, no man hath betrayed thee, but a woman. And she is such an one! Behold, is thy beard then shaking; for she shall loose thy skull and drink thy blood."

And it was true that the sun came forth and Ahmud stood at the ope and looked unto the market road's-way that led past. And at the high sun he still stood. And Abraham stirred him not, but sat within the dark of the pit wailing. And when he had stood long, Ahmud spake:

"Thanks be unto this God, whoe'er He be, that Ahmud's raiment telleth his tribe. For Abraham, thou hast a gentle smile, yet thy fingers and thy wisdoms tell the rogue."

And it was true that the road's-ways shewed Panda seeking. And when he had come unto the hall's place, behold, he stopped that he dry his brow. And it was true that he rested within the shade of the camel of Ahmud Hassan. And the voice of Ahmud cried out unto the camel:

"Welcome, brother, welcome! Shake! Be the Rome's men wise, or thy master o'er them?"

And the camel turned its neck slow and listed, and shook it nay, nay. And Ahmud wailed: "What! then the Rome's men are fools and still thy master not o'er them? What manner of beast art thou? Panda, brother, come unto the spot. What dost thou seek? Surely thou seekest not Ahmud; for thou shouldst know that he who might buy of rugs without a price may buy from out the hand of Rome without price. Doth Rome offer wisdoms, then Ahmud shall speak words that Rome knoweth not. 'Tis but one great fool that hath come forth that he lay hands upon Hassan. And list, Panda, he hath cast discus with Hassan and lost!"

And Panda looked sorrow-eyed unto the in of the pit's place and spake: "Ahmud, the tides shewed thee not and no word hath come, and Panda hath taken from out the mouths of men what hath been, and seeketh thee; for how may all things be right save that thou shalt be free? Word cometh out the byways that the man Jesus shall come unto Jerusalem, and Panda feareth, for it is told that Hatte is like a shadow beside Him."

And Ahmud spake: "Panda, thou then wouldst loose thy tongue, even though thine eyes have pierced not the place that containeth Ahmud? Behold, bend thee closer, brother. Thy loved brother, Abraham, beddeth yon."

And Panda spake: "What soundeth therein?"

And behold, the voice of Abraham sounded, wailing soft: "Threescore years and ten Abraham hath known the market's place at each morning's coming, and it hath forgot him! Threescore years and ten Abraham hath offered full price unto his brothers! Threescore and ten! Hath Abraham then offended the God? Hath his good work gone for naught? In ash hath he prostrated him and no ear harketh unto his crying out!"

And Ahmud laughed loud and spake: "Hark, Panda! He waileth e'en as a Jew at the wall o'er one already dead. Thou sayest Jesus Christus cometh unto Jerusalem? What bringeth Him?"

And Panda answered: "Ahmud, this man's wisdom is past all knowledge. He hath trod upon a shepherd's legs the ways of all men, rich and powerful. Wild like the winds of storms come the words of His healing, His ministering, His wonderworks. Ahmud, He hath come not only unto the bypaths but unto Jerusalem, even so unto the Jews, and all-powerful unto Rome! Ahmud, one who rode the paths yester, brought forth words that He hath spoken with them He ministered unto and had foretold that Jerusalem should be laid low like unto the sands before the winds; that His hands might cast a stone, yea, would cast a stone, that should cause the tabernacles to tremble and the temple's stones to fall. And this stone within His hand is builded but of bread. Even so, He spake, was the might of His Father. Hassan, hark! hearest thou any step that might betray thee and shew Panda unto the eyes of Rome?"

And Hassan answered: "Nay, brother, tell on."

And Panda spake more, saying: "Thou knowest, Hassan, the Jew's temples are defiled by the barting of Rome. Rome hath set glut within the Jews; hath set her goods upon the temple steps within the hands of Jews. Rome defileth them, yet in their submission they fall down before her as children. Even this man who *is* their King they fear to lift up before the face of Rome; for what man hath aught that he may lift up against Rome? Rome, like a serpent, jewel circleted, beauteous, crawleth upon her belly even unto the inner places of their temple. And list, Hassan! the fangs of this serpent shall split the holy veil! It is upon us! Rome hath thee beneath her heel, and who is Panda? Panda hath naught but his loving, and Rome careth not for this. Panda's goods are of the Jews, for he hath abided their lands. The Jews are his brothers, yet he may not lift his hand. Behold Levi, Hassan—Levi, who fell to seal the pit unto Rome, and his flesh. Look what hath befallen Theia."

And a wailing set up: "Threescore and ten——" And Hassan spake: "Wail on, Abraham, wail on! Thou shalt know Rome is not the market's place. Ah, but thy coming hath woven such a thong!"

And Panda leaned him o'er the light's ope and said: "Hassan, Hassan, list! for Panda shall not tarry longer. Look what hath befallen Theia, yea, and Phaeton and Caelius, yea, even Peter and Simeon. They fell like dry leaves before Rome, or by Jews through Rome. Panda hath but one land, Hassan, and it is smitten. Where to, where to, brother? Panda feareth. My son, the young shepherd, went the long way, proud, yea, and unbroken. But Hatte is smitten. Hassan, she waiteth, she waiteth! She hath looked the East way and her teeth are dull from the grinding of her faith. Hassan, it must not be! Rome shall not touch him save o'er Panda. This is all Panda hath, his love."

And Hassan said: "Panda, Nada!"

And Panda whispered: "I have spoken it unto Nada. Panda spake: 'Nada, Panda heareth his land.' And Nada answered: 'Go thou.'"

And the slim hand of Hassan slipped through the ope and he whispered: "Thy hand, brother, thy hand! Go!"

And Panda prodded the camel and went his way, his face even so empty as the vasts of the desert's sands. And Abraham started up and spake: "Hassan, thou art of Rome. Thou hast favor within the eyes of Rome. Leave thy aid unto Abraham. Give him succor. What price wouldst thou demand of him? Speak and it is thine."

And Hassan looked upon the shrinking Abraham and said: "Who hath told thee that Hassan hath favor? If thou art filled of this, who knoweth what thing thou knowest?"

And Abraham spake: "Oh, that Abraham's tongue might wither! Oh, that Abraham might feel a skin beneath his hands and pluck wools!"

And Hassan said: "What wouldst thou give—thy silence?"

And Abraham raised meek eyes unto Hassan and spake: "Yea, Abraham knoweth naught!"

And Hassan said: "List! woman is the pit, Abraham. Even Rome tottereth at the feet of woman. Indra is like unto the mighty one's flesh, lustful. Behold, Herodias lusteth o'er the flesh of John, and look unto the woe! Even so Indra lusteth. Such is the play of Rome's women. They love—O ye Prophets!—they love, unto the sinking of weakness, and then they kill. This is the topmost pinnacle of loving; it is finished. And Indra loveth thee, Abraham. List! do they bring her up, her soft eyes shall be upon thee, her sweet tongue shall woo thy words. Aye, and when thou dost fall short, thinkest thou Indra shall embrace thee? Nay; her fair arms would know a full man's strength. She then would commend thee unto the gentle arms of the rack, or—but Hassan doubteth this—she would swing thee free upon some silver cord. Abraham, lay thy hands upon the throat of Hassan. It is short and thick, and thine long and thin. It is said that he who hath a long neck dieth long."

And Abraham fell upon his knees and cried out: "What hath befallen Abraham? For threescore and ten years hath he loved his brothers! Hassan, the bin is thine, the lands of Abraham—all things, but lend thine aid!"

And Hassan sat him down and spake: "Abraham, the price is the lone half of thy beard. This Hassan shall sever before Rome when thou goest free."

And Abraham fell upon his face and cried out: "Even this! Speak thine aid is Abraham's."

And Hassan answered: "Yea, but a man who hath no ass must walk, and he may not lend his ass. Ahmud hath none. His mightiness, Tiberius, thinketh naught of ministering draughts of poison unto any man who offendeth, or who be one o'er the many of office he hath for to offer. He hath done unto his people that that no thief would do unto his brother, and e'en the cloth of his doings would be unfit for a beggar's bed. Abraham, Ahmud feeleth a sharp steel's point upon his belly. It is thee and me against one woman and one who loseth at discus."

And Abraham cried out: "But look! did not Abraham with his wisdoms set Indra among the Romans? Is she not royal at his words? Indra hath for to pay."

And Hassan laughed and spake: "Nay, nay; this is not the day's way. Thou mayest give unto a babe the sword of a war's man and he may fell an ox. But he will wail and know thee not when thou wouldst unblade him," and he shrugged. "Thou didst put within the hands of Ahmud a scourge that hath caused thy woe. Didst thou deny all unto Indra?"

And Abraham wailed: "She set no price upon the word of Abraham, and Abraham might bart his goods."

And Hassan answered: "Yea, the skin Indra offered was filled of holes."

And it was true that the hours that filled up the days slipped slow, and no man came unto the pit's place save them that ministered sup and eat. Nor did Panda seek, for the lips of Hassan had said " Go," and the go had no beckoning hand upon it.

And it came unto Jerusalem that Jesus Christus was upon His way thereto, and word came unto the market's place that there had been wild things afoot within the ways leading out from Nazareth. For a man had been found whose throat had been oped, and grain's sacks had been slit and the grains scattered in waste, even so that men feared that devils beset the paths; for no man knew when he bedded that his sheep would be a whole flock at the morn. And the oxen of some had been slit upon the withers and the necks of them oped, and no man might lay his hand upon the thing that did these things. But shadows flitted and sunk unto the dark, and tracks shewed upon the earth, and stains upon the stones.

And lo, at a later tide, a morn broke when the mists hung and it had been true that no thing had been done of the wild things. And afar from Nazareth, within the hill's-ways, upon a high summit, Hatte sought, and Aaron followed. And they were weary—spent and hungered like unto wild things. And no word spake Hatte but had sunk unto the manner of making known that was Aaron's.

And it had been days and nights and nights and days since the lips of Hatte had spoken one word. And his eyes shewed swift, fevered, and his legs long and thin, and he limped sore. And they sought o'er

the rugged places unto the highest spot, whereon stones were heaped.*
And Hatte stood him up tall and dropped his staff and cast his sweeping glance o'er the valley way. And he sobbed:

"Bethlehem, I am come! Where is she? Thou art veiled in mists
of sorrow. Lift up thine eyes and speak! Where is she? I am come,
Simeon. Dost thou hear? I am come, like all things that be hers—
smitten! Within thee was brought forth her flesh, oh Bethlehem! And
He, He, the Seeker, Jesus, even so. Didst thou, oh mother city, deliver
unto His hand bread, and unto mine a stone?"

And Aaron stood dumb, looking upon his strands of nets, and his eyes
looked thence unto Hatte, and, seeing his woe, behold he sped unto him
and pealed laughter. And Hatte shrieked loud and fell upon his face
upon the stones even so that they cut his flesh.

And the day wore it on, and still he lay fevered. And Aaron stood
him o'er, watching, watching and waiting, and the silence was but
broken by his soft laughter, and soft the deep breath of Hatte, like unto
sobs. And when the sun was high and had passed unto the mid of eve,
his lips murmured:

"I shall not look until the star hath come!"

And the eve sunk, even though the mists still clung the valley, and
the sun was dimmed. But the gold took from out the eve the silvered
mists to wrap its brightness and left the sky a silver green. And lo, the
star came!

And when it was the time, Hatte started up, slow, for weariness
had o'ercome him, and he turned like to one in a dream unto the star's-
way and stood, his eyes started forth unto the shewing of the whites,
and his swelled lips spake:

"And thou didst come? Is there no cloud to hide thee?" and he
put his hands o'er his eyes and looked once more, and behold, he threw
his arms up and fell upon the neck of Aaron, laughing, laughing, and
weeping, weeping!

And when the morn had come, lo, within Bethlehem sheep had been
felled, and grains had been waste, and an ox had been oped at the neck,
and a beggar found smitten.

* The grave of Simeon.

CHAPTER XVI

AND it was true that afar and near the fame of Jesus Christus spread forth, and it shewed within the byways and highways that He need not trod that He be known. And where'er He sought unto, behold, His fame went before, even as the lightnings foretell the storm. And at a later tide, word went forth that He would seek out Jerusalem even though them that loved Him feared His going thereto. For the word of the mighty one * had gone forth since the fame of Jesus had spread, that he feared His might, and that he believed Him the risen John. Even did the words speak that He was a prophet of old and arisen. And it filled them that followed the teachings of Jesus full of fear, and they spake unto Him, saying:

"It is well that thou shouldst not seek Jerusalem, inasmuch as thy fellowmen speak o'er that they should of thee." For Jesus had chided them that they spread not His words, save unto them that hungered, and not unto them whose ears deeped for the filling. And He had looked upon them not but gazed afar and answered them:

"Why fear? For it is written upon the sky that the Son of Man shall be delivered unto the people. Yea, that He shall arise and shew His flesh even before their eyes, for no man may destroy Him."

And they took not in that that He spake unto them, and answered Him, saying: "Look thou, Master, the multitudes press upon us. See! they come like unto the waves of water unto the shore, even to be stopped by thy smile, even as the tides follow the sun's and moon's going."

And behold, they pressed upon Him, and they that loved Him clung close unto His side and made that they send them away from the side of Him, crying out: "How may we proceed when thou dost press upon us?"

And it was true that Jesus spake: "Who hath touched me?"

And they answered: "Behold, how may we tell unto thee who hath touched thee? Even as a tree that swayeth within the winds, thy body doth sway with the press."

And He spake once more: "Who hath touched me?" And His

* Herod, the tetrarch.

577

eyes fell upon a woman who knelt at His feet, crying out: "Behold me, Lord! I am before thee."

And He said: "I have answered thee. Inasmuch as thou hast touched me and thy touch fell in faith, it is done. Arise! Thou shalt be whole, for behold, the new light sheweth no shadows."

And the loved of Him spake: "Lord, they have followed and are wearied upon the way. How then mayest thou speak unto them or yet minister when their bodies hunger and their bellies cry out for meat and breads?"

And He answered: "And thou art then chosen that thou shalt build up faith!"

And they said: "Then wouldst thou that we go forth and buy of meats and breads for all of these?"

And He answered: "Nay. Leave me that I speak with them."

And behold, He sent up His silvered voice, saying: "Depart ye and set down that we feast." And He spake unto them that He loved: "Go thou and set them down within tribes, fifty unto the tribe."

And there were many, and behold, the loved cried out: "Master, this is folly, for behold, there is naught save two fishes and a loaf."

And Jesus smiled and spake: "Do thou as I have spoken."

And they did the thing, and behold, they sought out a stone that stood high, and Jesus went Him up unto its summit and sat, and they came unto Him, saying:

"Master, it is done. Thou didst speak that we set them down and it is done. Yet here are the fish and the loaf."

And Jesus took out of their hands the fish and the bread, and, holding it up high, spake words of supplication unto the Father. And behold, them that looked upon Him harked. And He broke the fish, even so the bread, unto many bits. And lo, He sat and His voice lifted up, and He taught them in parables, speaking of days as ships, of men as grains, of earth as fields, of love as water, and of the Father's love as bread. And they harked, and were full of the spirit. Even did their eyes fill up of brightness and their faces shew the bathing of the spirit, and no man among them hungered. Even did they cry out: "I am full. Yea, Lord, why hunger? We are feasted."

And He spake on, and the twelve that He loved were as baskets that plucked up the broken crumbs that they hold them for the feeding of yet more of hungered. And it wore unto the coming of the eve and still they sat. And some among them pressed upon Him and spake:

"Master, it is told that thou hast been found shining like unto some white light even as thou didst pray. Yea, eyes that have looked upon thee have lended their seeing unto lips that have told it."

And He answered: "No thing is wondrous. Behold, the words that build, of earth's waters, wines, may make light of darkness. No thing may hunger that is filled of the spirit of the Father; for the body crieth out only when the spirit is barren. For upon earth standeth men whose bodies are fatted and their spirits wasted racks."

And they listed unto His words, and when they had taken them in, behold, they knew not of what He had spoken. And it was true that one among them drew nigh and spake:

"Master, what is the Father's labor that He set such as yon multitude upon earth, for there be not one man within ten that the earth hath need of."

And He answered the one, saying: "Behold, the Father manifesteth Himself in them all, and within their atoms is builded up great things. From out their blood cometh new men of office. Out of their bone is the bone of earth renewed. Yea, and their love is a mighty thing that may build from out itself a mightier work. For all of these hold them lowly, thereby, e'en though they know not their God, they deny Him not. Even so He dwelleth within them and they welcome Him.

"The Father is like unto an everlasting stream. He poureth Him about the universe. Yea, He is that upon which the universe hangeth. Behold yon multitude! They know not this thing, yet there be men among them whose hands up and down in labor for the Father, their eyes blinded and their ears not oped, yet He is within them, and thou mayest see Him within their eyes.

"He who denieth me denieth not the Father, inasmuch as his flesh is weak and his eyes oped but unto that his forefathers hath seen. Yea, and doth his lips deny me and his heart love my flesh, even so hath he acclaimed the Father.

"Man's words are but the scales upon the flesh of him, like unto the scales of fishes. Yea, and men of earth should cast the scales unto waste and eat the flesh. Doth a man deny me, he denieth not the Father, inasmuch as I am not Him, but of Him, even as my brother.

"Go I unto him calling out that he acclaim me, and he denieth me, it is well, and he hath *not* denied the Father. Go I unto my brother once more crying out that he acclaim me, and he denieth me, but holdeth within him his counsel of his God, thereby again he hath not denied the Father. Go I unto him thrice crying out that he love me as his brother, but o'er me his God, and he denieth me the love, then hath he denied the Father. Go I unto him crying out that he love the Father and thereby share of his love with me, his brother, and he doeth this, behold, his spirit is cleansed and the Holy Ghost is born. Yea, like unto a white dove shall it descend unto thee, bearing the Sign, which is peace within thee.

"Thereby the Holy Ghost is not the Father and the Son within thee, but thee within the Father and the Son. Oh, ye sons of men! think ye upon this and ponder it within thy hearts. Within thy hand is the taper that may light the Great Light. He, the Father, or yet the Son, may not proceed unto thee. Nay, but thou shalt proceed upon the path of love unto the Father and the Son. The High Throne waiteth thy coming, and even though the ages have preceded thee, still it standeth empty for thee! The Father's arms ope; wilt thou tarry?

"Look ye! *man* is not complete. Behold, he is like unto a river that seeketh the sea and is beat and bruised waters that fret to find the sun. And the sun is even as the Father, for it taketh all the waters of earth back unto the source wherefrom it hath fallen. How know ye but that the waters of the earth be the tears of angels shed in sorrow, yet in mercy causing beauteous things to spring up?

"Man is not complete. Behold, how may he then take in all things? He is new, when the ages are old. Yea, and a new vat holdeth not well the wine. Then would the vine's man rebuke his vat? The sons of men have been set upon His lands and it is not the Father's will that he fail.

"Behold, I bring ye naught but the thing thou mayest balm all bruises with—*Love*. Nor do I cry out 'follow me,' but 'follow the way unto Him.' Oh, brothers! Do ye not receive me, remember, within thee keep the counsel of thy God! Cry out unto Him: 'Father, hath my brother passed and I lifted not up mine eyes but saw thy light, forgive me, for I knew Him not. Hark, hark, oh, Father, hark!'

"Do this in contriteness and I promise ye the Son shall pass e'en so close that thou shalt see His smile. Oh, the blood of the tribe of David shall weep! Yea, and the tribes of Judea wail, for they shall be cast down. Among them shall I have trod, yea, ministered unto them in loving. Judea is full of loving within their hearts, but behold, the Son of Man shall be delivered unto the hands of glut. Yea, His blood shall make the tabernacle like unto an isle sunk afar. And ages shall cast stones at her,* and sail new ships that bear new bread unto her people. Yet shall she stand! For she is not walls and stones, but the heart of the Jews! I say unto thee: Look unto what hath been. O'er the sea of blood shall the Son of Man walk, even upon its waters, unto the

* Judea.

tabernacle, even within the holy spot. And the priests *shall* fall down and cry out: 'Christ!' Cease thy waiting, oh, Judea! Seek that thou dost make born the Holy Ghost!"

And they that harked marveled, and the words sunk within their hearts, but they feared, and some among them that listed would to know but might not know the fullness of the words. And no man arose that he depart.

And when the sun had sunk, lo, Jesus stood Him up and looked unto the way unto Jerusalem and spake: "Jerusalem, thou shalt stone me! Ye will not of the water and I would offer it, for a hand shall dash the cup."

And He withdrew, and His loved followed. And they spake unto the multitude: "Depart! It is finished. Peace be with thee!"

And the multitudes departed, and Jesus sought with His loved unto a new spot upon the way.

CHAPTER XVII

AND within Jerusalem came word from all ways that shewed that the Nazarene who had trod Jerusalem's pathways might set the high places * before her men. Yea, the market's-ways whispered His might and the Jew's eyes glisted in their knowledge, for out from them had arisen a One whose wisdom was o'er might. Men whose wisdom was great had fallen before Rome. Yea, the Jews had suffered their tribesmen of high office to be delivered up. Even the priests within the temple had betrayed them unto the hands of Rome for glut. And unto Rome's ears crept all of this. Even did Rome's eyes take in that the Jews but waited the trumpet's blast that they fall them upon the men of Rome and of office, that they hold their own.

Behold, sacks of grain had been found thick-strewn of blades, and packs of skins held, binded within them, blades and slings. Even the young Jews busied at the sharping of stones within their abodes. And the eyes of the Jews had taken in the dealings of Rome unto Levi and his flesh; the felling of the brother of Levi, who had been delivered for no offense save that his blood was the blood of Levi. The eyes of the Jews had looked upon the setting of Rome's ones upon their brothers, and the spatting within the temple places. All of this had filled them up of angers. And behold, all Jews had known of the deliverance of the flesh of Flavius † unto slave's days; even that Flavius, the brother of the Rome's men, was, within their hands, but a cloth from which they would wring the blood of the one they sought.

The tongue of Abraham had given forth o'ermuch of the going of Arminius and Mary. Even did the Jews take in the truth of the words that had come unto them of Indra; that her tongue crept among the Rome's men like unto a greened serpent. Yea, the Jews who had taken in marriage and lived unto the laws of the prophets looked upon the bart of woman's flesh as defilement, for behold, was a woman a wanton and taken in marriage and did her husbandman then perceive this thing, she was brought forth and stoned, even before the eyes of the people.

* Might fill the places of authority; might be the promised King.
† Mary.

Yet the flesh of the Jews had been taken forth and slaved unto underlings, even them that bended unto the feet of slaves. Flesh that stood high had been binded up unto the grister * and their backs bended unto an oxen's labor. And behold, Jerusalem waited like unto a she-wolf who hath young within a cave.

And lo, it had come to pass there had ridden forth from out Jerusalem men who sought. For word had come that they should bring forth a woman who had gone from hence. For it was spoken that she held the knowing that Rome would have. Even did they seek Arminius, who was afar, with offer of renewed favor of office, and the giving unto the hands of Flavius of his flesh. And Jerusalem had harked unto this and knew it had been. And they waited, for within them rested the knowing that Rome did this not in loving, and it set up a hate that flamed.

And it was true that they also knew the taking of Abraham and that Abraham would even betray them unto the hands of Rome, was this for the saving of Abraham. And it was true that the first hand that had set the Jews unto the taking up of their tribe's honor had been Levi. And it had been true that he had spoken that the Promised One was born and abided even then among them; that he had even spoken that one of the Nazarenes was He. And the Jews had seen the falling of Levi, and knew that he fell and shed his blood that his brothers might sup. They knew that the lips of Levi were the first lips of the Jews to call out " Messiah." They knew that Rome had laughed and cried out: " A fitting King for fools! Born within an ass's bed."

And it was true that among them they whispered. And Isaac, the young Jew, had filled up of all of this and had taken in that there was within Rome a thing that divided them: for some among them looked unto the Nazarene and others looked unto the lad called Hate. And wonders set among the Jews that this thing might be, for they had known that Hate was the ill-begotten flesh of Tiberius. The Jews knew this, and that this was like Rome, to cloak her wrongdoings with the fairest cloth wove of Jews.

And they waited, like a she-wolf waiteth. And they knew that he who sought would stop not before them but would eat the young and slay them.

And they waited. And among them went forth a sign, and this was the sign: that did Rome beset the Nazarene no man would bow unto Rome. But among them were a few who glutted and played the gaming of Rome. These the Jews looked not upon as brothers. And it

* Turning the grinding stones of the mill.

was spoken among the faithful that did Rome smite and no man's hand might aid, then they would withdraw and lay them down within ashes before the face of God.

And they waited. And word went up that Mary had been brought forth, and Arminius even so. And it was true that they waited the what of this. And lo, the priests of the temples shook before the power of Him who unraimented them, who held God up unto the people, even lifted up the Holy Veil. They spake against this unto the tribes and called it the work of an heretic against the people. And still the tribe's men saw their God within the words of the Nazarene. The Jews and the Rome's men were filled of the wonders He had done. Word had come that before Him multitudes bended low, that beneath His hands all sorrow vanished, the eyes of the weeping smiled; that no man who passed Him upon the road's-way might pass unknowing that he had met the God. For His words were like unto no man's. His wraths were anguish bathed of mercy, His sorrow was the tears of happiness, His wisdom like unto a breaking day, faint unto thee, and as the tides swept, fairer, brighter; and when thou hadst wearied, behold, His wisdom was like unto the night's rest.

And it had come that multitudes had cried out: "Master, who among us is greatest?"

And He had taken unto His breast a babe and let His blessed lips to lay upon the golden crown and had spoken: "Behold the undoer of Heaven! I say unto ye, no man whose faith is not like unto one of these may know the Father. The fields of earth are like unto man, o'erfull of grain. Then how may ye become greater who are already full? Behold ye, he who filleth up on mighty things may forget bread! But the babe thirsteth for its mother's breast and knoweth not why nor yet whither from the fount. Except as thou becomest as one of these, thou mayest not see the Father. Behold ye the eyes of this one! unto all earth it turneth fearful, yet unto its mother, knowing. Even so the son of man shall be.

"Oh, the folly of man! He plucketh up the sea's drift and storeth it, when, behold, the waters sing the song of knowing. Fill ye not up of wisdom, but of righteousness and mercy, for this is the bread of wisdom. The sea of wisdom rocketh upon a foundation of faith. Yet men there be who would know the foundation, and they shall drown! All that be of the Father be, like unto Him, of all, in all, yet not therein for the laying on of hands. Should then the Father be delivered unto man that he might lay hands upon Him, behold, he would set him down and play with Him like unto stones that he might cast.

Yea, and at some morrow, behold, like unto a babe who hath no wisdom, would he cast Him!

"The river must seek a sea, the brook the river, the mountain the sky, and man his God. Else there is no going upon the way, but the end of all things. The Father is the mighty river that circleth the universe. Seek Him! Seek Him! Seek Him! And be empty for the thirst for Him! Earth's wisdoms are but the smiting that causeth thee to be greater cups for the filling. Care ye not for the wisdom that smiteth thee. Leave it for to smite, and remain thee but the cup. Forget not that thy hand shall bear the cup unto the River."

All of this had come and Jerusalem knew the fullness of such wisdom. And lo, it was true that word came that Jesus Christus was upon His way thereto, and much wonder spread among the people. Even though His feet had known the streets of Jerusalem, Jerusalem knew Him not, for the wick of His wisdom was then not yet lighted.

And it had been that there had sped days that had been full of His coming. And upon a morn, behold, within the street's-way, at the side of the pool of cleansing, had been found Jacob, his throat oped. And behold, the men of Rome came upon him at the early hour, and he was not yet dead but his lips might not speak. And behold, he had given up the ghost even before he had been delivered unto his son, Samuel. And Jerusalem rocked of all of this. And some spake that evil had been upon the lands, and that the Nazarene, whose tongue was honeyed, was beset of devils by night.

And within the Rome's place Indra had smiled, and had spoken within the listing ears of Rome: "Nay, this is no work of the Nazarene. Bring ye forth Abraham and the desert's man, Hassan."

And when the noon of the day had come, lo, Panda shewed within the market's place, and his eyes told naughts, but his ears heard all things. And a one of the roadway had brought forth the telling of the wasted grain and the slain oxen and sheep upon the way unto Bethlehem. And from out Nazareth way had come the same word. Thereby they pointed unto the Nazarene. And yet among them came a one who told this was not the labor of one, but that two had lent their hands unto it, for had his eyes not seen their shadows? And one was lame! And the night's men had spoken that there had sounded out a cry that sounded as the cry of an owl or some nightbird that laughed, for it sounded "Ha-a! Ha-a!" and would echo far, then near, and sink to naught. And, behold, they spake that they should fashion out a snare wherein to bring the thing forth.

And Panda harked unto this, and his hands pressed the thong that held the neck of the camel of Hassan unto the shewing of the nail's yellow. And, behold, he went his way back unto the without of Jerusalem and on unto the hut.

And he spake unto his own listing: "Panda, what doest thou? Thy ram * is within the hands of Rome, and thy sheep † strayed. Panda, thou art no war's man but a slave. Thy wisdom is not the wisdom of victory, but the wisdom of waiting."

And lo, he sought the hut, and supped, and told unto Nada what had been within Jerusalem. And when the dark had come, behold the roadway shewed Panda, in whose hands were a jug of wine, and bread, seeking, seeking. And his soft voice sung: "Hatte! Hatte!" and no answering sounded. And he went unto the way unto Bethlehem wherefrom the word had come, and still he called amid the dark: "Hatte! Hatte!" And the darkness made no answer.

And Panda spake: "This is like unto the seeking of the God. He answereth not without faith. Hatte! Hatte!"

And he wearied upon the way. And it was pit dark, and he sought the lone spots off the roadways where no tribesmen dwelled, and no answer came. Still sought he, calling, calling: "Hatte! Hatte!" And behold his ears took in a sound like unto a dog that had run o'er its strength, its breath coming fast. And Panda sought and fell o'er what he came upon. And lo, he bended down, and his eyes might not see. And he spake: "Answer thou me, Hatte! Hatte!"

And no word came, but the laugh of Aaron. And Panda started, and sought the dark, for he knew that the ears of Aaron heard not. And no answer came from Hatte, and still he called and sought. And once more he fell, and lo, he touched a thing that quivered. And he spake: "Hatte!"

And whispered word answered: "He is gone!"

And Panda spake: "Arise!" And Aaron's laugh sounded soft, soft, like unto some glutting thing. And Panda said: "Arise!"

And Hatte whispered: "Who art thou?"

And Panda answered: "Hatte, Hatte, it is Panda, thy loved Panda."

And Hatte said: "He is no more. Panda is gone. Rome hath eaten him."

And Panda spake: "Come!" And Hatte answered: "Nay, wait thou, wait! and when the light cometh I shall arise."

And Panda, knowing that he was filled of his folly-wine, sat him, waiting the light. And when it had come, behold, he started up within

* Hassan.   † Hatte.

the first graying and cried aloud, for the hand of Hatte was within the snare, crushed. And Panda wept, and made that he free the smitten thing. And Hatte's lips curled bitter, and he spake:

"Leave it! for I did offer it unto my brothers and they would not of it. It is well."

And he leaned o'er the hands of Panda that busied at the freeing, and spake: "Look! it is done! It is a dead thing!"

And Aaron laughed, laughed. And Panda's mantle shewed red of the blood of Hatte, and his hands, like unto a woman's, freed him. Even his mantle stripped he to bits and binded up the wound. And his cheeks were wet. And behold, when he had done Hatte had fallen like unto one dead. And Panda fell down unto his knees and lifted up his voice, crying out: "Oh, thou God of Theia, forsake him not!"

And he arose and took up the form of Hatte and set him upon his way, swift, that he make way before the coming of the light unto the full. And Aaron, seeing, followed, chattering naughts and dragging the knotted strands of his nets.

And as the light came, Panda labored on with his pack, and within him came back the path from Bethlehem unto Jerusalem, and he smiled, for the hand of Nada had soothed his weariness. And his lips moved and he spake: "Speak thy name!" And he answered his own wording: "Nada." And he stumbled upon the way, and his weariness made him that he rest, and he lay his burden down and rested the weary head of Hatte upon his breast and spake:

"The wolves seek thee, oh, my lamb! Oh, that I might hide thee within this bosom!"

And his gentle hand fell upon the matted locks of Hatte, and he touched the withered leg, and behold, he raised up the smitten hand and kissed it, and his eyes raised and he spake: "Oh, thou God of Theia, is this thy wisdom?"

And behold, the pale lips of Hatte smiled! And Panda started and murmured:

"Then unbuilding thou art building, and building thou art unbuilding! Panda is a slave and boweth!"

And he arose and took up his burden. And no man came upon them when he found the hut and went within. And Aaron followed.

And when this had been it was young day and Panda tarried not, but delivered Hatte unto the ministering of Nada and went forth seeking Paul within the hills where he tended the flocks. And he came unto him and spake:

" Paul, take thou the camel of Hassan and this," and he took forth all the earnings he was possessed of that were not land or sheep, " and go unto Rome., Go! Say ye one word: ' Come '! "

And when the morn had come of the next light, behold, the market's place knew of what had been, and behold, the men sat them among their wares speaking words of the undoing of Jacob. And it was known that the nights had shewed shadows that no man might follow when they had set the snares their tongues had spoken of. And at the noon's coming, behold, Panda shewed among them, and he took in what they spake nor oped he his lips. And he sought out the bin of Jacob, wherein Samuel sat and offered wares at the tide when others supped and rested, for was it not the time when grief was upon him that he should offer unto the multitudes and make fuller price?

And it was true that they held their words up that all men hark, and they spake them loud of the falling of Jacob. And Samuel leaned far out of the bin's place and took in their words nor forgot that he offered wares. And Panda sought out Samuel and spake not, but sat him down beside the bin and waited the coming of the market's men. And they sought and barted them for goods. And one among them spake that it was told by one who had ridden the roadways that a man whose hut had stood upon the roadway to Bethlehem had set up a snare, and behold, when the morn's light had come he had sought out the spot whereon he had stored his grains, and lo, it had shewed the snare fallen and stained o'er of bloods, and the earth about had given sign that the feet, not of one, but of a twain or more had trod thereon. And it had been shewed unto him that one of these had borne away a thing, for the trodding of one had not been seen past a short way and the steps of one had been sunk deeper of weight.

And Panda took in this thing but spake not, and at a later tide one came forth who told of coming upon a twain amid the hills, and one was a fool who dragged of shreds of nets, and a one who stepped with him who was like unto a wild thing, thin and wasted unto the bone. And Panda listed unto this and spake not.

And the market's men spake no more of the nights and the wasting of grain and smiting of sheep, nor of shadows nor fools, but brought forth word that the Nazarene, Jesus Christus, was upon the way unto Jerusalem, but ministered as He came. And they told that before Him went His loved unto the spots He would seek, and brought forth word of His coming. And their words filled the people up of the ministering of Jesus, even so that when He came unto the spot He sought, lo, multitudes came forth to meet Him and cried out " Lord " and " Master." Even did they bow down.

And the market's men laughed and spake: " He is a great fool if these fools acknowledge Him! "

And they told that within a certain spot that was walled, Jesus had sought, and lo, the multitudes had pressed upon Him even so that there was one man that might not see but had gone him unto a tree top that he might look upon Jesus. And Jesus had called his name and brought him down, and they that had looked upon this had marveled, and their words sounded out falsely, for they told of wonders that His hand had not wrought and they forgot them that He had wrought.

And at a later tide there came forth one from the Rome's place who told that the woman Mary and Arminius had been brought forth even though they would not and were in the hands of Rome for the emptying. And word crept out that Tiberius had taken a slave's woman who was the chattel of his glut, the noble blood of Greece that had fallen unto his hand, and this thing had wrought him feared, for within Greece were them that knew this thing, and even did they arise to bring forth the son that had been brought out of Greece's blood. This thing sat upon the dreams of Tiberius and set him that he seek this son.

And it was spoken that the Nazarene's wisdom struck the brasses of jealousy within Tiberius and he had caused that they seek Him out. And even upon the ways that Jesus Christus trod Rome followed. And they did speak that this man Jesus ministered sweets amid the day, and in the nights was He possessed of devils that wrought havocs. And this was the filling of the mouths of all save the Jews who knew Him. And word went forth among them that the one who had slit the throat of Jacob was one who had hate against him, and they looked unto Abraham who had barted 'gainst the barting of Jacob. Jerusalem was full of this, and Panda listed unto it. And he sought, at a later tide, unto the Rome's halls, but no sign shewed of Hassan, nor no word came forth that might tell of aught. And he went him hither unto the hut's place.

CHAPTER XVIII

AND the morrows sped unto a certain morn when the out-ways shewed the multitudes pressing upon Jesus, and His loved following Him. And behold, He rode upon an ass, and within His hand was the branch of a fig, the sign of the fruiting. And they followed Him, crying out: " Messiah! Lord! King of kings! " Even did they unloose their head-bands and their mantles and cast them down before Him that His ass walk o'er their cloth. And the gate's man, even of Rome, cast the gate ope that He go therein unto Jerusalem's heart, even though He should find not rest.

And it was true that when they had come within, the multitudes of the city's people came unto Him, and He sat upon the ass and spake unto them of Jerusalem and the Jews, for His blood lay close unto Him, yea, sorrowed Him. And they spake unto Him, saying:

" Master, Rome is within the land of the Jews. Yea, even Jerusalem hath she filled up of Rome."

And He answered them, saying: " Weep thou, oh, brothers, weep! Leave thy tears to flow for the tribes to come, for Rome shall slay their sheep of sacrifice, and betray them."

And they cried out: " Ope up thy mouth and leave forth words unto the Father that He make fire to descend upon them."

And Jesus answered them: " I am not come to destroy man but to deliver him from the serpent that crusheth. I am not come to unbuild, but to build up. No man shall call unto the Father that He send destructions. Nay; man shall not look unto Him for aid in such prayer. He who shall unbuild evils, doth build. Ye may not undo by undoing, save that the unbuilding be done in truth and not by evil intent.

" Oh, ye of Jerusalem, hark! What is the law? Thou shalt not kill! Would ye then blade ye? For blade hungereth that it clatter upon its brother. The undoing that shall build shall be born of bloods.* This thing shall be. Even the Son of Man shall write the law, Thou shalt not kill, in His own blood. Yea, and this is the first seed for a greater harvest. Even so shall there be hosts that shall write upon the earth's sides, ' Thou shalt not kill,' in their bloods. Aye, and from

* By the shedding of blood.

out the flood of birth-blood shall come forth the thing that shall unbuild and thereby build!"

And they harked, but took not in the fullness of this, and cried out: "Nay, Master, who would destroy thee or yet slay thee?"

And He smiled Him sorry upon them and spake: "The sun that hangeth o'er Jerusalem shall look upon the thing I have spoken."

And they asked of Him: "Goest thou unto the temple?"

And He answered: "Yea, after the manner of my tribe, for I am what I am, a Jew."

And it was true that they were filled of what was within Him, for His eyes shone, and His lips smiled soft and wistful, and His words fell sorried, even as though they came from out a throat that knew tearful eyes. And it was true that the coming together of the people brought forth ones of Rome who listed, and the bladesmen gathered them that they watch what would come to pass. And them within the market's bins came forth and joined unto them that followed Him, the Nazarene, and He went His way upon the ass unto the temple.

And behold, it was high noon, and the pool shewed bright, and the temple's doves wheeled within the sky and circled back unto the temple as the people came unto the spot. And lo, upon the steps unto the temple's doors squatted beggars. And men lay upon their sides upon the stones, and before them lay their wares. And the day was filled of their crying out. Even amid the chants of the priests within the temple place came floating, to echo against the altars, the crying out of wares. Even did the waresmen seek within the very threshold, barting with them that came without. And the priests looked not upon this, for unto the priests' hands they that barted delivered a sharing of what fell unto them, and thereby the priests took out of the people of their gains. And Rome knew this thing, and took of the priests a sharing of the sharing.

And it was the time when the martsmen cried loud that Jesus Christus came unto the temple and came Him off the ass and walked among them that beset the steps unto the temple's place. And when He had come unto the topmost stone of the temple's way, behold He turned. And the Rome's men stood at the base looking upon Him, for it was feared that the Jews, beneath the sound of His voice, would break forth. And when the eyes of Jesus fell upon the men of Rome He drew Him up unto His utmost, and wraths mounted His eyes even so that they looked heavy and fulled of sorrow, and His hands shook as He held them forth and spake and pointed unto the Rome's men, saying:

"It is written that the Father's house should be the house of prayer, and prayer is the puring waters of the soul, and thou hast made it a den of thieves! Thinkest thou that the blade of office shall set fear within me? Nay! Hark ye!" And His voice rang clear and He took up a lash of knotted thongs and let it free upon the air and brought it down upon the back of a Jew who offered wares, crying out: "Begone! Cast thee down within the dusts, for thou hast offended the God!" And He swept unto another and let fall the lash, crying out: "Who art thou who may bring forth bart unto Him who barteth not?" And He swept him on, and His cheeks flamed, and He cut upon the flesh of one who begged, and spake: "Go thou! for thou art come begging unto Him who giveth freely!"

And He passed Him on unto one who offered many colored stuffs, crying out: "Get thee gone! For who art thou who offereth vainglorious stuffs before His face who knoweth no thing that is vainglorious! Oh, my brothers! Where art thou, that thou wilt leave ones to deliver unto thy hands stuffs to set before the face of God?"

And it was true that as He smote the mart's ones upon the stoned way, there came forth a one whose robes shewed him of high office among the Jews, and he stepped him down unto the spot and looked at what was. And the eyes of Jesus saw this thing. And lo, there came forth a woman from out the temple's place. And she was of the hosts,* nor was she clothed in raiment that told her a man's woman, but within the sign of mourning. And he of high office seeing her, drew him away that she pass. And the eyes of Jesus looked upon this thing, and He cried aloud unto them that listed as He brought down the lash upon the back of the man of office:

"Look ye! it is far o'er an easier task that a camel may pass through the eye of the Needle than that a rich man may enter the Kingdom of Heaven."

And the Jews harked, for they knew of the gate which was called of this name, and the camel men came them and the camels kneeled that they pass through.

And Jesus cried aloud: "Look ye! a camel is for the pack, and no man who hath o'er his world's goods may stand him unpacked of follies. Behold her yon!"—and he pointed unto the sorrowed woman,—"she hath brought forth a coin which is mightier unto the sight of the Father than the camel's pack."

And the man of office looked upon Him, and even though he was sorely tried, he cried not out but stopped that he list, being full of what was within Jesus that would come forth.

* A woman of the people, unmarried, and clothed in the garb of mourning.

And the loved of Him cried out: "Hosannah!" "Lord!" "King!" And the Rome's men spake unto them in a loud voice, saying: "Cease! Cease ye!" And the Jews spake unto Jesus, saying: "Speak unto them. Say that they should not cry out aloud, for it is fearful unto us."

And the voice of Jesus arose, crying out aloud: "It may not be! For dost thou, oh Rome, cease their tongues, the stones shall cry aloud. The bone is builded by the Father and man shall make new flesh for the bone, but the tides shall sweep, and the man-wrought flesh shall drop unto dusts and the bone remain. Ye may not stop the crying out of the stones, oh Rome! This is the bone. Thou mayest strip their throats of tongues but their bone shall remain, and the ages shall build them up and unbuild them and build them up once more, for they may not destroy them. New prophets shall take their places and offer new bread, but these prophets are false. Many shall come that shall speak out they are the Christ, even so that they are given the prophet's tongue. And I say unto ye, haste ye not forth that ye greet them, but wait the renewing of the old prophets. The hand of Rome is not upon the arm of God!"

And the Rome's men laughed, and the Jews were fearful, for this was against Rome and Jerusalem already smarted 'neath the lash. And Jesus stood Him higher upon the base of a pillar, and within His hand hung the lash. And behold, He held it up unto the seeing of the Rome's men and cast it o'er the multitude until it fell at their feet, and He cried aloud:

"See! The Son of Man cometh uncrowned unto Rome's hands; yea, unbladed unto Rome's war. Yet Rome's foundation shall shake, and not one stone of the temple be left upon its brother! The precious stuffs of the holy places shall be ground unto dusts beneath the mighty stones that fall. Yea, hark ye, my brothers of Jerusalem! Rome may unbuild ye, but she may not build ye up."

And tears flowed His eyes, and He raised them up unto the sky, and His hands spread forth, and He cried: "Oh, Jerusalem, how would I have succored thee! How would the Son of Man have lain upon thy bosom; but thine eyes are blinded by the dusts of higher office. Oh, Jerusalem, Jerusalem the golden city, walled by the hands of the tribes that have found the promised land, I see thy very stones drop drops! Yea, Jerusalem, Jerusalem, the God hath knocked and thou didst not slumber, but, fearful, let Him go! Yet say I unto ye, my brothers, the breasts of Jerusalem shall spurt new milk and the Son of Man shall nurture by it. The Jew's tribes brought forth the flesh of the

Father, the Son of Man. Yea, and they shall fall unto child-bed again! For within their hearts shall He be born anew."

And His voice shook in sorrow, and He spake on: "Yea, when the Son of Man hath trod the path of ages and seen His hosts vanquished, seen His brothers broken against the day, and they upon the earth who have called Him brother forget Him and eat them lone the Father's bread, casting their bodies one 'gainst the other that they take their sharing, and He standeth waiting that they see Him, the new birth shall shew them!"

And He called: "Hark! Hark! Hark! Hark! Oh, Jerusalem, look ye! I am calling not thee now, but ever! For I am what I am, a Jew!"

And it was true that He came down among the Jews, and they fell upon Him, their eyes lighted with a new light and they spake: "We are answering thee!"

And He smiled and said: "Oh, ye beloved, I may not list, for I know!"

And the Rome's men came through the people and sought Him out and spake: "Thy hand doeth no service. Thou art even as a beggar. Thy followers are fed out of the bounty of the people. What manner of authority hast thou?"

And He answered them: "Look ye unto yon sun! Ask him this."

And they marveled at this, that a man of no office should speak so, and they spake unto Him: "Knowest thou that among the Jews there be them that hate thee?"

And Jesus smiled and answered: "Look ye unto yon well! Know ye that beneath its waters are stones?"

And they spake: "But thy hands do no labor."

And He answered them, saying: "What wouldst thou?"

And they pointed unto a roadway, past and about the market's-way, wherein an ox stood fast with his wheeled pack. And they spake: "Go and deliver the ox unto its master out of the mires."

And He went unto the spot, and the people followed Him. And behold, He laid His hand upon the ox and it came forth. And He drove it thence out of Jerusalem's walls unto its master's abode. And they followed not His going without.

And lo, the eve came, and forth from out Jerusalem went the Jews bearing palms and singing, their babes before them. And they went that they meet Jesus, who came unto Jerusalem from the labor Rome had set. And they brought with them a white ass, and its neck was girded with palms. And they sang as a host, and brought Him forth unto the heart of Jerusalem triumphant.

And Rome watched, and knew that the Jews knew their King, even though the king's seat was filled.* And the Rome's men fell upon the Jews that they drive them forth from the listing unto Jesus, and even did they make that they lay their hands upon Jesus, nor rebuked He them. And the Jews, being full of Rome and Rome's day, spake unto the blade's men, saying:

" How do ye do this, when thou knowest thy Emperor hath flesh that is cast forth as waste? It is known among the Jews that Jerusalem hath housed him. Shame be upon the mighty flesh for these things! He would pluck the flower of the Jews and cast his own bud."

And they took this unto the ears of Rome and them of office.

And it was true that Jesus knew the street's-ways of Jerusalem and spake unto the people—even ministered He within the temple.

* By the Roman procurator.

CHAPTER XIX

AND Rome watched. And the days sped. And Panda watched, and knew the words of Jesus, and stepped the shadows of the Rome's halls. And it was true that no word came out of them of Hassan. And the Jews knew not of Abraham. Yet even the coming of Jesus had not stilled the Jews' tongues of the laying low of Jacob, and they sought him who had done the thing. And the tongue of Samuel spake unto to the Jews:

"Deliver this one, the son of Tiberius, up unto Rome. Give him unto Rome. Lift him up, for he is broken and is waste."

And Samuel knew not that Hatte was within the shadows of Jerusalem. And lo, words came within the walls that the nights shewed no havocs and the evil thing had gone. And Panda smiled. But at a certain morn, lo, he waked and Hatte and Aaron were not. And Panda arose and made way unto Jerusalem, where, within the market's places, high words ran that they had taken the ones who had done the evils. And they brought forth Hatte, and Aaron, who looked empty unto them and laughed. And they went past the bin of Samuel, and Samuel arose and pointed unto Hatte, crying out:

"This is the son of Tiberius! This is the high flesh of Rome! Deliver him up!"

And they spake unto Hatte, saying: "Art thou the son of Tiberius?"

And he answered not, but his head fell upon his bosom and his teeth ground.

And Samuel cried aloud: "His tongue-lagging covereth him not."

And they spake: "Then make ye a proof."

And Samuel fell silent, but looking unto the people saw Panda, and cried out: "Look ye! yon man knoweth him, and he is called Hatte."

And they brought up Panda and said: "Knowest thou this man, or yet the fool?"

And Panda answered: "I know not this man as a fool, nor this man thou hast taken. He is a broken man. What wouldst thou of him?"

And they told him of the slaying of Jacob. And Panda answered them, saying: "Then had Jacob no man who was his enemy?"

And they laughed. And Samuel wailed that this man was the one who had done the evils. And Hatte looked not up nor spake he. And Panda said: "Leave him go! Thou hast heard the words of Jesus and are filled of mercy. Leave him go!"

And they did this thing. And lo, they looked not upon him, and listed not unto the crying out of Samuel, for they believed him not. For how might this man, even worse than a beggar, lame and smitten, be of noble flesh? And behold, they forgot him, and sought their ways. And Panda led him back, and Aaron followed, unto the hut.

And the sun sunk and the night came thrice. And Jerusalem became a babel; for out of the temple the holy things were taken. And word came from out the mighty place that he who had done this thing should fall.

And the priests had listed unto the ministering of Jesus and had called upon Him that He make known His authority. And He had confounded them with His learning, and filled up the people with His teachings. And there fell among the priests the wish that they might undo Him, for they feared the free-giving of the God would leave the temple bare. And they spake among them:

"This, then, shall we hold as His work. For His hands labor not and His followers even so. They go forth and cast the God unto the fields and roadways, and deliver Him unclothed unto the hands of the people. This, then, shall we call His work."

And it was true that the golden candlesticks that burned upon the altar of sacrifice were gone. And they sought Jesus and spake: "Hast thou done this thing? The lights are gone out of the temple."

And Jesus answered them, saying: "Wherefore hast thou need of light?"

And they said: "The bowls of office are gone also."

And He answered: "Wherefore hast thou need of bowls? for ye may not measure God."

And they spake: "The ashes of sacrifice are strewn."

And He answered them, saying: "It is well, for ashes are a dead thing, and the God a living thing. Hark ye! No Jew hath done this thing, for the temple is walled with his heart. Yet, I say, even so his heart is the temple, and no thing of office needeth he."

And they ceased. And Rome heard of this. And it was true that the wrath of the Jews was high, and they sought him who had defiled the temple. And Samuel had whispered unto them: "Rememberest thou the one that was within thy hands?" And they sought.

And afar there sounded the calling of Hatte, amid the high spots: "Hatte! Hatte! Hatte! Hatte!" And then naught, to break forth once more: "Hatte! Hatte! Hatte!" And they who sought heard, but when they came unto the spot wherefrom the sound had come, behold it was yon.

And the night came upon them, and they lighted brands and sought the highways and hill's places. And behold, within a sink amid the rock, they came upon Hatte, spent, weary unto the sinking, and within his hand a golden candlestick! And they lay hands upon him, crying out:

"Here is the offender! Bear him before the officials that they mete out the rightful unto him, for it is well that we slay not, knowing within us what we know." And they cried out: "Deliver him up!"

And Hatte waked, and they cast the light of the brands unto his face and he looked unto them, speaking:

"Oh, hast thou sought me? No man hath e'er sought me! I am glad! I would give thee my hand but it is dead! Ye would not of it, for no man would have it whole."

And lo, a burning brand shewed, and wild eyes shewed beneath the gleaming like unto bared wolf's fangs! And this was Panda, and his hand clutched a blade that gleamed. And he cast him upon the form of Hatte and turned. And they that watched saw that they looked upon one who burned of wrath. And Panda's shoulders heaved, and he panted and spake:

"Smite! Smite! Take him not! See, he is already dead! He may not enjoy the smiting, but this flesh is new! May the God wreak His curse upon ye, ye maggots of filth! May He make thy tongues dust! May He fell ye low, for ye will not eat thy bread, and He is not thine! Oh, ye shall pay! Ye shall pay upon thy knees! Thou shalt lay beneath the sneers of earth and they shall speak out, 'Thou hast smitten love,' when I say unto thee thou hast tortured hate, and love is everlastingly renewed of strength and hate is dead! Would ye persecute a dead thing? This is mocking God's smile. Smite!"

And one among them that had sought, caught the hand of Panda and lay his palm ope, and Panda raised his blade within the streaming hand and split ope the eye of the one, saying: "This, that thou shalt see!" And he raised up his hand once more and split the other eye and cried: "In the darkness seek your God, like unto him here!" and he pointed unto Hatte.

And they fell upon Hatte and bound the hands of Panda. And he bit the airs and cried: "Oh, thou God of her, when Panda's spirit is free wilt thou bind his hands?"

And they listed not but brought them on unto Jerusalem's way.

And when they had passed the crossroad, lo, standing like unto a frighted thing, a brand lighted and held high, was Nada, waiting. And she saw what had been and called out: " Panda, I have waited thee, but I know thy sheep hath called."

And she flashed her smile and made the sign unto the East. And they bore on toward Jerusalem. And Nada watched their going, night-eyed, silent, smiling.

And afar within the spot where Hatte had sunk lay the one who had fallen at the hand of Panda. And there sounded the step of one who sought, and the sound of laughing, and behold, the one passed into the dark laughing, laughing. And there sounded naught. And once more returned the one, seeking, seeking. And when the light came, behold, it shewed Aaron, looking afar and seeking a thing, and laughing.

And when morn came upon Jerusalem Hatte was within the hands of Rome. And his lips spake naught save the gladness that they had sought him. And he looked upon the golden candlestick and knew it not, and spake:

" Nay, this hand is dead. How might it do this? "

And they said: " Then the fool, who is thy brother—did he this thing? "

And Hatte looked unto them troubled and spake: " Nay, nay, I have done it. Behold, the holy thing fell upon me and crushed me. This was the sign of the God upon me."

And he shut his lips, nor oped them e'er, though they would much of him.

And Panda was brought forth and they shewed Hatte unto him, saying: " Is it true that this one is of high birth? "

And Panda spake: " Look upon him. He suffereth as one who was brought forth out of the filth of Rome, doth he not? "

And they said: " This hath not answered. Is he that that is spoken? "

And Panda answered: " Where is thy mirth? What woeful merry-making! Ye seek a sheep that is sore smitten to fell for feasting. Oh, the deserts may be dumb, but they speak a truer tongue! "

And they spake once more unto Panda, saying: " Thy words mean naught that a man may know as yea or nay."

And Panda said: " All ' wisdom ' is like unto this."

And they waxed wrathed at the words of Panda, and turned unto Hatte, speaking out: " Who art thou? "

And lo, Hatte burst forth in laughing, and the walls rung of the wildness of the laugh, and he leaned far unto the mighty-seat and whispered: "Ask Rome!" And he laughed more and spake amid his laughter: "Ask Rome!"

And they spake: "Then thou art of Rome?"

And Hatte answered: "Rome hath not spoken it."

And they said: "Who art thou?"

And he answered them, saying: "Hast thou heard the thud of a blade upon flesh? I am the thudding. Hast thou e'er seen an evil cloud come forth and mar the beauteous sky? I am that cloud. Wait! I will tell thee this. I am gone! I am not! The wine hath flown from me. Rome hath drunk it. Let Rome then dance in her drunkenness. Hast thou seen me upon the hill's-ways? See! I am gone out of me. All that is me is gone and I am replaced by Rome. Look! man's building is not lovely. Nay, the gods refuse that they look upon it. Wait! Wait!"—and he tore at the smitten hand and lo, it ran forth blood. And he looked upon it and spake: "I thirst! Ah, I thirst! Nay, bring not forth Rome's water! I shall drink my blood! See!"—and he held forth the hand quivering—"it is dead! Its heart is stopped! It is Caanthus, broken!"

And he shook like one fallen unto the chill of death. And Panda's eyes looked as fires that lay beneath ash.

And the Romans tired of this, and spake one unto the other among them, saying: "Make ye sure this is he. Slay not, for within us we know what we know." And they spake: "Bring forth the man, Hassan, and the Jew, Abraham."

And behold, Panda started. And they went forth and brought unto the spot Hassan and Abraham. And they pointed unto Hatte and spake unto Hassan: "Knowest thou this man?"

And Hassan answered: "Yea, a beggar's waste."

And it was true that he knew not what had befallen. And the Romans pointed unto Panda, speaking: "Knowest thou this man?"

And Hassan said: "Doth the sand know its brother grains?"

And they spake unto Panda: "Knowest thou this man?"

And Panda answered slow: "Why askest thou this? He knoweth not that this one hath been accused of taking out of the temples the sacred things. Neither knoweth he that his brother is beneath thee for the slaying of one of thee."

And Hassan's smiling lips shewed thin and ceased their smiling. And they spake unto Hassan, saying: "Tell thee all thou knowest, for it is true that Rome, the mighty one o'er all, bids this."

And Hassan spake not. And they turned unto Abraham, saying: "What knowest thou? For thy oil may loose his tongue."

And Abraham lifted up his beard and wailed loud: "Three-score years and ten hath Abraham dwelt in peace within the heart of Jerusalem. Abraham knoweth naught of the filth of the street's-ways."

And the eyes of Hassan narrowed, and the voice of Abraham wailed of skins, of his bin's place, of the woe that had befallen him, and no word came that told aught.

And they spake: "Go, bring forth Indra!"

And they did this thing, and when Indra had come among them, lo, they said: "Who is this man?"

And she answered: "He is called Hatte by the Jews, yet his name is Hate. He is he whom thou seekest."

And they spake: "How may we know this?"

And Indra plucked forth from her bosom the golden scourge of the locks of Theia and held it before the eyes of Hatte, and he looked upon it dull-eyed. And she said: "This is thine."

And he answered slow: "Nay, it, too, is a dead thing."

And Indra spake: "Look! knowest thou not Indra, the babe of Joel?"

And Hatte spake not, but pressed the hand that was whole upon his brow, and his great eyes looked like unto bottomless wells wherein a star reflected. And he spake naught but fell unto plucking at the smitten hand and making that he stay the flowing. And his knees sunk, and he called out: "See, my wine is gone!"

And Panda swept unto him and took him up and cried: "Look! this man is sinking. Bring forth a thing that he rest upon it, if Rome must drain him."

And they brought forth sacks filled of cloths, and a rug and spread it, and Hatte sat upon it, and his lips worked and spake words that he knew not. And Indra went up unto the Rome's men and spake unto them. And it was true that they withdrew, and as they waited their words the door's-way shewed the form of Mary. And no man spoke. And she looked about the spot and her eyes leaped as she looked upon Panda. And she saw the form of Hatte, bowed and sunk upon the rugs, and came unto him and looked her keen. And her eyes started forth, and her cheeks paled, and the lips trembled, and she fell upon him, crying out: "Hatte, my brother!"

And Hatte turned, like unto a startled thing, and arose, and his vacant eyes leaped. And he stood mute before her long, and sudden, behold, he thrust forth his arms and his face was bathed with beauteous light, and the scar upon his cheek twitched, and his eyes were lighted with a great light. And he spake in a voice like unto a silver trumpet, blown soft: "Theia!"

And the Rome's ones left his tongue to speak, and he swayed, his lips smiling like unto the smile that greeted the day of Bethlehem, and he spake: "Ah, it is o'er! My dream hath come true! Ah, I have seen thee in the clouds, Theia. I have heard thee in the winds. They wailed unto me: 'Hatte! Hatte!' and it was thee, calling, calling! And when they sunk they breathed: 'Theia! Theia! Theia!' Ah, leave me touch thee!"

And Mary's eyes were wet of tears, and she lay her hand of soothing upon his fevered brow and her cool arm about him. And he sunk his weary head upon her soft breast and sighed: "Ah, dreams, begone! This is mine at last!"

And the voice of Mary soothed him like unto a woman o'er a babe, and she spake: "Thou art broken, brother. Hath the day done this?"

And he answered: "Nay, I am whole. I am a noble. Wouldst thou see my treasures, Theia?" And he raised up his head and touched her locks and spake: "This is my gold. These my sapphires, the jewels of my crown, thine eyes. These the royal rubies, thy lips. This the alabaster, thy flesh. Theia, mother, say thou lovest me! Ah, the night hath been long but the day hath come! Say thou lovest me!"

And Mary whispered: "I have spoken it at the morn, at the eve, at the night, ever, ever!"

And he answered: "Aye, and I have heard thee. But Rome would not cease her dancing, and I forgot thee. Theia, it is upon me! Ah," and he swayed, "I see thee, spent, worn, white-faced, thy locks whited, thy breast shrunk, and but two great eyes that speak love! It is not thee! Thou art lovely! Fresh as the early morning. Thou mightest dance among the stars and seem but some rose-tipped cloud. Yea, thou mightest be but a lovely thing—yet, what is this? The long, long path and then—the slaying! the slaying!"

And he threw high his hands and fell upon the stones as one dead.

And Rome looked upon this nor spoke aught. And it was true that their manner shewed unto all that looked upon it that no man should ope his lips. And Mary had forgot that Rome e'en was. And she sunk upon her knees and her soft hands fluttered o'er the matted locks of Hatte, and the glistening tears fell upon him even as jewels upon his head. And lo, her eyes fell upon the scarred flesh of his cheek and her throat throbbed, and she touched it and shut her eyes and left her head to stoop close, even so that her cheek lay upon the cheek of Hatte.

And her lips spake: "Oh, my brother of the hills, where hath the sunlight gone? Hast thou found her? Is it true that thou believest Mary is she? The God is o'erkind. Mary might not be unto thee as she. Nay, it is true, Hatte; she knoweth it, for thou hast dreamed her. Yea, thou hast breathed of her and known but her within thy heart, and there is no room therein for Mary. But she is gone, and thou, oh, my brother! didst see her within the flesh of Mary. Ah, madness, thy love is mine, even though I have drunk it from out her chalice!"

And she took up the withered form of Hatte unto her, and her hands smoothed o'er his locks, and she kissed him upon his lips and, weeping, crushed him unto her.

And Rome smiled. And Indra's eyes gleamed as a she-lion's. And of a sudden Mary arose, leaving the form of Hatte soft down upon the floor that it rest, and her eyes looked wild, and she turned unto the officials of Rome and the mighty one, and unto Indra, and spake:

"It is finished! I am emptied! Ah, sires,"—and she raised her hands unto the mighty-seat,—"it is done! Mary let her heart to wing out of the walls of humandom. Look! here is the flesh of Mary, but she is gone. Her heart hath found the heart of the sun and thine eyes shall be blinded do ye seek it. Look upon this!"—and she bended o'er Hatte—"hast thou seen the temple doves? Such was he. Hast thou known the pure of morning? Such was he. Hast thou known a young flesh, filled of the wine of the gods that chafeth him unto mighty tasks? Such was he. The great God builded him up, and Rome hath unbuilded him. What hath he done but loved? Yet look ye! his love hath turned like a sickle back upon him, and Rome turned it! See! he is mad. I am Rome's. Leave Rome take me. Mete unto the flesh of Mary what ye will, but, sires, in the name of the God the Nazarene weepeth that ye see, leave him go."

And she turned unto all that stood, and they looked not upon her, but the eyes of Hassan were shut, and Panda looked unto her as a sorrowed mother. And it was true that they of Rome waited.

And Hatte waked and looked upon Mary weeping, and his lips moved and he spake: "Weep not, Theia! Suredly the bottom of the well of thy tears is fully dried. Think ye! The morning cometh. Thou shalt dance upon the dews so that they bathe thy rosed feet. Thou art pure as the sacred vessels! Theia! Theia!" and his voice rung clear, "Behold thy son!" And he rose, weak, and held unto the flesh of Mary that he make him straight, and he cried out: "Behold thy son, Theia!"

And he stood, sobbing, broken, and turned vacant eyes unto all that saw. And his lips spake: "Nay, I am dead. I am no more. The pitcher of flesh hath gone unto the well of sorrow o'ermuch and is broken." And he flung him upon the breast of Panda, crying out: "Panda, hide thou me! They look upon my breaking, and I would be whole. Hide thou me!" And his sobbing filled the great hall.

And Panda whispered: "Hide thee, Hatte, within silence."

And Hatte looked wide-eyed, hunger-eyed unto Panda, and spake: "Panda, where is the Nazarene? Hatte would tell unto Him all his breaking. Thinkest thou that even so He would make him whole? He hath done this. Panda, what spilleth my wine?"

And Panda answered: "Silence! Silence, Hatte! It is the key to the without."

And Mary stood looking, frighted, for within her she knew she had undone him she loved. And the Rome's men spake among them: "He is he whom we have sought. Why then lay hands upon this man, Abraham? He is a Jew and hath done naught that maketh mete for to keep him, since his tongue leadeth not unto the path we sought. And the man, Hassan, he hath offended; for inasmuch as he hath befriended the woman and is her mouth's-piece and the mouth's-piece that beareth unto her that she would of, he hath offended, thou knowest, the will of Tiberius."

And Hassan listed and his lips smiled. And they spake unto him: "Thine hour hath come. Make ye ready, for thou hast betrayed unto the woman that that hath displeased Tiberius. This thou knowest, and furthermore, thou hast come unto Jerusalem that ye seek out the woman's flesh yon and free him out of Rome's hands."

And Hassan answered not but smiled. And they asked of him: "Hast thou aught to say?"

And he answered: "Nay; the day is for a man's tongue to speak, and thou sayest the night of Hassan's day hath come. Then Hassan shall rest."

And they spake: "Thou mayest speak then all that thy heart may bid, for it is the all."

And Hassan stood him tall, and his eyes flashed, and he said: "Unto Rome, naught; not e'en thank. Unto thee, brother," and he turned unto Panda, "I commend the trust. Wait thee. Remember, the sun ever riseth o'er the sands, and the steed of Hassan awaiteth at the sky's edge. He seeth her, her nostrils spread and her hoofs pawing the sands to away! Already he feeleth his mantle free upon the winds. Tell this unto thy heart, for Hassan knoweth where thy heart speaketh. Go, brother! ask the camel is Rome wise?"

And Abraham fell, quaking, and his flesh shewed ashen. And Hassan, seeing, spake: "Fear not, oh Abraham! thy beard shall grow anew and thy neck—it is not worthy the snapping." And he turned unto Indra and bowed him in obeisance, saying: "Dream ye, Indra, sweet dreams, wherein the evil spirits of thy dead play with thy rotting flesh." And he stood him up and looked unto the eyes of Panda and spake: "Unto thee, brother, I commend the trust."

And Panda cried aloud: "Brother! Hassan!" And Rome cried: "Stop!"

And Panda ceased his words, but sunk upon his knees and made the sign unto the East and sung the chant. And the voice of Hassan made answer in chanting as they bore him away. And when he was gone the words came back: "Ask the camel is Rome wise?"

And Mary fell. And Indra came up unto her that she lend her aid, and Mary rose and hissed: "Nay, touch me not! Thy hands are filthed! For upon thee is the blood of Hassan and of him who lieth here, do they slay him! Thou hast led Mary unto the slaughter that she pluck forth the sheep of sacrifice!"

And she shrunk from Indra. And the Rome's men made the sign that the women be gone, and they departed, Mary weeping and Indra making play with the scourge of Hatte.

And they bade that Hatte be cast into the pits. And Panda they bade go free, for within them they knew he would lead the way unto Theia. And Abraham, wailing, sought the without, and Panda, bowed, went slow, holding his smitten hand, seeking the byways unto the hut's place.

And it was eve when he came thereto, and within, upon a rug, sat Nada. And she had made the smokes and chanted, and the door was ope. And Panda sought within and sunk upon the rug, and they bowed in obeisance unto the East, and their locks mingled. And when it was o'er, Nada spake:

"Panda, what chilleth Nada's heart?"

And Panda answered: "Hassan is no more, Nada."

And Nada looked wide-eyed unto Panda and spake: "And Hatte, Rome hath him?" And Panda answered: "Yea."

And Nada said: "Then, Panda, what is for us to do?"

And Panda spake: "Nada, rememberest thou the wisdom of waiting? How know ye that we are not the things that shall write a script for troublous tides to read? Know ye not that more of bitter maketh bitter less?"

And Nada said: "Come, Panda! Thinkest thou that we may see the swallow's wings?" And Panda answered: "Yea."

And they sought the without, and the moon shone upon their waiting.

CHAPTER XX

AND Jerusalem was full of what had been, for the Jews had taken in that Hatte was not of the hosts, but a noble; that he was the flesh of Tiberius, an ill-begotten flesh.

And Jesus Christus had taught within the temples, and the people were swayed as tall grass before the wind at His words. And He had spoken unto them of mighty signs, and had told once more that it was written that the Son of Man should be delivered unto the hands of sinful men and delivered up thence unto the hands of office, and should be slain and come forth at the third day, whole. And they marveled at all of this and spake within their beards:

"This is in truth the Messiah. Yea, the Son hath come. Hath not His hands done wonders and His lips spoken the confoundment of the priests? Is not all of this foretold within the words of the prophet? Is it not written within the psalms of David, His glorification?"

And it had been true that Jesus had spoken unto them at a certain day, saying: "Ye shall see mighty signs writ upon the skies, and nations shall fall upon nations. Yea, and the skies shall spit forth fires; even so shall sea monsters ride upon roaring waves, yea, and wallow in their blood. And ye shall know this is the sign that the Kingdom shall come. Yea, Jerusalem shall be beneath the heels of the Gentiles. The waters of the tribes shall be dried up and they shall be cast unto the four corners of the earth. By all of this ye shall know the Kingdom is not by ye at the morrow, but by ye now. Oh, hark ye, my brothers of the blood!—for I am what I am, a Jew—it shall be within this dark day that the tribes shall be scattered as I have spoken, and the earth shall hold them up before their faces that the stones of the universe shall slay them. And I say me, this shall not be for Jerusalem, nor for the Jews, but that the Kingdom shall come.

"Behold, at a morn they shall awake and the Kingdom shall shew oped unto them, and the Son of Man shall shew, verily, even so that they shall see Him within them."

And they spake unto Him, saying: "Who then among us shall be greatest in the Kingdom?"

And He answered: " It is written, yet shall I speak it."

And it was true that it was the feast of the Passover. And He spake unto them: " I would that I break this bread with thee, for know ye, this shall be the last bread before the coming of the Kingdom."

And they said: " But, Master, there is no household open unto us."

And He answered: " Go ye forth! Did I not send thee unpursed unto the byways, unscripted and without goods, and do ye lack aught? "

And they said: " No thing, Sire."

And He said unto them: " Then go ye forth, and ye shall come upon a man who beareth water and ye shall speak unto him, saying: ' Where within thy household is the feasting hall? The Nazarene hath sent us forth that ye make ready.' And he shall ope unto ye and therein shall ye eat."

And the Jews spake: " See! He hath prophesied." And they followed the loved of Jesus upon the way. And behold, they *did* come upon a man who bore water and they spake unto him as they were bidden, and he oped his house. And some among them departed that they bring forth Jesus Christus, and as they went thereto, Jesus turned unto Peter and spake:

" Peter, the Lord God hath chosen that He cast my loved even as grains within a sieve that He find the tare. I have prayed that thy faith hold."

And Peter said: " Oh, my beloved! I would follow thee upon thy way, even though it led unto death."

And Jesus spake, and His eyes looked troubled: " Nay, Peter; before the cock crows thrice thou shalt deny me thrice."

And Peter denied this be true, and the disciples believed it not, nor did they that harked.

And it was true that they went unto the abode of the houseman, and they brought forth bread and wine and sat that they eat. And behold, the doors were shut, for Jesus Christus spake: " This would I with ye."

And when they had sat, behold He took up a loaf and broke it and spake: " This is my body that ye may feed upon it, for a man *must* have *bread* that he *know* the day. Take ye this in sign of this, for I go from thee."

And they spake: " Master, what speakest thou? This bread is thy body? "

And He answered: " Yea, for the flesh is the chalice that shall hold the wine of wisdom. Look ye unto it. Have I not builded my flesh as thine and dealt ye wisdom freely? Even so this flesh fed upon bread. This is the sign of the commonness of the flesh."

And He broke it up and eat therefrom. And they looked upon Him, and He delivered unto their hands the breaking, saying: " Take; eat in the sign."

And He sat and meditated long, and His lips moved and He spake unto them, saying: " The tribes to come shall pluck forth from the bowels of earth stuffs for the destruction of the building of God. With their own hands shall they fashion them, with their own strength shall they hurl them, with their own hate shall they cast them, dyed of poisonous stuffs. And they shall cry out: ' This is the wisdom of God.' I speak me, man's building, man's hurling, man's hating, is not of God. Man alone may beget hate or nurture it, for within the Kingdom it hath no rooting spot. Yea, and the earth shall shriek out against God, and this shall be near the Kingdom's coming. These tribes shall build up a mighty thing that shall stalk the earth, hideous of wrath, and I say me, beneath its feet shall be mankind. And when they have finished the building of this they shall call it a name, and behold, its flesh shall fall unto dusts before their eyes. And this is their folly. And the bones shall remain, and this is the bone of the righteous upon which the follied builded. And the falling away of the flesh shall leave it empty for the filling up of the Kingdom.

" All of this I have spoken unto thee, and it shall be ash unto the earth when this shall come, but beneath the ash shall the flame of my tongue burst forth."

And * the shades fell from beneath the tapers' lights and swept the walls. And His loved harked nor spake; and the bread was within their hands, for they listed and ate not. And He looked upon them, and behold, the head of John bowed, and he lay it upon the blessed breast and wept. And Jesus raised His arms and took him unto His bosom.

And it was true that His loved sat waiting, each hanging upon His word, and o'er their faces played the light and shadow like unto the foreshadows of the coming ages.

And He spake: " The spirit moveth me to tell thee all. Thou hast asked who among ye should be greatest. I answered ye I yet

---

* Patience prefaced the sitting commencing with this paragraph with a little prayer, which follows: " Oh, my Beloved, give tongue to me to sing thy sorrows like unto a gladsome song! For I see thy bloody sweat like rubies gleaming in their triumph. I see thy crown of thorns bejeweled of them, and their glory fades beside the radiance of thy smile. Leave me, oh my Beloved, thy smile! "

should speak. List! Let he who is greatest become as him that serveth, and let he who is least among ye become as him who eateth the meat served at the hand of him who serveth. Look ye! Am I not He whom thou knowest, and bear I not the Father's bread with mine own hands? Thereby am I among ye. Hark! this say I: One among ye shall, with the sign of loving, deliver me up. And he is with me now, his hands upon the table. For this am I deeply sorrowful, for woe is he who denieth his God, for he is empty and shall seek his filling. For he *shall* come unto the Kingdom full laden."

And He arose and spake: "What! thou hast not eaten? This is the sign. Earth shall tarry. Yet I have sung unto the empty hills, unto my brothers; I have trodden their paths; I have known the stones; I have known the hunger of the flesh, that ye shall know the God is a jealous God and denieth not His Son His brother's dealing. Ponder this within thy hearts.

"Let him who is without purse seek one; let him who hath no sword strip him and purchase one—yea, a purse of wisdom of the Father, and the sword of righteousness. I am filled of the bread for ages. Yea, this leaven I put within thee. Make ye it threefold fruitful. Look ye unto it! I shall give ye the tongue of confoundment. They shall persecute ye, and among ye are they that shall suffer death. Thy tears shall write scripts for new men. Thy blood shall buy the birth of newness within wisdom-old hearts, for the God, the Father, is ever new, and no wisdom of Him is ever old.

"Through the bond of flesh am I earth's. Nor shall I forsake her, neither my blood. When I shall look upon the blood of the tribes * persecuted, behold, shall I stand beside them waiting. Yea, when the earth shall seem for to deny me and decry my Father, there beside her shall I wait. For earth hath an end, even so tribe, even so mankind; but the Kingdom hath not an end. Behold, the riven fields *shall* heal; the split mountains *shall* fall; the sea's water *shall* dry; mankind *shall* cease; yet shall I wait, for the eternities are ever waiting.

"All things shall be complete therein, then renewed and completed. Thereby the complete awaiteth renewing and the renewed awaiteth the completing. Behold, the hour is upon us!"

And they harked, and He commanded them: "Eat, for ye shall remember me in bread!"

And they ate slow. And He took up a vessel of wine and poured forth a cup and spake: "Behold thou this! This is the covenant of

* The Jews.

blood—the sign of birth, not death; not many cups, but one, thereby shewing the Son of Man is one of ye."

And He held it high and spake: "Father, behold thy Son!" And He supped the cup, and with His wet lips kissed its brim for His brothers. And lo, the spot was bright of a new light that shone from Him like unto a radiance. It streamed His eyes like the beams of a star, and His hands seemed for to stream gentleness. And they that looked upon Him were filled, not of wine but of spirit.

And He breathed: "This is the Holy Ghost, the sign of peace within thee!"

And they fell silent before Him. And He stood long, wrapped, like unto an illumined chalice that poured living wine. And His loved knew within them the tide and the day had come, and saw the shadow that man cast upon Him.

And He was sorrowful. And they came unto Him, and He passed unto their hands the cup, saying: "Drink, in the sign!"

And they sat and waited His words, for He seemed that His flesh chafed and His spirit would flee.

And when they had waited long, behold, He arose and spake: "Unto thee do I deliver the watchword of the Kingdom—Mercy. Unto thee do I deliver the key—Faith. Unto thee do I deliver the Kingdom—Love."

And they arose and bowed before Him and He said: "Peace be with ye, yet I know it shall forsake ye."

And it was late hour, and afar the sounds of Jerusalem sounded through the dark. And He spake unto them, saying: "I would go up into some spot where I may hear the stillness."

And they said: "Unto the mount, Master? Unto the garden?"

And He answered: "Yea, for upon the mounts sound the heights of earth's sounds, and I would know the stillness that I hark unto the small voices."

And they departed unto the garden. And He withdrew from them, even though they would follow Him.

And they spake unto Him, saying: "Shall we make ready swords to defend thee and stand waiting, fearful of them that might seek?"

And He answered them: "Nay. The Kingdom of Love is complete; it is the fearfulness *and* the sword. Await!"

And He departed within the garden's place. And they harked long unto His voice, raised up like unto a song, wooing, tender, pleading, gladsome, fretting to away! And His form shewed touching the earth with His hands, pressing the green things unto Him, looking unto the skies, turning all ways. And once more His voice arose like a mighty wind speaking monstrous * things, filling the emptiness of all things till it seemed that the dead stones had taken Him in.

And He knelt Him down and looked up on high, and behold, no light was there. And His voice sounded amid the dark: " Father, behold thy sons!" And He spake more unto the heavens, saying: " If it be thy will, the bitter *shall* be sweet! If it be thy will, leave the bitterness unto me and by my supping sweet the cup. May it pass from me, sweet, unto thy sons!"

And from the East shewed the new day's coming. And He arose and held His arms wide to greet her, and His lips spake: " Father!"

And He sought slow through the thick growth, pausing to pluck a branch and kiss it, plucking up a stone, to smile and leave it fall. And the dews of night glistened upon His raiment. And He sought His loved, bathed of the Holy Ghost.

And lo, He came upon them, and they had wearied and slept. And He stood within the young light and looked upon them and smiled, and spake: " Sleep, oh earth! Ye *shall* wake! The day knocketh thee. The stars have fallen out of the heavens and given place unto the sun of Love. Awake! Do ye tarry? Then sleep, for thy waking surely cometh. The Son of Man hath not a spot whereon to lay His head save the bosom of Heaven."

And it was true that there shewed men of Jerusalem who sought the spot, and Jesus looked upon their coming like unto one who awaited them he knew.

And He said: " Where hath Judas gone from among ye?"

And His loved answered: " He sought the temple that he make his praying. He hath gone unto the priests for to pray."

And behold He smiled and spake: " The tare. Within thee forgive him."

And it was true that as the men of Jerusalem came unto the spot they shewed to be men of office and some of the priests. And it came to pass that Judas came from out their midst and fell upon the shoulders of Jesus Christus and kissed Him. And Jesus turned and held His oped hands unto them that came and spake: " By the sign of love is love delivered up."

And they that sought called out against Him as a tongue that drove the people out of the temple. And it was true that the loved looked upon Judas and knew that the prophecy had come. And Judas looked not unto them but departed among them that sought.

* In the sense of tremendous.

And they spake unto Jesus, saying, for there were men of office that listed unto His words for heresy: "Art thou the Son of God?"

And He answered not, knowing their meaning. And they said: "Make thee a wonderwork, since thou canst do these things."

And He answered them not, but stood looking far; nor sought He out with His sorrowed eyes, Judas.

And they spake unto Him, saying: "Thou hast perverted the people and driven them forth out of the temple."

And the priests bore upon Him charging all of this. And He spake unto them in answering: "Whyfore hast thou not lain thy hands upon me within the temple? For have I not taught among ye and abided within the temple?"

And the priests took this in and spake unto Him, saying: "But thou hast o'ercome the words man should speak of the God, for do ye deliver the God unto the people that they may eat them as bread, lo, He shall become as a naught."

And Jesus answered them, saying: "Nay; doth the God be delivered unto the people, they shall fat and thou shalt lean."

And the Romans harked unto what the priests had spoken, and they urged them that they decry Him. And lo, they binded up His eyes and smote Him upon His flesh, crying out: "What thing hath smitten thee? Prophecy! thou canst then tell!"

And He answered not. And His loved drew nigh that they defend Him, and, behold, the Rome's men lay lash upon them and drove them forth before them. And they made fast the hands of Jesus and sought the way unto Jerusalem's heart. And lo, as they passed upon the way through the street's-ways the Jews looked upon Him and went unto their households and shut up their doors, even so that no Jew shewed.

And it was true that they of office, who were banded together beneath the loved of Him, sought out the priests at a later hour, speaking out: "Hast thou then brought Him forth unto the temple, before the high priests, that they cast their judgment upon Him?"

And they answered: "Yea; when the sun is high this shall be."

And they that sought spake: "Thou art delivering up the thing that is the most precious thing of the Jews. Thou art betraying the King. Thou hast brought forth the lamb of sacrifice out the tribe of David, and woe shall befall ye!"

But their words found not harking within the temples. And lo, they banded together and sought out the Rome's hall wherein the mighty one of Rome sat at judgment. And they brought forth word that Jesus Christus had fallen within the hands of the Romans but had been delivered up, first unto His own blood at the temple in accord with the respect of the Jew's right.

And they spake: "Look ye! is He delivered unto thy hands? It is abroad that Rome shall slay Him, for all the Jews know the thing that hath set Rome as His shadow."

And he of Rome harked and spake unto them: "This man hath done naught punishable by death."

And they said: "Then thou wilt so declare?"

And he answered them not, for within him he knew that Jesus Christus was sought out by Rome for cause of the glut of Tiberius. Yea, he was full of all that had come forth of the seeking of the flesh Tiberius coveted. Yet within him was no thing that bid that he up the blade.

And the Jews, seeing that he withheld his word, spake: "Look ye! Think ye not the Jews know this one who is within thy hands? It is true that do ye offer up as sacrifice this man of the Jews, and withhold the smiting from the flesh that the Jews *know* is the flesh of Rome, then woe be upon thee!"

And the mighty one answered them, saying: "Who hath spoken all of this unto the ears of Jerusalem and Judea?"

And they answered: "Hark, oh sire! It is known among us that our brother Abraham hath, with Samuel, delivered Him up unto the priests; that they too have made bart between the priests and ye of Rome. And the man, Helios, who hath come, hath come for to lift up the flesh of Tiberius o'er us, mayhap for to cast down the blood of Herod and lift him up, calling him King. It is known, and woe unto ye do ye this!"

And they departed. And word ran high within the Rome's walls, for there had come forth word that Hatte should be offered up, and the Jew, Jesus, taken from the midst of His people and brought down. For inasmuch as the son of Tiberius was broken, and one rose up among the Jews as mighty, it was well to fell him, lest Jerusalem uprise. And they spake that all among them knew that Helios had come from Rome, yea, from the mighty one, and his words had sought among the people and he had bethought him that the Jew, Jesus, was the son of Greece. Thereby had he sought not as from the mighty one, save by his order, but by his pledge unto Theia, the noble of his land. And when he had found the son was broken, behold, he had spoken that Tiberius might do the thing; that he had given up his blade against the word of Tiberius.

And when this had been known amongst the Romans, it was the

tide that Hassan had been delivered unto them, and the Rome's hall was full of the word that Helios had been found oped, and Hassan gone. And they that had borne Hassan thence that they undo him, told that they knew not what had been, so swift, as the darts of a hawk, was the thing o'er. And within the hands of one was hair of the beard of Hassan.

And within the market's place, at the next morn, unto the hands of Abraham had come a skin filled of holes. All of this Rome knew; but they knew not whereto Hassan had flown, for no spot had shewn him.

CHAPTER XXI

ALL of this filled up the morn. And it was true that Jesus Christus had been taken forth unto the temple and thence unto Rome's hall. And the mighty one had known that the Jew, Jesus, was of Galilee, and behold, he had builded up within him a thing for to do that Rome fall not within the displeasure of the Jews. Then would he deliver Him up unto him who sat upon the seat of judgment for His land;* thereby Rome should be clean. And when they had brought forth Jesus Christus, behold, they told that He had spoken treasons against Caesar, and would do no homage before the name of Caesar, speaking out that His Father sat o'er the kingdoms of the earth, and no man might call his name Caesar and cause the son of such a Sire for to make homage. And the mighty one harked but spake not. And they made more of words, saying that He was causing wrath among the Jews, for He spake that He was the Son of the God, and this was blasphemy. And they made much of this, speaking: "This is an offense worthy of death."

And the mighty one said: "Art thou the Son of God?"

And Jesus answered: "Thou hast spoken it. Should my lips have spoken it thou wouldst not believe."

And the mighty one spake: "What manner of words tellest thou the people that setteth them against thee?"

And Jesus answered him: "I am come to lift them up, and they exalt themselves from the earth unto the lifting up. Yea, from the prostration upon their faces they look for the coming of a new day."

And the mighty one made more of words, and in answering got no thing that might wax his wrath.

And he turned unto them that had brought Him and said: "I will not of this barting. Seek ye unto the spot where the judge of His land abideth. I have found no thing that might cause Rome to slay Him."

And they took their words unto the judge of the land of Galilee, and lo, as they sought therefrom, no Jew shewed upon the way save

* Herod Antipas.

616

them that had been at the barting. And when they had come unto the spot, they cast the form of Jesus before them and pressed upon Him unto His bearing down, and tore at His raiment. E'en did they spat upon Him, for the Rome's men had seen His teachings and were filled with the wild words that told that from the lowly would He be lifted up. And believing that He, or yet Hatte, was the flesh of Tiberius, lo, they thought them to shew their hate of Tiberius in the smite of anything of him.

And lo, it was true that they drove Him up unto the foot of the mighty-seat whereon sat the judge of Galilee's land.* And they brought Him unto His knees before the mighty-seat and cried: "Make ye homage!"

And He moved not. And they smote Him, and His flesh shrunk, yet moved He not. And they brought Him down even upon His face before the mighty one, crying out: "Make ye homage!"

And He arose before the mighty one and stood Him up, nor bowed He His head.

And they spake unto the mighty one, when they had fallen upon their faces before him: "This man hath offended the Jews, for He calleth Him the Son of God, and this waxeth wrath among them."

And it was true that the mighty one had been filled of the teachings of Jesus Christus, and had taken in the words that had spoken that He had begotten wonders before the eyes of men, that had set wondering among the sages of the land; and he was filled of the desire that he look upon the man Jesus that he fill up of Him, thereby to know was He the flesh of Tiberius, as it had been told within the beards of men. And he took in that the man Jesus was a Jew, for upon Him was the sign of the blood.

And he spake unto Him, saying: "Is this thing true?"

And He answered: "Thou hast spoken it. Have I not taught within the temple's places, among the priests, and they reached not forth their hands nor laid them upon me?"

And the mighty one spake: "But thou hast answered not. Art thou the Son of God? For mine eyes look upon thee and my lips would speak out, 'A Jew.'"

And Jesus Christus stood before him, His hands locked one unto the other before Him, and His head high, and He spake: "Thou hast spoken it. I am a Jew."

And the mighty one said: "But thou hast not answered. Once more, art thou the Son of God?"

* Herod Antipas.

And Jesus Christus spake: "Is this the mighty one who asketh this thing? Sire, thou knowest do I answer thou wouldst not believe."

And the mighty one spake: "Whyfore among the Jews wouldst thou defile the temple?"

And Jesus answered: "Nor have I done this thing. Within the temple is no thing that is not wrought of man. How then doth defile-ing be?"

And the mighty one knew that this was fearful, for the Jew's priests harked, and even though Jesus Christus swayed their people upon His words, their tongues sat within the throats of the people.

And he spake: "What manner of man art thou, for knowest thou not that thy words are the defilement?"

And Jesus answered: "Nay; my words are the light. E'en though my blood shut the temple, yea, seal it up, it is man-wrought and shall crumble and the light enter."

And they harked, and the priests cried out: "Seest thou, O mighty sire, He hath uttered the defilement! For He knoweth not a temple, but taketh His God among the unclean! Yea, nor doth He look Him unto the sacred rites of the Jews nor payeth He tribute unto the sect, but maketh Him free among all men!"

And it was true that the mighty one harked unto them, for he was filled of pride that the man of Rome should deliver up his right unto him. Yet he was filled of the Jews and knew that their eyes burned living fires, that their hearts were full of this man, Jesus Christus, that they but awaited His word to arise, and he would not that their wrath fall upon him. And it was true that when he had spoken long and brought forth no thing save that that might offend the Jews, he turned unto them that had sought and spake:

"Return ye! Go ye unto the Sanhedrin."

And it was true that one of the priests said: "Yea, bring Him forth before the temple's judges. Make Him utter the defilement."

And they bore Him out among them and mocked Him. Even did the servants of the mighty one bring forth tattered raiment of beau-teous color and they arrayed Him. And lo, like unto the white moon that had come unto some glaring noon looked He! And yet His flesh bore the mocking even as a noble might take homage. And they called Him names of ribaldry, and His lips smiled. And they wondered among them that He breaked not nor wrathed.

And among them they spake: "This is the flesh of Tiberius."

And the Rome's men said: "Yea, this is true. Look ye! He knoweth His sire will lift Him up."

And they spake unto Him: " Is it true that thy sire shall lift thee up? "

And He cried: " Upon earth's folly am I exalted."

And they bore Him unto the household of one of the priests. And behold, within the court was kindled a burning heap whereby stood the servants that they make lights for the lighting up of the household at the later tide. And they brought forth skins and left before the fires unto the tide that they shewed hard and dried. And these they stripped into narrow thongs for wicking; thereby the scent of the green skin was gone. And they brought Him forth unto this spot.

And it was true that His loved sought Him out, fearful. And a one, a servant, looked upon Peter, who came unto the court seeking, saying: " Yon is he who is of this man's tribe. He is one of Him."

And it came to pass that they drew up unto Peter and spake: " Is this man He whom thou knowest and art thou of Him? "

And Peter, knowing that woe was upon him, answered: " Nay, I know Him not."

And lo, he withdrew unto the outer spot from the court. And one of the men servants spake unto him, saying: " Thou art one of His teachers. Thou knowest this man, Jesus Christus? "

And Peter said: " I know Him not."

And he came back unto the spot whereon stood Jesus Christus within the hands of the Romans and the priests and them that would lead Him unto sacrifice, and he looked upon Him. And one of the priests spake: " Is this man Jesus Christus? "

And Peter answered: " I know not."

And the cock crew thrice, and behold, Peter's eyes started ope, and Jesus Christus lifted His sorrow-heavy eyes and spake: " And unto thee, Peter, did I deliver the stone of my foundation. Yea, unto thy hands did I commend the very foundation of the temple I am come to shew—Faith; unto thee have I delivered the kingdom—Love, and thou art faithless."

And Peter fell upon his face, weeping. And they looked upon what had been and spake: " This man doth know Him."

And Jesus Christus said unto them: " Nay, he knoweth me not. His eyes are sealed, yet his heart shall ope them, for he hath the key."

And they brought Peter up unto Him and spake: " What manner of man denieth one he loveth? This is one thou wouldst claim as thy loved."

And Jesus Christus answered: " What manner of man denieth

one he knoweth? Flesh *is* flesh. Flesh is flesh, and may thereby err. He who denieth me not his love, denieth me not. His lips have uttered words like unto scales upon the meat of fish."

And they spake: "What wouldst thou of him—that he acknowledge thee?"

And Jesus spake: "Look unto him! He doeth this."

And He took Peter unto Him and kissed him upon the cheek. And they that had looked upon all of this marveled, for the man broke not, and they fell unto words among them.

And the Rome's man took out of the servant's hands the skins that were green and slitted them, thereby making of them thongs, in which they tied knots, knotted o'er stones. And they made of these lashes, and lo, they laid them upon the frail form of Him, and they shouted, crying out:

"This is the Son of God! Behold ye, O ye Jews!"

And the Rome's men brought down the thongs upon Him and drove Him through the street's-ways and thence through the byways that they might shew the Jews what had been. And behold, the households were shut. And as they shewed, the bin's men that had remained put up the bin's cloths and hid. And they brought Him up unto the temple, and the Rome's men spake:

"What manner of judgment may thy priests speak upon Him, for they have not the power that they may slay?"

And they spake among them that they should seek out the Rome's court and make known that it was the wish of the people that the man be delivered up unto the priests.

And it was true that a certain man called Joseph had banded together ones that loved Jesus Christus, and sought out the Rome's halls and called audience with the mighty one. And Joseph had spoken words, pleading that the man, Jesus Christus, be left unto the people. And he had told them the wrath of the Jews was high, for they knew that there was among them a man called Hatte, who was ill-begot of Tiberius, and no man raised his hands against him. Even had he spoken evil among the people and set them against the man Jesus. Even more spake he, that this man Hatte had oped the throat of Jacob, had oped the sacks of grain and felled the sheep. Yea, and had wrought havoc among the hill's-ways and even afar upon the ways unto Nazareth; even within the spot called Bethlehem had he done havocs, and yet, though he was taken unto Rome's pit, no thing had been done. And he spake that it should be done unto this one even before the flesh of Jesus had suffered, else he would rouse the Jews.

And the mighty one harked unto him and filled up of all that he spake. And it had been true that one had come forth from out Rome, bearing swift word that they should rid the lands of them that spake of the mighty one o'er all as their flesh, seek out the Jew and him that they had known had fellowed with the man, Hassan. Make end of o'er-much word; for in this thing lay woe.

And the mighty one of Jerusalem knew that the thing that filled up the one o'er all was not that this was the son of a slave, but that the woman was noble, and it had made vengeance living among Greece. The noble blood was hot of anger that Rome should ride the lands and take the blood of Greece to drain and then cast unto naught. All of this the mighty one knew, and he awaited the coming of this messenger that he mete unto the flesh of Hatte.

And even as Joseph spake with the mighty one, lo, the sound of the coming of them that bore Jesus Christus sounded out, and they cried amid their laughter and shouting: "Crucify Him! Spread Him ope! Shew the men of Jerusalem their King, who hath called Him the Son of God!"

And they laughed and cast filth upon the tatters of Jesus Christus. And He walked among them, beaten as some waste upon a wave, seeing not, hearing not. And they came unto the walls of the Rome's halls, and they swept Him through the great gate unto the inner courts, thence unto the hall, even among the slaves and men of office, for they were hot of wines and wicked of heart. And the priests of the Jews fell fearful before such a sight, and they spake not nor cried out against Him.

And within the halls stood Indra and a he-one of Rome, whose lusts bought his spirit and left his body empty that he fill of evil. And this man was he who had come forth from out Rome.

And Indra leaned unto him, saying: "Indra is thine dost thou bring Him down. Look ye! this is the Jew, and the man Hatte hath gone unto the temples and brought forth their sacred things. Bring him down! The mother of the Jew is within the house of Isaac, and the woman, Mary, hath fled unto her, for she loveth the flesh of the Rome's man, Hatte, and the spirit of Him yon."

And the Rome's man laughed and spake: "And Arminius, the Roman, who hath assumed new office?"

And Indra laughed and cried: "What! thou wouldst call him a Roman? Nay, he is a vestal virgin!" And they leaned one upon the other and laughed.

And the men of office sought the side of the mighty one, and among them stood Arminius. And they that bore the form of Jesus Christus cast Him before them, and smote Him as they bore Him on. And they came them up unto the ope of the mighty hall and craved entrance. And it was true that they were left to come therein.

And they cried aloud: " Behold, sire, we have come forth from the judge of Galilee, and yet of the priests, with this man. He is a perverter of the people and is filling up the land with treasons against Rome."

And the mighty one looked upon Jesus Christus, whose flesh shewed the white bite of the lash and the blush beside it, and he was troubled. And he spake: " Thou hast brought Him forth and I have found Him not an offender, and even so, thou speakest, hath done the judge of Galilee. What then wouldst thou of me? "

And they cried out: " Hark, sire! Offer Him up beside the flesh of the man, Hatte. Give Him unto the hands of thy people, for the Jews are full of wrath against the man Hatte, and they hold him up. It is spoken that he is even the blood of Tiberius. This is a common thing. Rome is derided before Jerusalem. Make them lap up their words in blood! The priests have spoken words to undo Him and *they* are the law. The Jews dare not arise. Bring Him down! "

And it was true that the mighty one looked unto Jesus Christus and said: " What sayest thou? "

And He turned unto the priests and spake: " This day hast thou emptied the temple and stripped the tabernacle. Rome hath thee! Thou art as clay within her hands. Ye may not undo that that thou hast done. Oh weep, Jerusalem, for thou shalt cry unto the heavens to fall and cover thee! I say me, in the jealousy for thy God thou art consumed. In thy glut thou art stricken, for ye would feed the temple and make hungry the great God's hosts. Hereby thy blade of jealousy hath slain the lamb of sacrifice for the feeding of the tribes of ages. And Rome shall undo thee! Oh, ye priests of the temple, thou hast o'erturned thy urns of wisdom upon this people, and I say they have not drunk it! By thy hands of office is the altar made. Yea, and by thy blade the lamb is slain. Yea, but the brand of Rome lighteth the fire of sacrifice, and the stone of Rome hath keened the blade! Begone! for the voices of the priests of ages shall arise in an endless praying, and Rome shall stand holding up thy God for men to laugh upon, for He shall be dead within Rome's hands, by Rome's hands and thy blade! Go! Go! "

And He towered tall and pointed unto the way out the hall. And they followed His shewing.

And He turned slow unto the mighty one, saying:

"No Jew is beneath thee, but Jesus Christus. Do the thing! He awaiteth."

And the hall was silent. And He stood, robed in tatters and the stripes of the thong, regal. And Rome cowered before Him.

And when He had stood long so, He turned, unto them that had taunted Him, a smile like unto a young sun of morning. And they feared Him. And the mighty one arose and spake naught, but bid that they bear Him thence, delivered unto the blade's men. And they bore Him from the great hall unto the pits' places.

And they that had come set their tongues living once more. And they spake like wild things: "Crucify Him! Crucify Him! Lay Him low! Bring forth the flesh of the man that oped the Jew's temples, and slay him! Yea, upon the feast day make ye merry, oh sire! Offer up sacrifice before the eyes of the Jews, lest they arise. Shew them Rome's heel!"

And the mighty one spake: "I will not of it."

And they made louder noises, even did they fall one unto the other. And the men of office of Rome spake unto him: "Seest thou? These men are of Rome, but they abide in Jerusalem and they shall raise up the Jews. It is a fearful tide. Deliver the man up."

And the mighty one arose and stood and bade that the slaves bring forth a cup, and he drank it slow and pondered. And he called that a slave bring forth a fount, and Indra went forth and returned with a bowl of gold and jade. And she offered it, and the mighty one arose and bathed him therein, saying: "This is a sign I will not of it."

And the men of office looked unto him, and he spake: "Do as thou wilt."

And they that had sought departed, filled up of the words of the men of office that they would deliver these up unto their hands upon the feast day.

CHAPTER XXII

AND the night came, and the streets of Jerusalem were filled of Jews who beat their bosoms. And they sought one unto the other's households, and within their house-walls sounded the voices of praying. And there were among them ones who feared the heavens would fall. And the priests waked through the night's hours, nor did one among them sleep. And the Rome's hall was skirted of Jews who sought, fearful, beating their bosoms.

And they spake: "What hath the man done? And this flesh of Tiberius, he is mad! Woe is upon us! Woe is upon us!"

And they made the sign among them.

And when the hour was late, behold, within the Rome's walls the pits' places were dark, and there had sounded out the step of them that brought one forth even unto the spot, and this was Jesus Christus. And they oped the pit and left Him therein. And He stood amid the dark, still, silent, still. And there sounded a voice speaking soft:

"He shall come! Theia hath spoken it."

And a form arose and sought the pale gray spot that shewed the ope, and it strained that it reach up and look without, and he spake: "He tarrieth! Yon is the East, and it is dark."

And the Beloved One spake soft: "Brother!"

And Hatte cried aloud: "Panda! I knew thou wouldst come!"

And he sprang unto the bosom that was bruised by the hand of man. And the loving arms gathered him in.

And He whispered: "Brother!"

And Hatte spake: "It is dark—dark—dark!"

And the voice answered: "Nay, the darkness is without thee. Look within."

And Hatte started and spake: "I fear not, for I am the son of a noble. I am Rome's man. Let Rome deny me."

And Jesus Christus spake not. And Hatte listed long and questioned: "Who art thou?"

And He answered: "I am thy brother, even as thou art mine."

And behold, Hatte sprang upon Him like unto a wild thing, crying out wild cries, as a bird of night lost amid some storm. And he smote His flesh, speaking out:

"Thou liest! Thou art Him of the hills! Thou hast spread thy honey upon the hills and I have eaten gall! Where is she? If thou art a god, answer thou me! Why doth thy Father sleep when I call? Why are the hills empty? Why do all men turn unto thee and speak me naught save their taunting, their curses, their hate? I am ridden by Rome! Yea, Theia is gone. I am a dead thing. Make me whole! Cry out unto thy God! Make Him hear! Ha, ha, ha! I am the son of Tiberius and he is mightier than thy God, for he shall slay thee and thy God shall not save thee! I am nobler than the Son of God thereby!"

And the gentle hands fell upon the frenzied writhing of Hatte, and His words sounded soft: "Hark! Hark! Oh, brother, by thy own dinning thou mayest not hear thy God. I *am* thy brother, even as thou art mine."

And Hatte spake: "Thinkest thou they will offer up the flesh of Tiberius? Rome doeth such things." And he turned unto Jesus Christus, speaking: "Fear not! My sire shall come. He shall come upon a whited camel out of the East way, for thee and me. For I shall speak thee my brother, releasing thee. Fear not! Fear not!"

And Jesus Christus spake not. And Hatte waited long, beating his hands one upon the other. And upon his thumb was the copper ring of vanities. And when it was darker, and they had sat long silent, there sounded a whisper, hoarse: "Hatte! Hatte! Hatte!" And he arose and ran unto the sound, and behold, it was Mary. And she slipped her hands through the ope and smoothed the fevered brow, and Hatte whispered:

"He is here, the Nazarene. He is here, Theia. He hath a new Kingdom and He would that I seek with Him. Theia! Theia! Oh, wondrous one who hath poured the wine of hate for thy son, hark; he hateth all things but loveth thee; Theia, Theia, mother—I shall bear me as the son of Tiberius! I am noble, yea, noble!"

And Mary wept soft and spake: "Oh, my beloved! I would leave my tongue to flow like waters scented of sweet herbs, filled of all things, unto thee. I would fill thee up of me, of me, of me! Yea, and I would fill up of thee, of thee, of thee!" And she wept sorrowful. "Remember thou, Theia loveth thee. Theia's arms have ached as thou hast craved her bosom. This was thy answer. Theia's throat ached full, when thou didst call her. This was thy answer. Theia's eyes saw thee proud, royal, regal, her son, and the son of Tiberius. Theia loveth thee!—loveth thee!—loveth thee!—loveth thee! Oh, my loved! hast thou seen the dove's wings lap the sweet airs? Such would be Theia's kisses. Oh, my loved! hast thou seen some tall reed lapped by the waters? Such would be Theia's embracing. Oh, my loved! hast thou seen the young Spring split ope with a vagrant bolt? Such would be the pinnacle of Theia's love! Oh, my loved! hast thou seen the meadows lay beneath a silver veil? Such would Theia be without thee, for the sun would forsake her. Oh, my loved! knowest thou the heart of the lily? This is the chalice Theia offereth thee for to drink her wine! Even though it be hate, thereby shall it sweet."

And she held unto the flesh of Hatte's hand. And he was stricken of a quaking, and he cried: "Stop! Stop! What is the blade that hath touched me? Ah! Doth the God sleep? Nay! Theia! Theia! Theia!" And he shrieked: "Hatte! Hatte! Hatte!" and fell.

And lo, the voice of Jesus Christus sounded soft, calling: "Brother! Brother!" And he leaned o'er the fallen one.

And behold, Hatte arose and his voice answered, slow, clear, like unto a trumpet: "Brother!"

And Mary cried out: "Jesus Christus, he is broken. Unto thy hands do I commend him." And she departed, weeping.

And Jesus Christus stood holding the hands of Hatte and spake: "Long have I called."

And Hatte murmured like unto a weak child: "I see the hills! Ah me, I hear the sheep! I am chilled. The earth called unto me, 'Who! Who! Who!' and I was Caanthus of Rome, broken. Before me cometh the morn when the ass sought the byways, and the woman and her husbandman and the Seeker, the young youth who spake me 'brother.' I see me now, pleading for to leave my head upon his mother's breast, and then, and then—ah, I am broken!"

And He, the Beloved, spake: "Leave thy heart to flow out of thee. Give forth love. This is the mending. Speak! Speak love!"

And Hatte murmured: "Theia!"

And the voice of Jesus Christus cried out: "Leave it flow! Leave it to mount up unto monstrous * waves! Bathe within it! Leave it flame! Burn thee within its puring flame! Leave thy throat to call it loud, for thou hast spoken it! Thou hast spoken it and it is thy mending! Speak ye out love."

And Hatte answered: "Theia!"

And the first gray of day shewed.

And without, men sought amid the dark with lighted brands, and their voices sounded loud about the Rome's halls, and they spake fear-

* Great, tremendous.

fully. For some of them were Jews who watched, and some were of various tribes, and some were of Rome. And they of other tribes were Rome's. And they spake:

"They shall be delivered up. This day shall they fall into the hands of them that seek them."

And amid the calling sounded out the words: "The Son of God!" "The King of the Jews!" "The Son of Tiberius!" "A swine-noble!" "Crucify them!" "Crucify them!"

And the ways ran of men who breathed fast, and dogs barked, and asses brayed, and the sounds of morning were wild.

And the voice of Jesus Christus arose once more speaking out: "Call thou this name! It is thy cloak. No noble e'er wore more regal garment."

And Hatte spake: "Theia!" And his voice was like unto a child's, peace-filled.

And Jesus Christus said: "Call thou!"

And Hatte spake soft, trusting-soft: "Theia! Theia! Theia!"

And behold, the light shewed, and the face that turned unto the ope was illumined with the young sun. And it was the face of Caanthus!

And behold, he stood him up tall, and drew up his arms, saying: "I am strong!"

And afar, afar, upon a valley spot, where the road's-ways were stoned and still dark from the sun, sagged a camel. And from out its trappings sounded out a voice: "Oh—e—e—e——!" And within a woman beat her hands one upon the other.

CHAPTER XXIII

AND it was true that the early light was dimmed of white mists within Jerusalem. It hung like unto a filmed veil, close, close, and the burning brands leapt like tongues of flame within the silver. And the Jews were filled up of wraths and fears, and the early tide found the temple stones wet of the trodding of many feet that sought for to pray. And no dove shewed, and the pools were hid within the mist. Yea, it seemed that one Jew had hid from his brother within the circling white.

And within the Rome's halls, at the very earliest hour, behold, men arose and they held an audience before the mighty one, speaking out of the Jews who trod the road's-ways. And they pointed unto the brands and harked unto the outcries among the men without, and they spake:

"Behold these people! They hunger for to mount up unto wraths. This is their feast day. Yea, and behold, they shall come them from off every road's-way unto the temples and meet with their tribesmen. This, then, is the time to offer up their King. It is in accord with the law that we free one unto them. Do this thing! Offer up the Jew who hath slain and is within the hands of Rome. Give him up and make a feasting before their eyes. Make merry before them. Offer up their King as Rome's sacrifice. Shew them Rome's power before their tribes. They have come for the sign of blood. Give it unto them! Behold thee," and they spake unto the mighty one, "it is spoken unto thee that thou shalt offer up the flesh ill-begotten of Rome. Do thou this. Seest thou not thou mightest speak it is not beneath thine hands? for it is the priests who abide Jerusalem's temples that hungered that the man Jesus Christus be offered up before the face of the people, and thereby their tongues are silenced. Yea, and more; the man Hatte hath gone unto the holy places of the Jews and stripped their holy vessels from out the walls, thereby offending them. They have decried him and made known that they would have him offered up."

And they worded long, and it was true that the mighty one spake: "Do that thou wilt."

And the Jews came forth at the coming of light. And it was true

that the mists had given place to hanging gray of cloud that seemed
filled up of drops and hung like unto the bellies of swine o'er the skies.
And the airs were heavy, and wets slipped the stoned walls, and the
sky's rim rumbled, and lightnings played amid the far clouds. And all
men of the road's-ways seemed filled up of a thing they scarce might
hold.

And the Jews came unto the Rome's hall and demanded that that
was custom. And they delivered up the transgressor who had slain.
And they looked upon him and were filled up of wrath against him and
spake:

"He is an offender of the law of Moses. He hath forsworn the
prophet's words. Make him, before the eyes of our brothers, to acclaim
his wrong!"

And they lay upon the one and made words unto him, speaking
out: "Thou shalt acknowledge before the face of the temple and the
judge thy wrong and shall be delivered up for the atonement." And
they cried out among them: "Crucify him!"

And wrath ran high. And it was true that the war's men of Rome
sought out the Jews and listed unto all that should befall this one.
And they spake unto them, saying: "Before thine eyes shall be finished
with the offering up of this one, lo, Rome shall do thy bidding and bring
low, even as thou ministereth unto this one, the man Hatte, who hath
defiled thy temples."

And they spake: "But the man is mad!"

And the Rome's men said: "This is not true. He is cunning."

And among them word ran that told that the man Hatte would be
crucified even as the offender against the law of Moses.

And lo, within the pit's place the lightnings shewed. And behold,
the clouds gave up their heavy-ladenness of drops, and it swept Jerusalem. And within the pit lay Hatte, his head at rest upon the bosom of
the Shepherd, Jesus Christus.

And he stirred and spake: "Hark! What is without?"

And Jesus Christus answered not. And Hatte arose, and his face
was troubled, and he spake: "It is upon me—the hand of Tiberius!
This day undoeth Hate."

And Jesus Christus said: "Yea, the undoing of Hate is the freeing of Love."

And Hatte looked upon Him and he spake: "So. It mattereth not
what the path, be it the valley's among the sheep and the gentleness of
shepherdom, or yet the hill's-ways among the tares and stones, it leadeth
unto a common thing. I am the son of a noble. Speak!—thou hast not

one whit for to gain or lose—speak, brother, unto me! This is thy day and mine. Art thou the son of a noble? Hath he betrayed thee?"

And Jesus Christus arose and said: "I am the Son of a noble. And it is true that flesh may be betrayed unto death, but truth within the flesh is blind unto betrayal, blind unto sin, blind unto all things save the Father. Thereby the betraying of flesh unto death is the unloosing of truth."

And Hatte spake: "Rome shall strike. Without, yon upon some height, is an empty man.* He hath naught save his folly, for he hath lost hate. Herein is Hate and he hath left folly rove the hill's-ways. I am the son of Tiberius. It mattereth not doth earth know this consumes me. I shall fall his son, yea, the son of Theia. It is empty. There is no thing for to come. Sire, if thou art the Son of God, make ye a sign."

And Jesus Christus stooped close and spake: "It shall be so." And He spake more, saying: "Thou art the son of Tiberius, and who begat Tiberius and his kind and tribes since ages? The Father. Thereby art thou His son."

And Hatte cried: "But He knoweth me not! He hath ne'er harked unto my crying. He hath stopped His ears that He hear not Theia's calling. Let Him shew His power!"

And Jesus Christus said: "Keep within thee faith and it shall be."

And Hatte spake: "Then thou wouldst leave me but faith, the thing that fishermen cast within the sea with their nets?"

And it was true that their words were stopped by the bolts from heaven that roared like monsters from o'erhead. And Jesus Christus said: "Let Tiberius speak such a tongue!"

And Hatte sank upon the stones and looked not up unto the ope, nor yet unto Jesus Christus.

And the storm broke and loosed, and a cool set the land, and men came forth, and the sun even so. And when the tide had come when the street's-ways were fulled of Jews, lo, the Rome's men came forth bearing up the golden candlestick of the temple, and crying out of the offender before the Jews. And they went them up unto the temple, even before the door's-ways, and shewed the thing unto the eyes of all Jews that entered therein.

And they mocked them and spake: "The Son of God is within the pits of Rome. Let Him set them quaking and come forth!"

And they derided them and called them loud the followers of a false prophet. And they cried: "Look ye! if He hath done that the

* Aaron.

tongues of men speaketh, why then doth not the God split ope the Rome's halls and deliver Him up?"

And the priests feared, for the words of the Romans made the Jews rise up and come unto them, bearing word of what they suffered. And they spake unto the Romans: "Make ye Him deliver Himself up, or take Him unto ye."

And it was true that they made ready that they should crucify the transgressor, and the spirit of evil mounted the rabble. And it was true that Rome unloosed skins of wines among them. And at the high hour, behold, the streets cried out like wild things. Men ran thither and yon, laughing or shrieking, bearing stones and sticks of broken woods. And Rome sat, fatted, comfort-full, and smiling.

And behold, the pits were oped, and they delivered unto the hands of the war's men, and they whom Rome had set mad, Jesus Christus and the son of Tiberius! And it was true that Rome had shut up her doors and left be that that would. And the sun was o'erclouded and shone but to hide. And the blade's men bore forth Jesus Christus, whom they had stripped naked, and He shrunk beneath their eyes and cast His eyes down. And lo, they laid hands upon Hatte and stripped him, and the women that looked upon this withdrew and hid.

And they cried out: "Who art thou, thou thief of the temples? Who art thou?"

And Hatte stood like unto one who wandered upon some far height. And they cried aloud: "Behold the son of Tiberius! Behold him!"

And they laughed and cast stones and bits of stone wares and rotted fruits and filths of the street's-ways. And Hatte stood, empty. And Jesus Christus spake not. And they decried Him, crying out: "Behold the King of the Jews! He is the son of who! He is a false prophet! Stone Him! Stone Him!"

And they lay hands upon them and beat them on the path's-way, even as wastes upon waters. And their flesh was torn and the hairs of their heads torn out, and lo, blood shewed upon their faces and their naked flesh. And the chill of the after-storm was upon Jerusalem, and they shook in cold quaking. And they that taunted them brought forth waters and cast o'er them; even did they bring forth heated brands and put unto their flesh.

And lo, among them stepped the Son of God, silent. They knew Him not. And Hatte held his head high and stepped regal, even though his withered leg gave way and was dragged at his stepping, for the weighting down of them that beset him was o'ermuch.

And they wearied of their taunts, for no manner of outcry came there for to feed their madness. And they cried out: " Crucify them! Spread them ope! Shew unto all men that enter the city, the Son of God and the son of Tiberius! Ha, ha, ha! Down the flesh of Rome beneath all men! Crush the blood of Tiberius beneath the heels of men where he hath crushed the flesh of our tribes! "

And it was true that the Jews were mad, and, mingled with the Romans within one cup, had they fallen. And when the cry had gone up " Crucify them! " behold, Hatte looked unto Jesus Christus, whose body was sagged of weakness, and with his own arms did he cast off them that clung, and tear him through flesh unto His side and lift Him up. And his lips spake:

" Seest thou? It is the end of the paths. Thine of love and mine of hate lead thee unto a common thing."

And Jesus Christus lifted up His head, and behold, through the blood, through the sears of torment, through the agony of flesh, broke forth the smile of God. And Hatte looked upon His face, and his thin lips spread in smiling.

And they that looked upon this waxed wrathed o'er their filling and beset one the other. Men fell upon their brothers, even did they deal flesh wounds one unto the other, so that blood was upon them as a hideous cloak.

And it grew dark, and lo, clouds rolled up like smokes of wrath, and the heavens flamed licking fires, and the thunders pealed upon them. And this but set the wraths frenzied more, and they went forth and brought unto the spot young trees and binded them up with thongs into rude crosses. And these were the work of wrath, and the woods were rough and the barks sharp. And lo, these they laid upon the backs of Jesus Christus and the son of Tiberius.

And Hatte took it upon him and he murmured: " Is the God sleeping? " And he looked unto Jesus Christus, who sagged beneath the new weight, and he spake: " Thou, too, even as Tiberius, hath betrayed thy Son."

And behold, the flesh of Jesus gave way, and He sunk. And they lay scourges upon Him, and He might not arise, for the wine of the flesh was gone; His spirit chafed that it flee.

And Hatte called out loud: " Brother! Brother! I am calling! " And Jesus arose, and lo, upon His face was the smile.

And the heavens roared like monstrous caves filled of wraths of ages. And the lightnings licked the earth, and the winds arose and blew like wild voices o'er the hill's-ways and valleys.

And they drove them upon the way unto a high spot, barren of

shade, where the sun might bite. And it was true that there sounded
out a wail of anguish, and it was the voice of Hatte, for he was broken.
And from out the throngs sped a woman, crying: " Hatte! Hatte!
Hatte! " And this was Mary, who followed with the mother of Him.
And lo, they wept, and were cast among the men as wastes, and beaten
and trodden, yea, and bruised. And the cheek of Mary was white and
stained; yea, even the things they had cast at the flesh of Jesus Christus
and Hatte had smitten her and the holy bearer of Him. And lo, at
the calling: " Hatte! Hatte! " Hatte arose and cried aloud:

" Theia, behold thy son! This is the long dark path, but the
fleeing is no more! It is come! The hand of Tiberius hath fallen! "

And Mary came her up and with her frail hands made that she
bear the cross, and wept and spake soft words, saying: " Wait! Wait!
Rememberest thou? He shall come! "

And Hatte spake: " It must be true, for true as hate hath followed
me hath this."

And lo, they swept them apart and trod down the women, leaving
them, and bore them upon the way.

And when they had come unto the high spot, lo, already stood one
cross made living! And they cast down Hatte and lay the cross upon
the earth and brought forth irons. And they made him ready, and
through the living flesh they set man's wrath to prison man's flesh unto
God-wrought wood.

And they took up the smitten hand and made ready. And Hatte
laughed and spake: " It is dead! " And they brought forth the whole
hand, and Hatte whispered hoarse: " It is whole! Behold, earth, I
offer it unto thee! " And they made it fast and he cried: " Ye—oh!—
will not! " And they fastened his feet. And his lips stopped, locked
of agony, and his eyes spake empty.

And they cast down Jesus Christus. And behold, they had brought
forth the tatters within which He had been clothed and they spread them
forth and cried: " Behold, the raiment of a King! " And they took
bits among them and cried aloud in mockery. And it was true that one
who stood holding of the cloth saw it not. And this was Flavius.

And they lay upon Jesus Christus, and behold, Hatte's lips twisted
that he speak, and the word was the watchword, " Mercy! " And he
whispered: " God, if thou art God, mercy! "

And behold, the form of Jesus fell empty, knowing not, and they
pierced the chalice that let flow the living wine. And they raised up
the crosses and made them fast. And lo, the clouds sunk even upon the
earth, sweeping the hills and breaking down the trees in wrath of the

winds. And the tempests rang the wraths that should fall upon ages of them that did this thing.

And it was true that they stood beneath the crosses and beat upon the pierced feet, and the flesh quivered like unto a host of maggots beneath the skin. And behold, the ribs stood out even so that it seemed they would burst the flesh, and their bellies panted, and the eyes rolled from side unto side in anguish.

And when they had stood looking upon this long they lay hands upon the two women who sought. And it was true that women of the town had come that they lend their succor unto them that sorrowed. And they that had borne them up upon the crosses laid hands upon them and brought them up unto the foot of the crosses and cried:

" Look upon the King of the Jews, women! Look upon Him! Look upon the flesh of Tiberius! "

And Mary sunk and tore unto shreds her mantle, crying out the while, and made that she bind up the wounded feet. And behold, their lips were stained of blood where they had kissed their loved flesh!

And the legs had split up unto the knees with the weighting down and the flesh-quaking which tore at the throbbing. And behold, there was a sound of anguish, and the body of Hatte fell forward, crushing, the hands torn loose and the knees broken. And they that looked sent up a shout of victory. Yea, their voices shrieked and mingled with the on-sweeping torrents. And they laid hold of him and made the cross low and binded him up once more.

And it was the late sun, and it glowed anger-red below the bellied clouds.

And lo, there sounded out a voice calling: " Oh-e-e-e! " For it had been true that the camel had come unto Jerusalem, and they had taken in word that they had borne the son of Tiberius forth for to crown. And Theia had been full of what her heart held and had followed their pointing, and behold, when she had come unto the spot her eyes took in the multitudes and the cries and the storm and fear was upon her. And lo, she came upon His loved, who stood afar, praying, after the manner He had spoken. And she had leaned far and said: " Where is the crowning of the son of Tiberius? "

And they answered: " Yon."

And she had looked upon what shewed on high o'er the heads of the multitudes, and behold, her throat swelled, and she tore at her locks and her hands she beat one upon the other, speaking: " It *shall* be! " And lo, she sprang off the camel and ran swift. Like unto a bounding deer her feet sped in the beauteous steps of the dance. And she loosed

her locks and brought forth the cloths and spread them, tearing off the
mantle of coarse stuffs, and her lips speaking: " It shall be! It shall
be!"

And lo, she came up unto the things that stood, dead things, empty
chalices that dropped drops and that still made flesh sounds. And
behold, the hands were swelled unto the blackening, and the lips were
black of blood, and the heads sunk. And they that looked upon them
called out:

" Behold, the Son of God and the King of the Jews!"

And they brought forth a white script and with the wet blood wrote:
" The King of the Jews." And this hath ne'er been wiped whither.
And they cried out:

" See the son of Tiberius! He is broken! He is no more! Crown
him! Crown him! Yea, and the King, for their heads are still free and
may suffer!"

And they brought thorned branches and wove crowns and with
their hands pressed them down unto the deep of the flesh. And lo,
they cried not out.

And the flesh of Hatte shook, and he made that he wet his lips with
his tongue, and his throat made a hollow sound. And he turned his
head unto Jesus Christus and called: " Brother, the sign!"

And no sound came. And the voice of Jesus, at a later time, cried
out: " My God! My God! Hast thou forsaken me?"

And lo, Hatte bended his body like unto a bow and cried:

" Behold the palms wave! The sands gleam! The caravan cometh,
and it is led by a camel white as goat's milk, whose eyes are like unto
rubies, and upon it—Jesus Christus! And before it danceth Theia!
And one limpeth—Simeon! Simeon! Caanthus, I am strong!"

And he gave up the ghost.

And upon the cross still suffered He, for the transgressor of the
Jews beside Him lived. And they that watched laughed, and behold,
they saw that they stirred and they brought forth vinegar, the wine of
the people, and offered it that He might live long to suffer.

And it was true that the Jews had fallen fearful, and one and another departed unto the temples to pray and hide. And Rome remained
to glut upon the feast. And they had called out against the Son of God,
and fallen weary of His words, for He forgave them, and spake in tones
to the heavens, crying out that the Father forgive, for the Jews knew
that Rome had lain their backs ope.

And the transgressor cried out long in his agony, and he turned unto

Jesus Christus, speaking out: "Mercy!" And the Rome's men spake unto Him: "If thou art the Son of God, save thyself and him."

And the transgressor spake: "Why do this unto Him? He hath done naught unto thee, and I have perverted the laws and undone them."

And Jesus Christus turned His head slow unto the transgressor and spake: "Behold, thou shalt enter the new land this day and be with the Father even as I."

And lo, they looked upon Him at this, for He was uttering prophecy even in death.

And He hung, His beauteous head wet of blood and crowned of thorns, even as man had made His days thorned, and His precious flesh was illumined with the flames of the lightning.

And behold, the earth quaked. And it was true that the tombs gave up dead. Their bodies were shaken free. And when the mighty peal had fallen like a trumpet, like a bird that flees singing, sounded out: "It is finished!"

And His head sunk, and He turned unto the withered form of Hatte, hanging limp and broken, and the smile of God broke upon His countenance, and it was o'er.

And lo, a shrieking sounded, and the voice of Theia called: "Jehovah! Jehovah! Unto thy fires I commend him!" And she fell upon her face.

And the multitude had departed save for a few of the Romans who were deep in cup. And they, too, seeing all was o'er, departed.

And at the foot of the crosses, upon their knees, were Mary and the precious mother, weeping. And lo, His loved sought, for it had been that He had commended her unto His most loved, and he came that he lend succor, and bore them away.

And Theia arose, and no thing looked upon her, nor they that had gone from out the empty flesh that hung. And she crept her slow, fearful-slow, gasping, fearful, and touched the flesh. And behold, she stood her up and spake:

"It is written in blood upon the ages. Tiberius, I wait; for it hath been—the thing within me! And it shall be—the thing yet to come! See!" and she dipped within the blood her finger and wrote upon a bit of her mantle: "The Son of Tiberius."

And lo, she looked upon it and cried: "Ah, ye coming ages! Ye shall read this!"

And she watched the wind's havoc, and turned all ways, and it was empty. And she spake: "Theia, where to?" And lo, she spread her locks and danced before the dead things, telling upon the winds her anguish, weeping not, but uttering sounds that chilled the echoes into phantoms. And she danced long, and long, and long, and long. And when it was dark, behold, she fell, to arise and step once more. And lo, at the deep of dark she crept, like unto a wounded thing, unto the cross upon which Hatte hung, and lay her down.

And lo, the night was long, and when the morn had come, behold, the first rays broke rosed, and bathed the wrath of man in God's mercy. And o'er the naked bodies had swept the torrent blood, and within the light it shewed royal, the purple of the son of a noble! And upon the form of Theia the purple shewed. And she was no more.

CHAPTER XXIV

AND lo, the light shewed o'er the hill's-ways without Jerusalem. And one sought the road's-way unto the hut of Panda, and he stepped swift, for he was full of what had been within the city. And behold, he came upon the spot and no thing shewed. And he went up unto the door's-way and made the sound that he would enter, calling: "Panda! Panda!"

And lo, Panda swept swift without, holding his arms wide and speaking: "Where is she? Hath she come?"

And it was true that the one, who was Paul, let his head bow and spake not. And Panda spake: "Hath she then not come?"

And Paul answered: "Panda, I am come empty. The trust thou didst deliver me is undone. The land is swept with wrath. Jerusalem is mad. Go ye unto the city and thou shalt hear the wailing of the Jews who weep within their households. Yea, they have scattered ash before their door's-ways, yea, beat their bosoms, for they have delivered up the Nazarene, Jesus Christus. Yea, they have crucified Him."

And Panda stood mute before this, then cried: "Paul, speak! Thou knowest more."

And Paul shook before the eyes of Panda and answered: "Hatte is beside Him."

And Panda reached forth and touched the flesh of Paul and spake: "Then she is beneath the cross. Tiberius, thou hast written and thou mayest not wipe it awhither!"

And Paul said: "Panda, look!" And he shewed many wounds upon his flesh whereon he had been bruised by the multitudes, and he spake: "I was felled beneath their feet, and sought her but found her not until the morn's coming. Hark! The flesh hangeth upon the crosses, and she is beneath them, and no Jew will lend a hand to take off the uplifted. Yea, and Rome laughs, and will not lend aid."

And Panda said: "Speak ye not of these things. Wait!" And he went within. And behold, upon the rug's-cast lay Nada, and upon her breast a babe. And he knelt before her, speaking out: "Nada, Hatte is gone. He is no more. Hate is dead."

And Nada spake: "I have harked, Panda, I have harked." And

she lifted up her babe and said: "Behold, in the name of Theia, I call thee Hate! Hark, Panda, hate is but a word, not a thing! Hate is no more. The Nazarene hath uprooted it, yea, and left His blood unto the nurturing of a new root. Thereby the coming hates of earth have the bread of His love for their nurturing, and the flesh of hate shall be made love. Here is Love." And she pressed her lips upon her love-born.

And Panda spake: "Nay, nay, Nada, hate is hate."

And Nada answered: "Go thou, Panda; look upon the dead face of Hatte who hangeth beside Him, and thou shalt find thy words undone."

And Panda stood him up, and his breast heaved, and he spake: "Panda hath left his fold to scatter. Panda, thou art free. No more art thou slaved, yet art thou bound even as the slave; for love may not die and weigheth heavily even after the flesh is gone."

And he said: "Nada, this day is fearful. We may not tarry. Lo, it is well, for he who knoweth the sands knoweth that a man must rise at the end of the long night and trod the new day." .

And he leaned o'er her, and behold, the lips of the new-born Hate were smiling.

And within Jerusalem had been much wording. For Abraham had given up unto the hands of Rome the men that hung before their eyes, and it was true that the Jews beset him and offered him up, and no man knew who had upped the blade. And the house of Samuel was sacked, and his goods oped and thrown unto the street's-ways, and the Jews cried aloud: "Unclean! Unclean!"

And within the Rome's halls the word was given forth that the morn should give unto their hands the man Panda, that they shut his wording. And Jerusalem seethed within her walls like unto a boiling pot. Wraths crept o'er her walls and ran the sides of the earth. Yea, and still it spreadeth!

And it was true that the loved of Jesus Christus had gone unto the Rome's spot and asked that they deliver the body of Jesus up unto them, and they had laughed and made no answer. And at a later tide, one who loved Him and held office among the Romans, yet was of the Jews, had sought out the Rome's hall and craved of them the body, and it was given up unto him. And they had let him take it forth. And lo, no man dared that he seek the body of Hatte, for it was of Rome, and Rome would not of it.

And it was true that the dark came, and the dead things hung silent, leaving silence to be filled by the tongues of the coming ages.

And when it was deep dark, lo, the moon arose not, but o'er the dark one star gleamed! And a shepherdless fold sought out the silent spot and lay it down at the foot, beneath Death.

And when it was late hour came forth Panda and Paul and one who spake not but lended aid, and they did the thing unto the empty flesh that waited. Upon the breast of Joel they lay them. And the night's winds sounded out like unto a wail: "Waiting! Waiting!"

And the moon arose, and the clouds cast their shadows upon the fields and hill's-ways like unto phantoms that trod the ways. And among the sheep upon the hills sounded the echoes of the winds' sighing, and they started, e'en as though they harked unto their shepherd.

And there shewed upon the out-roads a camel, seeking, and asses laden, and upon the camel was a trapping whereon Nada rested, with Hate nurturing at her bosom. And Panda followed, and one leaned close unto the side of Panda as he drove the laden ass, speaking:

"The sands, brother, the sands! Ask the camel is Rome wise." And he laughed and said: "Hassan speaketh Rome's wisdom hath bathed in folly and is drunk." And he made the sound: "E-e-e-e-oh! E-e-e-e-oh!"

And they rode them unto the up-coming moon, whereon the swallow's wings were spread.

And afar, upon the breast of Arminius, who soothed, Mary wept, and her lips spake: "I am empty, Arminius, empty."

And he answered: "Nay, Mary, sorrow is the bread of love."

And the long-night waited the new day, and when it came, behold, the sun shewed o'er the filmed cloud its gold, and it streamed like unto the spread locks of Theia, and the clouds danced upon the breeze.

And still earth slept, and no sound came from out Jerusalem, and within the shadow of the wall crouched one who held within his hand a golden candlestick, and laughed, laughed.

And upon the hill's spot shewed the empty crosses—dead, empty. And the new sun mocked them. And o'er the stillness sounded the wailing winds: "Waiting! Waiting!"

And Jerusalem's day had come, and sped, and swept unto the eve. And afar the hills of Bethlehem shewed, sunk within the silvering eve. And o'er the heights, the Star!

And the road's-ways shewed Aaron, seeking, seeking, dragging his nets, and laughing, laughing.

THE END

APPENDIX

1. There is no reference in the Bible to the appearance of a star at the time of the birth of Jesus. Few subjects, however, have been more generally discussed than the star which appeared to the magi, and some have thought that this star became visible before or at the time of the birth. Foundation for this belief is derived from some of the Apocryphal gospels, notably the "Protevangelium of James," believed to be the oldest of these apocrypha, and the "Gospel of Pseudo-Matthew." "Moreover, a great star called Keryoun, larger and brighter than all that were before it, shone over the cave with inexpressible light from the evening until the morning." And again: "Some shepherds, whose names were Misael, Acheel, Cyriacus and Stephanus, wondered at the star which had appeared" (Donehoo's Apocryphal and Legendary Life of Christ). Cruden's Concordance mentions ancient authors who take it for a kind of comet, which appeared preternaturally in the air. Apparently a comet is meant by the description given by Ajax—"trailed a beard like a priest's beard, long and bright." The Chronicles of the Saxons mention a comet appearing in 1066 which "some men calleth the long-haired star."

2. The title "Jehovah" is said to be an erroneous and comparatively modern rendering of the Hebrew "Jhwh," which the Jews were forbidden to pronounce except in the service in the temple, and there by none but the priests. In the synagogues, and when reading the scriptures anywhere, a substitute, usually "Adonai" (Lord), was uttered, if the ineffable name appeared. The correct pronunciation is now supposed to have been Yahweh or Jahweh. But in this narrative Patience permits Jews as well as Gentiles to use the word "Jehovah," and does so for the reason that it was necessary to have a distinctive title for the God of Israel to distinguish Him from pagan gods, and to be a title familiar to readers of the present day. Patience was asked about this and she answered: "Thy handmaid setteth her so that she be not robing a one for the Jew nor yet for the Gentile, nor yet for him who worshipeth his god, be it a sun, or yet a moon, or yet a graven one. Nay, this would she put into the hands of the multitudes even as manna, not of grains they know not but builded in their tung. How be it a man may speak a word that meaneth God and hideth him? 'Tis God; then Jehovah belongeth not to the priests, and tides have (time has) swept the veil even out the holy place."

3. Fish formed a staple article of food among the Jews. Jerusalem derived its supply principally from the Mediterranean, and had a gate known as the "fish gate," probably near a fish market. Fresh fish, no doubt, as well as salt, were brought from the coast and, perhaps, from Galilee. Nehemiah speaks of the men of Tyre "which brought fish." So there is nothing improbable in the appearance of Peter at Bethlehem, so far away from fish-producing waters.

4. Was Bethlehem, in the time of Christ, a walled town? Patience Worth, in this story, has it so. There is nothing in the gospels, nor in the apocryphal legends, that indicates walls or the lack of them. Modern Bethlehem tells nothing, for the town was utterly destroyed by Hadrian in 130 A.D., and a pagan grove planted upon its site (Jerome), the town vanishing, with many other places that felt the ruthless vengeance of that emperor. It is only from the Old Testament that any information upon this point seems

to be obtainable, but this apparently supports the assertions of Patience Worth in this particular. It was at the "gate" of Bethlehem that Boaz announced the purchase of Ruth the Moabitess to be his wife, "and all the people that were in the gate and the elders, said, We are witnesses." And David, when the Philistines were in possession of Bethlehem, "longed, and said, Oh, that one would give me drink of the water of Bethlehem, which is by the gate" (Samuel 23:15). Gates presuppose walls. Later on, King Rehoboam "built cities for defense in Judah," among which was Bethlehem, "and he fortified the strongholds" (2 Chronicles 11:5-11). All this, it is true, was centuries before Christ, but it is a reasonable presumption that the walls were not permitted to disappear during a period when walls were always a desirable, if not an absolutely necessary, protection.

5. Herod, at this time, was near the end of his days, an old man whose passions and cruelties had made him hated throughout the land. The terrible diseases from which he suffered are described by Josephus, who says the diviners declared they were "a punishment upon him for what he had done to the Rabbins." But it is more likely that they were, as Patience intimates, the natural consequences of what he had done to himself. The palace which is the scene of this picturesque episode was built by Herod, one of the many splendid edifices with which he adorned all Judea. It was situated in the western part of the "upper city," was surrounded by a wall thirty cubits in height, and contained columned halls of great magnificence (Josephus).

6. Luke, the only one of the gospel writers who records this incident, does not mention the priests, but speaks of Simeon and Anna, the prophetess, who acknowledged Christ. The temple, begun and, for the greater part, built by Herod, was not yet finished. Commenced about 17 B.C., John says it was "forty and six years" in building (John 2:20), but it is not understood that it was even then complete, the final work upon it being done in A.D. 64. Whether the line (the soreg) beyond which a Gentile could not go had been fixed at this time would be difficult to say definitely. Doubtless it was. The court of the Gentiles, in which those who were not Jews could move freely, was within the temple walls and surrounded the temple proper, from which Gentiles were rigidly debarred; from which women, too, were excluded, except from the "Court of the Women" which opened upon the court of the Gentiles. Through the gate of the Court of the Women, Theia seems to have observed the meeting of Mary with the priests and Anna. However, the clairvoyant power attributed to Theia might very well be considered a sufficient answer to the question that arises in connection with this scene.

7. The leprosy of ancient Palestine, so frequently referred to in the Bible, is said to have been a disease quite different from that modernly known by that name. According to the Levitical text, the features of leprosy were: (1) bright white spots or patches on the skin, the hair on which also was white; (2) the depression of the patches below the level of the surrounding skin; (3) the existence of "quick raw flesh"; (4) the spreading of the scab or scoll (Jewish Encyclopedia). It was looked upon by the Jews as a divine visitation and those who were afflicted with it were morally, as well as physically, outcast. But recovery was possible and apparently not infrequent, for the Levitical laws provided for the restoration to the communion, as well as to the ordinary rights of citizenship, when the disease had run its course.

8. According to history, Tiberius voluntarily exiled himself because of the conduct of his wife, Julia, the daughter of Augustus, and resided quietly at Rhodes from B.C. 6 until A.D. 2. If he left the island at any time during the period it is not recorded. The story, however, has him privately recalled to Rome by Augustus and sent upon a secret mission to a far country, which involved a journey across sea and desert. Theia accompanied him and remained with him until his recall, when she was discarded.

9. From its proximity to the East gate this palace is presumably the fortress of Antonia, so named by Herod, who rebuilt the citadel of Baris at the north of the temple and gave it the new title in honor of Mark Antony. "Nor was it other than a palace," says Josephus, although it was primarily a fortress.

10. The word "belly," not now permitted in polite literature or conversation, is frequently used in this work, both as a noun and as a verb, and its use is in harmony with the character of the language of the composition. Literally, it has a broader significance than its Latin substitute, and it has figurative values wholly lacking in the modern "abdomen." It would be an absurd affectation to use the accepted synonym where the older and stronger Saxon term is found in this story, even when they are really synonymous terms, but there are many places where the Latin word would have little or no relation to the meaning conveyed by the text as it stands. "Belly," in the Stuart period of English literature, was a perfectly proper word. It appears about fifty times in the authorized version of the Bible with various significance, sometimes referring to the abdomen specifically, sometimes to the whole trunk, sometimes used literally and at others figuratively. Shakespeare uses it whenever it serves his purpose and its broad application is discerned in the phrase, "With hearts in their bellies no bigger than pins' heads."

11. Very little is known of the religion of the Arabs before Mahomet, but from time immemorial the title "Allah" seems to have been given to a shadowy deity of indefinite attributes, whose worship, at some remote period, centered about the holy stone enshrined in the Kaaba at Mecca. The "hosts of heaven," the sun, moon and stars, but particularly the moon, were perhaps the earliest objects of adoration, and later times developed innumerable tribal and tutelary deities, some of them imaged in stone or metal. There are indications that temples of a sort existed and officiating priests. That form of demonism which peoples the air with jinns appears to have been far older than Islamism. Allah, however, was apparently the supreme god, at least among the Koreishites, to which tribe Mahomet belonged. How long his worship had existed and to what extent, no one can say. The Arab tradition has it that the seal of Solomon was engraved with the name. The Arabs in this story seem to have a common understanding of certain simple rites and symbols and use the rug ceremonially. Whether these things are true to the time is a question that may or may not be answerable. No authority within reach of the editor reveals the slightest positive information. They seem, however, to be in accord with the customs of the Arabs from the beginning of history. There is no doubt that rug making was an established industry in the Orient centuries before Christ, and it is probable that their original use was religious rather than utilitarian (Mumford).

The symbol of the crescent, mentioned several times, is puzzling. The crescent, in its modern use, is an emblem of Turkish nationality rather than of the Mahometan religion, and, according to some authorities, was derived from the Byzantines. If the references were to this symbol they would be, of course, anachronistic. But it is more likely that they are founded upon the general worship of the heavenly bodies, and the special attraction which the new moon held for most of the Semitic race. The Israelites offered burnt offerings in the new moons, and for a long time the forbidden practice of making sacrifices to the moon (the Queen of heaven) in worship was continued by them (Jer. 7:18; 44:17). "The moon-shaped ornaments, which adorned the necks of the Midianite camels in the time of Gideon, were probably results of the same idolatrous tendency" (Jewish Encyclopedia). The Midianites were Arabians, who, it seems probable, were moon worshipers from the earliest times. "The moon god," says Dr. Jastrow, "is par excellence the god of nomadic peoples, their god and protector at night when, during a great part of the year, they undertake their wanderings, just as the sun god is the chief god of an agricultural people." And this same eminent authority says, "We are justified in supposing that the cult of the moon god (Sin) was brought into Babylonia by Semitic nomads from Arabia. Sin was the chief god of the pantheon of Babylonia and Assyria for a considerable period, and the symbol of Sin was the crescent. Modern scholars are of the opinion that Mount Sinai, the Biblical "Mountain of God," derives its name from Sin (M. Seligsohn), and Antoninus Martyr, writing in the sixth century A.D., tells of the heathen Arabs celebrating a moon feast there (Dr. Socin). So it seems reasonable to assume that the crescent is correctly used as the symbol of an Arabian deity in the time of Christ.

12. Patience discussed this theme at greater length. "Ye see," she said, "there be them that seek o' brothers athin (within) their days. Yea, and call these friends. And behold, unto the measures o' these deal they their love. So. And some do for to seek o' the perfect bowl, and find not a storing place for love. And then there be them that take o' the bowls e'en as they be offered, and doth the bowl be cracked or yet broken, even so they deal unto that that remaineth, and thereby fill up the broken bowls unto the many. And, so by, earth hath much o' their love, and they do for to take of a full o' loving from out the earth's days. When lo, he who seeketh perfect measure falleth short that he find, and thereby earth loseth, and he falleth short of brothers, yea, and friends. For behold, the broken bowls still hold sweets."

13. The identity of the woman who anointed the feet of Jesus, as described in the seventh chapter of Luke, and the origin and meaning of the word "Magdalene" that distinguishes one of the Marys, have been matters of controversy through ages. Luke does not say that this was Mary Magdalene, and many persuasive arguments have been presented against the long established belief that it was she. But arguments that seem to be fully as convincing are urged in favor of the accepted tradition, and this position is supported by the story. Most commentators accept the theory that the word "Magdalene" is derived from the town of Magdala, or Magadan, on the shore of Galilee, mentioned once in the Bible (Matt. 15:39). "According to the Talmud," says the Catholic Encyclopedia, "Magdala was a wealthy town and was destroyed by the Romans because of the moral depravity of its inhabitants," which if true would make it unique in Roman annals. But the same authority (C. E.) speaking of Mary Magdalene says she was "so called either from Magdala or possibly from a Talmudic expression which the Talmud explains as of an adulteress." Another authority (Dictionary of the Bible—Scribner's) says that "Lightfoot, following some of the Rabbinical writers, gives a different derivation, according to which the name would mean a plaiter of hair, a phrase sometimes used of a woman of light character." In the story the word seems to be used specifically as a term of opprobrium, and therefore to accord more nearly with the Rabbinical interpretation.